D1096248

SELECT EDITIONS

Selected and Edited by Reader's Digest

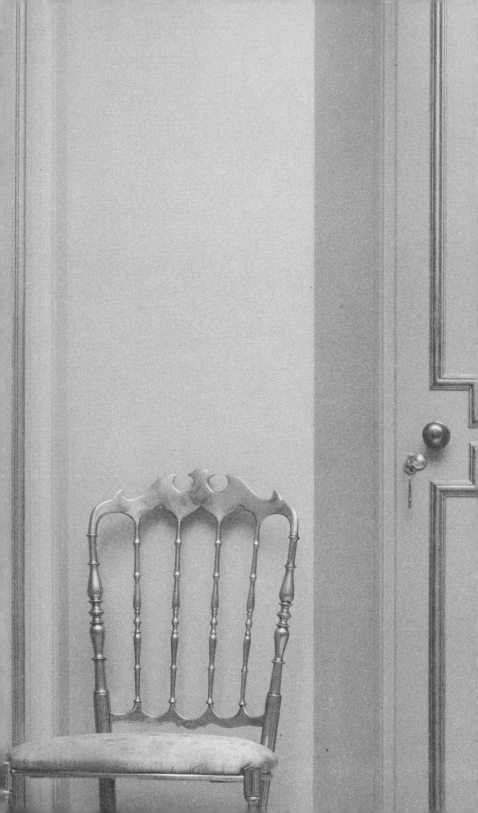

SELECT EDITIONS

Selected and Edited by
Reader's Digest

 New York · Montreal

FROM THE EDITORS

Old pros know their stuff. When in the hands of a seasoned author, readers can trust that the story they're about to begin is worthy of their time and emotional energy. In this volume of Select Editions, we're celebrating authors who have appeared in our pages before. We hope you'll enjoy reconnecting with these fine writers.

Riley Sager's latest, *Lock Every Door*, is his third book, and the second that has appeared in our series. This terrific psychological suspenser features an elegant and mysterious apartment building in New York City that has many secrets to hide.

Linda Castillo's mysteries starring chief of police Kate Burkholder have become something of a staple for us in recent years, with *Shamed* as her latest. We love this series not only for its outstanding plots but also because of Castillo's ability to immerse us in the fascinating world of the Amish.

Our third selection, *The Whispers of War*, is a poignant historical story of friendship, loyalty, and bravery set in wartime London. This is the second appearance of author Julia Kelly, and we're thrilled to have her back.

Finishing up the volume, we've got *Careful What You Wish For* by Hallie Ephron, a repeat author who combines a wonderful sense of fun with her whodunits. Who says murder and mayhem can't offer a few laughs along the way?

So there you have it—old pros doing their thing. Enjoy!

Inside

SELECT EDITIONS

NEW YORK TIMES BESTSELLER

LOCK EVERY DOOR

a Novel

"Move over, *Rosemary's Baby*, urban paranoia has
a deliciously Gothic new address." —RUTH WARE

RILEY SAGER

Ginny gazed up at the building, her feet planted firmly on the sidewalk but her heart as wide and churning as the sea. Not even in her wildest dreams did she ever think she'd set foot inside this place. To her, it had always felt as far away as a fairy-tale castle. It even looked like one—tall and imposing, with gargoyles gracing the walls. It was the Manhattan version of a palace, inhabited by the city's elite.

To those who lived outside its walls, it was known as the Bartholomew.

But to Ginny, it was now the place she called home.

—Greta Manville, *Heart of a Dreamer*

Now

Light slices the darkness, jerking me awake.

My right eye—someone's prying it open. Latex-gloved fingers part the lids.

There's more light now. Harsh. A penlight, aimed at my pupil.

The same is done to my left eye. Pry. Part. Light.

The fingers release, and I'm plunged back into darkness.

Someone speaks. A man; a gentle voice. "Can you hear me?"

I open my mouth, and hot pain circles my jaw. "Yes."

My voice is a rasp. My throat is parched. So are my lips, save for a single slick spot of wet warmth with a metallic taste.

"Am I bleeding?"

"You are," says the same voice as before. "Just a little. Could have been worse."

"A lot worse," another voice says.

"Where am I?"

The first voice answers. "A hospital, honey. We're taking you for some tests. We need to see how banged up you really are."

It dawns on me that I'm in motion. I can hear the hum of wheels on tile and feel the slight wobble of a gurney. I try to move but can't. My arms and legs are strapped down. Something is pythoned around my neck, holding my head in place.

Others are with me. The two voices, and someone else pushing the gurney. Warm huffs of breath brush my earlobe.

"Let's see how much you can remember." It's the first voice again. "Think you can answer some questions for me?"

"Yes."

"What's your name?"

"Jules. Jules Larsen."

"Hi, Jules," the man says. "I'm Bernard."

I want to say hello back, but my jaw still hurts. As does my entire left side from knee to shoulder. As does my head.

"How old are you, Jules?" Bernard asks.

"Twenty-five." I stop, overcome with a fresh blast of pain. "What happened to me?"

"You were hit by a car, honey," Bernard says.

This is breaking news to me. I don't recall anything.

"When?"

"Just a few minutes ago."

"Where?"

"Right outside the Bartholomew."

My eyes snap open, this time on their own.

I blink against the harsh fluorescents zipping by overhead as the gurney speeds along. Keeping pace is Bernard. He has dark skin, bright scrubs, brown eyes. They're kind eyes, which is why I stare into them, pleading.

"Please," I beg. "Please don't send me back there."

Chapter 1

Six Days Earlier

THE ELEVATOR RESEMBLES a birdcage. The tall, ornate kind—all thin bars and gilded exterior. I even think of birds as I step inside. Exotic and bright and lush.

Everything I'm not.

But the woman next to me certainly fills the bill, with her blue Chanel suit, blond updo, and perfectly manicured hands weighed down by several rings. She might be in her fifties. Botox has made her face tight and gleaming. Her voice is champagne bright and just as bubbly. She even has an elegant name—Leslie Evelyn.

Because this is technically a job interview, I also wear a suit.

Black. Not Chanel.

My shoes are from Payless. The brown hair brushing my shoulders is on the ragged side. Normally, I would have gone to Supercuts for a trim, but even that's now out of my price range.

I nod with feigned interest as Leslie Evelyn says, "The elevator is original, of course. As is the main staircase. Not much in the lobby has changed since this place opened in 1919."

Leslie and I stand shoulder to shoulder in the surprisingly small elevator car. There's red carpet on the floor and gold leaf on the ceiling. On three sides, oak-paneled walls rise to waist height, where they're replaced by a series of narrow windows.

The elevator car has two doors—one with wire-thin bars that closes by itself, plus a crisscross grate Leslie slides into place before tapping the button for the top floor. Then we're off, rising slowly but surely into one of Manhattan's most storied addresses.

Had I known the apartment was in this building, I never would have responded to the ad. I would have considered it a waste of time. I'm not a Leslie Evelyn, who carries a caramel-colored atta-ché case and looks at ease in a place like this. I'm Jules Larsen, the product of a Pennsylvania coal town with less than five hundred dollars in my checking account.

I do not belong here.

But the ad didn't mention an address. It simply announced the need for an apartment sitter and provided a phone number to call if interested. I was. I did. Leslie Evelyn answered and gave me an interview time and an address. Lower seventies, Upper West Side. I didn't know what I was getting into until I stood outside the building, triple-checking the address.

The Bartholomew.

One of Manhattan's most recognizable apartment buildings—a sliver of stone rising over Central Park West. The main reason for its fame is its gargoyles. The classic kind, with bat wings and devil horns. They're everywhere, from the pair that sits over the arched front door to the ones crouched on each corner of the slanted roof. More inhabit the building's facade. They sit on marble out-croppings, arms raised to the ledges above, as if they alone are keeping the Bartholomew upright.

Over the years, the Bartholomew and its gargoyles have graced a thousand photographs. I've seen it on postcards, in ads, as a back-drop for fashion shoots. It's been in the movies. And on TV. And on the cover of a bestselling novel published in the eighties called *Heart of a Dreamer*, which is how I first learned about it. Jane had a copy and would often read it aloud to me as I lay sprawled across her twin bed.

The book tells the fanciful tale of a twenty-year-old orphan named Ginny who, through a twist of fate and the benevolence of a grandmother she never knew, finds herself living at the Bar-tholomew. Ginny navigates her posh new surroundings in a series of increasingly elaborate party dresses while juggling several suit-ors. It's fluff, to be sure, but the wonderful kind.

As Jane would read, I'd stare at the book's cover, which shows an across-the-street view of the Bartholomew. There were no buildings like that where we grew up. It was just row houses and storefronts with sooty windows. The Bartholomew was worlds away from the tidy duplex we shared with our parents.

"Someday I'm going to live there," Jane often said.

"And I'll visit," I'd always pipe up.

Jane would then stroke my hair. "Visit? You'll be living there with me, Julie-girl."

None of those childhood fantasies came true, of course. This elevator ride is as close as I'm going to get.

The elevator shaft is tucked into a nook of the staircase, which winds upward through the center of the building. I can see it through the elevator windows as we rise. Between each floor is ten steps, a landing, then ten more steps.

On one of the landings, an elderly man wheezes his way down the stairs with the help of an exhausted-looking woman in purple scrubs. She waits patiently, gripping the man's arm as he pauses to catch his breath. As the elevator passes, I catch them taking a quick look just before the next floor blocks them from view.

"Residential units are located on eleven floors, starting with the second," Leslie says. "The ground floor contains staff offices and employee-only areas, plus our maintenance department. Storage facilities are in the basement. There are four units on each floor. Two in the front. Two in the back."

We pass another floor, the elevator slow but steady. On this level, a woman around Leslie's age waits for the return trip. Dressed in leggings, UGGS, and a bulky white sweater, she walks an impossibly tiny dog on a studded leash. She gives Leslie a polite wave while staring at me from behind oversize sunglasses. In that brief moment when we're face-to-face, I recognize the woman. She's a soap-opera actress. At least she used to be.

"Is that—"

Leslie stops me with a raised hand. "We never discuss residents. It's one of the unspoken rules here. The Bartholomew prides itself on discretion."

"But celebrities do live here?"

"Not really," Leslie says. "Which is fine by us. The last thing we want are paparazzi waiting outside. Our residents like their privacy.

A good many of them use dummy corporations to buy their apartments so the purchase doesn't become public record."

The elevator comes to a rattling stop at the top of the stairs, and Leslie says, "Here we are. Twelfth floor."

She yanks open the grate and steps out, her heels clicking on the floor. The hallway walls are burgundy, with sconces placed at regular intervals. We pass two unmarked doors before the hall dead-ends at a wide wall that contains two more doors. Unlike the others, these are marked—12A and 12B.

"I thought there were four units on each floor," I say.

"There are," Leslie says. "Except this one. The twelfth floor is special."

I glance back at the doors behind us. "Then what are those?"

"Storage areas. Access to the roof. Nothing exciting." She reaches into her attaché to retrieve a set of keys, which she uses to unlock 12A. "Here's where the real excitement is."

The door swings open, and Leslie steps aside, revealing a tasteful foyer. There's a coat rack, a gilded mirror, and a table containing a lamp, a vase, and a small bowl to hold keys. My gaze moves past the foyer into the apartment proper and a window opposite the door. Outside is one of the most stunning views I've ever seen.

Central Park. Late fall. Amber sun slanting across orange-gold leaves. All from a bird's-eye view of one hundred and fifty feet.

The window providing the view stretches from floor to ceiling in a formal sitting room on the other side of a hallway. I cross the hall and head to the window. Straight ahead are Central Park Lake and the graceful span of Bow Bridge. To the right is the Sheep Meadow, its expanse of green speckled with people basking in the autumn sun. Belvedere Castle sits to the left, backdropped by the stately gray stone of the Metropolitan Museum of Art.

I take in the view, slightly breathless.

I've seen it in my mind's eye as I read *Heart of a Dreamer.* This is the exact view Ginny had from her apartment in the book.

For a brief moment, it's my reality. In spite of everything I've gone through. Maybe even because of it. Being here has the feel of fate somehow intervening, even as I'm again struck by that all-consuming thought—*I do not belong here.*

"I'm sorry," I say as I pry myself away from the window. "I think there's been a huge misunderstanding."

Leslie tilts her head, giving me a confused look.

"You don't like the apartment?" she says.

"I love it. But I'm not looking for an apartment. I mean, I am, but I could save every penny until I'm a hundred, and I still wouldn't be able to afford this place."

"The apartment isn't available yet," Leslie says. "It just needs someone to occupy it for the next three months."

"There's no way someone would willingly pay me to live here. Even for three months."

"You're wrong there. That's exactly what we want."

Leslie gestures to a sofa in the center of the room. Upholstered in crimson velvet, it looks more expensive than my first car. I sit tentatively. Leslie takes a seat in a matching easy chair opposite the sofa. Between us is a mahogany coffee table on which rests a potted orchid, its petals white and pristine.

The entire sitting room is done up in reds and wood tones. It's comfortable, if a bit stuffy. Grandfather clock ticking away in the corner. Velvet curtains and wooden shutters at the windows. Brass telescope on a tripod, aimed not at the heavens but at Central Park.

The wallpaper is a red floral pattern—an ornate expanse of petals spread open like fans and overlapping in elaborate combinations. At the ceiling are matching strips of crown molding, the plaster blossoming into curlicues at the corners.

"Here's the situation," Leslie says. "Another rule at the Bartholomew is that no unit can stay empty for more than a month. It's an old rule and, some would say, a strange one. But those of us who live here agree that there's security to think about. If word gets out that a place in the Bartholomew is going to be empty for a few months, there's no telling who might try to break in."

"So you're looking for a guard?"

"We're looking for a *resident*," Leslie says. "A person to breathe life into the building. For example, the owner of this place recently passed away. She was a widow. Had no children of her own. Just some greedy nieces and nephews in London currently fighting over who should get the place. Until that gets resolved, this apartment will sit vacant."

"Why don't the nieces and nephews just sublet?"

"That's not allowed here. There's nothing to stop someone from subletting a place and then doing who-knows-what to it."

I nod, understanding. "By paying someone to stay here, you're making sure they don't do anything to the apartment."

"Think of it as an insurance policy," Leslie says. "One that pays quite nicely, I might add. In the case of 12A, the family of the late owner is offering four thousand dollars a month."

My hands, which until now had been placed primly on my lap, drop to my sides. The pay is staggering—more than enough to tide me over while I put my life back together.

"I assume you're interested," Leslie says.

Every so often, life offers you a reset button. When it does, you need to press it as hard as you can.

Jane said that to me once. Back in our reading-on-her-bed days, when I was too young to understand what she meant. Now I do.

"I'm very interested," I say.

Leslie smiles. "Then let's get on with the interview, shall we?"

LESLIE conducts the rest of the interview during a tour of the apartment. First stop is the study, to the right of the sitting room. It's very masculine. All dark greens and whiskey-colored woods. The wallpaper pattern is the same as in the sitting room, only here it's a bright emerald.

"What's your current employment situation?" Leslie asks.

I could—and likely should—tell her that this time two weeks ago I was an administrative assistant at one of the nation's biggest financial firms. It wasn't much—just lots of photocopying and coffee fetching. But it paid the bills and provided me with health insurance. Until I was let go along with 10 percent of the staff. *Restructuring.* My boss thought that sounded nicer than *layoffs.*

"I'm currently between jobs," I say.

Leslie reacts with the slightest of nods. I don't know if that's a good sign or a bad one. The questions continue as we return to the main hall.

"Do you smoke?"

"No."

"Drink?"

"An occasional glass of wine with dinner."

Except for two weeks ago, when my best friend, Chloe, took me out to drown my sorrows in margaritas. I ended the night puking in an alley. Another thing Leslie doesn't need to know.

The hallway makes a sudden turn to the left. Rather than follow it, Leslie steers me to the right, into a formal dining room so lovely it makes me gasp. The hardwood floors have been polished to a mirror shine. A chandelier hangs over a long table that can easily seat twelve. The busy floral wallpaper is light yellow. The room is situated on the corner of the building, offering views of Central Park on one side, the building next door on the other.

I circle the table, running a finger along the wood as Leslie says, "What's your relationship status? While we don't exactly frown on having couples as apartment sitters, we prefer people who are unattached. It makes things easier from a legal standpoint."

"I'm single," I say, trying hard to keep bitterness from seeping into my voice.

Left out is the fact that on the same day I lost my job, I returned home early to the apartment I shared with my boyfriend, Andrew. At night, he worked as a janitor in the building where my office was located. During the day, he was a part-time student at Pace University majoring in finance and, apparently, having sex with one of his classmates while I was at work.

That's what they were doing when I walked in with my little box of things hastily cleared from my cubicle. They hadn't even made it to the bedroom.

I'd be sad about the whole thing if I wasn't still so angry. And hurt. And blaming myself for settling for someone like Andrew.

Leslie leads me into the kitchen, which has two entrances—one from the dining room, one from the hall. I rotate slowly, dazzled by its pristine whiteness, its granite countertops, its breakfast nook by the window. "It's massive," I say, awed by its sheer size.

"It's a throwback from when the Bartholomew first opened," Leslie says. "It used to be the kitchen and servants' quarters for a much larger unit below. See?"

Leslie moves to a cupboard with a sliding door that's tucked between the oven and the sink. When she lifts the door, I see a dark shaft and two tendrils of rope hanging from a pulley above.

"Is that a dumbwaiter?"

"It is. But it hasn't been used for decades." She lets the dumbwaiter door slam shut, suddenly back to interview mode. "Tell me about your family. Any next of kin?"

This one's harder to answer, mainly because it's worse than losing a job or being cheated on. Whatever I say could open the floodgates to more questions with even sadder responses.

"Orphan," I say.

It's almost the truth. My parents were the only children of only children. There are no aunts, uncles, or cousins. There's only Jane.

Also dead. Maybe. Probably.

"Since there's no next of kin, whom should we contact in case of an emergency?"

Two weeks ago, that would have been Andrew. Now it's Chloe, I guess, although she's not officially listed on any forms.

"No one," I say, realizing how pathetic that sounds. So I add a slightly hopeful caveat. "For now."

Eager to change the subject, I peek through the door just off the kitchen. Leslie gets the hint and ushers me into another hallway. It contains a guest bathroom she doesn't even bother to show off, a closet, and—the big surprise—a spiral staircase.

"Oh, my. There's a *second floor?*"

Leslie gives a happy nod. "It's a special feature exclusive to the two units on the twelfth floor. Go ahead. Take a look."

I bound up the steps to a bedroom that's even more perfect than the kitchen. Here the floral wallpaper actually works with the room. It's the lightest shade of blue. The color of a spring sky.

Like the dining room directly below, it's located on a corner of the building. The massive bed's been placed so that whoever is in it can gaze out the windows flanking the corner. And just outside those windows is the pièce de résistance—a gargoyle.

It sits on the corner ledge, its wings spread so that the edge of one can be glimpsed through the north-facing window and the other through the one pointing east.

"Beautiful, isn't it?" Leslie says, suddenly behind me. I hadn't even noticed her come up the steps. I was too taken with the gargoyle, the room, the whole idea that I could get paid to live here.

"Yes, beautiful," I say, awed by it all.

"Once upon a time it housed several servants," she adds. "They lived here, cooked downstairs, worked a few floors below."

I cross the room on white carpet so plush I'm tempted to kick off my shoes and see how it feels on bare feet. The wall to the right bears two doors. One leads to the master bath. A quick look inside reveals a shower encased in glass and a claw-foot bathtub. Through the other door is a massive walk-in closet.

"This closet is bigger than my childhood bedroom," I say. "Scratch that. It's bigger than every bedroom I've ever had."

Leslie, who's been checking her hair in the mirror, turns and says, "Since you've brought up living arrangements, what's your current address?"

Another tricky topic. I moved out the same day I found Andrew with his classmate. For the past two weeks I've been crashing on Chloe's couch in Jersey City.

"I'm between apartments," I say.

Leslie blinks rapidly. "*Between* apartments?"

"My old place went co-op," I lie. "I'm living with a friend until I can find something else."

"Staying here would be very convenient for you, I imagine," Leslie says tactfully.

In truth, living here would be a lifesaver. It would give me a home base from which to search for a job. And when it was all over, I'd have twelve grand in the bank. Mustn't forget about that.

"Well, then, let's finish up and see if you're the right fit."

Leslie leads me out of the bedroom, down the steps, and back to the crimson sofa in the sitting room. There, I resume my hands-in-lap seated position.

"Just a few more questions and we'll be done," Leslie says as she opens her attaché case and pulls out a pen and what looks to be an application form. "Do you have any illnesses or health conditions we should be aware of?"

"Why do you need to know that?"

"Emergency purposes," Leslie says. "Because there's currently no one we can contact if, God forbid, something happens to you while you're here. It's standard policy, I assure you."

"No illnesses," I say.

Leslie's pen hovers over the page. "So no heart problems or anything of that nature?"

"No."

"And my last question: Would you consider yourself to be an inquisitive person?"

Inquisitive. Now, there's a word I never expected to hear during this interview. "I'm not sure I understand," I say.

"Then I'll be blunt," Leslie replies. "As you probably know, the Bartholomew has a reputation for secrecy. People are curious about what goes on inside these walls. In the past, some apartment sitters have arrived looking for dirt. About the building, its residents. So if you're here for gossip, it's best we part ways now."

I shake my head. "I don't care what happens here. Honestly, I just need some money and a place to live for a few months."

That ends the interview. Leslie stands, smoothing her skirt. "The way it usually goes is that I'll tell you to expect a phone call if we're interested. But I see no point in making you wait. We'd love for you to stay here."

At first I think I've misheard her. I give a blank stare.

"You're joking," I say.

"I'm as serious as can be. We'll need to run a background check, of course. But you seem like a perfect fit."

That's when it hits me: I get to live *here.* In the Bartholomew, of all places. In an apartment beyond my wildest dreams.

Even better, I'll be paid to do it. Twelve thousand dollars.

Happy tears form in my eyes. "Thank you," I say. "Truly. It's the opportunity of a lifetime."

Leslie beams. "It's my pleasure, Jules. Welcome to the Bartholomew. I think you're going to love it here."

"THERE'S a catch, right?" Chloe says before taking a sip of Two-Buck Chuck from Trader Joe's. "I mean, there has to be."

"That's what I thought," I say. "But if there is, I can't find it."

The two of us are in the living room of Chloe's non-luxury apartment in Jersey City, seated around the coffee table that has become our regular dining spot since I started crashing here. Tonight it's scattered with cartons of cheap Chinese takeout.

"It's not like it's some kind of vacation," I say. "It's a legitimate job. I have to take care of the place."

Chloe pauses mid-bite. "Wait—you're not actually going to do this, are you?"

"Of course I am. I can move in tomorrow."

"*Tomorrow?* Jules, you know I'm not paranoid, but this is ringing alarm bells. You don't know these people. Did they even tell you what happened to the woman who lived there?"

"She died."

"Did they say how?" Chloe says. "Or where? Maybe she died in that apartment. Maybe she was murdered."

"You're being weird."

"I'm being cautious. There's a difference." Chloe takes another gulp of wine, exasperated. "Will you at least let Paul take a look at the paperwork before you sign anything?"

Chloe's boyfriend is currently clerking at a big-time law firm while prepping for the bar exam. After the bar, they plan to get married, move to the suburbs, and have two kids and a dog.

"I already signed it," I say. "A three-month contract."

That last part is a bit of an exaggeration. It was a letter of agreement instead of a contract. I say it because Chloe works in human resources. Contracts impress her.

"What about tax forms?" she says. "Did you fill one out?"

To avoid answering, I poke my chopsticks into my fried rice.

"Jules, you cannot take a job that pays you under the table. It's illegal."

"All I care about is twelve thousand dollars. I need that money."

"I told you, I can loan you money."

"That I won't be able to pay back."

"You *will*," Chloe insists. "Eventually. You're my best friend going through a rough patch, and I'm happy to let you stay as long as you need. You'll be back on your feet in no time."

Chloe has more faith than I do. I've spent the past two weeks wondering just how, exactly, my life has gone so spectacularly off the rails. I'm smart. A hard worker. A good person. At least I try to be. Yet all it took to flatten me was the one-two punch of losing my job and Andrew being a garbage human being.

"I need to do this," I tell Chloe. "Is it unusual? I admit it is. But sometimes good things happen to good people, right when they need it the most."

Chloe scoots next to me and pulls me into a ferocious embrace, something she's been doing ever since we ended up being freshmen roommates at Penn State.

"I'd feel better if it was any building but the Bartholomew."

"What's wrong with the Bartholomew?"

"I've heard"—Chloe pauses, seeking an appropriately ominous word—"stuff. My grandparents lived on the Upper West Side. My grandfather refused to walk on the same side of the street as the Bartholomew. He said it was cursed."

I reach for my lo mein. "I think that says more about your grandfather than it does the Bartholomew."

"He believed it," Chloe says. "He told me the man who built it killed himself. He jumped right off the roof."

"I'm not going to turn this down just because of something your grandfather said."

"All I'm saying is that it wouldn't hurt to be a little cautious while you're there. If something feels off, come right back here. The couch is always open."

"I appreciate the offer," I say. "I do. And who knows? I might be right back here three months from now. But cursed or not, staying at the Bartholomew is the best way out of this mess."

Not every person gets a do-over in their life. My father certainly didn't. Neither did my mother. But I now have that chance.

Life is offering me a building-size reset button.

I intend to press it as hard as I can.

Now

I WAKE with a start, confused. I don't know where I am, and that terrifies me. Lifting my head, I see a dim room, brightened slightly by a rectangle of light stretching from the open door. Beyond the door is a glimpse of a hallway, the sound of hushed voices, the squelch of sneakers on a floor.

The pain that had screamed along my left side and in my head is now only a slight murmur. I suspect I have painkillers to thank for that. My brain and body feel like I've been stuffed with cotton.

Panicked, I take stock of all the things that have been done to me while I was unconscious. IV tube attached to my hand. Bandage wrapped around my left wrist. Brace around my neck. Bandage at my temple, which I press with curious fingers. The pressure sends up a flare of pain.

A light flicks on, revealing white walls, a chair in the corner, a Monet print in a cheap black frame.

A nurse enters. The same one from earlier. The one with the kind eyes. Bernard. "Hey there, Sleeping Beauty," he says.

I look around the room. It's windowless. "Where am I?"

"A hospital room, honey."

Relief washes over me. The kind of blessed relief that brings tears to my eyes. Bernard grabs a tissue, dabs my cheeks.

"There's no need to cry," he says. "It's not that bad."

He's right. It's not bad at all. In fact, it's wonderful. I'm safe.

I'm nowhere near the Bartholomew.

Chapter 2

Five Days Earlier

IN THE MORNING, I give Chloe an extended hug goodbye before taking an Uber into Manhattan. A splurge while carrying my belongings. Not that I have much. I allowed myself exactly one night to move out of the apartment after I found Andrew and his "friend." I simply said, "Get out. Don't come back until morning. I'll be gone by then."

Andrew didn't argue, which told me everything I needed to know. While he was gone, I methodically packed, choosing what could stay and what I couldn't live without. My entire life now fits into a suitcase and four fifteen-by-twelve-inch storage boxes.

After the car pulls up to the Bartholomew, I slip out and gaze at the facade of my temporary home. The gargoyles over the doorway stare back. With their arched spines and open wings, they look ready to hop from their perch to greet me. That duty instead goes to the doorman standing directly beneath them. Tall and bulky, with ruddy cheeks and a Fuller Brush mustache, he's by my side the moment the Uber driver pops the trunk.

"Let me get those for you," he says, reaching for the boxes. "You must be Miss Larsen. I'm Charlie."

I grab my suitcase, wanting to make myself at least a little bit useful. "Nice to meet you, Charlie."

"Likewise. And welcome to the Bartholomew. I'll take care of your things. You go on inside. Miss Evelyn is expecting you."

Sure enough, Leslie is waiting in the lobby. She wears another Chanel suit. Yellow instead of blue.

"Welcome, welcome," she says cheerily, punctuating it with air kisses on both of my cheeks. Spotting the suitcase, she says, "Is Charlie taking care of the rest of your things?"

"He is."

"He's a dream, that Charlie. If you ever need him, he'll either be outside or right in there."

She points to a small room just off the lobby. Through the doorway, I glimpse a chair, a desk, and a row of security monitors glowing blue-gray. One of them shows an angled image of two women paused in the lobby. It takes me a second to realize I'm one of them. Leslie is the other.

I follow her to a wall of mailboxes on the other side of the lobby. There are forty-two of them, beginning with 2A. Leslie holds up a tiny key on a plain ring marked 12A.

"Here's your mail key." She gives it to me the way a grandmother hands out hard candy—dropping it directly into my open palm.

"You're expected to check the mail every day. The late owner's family requested that whatever does arrive be forwarded to them. As for your own mail, we recommend getting a post-office box. Receiving personal mail at this address is strictly prohibited."

I give a quick nod. "Understood."

"Now let's get you up to the apartment. On the way there, we can go over the rest of the rules."

She crosses the lobby again. Trailing behind her with my suitcase, I say, "Rules?"

We stand by the elevator, which is currently in use. Through the gilded bars, I see cables in motion, slithering upward. A few floors above us, the elevator car hums as it descends.

"No visitors," Leslie says. "That's the biggest one. And when I say no visitors, I mean absolutely no one. No friends. No family members. And definitely no strangers. I can't stress this enough."

My first thought is Chloe, to whom I had promised a tour tonight. She's not going to like this. She'll tell me it's a sign—another alarm bell. Not that I need Chloe's help to hear this one.

The elevator arrives, bringing with it a man in his early twenties. He's short but muscular, with a broad chest and big arms. His hair—black, obviously dyed—flops over his right eye. Small ebony disks rest in both earlobes.

"Well, isn't this marvelous?" Leslie says. "Jules, I'd like to introduce you to Dylan. He's another apartment sitter."

I had already intuited this. His T-shirt and baggy black jeans, frayed at the cuffs, gave it away. Like me, he doesn't belong in the Bartholomew.

"Dylan, this is Jules."

Rather than shake my hand, Dylan shoves his hands into his pockets and gives me a half-mumbled hello.

"Jules is moving in today," Leslie tells him.

"Nice meeting you, Jules. I'll see you around," Dylan says, his eyes aimed at the marble floor between his sneakers.

He pushes past us, his hands still shoved deep into his pockets.

"A nice young man," Leslie says once we're in the elevator. "Quiet, which is what we like around here."

"How many apartment sitters currently live here?"

Leslie slides the grate across the elevator door. "You make three. Dylan's on eleven, as is Ingrid."

She hits the button for the twelfth floor, and the elevator again creaks to life. As we rise to our destination, she goes over the rest of the rules. Although I'm allowed to come and go as I please, I must spend each night in the apartment. It makes sense. That is, after all, what I'm being paid to do. Live there. Occupy the place.

Smoking isn't allowed, of course. Nor are drugs—another no-brainer. Alcohol is tolerated if consumed responsibly, which is a relief, seeing how there are two bottles of wine Chloe gifted me in one of the boxes Charlie's set to deliver to my door.

"You're to keep everything in pristine condition at all times," Leslie says. "You need to leave the place looking exactly the way it did when you arrived."

Other than not allowing visitors, none of this sounds unreasonable. But then Leslie adds another rule.

"One last thing. As I mentioned yesterday, the residents here enjoy their privacy, and we insist that you don't bother them. Speak only if spoken to. Also, never discuss residents beyond these walls. Do you use social media?"

"Just Facebook and Instagram," I say. "And both very rarely."

For the past two weeks, my social media usage has consisted of checking LinkedIn for potential job leads.

"Be sure not to mention this place there. We monitor our apartment sitters' social media accounts, again for privacy reasons. If the inside of the Bartholomew shows up on Instagram, the person who posted it is forced to leave immediately." The elevator shimmies to a stop on the top floor. Leslie throws open the grate and says, "Do you have any other questions?"

I do, only I'm afraid to ask for fear of sounding indelicate. But then I think about my checking account and decide I don't care.

"When do I get paid?" I say.

"A very good question that I'm so glad you asked," Leslie replies, tactful as always. "You'll receive your first payment five days from now. A thousand dollars. Cash. Charlie will hand-deliver it to you at the end of the day. He'll do the same at the end of every week you're here."

My body practically melts with relief. I was afraid it wouldn't be until after my three months were up.

"I'll let you get settled in." Leslie holds up a key ring. Attached to it are two keys, one big, one small. "The big one is to the apartment. The small one opens the storage unit in the basement."

Instead of dropping it into my hand, she places the key ring in my palm before gently curling my fingers around it. Then with a smile and a wink, she returns to the waiting elevator and is lowered out of view.

Alone now, I turn to 12A and take a deep, steadying breath.

One thousand dollars every week. Money I can use to erase debt and save for a future that's suddenly far brighter than it was a day ago. A future that's just on the other side of that door.

I unlock it and step inside.

I NAME the gargoyle outside the window George.

It comes to me as I haul the last of my boxes into the bedroom. Standing at the top of the staircase, I look out the window, drawn to that sumptuous view of the park. Late morning sunlight pours through, silhouetting the curve of wings just beyond the glass.

"Hi, George," I say. "Looks like we're roommates."

The rest of the day is spent making this deceased stranger's apartment feel like my home. I transfer my wardrobe to the closet and arrange my meager beauty products on the bathroom counter.

In the bedroom, I personalize the nightstand with a framed photo of Jane and my parents. The picture, taken by fifteen-year-old me, shows them standing in front of Bushkill Falls in the Poconos. Two years later, Jane was gone.

Two years after that, so were my parents. Not a day goes by when I don't miss them, but today that feeling is especially acute.

Joining the photo on the nightstand is my battered copy of *Heart of a Dreamer*. The very copy Jane read to me.

"I'm totally a Ginny," Jane said during that first read, referring to the book's main character. "Hopeful, tempestuous—"

"What does that mean?" I had asked.

"That I feel too much."

That definitely summed up Ginny, who experienced everything with a combination of joy and ecstasy. And the reader is swept right along with her, experiencing her lows and her highs. It's why *Heart of a Dreamer* has become a touchstone for generations of girls. It's the life many dream of but few get to experience.

I stare at *Heart of a Dreamer*'s cover, once again not quite believing I'm now inside the same building pictured there. I even spot the window of the very room I'm in. And right next to it is George. Perched on the corner of the building.

I touch the image of the gargoyle and feel a pang of affection. For the next three months, George is mine. It's my window he sits outside, and thus he belongs to me.

With the book in its rightful place, I sit beside George at the bedroom window with my phone and laptop. First, I text Chloe, canceling the plan for her to visit the apartment tonight.

Chloe's reply comes three seconds after I send the text.

Why can't I come over?

I start to type that I'm not feeling well but think better of it. If I know Chloe, she'll be at the door in an hour with a gallon of chicken soup and a bottle of Robitussin.

Job hunting, I text back.

So when can I see the place? Paul wants a tour, too.

I have no more excuses at the ready. I need to tell her the truth.

You can't.

Chloe's reply is immediate. *Why not???*

No visitors. Building policy.

I've barely finished sending the text when my phone rings.

"No visitors?" Chloe says as soon as I answer. "I've never heard of a building telling residents they can't have guests."

"But rich and important people live here. Emphasis on the *rich*. And they're big on privacy. I can't really blame them."

"Between this no-visitors thing and what Paul has told me about the place, I'm starting to get freaked out."

"What did Paul say?"

"Just that it's all so secretive," Chloe says. "He said it's next to impossible to live there. The president of his firm wanted to buy there. They wouldn't even let him inside the building. They told him nothing was available but that they could put him on a ten-year waiting list. And then there's the article I read."

My mind is starting to spin. "What article?"

"I found it online. I'm going to email it to you. It talks about all the weird stuff that's happened at the Bartholomew. Illnesses and strange accidents. A witch lived there, Jules. An actual witch. I'm telling you, that place is shady."

"It's the complete opposite of shady."

"Then what would you call it?"

"I call it a job." I look out the window, taking in George's wing, the park below. "A dream job. In a dream apartment. Why should I give that up? Just because the people who live here are private?"

"What you really should be asking is *why* they're so private," Chloe says. "Because, in my experience, if something seems too good to be true, that's because it is."

The call ends with our agreeing to disagree. We make plans to have dinner soon, even though I can't afford it until next week.

That task out of the way, I go about looking for a job. I wasn't lying to Chloe about that. It's how I plan to spend today—and all the days after it. I grab my laptop and check the latest postings on a half dozen different job sites. There are plenty of openings available, just not for me. The curse of being your basic office drone. I'm a dime a dozen, and everyone is looking for a quarter.

Still, I make a note of all the jobs that land within my narrow window of qualifications and compose cover letters for each of them. I send them off with my résumé.

My expectations of hearing back from them aren't high. Lately I've found it best not to get my hopes up. My father was the same way. *Hope for the best, prepare for the worst,* he used to say.

By the end, he ran out of hope, and nothing could have prepared him for what lay in store.

With the job search, such as it is, out of the way, I open a spreadsheet on my laptop and try to come up with a budget for the next few weeks. It's frighteningly tight. All I have to live on is what's in my checking account, a figure that makes my heart sink.

I have only four hundred and thirty-two dollars to my name.

Thanks to a wretched cell phone contract that I can't escape for another year, another hundred and ten bucks is gone in an instant.

I now have only three hundred and twenty-two dollars.

I console myself with the fact that an unemployment check will be automatically deposited into my account at the stroke of midnight. It's cold comfort. I'd rather be receiving an employment check for an honest week's work.

I decide to clean, even though the apartment's already sparkling. I start in the upstairs bathroom, wiping down the spotless countertops and spraying the mirrors with glass cleaner. Then it's on to the bedroom, where I dust and sweep the carpet with a sleek vacuum I found in the hall closet.

The cleaning continues in the study, where I run a feather duster over the desk, the top of which has been cleared of the previous owner's belongings. It strikes me as odd that so much of what she owned remains in the apartment. Her furniture. Her dishes. Her vacuum. Yet anything that could identify her has been removed.

I look around the study, acutely aware that I've moved from cleaning to snooping. But not in a prurient way. I have no interest in any of the dead owner's dirty secrets. What I'm after is a hint of who she was.

I search the bookshelf first, scanning the rows of volumes for signs of the dead owner's profession. The books are either classics bound in faux leather or bestsellers from a decade ago. Only one catches my attention—*Heart of a Dreamer*.

It's a hardcover, in perfect condition. So unlike my beloved paperback. When I flip the book over, the author stares back at me.

Greta Manville.

It's not an entirely flattering picture. Her face is made up of harsh angles. Sharp cheekbones. Pointy chin. Narrow nose. On her lips is the barest hint of a smile. It's as if she and the photographer shared a private joke right before the shutter clicked.

I put *Heart of a Dreamer* back on the shelf and move to the desk. Its contents are disappointingly generic. Paper clips and Bic pens in the top drawer. A few old copies of the *New Yorker* in the bottom ones. Definitely no documents with names on them.

But then I notice the address labels stuck to the magazine covers. All of them bear not only the Bartholomew's address and this apartment number but also a single name: Marjorie Milton.

I can't help but feel let down. I've never heard of her.

Disappointed, I drop the magazines back in the desk and continue cleaning, this time in the sitting room. I hit the biggies—carpet, windows, coffee table—before running a dust mop across the crown molding, my nose mere inches from the wallpaper.

The pattern is even more oppressive up close. All those flowers opening like mouths, their petals colliding. The oval spaces between them remind me of eyes.

I take a step back and squint. My hope is that it'll erase the impression. It doesn't. Not only are the eyes still there, but the spreading petals also take on the shapes of faces. Grotesque ones with warped noses and elongated jaws that make it look as though they're talking. But these walls don't talk. They observe.

Yet something inside the apartment is making noise. I hear it from my spot in the sitting room—a muffled creak. The creak is accompanied by the groan of something being forced into motion. It brings to mind rusty cogs and stiff joints.

I follow the sound to its point of origin in the kitchen, at the cupboard between the oven and the sink. The dumbwaiter.

I throw open the cupboard door, revealing the empty shaft behind it. The ropes that hung lazily when Leslie showed me the dumbwaiter during my tour are now taut and in motion. Above, the pulley turns, stopping and starting with each tug of the rope.

I peek into the shaft. At first I see nothing. Just inky darkness. Then something emerges from the black, rising to meet me. Soon I can make out the top of the dumbwaiter itself.

The pulley turns and squeaks. When it finally stops, the once-empty space is filled with the dumbwaiter. It's a perfect fit. A casual visitor opening the cupboard door wouldn't even know it was a dumbwaiter. It's a plain wooden box, just like any cupboard.

Resting on the bottom is a piece of paper. Its left edge is slightly ragged, indicating it was torn from a book. Printed on it is a single poem. Emily Dickinson. "Because I Could Not Stop for Death."

I turn the page over and see that someone has written on the back, the letters large and in all caps: *HELLO AND WELCOME!*

Beneath it is the messenger's name—*Ingrid*.

I search the kitchen for a pen and paper, finding both in a junk drawer. I write my response—*Hi and thanks*—before placing it inside the dumbwaiter and giving the rope a tug.

The dumbwaiter shimmies. The pulley above it creaks.

It's not until the dumbwaiter begins to descend that I realize how big it really is. The same size as an adult male and almost as heavy. As it descends, I count how far I think it's traveled.

Five feet. Ten feet. Fifteen. Just before I hit twenty, the rope goes slack. The dumbwaiter has been lowered as far as it can go, which by my estimate means the apartment directly below—11A.

Home of the mysterious Ingrid. Even though I have no idea who she is, I think I like her already.

IN THE afternoon, I head out to buy groceries, taking the elevator from the silent twelfth floor past levels that are louder and livelier than my own. On the tenth floor, Beethoven drifts from an apartment down the hall. On the ninth, I spy the swing of a door being closed. With it comes a nose-stinging waft of disinfectant.

On the seventh, the elevator stops completely to pick up another passenger—the soap opera actress I saw during yesterday's tour. Today, she and her tiny dog wear matching fur-trimmed jackets.

"Room for two more?" she says.

"Of course."

I open the grate and nudge to the side so the actress and her dog can enter. Soon we're descending again.

The actress looks different up close. Maybe it's the abundant makeup she wears. Or it could be the saucer-size sunglasses she's once again wearing, which cover a third of her face.

"You're new here, aren't you?" she says.

"Just moved in," I reply, debating whether I should add that I'm getting paid to be here. I choose not to.

"I've been here six months," she says. "Had to sell my house in Malibu, but I think it'll be worth it. I'm Marianne, by the way."

I already know this, of course. Marianne Duncan, whose fashionable bitchery on the small screen was as much a part of my adolescence as reading *Heart of a Dreamer*. Marianne holds out the hand not currently occupied by a dog, and I shake it.

"I'm Jules." I look to the dog. "Who's this adorable guy?"

"This is Rufus."

I give the dog a pat. He licks my hand in response.

"Aw, he likes you," Marianne says.

Lower we go, passing two other presences from my first tour— the older man struggling down the stairs and the weary aide by his side. This time the man offers us a smile and a trembling wave.

"Keep it up, Mr. Leonard," Marianne calls to him. "You're doing great." To me, she whispers, "Heart trouble. He takes the stairs every day because he thinks it'll prevent another coronary. Then again, he used to be a senator. I'm sure that alone caused a heart attack or two."

In the lobby, I say goodbye to Marianne and Rufus and head to the mailboxes. The one for 12A is empty. No surprise there. As I turn away from it, I see someone else entering the lobby. She looks to be in her early seventies and makes no attempt to hide it. No forehead-smoothing Botox or caked-on foundation. Her face is pale and slightly puffy. Straight gray hair brushes her shoulders.

It's her eyes that really catch my attention. Bright blue even in the dim light of the lobby. We make eye contact—me staring, she politely pretending that I'm not. But I can't help it. I've seen that face a hundred times, staring at me from the back of a book cover.

"Excuse me, but are you Greta Manville? The writer?"

She gives me a Mona Lisa smile. "That would be me," she says, her voice polite but wary.

There's a flutter in my chest. "I'm Jules," I say.

Greta Manville makes no attempt to shake my hand, instead edging around me on her way to the mailboxes. I make note of the apartment number—10A. Two floors below me.

"Pleased to meet you," she says, sounding anything but pleased.

"I love your book. *Heart of a Dreamer* changed my life. I've read it, like, twenty times." I stop myself, aware that I'm gushing. I take a breath and say, as calmly as I can, "Reading it is why I moved to New York. And now I'm here. Temporarily, at least."

Greta turns away from her mailbox. Slowly. Not too curious, but enough to study me with those keen, inquisitive eyes.

"A temporary tenant?"

"Yes. Just moved in."

This prompts a slight nod from Greta, who says, "I imagine Leslie went over the rules."

"She did."

"Then I'm sure she told you about not bothering residents. You might want to keep that in mind."

Greta shuts the mailbox and edges past me again, our shoulders brushing. I shrink away. In a voice no louder than a murmur, I say, "Sorry for bothering you. I just thought you'd like to know that *Heart of a Dreamer* is my favorite book."

Greta spins around in the middle of the lobby, an armful of mail clutched against her chest. Her blue eyes have turned ice cold.

"If that's the case," she says, "then you need to read more."

The words have the impact of a slap—hot and stinging. Greta strides to the elevator, not bothering to see my reaction.

But then I turn toward the front door and see Charlie standing just inside the lobby. I think he saw enough of my conversation with Greta to know why I appear so rattled.

Tipping his cap, he says, "While I'm not allowed to speak ill of the residents, I'm also not supposed to turn a blind eye when one of them is rude. And she was very rude to you, Miss Larsen. I apologize on behalf of everyone at the Bartholomew."

"It's fine," I say. "I've been treated worse."

"Don't let it get you down." Charlie smiles and holds the door open for me. "Now go out and enjoy the beautiful day."

I step outside. On this patch of busy Manhattan sidewalk, in addition to tourists, I see dog walkers, nannies pushing strollers, harried New Yorkers doing the sidewalk slalom around them.

I join them all at the corner two blocks away from the Bartholomew, waiting for the light to change. The streetlamp there bears a taped flyer that's come loose at one edge, the paper flapping. I get glimpses of a woman with pale skin, almond-shaped eyes, and a mane of curly brown hair. Above her photo, in siren-red letters, is one dreadfully familiar word: MISSING.

Memories lurch out of nowhere, leaping on top of me until the sidewalk turns to quicksand beneath my feet. All I can think about are those first fraught days after Jane vanished.

She was also on a flyer, her yearbook photo placed under the word MISSING, which was colored a similarly urgent red. For a few weeks, that picture was everywhere in our tiny town.

I'm relieved when the light changes a second later, sending the dog walkers, nannies, and weary New Yorkers into motion across the street. I follow, my footsteps quick, putting as much distance between me and the flyer as possible.

Chapter 3

I NOW HAVE ONLY two hundred and five dollars to my name.

Grocery stores in Manhattan aren't cheap. Especially in this neighborhood. It doesn't matter that I bought the least expensive things I could find. Dried pasta and generic red sauce. Off-brand cereal. An economy-size box of frozen pizzas. My only splurge was the handful of fresh fruits and vegetables I bought to keep me from being malnourished. It's mind-boggling to me how a few oranges can cost the same as five pounds of boxed spaghetti.

I leave the store with more than a week's worth of meals carried in two sagging paper bags. They're an unwieldy pair, which shift with every step I take. But when I reach the Bartholomew, there's Charlie, who sees me coming and holds the door wide open.

"Let me carry those for you, Miss Larsen."

"I've got them. But I won't say no to being helped with the elevator."

I look across the lobby and see the elevator car descending into its gilded cage. I dash forward, hoping to catch it, when I spot a young woman flying down the stairs right beside it. She's in a hurry. Legs churning. Head down. Eyes on her phone.

"Whoa! Look out!" Charlie shouts.

But it's too late. The girl and I collide in the middle of the lobby. The girl stumbles backward. I fall completely, slamming against the floor as both grocery bags spring from my grip. Although a sharp pain shoots through my elbow and down my left arm, I'm more worried about my groceries. Thin sticks of dried spaghetti cover the floor like strands of hay. Nearby is a shattered jar oozing sauce. Oranges roll through the puddle, leaving trails of red.

The girl is by my side in an instant. "I'm so sorry! I can't believe I'm so clumsy!"

Even though she tries to help me up, I remain on the floor, scrambling to shove my groceries back into the bags. But the collision has already drawn a small crowd. There's Charlie, who hurriedly gathers the fallen groceries, and Marianne Duncan returning from taking Rufus for a walk. She stands in the doorway as Rufus yaps. The commotion brings Leslie Evelyn rushing out of her office to see what's happened.

Mortified, I continue to collect my groceries. When I reach for one of the oranges, another bolt of pain zaps through my arm.

The girl gasps. "You're bleeding."

I sneak a glance at my arm and see a long gash just below my elbow. Blood streams from the wound in a thick rivulet. Charlie yanks a handkerchief from his pocket and presses it to the wound.

Looking around, I see chunks of broken glass scattered across the floor. I can only assume one of them dug into my arm.

"Sweetie, you need to see a doctor," Leslie says. "Let me take you to the emergency room."

That would be a fine idea if I could afford it. But I can't.

"I'm fine," I say, even though I'm starting to think I'm not. The handkerchief Charlie gave me is already crimson with blood.

"You should at least see Dr. Nick," Leslie says. "He lives here—twelfth floor, same as you."

Charlie stuffs the last of my groceries into the bags. "I'll take care of these for you, Miss Larsen. Go on up and see Dr. Nick."

Leslie and the girl help me to my feet, lifting me by my good arm. Before I can protest, they're ushering me into the elevator. Only two of us can fit, which means the girl remains outside.

"Thank you, Ingrid," Leslie says before sliding the grate shut.

I stare at the girl through the grate, surprised. This is Ingrid? Although we look to be roughly the same age, she's dressed like someone younger. Oversize plaid shirt. Distressed jeans that reveal pink knees. Converse sneakers with the laces coming undone. Her hair is dark brown but had previously been dyed blue. A two-inch strip of color fans out across her back and shoulders.

Ingrid catches me staring, bites her bottom lip, and gives me an embarrassed wave, her fingers wiggling.

Inside the elevator, Leslie hits the button for the top floor, and up we go. "I'm so sorry about this," she says. "Ingrid's a lovely girl, but she can be oblivious to what's going on around her. But don't worry. Dr. Nick will fix you right up."

Soon we're at the door to 12B, Leslie giving it a series of rapid knocks while I continue to press Charlie's handkerchief against my arm. Then the door opens, and Dr. Nick stands before us.

I was expecting someone older but distinguished. Gray hair. Moist eyes. Tweed jacket. But the man at the door is a good forty years younger and a lot better-looking than the doctor of my imagination. His hair is auburn. His eyes are hazel. His outfit of khakis and a crisp white shirt reveals a tall, trim physique.

"What do we have here?" he says, his gaze moving from Leslie to me and my bloody arm.

"Accident in the lobby," Leslie tells him. "Do you think you could take a look and see if Jules here needs to go to the ER?" She nudges me gently toward the door. "Go on, sweetie. I'll check on you tomorrow." Then she hurries to the waiting elevator and descends out of sight.

I turn to Dr. Nick, who says, "Don't be nervous. I don't bite."

Maybe not, but the situation makes me uncomfortable all the same. Handsome doctor rich enough to live at the Bartholomew. Eligible girl paid to live right next door. In the movies, they'd banter, sparks would fly, and a happy ending would ensue.

But this isn't a movie. It's cold reality.

"I'm really sorry about all this, Dr. Nick."

"Don't be," he says. "Leslie was right to bring you here. And please, call me Nick. Now let's get that arm looked at."

THE apartment is almost a mirror image of 12A. The decor is different, of course, but the layout is the same, only flipped. The sitting room is straight ahead, but the study is to the left and the hallway leads to the right. I follow him past a dining room situated on the corner, just like the one in 12A. The table here is round and surrounded by red chairs.

Dr. Nick guides me into the kitchen and gestures for me to sit on a stool by the counter. "I'll be right back," he says before disappearing down the hall.

I have a look around in his absence. Our kitchens are roughly the same size and of similar layout, although Dr. Nick's has an earthier vibe. Pale brown tile and countertops the color of sand. The only splash of brightness comes from a painting that hangs over the sink. It depicts a snake with its mouth clamped down on its tail, its long body curled into a perfect figure eight.

I approach the painting, curious. It looks old, the surface spiderwebbed with a hundred tiny cracks. But the paint remains vibrant. The scales on the snake's back are scarlet. Its belly is seasick green. The one visible eye is a deep shade of yellow.

Dr. Nick returns with a first-aid kit and a medical bag.

"Ah, you've noticed my ouroboros," he says. "I picked it up during my travels abroad. Do you like it?"

That would be a definite no. It reminds me of a Mexican restaurant Andrew once took me to that had brightly decorated skulls staring from the ceiling. I spent the meal shifting with discomfort.

I do the same once I return to the stool, the snake watching me with his blazing eye. "What's its meaning?"

"It's supposed to represent the cyclical nature of the universe," Dr. Nick says. "Birth, life, death, rebirth."

I stare at the snake's eye one second longer as Dr. Nick washes and dries his hands, slips on latex gloves, and gently peels the handkerchief from the wound.

"What happened here?" he says.

"Two women colliding in spectacular fashion and a broken jar of spaghetti sauce. I'm sure it happens here all the time."

I hold still as he cleans the wound with peroxide, trying not to flinch at the sudden cold bite of pain. Dr. Nick notices and does his best to distract me with small talk.

"Tell me, Jules, how do you like living in the Bartholomew?"

"How do you know I live here?"

"I assumed that if Leslie brought you to see me then you must be a tenant," he says. "Am I wrong?"

"Partially. I'm a—" I search for the term Leslie had used earlier. "Temporary tenant. Right next door, in fact."

"Ah, so you're the lucky apartment sitter who snagged 12A. Let me officially welcome you to the building," he says.

"What kind of doctor are you?"

"Surgeon."

I glance at his hands as he attends to my arm. They're surgeon hands, with long, elegant fingers that move with steady grace. When he removes them, I see that the cut looks less severe now that it's been cleaned. Just a two-inch gash that's quickly covered with a rectangle of gauze and sealed in place with medical tape.

"That should do it for now," Dr. Nick says as he peels the latex gloves from his hands. "It's a good idea to keep the bandage on until morning. When was your last checkup?"

"Um, last year," I say, when in truth it's another thing I can't remember. My approach to health care is not seeing a doctor unless I absolutely need to. "Maybe two years ago."

"Then I'd like to check your vitals, if you'll let me. The heart can sometimes beat erratically after a fall or loss of blood." Dr. Nick digs a stethoscope out of the medical bag and presses it to my chest, just below the collarbone. "Take a deep breath."

I do and get a whiff of his cologne in the process. It has hints of sandalwood and citrus and something else. Something bitter.

"Good," Dr. Nick says as he moves the stethoscope an inch, and I take another deep inhalation. "You have a very interesting name, Jules. Is that short for something? A nickname?"

"No nickname. Most people think it's short for Julia or Julianne, but Jules is my given name. My father used to say that when I was born, my mother took one look into my eyes and said they sparkled like jewels."

Dr. Nick peers into my eyes. It lasts only a second, but it's still enough to make my pulse quicken. I wonder if he can hear it, especially when he says, "For the record, your mother was right."

I will myself not to blush. "And Nick is short for Nicholas?"

"Guilty as charged," he says while wrapping a blood pressure cuff around my upper right arm.

"How long have you lived at the Bartholomew?" I ask.

"Actually I've lived here my whole life. This apartment has been in my family for decades. I inherited it after my parents died, five years ago. They were both killed in a car accident."

"I'm sorry," I say, wishing I had just kept quiet.

"Thank you. Losing them both so suddenly was hard. In some ways, I feel like I'm also an apartment sitter. Just watching this place until my parents come home."

Dr. Nick finishes taking my blood pressure and says, "One twenty over eighty. You seem to be in excellent health, Jules."

"Thanks again, Doc—Nick. I appreciate it."

"It was no problem at all."

He leads me back into the hall, where I get turned around by the layout. Instead of making a right, I go left, accidentally taking a few steps toward a door at the end of the hallway. It's wider than the others, locked in place with a dead bolt. After a quick spin, I'm back on track, following Nick to the front door.

"I'm sorry for being nosy about your apartment," I tell him once we're in the foyer. "I didn't mean to bring up bad memories."

"There's no need to apologize. I have plenty of good memories. Besides, I think every family has at least one big tragedy."

He's wrong there. Mine has two.

MY PHONE buzzes as I leave Nick's apartment. It's an email from Chloe, which I give a cursory glance while unlocking the door to 12A. The subject line prompts an annoyed sigh: *Scary stuff.*

There's no message. Just a link to an article with a headline that's ominously blunt: THE CURSE OF THE BARTHOLOMEW.

I shove the phone back into my pocket and push into 12A, where I toss my keys into the bowl on the foyer table. Only my aim is off, and the keys end up hitting the edge of the table before clattering onto a heating vent in the foyer floor. An antique grate covers the vent—all cast-iron curlicues with gaps between them wide enough for the keys to tumble right through. Which they do.

I drop to my hands and knees and peer into the grate, seeing mostly darkness within. This isn't good. Not good at all.

I still have my face pressed to the grate when there's a knock on the door. Charlie's voice rises from the other side.

"Miss Larsen, you in there?"

"I'm here," I say as I lift myself off the floor. I whip open the door to see Charlie, two large grocery bags in his arms.

"I thought you might need these," he says.

I take one of the bags and carry it to the kitchen. Charlie follows with the other. Inside are replacements of every item damaged in my collision with Ingrid. There's even the addition of a bar of dark chocolate. The decadent, expensive kind.

"I tried to salvage what you had bought, but I'm afraid not much survived," Charlie says. "So I made a quick trip to the store."

I stare at the groceries, touched beyond words. "Charlie, you shouldn't have."

"It was nothing," he says. "I have a daughter around your age. I hate the thought of her going hungry for a few days."

"How much do I owe you?"

To my relief, he shoos away the offer as if it's a pesky fly. "No need to worry about that, Miss Larsen. It makes up for that unfortunate incident in the lobby."

I unwrap the edge of the chocolate bar, snap off a square, and offer it to Charlie. "I feel like I should repay you somehow."

"Just perform a good deed for someone else," he says. "That'll be payment enough."

"I'll do two good deeds," I say. "Because it seems I need yet another favor. My keys, um, sort of fell into the heating vent."

Charlie tries to stifle a chuckle. "Which one?"

"Foyer," I say. "By the door."

A minute later we're back in the foyer. Charlie presses his formidable stomach against the floor. In his hand is a pen-shaped magnet stick, the end of which he lowers through the grate.

"I'm so sorry about this," I say.

Charlie wiggles the stick. "Happens all the time. These grates are notorious. They'll eat up anything that comes their way. Even cell phones, if one falls at the right angle."

Carefully, he removes the stick from the grate. Dangling from the end is my key ring. Charlie gently places it into the bowl on the foyer table. The magnet stick goes back into his jacket pocket.

"If it ever happens again, just grab a screwdriver," he says. "The grate comes off real easy, and you can reach right in."

"Thank you," I say with a sigh of relief. "For everything."

Charlie tips his cap. "It was my pleasure."

After he leaves, I return to the kitchen and unpack the groceries. I've just put away the last of them when I hear a telltale creak rise from the cupboard. The dumbwaiter on the move.

I lift the cupboard door as it rises. Inside is another poem.

"Remember" by Christina Rossetti.

Seeing it causes a slight hiccup in my chest. I know this poem. It was read at my parents' funeral.

Remember me when I am gone away. Ironic, considering how I long to forget sitting in the front pew of that church, Chloe by my side, a smattering of mourners mute behind us.

On the back Ingrid has left me another note: *SORRY ABOUT YOUR ARM.*

With the same pen and paper I used earlier, I write my response: *It's fine. No worries.*

I put it in the dumbwaiter and send it to 11A, having an easier time this go-round. I receive a response five minutes later. Inside is a fresh poem. "Fire and Ice" by Robert Frost.

Some say the world will end in fire.

On the back, Ingrid has written not another apology but a command: *CENTRAL PARK. IMAGINE. 15 MINUTES.*

As instructed, I'm at the Imagine mosaic fifteen minutes later, looking for Ingrid among the usual crowd of tourists and grungy buskers playing Beatles songs. It's a beautiful afternoon. Mid-sixties, sunny and clear. When I finally spot Ingrid, I see that in her hands is a hot dog, which she holds out to me.

"An apology gift," she says. "I've always hated those people who look at their phones instead of where they're going. Now I've become one. It's inexcusable. I'm the lowest of the low."

"It was just an accident."

"A stupid, preventable one."

We start to move deeper into the park. I can't help but notice our height difference as we stop at the edge of Central Park Lake. I've got about six inches on Ingrid, which means she barely clears five feet. Then there's her thinness. She's nothing but skin and bones. In all ways, she looks hungry. So much so that I give her my hot dog and insist that she eat it.

"I couldn't possibly," she says. "It's my apology hot dog."

"I just had lunch," I say. "And your apology is accepted."

Ingrid takes the hot dog with a grand curtsy.

"I'm Jules, by the way."

Ingrid takes a bite, chewing a bit before saying, "I know. And I'm Ingrid Gallagher in 11A, who knows her way around a dumbwaiter. Never thought I'd learn that particular life skill."

She plops onto the nearest bench to finish the hot dog. I remain standing, staring at the rowboats on the water.

"How do you like the Bartholomew?" Ingrid says before popping the last bit of hot dog into her mouth. "It's dreamy, right?"

"Very."

"I've been here two weeks now," she says.

"Where did you live before that?"

"Virginia. Before that, Seattle. I'm originally from Boston." She lies on the bench, her blue-tipped hair fanning out around her head. "So I guess I don't live anywhere now. I'm a nomad."

I wonder if that's on purpose or out of necessity. A constant flight from poor choices and bad luck. Someone not unlike me.

"I left Boston two years ago," Ingrid tells me. "I came here to New York. Then it was off to Seattle, where I waitressed a bit. So awful. This summer I went to Virginia and got a job bartending at a beach bar. Then it was here. I had literally no idea where to go next when I saw the ad for the Bartholomew. The rest is history."

Ingrid sits up and pats the spot on the bench beside her. "And how did you end up at the Bartholomew? Tell me everything."

I take a seat and say, "There's not too much to tell. I mean, other than losing my job and my boyfriend on the same day."

Ingrid displays a stricken look. "He died?"

"Just his heart," I say. "If he ever had one."

"Why do boys totally suck? I'm starting to think it might be in-grained in them. That's the reason I left New York the first time. A stupid boy."

"What about your family?" I say.

"I don't have any." Ingrid examines her fingernails, which are painted the same shade of blue as the tips of her hair. "I mean, yes, I had a family. Obviously. But they're gone now."

Hearing that word—*gone*—jolts my heart for a few swift beats.

"Mine, too," I say. "Now it's just me, even though I have a sister. Or had one. I don't really know anymore."

I don't intend to say it. The words simply slip out, unprompted.

"She's missing?" Ingrid says.

"Yes."

"For how long?"

"Eight years." It's hard to believe it's been that long. The day re-mains vivid in my memory. "I was seventeen."

"What happened?"

"According to the police, Jane ran away. According to my father, she was abducted. And according to my mother, she was most likely murdered."

"What's your theory?" Ingrid says.

"I don't have one." To me, it doesn't matter what actually hap-pened to Jane. All I care about is the fact that she's gone.

It was February when it happened. A cold, gray month of con-stant clouds. Jane had just finished her shift at McIndoe's, the pharmacy that sat on the last thriving corner of our town's Main Street. She had worked as a cashier there since graduating from high school a year and a half earlier. Saving money for college, she told us, even though we knew she wasn't the college type.

The last person known to have seen her was Mr. McIndoe himself, who watched from the store's front window as a black Volkswagen Beetle pulled up to the curb. Jane, who had been wait-ing beneath the pharmacy's awning, hopped inside.

There wasn't a struggle. Nor was the person behind the wheel a stranger to Jane. She gave the driver a little wave through the window before opening the passenger door. Mr. McIndoe never got a good look at that person.

Then the Beetle drove away. Jane was gone.

In the days following her disappearance, it became clear that none of Jane's friends drove a black Beetle. Nor did any friends of those friends.

Mr. McIndoe didn't think to make a note of the car's plates. He had no reason to. When asked by the police, he couldn't remember a single letter or number. A lot of people in town held that against poor Mr. McIndoe, as if his weak memory was the only thing keeping Jane from being found.

My parents were more forgiving. A few weeks after the disappearance, my father stopped by the store to tell Mr. McIndoe there were no hard feelings.

I didn't know this at the time. It was told to me a few years later, by Mr. McIndoe himself, at my parents' funeral.

That, incidentally, was the day I realized Jane would never return. Until then, I had held a sliver of hope that she might find her way home. But my parents' deaths made the news. And if Jane had heard about it, she'd surely have come back to see them buried. When she didn't, I stopped thinking she was still alive.

"I'm sorry," Ingrid says, adding nothing after that. I've saddened her into silence.

We spend the next few minutes looking out at the lake and feeling the breeze on our skin. It rustles the trees, their golden leaves quivering. Quite a few drift to the ground like confetti.

"Do you really like it at the Bartholomew?" Ingrid eventually says. "Or were you just saying that because you think I do?"

"I like it," I say. "Don't you?"

"I'm not sure." Ingrid's voice has grown quiet. "I mean, it's nice there. But something about the place seems . . . off."

"It *is* an old building," I say. "They always feel strange."

"But it's more than that." Ingrid pulls her knees to her chest, a pose that makes her look even more childlike. "It . . . it scares me."

"I don't think there's anything to be scared of," I say, even as that disconcerting article Chloe sent me creeps into my thoughts.

"Have you heard about some of the things that have happened there?" Ingrid says.

"I know the owner jumped from the roof."

"That's, like, the least of it. There's been worse. A lot worse."

Ingrid turns around and looks past the treetops, to the Bartholomew looming beyond them. On the northern corner is George, looking down over Central Park West. Seeing him makes my chest swell with affection.

"You don't have to stay there," I say. "I mean, if it makes you so uncomfortable."

Ingrid shrugs. "Where else am I going to go? I need the money."

There's no need for her to say anything else, a sign that she and I might have more in common than I first thought.

"I need the money, too," I say, in what is surely the understatement of the year. "I couldn't believe how much the job paid. When Leslie told me, I almost passed out."

"You and me both, sister. And I'm sorry for getting all creepy on you just now. I'm fine. The Bartholomew is fine. I think I'm just lonely, you know? I'm on board with all the rules except for the one about not having visitors. Sometimes it feels like solitary confinement. Especially since Erica left."

"Who's Erica?"

"Oh, Erica Mitchell. She was in 12A before you."

I look at her. "You mean the owner? The woman who died?"

"Erica was one of us—an apartment sitter," Ingrid says. "She was nice. We hung out a little bit. But then she left a few days after I got there. Which was strange, because she told me she had at least two months left."

I'm surprised Leslie never mentioned there had been an apartment sitter in 12A before me. She had made it sound like the owner had just died. "Are you sure she was in 12A?"

"Positive," Ingrid says. "She sent me a welcome note down the dumbwaiter. When you arrived, I thought it would be fun to do the same thing."

"Did Erica tell you why she left early?"

"She didn't tell me anything. I was bummed because it was nice to have an upstairs neighbor to hang out with." Ingrid's face brightens. "Hey, I have an idea. We should do this every day. Lunch in the park until our time is up. I've been so bored in that building, and there's a great big park to explore. Think about it, Juju. That's what I've decided I'm going to call you, by the way."

"Duly noted," I say, unable to conceal a smile.

Ingrid begins to count on her fingers. "Think of all the fun things we could do. Bird watching. Picnics. Boating. All the hot dogs we can eat. What do you say?"

She gives me an expectant look. Hopeful and needy all at once. And lonely. As lonely as I've felt the past two weeks. Maybe Ingrid is the person who'll reverse that tide.

"Sure," I say. "I'm in."

Ingrid claps excitedly. "Then it's settled. We'll meet at noon in the lobby. Give me your phone."

I pull it from my pocket and hand it to her. Ingrid enters her number into my list of contacts. I do the same with her phone.

"I *will* be texting if you try to ditch me," she warns. "Now let's seal the deal with a selfie."

She holds up my phone and squeezes against me. Our faces fill the screen. I smile because for the first time in a long while, things don't seem so bad.

"Perfect," Ingrid says.

She taps the phone, and with a click, our pact is complete.

I SPEND my first night at the Bartholomew joyfully confounded over how I ended up here. The evening progresses in sequence.

First, I fill the claw-foot tub in the master bathroom, pour in some pricey lavender-scented bubble bath I discover beneath the sink, and soak until my skin is rosy and my fingertips are pruned.

After the bath, I microwave a frozen pizza and plop it onto a china plate so beautiful and delicate that merely touching it makes me nervous. I find a box of matches in the kitchen junk drawer and light the candles in the dining room. I eat as the flickering candlelight reflects off the windows.

When dinner is over, I open one of the bottles of wine Chloe gave me and plant myself at the sitting room window, drinking as night descends over Manhattan. I empty the glass. I refill it.

Time passes. Hours. When my third glass of wine has been emptied, I retreat to the kitchen and linger there, rinsing the wineglass and wiping down the countertops. I'm oddly happy, content, and, for what feels like the first time in forever, hopeful.

Without thinking, I grab the matches off the counter, swiping one against the box until a flame flares at its tip. I then hold my left hand several inches above the flame, feeling its warmth on my open palm. I slowly lower my hand toward the flame. As I do, I think of my parents. The warmth on my palm soon gives way to heat, which is quickly usurped by pain.

But I don't move my hand yet. I need it to hurt a little more.

I stop only when my hand twitches and self-preservation kicks in. I blow out the match, the flame gone in an instant.

I light another, intent on repeating the process, when a strange noise rises from the dumbwaiter shaft. Although it's muffled slightly by the closed cupboard door, I can tell the sound isn't the dumbwaiter itself. There's no slow turn of the pulleys, no almost imperceptible creak. This noise is different.

Louder. Sharper. Clearly human.

It sounds, I realize, like a scream from the apartment below.

Ingrid's apartment.

I stand frozen in the kitchen, my head cocked. When the lit match reaches my fingers—a hot flash of pain—I yelp, drop the match, watch the flame wink out on the kitchen floor.

The burn spurs me into action. Soon I'm out of 12A, moving down the twelfth-floor hall on my way to the stairs.

The scream—or at least what I thought was a scream—replays in my head as I descend to the eleventh floor. In the stairwell, the only thing I hear is the whisper of my own cautious footfalls.

I check my watch when I reach the eleventh floor: 1:00 a.m. Another cause for concern.

At the door to 11A, I pause before knocking, hoping I'll hear another, happier sound that will ease my mind. Instead, I hear nothing, which prompts me to knock.

"Ingrid?" I say. "It's Jules. Is everything okay?"

Seconds pass. Ten of them. Then twenty. I'm about to knock again when the door cracks open and Ingrid appears. She looks at me, eyes wide. I've surprised her.

"Jules, what are you doing here?"

"Checking on you." I pause. "I thought I heard a scream."

Ingrid pauses, too. A seconds-long gap during which she forces a smile. "It must have been your TV."

"I wasn't watching TV. It—"

I stop, concerned. Something about Ingrid seems *off*. Her voice is flat and reluctant. I can see only half her body through the gap in the door. She's dressed in the same clothes as earlier, her right hand shoved into the front pocket of her jeans, as if searching for something.

"It sounded like *you* screamed," I say. "I got worried."

"It wasn't me," Ingrid says. "I'm fine. Really."

Her face says otherwise. Besides her rictus grin, there's a dark glint in those widened eyes. She looks, I realize, afraid.

I stare directly into her eyes. "Are you sure?" I whisper.

Ingrid blinks. "Yes. Everything's great."

"Then I'm sorry for bothering you," I say, forcing my own smile. "Are we still on for tomorrow?"

"Noon on the dot," Ingrid says. "Be there or be square."

I give her a wave and take a few steps down the hall. Ingrid doesn't wave back. Instead, she stares at me a second longer, her smile fading to a grim flat line just before she closes the door.

At this point, there's nothing left for me to do. If Ingrid says she's fine, then I need to believe her. But as I climb two sets of steps—one to the twelfth floor, the other to the bedroom of 12A—I can't shake the feeling that Ingrid was lying.

Now

Bernard leaves. A doctor enters.

He's older. Snowy hair and strong jaw and tiny glasses perched in front of hazel eyes.

"Hello there. I'm Dr. Wagner." *He pronounces it the German way,*

*with a V instead of a W. His accent is at once rough and charming.
"How are you feeling?"*

*I don't know enough to give an answer. I remember being told I was
hit by a car, which should make me feel lucky I'm not dead.*

"My head hurts," I say.

*"I imagine it does," Dr. Wagner tells me. "You banged it up pretty
good. But there's no concussion, which is fortunate. All things considered,
it could have been much worse."*

I try to nod, the motion stymied by the neck brace.

"Now I need to ask you a few questions," Dr. Wagner says.

I attempt another neck-brace-shortened nod.

"How much do you remember about the accident?"

*"Not much," I say. I recall a screech of tires. A blast of car horn. Pain.
Darkness.*

*It's the same with my arrival in the hospital. I can't recall how I got
here or what, exactly, I said when I arrived.*

*"Let's try another question," Dr. Wagner says. "A witness said he saw
you burst out of the Bartholomew and run right into oncoming traffic.
He said you didn't stop. Not even for a second."*

That I remember. "That's right," I say.

*The doctor casts me a curious look from behind his tiny frames. "That's
not exactly normal. It sounds to me like you ran away."*

"No," I say. "I escaped."

Chapter 4

Four Days Earlier

I DREAM OF MY FAMILY.

My mother. My father. Jane, looking exactly like the last time I
laid eyes on her. Forever nineteen.

The three of them walk through Central Park. It's night, and the park is pitch-black, all its lampposts snuffed out. Yet my family glows a faint greenish gray as they traverse the park.

I watch their progress from the roof of the Bartholomew, where I sit next to George, one of his stone wings folded around me in a gargoyle semi-embrace.

My parents see me and wave. Jane calls to me, glowing hands cupped around her mouth. "You don't belong here!" she shouts.

As soon as the words reach me, George moves his wing.

No longer hugging. Shoving.

Soon I'm falling, twisting, as I plummet to the sidewalk below.

I wake with a scream in my throat. I gulp it down, coughing in the process. Then I sit up and eye George through the window.

"Not cool, dude," I say.

My words have barely faded in the cavernous bedroom when I hear something else.

A noise. Coming from downstairs.

I'm not even sure it qualifies as a noise. It's more like a sensation. An ineffable feeling that I'm not alone. If someone asked me to describe it, I wouldn't know how. Not tapping. Not even a rustle, although that's the nearest comparison I can think of.

Motion. That's what it sounds like. Something moving through space and leaving a slight whisper in its wake.

I slip out of bed, throw on my tattered terry-cloth robe, and whisk downstairs. But when I get there, I find the apartment empty. The door is locked and dead-bolted, and the chain remains undisturbed. The noise or presence or whatever you want to call it was just my imagination. The foggy remnants of my nightmare.

Exhausted but too jumpy to go back to sleep, I head to the kitchen to make coffee. As it brews, I try to shake off the nightmare. What a strange, awful dream.

Part of me worries that if I look out the window into Central Park, my family will still be there, glowing their way across Bow Bridge. So I spend the morning looking at clocks.

The digital alarm clock in the bedroom as I dress for the day.

The clock on the microwave as I pour the coffee that I brewed.

The grandfather clock as I drink my coffee in the sitting room, counting the pairs of eyes in the wallpaper. My tally stands at sixty-four when the clock bongs out the hour. My heart sinks. It's only nine o'clock.

Kill time before it kills you.

My father told me that, not long after my mother got sick and he lost his job. So I do another job search, finding no openings I haven't seen before. Then I do a little cleaning, even though nothing needs it. When the grandfather clock announces noon's arrival, I leave the apartment.

Since Ingrid's not in the lobby yet, I go to the mailboxes to see if anything's been sent to 12A. It hasn't. I close the mailbox and check my watch. Five minutes past noon. Ingrid is late.

When my phone rings, I reach for it, thinking it might be her. My stomach tightens when I see who's really calling.

Andrew. I ignore the call. A minute later, a text arrives: *Please call me.* It's followed by a second one: *Can we just talk?*

Then a third: *Please????????* I don't reply.

Ingrid is now ten minutes late. It occurs to me that maybe I got our meeting location mixed up. I send a text. *Were we supposed to meet in the park?*

When two minutes pass without a response, I decide to walk to the park and see. On my way out of the Bartholomew, I look for Charlie to ask if he saw Ingrid leave the building. Instead, I find one of the other doormen—a smiling older man. He tells me Charlie worked the night shift and called in sick for his shift later today.

"Family emergency," he says. "Something about his daughter."

I thank him and move on, crossing to the park side of the street. It's more overcast than yesterday, with a slight chill that foreshadows winter's rapid approach. Soon I'm by the Imagine mosaic. Ingrid isn't there.

I check my phone again. Still nothing.

I move on, heading toward the lake and the bench we occupied yesterday. I take a seat and send another text. *I'm in the park now. Same bench as yesterday. Is everything OK?*

Something about the situation doesn't sit right with me. I think about last night—the scream rising from her apartment, the uncomfortable delay between my knocks and her opening the door, the dark glint in her eyes.

I check my phone again and see that it's now quarter to one.

I leave the park, worry tugging at me. On my way back to the Bartholomew, I send another text simply asking Ingrid to please respond. I know I'm overreacting. I don't care.

Inside the building, I pass Dylan, the other apartment sitter. He's dressed for a jog in the park. Sweats. Sneakers. Electric guitar screeching from his earbuds. I enter the elevator he just vacated and almost press the top button but instead hit the one for the eleventh floor. I tell myself it won't hurt to check on Ingrid. I close my eyes and recall the flatness of her voice, that plastered-on smile, the way that smile vanished just before she shut the door.

Once I'm standing outside 11A, I knock. Two gentle raps. As if this is a casual drop-in. The door swings open.

Just beyond it stands Leslie Evelyn in another of her Chanel suits. There's a harried look on her face. A strand of hair has escaped her updo and curls down her forehead.

"Jules," she says, not quite hiding her surprise to see me. "How's your arm?"

I absently touch the bandage under my jacket and blouse. "It's fine," I say, glancing into the apartment. "Is Ingrid here?"

"She's not," Leslie says with a noticeable sigh. "Ingrid is gone."

JANE is gone.

That was how my father put it a week after my sister failed to come home. It was almost midnight, and the two of us were alone in the kitchen, my mother having taken to her bed hours earlier. By this point the police had talked to Jane's friends, and her picture had appeared on every telephone pole and storefront in the county. My father took a sip of the black coffee he'd been mainlining for days and said, simply and sadly, "Jane is gone."

I remember feeling more confused than sad. I feel that same confusion now as I watch Leslie swipe the rogue curl of hair back into place.

"Gone? She's no longer living here?"

"She is not," Leslie says with a disdainful sniff.

I think of the rules. Ingrid must have broken one. A big one. "Did she do something wrong?"

"Not that I'm aware of. She wasn't kicked out, if that's what you mean. She just slipped out in the middle of the night."

"Did anyone see her leave? Who was the doorman on duty?"

"That would be Charlie," Leslie says. "But he was in the basement at the time. The security camera down there wasn't working properly, so he left his station to try to fix it. When he returned, he found the keys for 11A right in the middle of the lobby. That's where Ingrid dropped them on her way out."

"What time was this?"

"I'm not sure. You'd have to ask Charlie."

Leslie tilts her head, the unruly curl on the verge of breaking free again. "Why are you so interested in Ingrid?"

I could give her several reasons, all of them true. That Ingrid was friendly and fun and I liked being around her. Instead, I tell Leslie the biggest cause of my concern.

"I thought I heard a scream last night."

Leslie gives an exaggerated blink of surprise. "In 11A? When?"

"Around one a.m. I came down to check on Ingrid, but she told me I was just hearing things."

"None of the other residents reported hearing anything like that," Leslie says. "That kind of thing would be noticed in a building as quiet as this one."

"I'm just worried about her," I say.

"She left, sweetie," Leslie says dismissively. "Like a thief in the night. Which was my initial thought, by the way. I thought for sure I'd find this place completely cleaned out. But Ingrid took only her belongings."

"And she didn't leave anything behind?"

"Not to my knowledge," Leslie says. "If she did, it would be in the basement storage unit. I haven't checked there yet because it seems that Ingrid lost the key to it. It's missing from the key ring Charlie found in the lobby."

Which means Ingrid probably never used it. I've certainly had no need to visit 12A's storage unit. The bedroom closet is big enough to hold everything I've ever possessed.

Leslie touches my shoulder and says, "I wouldn't be too worried about Ingrid. I'm sure there's a good reason why she left. And quite frankly, I'd love to hear it."

As would I. Because right now, nothing about this makes sense. A renewed sense of worry clings to me as I climb the stairs to the twelfth floor. Back inside 12A, I crash on the sitting room sofa, my brain clouded by confusion. Why would Ingrid want to leave the Bartholomew? She made it clear that she had no money and nowhere else to go. Something about her situation must have suddenly changed. Quite literally overnight.

I dig my phone from my jacket pocket. When I scroll through the texts I sent her, I see that she hasn't read a single one.

Rather than text again, I decide to call, tapping her all-caps name and listening as the call goes straight to voice mail.

"Hey, Ingrid," I say, trying to keep my tone pitched somewhere between casual and concerned. "It's Jules. From the Bartholomew. Leslie just told me you moved out during the night. Is, um, everything okay? Call or text to let me know."

I end the call and stare at the phone, unsure of what to do next. The only thing that will assuage my worry is hearing from Ingrid herself. But to do that, I need to first find out where she went.

I grab my laptop and start searching for Ingrid's social media accounts, beginning with Facebook. I try to remember all the places she told me she's lived in the past two years. I narrow the search to New York, Seattle, and Boston, finding two Ingrid Gallaghers. Neither is the one I'm looking for.

I move on to Twitter, with similar results. Lots of Ingrid Gallaghers. None resembles the one I know.

Next up is Instagram, which I open using the app on my phone. At last, success. Ingrid Gallagher has an account.

Her hair is all blue in her profile picture. A too-bright shade that reminds me of cotton candy. But then I see that the most recent picture is a selfie Ingrid took in Central Park, a bit of the Bartholomew visible over her left shoulder.

It was taken two days ago, probably around the same time I was getting a tour of 12A. The photo received fifteen likes and one comment from someone named Zeke, who wrote, *cant believe ur in NYC and havent hit me up.*

I take a look at Zeke's profile picture. The scraggly beard and scuffed skateboard raised conspicuously into the frame tell me all I need to know about the guy. I send him a message just in case she decided to, in his words, hit him up.

> *Hi. I'm a neighbor of Ingrid's. I'm trying to get in touch with her. Have you heard from her recently? If not, do you have any idea where she might be? I'm worried about her.*

I leave my name. I leave my number. I ask him to call.

After that, it's back to Ingrid's Instagram account, where her older pictures might offer clues about where she could have gone.

The photo before the park selfie grabs my attention. Taken eight days ago, it's a close-up of Ingrid's hand. The fingernails are light pink. Her hand rests atop a book. Glimpsed in the spaces between her fingers is a familiar image—George perched at the corner of the Bartholomew. In addition to that are scraps of a familiar font spelling out an equally familiar title: *Heart of a Dreamer.*

The caption is even more surprising: *I met the author!*

I've also met the author, and she wasn't too happy about it. Still, this photo seems to suggest that Greta and Ingrid were, if not friends, at least acquaintances. Which means there's a small chance she might know where Ingrid went.

With a sigh, I grab the last bottle of wine Chloe gave me, leave the apartment, and make my way to the stairwell. I'm going to see Greta Manville, no matter how much it's sure to annoy her.

MY INITIAL knock on the door to 10A is so tentative I can barely hear it over the sound of my thudding heart. So I rap again, using more force. Behind the door, footsteps creak over the floorboards, and someone shouts, "I heard you the first time."

When the door finally opens, it's only a crack. Greta Manville peers through it with narrowed eyes. "You again," she says.

I raise the wine bottle. "I brought you something."

The door opens wide enough for me to see her outfit of black slacks and a gray sweater. On her feet are pink slippers. The left one taps with impatience as she eyes the bottle.

"It's an apology gift," I say. "For bothering you in the lobby."

Greta takes the bottle and checks the label. It must be a decent vintage, because she doesn't grimace. She opens the door wider. "You can come in or leave. It makes no difference to me."

I decide to enter. Greta turns and moves wordlessly down the hall. I follow, sneaking glances at the apartment. Books are everywhere. Filling the shelves of the room opposite the door. Sitting on end tables. Rising from the floor in tilted, towering stacks.

"Who are you again?" Greta says as she retrieves a corkscrew from a drawer in the kitchen.

"Jules," I say.

"That's right. Jules. And my book is your favorite and so on and so forth."

Greta caps the comment with a mighty pull of the cork. She then fetches a single wineglass, filling it halfway before handing it to me. "Cheers," she says.

"You're not having any?"

"Sadly, I'm not allowed. Doctor's orders."

"I'm sorry," I say. "I didn't know."

"You couldn't have," Greta says. "Quit apologizing and drink."

I take an obligatory sip, mindful about not drinking too much too fast. It could easily happen, considering how anxious I am.

"Tell me, Jules," Greta says. "Why did you really stop by?"

I look up from my glass. "Do I need an ulterior motive?"

"Not necessarily. But I suspect you have one. In my experience, people don't arrive bearing gifts unless they want something."

I pause to fortify myself with more wine. "You're right. I came here for a reason. I came to ask you about Ingrid Gallagher."

"Who?" Greta asks.

"She's an apartment sitter. In the unit above you. She left last night. And no one knows where she went. And since she mentioned on Instagram that she met you, I thought that possibly the two of you were friends and you might know."

Greta gives me a tilted-head gaze, curiosity brightening her eyes. "Are you referring to that girl with the ghastly colored hair?"

"Yes."

"I met her twice," Greta says. "Leslie first introduced us as I was passing through the lobby."

"When was the second time?"

"Two days ago. She came by to see me." Greta gestures to the open bottle on the counter. "*Without* wine."

"What was *her* ulterior motive?"

"Now you're catching on," Greta says with an approving nod. "She wanted to ask me about the Bartholomew. She was curious about some of the things that have happened here. I told her that if she was looking for gossip, she should try the internet. It was a two-minute conversation at best."

"And you haven't talked to her since?"

"I have not. Is she missing?"

"Maybe. I've been trying to reach her all day. She hasn't responded. And the way she left, well, it concerns me."

"Why?" Greta says. "She's free to come and go as she pleases."

"It's just . . . you didn't hear anything unusual last night, did you? Like a strange noise coming from the apartment above you?"

"I didn't," Greta replies. "And I was awake most of the night. Insomnia. The older I get, the less sleep I require. So if there had been a strange noise from upstairs, I would have heard it."

I take another sip of my wine.

"If you'd like, you may ask me one question about that book," Greta says.

Only one? I have a hundred. But I noticed the pronoun she used. Not *my* book. Or *the* book. It tells me she'd rather talk about anything other than *Heart of a Dreamer.*

"Why did you stop writing?"

"The short answer is because I'm lazy. And I have no financial need to write. My family was wealthy. The book made me wealthier. It generates enough income to allow me to live comfortably."

"Have you lived here long?"

"If you're asking if I lived here when I wrote *Heart of a Dreamer*, the answer is yes," Greta says.

"In this apartment?"

Greta gives a quick shake of her head. "Elsewhere. It was my parents' apartment. I grew up there, moved out after getting married, and moved back following my divorce. I was aimless and bitter and suddenly had a lot of time on my hands. I decided to fill it by writing what I wished my life to be like. When the book was finished, I moved out again."

"Why?" I ask, still unable to comprehend why anyone would choose to leave the Bartholomew.

"Why does anyone move?" Greta muses. "I needed a change of venue. Besides, people get tired of living with their parents. And I'm a very different woman now from the one I was when I wrote the book. I was so in need of fantasy that I failed to do the one thing all good writers are supposed to do—tell the truth."

I down the rest of the wine, preparing myself for something I never thought I'd have to do—defend a book to its own author.

"You're forgetting that readers need fantasy, too," I say. "My sister and I used to lie on her bed, reading *Heart of a Dreamer* and picturing ourselves in Ginny's shoes. The book showed us there was life outside our tiny dying town. The book gave us hope."

"But what about the real world?" Greta says.

"That sister I mentioned? She disappeared when I was seventeen. My parents died when I was nineteen. So frankly, I've had enough of the real world."

Greta lifts her hand, places her palm to her cheek, and spends a good ten seconds sizing me up. Caught in her stare, I freeze.

"You strike me as a gentle soul," she says.

I've never thought of myself as gentle. Fragile is more like it.

"I don't know. I guess I am."

"Then you need to be careful," she says. "This place isn't kind to gentle souls. It chews them up and spits them out."

"Do you mean New York or the Bartholomew?"

Greta keeps staring. "Both," she says.

GRETA'S WORDS STAY WITH ME as I climb the stairs from the tenth floor to the twelfth. Not just the part about being chewed up and spit out but also the reason Ingrid came to see her. Why would Ingrid be asking about the Bartholomew and its past?

It . . . it scares me.

That's what Ingrid had said about the Bartholomew. And I believed her. That little stutter seemed to me like a confession.

I pause on the eleventh-floor landing to check my phone. Ingrid still hasn't read my texts. Which means she also likely hasn't listened to the voice mail I left.

I shove the phone back into my pocket and am about to continue up the steps when Dylan, the Bartholomew's other apartment sitter, leaves 11B. He's dressed similarly to yesterday. Same baggy jeans. Same black disks in his ears.

My presence on his floor clearly surprises him. His eyes widen behind a veil of floppy black hair. "Hey," he says. "You lost?"

"Trying to find someone," I say. "Did you know Ingrid at all?"

"Not really."

I find that surprising. "Not at all? You never hung out?"

"If saying hi to each other means hanging out, then, sure, we hung out. Otherwise, no. Why do you want to know?"

"Because she moved out last night, and I'm trying to reach her."

Dylan's eyes go even wider. "Ingrid's gone?"

"Why do you seem so surprised?"

"Because she just got here. I thought she'd have stayed longer."

"How long have you been here?"

"Two months," Dylan says. Then he adds abruptly, "Are we about done with the questions? There's somewhere I need to be."

Rather than wait for the elevator, Dylan opts for the stairs. He's either very late for something or extremely eager to be rid of me.

I call after him. "Just one more thing."

Dylan pauses on the landing between the tenth and eleventh floors, looking up at me with his head askance.

"Did you hear any strange noises last night?" I say. "From Ingrid's apartment?"

"Last night?" he says. "No, sorry. Can't help you there."

Then he's off again, speeding around the landing and down more steps before I can ask him another question. I use the stairs as well, slower than Dylan, going up instead of down.

A few floors below me, the elevator grate slides shut with a clang. When it comes into view, I see Nick inside, a stethoscope draped around his neck. Seeing me through the elevator window, he gives a friendly wave. I wave back and hurry up the remaining steps to the twelfth floor, which we reach in unison.

"Hey there, neighbor," Nick says as he leaves the elevator. "How's the arm?"

"It's great. Thanks for, you know, fixing it."

I cringe at my tone. Could I be any more awkward? I blame Nick's whole handsome-doctor vibe, which is intimidating.

"Making a house call?" I say, gesturing to the stethoscope.

"Yes, unfortunately. Mr. Leonard was having heart palpitations. He swore the big one was coming. I made him take an aspirin and told him to call nine-one-one if it gets any worse. Knowing him, he won't. And where are you coming from?"

"The tenth floor."

"Making friends with the neighbors?"

I hesitate. "I went to visit Greta Manville."

"Now, that's a surprise. Greta doesn't strike me as being very social. How on earth did you manage to charm her?"

"I didn't," I say. "I bribed her."

Nick laughs, and I realize he's enjoying this conversation. I am, too. I think we might be flirting.

"I needed to talk to her about Ingrid Gallagher."

Nick frowns. "Ah. The runaway."

"So you've heard," I say.

"Word travels fast in this building."

Just like that, I realize Ingrid made a mistake when she approached Greta Manville about the Bartholomew's past. She should have asked someone else. Someone friendly. And handsome. And who has lived here all his life.

"I bet you know a lot about this place," I say.

Nick shrugs. "I've heard some things over the years."

I bite my bottom lip, not quite believing what I'm about to say next. "Would you like to get coffee? Or maybe a bite to eat?"

Nick gives me a surprised look. "What did you have in mind?"

"You pick. After all, you know the neighborhood."

And, I hope, he also knows a lot about the Bartholomew.

Chapter 5

INSTEAD OF GOING OUT to eat, Nick suggests retreating to his apartment. "I have leftover pizza and cold beer," he says. "Sorry to be so simple."

"Simple is good," I say. So is free, considering I don't really have the money to buy my neighbor dinner.

Inside 12B, Nick hands me a bottle of beer before returning to the kitchen to heat up the pizza. In his absence, I sip my beer and roam the sitting room, checking out the photographs that fill the walls. Some of them are of Nick in a variety of far-off locales. Versailles. Venice. A savanna in Africa lit by the rising sun.

On the coffee table is a leather-bound photo album similar to one my parents owned. It's long gone now, like most of their belongings. I think of the framed photo currently on the nightstand in the bedroom of 12A. It's the only picture that remains of my family. I envy Nick and his entire album of family photos.

The first photograph in the album is also presumably the oldest—a sepia-tinted image of a young couple standing in front of the Bartholomew. The woman has an opaque look; the man with her is a handsome devil, though. Familiar, too.

I carry the album into the kitchen, where Nick is pulling slices of reheated pizza from the oven. Just behind him, the painting of the ouroboros stares at me with its single flamelike eye.

"Is this your family?" I ask.

Nick leans in to get a better look. "My great-grandparents."

I examine the picture, noticing the ways in which Nick resembles his great-grandfather—same smile, same granite jaw—and the ways he does not. Nick's eyes are softer, less hawkish.

"They also lived in the Bartholomew?"

"This very apartment," Nick says.

I continue flipping through the album. A color photo of a young Nick sits beside a black-and-white image of two people huddled together in a snowbound Central Park.

"My grandparents," Nick tells me. "Nicholas and Tillie."

On the next page is a striking photograph of an even more striking woman. Her gown is satin. Silk gloves reach her elbows. Her face is made up of sharp angles that, when joined together, merge into something arresting, even beautiful.

She stares at the camera. I've seen that look before. "This woman looks a bit like Greta Manville," I say.

"That's because it's her grandmother," Nick says. "Her family and mine were friends. She lived in the Bartholomew for years. Greta's whole family has. She's what we call a legacy tenant."

"Just like you."

"I suppose I am."

He transfers the pizza onto two plates and carries them to the table in the dining room. We sit side by side, positioned so both of us can look out the window at twilight settling over Central Park. The arrangement gives it the feel of a date, which makes me nervous. It's been a while since I've done anything resembling a date. I had forgotten what it feels like to be a normal single person.

I take a bite of pizza. "Tell me about yourself," I say. "Did you always want to be a surgeon?"

"I didn't have much of a choice," he says. "I come from a long line of surgeons, beginning with my great-grandfather. All my life, I knew how proud they were of their work. It's like they were mystics—bringing people back from the dead. Looking at it that way, I was all too happy to join the family business."

"And business must have been booming if they could afford an apartment in the Bartholomew."

"I'm very fortunate," Nick says. "But honestly, this place never felt special. Growing up, it was just home, you know? It wasn't until I went away to college that I finally realized most people don't get to live in a place like the Bartholomew."

I pick a slice of pepperoni off my pizza and pop it into my mouth. "That's why I can't understand why someone like Ingrid would want to leave. You didn't know her at all, did you?"

"We met briefly. Just a quick hello the day she moved in."

"She and I made plans to hang out. And now . . . the way she left strikes me as weird."

"I don't think it's weird, necessarily," Nick says before taking a sip of his beer. "Apartment sitters have left before, you know. The person who was in 12A before you did that."

"Erica Mitchell?"

Nick looks at me, surprised. "How do you know about her?"

"Ingrid mentioned her," I say. "She left two months early."

"That sounds right. She was here around a month before telling Leslie she wasn't comfortable with the rules. I suspect it was the same with Ingrid. The Bartholomew's not for everyone."

"When I talked about it with Ingrid, she seemed frightened."

"Of the Bartholomew?" Nick's voice is thick with disbelief.

"I don't know if it was the building itself or something inside it," I say. "But she was definitely afraid."

"I wish Ingrid had come to me about this. I could have put her mind at ease." Nick runs a hand through his hair, more exasperated than annoyed, although I sense some of that as well. "Trust me, there's nothing here to fear. You do like it here, don't you?"

"Of course." I flick my gaze to the expanse of Central Park outside the window. "There's a lot to like."

"Good. Now promise me something. If you get so creeped out that you feel the need to leave, at least come and talk to me first."

"So you can talk me out of it?"

Nick's shoulders rise and fall in a shy shrug. "Or at least so I can get your phone number before you go."

And it's official: he and I really are flirting.

"My number," I say with a coy smile, "is 12A."

FIFTEEN MINUTES LATER, I'm back in my apartment. Even though Nick showed no signs that I was overstaying my welcome, I felt it best to leave sooner rather than later. Especially once it became clear he had no intention of sharing any of the building's secrets.

I sit by the bedroom window, George a faint outline against the night-darkened sky. With me are a mug of tea, the remainder of the chocolate bar Charlie bought for me, and my laptop, open to the email Chloe sent yesterday: THE CURSE OF THE BARTHOLOMEW.

I click the link. The first thing that greets me is a photo of the Bartholomew itself, taken on a day that couldn't be more picture-perfect. The image stands in stark contrast to the article itself, which drips with menace.

> From the moment it opened its doors to residents, New York City's Bartholomew apartment building has been touched by tragedy. The Spanish flu pandemic that spread across the globe in 1918 had already done its worst when the Bartholomew opened to great fanfare in January of the next year. Therefore it was a surprise when, five months later, the disease swept through the building, killing twenty-four residents. Most of the victims were servants, whose close quarters allowed the illness to rapidly spread.

I look up from the screen, unnerved. Because 12A was originally servants' quarters, some of those flu victims could have slept in this very room.

A horrible thought, made worse by the photo just below that paragraph. It shows the Bartholomew's facade, this time rendered in grainy black and white. A small crowd has gathered on the street. High above them, alone on a corner of the roof, is a man in a black suit. A thin silhouette against the sky.

The building's owner. Moments before his very public suicide. The text under the photo confirms it.

> Doctors determined that the flu deaths were caused by poor ventilation in the servants' quarters. This greatly upset the man who designed and paid for the construction of the building,

Thomas Bartholomew, a doctor himself. He became so distraught by the incident that he leaped from the roof of the structure that bore his name.

According to the article, witnesses made a point of stressing the fact that the man jumped. This was no accidental fall. Dr. Bartholomew killed himself, leaving behind a young wife, Louella, and a seven-year-old son.

This is how I work for the next few hours, using the article Chloe sent as a sort of Rosetta stone of Bartholomew history. I learn that the 1920s and 1930s were relatively quiet, marked only by a few incidents. A man tumbling down the stairs and breaking his neck in 1928. A starlet overdosing on laudanum in 1932.

And I learn that on the first of November in 1944, as World War II neared its end, a nineteen-year-old girl who worked at the Bartholomew was found brutally murdered in Central Park.

Her name was Ruby Smith, and she was the live-in maid of former socialite Cornelia Swanson. According to Swanson, Ruby liked to walk in the park before returning to wake her at seven o'clock each morning. When that didn't happen, Swanson went to the park to look for the girl and found her lying in a wooded area directly across from the Bartholomew.

Ruby's body had been cut open and several vital organs removed, including her heart. The murder weapon was never found. Neither were Ruby's organs.

Because there were no defensive wounds or signs of a struggle, the police concluded that Ruby had known her attacker. A lack of blood around the crime scene told them the ill-fated maid hadn't been killed where she was found. But police *did* find blood inside Ruby's small bedroom, located in Cornelia Swanson's apartment.

Cornelia Swanson immediately became the police's sole suspect. Their investigation uncovered an unsavory period from Swanson's past. In the late 1920s, she lived in Paris and became enamored of a mystic named Marie Damyanov, the leader of an occult group known as Le Calice D'Or—the Golden Chalice.

This information led police to charge Cornelia Swanson for the murder of Ruby Smith. In the arrest report, police noted the date of the murder—Halloween night.

The case ended up never going to trial. Swanson died of an undisclosed illness in March 1945, leaving behind a teenage daughter.

Not counting the inevitable heart attacks and strokes and slow succumbings to cancer, there have been at least thirty unnatural deaths at the Bartholomew. Although that seems like a lot, I also know that bad things happen everywhere, in every building. It's absurd to expect the Bartholomew to be any different.

I close the laptop and check my phone. Still nothing.

What bothers me most about Ingrid's silence is that she's the one who threatened to send pestering texts if I was a no-show. Even our first encounter—that messy and humiliating collision in the lobby—happened because she was looking at her phone.

Only now that I think about it, that wasn't our first encounter. Technically, we had met an hour earlier, in a most unusual way.

I rush from the bedroom and twist down the stairs to the kitchen. Since the dumbwaiter is how Ingrid introduced herself, I can easily see her saying goodbye the same way. And sure enough, when I fling open the door, I find another poem.

Edgar Allan Poe. "The Bells." Sitting on top of it is a key.

I pick it up and examine it. It's smaller than a regular house key. Yet I know exactly what it opens. I have a similar key hooked to the ring that currently occupies the bowl in the foyer.

It's for the storage unit. The very key Leslie said was missing from the others Ingrid had discarded on the lobby floor.

Why she put it in the dumbwaiter eludes me. My only guess is that she left something behind, possibly with the hope I'd retrieve it and give it to her at a later date.

I shove the key into my pocket, my mind quickly easing. I grab the poem, certain that when I flip it over I'll find an explanation.

But one look at what Ingrid wrote sends me plummeting into a deep well of worry: *BE CAREFUL*.

To GET to the basement, I have to take the elevator past the lobby and into the depths of the Bartholomew. Compared with the rest of the building, the basement is downright primitive, with walls of bare stone and support beams of concrete. A rush of frigid air hits me as soon as I step out of the elevator. Ingrid's message scrapes at my nerves like sandpaper. *BE CAREFUL.*

It doesn't help that the basement bears a cryptlike quality. Dank and dark. Yet here I am, palming the key Ingrid left behind and hoping whatever's in that storage unit tells me where she's gone.

Hanging from the support column opposite the elevator is a security camera. The one Leslie said wasn't working when Ingrid left last night. I peer up at it and wonder if I'm being watched.

I move deeper into the basement. Everywhere I look are cages of steel mesh. One behind the elevator that contains its ancient equipment. Inside another are the furnace, water heater, and air-conditioning unit. All of them hum—a ghostly sound.

Another sound joins them. A ragged swish that quickly gets louder. I spin toward the noise and see a bulging trash bag plummet into a dumpster the size of a double-wide trailer. The entire area is surrounded by a chain-link barrier.

I'm not surprised. Down here, even the lightbulbs are caged.

I round the dumpster, startling Mr. Leonard's aide, who stands on the other side. She startles me right back. We both suck in air—simultaneous gasps that echo off the stone walls.

"You scared me," she says. "I thought you were Mrs. Evelyn."

"Sorry," I say. "I'm Jules."

The woman nods coolly. "Jeannette."

"Nice to meet you."

Jeannette's dressed for the basement's chill, her purple scrubs covered by a ratty gray cardigan with gaping pockets. She keeps her other hand behind her back in an attempt to hide the lit cigarette she's holding. When it becomes clear that I've seen it, she lifts the cigarette to her lips and says, "You're one of those apartment sitters, aren't you? The newest one?"

"I am."

Jeannette stares at me a moment. "You're not going to narc on me, are you? Smoking's not allowed in the Bartholomew."

"I won't tell," I say.

"I appreciate that."

Jeannette takes one last puff before stubbing out the cigarette on the concrete floor. When she bends down to pick it up, a lighter falls from a pocket of her cardigan. I grab it while she drops the butt into a coffee can at her feet and slides it into a corner, where it blends in with the shadows.

"You dropped this," I say, handing her the lighter.

Jeannette stuffs it back into her cardigan. "Thanks."

"I was wondering if you could help me. One of the other apartment sitters left last night, and I'm trying to reach her. Her name is Ingrid Gallagher. She was in 11A."

"Never heard the name."

Jeannette shuffles to the elevator. I follow, pulling out my phone and swiping to the picture of Ingrid and me in Central Park. I hold it in front of her. "This is her."

Jeannette presses the button for the elevator and gives the photo a brief glance. "Yeah, I saw her once or twice. Why?"

"I haven't heard from her since she left," I say. "I'm worried."

"Sorry I can't help you," Jeannette says. "But I've got enough to deal with. Sick husband at home. Mr. Leonard convinced he's going to keel over every minute of the day."

The elevator arrives. Jeannette steps inside. "Listen, Julie—"

"Jules," I remind her.

"Jules. Right." Jeannette brings the grate across the elevator door. "In the Bartholomew, it's best to mind your own business. I don't go asking a lot of questions. I suggest you follow my lead."

She hits a button, and the elevator takes off, lifting her out of the basement and out of view.

I FOLLOW the string of exposed bulbs inside their red-wire confines to the storage units, which line both sides of a mazelike corridor. Each chain-link door bears the number of its corresponding apartment, beginning with 2A.

My phone blares suddenly from deep in my pocket. Thinking it might be Ingrid, I grab it and check the number. Even though it's one I don't recognize, I answer with a distracted "Hello?"

"Is this Jules?" It's a man calling, his voice lazy and light, with a noticeable stoner drawl.

"It is."

"Hey, Jules. This is Zeke."

Zeke, Ingrid's friend from Instagram, calling me at last.

"Zeke, yes. Is Ingrid with you?"

I start my way down the corridor, sneaking glances into units as I pass. Most of them are too tidy to be interesting.

"With me?" Zeke says. "Nah. We're not that close. We met a few years ago and only hung out a few times since then."

"Have you heard from her? It's important that I talk to her."

Not even Zeke's slacker voice can hide his growing suspicion. "How do you know Ingrid again?"

"I'm her neighbor," I say. "Was her neighbor, I guess."

"She moved out of that fancy building already?" Zeke says.

"How do you know she was living at the Bartholomew?"

"She told me."

The corridor makes a sudden turn to the left. I follow it, noting the numbers: 8A, 8B. Inside the one for 8C is a dialysis machine on wheels. I move past the machine, quickening my pace until I reached the other side of the building.

"What did she say?" I ask Zeke.

"I'm not sure I should tell you anything else," he says. "I don't know you."

"Listen, Ingrid might be in some kind of trouble. But I won't know until I talk to her. So please tell me what happened."

The corridor makes another turn. When I round it, I find myself staring at the storage unit for 10A. Greta Manville's apartment.

The cage is full of cardboard boxes. Each marked not with its contents but its worth. *Useful. Useless. Cheap sentiment.*

"She came to see me," Zeke says. "I, uh, procure things. Herbal things, if you catch my drift."

I do. Color me unsurprised. "So Ingrid came to buy weed?"

Across from Greta's storage cage is the one for 11A. The only thing inside is a single shoebox. It rests on the concrete floor, its lid slightly askew, as if Ingrid left it there in a hurry.

"That's not what she was looking for," Zeke says. "She wanted to know where she could buy something I don't deal with. But I know someone who does and told her I could be the middleman between them. She gave me the cash; I made the exchange with the supplier and brought it back to Ingrid. That was it."

Fumbling with the phone in one hand and the key in the other, I unlock the cage. "Who was the supplier?"

Zeke scoffs. "I'm not giving you his name."

I step into the cage and move to the box.

"Then at least tell me what Ingrid bought."

I get the answer twice, both of them arriving in unison. One is when Zeke blurts the word over the phone. The other is when I lift the shoebox's lid.

Inside, nestled on a bed of tissue paper, is a gun.

THE gun sits on my bed, a deep black against the comforter's cornflower blue. Beside it is the full magazine, also found in the shoebox Ingrid left behind. Six bullets, ready to be loaded.

It took all the courage I could muster just to carry the shoebox from the basement to the elevator. I spent the long ride to the twelfth floor in terror, and when I finally did remove the gun and magazine, I used only my thumb and forefinger.

It was the first time I'd ever touched a gun.

Thanks to Google and a soul-deadening number of websites devoted to pistols, I have learned I'm now in possession of a nine-millimeter Glock G43.

During the rest of my conversation with Zeke, he told me that Ingrid said she needed a gun. Fast. She gave him two grand in cash. He took it to his associate and came back with the Glock. "It took an hour, tops," he said. "It's the last time I heard from her."

What I still don't know is why Ingrid felt as though she needed a gun. And why she bequeathed it to me when she left.

And why she still isn't responding, even after I've sent a half dozen texts, all of which were versions of *WHAT IS GOING ON? WHERE ARE YOU? WHY DID YOU LEAVE ME A GUN?!?!?!*

I return the gun and the ammunition to the shoebox the same

way I removed them—cautiously. I then cover the box with its lid and carry the whole thing downstairs to the kitchen, where I shove it in the cupboard under the sink.

I check my watch. It's now almost eleven. Roughly ten hours since I found out Ingrid was gone. Something about this situation is very, very wrong. And the only thing I know is that if I'm going to find Ingrid, I'll have to do it all on my own.

ANOTHER night, another bad dream.

My family again. They're still in Central Park, occupying Bow Bridge, all of them holding hands and smiling up at me.

This time, though, they're on fire.

I'm once more perched on the roof, nestled inside one of George's open wings. I watch the fire engulf each of them. Jane waves to me. "Be careful," she calls out as smoke pours from her mouth.

It's thick smoke. Black and roiling and so strong I can smell it.

I look at George, his beaked face stoic. "Don't push me," I say.

His beak doesn't move when he answers. "I won't."

Then he uses a stone wing to nudge me off the roof.

I wake with a jerk on the crimson sofa in the sitting room, the nightmare clinging to me like sweat. I can still smell the smoke. It tickles my nose and throat. I cough.

That's when I understand what's going on. This isn't a dream. It's really happening. Something in the Bartholomew is on fire.

The smell of smoke drifts into the apartment. Out in the hallway, the fire alarm blares. Contained inside that incessant clanging is another sound—pounding. Someone is at the door.

In between those rattling knocks comes Nick's voice.

"Jules?" he shouts. "You in there? We need to get out of here!"

I fling open the door and see Nick standing in a T-shirt, sweatpants, and flip-flops. His hair is mussed. His eyes are fearful.

"What's going on?" I say.

"Fire. Not sure where."

I yank my jacket from the coatrack and shove it on, even as Nick starts to pull me out of the apartment. I shut the door behind me because I read that's what you're supposed to do.

Nick pulls me into the hall, where a thin haze of smoke is made more pronounced by the bright strobe of the emergency lights on the wall. "We have to take the stairs," he shouts over the alarm.

The stairwell pumps out smoke like a chimney. Soon we're descending, Nick moving at a quick, steady pace.

The smoke is thicker on the eleventh floor—a foglike undulating wall. I lift my jacket to cover my nose and mouth. Nick does the same with his T-shirt. "Go on ahead," he says. "I want to make sure no one else is still up here."

I don't want to go down alone. "I'll come with you," I say.

Nick shakes his head. "It's too dangerous. Keep going."

I grudgingly oblige, stumbling down the steps to the tenth floor. On the landing, I peer down the hall, squinting against the smoke in search of Greta Manville's apartment. The door is barely visible through the haze.

I make my way down the hall toward 10A, where I pound on the door. It opens immediately. Greta stands in the doorway, covered in a flannel nightgown and the same slippers she wore earlier. "I don't need you to rescue me," she says.

Only she kind of does. When she sets off down the hall, it's at a snail's pace. Her breath gets heavy before we even reach the stairs. When I try to ease her down the first step, her legs sway like wind-blown palms.

I clutch her hand. We both know we're not going to make it down those steps. Greta's too weak. I'm too terrified.

"The elevator," I say, hauling her back up that one meager step.

"You're not supposed to use an elevator during a fire."

I know that. Just like I knew about closing the apartment door.

"There's no other choice," I snap.

I head to the elevator, dragging Greta the same way Nick dragged me. I can feel her wrist twisting beneath my fingers, resisting my pull.

The elevator isn't stopped on the tenth floor. I'm forced to pound the button and wait. I keep coughing, and my eyes keep watering. Fear clangs in my skull. Louder than the alarm.

When the elevator finally arrives, I push Greta inside, following behind her. I close the grate and press the button for the lobby. With a rattle and a shudder, we start to descend.

The smoke is heavier on the ninth floor.

And still worse on the eighth.

We keep descending. When we reach the seventh floor, it's clear that this is the source of the fire. The smoke here is sharper, stabbing the inside of my throat.

I see firefighters coming and going along the seventh-floor hall with hoses that have been carried up the steps so that they spiral around the elevator shaft like pythons.

Just when we're about to move past the seventh floor, I hear a sharp bark, followed by the skitter of claws on tile. A furry blur darts past the elevator. I slam the emergency-stop button. The elevator comes to a quivering halt as Greta gives me a fearful look.

"What are you doing?"

"There's a dog," I say. "I think it's Rufus."

He barks again, and the noise pierces my heart. I pull open the grate. After that comes the thin-barred door. It takes both hands and an extra-hard tug to pry it open.

The elevator has stopped three feet below the landing, forcing me to pull myself up onto the seventh floor. I then crawl along the floor to evade the smoke—another of those things-to-do-in-a-fire facts I never thought I'd use.

While crawling, I cough out Rufus's name, the sound lost in all the noise. I see firefighters stomping into 7C, their voices muffled under helmets and face masks. Through the open apartment door comes a hot glow.

Flames. Pulsing and bright, a hypnotic orange-yellow.

I climb to my feet, drawn to it. I'm no longer afraid. All I feel now is curiosity. I take a step down the hall, coughing as I go.

"Jules," Greta calls. "Grab the dog and let's get out of here."

I ignore her and take another step. Although I suspect I have no choice at all in the matter. I'm being compelled.

I keep walking until there's a noticeable warmth on my face. The heat of the flames caressing my skin. I close my eyes against the smoke. I take a breath, sucking it in until I start to cough.

I experience a jolting moment during which I have no idea where I am, why I'm here, what I was just doing. But then I hear a bark behind me, and I whirl around, spotting a familiar shape.

Rufus. Panicked and lost.

Blindly, I drop to the floor again and pull him into my arms as he barks and struggles and paws my chest in agitation. Rather than crawl back to the elevator, I inch forward on my behind, scooting awkwardly until I reach it. Carefully, I drop the three feet back into the cage and, clutching Rufus in one hand, slam the grate shut with the other. Beside me, Greta shoots me a startled, fearful look before hitting the down button.

Lower we go, into the bottom half of the Bartholomew, the smoke getting lighter the farther we descend. By the time we reach the lobby, it's been reduced to a light haze.

As Greta and I leave the elevator and make our way across the lobby, we encounter a trio of EMTs on their way into the building. With them is a stretcher, its wheeled legs folded.

We step outside to a street painted red by the lights of two fire trucks and an ambulance stopped at the curb. The block has been closed to traffic, allowing people, many of them members of the media, to gather in the middle of Central Park West.

As soon as we hit the sidewalk, reporters push forward. Camera lights swing our way, blindingly bright. A dozen flashbulbs pop like firecrackers. A reporter shouts a question that I can't hear.

Rufus, as irritated as I am, barks. This draws Marianne Duncan out of the milling crowd. She's dressed in a flowing caftan, turban, and cat's-eye sunglasses. Her face is smeared with cold cream.

"Rufus?" She rushes toward me and lifts Rufus from my arms. "My baby! I was so worried about you." To me, she says, "Rufus got spooked and jumped out of my arms. I wanted to look for him, but a fireman told me I had to keep moving."

She's started to cry. Streaks appear in the cold cream, plowed by tears. "Thank you," she says. "Thank you, thank you!"

I can only muster a nod. I'm too dazed by the flashbulbs and the smoke, which continues to roll like a storm cloud in my lungs.

I leave Greta with Marianne and push my way through the crowd.

I spot Dylan in pajama bottoms and sneakers, looking impervious to the cold. Leslie Evelyn wears a black kimono, which swishes gracefully as she and Nick do a head count of residents.

When EMTs emerge with Mr. Leonard strapped to the stretcher and his face covered by an oxygen mask, the crowd breaks into applause. Mr. Leonard gives a weak thumbs-up.

By then I'm on the other side of Central Park West. I walk north a block, drop onto a bench, and sit with my back to the stone wall bordering Central Park.

I cough one last time. Then I allow myself to weep.

Chapter 6

Three Days Earlier

I WAKE JUST AFTER SEVEN to the same sound I heard my first night. The noise that's not a noise.

Although this time I no longer think someone's inside the apartment, I'm still curious about what it could be. So I force myself out of bed, shivering in a bedroom whose windows have gaped open all night. A necessity after the fire.

Padding downstairs in bare feet and flimsy nightclothes, I stop every so often to listen—really listen—to the sounds of the apartment. I hear noises aplenty, but nothing that matches *the* noise. That specific sound has suddenly vanished.

In the kitchen, I find my phone sitting on the counter, blaring out the ringtone reserved for Chloe. Worrisome, considering the two of us instituted a no-calls-until-coffee rule in college.

"I haven't had my coffee yet," I say upon answering.

"The rule doesn't apply when a fire is involved," Chloe says. "Are you okay?"

"I'm fine. The fire wasn't nearly as bad as it seemed."

The blaze itself was confined to 7C, Mr. Leonard's apartment. It turns out the heart palpitations Nick told me about earlier had returned. Rather than call 911, Mr. Leonard ignored the warning signs. Later, while he was cooking dinner, a heart attack arrived.

The fire started when Mr. Leonard dropped the pot holder in his hands as the coronary struck. It landed on the stovetop, where it quickly ignited.

It was Leslie Evelyn, also a seventh-floor resident, who called 911. She smelled the smoke, went into the hall to check, and saw the plumes rolling from Mr. Leonard's door. Because of her quick thinking, the rest of the Bartholomew remained mostly unscathed.

I learned all this once residents were allowed back in their apartments two hours later. Because the elevator can fit only so many people at a time, a gossipy crowd formed in the lobby. Some of them I recognized. Most of them I didn't. All of them, save for Nick, Dylan, and me, were well past sixty.

"How did you find out about it?" I ask Chloe.

"Your picture's on the front page of the newspaper."

"Wasn't there anything else to put on the front page? You know, like real news?"

"This *is* news," Chloe says. "Most New Yorkers see the Bartholomew as the closest thing to heaven on earth. But what a strange alternate universe you've stumbled into."

I move from the kitchen to the sitting room, where I'm greeted by the faces in the wallpaper. I instantly turn away.

"Trust me, this place is far from perfect."

"So you read that article I sent you," Chloe says. "Scary, right?"

"It's more than the article that's bothering me."

I tell her about meeting Ingrid, our plan to hang out each day, the scream from 11A, and Ingrid's insistence it was nothing. I finish with how Ingrid is now gone and not answering her phone and my suspicions that someone caused her to flee. Left out are all the worrisome parts—specifically, the note and the gun.

"You need to stop looking for her," Chloe says. "Whatever her reason for leaving, it's none of your business."

"I think she might be in some kind of trouble."

"Jules, listen to me. If this Ingrid person wanted your help, she would have called you. Clearly, she wants to be left alone."

"There's no one else looking for her," I say. "If I vanished, you'd look for me. I don't think Ingrid has a Chloe in her life."

There's silence on Chloe's end. I know what it means—she's choosing her words carefully in an attempt not to upset me.

"I think this has less to do with Ingrid and more to do with your sister."

"Of course my sister has something to do with it," I say. "Maybe she'd be here now if I hadn't stopped looking for her."

"Finding Ingrid won't bring Jane back."

No, I think, *it won't. But it* will *mean there's one less lost girl in the world. One less person who vanished into thin air.*

"I think you should get away from the Bartholomew," Chloe says. "Just for a few days. Crash at my place."

"I can't."

"Don't worry about imposing. Paul is taking me to Vermont for the weekend."

"It's not that," I say. "I'm not allowed to spend any nights away from the apartment. You know I need the money."

"And *you* know I'd rather loan you some cash than see you be held prisoner in the Bartholomew."

"It's a job," I remind her. "Not a prison. And don't worry about me. Go to Vermont. Have fun."

"Call me if you need anything," Chloe says. "I'll have my phone with me the whole time, even though our B-and-B is, like, in the middle of nowhere. There might not be cell service."

"I'll be fine."

When the call ends, I remain in the sitting room, staring at those faces in the wallpaper. They stare back, eyes unblinking, mouths open but silent, almost as if they want to tell me something.

Or maybe they're just flowers on wallpaper and, like Ingrid's departure, the Bartholomew is starting to get to me.

At twelve thirty, there's a knock on my door.

Greta Manville.

A surprise, although not an unpleasant one. Even more surprising is that she's dressed for an outing. Black capris and an oversize shirt. Sweater preppily tied around her neck.

"To thank you for your assistance last night, I will allow you to escort me to lunch."

She says it with benevolent pomp. Yet I detect another emotion lurking in the back of her throat—loneliness. I suspect that deep down, Greta likes my company.

I loop my arm through hers. "I would be happy to escort you."

We end up at a bistro a block away from the Bartholomew. A red awning covers the door, and lights twinkle in the windows. Inside, the place is bustling. But upon seeing Greta, the hostess leads us to a corner booth that's remained conspicuously empty.

"I called ahead," Greta says as she picks up one of the menus left for us on the table. "Also, the owner values loyalty. And I've been coming here for years, since the first time I lived at the Bartholomew."

"How long has it been since you moved back?" I ask.

Greta gives me a stern look across the table. "We're here to have lunch. Not play twenty questions."

"How about two questions?"

"I'll allow it," Greta says as she beckons the nearest waitress. "But let me order first. If I'm going to be interrogated, I'd like to make sure sustenance is on the way."

She orders grilled salmon with a side of steamed vegetables. Even though I assume she's treating, I get the house salad and a water. Frugal habits die hard.

"The answer to your first question," Greta says once the waitress departs, "is almost a year. I returned last November."

"Why did you come back?"

Greta sniffs, as if the answer is obvious. "Why not? It's a comfortable place with close proximity to everything I need."

"I heard it was difficult finding an open apartment there," I say. "Isn't the waiting list huge?"

"That's your third question, by the way." There's a noticeable upturn to her lips that she tries to hide by taking a sip of water. "The answer is yes, there is a waiting list. But there are ways around it if one knows the right people. I do."

When the food arrives, Greta's meal looks scrumptious, the salmon steaming and smelling of lemon and garlic. My salad is nothing but limp romaine lettuce smattered with tomato slices.

Greta takes a bite of fish before saying, "Has there been any news regarding your recently departed apartment-sitter friend? What was her name again?"

"Ingrid."

"That's right. Ingrid with the abominable hair. There's still no indication where she went?"

I shrug. "At first, I thought she was afraid to stay in the Bartholomew any longer."

Greta reacts the same way Nick did—with muted shock. "Why on earth would you think that?"

"You have to admit something feels off," I say. "There are entire websites devoted to the bad things that have happened there. The servants killed by Spanish flu. Dr. Bartholomew jumping from the roof. That doesn't happen at average buildings."

"The Bartholomew isn't an average building. And because of its notoriety, things that happen there become exaggerated to the point of myth."

"Is Cornelia Swanson a myth?"

Greta, who had been lifting a forkful of salmon to her mouth, halts mid-bite. She lowers her fork and says, "Cornelia Swanson was a lunatic. As for all that nonsense—that she consorted with that Frenchwoman and sacrificed her maid in some occult ritual— it's nothing more than conjecture. In fact, the strangest thing I've seen at the Bartholomew lately is the behavior of a certain young woman who helped escort me from the building last night."

I stab my fork into the salad, saying nothing.

"When the elevator was stopped on the seventh floor, you acted . . . unusual. Would you care to explain what happened?"

I should have seen this lunch for what it really is—an attempt to understand what she witnessed. Although I don't necessarily need to talk about it, I find myself wanting to.

"When I was a freshman in college, my father got laid off from the place he had worked for twenty-five years," I begin. "After months of searching, the only job he could get was the night shift stocking shelves at an Ace Hardware three towns away. My mother worked part-time at a real estate office. To make ends meet, she got another job waiting tables at a local diner on weekends. I tried to lighten their load by getting two jobs myself. That kept us afloat for the better part of a year."

But then, at the start of my sophomore year, my mother was diagnosed with non-Hodgkin's lymphoma, which spread to her kidneys, her heart, her lungs. My mother had to quit her jobs. My father cared for her during the day while still going to work at night. I offered to leave college for a semester to help. My father refused, telling me that if I quit, I'd likely never return.

My mother's medical expenses soared. And my father's meager health insurance plan covered only so much. Then the Ace Hardware my father worked at closed its doors. There went his job and health insurance.

"Not long after that, my parents died," I say.

Greta gasps. A shocked, sorrowful sound.

I keep talking, too far into the tale to stop now. "There was a fire. It was the middle of the spring semester. The phone rang at five in the morning. The police. They told me there had been an accident and that both of my parents were dead."

Later that day, Chloe drove me home, although there was nothing left of it. Our side of the duplex was a charred ruin.

"Smoke rose from the wreckage," I tell Greta. "It was an awful throat-coating smoke I hoped I'd never smell again. But I did. Last night at the Bartholomew."

The only thing that survived was my parents' Toyota Camry. On the driver's seat was a ring with three keys on it. The instant I saw them, I knew the fire hadn't been an accident.

One key was for the Camry itself. The other two opened storage units at a facility a mile outside of town.

One unit contained my belongings. The other held Jane's.

My father had emptied both our bedrooms, which told me that even in their darkest hours, my parents still clung to a sliver of hope that Jane would be found. That things would turn out okay for us.

Arson investigators concluded that on the night of the fire, my father and mother shared a bottle of my mother's strongest pain-killers. They said the fire began in the hallway outside my parents' room, spurred by lighter fluid and some newspapers. My mother died from the overdose. My father was killed by the smoke.

"I tried to be mad at them," I say. "But I couldn't. Because even then I knew they did what they thought was right."

I don't tell Greta that sometimes I get the need to flirt with fire. To feel its heat on my skin. To know what it feels like, so I can understand what my parents went through.

Greta slips her hand over mine. "I'm sorry for your loss. I'm sure you miss them greatly."

"I do," I say. "I miss them. I miss Jane."

"Jane?"

"My sister. She vanished two years before the fire. There's been no trace of her since."

I've slumped noticeably in the booth, my arms at my sides. Talk-ing about my parents and Jane doesn't make my grief better or worse. It simply remains.

"Now I see why you're so keen to find Ingrid," Greta says.

"I just can't shake the feeling she's in trouble," I say. "She specifi-cally told me she had nowhere else to go."

This elicits a sympathetic sigh from Greta. "If I were you, I'd call some of the hospitals in the area. If that doesn't work, I'd look around the neighborhood. There's a chance she's out on the streets. Have you checked any homeless shelters?"

"You think I should?"

"It certainly couldn't hurt," Greta says with a firm nod. "Ingrid Gallagher might be there, hiding in plain sight."

THE nearest homeless shelter for women is twenty blocks south and two blocks west of the restaurant. After making sure Greta can get back to the Bartholomew on her own, I go there on the slim chance that she's right and Ingrid is living on the streets.

The shelter is housed in a building that's seen better days. The exterior is brown brick. The windows are tinted. It used to be a YMCA, as evidenced by the ghost of those letters hovering to the right of the main entrance.

I make my way into the building. Just inside the door is a registration desk behind a shield of scuffed reinforced glass.

"Excuse me," I say to the woman at the desk. "I'm looking for someone. A friend."

I press my phone against the glass so she can see the selfie of Ingrid and me in Central Park. After a moment's contemplation, she says, "She doesn't look familiar. But I'm only here during the day. This place fills up at night, so there's a chance she's here then and I just missed her."

"Is it possible to talk to someone who *is* here at night?"

She gestures to a pair of double doors opposite the desk. "There's a few of them still here. You're welcome to take a look."

I push through the doors into a gymnasium that's been turned into a space for two hundred people. Identical cots have been spread across the floor in untidy rows of twenty each.

I walk among the cots, seeking out the few that are occupied just in case one of them is Ingrid. At the end of one row, a woman sits straight-backed on the edge of her cot. She stares at an inspirational poster taped to the wall. A field of lavender swaying in the breeze. At the bottom is a quotation from Eleanor Roosevelt.

With the new day comes new strength and new thoughts.

"Every day, before I leave for work, I sit and stare at this poster, hoping that Eleanor is right," the woman says. "But so far, each new day only brings the same old crap."

"It could be worse," I blurt out. "We could be dead."

"Gotta say, I wouldn't mind seeing *that* on an inspirational poster." The woman slaps her thigh and lets out a raucous laugh. "I haven't seen you before. You new?"

"Just visiting," I say.

"Lucky you."

I take that to mean she's been here awhile. A surprise, seeing how she doesn't look homeless. Her clothes are clean and well-pressed. Khaki pants, white shirt, blue cardigan. All of them in better condition than what I'm wearing. My sweater has a hole at the cuff that I cover with my left hand as I hold out my phone with my right.

"I'm looking for someone who might be staying here. This is a recent picture of her."

The woman eyes the photo of Ingrid and me with curiosity. "Her face doesn't ring any bells. And I've been here a month."

"She would have been here in the past day," I say. "Her name is Ingrid. I'm Jules."

The woman looks up from the photo and smiles. "I'm Bobbie."

She pats the space next to her, and I join her on the cot. "It's nice to meet you, Bobbie."

"Likewise, Jules." She plucks the phone from my hand to study the photo once more. "Is Ingrid in trouble?"

"That's what I'm trying to find out. If she is, I want to help her."

Bobbie sizes me up. I suspect she sees a kindred spirit, because she says, "I'll keep an eye out for her if you want. Can you send me the picture?"

"Sure."

Bobbie gives me her phone number, and I text her the photo.

"I'll save your number," she says. "So I can call you if I run into her."

"Thanks. I hope life gets easier for you very soon," I say.

"And I hope you find your friend," Bobbie says. "Doing good deeds makes this rotten world just a little bit better."

WHEN I return to the Bartholomew, at three o'clock, Charlie greets me outside, a dark look of concern in his eyes.

"Someone's here to see you," he says. "A young man. He's been here awhile. After an hour, I told him he could wait inside."

Charlie opens the door, and my stomach drops.

There, standing just inside the lobby, is Andrew.

His unexpected—and unwanted—presence makes me see red. I march through the door. "What the hell are you doing here?"

Andrew looks up from his phone. "You haven't responded to my calls or texts."

"So you just showed up? How did you even know I was here?"

"I saw your picture in the paper," Andrew says. "It took me a minute to realize it was you. You're much prettier in person."

Andrew flashes his seductive grin. The one that made me weak-kneed when we first met. It's a dazzling smile, and he knows it.

"What do you want, Andrew?"

"To apologize. I truly hate how we ended things. The way I treated you was awful. There's no excuse for it."

"You should have said all this two weeks ago," I tell him.

"I never meant to hurt you, Jules. I need you to know that."

He moves in and attempts to tuck a lock of hair behind my ear. Another of his surefire moves. He did it right before our first kiss.

I slap his hand away.

"You have every reason to be angry and hurt," he says. "I just wanted to tell you that I regret everything. And that I'm sorry."

He stands in place, as if waiting for something. I think he wants me to forgive him. I don't plan on doing that anytime soon.

"Fine," I say. "You've said your apologies. Now you can go."

Andrew doesn't budge.

"There's something else," he says, growing quiet.

I cross my arms and huff. "What else could there possibly be?"

"I need—" Andrew looks around the lobby until he's certain there's no one else around. "I need money."

I stare at him, stunned. "You can't be serious."

"It's for the rent," he says, his voice a whisper.

"What makes you think I have any money to give?"

"Because you live *here*." Andrew spreads his arms wide, gesturing at the grandiose lobby. "I don't know what racket you've got going, Jules, but I'm impressed."

Just then, Nick enters the lobby, looking particularly dashing in a fitted gray suit. Even better, he looks rich, which prompts Andrew to eye him with undisguised contempt. Seeing it makes me feel petty. Vindictively so. Which is why I rush to Nick and say, "There you are! I've been waiting for you!"

I pull him into a hug, whispering desperately into his ear, "Please go along with this."

Then I kiss him. More than just a quick peck on the lips. It's a kiss that lingers—long enough for me to feel the jealousy radiating from Andrew's side of the lobby.

Nick, thankfully, continues the charade. Throwing an arm over my shoulder, he says, "Who's this?"

"This is Andrew," I say.

Nick steps forward to shake Andrew's hand. "A pleasure to meet you, Andrew. I'm Nick. I'd love to stay and chat, but Jules and I have an important thing to get to."

"Yes," I add. "Very important. I suggest you run along as well."

Andrew hesitates a moment, his gaze switching between Nick and me. His expression is a mixture of insult and injury.

"Bye, Andrew." I give him a weak wave. "Have a nice life."

With one last regretful look, Andrew slips out the door and, I hope, out of my life. Once he's gone, I pull away from Nick, humiliation burning my cheeks.

"I am *so* sorry about that. I needed him to leave and couldn't think of a better way to make that happen."

"I think it worked," Nick says while absently touching his lips. "I'm guessing Andrew is an ex-boyfriend?"

We make our way to the elevator, cramming ourselves inside. Standing shoulder to shoulder with Nick, I'm exposed once again to his cologne. That woodsy, citrusy scent.

"He is," I say as we begin our ascent. "Unfortunately."

"It ended badly?"

"That would be an understatement."

The elevator reaches the top floor. Nick moves the grate aside, allowing me to exit first. As we walk down the hall, he says, "I'm glad I ran into you. And not just because of the way you greeted me in the lobby. I wanted to know if you'd heard from Ingrid."

"Not a peep."

"That's disappointing. I was hoping you had."

I could tell Nick about the gun. Or the note Ingrid left that I try not to think about: *BE CAREFUL.*

I don't mention them for the same reasons I didn't tell Chloe. I don't want Nick to think I'm being overly worried, even paranoid.

"I know she's not in the homeless shelter I just returned from visiting," I say.

"That was some smart thinking to look for her there, though."

"I can't take credit. It was Greta Manville's idea."

Nick's brows lift in surprise. "Greta? If I didn't know any better, I'd say the two of you are becoming friends."

"I think she just wants to help," I say.

We reach the end of the hallway, pausing in the wide space between the doors to our respective apartments.

"I'd like to help, too," Nick says. "Seriously, if you need anything at all, let me know. Especially if Andrew comes back."

He gives me a wink and heads to his apartment. I do the same, pausing in the foyer as soon as the door is closed behind me. I feel slightly dizzy, and not just because of Nick. The past twenty-four hours have been bordering on the surreal. Ingrid going missing. The fire. Having lunch with Greta Manville.

Chloe was right. It is indeed a strange universe I've stumbled into. I just hope she's wrong about something else she told me: that it's all probably too good to be true.

Chapter 7

I SPEND THE NEXT TWO HOURS following Greta's other suggestion and calling every hospital in Manhattan. None of them is aware of an Ingrid Gallagher or a Jane Doe matching her description being admitted within the past twenty-four hours.

I'm about to start on hospitals in outer boroughs when there's another knock on my door. It's Charlie this time, standing in the hall with the largest flower arrangement I've ever laid eyes on. It's so big that Charlie himself is practically invisible behind it.

"Charlie, what will your wife think?"

"Cut it out," Charlie says, a blush in his voice. "They're not from me. I'm just the deliveryman."

I gesture for him to set down the arrangement on the coffee table. As he does, I count at least three dozen blooms. Roses and lilies and snapdragons. Tucked among them is a card: *Thank you for saving my beloved Rufus! You're an angel!—Marianne*

"I heard you were quite the hero last night," Charlie says.

"I was just being a good neighbor," I say. "Speaking of which, how's your daughter? One of the other doormen told me there was some sort of emergency."

"She's fine now. But it's nice of you to ask."

I take a sniff of the flowers. They smell heavenly. "She's lucky to have a dad like you."

Charlie drifts toward the door, seemingly unsure about whether to leave. But then he says, "I heard you were asking about that other apartment sitter. The one who left."

"Ingrid Gallagher. Leslie told me you were the doorman on duty the night she left but that you never actually saw her leave."

"I didn't. I had to step away from the door to deal with the security camera in the basement—it was disconnected. A wire had come loose. It was an easy fix."

"When did you notice it was out?"

"A little after one a.m."

My body freezes. That was around the time I heard the scream and went to check on Ingrid.

The timing seems too convenient to be a coincidence. My first thought is that Ingrid disconnected the camera herself so she could leave unnoticed. But there's no rule requiring apartment sitters to remain at the Bartholomew if they don't want to.

"Did you see anyone going to the basement before you realized the camera was out?"

"I didn't. I was outside, attending to another resident."

"At that hour? Who was it?"

Charlie straightens his spine. "I don't think Mrs. Evelyn will like that I'm telling you so much. I want to help, but—"

"I know, I know. The building's big on privacy. But if your

daughter were missing, you'd be asking a lot of questions, too."

"If my daughter was missing, I wouldn't rest until I found her."

"Don't you think Ingrid deserves the same treatment?" I say. "You don't have to tell me a name. Just give me a little hint."

Charlie sighs and looks past me to the flowers on the coffee table. A hint almost as massive as the bouquet itself.

"She took the dog out a little before one," Charlie says. "That's not the hour a woman should be on the street alone. Once Rufus did his business, we went back inside. She took the elevator to the seventh floor, and I peeked at the security monitors. That's when I saw the camera in the basement was out."

"Thank you, Charlie." I snap off a rose from the bouquet and place it in the buttonhole on his lapel. "You've been a huge help."

With a tip of his cap, Charlie opens the door to leave. Before he can make it all the way out, I toss him one last question.

"What apartment does Marianne Duncan live in?"

"Why?"

I flash him an innocent smile. "So I can send her a thank-you note, of course."

I'm certain Charlie doesn't believe me. He looks away, gazing into the hallway, then tosses an answer over his shoulder.

"Seven A," he says.

THE seventh floor is as busy now as it was last night. Only instead of firefighters, it's contractors moving through the smoke-stained halls. The door to Mr. Leonard's apartment now leans against a wall stippled with smoke damage. Next to it is a section of kitchen counter, its surface covered with burn marks. Soot spreads across the tile floor like black mold.

I move in the opposite direction, toward the front of the building. At 7A, I give two short raps on the door.

Marianne answers in a rush of perfume-scented air. "Darling!" she says, pulling me in for a hug and an air kiss. "I was hoping I'd see you today. I can't thank you enough for rescuing my Rufus."

I'm not surprised to see Marianne carrying Rufus in her arms. What is a surprise is that both of them are wearing hats. Hers is black with a wide, floppy brim. His is a tiny top hat held in place with an elastic band.

"I just stopped by to thank you for the flowers," I say. "They're beautiful. But you really didn't need to go to all that trouble."

"Of course I did. You were a complete angel last night."

"And how's Rufus?" I say. "All better after last night, I hope."

"He's fine. Just a little scared. Isn't that right, Rufus?"

The dog nuzzles the crook of her arm, trying in vain to free himself of the tiny top hat. He stops when a sudden bang echoes up the hallway from 7C.

"Horrible, isn't it?" Marianne says of the noise. "I'm sorry about what happened to Mr. Leonard, and I wish him a speedy recovery. But it's quite an inconvenience for the rest of us."

"It's been an eventful few days. What with the fire and that apartment sitter leaving so suddenly."

I hope the mention of Ingrid sounds less calculated to Marianne than it does to me. To my ears, it clangs with obviousness.

"What apartment sitter?" Marianne's face remains obscured by her hat, making her expression unreadable.

"Ingrid Gallagher. She was in 11A. Then two nights ago, she suddenly left without telling anyone."

"I wouldn't know anything about that."

Marianne's voice isn't unkind. Her tone hasn't changed. Yet she peeks into the hallway, checking to see if anyone else is around. Only one is—a workman outside Mr. Leonard's door.

"I heard you and Rufus went to the lobby the night she left," I say. Again, it's not the subtlest of transitions. But there's no telling how long Marianne's sharing mood is going to last. "Did you see or hear her go?"

"I—" Marianne stops herself, changing course. "No. I didn't." She's got one hand on the door now. When she raises her other hand to the brim of her hat, I see it's trembling. She gives the hallway another up-and-down glance and says, "I need to go."

"Marianne, wait—"

She tries to close the door, but I slide my foot against the frame, blocking it. I peer at her through the six-inch gap that remains.

"What aren't you telling me, Marianne?"

"Please," she hisses, her face still hidden in shadow. "Please stop asking questions. No one here is going to answer them."

Marianne pushes the door against my foot, forcing me to pull it away. Then the door slams shut in another perfume-soaked rush.

Twisting away from Marianne's door, I see Leslie Evelyn standing a few yards down the hall. She's just returned from a yoga class. Lululemon tights. Rolled-up mat under her arm. Thin line of sweat sparkling along her hairline.

"Is there a problem here?"

"No," I say, even though she clearly saw Marianne slam the door in my face. "No problem at all."

"Are you sure? Because it looks to me like you're bothering one of the tenants, which you know is strictly against the rules."

"Yes, but—"

Leslie silences me with a raised hand. "If I see you bothering Marianne, or any of the residents, again—about anything—I'm afraid you'll have to go."

"I understand," I say. "And I'm sorry. It's just that I still haven't heard from Ingrid, and I'm worried something bad happened."

"Nothing bad happened to her," Leslie says. "At least not within these walls. She left willingly."

"How do you know that for sure?"

"Because I was in her apartment. There were no signs of a struggle. Nor was anything left behind."

Only she's wrong about that. Ingrid did leave without something—a Glock that's now stowed under the kitchen sink in 12A. Which means Leslie could also be wrong about Ingrid not leaving other things behind.

I apologize to Leslie once more and hurry away, suddenly seized with the idea that some of Ingrid's things could still be in 11A. Shoved in the back of a closet. Under a bed. And among those items could be something indicating not only where Ingrid went but also whom she was running from.

I won't know unless I look for myself. Not an easy task. Adding to the difficulty is that it needs to be done quickly and quietly.

Because now I have another, unexpected worry to contend with. Leslie is watching my every move.

"I REALLY don't think this is a good idea," Nick says.

The two of us are in the kitchen of 12A, staring into the open dumbwaiter. Nick scratches his neck, charmingly uncertain.

"You know of a better way to get into Ingrid's apartment?"

"You could just ask Leslie to let you in. She's got a key."

"I'm on her bad side at the moment."

I give him a quick rundown of the past hour, from Charlie's flower delivery to Marianne's skittishness to the idea that 11A might still contain some clue regarding what happened to Ingrid.

"With Leslie unlikely to cooperate, it's the dumbwaiter or nothing," I say. "You lower me down, I look around, you pull me back up."

Nick continues to eye the dumbwaiter with skepticism. "There are, like, a hundred ways in which your plan can go wrong."

"Please, Nick. Just a quick look. Down and back."

"Down and back," he says, giving the rope a tug to test its strength. "How much time do you plan on spending down there?"

"Five minutes. Maybe ten."

"I told you I'd help, so I will," Nick says, shaking his head, as if he can't quite believe he's agreed to this. "What's the plan?"

The plan is for me to climb into the dumbwaiter with my phone and a flashlight. Nick will lower me into 11A. As soon as I'm out, he'll raise it back to 12A, in case Leslie keeps tabs on this kind of thing. I'll then search the apartment while Nick keeps watch on the stairwell landing between the eleventh and twelfth floors. If it looks like someone is approaching, he'll alert me with a text. I'll then leave immediately, using the door, making sure it locks behind me.

We hit our first hurdle as soon as I try to climb into the dumbwaiter. It's a tight fit, made possible only by curling into a fetal position. The dumbwaiter starts creaking as soon as I'm inside, and for a fraught, fearful moment I think it's going to collapse under my weight. When it doesn't, I give Nick a nervous nod.

"We're good," I say.

Nick gives the rope a tug, freeing it from the locking mechanism on the pulleys above. The dumbwaiter immediately drops several inches. Startled, I let out a whimpered half shriek, prompting Nick to say, "Everything's okay. I've still got you."

"I know," I say.

I grip the twin strands of rope running through the dumbwaiter. Now they're on the move, sliding through my clenched fists. I descend, the bottom of the cupboard level first with my thighs, then my chest, then my shoulders. When it reaches eye level, only a two-inch gap remains. Nick gives the rope a heave, and the gap closes completely, plunging me into darkness. I become convinced the dumbwaiter is getting smaller, shrinking ever so slightly, forcing me into a tighter ball.

I flick on the flashlight. A terrible idea. In the sudden glow, the dumbwaiter's walls remind me of the inside of a coffin.

I turn off the light. Thrust once more into darkness, I notice the sudden lack of noise around me. The dumbwaiter has stopped.

But then my phone lights up. A text from Nick: *You're lowered.*

I elbow the wall to my left, realizing it's not a wall at all.

It's a door. A cupboard door, to be precise. One that slides upward just like its twin in 12A. I lift it and slide out.

In the darkened kitchen of 11A, I text Nick back: *I'm in.*

Two seconds later, the dumbwaiter begins to move. Watching its rise, I close the cupboard door and turn on the flashlight.

There's no turning back now. Time to start searching.

I begin in the kitchen, shining the flashlight into every cupboard and drawer. Nothing looks out of place. Nor does anything look like it once belonged to Ingrid. The phone brightens in my hand. Another text from Nick: *On the landing now. All is clear.*

I continue the search, going through the hallway, the living room, and the study, all of which follow the same layout as 12A. There's even a desk and bookshelf in the study, although they're as devoid of information as the ones directly above them. The desk is empty. The bookshelf mostly is, too.

I move to the other side of the apartment, the one that doesn't follow the same layout as mine. Here I find a bathroom and two small bedrooms across the hall from each other.

At the end of the hall is the door to the master bedroom. While not as grand as the one in 12A, it's still impressive. There's a king-size bed, an eighty-inch flat-screen TV, a master bath, and a walk-in closet. That's where I go first, aiming the flashlight over bare carpet, empty shelves, dozens of wooden hangers holding nothing. I go to the bathroom next, finding it equally empty.

There's clearly nothing of Ingrid's left in this apartment. I haven't seen a single box or suitcase. But I also don't want to leave without checking every square inch of the place.

I do a quick check under the bed, sweeping the flashlight back and forth across the carpet. Nothing.

I go to the nightstand on the left side of the bed. Nothing.

I then check the one on the right. Something.

A book, resting at the bottom of an otherwise empty drawer.

A new text arrives from Nick. *Someone's in the elevator. It's moving up.*

I aim the flashlight at the book in the drawer. *Heart of a Dreamer.* I'd recognize that cover anywhere. When I pick it up, I find a bookmark with a red tassel tucked among its pages.

I've seen this book—and bookmark—before. In a photo Ingrid posted on Instagram. I've finally found something she left behind.

I slide the bookmark from its place and flip backward through the book, checking for notes in the margins. There's nothing until I get to the title page, which bears an inscription.

> *Darling Ingrid,*
> *Such a pleasure! Your youthfulness gives me life!*
> *Best wishes,*
> *Greta Manville*

My phone lights up. I see four missed texts from Nick, each one more frightening than the last: *Elevator stopped on 11. It's Leslie! Someone's with her. They're heading to 11A!!* The last text, sent mere seconds ago, makes my heart rattle: *HIDE.*

I drop the book back into the nightstand drawer and push it shut. Then I rush to the hallway just in time to hear the sound of a key turning a lock, the door opening, and, finally, the voice of Leslie Evelyn filling the apartment.

"Here we are, sweetie: 11A."

LESLIE AND HER GUEST ARE roaming 11A, their voices low, conversational. So far, they've stayed on the other side of the apartment. The study. The sitting room. Right now they're in the kitchen, Leslie saying something I can't quite make out.

I remain in the master bedroom, where I've stuffed myself beneath the bed. I lie on my stomach, the phone shoved under me to block the glow if Nick texts again.

Outside the bedroom, Leslie's voice gets louder, clearer, which means she's left the kitchen and is getting closer.

"This is one of the Bartholomew's nicest units," she says.

The person with her is a woman, young and chipper. I notice a quiver in her voice when she says, "It's an amazing apartment."

"It is," Leslie agrees. "Which means staying here is a big responsibility. We need someone who'll watch over the place."

Ah, so this is an interview for Ingrid's replacement.

"What's your current employment situation?" Leslie says.

"I'm an actress," the girl says. "I'm waiting tables part-time until I get my big break."

She lets out a nervous chuckle, making light of the idea. I watch their shadows glide along the hallway wall. A moment later they're in the bedroom, Leslie flicking on the overhead light. They cross the room. Then approach the bed.

Then stop so close that I can see their shoes. Black pumps for Leslie. Scuffed Keds for the girl. I hold my breath, my heart pounding so loud in my chest that I'm certain they can hear it.

"What's your relationship status?" Leslie asks.

"I, um, have a boyfriend. Will that be a problem?"

"For you, yes," Leslie says. "There are certain rules temporary tenants must follow. One of them is no visitors. Another is no nights spent away from the apartment. So if you're approved, I'm afraid you won't be seeing much of your boyfriend."

"I'm sure it won't be a problem," the girl says.

"I've heard that before," Leslie says. Her black pumps are mere inches from my face. "Tell me about your family. Any next of kin?"

"My parents live in Maryland. Same with my younger sister. She wants to be an actress, too."

"How lovely for your parents." Leslie pauses. "Shall we return to the lobby?"

They leave the bedroom, Leslie flicking off the lights on her way. Soon I hear the front door close and the key click in the lock.

Even though they're gone, I wait before moving.

One second. Two seconds. Three. I slide my phone out from under me and check for a text from Nick.

It arrives thirty seconds later. *They're in the elevator.*

I crawl out from under the bed and move into the hall on tiptoe. At the door, I undo the lock and peek outside, making sure they're really gone. Seeing no one, I lock the door again, close it behind me, and sprint to the staircase.

Nick is still on the landing, his expression changing from fraught to overjoyed when he sees me running up the steps.

"That was nerve-racking," he says.

"You have no idea."

My heart continues to hammer in my chest, making me light-headed. Nick is gripping my hand, his palm hot as he quickly pulls me up the steps to the twelfth-floor landing.

We head to his apartment—running, giggling, shushing, both of us riding the high of getting away with something. Inside, Nick leans against the door, his chest heaving. "Did we just do that?"

I'm also out of breath, answering in huffs. "I think . . . we did."

Nick, his hand still holding mine, pulls me into a giddy embrace. Adrenaline leaps off him like an electrical current, passing straight into me until I'm so dizzy the room spins.

I look into Nick's eyes, hoping that will steady me. Instead, I only feel increasingly unmoored. Caught in a wave of euphoria, I press myself against him until our faces are inches apart.

Then I kiss him. A quick, impromptu peck that makes me instantly recoil in shame. "I'm sorry," I say.

Nick stares at me, a flash of hurt in his eyes. "Why? Did you not want to kiss me?"

"I did. It's just—I wasn't sure if you wanted me to."

"Try it again and see."

I kiss Nick again. Slowly this time. Anxiously. It helps that Nick's an amazing kisser. An expert. I willingly lose myself in the sensation of his lips on mine, his heart thundering beneath my palm, his hand on the small of my back.

The two of us say nothing as we move down the hallway on swaying legs, kissing against one wall before breaking away and reconnecting a few steps later. I follow him up the spiral steps to his bedroom, his white-hot hand brushing mine.

I pause for a moment at the top, a meek voice in the back of my brain telling me this is all happening too quickly. But then Nick kisses me again. On my lips. On my earlobe.

On the nape of my neck as he starts to undress me.

When my clothes fall away, all my worries go with them.

Relieved, I let Nick guide me to his bed.

Now

DR. WAGNER *stares at me expectantly, waiting for me to continue.* "Escaped?"

"That's what I said."

I don't mean to be standoffish. But I'm not ready to trust anyone at the moment. A by-product of living at the Bartholomew.

"I want to talk to the police," I say. "And Chloe. My best friend."

"We can call her," Dr. Wagner says. "I'll have Bernard look through your things and find the number."

I let out a relieved sigh. "Thank you."

"Why did you feel the need to escape from the Bartholomew?"

I'm going to have to tell him everything. This time, it's not a matter of trust. It's a matter of how much I think he'll believe.

"I met a girl on my first day. She later disappeared."

I sound calm now, even though on the inside I'm at full panic.

"She was there one minute, gone the next. As if she had died."

I pause, giving the statement enough time to settle over Dr. Wagner. When it does, he says, "It sounds to me like you think someone at the Bartholomew was murdered."

"I do," *I say before adding the stinger.* "Several people."

Chapter 8

Two Days Earlier

WHEN I WAKE, it's not George I see outside the window but a different gargoyle. His twin. The one that occupies the south-facing corner. I eye him with suspicion. But then I realize I'm not alone.

Nick is asleep beside me, his face buried in a pillow, his broad back rising and falling. Which explains the different gargoyle.

And the very different bedroom, which I'm just now noticing. The previous night comes roaring back. The mad dash from 11A. Kissing downstairs. Then kissing upstairs. Then doing a lot more upstairs. Things I haven't done since before Andrew and I moved in together.

I sit up to check the nightstand clock. Ten minutes after seven.

I spent the entire night here and not in 12A. Yet another Bartholomew rule I've broken.

I slip out of bed naked, shivering in the morning chill and feeling suddenly shy. I've barely slipped on my panties when Nick's voice rises from the bed. "Are you leaving?"

"Sorry, yeah. I need to go," I say, pulling on my blouse.

Nick sits up. "Why the rush?"

I gesture to the clock. "I didn't spend the night in 12A. I broke one of Leslie's rules."

"I'm not going to tell anyone, if that's what you're worried about." Nick gets out of bed, displaying none of my shyness. He moves to the window and stretches, showing off a body so beautiful my knees go weak. He toes a pair of plaid boxers on the floor, deems them acceptable, and slides them on.

"I'm worried about losing twelve thousand dollars."

I step into my jeans and give him a quick, closemouthed kiss, hoping he can't detect my morning breath. Then, with my shoes in hand, I scamper barefoot down the stairs.

"I had a great time," he says as he trails behind me. "I'd like to do it again sometime." He flashes a grin the devil would envy.

Heat rushes to my cheeks. "Me too. But not now."

Nick grips my arm, not letting me leave. "Hey, I forgot to ask. Did you find anything in 11A? I meant to ask last night, but . . ."

"I found a book. *Heart of a Dreamer.*"

"Not surprising. Copies of that are everywhere in this building. Are you sure it was Ingrid's?"

"Her name was in it," I say. "Greta signed it for her."

I'd love to tell Nick more. But I really, really want to get back to 12A, just in case Leslie Evelyn decides to drop by.

"We'll talk later," I say. "Promise."

I give him one last kiss, then rush into the hallway and make a barefoot dash from 12B to 12A.

Once inside, I drop my shoes on the floor and toss my keys toward the bowl. But my aim is off yet again, and the keys end up on the heating vent, where they skitter, slide, and drop through.

Sigh.

Wearily, I head to the kitchen. Since I don't have one of those handy magnet sticks Charlie used, I search the junk drawer for a screwdriver. I end up finding three. I grab all of them, plus a penlight that's also in the drawer.

While I unscrew the grate, I think about Nick. Mostly I think about what he thinks of me. That I'm easy? Desperate? I harbor no illusions that he and I are going to get married and live out our days on the top floor of the Bartholomew. That only happens in fairy tales. In three months, it'll be back to reality for me.

I'm pleased to see that Charlie was right about the grate being easy to remove. I loosen the screws and remove the covering without a problem.

I aim the penlight into the vent and immediately spot the keys. Surrounding them are other items that have fallen in and been forgotten. Two buttons. A rubber band. A dangly earring.

I grab the keys and leave everything else. Before replacing the grate, I sweep the light across the bottom, just in case something valuable has fallen in there. Like cash. A girl's allowed to dream.

Seeing nothing of value, I'm about to turn off the penlight when it catches the edge of something shiny wedged in the corner. I move in for a closer look. Although not cash, it's something just as unexpected: a cell phone.

I grab it and turn it over in my hands. When I try to turn it on, nothing happens, surely because the battery is dead. It might have been down there for months.

This phone is the same brand as mine. Although the one I have is older, my charger fits it all the same. I go upstairs and plug it in, hoping that after it charges I'll be able to figure out who it belongs to and eventually return it.

While the phone charges, I replace the grate over the vent and then take a shower. Freshly scrubbed and dressed, I return to the phone and see it now has just enough juice to be turned on. When I do, the screen displays a photograph, presumably of its owner.

Pale face. Almond-shaped eyes. Brown hair in unruly curls.

I swipe a finger across the screen, seeing that the phone is locked—a security feature. Without a passcode to unlock it, there's no way of knowing whose phone this is. Or was.

I swipe back to the first screen, staring again at the woman pictured on it. A realization bubbles up from the well of my memory.

I've seen this woman before. In a different picture.

In an instant I'm out of 12A and inside the elevator, which shuttles me to the lobby with excruciating slowness. Outside the Bartholomew, I pass a doorman who isn't Charlie and make a right.

I practically run down the sidewalk until I'm two blocks from the Bartholomew. There, at the corner streetlamp, is a piece of paper hanging on by its last bit of tape.

In the dead center is a photograph of the woman whose phone I found. Above it is that red-lettered word that so repelled me the first time I saw the flyer: MISSING.

Beneath it is the woman's name. One I also recognize.

Erica Mitchell. The apartment sitter who was in 12A before me.

BACK AT 12A, I SLAP THE FLYER flat against the kitchen counter and stare at it, my heart buzzing.

Erica and Ingrid. Both were apartment sitters at the Bartholomew. Both are now missing. That can't be a coincidence.

Next to Erica's photo is a line of text: LAST SEEN OCTOBER 4.

That was twelve days ago. Just a few days after Ingrid moved into the Bartholomew. At the bottom of the page is a number to call if anyone has information regarding Erica's whereabouts.

I grab my phone and dial. I have no doubt that whoever put up that flyer will be very interested to know I found Erica's phone.

The call is answered by a man with a distinctly familiar voice.

"This is Dylan."

I pause, surprise rendering me temporarily mute.

"Dylan the apartment sitter at the Bartholomew?"

Now it's his turn to pause. "Yes. Who is this?"

"It's Jules," I say. "Jules Larsen. In 12A."

"How did you get my number?"

"From the missing poster for Erica Mitchell."

The line goes dead. I'm about to call back when the phone buzzes in my hand.

A text from Dylan: *We can't talk about Erica. Not here.*

I text him back. *Why not?*

Several seconds pass before his next message appears. *Someone might hear us.*

I'm alone.

Do you know that for certain?

I start to type my reply, but Dylan beats me to the punch. *Why are you calling about Erica?*

Because I found her phone.

My own phone rings suddenly. It's Dylan calling, likely too shocked to text. "Where did you find it?" he says when I answer.

"In a heating vent in the floor."

"I want to see it," Dylan says. "But not here. The Museum of Natural History. Meet me at the elephants at noon. Come alone, and don't tell anyone about this."

I end the call with a queasy feeling in my gut, anxiety gnawing at my insides. Something very wrong is going on here. Something I can't begin to comprehend.

I LEAVE the Bartholomew at the same time Mr. Leonard makes his return. It's a surprise to see him out of the hospital so soon, mostly because he looks like he could use another day there. It requires the assistance of both Jeannette and Charlie to get him out of the cab and across the sidewalk.

When I get to the Museum of Natural History, I'm delayed by the busloads of students swarming the front steps. I nudge my way through them, jealous of their youth, their happiness, their drama and chatter. Life hasn't touched them yet. Not real life.

Once inside the Theodore Roosevelt Rotunda, I pass beneath the skeletal arms of the massive barosaurus and head to the ticket counter. The woman asks if I want to pay the suggested donation. I give her five dollars and get a judgmental look in return.

After that bit of humiliation, I enter the Akeley Hall of African Mammals. Or, as Dylan put it, the elephants.

He's already there, waiting for me on a wooden bench. His attempts to appear inconspicuous make him stand out all the more. Black jeans. Black hoodie. Sunglasses over his eyes.

"You're five minutes late," he says.

"And you look like a spy," I reply.

Dylan removes the sunglasses and surveys the packed hall. The schoolkids have started to ooze into the area, crowding around the nature dioramas. "Upstairs," he says, pointing to the hall's mezzanine level. "It's less crowded."

It is, but only marginally. After climbing the steps to the second floor, we stand before the only empty diorama. A pair of ostriches guarding their eggs from an approaching group of warthogs.

"Did you bring Erica's phone?" Dylan says.

I nod. It's in the front right pocket of my jeans.

"Let me see it."

"Not yet," I say. "I'm not sure I completely trust you."

Everything about Dylan seems jittery, from the way he jingles the keys in his pocket to his constant looking around the hall.

"I feel the same about you," he says.

I give him a wry smile. "At least we're on even footing. Now, tell me everything you know about Erica Mitchell."

"How much do *you* know?"

"That she was in 12A before me. She lived there a month before deciding to move out. Now she's missing and you're putting up posters looking for her. Care to fill me in on the rest?"

"We were . . . friends," Dylan says.

I note the pause. "You sure about that?"

We walk to another diorama. This one shows a pair of leopards. One of them keenly watches a nearby bushpig, ready to strike.

"Okay, we were more than friends," Dylan says. "I ran into her in the lobby on her second day at the Bartholomew. We started flirting, one thing led to another, and we started hooking up on a regular basis. As far as we knew, that wasn't against the rules. But we also didn't broadcast it."

I get a flashback to last night with Nick and can instantly relate. "How long did this go on?"

"About three weeks," Dylan says. "Then she left. There was no notice. One day, she was just gone. When I called, she never answered. When I texted, she never texted back."

"Did you ask Leslie what happened?"

"She told me Erica wasn't comfortable with all the apartment-sitter rules and decided to move out. But Erica never mentioned the rules to me. She never talked about being bothered by them."

"Do you think something changed?"

"I don't know what could have changed overnight," Dylan says. "I left her apartment a little before midnight. She was gone in the morning."

I note the similarities between her departure and Ingrid's. They're hard to miss. "Is that when you started looking for Erica?"

"You mean the posters? That was a few days after she left. I got worried. My hope was that someone would recognize her picture. I just want to know she's okay."

We move to another diorama. A pack of wild dogs hunting on the savanna, their eyes and ears alert for prey.

"Have you tried tracking down her family?" I ask Dylan.

"She doesn't have any. She was an only child. Her parents died in a car accident. Her only aunt raised her, but she died a couple of years ago."

"What about you? You have any family left?"

"None," Dylan says quietly, looking not at me but at the pack of dogs. Their own tight-knit unit. "My mom's dead, and my dad might be. I don't know. I had a brother, but he was killed in Iraq."

Dylan is yet another apartment sitter who doesn't have parents or family nearby. Between him, Erica, Ingrid, and myself, I'm sensing a trend. Either Leslie chooses orphans as an act of charity, or she does it because she knows we're likely to be desperate.

"One of the things Erica *did* talk about was the Bartholomew and how screwed up it seems. I thought she was being overly worried about the place. Now I think she wasn't worried enough."

"What do you mean?"

"Something weird is going on at the Bartholomew," Dylan says. "I'm sure of it."

The schoolkids have finally found their way upstairs. They ooze into the space around us, chattering and touching the diorama glass, leaving it riddled with sticky handprints. Dylan pushes away from them, moving to the other side of the room. I join him in front of another diorama. Cheetahs stalking the tall grass.

"Look, will you just tell me what's going on?" I say.

"A few days after Erica disappeared, I found this."

He reaches into his pocket and pulls out a ring, which he drops into my palm. The stone is purple, surrounded by etched letters proclaiming the owner to be a member of Danville High's class of 2014. Engraved on the inside of the band is a name.

Megan Pulaski.

"I found it behind a couch cushion," Dylan says. "I thought it might have belonged to someone who lived there. Or maybe another apartment sitter. I asked Leslie, who confirmed there was an apartment sitter named Megan Pulaski in 11B. She was there last year. Sounds normal, right?"

"I'm assuming it doesn't stay that way," I say.

Dylan nods. "I Googled the name. I found a Megan Pulaski who graduated from a high school in Danville, Pennsylvania, in 2014. She's been missing since last year."

I hand the ring back to Dylan, no longer wanting to touch it.

"It gets weirder," Dylan warns. "Three days ago, I went for a jog in the park. When I got back to the Bartholomew, I saw Ingrid in the lobby. I got the feeling she was waiting for me."

My stomach clenches. That's the same night Ingrid vanished. "So you were lying when you said you didn't know each other."

"That's the thing; I wasn't. We'd only spoken a few times before that, and one of them was when I asked her if she'd heard from Erica, because I knew they had hung out occasionally."

"What did she say that day in the lobby?"

"She told me she might have learned what happened to her," Dylan says. "She said she couldn't talk about it right then. She wanted to go somewhere private. I suggested we meet that night—in the basement."

"The security camera," I say. "You disconnected it."

Dylan nods. "Turns out it didn't matter. She never showed. I didn't find out she was gone until you told me the next day."

Now I know why Dylan acted so surprised that afternoon.

"And now I can't stop thinking that Ingrid's missing because she knew what happened to Erica," Dylan says. "It's almost like someone silenced Ingrid before she could tell me."

On the other side of the hall, one of the schoolgirls lets out a shriek. Not a scared one. A notice-me shriek, designed to get the attention of a nearby group of boys. Still, the sound is jolting.

"Have you seen what's on Erica's phone?" Dylan asks. "Maybe she was in contact with whoever caused her disappearance."

I remove the phone and hold it up for Dylan to see. "It's locked. Do you have any idea what her passcode was?"

"We weren't exactly at the password-sharing stage of our relationship," Dylan says. "Is there another way to unlock it?"

I turn Erica's phone over in my hand, thinking. Although I don't know the first thing about hacking into a cell phone, I might know someone who does. Grabbing my own phone, I scroll through the call history until I find the number I'm looking for. I hit the dial button, and a laid-back voice soon answers.

"This is Zeke."

"Hi, Zeke. This is Jules. Ingrid's friend."

"Hey," Zeke says. "Have you heard from her yet?"

"Not yet. But I'm wondering if you could help me. Do you know someone who can hack into a phone?"

There's a pause. Finally, Zeke says, "I do. But it will cost you."

"How much?"

"One thousand. That includes two hundred and fifty for me, as a finder's fee. The rest goes to my associate."

I go numb. That's an insane amount of money. But then I think about the possibility that a killer is living within the Bartholomew's walls. We could be next, Dylan and me.

I think Ingrid knew that. It's why she arranged to talk to Dylan. It's why she left me the gun and the note.

"You still there, Jules?" Zeke says. "Do we have a deal?"

"Yes," I reply, wincing as I say it. "Meet me in an hour."

I end the call and stare at the animals in the diorama in front of us. What a cruel afterlife they have. Dead for decades yet still gnawing, still fighting. Forever red in tooth and claw.

I NOW have only twenty-seven dollars to my name.

My latest unemployment check had left me with slightly more than five hundred dollars, but Dylan and I agreed that we should split Zeke's asking price between us. Five hundred from Dylan, five hundred from me.

With the cash in our pockets, we sit at the spot in Central Park where we're scheduled to meet Zeke—the Ladies Pavilion, a glorified gazebo with gingerbread trim. Dylan and I sit on opposite sides of the structure with our arms folded and scowls on our faces. We look like two people in the middle of a bad blind date.

It's an overcast afternoon, the clouds heavy and gray. Across from me, Dylan stares at a group of kids scampering up nearby Hernshead, a rocky outcropping that juts into the lake.

A lanky man with an unkempt beard appears on the path leading to the pavilion. Zeke. I recognize him from his Instagram photos. With him is a short girl with pink hair. She looks young. Barely-in-her-teens young. Her frilly white dress and Hello Kitty purse don't help matters. Nor does the fact that she never looks up from her phone, even as Zeke leads her into the pavilion.

"Hey," Zeke says. "I guess you're Jules."

I nod. "And this is Dylan."

Zeke gives Dylan a wary glance. "Hey, man."

Dylan responds with a brief nod.

The girl steps forward and holds out an open palm. "Cash first."

Dylan and I give the money to Zeke, my stomach roiling as it leaves my hand. Zeke passes it to the girl, who counts it before giving him his cut. The rest is shoved into the Hello Kitty purse.

"Now the phone," she says.

I give her Erica's phone. She studies it the way a jeweler does a diamond and says, "Give me five minutes. *Alone*, please."

The rest of us leave the pavilion, making our way to Hernshead. The children who were there earlier are now gone, leaving the whole craggy area to just Zeke, Dylan, and me.

I look over to the pavilion, where the girl sits on the bench I just vacated. Her fingers fly across the phone's screen.

"What do you think happened to Ingrid?" Zeke says.

I look to Dylan. Although the head shake he gives is tiny, his message is loud and clear. We need to keep this to ourselves.

"You're better off not knowing," I say. "But if you hear from her, please tell her to contact me. I just want to know she's okay."

Behind Zeke, the girl emerges from the pavilion. She thrusts Erica's phone back at me and says, "All done."

I swipe the screen and see all Erica's apps, not to mention her camera, photo gallery, and call log.

"I turned off the lock function," the girl says. "If it locks up again for some reason, I reset the passcode. It's 1234."

She walks away without another word. Zeke shakes my hand and gives Dylan a strange little salute. "Pleasure doing business with you," he says before hurrying to catch up with the girl.

Dylan and I return to the Ladies Pavilion, sharing a bench this time, the two of us crouched over Erica's phone.

"Where should we look first?" I ask.

"Her call log," Dylan says.

I swipe to the call history and scroll through a month's worth of Erica's outgoing calls. Nothing stands out. There are a few calls to Dylan. Some to a woman named Cassie and a man named Marcus. I'm not sure what I expected. A frantic call to 911, I guess. Or a goodbye call to Dylan.

I move on to Erica's incoming calls. The last one she received was from Dylan. Yesterday, 3:00 p.m. He didn't leave a message.

I search the text messages next. Dylan is well represented. He's sent dozens of them. There's even one from Ingrid, sent the day after Erica disappeared: *Where are you? I'm worried.*

I swipe back to the main screen, taking inventory of her most-used apps. Missing are the usual suspects. No Facebook, Twitter, or Instagram. "She didn't—" Dylan catches his use of the past tense and stops to correct himself. "She doesn't believe in social media. She told me it was a huge waste of time."

I go to the gallery of photos stored in the phone. It turns out she's an impressive cell phone photographer. She took dozens of well-composed shots of 12A's interior. The spiral steps. A view of the park taken from the dining room. George's right wing kissed by the light of dawn.

There are also two videos Erica took. I tap the oldest one first, and her beaming face fills the screen.

"Look at this place," she says. "Seriously."

The image streaks away from Erica to the bedroom window before swirling around the room itself, the visual equivalent of the dizzy euphoria she must have felt in that moment.

After two full spins around the room, Erica returns. Looking into the camera, she says, "If this is a dream, don't wake me up. I never want to leave this place." The video ends a second later.

I turn to Dylan, who's staring at the phone with a vacant look in his eyes. "Are you okay?" I ask.

"Yeah." Dylan then shakes his head. "Not really."

I slide my finger to the second video. The time stamp says it was taken on October 4. The night Erica vanished.

It begins in blackness. There's a rustling as the phone moves, giving a glimpse of darkened wall. The sitting room.

The phone stops on Erica's face, painted gray by moonlight coming through the window. Gone is the giddy grin she displayed in the other video. She whispers, "It's just past midnight, and I swear I heard a noise. I think something's inside the apartment."

I let out a gasp. I know the noise she's talking about. I've heard it as well. That ethereal sound, like the whisper of fabric.

On screen, Erica looks over her shoulder. Then she turns back to the phone. "I don't know what's going on here. This whole building. It's not right. We're being watched. I don't know why, but we are." She exhales. "I'm scared. I'm really scared."

A noise rises in the background. A single knock on the door.

Erica jumps at the sound. Her eyes become as wide as silver dollars. Fear sizzles through them. "It's *him*."

The screen suddenly goes black.

The video's abrupt end is jarring. Like a slap to the face. Yanked back to reality, I realize I'm holding my breath. Beside me, Dylan leans forward, as if he's about to be sick.

"Do you have any idea what she's talking about?" I say.

Dylan gulps before answering. "None. If she was feeling threatened by someone, she never told me about it."

Watching that video has shaken me to my core.

"Dylan, I think we're in real danger here," I say. "Especially if Ingrid vanished because she knew what happened to Erica."

Dylan stays silent, his face pensive, almost passive. Finally, he says, "We need to be careful. And smart. And quiet. We can't risk having what happened to Ingrid happen to one of us."

He steps out of the Ladies Pavilion and turns toward the Bartholomew. I join him and look up at George, keeping watch. The windows of 12A reflect the white-gray sky. They remind me of eyes. Similar to the ones in the wallpaper.

Wide. Unblinking. Staring right back at us.

Chapter 9

DYLAN AND I AGREED it was best not to head back to the Bartholomew together. All part of being careful, smart, and quiet. So we returned fifteen minutes apart, Dylan going first, his hoodie pulled over his head as he hurried away.

Now I'm in 12A, watching Erica's video on a loop. This current viewing is my sixth. I'm in the sitting room—the same place where the video was recorded. I'm even in the exact spot where Erica sat. The crimson sofa. Dead center.

"We're being watched. I don't know why, but we are."

Erica exhales. I do, too.

"I'm scared. I'm really scared."

A noise blasts from the phone. A knock.

That last wide-eyed, frightened utterance. "It's *him*."

When the video cuts to black, I continue to stare at the screen.

I think of Ingrid trying to warn me that afternoon we were together. I see her now, curled up on that park bench. *It . . . it scares me.* I should have believed her.

I start to watch Erica's video for a seventh time.

"It's just past midnight, and I swear I heard a noise."

As do I.

Two raps on 12A's door—as quick and jarring as gunshots.

My whole body jolts. The person who knocked when Erica was making that video could be on the other side of the door.

But when I walk to the foyer and peer through the peephole, I see Greta Manville. Standing with her cardigan and tote bag.

"I had a feeling you intended to check in on me at some point today," she says once I open the door. "I thought I'd spare you the trip and check on you instead."

"That's a pleasant reversal," I say. "Come in."

Having heard the magic words, she steps inside.

"Would you like something to drink?" I say before guiding her into the sitting room. "I have coffee, tea, and, well, that's pretty much it at the moment."

"Tea would be lovely. But only a small cup, please."

I retreat to the kitchen and put the kettle on the stove. When I return to the sitting room, I find Greta roaming its perimeter.

"I'm not being nosy," she says. "Just admiring what's been done to the place. It's less cluttered now."

"You've been here before?"

"My dear, I used to live here."

I look at her, surprised. "When you wrote *Heart of a Dreamer*?"

"Indeed."

I knew there were too many similarities for it to be a coincidence. Only someone who's spent hours gazing at the view from the window would be able to describe it with such accuracy.

Greta continues to roam, venturing to the brass telescope. "This is where I wrote the book, by the way. There was a rickety little table here by this window. I spent hours tapping away on an electric typewriter. The racket it made annoyed my parents no end."

"How long did they live here?"

"Decades," Greta says. "But it was in the family longer than that. My mother inherited it from my grandmother. I lived here until my first marriage, returning after its inevitable failure to write that book you so adore."

I follow Greta as she moves through the study and then back into the hallway. When the teakettle whistles, we both head to the kitchen, where Greta takes a seat in the breakfast nook. I pour two cups of tea and join her, grateful for her presence. It makes me far less jumpy than I was ten minutes ago.

"How much has the place changed since you lived here?" I say.

"In some ways, quite a bit. In others, not at all. The furniture is different, of course. And there used to be a maid's room near the bottom of the steps. But the wallpaper is the same. What do you think of it? Be honest."

I look into the teacup, my reflection shimmering atop the copper-colored liquid. "I hate it," I say.

"I'm not surprised," Greta says. "There are two types of people in this world. Those who would look at that wallpaper and see only flowers, and those who see only faces."

"Fantasy versus reality," I say.

Greta nods. "Exactly. I see both at once and decide which is more important to focus on," she says. "Today, I choose to focus on the flowers. Which is the real reason I stopped by. I wanted to give you this."

She digs through her tote bag, eventually removing a first-edition hardcover of *Heart of a Dreamer*.

"It's signed," Greta says as she hands it to me.

I'm touched beyond words. But that feeling—of friendship, of gratitude—lasts only a moment. Because when I open the book and see what Greta wrote on the title page, my blood turns cold.

"You don't like it?" Greta says.

I stare at the inscription. I want to be sure I'm not mistaken.

"I love it," I say, a bit too loudly, hoping the sound drowns out the voice of doubt that's now whispering in my ear. "I feel bad, that's all. You must get bothered all the time to sign copies. Especially by the apartment sitters."

"I haven't signed a copy for any other person at the Bartholomew. You're special, Jules. This is my way of showing you that."

I try to act flattered, pretending to be as thrilled as I would have been if Greta had done this a day or so ago. In truth, I want this book as far away from me as possible.

"I'm honored," I say. "Thank you from the bottom of my heart."

Greta continues to give me a concerned look. "Are you sure nothing's wrong?"

"To be honest, I'm not feeling well." Since faking enthusiasm didn't work, I might as well try an excuse that's slightly closer to the truth. "I think a cold is coming on. I thought the tea would help, but I think what I really need is to lie down for a bit."

If Greta sees through my attempt to get her out of the apartment, she doesn't show it. She simply downs the rest of her tea, hoists the tote bag onto her shoulder, and shuffles out of the kitchen.

At the door, she says, "Get some rest. I'll check on you tomorrow."

I force a smile. "Not unless I check on you first."

"Ah, so it's now a contest," Greta says. "I accept the challenge."

With that, she slips out the door, giving me a little wave on her way to the elevator. As soon as she's gone, I close the door and hurry down the hall to the bookshelf in the study. There, my heart exploding into jagged shards, I grab the copy of *Heart of a Dreamer* I found my first day here.

The title page bears the exact same inscription she wrote in two other copies—mine and Ingrid's.

> *Darling Erica,*
> *Such a pleasure! Your youthfulness gives me life!*
> *Best wishes,*
> *Greta Manville*

I TELL myself it means nothing.

That this is what Greta writes in every copy she signs.

That she certainly didn't befriend Erica and Ingrid, take them to lunch, and then—what? Kill them? Abduct them?

She's not capable of that. Not physically. Not mentally.

Then why did she lie?

I return to the crimson sofa with Erica's phone, scrolling once more through Erica's old texts, hoping to find a clue. But there's little of interest. Just routine exchanges with friends or arranging trysts with Dylan. It's the same with her call log.

I put down Erica's phone and pick up my own. I then text Ingrid on the unlikely chance that, of the dozens of texts I've sent in the past few days, this will finally be the one she sees and replies to.

> *If you're out there and can see this, PLEASE respond. I need to talk to you about the Bartholomew and Erica and what you know about both. It's important.*

I set my phone facedown on the coffee table and stare at the wall. The faces watch me passively, their dark mouths dropped open. Shifting nervously in their gaze, I close my eyes. Silly, I know. Just because I can't see them doesn't mean they can't see me.

My eyes snap open when my phone buzzes on the coffee table.

A text has arrived.

I pick it up, shock turning my body cold when I see it's from Ingrid: *Hi, Jules. Please don't be worried. I'm fine.*

Relief rushes through me. It starts at my hands and feet before coursing into my limbs, warm and glorious.

I send three texts in response, my still-warm fingers flying over the screen: *Where are you? Are you OK? What is going on?*

A minute passes with no response. After two more go by, I start to pace across the sitting room. I occupy myself by counting my steps. I get to sixty-seven before Ingrid sends her reply: *In Pennsylvania. A friend hooked me up with a waitressing job.*

I've been worried, I write. *Why didn't you call or text back?*

A reply comes immediately: *I left my phone on the bus. It took days to get it back.*

I wait for more, expecting a flurry of texts as exuberantly descriptive as the way Ingrid talked. But when her response arrives, it's the opposite. Staid, almost dull: *Sorry for any confusion.*

I text: *Why did you leave without telling me?*

I didn't have time, Ingrid texts back. *Short notice.*

But that makes no sense. I was at Ingrid's door minutes before she left. All she did was confirm our plans to meet in the park.

Then it hits me—this isn't Ingrid. All the relief I felt minutes ago is gone, replaced with pinpricks of dread across my skin.

I'm communicating with whoever made Ingrid disappear.

My first thought is to call the police and let them sort everything out. But in order for them to get involved, I need more than a hunch that this isn't Ingrid. I need proof. *Call me,* I type.

The reply is instantaneous. *Can't. Too noisy here.*

I need to be careful. My suspicion is starting to show. I need to think of a way to get whoever this is to definitively reveal they're not Ingrid—without realizing they're doing it.

What's my nickname? I finally type.

I hope against hope that when the answer appears, it will be the correct one: Juju. The name Ingrid gave me in the park that day.

The answer arrives, announcing itself with a buzz: *Trick question. You don't have a nickname. Jules is your real name.*

I yelp and throw the phone. A quick, frantic toss. It lands face-down on the sitting room carpet. I collapse onto the crimson sofa, my heart dripping like hot candle wax into the pit of my stomach. There's only one person who knows that. And it's not Ingrid. It's Nick.

MY PHONE buzzes again, the sound muted by the carpet.

I stay where I am. I don't need to see this new text to know the truth. I have my memory. Me sitting in Nick's kitchen, him making small talk, asking me if Jules was a nickname.

Most people think it's short for Julia or Julianne, but Jules is my given name.

Other than Chloe and Andrew, he's the only person who's been told the story behind my name. How stupid I was, basking in Nick's attention, enjoying that zap when he looked into my eyes.

The phone buzzes again. This time I move, approaching it with caution. Rather than pick it up, I flip it onto its back and read the texts I've missed: *Jules? You still there?*

I'm still staring at the words when there's a knock on the door. A single rap that makes me look up from the phone and gasp.

Nick's voice follows. "Jules? Are you home?"

It's him.

I don't answer. I can't. Nor can I say anything. A single tremulous word from me will tip him off that I know. About everything.

I turn and face the door. Then I see the chain dangling from the door frame. Just below it is the dead bolt, also in an unlocked position. In the center of the doorknob itself, the latch lies flat.

The door is completely unlocked.

I leap to my feet and rush toward the foyer, trying to make as little noise as possible.

Nick knocks again. I'm in the foyer now, inching closer to the door. I press my back against it, hoping he can't sense my presence. I can certainly feel his. A disturbance of air inches away.

"Jules," he says. "If you can hear me, I just want to apologize for this morning. I shouldn't have brushed off your concern about not being in your apartment all night. It was cavalier of me."

With my left hand, I reach out to touch the doorknob, my fingers sliding over the unlocked latch at its center.

"I also want you to know that I had a really great time last night. It was amazing. All of it."

I grasp the latch between my thumb and forefinger. Holding my breath, I turn it upward, my left arm twisting at an odd angle. I keep turning the latch, millimeter by millimeter.

"I don't want you to think I usually move so fast. I was—"

The lock slides into place with a noticeable click.

Nick hears it and stops, waiting for me to make another sound.

Beside me, the doorknob turns.

He's testing the lock, moving the knob back and forth.

After another breathless second, he resumes talking.

"I was caught up in the moment. I think we both were. Not that I regret it. I don't. I want you to know I'm not that kind of guy."

Nick departs. I hear his footsteps retreating. Still, I remain at the door, not moving, afraid he'll suddenly return.

But I heard what he had to say. He isn't that kind of guy.

I believe him. He's someone else entirely.

I PACE the sitting room, crossing back and forth in front of the windows. Outside, night settles over Central Park with silent swiftness. Bow Bridge has become a pale strip over black water.

I keep pacing, confronted by the faces in the wallpaper no matter which direction I turn.

Those faces. They know what Nick is. A serial killer.

I know how improbable that sounds. Yet a pattern has emerged. Of girls coming here. All of them desperate and broke and without family. Then they disappear without warning or explanation.

I know what I need to do—call the police.

And say what? I have no proof that Nick did anything to Ingrid or Erica. Even though I'm certain he has Ingrid's phone, it doesn't mean the police will think he's guilty of anything.

But staying here could be a point of no return. The beginning of my end. My mother swallowing those pills. My father striking a match outside the bedroom door. Jane climbing into that Beetle.

I'll go to Chloe's. To a place where I'll be safe.

I grab my phone and text Chloe. *I need to get out of here.*

I pause, breathe, type more. *I think I'm in danger.*

I put down the phone, resume pacing, return to the phone five minutes later. Chloe hasn't read my text yet. So I call her, reaching her voice mail. It isn't until I hear her recorded greeting that I remember she's out of town. Off to the Vermont wilderness with Paul. And me without a key to her apartment, which I returned the morning I left for the Bartholomew.

So Chloe's out. That leaves no one else I can turn to.

But I'm wrong. I have Dylan.

I call him next, again getting only voice mail. I consider leaving a message but decide against it. I'll sound crazy.

My only choice now is to grab my things, go to a hotel, and spend the weekend there until Chloe returns. But it all falls apart as soon as I check my bank balance. The twenty-seven dollars left in my account won't get me a night anywhere.

There's no other way around it. In order to leave, I need to stay.

I look across the hall to the foyer and the front door. The deadbolt and chain are in place, right where I left them.

I move into the kitchen, drop to my hands and knees, and open the cupboard beneath the sink. There, sitting between dishwasher soap and trash bags, is the shoebox Ingrid left behind.

I carry the box back to the sitting room and place it on the coffee table. Lifting the lid, I see the Glock and magazine exactly the way I left them. I remove both, surprised by how easy it is to slide the ammo clip into the gun itself. The two connect with a click that makes me feel if not strong, then at least ready.

With nothing else to do but wait, I take a seat on the crimson sofa and, gun in my lap, stare again at the wallpaper.

It stares back. Hundreds of eyes and noses and gaping mouths.

A few days ago, I had thought those open mouths meant they were talking or laughing or singing. But now I know better.

Now I know what they're really doing is screaming.

Now

DR. WAGNER *gives me a look that's one part shock, two parts disbelief.* "That's an alarming accusation."

"You think I'm lying?"

"I read the news," *the doctor says.* "There haven't been any murders at the Bartholomew. Not for a very long time."

Bernard, the nurse with the kind eyes, pokes his head into the room. "Sorry to interrupt," *he says.* "I saw this and thought Jules might like to have it in the room with her."

He holds up a red picture frame, the glass spiderwebbed with cracks. Behind them is a photograph of three people.

My father. My mother. Jane. I was carrying it when I ran from the Bartholomew. The only possession I thought worth saving.

"Where did you find it?"

"It was with your clothes," *Bernard says.* "One of the medics gathered it up at the scene."

That frame wasn't the only thing I was carrying. I had something else with me. "Where's my phone?" *I ask.*

"There was no phone," *Bernard says.* "Just your clothes and that picture."

"But it was in my pocket."

"I'm sorry. If it was there, no one found it."

Worry expands in my chest. Like a ball of dough. Rising.

Nick has my phone. Which means he can read my texts, see whom I've contacted. Including, I realize with a rib-shuddering gasp, Chloe. I think of those texts I sent Chloe and how much they've put her in jeopardy.

"Chloe," *I say.* "I need to warn Chloe."

I try to slide out of bed. The pain is so bad that I gasp for breath. I tear off the neck brace and drop it on the floor.

"Honey, you need to get back in bed," *Bernard says.*

"No! I need to talk to Chloe! He'll be looking for her!"

Bernard swoops toward me, his hands on my shoulders, pushing me back into bed. I try to fight him off, my legs kicking, arms flailing. The IV in the back of my hand feels like a jellyfish sting.

The nurse's eyes darken into something distinctly unkind. "You need to calm down," *he says.*

"But she's in danger!" *I'm still kicking, still writhing. He pins me against the bed, where I thrash beneath his weight. "You have to believe me! Please!"*

I feel a pinch on my upper left arm. Looking to the other side of the bed, I see Dr. Wagner with a syringe and the needle that's just been plunged into my flesh. "This will help you rest," he says.

My head lolls onto the pillow. When Bernard backs away from me, I realize I can no longer move my limbs.

I sink against the bed like someone plunging into a warm pool until I'm so far gone I wonder if I'll ever emerge.

Chapter 10

One Day Earlier

MY FAMILY IS DANCING across Bow Bridge. I sit in my usual spot next to George. Watching them. Wishing I could dance with them.

They twirl across the bridge in single file. My father is first. My mother's in the middle. Jane takes up the rear.

As they dance, I notice that their heads are lit from within by tiny flickering flames. Like jack-o'-lanterns. Tongues of fire lick from their mouths and leap in their eyes. Every so often, they look up at me with those fiery eyes and wave. I try to wave back, but something's in my hands. I haven't noticed it until now.

It's heavy, slightly wet, hot. I look down.

Sitting within my cupped hands is a human heart.

Shiny with blood. Still beating.

I wake up screaming. The sound blasts from my lungs, the sound reverberating off the walls. I clamp a hand over my mouth. But then I remember the dream, gasp, and pull my hand away.

I look at my surroundings. I'm in the sitting room, sprawled across the crimson couch. The grandfather clock ticks its way toward 9:00 a.m. When I sit up, something slides from my lap onto the floor.

The gun. I slept with it. But like a fickle lover, I no longer want to look at it now that I've held it all night. So it goes in the shoebox, which I put in its hiding place under the sink.

Back in the sitting room, I grab my phone, desperately hoping that Chloe and Dylan called me during the night. They didn't.

The fact that Nick has Ingrid's phone can mean only one thing: he killed her. A horrible thought. With it comes the gut-squeezing realization that I'm in the same situation she was. A person who might know too much. The only question now is how much *Ingrid* knew about Nick. Erica told her something. Of that I'm sure.

Quickly, I scroll through Erica's call log, checking to see if I missed something. And that's when I see that Erica had received a call from Ingrid on October 2. The time was shortly after noon. Ingrid even left a voice mail.

Hey, it's Ingrid. I just got the message you sent down the dumb-waiter. Which is super cool, by the way. Anyway, I'm confused. Am I supposed to know who Marjorie Milton is?

I stop the message, play it again, listen intently: *Am I supposed to know who Marjorie Milton is?*

I know that name. In fact, I saw it inside this very apartment.

I cross into the study, where I fling open the bottom desk drawer. Inside is the stack of magazines I found on my first day here. All those copies of the *New Yorker*, each marked with an address and a name: Marjorie Milton. The former owner of 12A.

I'm on the move again, winding up the stairs to the bedroom window, where both George and my laptop sit. I flip it open and Google Marjorie's name. Dozens of results appear.

I click on the most recent article, dated a week ago: CHAIR-WOMAN RETURNS TO GUGGENHEIM GALA.

The article itself is pure society-page fluff. A museum fund-raiser held last week in which businessmen and their trophy wives spent more per plate than what most people make in a year. The only item of note is a mention that the event's longtime coordinator was back after health issues forced her to miss last year's gala.

It includes a photo of a seventy-something woman wearing a

black gown and a proud, patrician smile. The caption below the picture gives her name: Marjorie Milton.

Which means only one thing. Marjorie Milton, the woman whose supposed death opened a spot in the Bartholomew for at least two apartment sitters, is alive.

I LOOK at my watch and sigh. Seven minutes past two.

I've entered the third hour of sitting on a bench just outside Central Park. I'm hungry, tired, and in dire need of a bathroom.

The park itself is behind me. In front of me, across the street, is the apartment building where Marjorie Milton currently resides.

Like much of what I know about Mrs. Milton, her address was discoverable online. Other things I've learned: she's the daughter of an oil executive and the widow of a venture capitalist. She has a Yorkie named Princess Diana. She gives generously to children's hospitals and the New-York Historical Society.

The biggest thing I learned, though, is that Marjorie Milton is alive and well and has been since 1943. I'm here on the bench in the hope that Marjorie will eventually come outside to take Princess Diana for a walk. According to a *Vanity Fair* piece about her that ran three years ago, it's one of her favorite things to do.

Once she does, I'll be able to ask not only why she left the Bartholomew, located a mere ten blocks south of her current address, but also why the people still living there claim that she's dead.

Finally, at half past two, a wisp of a woman in brown slacks and a teal jacket emerges with a leashed Yorkie by her side.

Marjorie. I've now seen enough photos of her to know.

I hurry across the street. When I get a few steps behind her, I say, "Excuse me—you're Marjorie Milton, right?"

"I am," she says. "Do we know each other?"

"No, but I live at the Bartholomew."

Marjorie looks me up and down, clearly pegging me as an apartment sitter and not a permanent resident.

"I don't understand how that's any concern of mine," she says.

"Because you also lived there," I reply. "At least that's what I've been told."

"You were misinformed."

She's in the midst of turning around and walking away when I reach into my jacket and produce the copy of the *New Yorker* that's been rolled up inside it. I tap the address label.

"If you want people to believe that, then you should have taken your magazines with you when you left."

Marjorie Milton glares at me. "Who are you?"

"I'm the person living in the apartment you used to own. Only I was told you were dead, and I'd really love to know why."

"I have no idea," Marjorie says. "But I never owned that apartment. I simply stayed there for a brief time."

She resumes walking, the Yorkie trotting several feet in front of her. I trail behind them, not content with the answers I've been given. "Apartment sitters are disappearing," I say. "Including the one who was in 12A after you and before me. If you know something about that, then you need to tell me right now."

Marjorie Milton halts. "If you don't leave me alone this instant, I'll give Leslie Evelyn a call," she says. "And trust me, you don't want that. I lived there, but I won't say anything else."

Then she's off again, Princess Diana pulling her along.

"Wait," I say. I grab the sleeve of her jacket, trying to keep her there. When she pulls away from me, the sleeve stays in my hand. The jacket falls open, revealing a white blouse underneath. Pinned to it is a tiny brooch. Gold. In the shape of a figure eight.

I let go of the jacket. Marjorie stuffs her arm back into it and pulls it closed. Before she does, I get one last look at the brooch, seeing that it's not a figure eight at all.

It's an ouroboros.

Two hours later, I'm in the main branch of the New York Public Library, one of many people occupying the Rose Main Reading Room. Late-afternoon sun slants through the arched windows.

I'm gripped with unease as I contemplate the stack of books in front of me. Old, dusty volumes about symbols and their meanings. But this ominous mood has been with me since the moment I glimpsed Marjorie Milton's brooch.

The snake eating its tail. Exactly like the painting in Nick's apartment.

I said nothing to Marjorie after I saw it. I simply backed away, leaving her standing with her dog on the sidewalk. I kept walking, as if the simple act of putting one foot in front of the other would somehow help everything make sense.

Which is why I ended up at the library, striding to the help desk and saying, "I need as many books on symbology as you can find." Now a dozen titles sit in front of me. I hope at least one of them will help me understand the meaning behind the ouroboros.

I grab one of the books at random and read.

The ouroboros is an ancient symbol depicting a serpent or dragon forming a circle or figure eight by eating its own tail. It symbolizes the cyclical nature of the universe—creation rising from destruction. Life rising from death.

I snatch another book and leaf through it until I come to an image of a card from a tarot deck. The Magician.

It depicts a man in red robes standing at an altar. Above his head, like a double halo, is a figure eight. An ouroboros.

The altar contains four objects—a staff, a sword, a shield adorned with a star, and a goblet made of gold. A chalice.

I lean in closer, studying first the shield, then the chalice.

Seeing it strikes a bell in the recesses of my memory. I leap from the table, leaving the books open across it. Back at the information desk, I summon the librarian who helped me earlier.

"How many books do you have on Satanism?" I say.

The librarian winces. "I don't know. A lot?"

"Give me all of them."

By five thirty I have, if not all of them, then at least a good sampling. Sixteen books now sit in front of me. I sort through this new stack, scanning the names in the hope one stands out.

One eventually does, in a scholarly text entitled *Modern Deviltry: Satanism in the New World*.

Marie Damyanov. I remember her from the article I read about the Bartholomew's tragic past. All those dead servants and Cornelia

Swanson's alleged murder of her poor maid. One of the reasons Cornelia seemed so guilty was because she had once consorted with Damyanov, an occult leader.

Le Calice D'Or. That was the name of her group of followers. I flip back, locating a passage about Marie Damyanov.

Damyanov believed that after forming the heavens and the earth, God abandoned his creations, allowing chaos to reign. To endure this, Damyanov advised her followers to appeal to a mightier deity—Lucifer—who could be summoned not with prayers but with blood. Thus began rituals in which young women would be cut, their blood caught in a golden chalice and poured over an open flame.

Years later, some of Damyanov's disillusioned followers hinted at more horrific practices. One wrote that Damyanov claimed the sacrifice of a young woman during a blue moon would summon Lucifer himself, who would grant those present good health and immense fortune.

I reread the passage, my sense of unease intensifying. I try to recall details of the Cornelia Swanson case. Her maid was cut open, her organs removed. Something like that is hard to forget. As is the fact that the murder took place on Halloween night. I can even remember the year: 1944.

I grab my phone and find a website that gives you the lunar phases for every month in any given year. It turns out that on Halloween in 1944, the sky was brightened by the second full moon of the month. A blue moon.

My hands start to shake as I do a new internet search, this time for a single name. Cornelia Swanson.

A flurry of articles appears, pretty much all of them about the murder. I click on one and am greeted by a photo of the infamous Mrs. Swanson. I stare at the picture, and the world goes sideways, as if the library has suddenly tilted. I grip the edge of the table.

Because the photo I'm looking at is one I've seen before. A sharp-featured beauty in a satin gown and silk gloves. Flawless skin. Hair as dark as a moonless night.

I saw it in the photo album in Nick's apartment. Although he identified the woman, he never used her name.

But now I know it. Cornelia Swanson.

And her granddaughter is none other than Greta Manville.

I TEXT Dylan from inside the library: *Call me ASAP! I found something!*

When he doesn't respond, I decide to call him. A theory is forming. One I need to share with someone else.

Outside, I lean against the base of one of the library's stone lions and dial Dylan's number. The call again goes straight to his voice mail. I leave a message, urgently whispering into the phone.

"Dylan, where are you? I think I know what's going on. Please, please call me as soon as you get this."

I turn around, about to head back inside the library, when a ring bleats from the phone, still held white-knuckled in my hand. Dylan calling me back at last.

But when I answer, it's an unfamiliar voice I hear. A woman, her tone tentative. "Is this Jules?"

"Yes."

A pause. "Jules, it's Bobbie. From the shelter."

And then I remember. Bobbie, the kind woman I spoke with two days ago. "How are you?"

"I'm okay. But as much as I like to gab, this isn't a social call."

My pulse revs up again. "You found Ingrid?"

"Maybe," Bobbie says. "A girl just came in. She looks a lot like the girl in that picture you gave me. But she doesn't talk much. When I tried to buddy up to her, she wanted none of it."

That doesn't sound like Ingrid. Then again, I have no idea what she's been through in the past few days. "What color is her hair?"

"Black," Bobbie says. "A dye job. A crappy one, too. She missed a spot in the back."

I grip the phone tighter. "Can you see her right now?"

"Yeah. She's sitting on a cot, not talking to anyone."

"That spot she missed in her hair—do you see any color there?"

"Let me look." Bobbie's voice becomes muted as she pulls away from her phone to get a better view. "Yeah, there's some color there. It looks to me like a spot of blue."

I exhale. It's Ingrid.

"Bobbie, I need you to do me a favor. Don't let her leave," I say. "Not until I get there. Do anything you can to keep her there. Hold her down if necessary. I'll be there as soon as I can."

Then I'm off, rushing down the library steps and turning onto Forty-Second Street. The shelter is ten blocks north and several long blocks west. Through a combination of jogging, speed walk-ing, and ignoring traffic lights, I make it there in twenty minutes.

Bobbie is waiting for me outside, still dressed in her work khakis and cardigan. We enter the building, her familiar presence allow-ing me to bypass the woman at the desk behind the scuffed glass. Tonight, the converted gymnasium is far more crowded than it was on my first visit. Nearly every cot has been taken.

"There she is," Bobbie says, pointing to a cot on the far side of the gym. Sitting on top of it, knees pulled to her chest, is Ingrid.

It's not just her hair that's changed. Everything about her is darker, dirtier. She's become a shadow of her former self.

Her hair hangs in greasy strings. Her shirt and jeans are the same ones she had on the last time I saw her, although they're now stained from days of wear.

Ingrid looks my way, recognition dawning in her bloodshot eyes. "Juju?"

She leaps off the cot and runs toward me, pulling me into a strong, scared embrace. "What are you doing here?" she says, showing no sign of letting me go.

"Looking for you."

"You left the Bartholomew, right?"

"No."

Ingrid breaks the embrace and collapses onto the nearest cot, her hands covering her face. "Juju, you need to get out of there."

"I plan to," I tell her.

"No, *now*," Ingrid says. "Run away as fast as you can. You don't know what they are."

Only I do. I think I've known for a while but wasn't able to completely comprehend it.

But now all the information I've gathered in the past few days is starting to make sense. It's like a photograph just pulled from a chemical bath. The image taking shape, revealing the picture.

I know exactly what they are. The Golden Chalice reborn.

Chapter 11

AT INGRID'S INSISTENCE, we go someplace secluded to talk.

"I don't want anyone to hear us," she explains.

At the shelter, that means commandeering the former men's locker room. Outside, Bobbie stands guard at the door, blocking anyone who might try to enter. Inside, Ingrid and I stroll past rows of empty lockers and shower stalls.

"I haven't showered in three days," Ingrid says, staring with longing at one of the stalls. "The closest thing has been a sponge bath at Port Authority, and that was yesterday morning."

"Is that where you've been all this time?"

Ingrid drops onto a bench across from the showers. "I've been everywhere. Port Authority. Grand Central. Anywhere there are crowds. Because they're looking for me, Juju. I know they are."

"But they're—" I stop myself before the rest of the sentence emerges. Because I now know they've been looking for her, too. Through me.

It's why Greta Manville suggested places for me to look. Why Nick lowered me down in the dumbwaiter to search 11A, hoping I'd find something of use. It's probably even why he slept with me. To keep me close, learn everything I had discovered.

"Why didn't you take a bus or train out of the city?"

"That's kind of difficult when you don't have any money," Ingrid says. "And I've got next to nothing. My meals have been fished out of trash cans. I had to shoplift this stupid hair dye. What little money I do have came from panhandling and stealing coins from fountains. So far I have, like, twelve dollars. At this rate, maybe I'll have enough to leave the country after a decade."

"We could go to the police," I suggest.

"And tell them that a bunch of rich people at the Bartholomew are worshipping the devil? Just saying it sounds ridiculous."

As does hearing it out loud, even though it's exactly what I think is happening.

"How did you figure it all out?"

"It was Erica who started it," Ingrid says. "She told me she found out that the person who was in 12A before her wasn't dead, which is what she'd been told. That freaked her out a little. So I did some research into the Bartholomew and learned about some of the stuff that happened there. That freaked Erica out *a lot*. So when she left, I assumed it was because she felt too creeped out to stay there. But then Dylan came by asking if I'd heard from her. And that's when I suspected something else was going on."

Ingrid's story is a lot like my own. The only difference is that she learned about Greta Manville's relationship to Cornelia Swanson much sooner than I did.

"I met Greta in the lobby during my interview with Leslie," Ingrid says. "And I thought it was cool to be in the same building as an author. At first, I thought she was nice. She even gave me a signed copy of her book. But when I read about Cornelia Swanson and noticed their resemblance, I knew what was up."

My apartment used to be Greta's apartment, which means that at one point it belonged to Cornelia Swanson. It's the same apartment where she murdered her maid.

I try not to think about how many others there have been. There'll be plenty of time to dwell on that later. Right now, I need to focus on extricating myself from the place.

"What happened after you talked to Greta?"

"I knew I didn't want to stay there, that's for sure." Ingrid stands and makes her way to the row of sinks along the wall. She turns on the tap and starts splashing her face with water. "At that point, I had two thousand dollars in apartment-sitting money. I also knew there'd be a lot more money coming if I stayed."

The cash. Dangled in front of us at the end of each week. Yet another way the Bartholomew trapped us.

"But I wanted to feel safe," Ingrid says, "so I—"

"Bought a gun."

Ingrid looks at me in the mirror above the sink, her brows arched. "So you found it. Good."

"Why did you leave it there in the first place?"

"Because something happened," Ingrid says, her voice getting quiet. "And if I tell you what it is, you're going to hate me." Ingrid uses a damp paper towel to clean her neck. "And I totally deserve it."

"Ingrid, just tell me."

"That gun cost me everything I had. That two grand I saved up? Gone, like that." She snaps her fingers. "So I asked Leslie if I could get an advance—nothing huge, just a week's pay early. She told me that wasn't possible. But then she said I could have five thousand dollars—no strings attached—if I did one little thing."

"What was it?"

Ingrid stalls by examining a strand of her black-as-pitch hair. When she looks in the mirror, there's disgust in her eyes. As if she hates every single thing about herself.

"To cut you," she says. "When we crashed in the lobby, that wasn't an accident. Leslie paid me to do it."

I recall that moment with vivid clarity. Me burdened with grocery bags. Ingrid rushing down the stairs, her eyes on her phone. Then the collision, the groceries falling, me suddenly bleeding.

"I had a Swiss army knife," Ingrid says, unable to look at me. "I held it against my phone, with just the tip of the blade exposed. And right when we crashed, I sliced your arm. Leslie told me it shouldn't be a big cut. Just enough to draw blood."

I back away from her. First one step. Then another.

"Why . . . why would they need you to do that?"

"I don't know," Ingrid says. "I didn't ask. By then, I had my suspicions about what she was. But I was too desperate to ask questions. All I could think about was that five thousand dollars."

I keep moving away from her until I'm on the other side of the bathroom, sinking into an open stall and dropping onto the toilet seat. Ingrid rushes toward me and drops to her knees. "I'm so sorry, Juju," she says. "You have no idea how sorry I am."

A bubble of anger rises in my chest, hot and bilious. But it's not directed at Ingrid. I can't blame her for what she did. She was broke and desperate and saw an easy way to make a lot of money.

No, my anger is reserved for Leslie and everyone else in the Bartholomew for exploiting that desperation and turning it into a weapon. "You're forgiven," I tell Ingrid. "You did what you needed to do to survive."

She shakes her head and looks away. "No. I'm an awful person. Truly awful. And right after it happened, I decided I needed to leave. Five thousand dollars was more than enough. I didn't want to stay there and see how much lower I could sink."

"Why didn't you tell me all this that day in the park?"

"Would you have believed me?"

The answer is no. No one in her right mind would believe there was a group of Satanists occupying a building like the Bartholomew. That, of course, is how they managed to go undetected for so long. The preposterousness of their existence is like a shield.

"In my mind," Ingrid says, "the best thing I could do was try to warn you by giving you some idea about what was going on there. I hoped it would at least make you think twice about staying."

"Which it did," I say. "But did you really run away?"

"Yes, but not the way I wanted to," Ingrid says, talking fast. "That night, I put that note in the dumbwaiter, trying to do everything I could to get you to leave. I left the gun for the same reason. I didn't leave immediately, because Leslie told me she'd be by at some point in the night to give me the five thousand dollars. Also, I had arranged to tell Dylan everything I knew, just in case it could help him find out what happened to Erica. My plan was to get the cash from Leslie, meet Dylan in the basement, grab my things, and give the keys to Charlie on the way out. That didn't happen, obviously."

"What went wrong?"

"They came for me," Ingrid says. "Well, *he* did."

My thoughts flash back to that video of Erica. *It's him.*

"Nick," I say.

Ingrid shudders at the name. "All of a sudden, he was there. *Inside* the apartment. I don't know how he got in. The door was locked. But there he was. I think he had been there for hours. Waiting. But the moment I saw him, I knew I was in danger."

Ingrid pauses, and I suspect she's replaying that moment in her head the same way I saw our collision in the lobby. Tears pool in her eyes as she croaks out a single, mournful sob.

"And I knew," she says as the tears break free and stream down her cheeks, "I knew that he was planning to kill me. He had a weapon with him. A stun gun. I screamed when I saw it."

And I heard that scream as I stood in the kitchen of 12A. Which means others probably heard it, too. Including Greta, who lives directly below that apartment.

"How did you get away?"

"You saved me." Ingrid wipes her eyes and gives me a warm, grateful smile. "When you came to the door."

"Nick was there?"

"Right behind me," Ingrid says. "I didn't want to answer the door, but when we heard it was you, Nick told me I had to open it or you'd get suspicious. He had the stun gun pressed against my back the entire time, just in case I tried to warn you. He told me he'd paralyze us—me then you."

That explains everything. Why it took Ingrid so long to open the door. Why she opened it only a crack. Why she wore that obviously fake smile and told me she was fine.

"I knew something was wrong," I say, surprised by my own tears. "I wanted to help you."

"But you *did*, Jules. I had pepper spray in my pocket. A tiny bottle attached to my key ring. Nick appeared so fast I didn't have time to reach for it. Then you came to my door. And you talked to me just long enough for me to reach into my pocket and grab it."

I remember that vividly. The way her right hand had been plunged into the pocket of her jeans, grasping for something.

"After you left, I hit him with the pepper spray," Ingrid says.

"Then I ran. I had to leave everything behind. My phone. My clothes. The only thing I had were the keys, which I threw onto the lobby floor because I knew I wouldn't be able to come back."

The locker room door opens, and Bobbie pokes her head inside.

"Ladies, you're going to need to wrap this up," she says. "It's getting packed out here, and someone's going to take my cot if I'm not in it soon."

Ingrid and I make our way out of the locker room into a shelter even more crowded than when we left it. It's a loud and bustling place, which makes me understand why Ingrid stuck to bus and train stations. There's safety in numbers.

But there's still one apartment sitter left at the Bartholomew. And he's all alone.

That realization prompts another thought. I pull out my phone and swipe through my search history, returning to the lunar calendar I looked at earlier. I type in this month. I type in this year.

When the results appear, I gasp so loud it makes others in the shelter stop and stare. "What's wrong?" Ingrid says.

"I need to go." I head to the exit. "Stay with Bobbie. Trust no one else."

Ingrid calls after me. "Where are you going?"

"The Bartholomew. I need to warn Dylan."

In a matter of seconds, I'm out of the gymnasium, then out of the building, then out on the street, where the moon still glows bright and round. It's a full moon.

The second one this month. A blue moon.

I TAKE a cab back to the Bartholomew, even though I can't afford it. My wallet is empty. So is my bank account.

But speed is the most important thing right now. I've allowed myself twenty minutes to get back to the apartment, collect what I can, meet up with Dylan, and then get the hell out of there.

Already I'm behind schedule. In five minutes, the cab's traversed only two blocks. I sit in the back seat, my hand shaking as I grab my phone and call Dylan.

I'm practically shouting. "Dylan, I found Ingrid. She's safe. But you need to get out of there. Right now. If you can, meet me outside. I'll explain the rest after we leave."

I end the call as the light changes and the cab speeds forward.

We zip by one more block. I check my watch. Ten minutes spent in this cab and I'm not even halfway there. Time to bail.

When the cab stops at the next light, I throw open the passenger door and leap out. The driver starts shouting at me, words I can't make out because I'm too busy scrambling past cars in other lanes on my way to the sidewalk. Behind me, the cabbie honks his horn.

I keep running, my pace quickening to a full sprint. Most people hear me coming and step out of the way. Those who don't are shoved aside. All I can focus on is getting to the Bartholomew as fast as possible.

As I run, I make a list of what to grab once I'm back in 12A. The photograph of my family. That's my main priority. Everything else can be replaced.

I keep running. My lungs are on fire. So are my legs. My heart pounds so hard I worry it might burst right through my rib cage.

I slow down once I near the Bartholomew. Approaching the building, I scan the sidewalk, looking for signs of Dylan.

He's not there.

The only person I see is Charlie, who stands at the front door, holding it open, waiting for me to come inside.

"Evening, Jules," he says, a good-natured smile widening beneath his bushy mustache. "You must have been busy. You've been out all day."

I look at him and wonder how much he knows. Everything? Nothing? I'm tempted to say something. Ask for his help. Warn him to leave. But it's a risk I can't take.

"Job hunting," I say, forcing my own smile.

Charlie tilts his head in curiosity. "Any luck?"

"Yes." I pause, stalling. Then it comes to me. My perfectly rational excuse for leaving. "I got a job. In Queens. But because the commute is so far, I won't be able to live here anymore. I'll be staying with friends until I can find a place."

"You're leaving us?"

I nod. "Right now."

When Charlie frowns, I can't tell if his disappointment is genuine or as fake as my smile. Not even after he says, "Well, I for one hate to see you go. It's been a pleasure getting to know you."

Inside the Bartholomew, all is quiet. There's no sign of Dylan here, either. No sign of anyone. The entire lobby is empty.

I hurry to the elevator. I step in, close the grate, and press the button for the eleventh floor. Once there, I push out and move quickly down the hall to Dylan's apartment.

I knock on Dylan's door. A quick trio of raps. "Dylan?"

I knock again. Harder this time, the door shaking beneath my fist. "Dylan, are you there? We need to—"

The door swings away, leaving my fist swiping at nothing but air. Then Leslie Evelyn appears. Filling the empty doorway. Wearing her black Chanel suit like armor. Wielding a fake smile.

My heart suddenly stops.

"Jules." Leslie's voice is sickly sweet. Honey laced with poison. "What a pleasant surprise."

I start to feel myself leaning to the side.

I'm too late. Dylan's been taken.

"Can I help you with something?" Leslie says, her eyelids fluttering in mock concern.

My mouth drops open, but no words come out. Instead, I hear Ingrid's voice. *Run away as fast as you can.*

I do. Away from Leslie. Down the hall. To the stairwell.

Rather than down, I go up. I have to. My only option is 12A. If I can get there, then I can lock the door, call the police, demand that an officer escort me from the building. If that doesn't work, there's always Ingrid's gun.

So I start to climb, even though my knees throb and my hands shake and shock has left me numb.

Finally on the twelfth floor, I hurry down the hall, winded and aching. Soon I'm inside 12A, almost weeping with relief.

I slam the door behind me and secure it. Lock. Dead bolt. Chain.

I slump against the door for a sliver of a second to catch my breath. Then it's down the hall, up more stairs.

In the bedroom, I go straight to the nightstand and grab the framed photo of my family. Everything else is expendable.

With the picture tucked under my arm, I descend the winding steps one last time. Soon I'll be in the kitchen, calling the police, digging out the gun, cradling it in my lap until help arrives.

At the bottom of the steps, I move into the hallway and stop.

Nick is there.

He stands straight-backed just beyond the foyer, blocking any attempt I might make to leave. Something's in his hand, held behind his back where I can't see it.

His face is expressionless. A blank slate.

"Hey there, neighbor," he says.

"How did you get in here?" I say.

A wasted question. I already know. Behind Nick, in the study, part of the bookshelf sits away from the wall. Beyond it is a passageway connecting one apartment to the other.

If I searched it, I'm sure I would find a small set of steps in the wall leading down to 11A and 11B, too.

Nick could have entered 12A anytime he wanted. In fact, I think he did. That noise I heard. The swishing sound, like socks on carpet or the train of a dress sliding across a table leg. That was Nick.

"Where's Dylan?" I no longer recognize my voice.

"Didn't Leslie tell you? He moved out."

Nick smirks. A slight upturn of his lips. I see it and know for certain that Dylan is dead. Nausea rushes through me in a wave.

"Please let me leave." I swallow hard, gasping for breath. "I won't tell anyone what's going on here."

Nick takes a step forward. I do the opposite, taking two backward. "Let's make a bargain," he says. "If you tell me where Ingrid is, then maybe—just maybe—we'll take her and spare you. How does that sound?"

It sounds like a lie.

"I guess that's a no," Nick says when I don't answer.

He takes another step and reveals what's been held behind his back. The stun gun, a blue spark dancing across its tip.

I sprint down the hall, cutting right, into the kitchen. Once inside, I drop to my knees, sliding across the floor, aiming for the cupboard under the sink. I fling open the door and grasp at the shoebox. It's empty.

I'm hit with a blast of memory. Me texting Ingrid about the gun. A text, I now realize, she never saw.

Behind me, Nick's voice rises from the hallway.

"I admire your survival instincts, Jules. But having a gun in the apartment is far too dangerous. I had to put it in a safe place."

He rounds the corner and steps into the kitchen. He's in no hurry. There's no need to be. Not when I'm trapped like this, armed with nothing but a framed photo of my family.

"This doesn't have to end violently, you know," Nick says. "Offer yourself up peacefully. It's easier that way."

I search the kitchen, desperately looking for a weapon. The wooden block of knives on the counter is too close to the spot where Nick is standing, and the utensil drawer is too far away.

Still, I have to try something. To my right is the closed cupboard tucked between the oven and sink. I fling it open, revealing the dumbwaiter behind it. Nick moves as soon as I start to clamber inside. I'm halfway into it by the time he reaches me, the stun gun sparking. I kick at him. Wildly. Savagely. Screaming as my foot connects with his chest. I see another blue crackle of the stun gun. I kick again, aiming at his face. Nick yelps and reels backward.

The stun gun blinks out and clatters to the floor.

I pull my leg into the dumbwaiter, suddenly reminded of how small it really is. Using both hands, I give the rope a tug. A second later, the dumbwaiter plummets, and I'm thrown into darkness.

I try to keep hold of the rope as the dumbwaiter drops, but it's zipping over my palms, slicing into them. I pull my hands away and clamp my knees against the rope, hoping to slow my descent.

A line of heat forms at my knees. Friction burning through the denim of my jeans. I part my knees and scream again, the sound consumed by the noise of the dumbwaiter as it smashes into the apartment below.

The impact blasts through my entire body. My head snaps backward. Pain shoots up my spine. When it's all over, I wonder if I'm too injured to move. Pain rings my neck, hot and throbbing.

But I can lift the dumbwaiter door and crawl out, careful not to jar my battered body. As I slide onto the kitchen floor of 11A, I'm surprised to see I can walk. I push through the pain, moving out of the kitchen and into the foyer, where I fling open the door.

Out of 11A, the pain lessens with each step. Fear, I think. Maybe adrenaline. As I approach the elevator, I see that—miracle of miracles—it's still stopped on the eleventh floor. The door sits open. I run toward it, suddenly aware of motion to my left.

Nick.

Coming down the steps from the twelfth floor, the stun gun zapping. Blood oozes from a cut below his right eye. I throw myself into the elevator and pound the button for the lobby.

Nick reaches the elevator as the outer door closes. He thrusts his arm between the bars, stun gun sparking like Saint Elmo's fire.

I reach for the interior grate and slam it into his arm, pinning it against the door. I pull back and do it again. Harder this time. So hard that Nick jerks his arm away, the stun gun falling from his hand and landing at my feet.

I slam the grate into place, and the elevator begins to carry me downward. Before I sink beyond the eleventh floor, I see Nick take to the stairs. Tenth floor.

He's flying down the steps. I can't see him yet, but his shoes slap against the marble, echoing down to me. Ninth floor.

He's getting closer. I get a glimpse of his feet crossing the landing between floors before the elevator slides out of view.

Eighth floor. Seventh floor.

I spot Marianne standing on the landing, watching. No makeup. No sunglasses. Her skin a sickly yellow. Sixth floor.

Nick speeds up after passing Marianne. He's in full view now, descending almost at the same speed as the elevator. Fifth floor.

I bend down and scoop up the stun gun. Fourth floor.

I press the button on the side of the stun gun, testing it. The tip sparks in a single, startling zap. Third floor.

Nick continues to keep pace with me. I rotate in the elevator car, watching out the windows as he moves. Ten steps, landing, ten more steps. Second floor.

I stand with my hand on the grate, ready to fling it open as soon as the elevator stops. Lobby.

I burst out of the elevator just as Nick starts down the staircase's final ten steps. I've got roughly ten feet on him. Maybe less.

I cross the lobby in frantic strides, not daring to look back. My body hurts so much that I can't feel the stun gun in my hand or my family's photo still tucked under my arm. My vision narrows so that all I can see is the front door ten feet from me.

Safety's just on the other side of that door. Police and pedestrians and strangers who'll have to stop and help.

I reach the door. I push it open.

Someone shoves me away from the door. My vision expands, taking in his cap, his uniform, his mustache. Charlie.

"I can't let you leave, Jules," he says. "I'm sorry. They promised me. They promised my daughter."

Without thinking, I fire up the stun gun and jab it into his stomach, the tip sparking until Charlie is doubled over in agony.

I drop the stun gun, push out the door, zoom across the sidewalk and into the street. Charlie calls out behind me, "Jules, look out!"

Still running, I risk a glance behind me and see him still doubled over in the doorway, Nick by his side.

There's more noise. A cacophony. The honk of a horn. The screech of tires. Someone screams. It sounds like a siren.

Then something slams into me, and I'm knocked sideways, flying out of control, hurtling into oblivion.

Now

When I wake, it's with jolting suddenness. I go from darkness to light in an instant.

I understand the situation with neon clarity. Chloe is in danger. Ingrid, too, if they ever find her. I need to help them. Right now.

I look to the open door. The room is dark, the hallway silent.

"Hello?"

No one answers. The hall, for the moment, appears to be empty.

I search the table by the bed for a phone. There isn't one. Nor is there a call button with which to summon a nurse.

I slide out of bed, relieved to discover I can walk, although not well. Soon I'm out of the room and into a hallway, a dim corridor with doors leading to two other rooms and a small nurses' station that's currently empty. There's no phone there, either.

"Hello?" I call out. "I need help."

Another door sits at the end of the hall, closed tight.

It's white. Windowless. And heavy, a fact I learn when I try to pry it open. It takes a pain-flaring grunt to finally get it to budge.

I pass through it, finding myself in another hallway.

One I think I've seen before.

To my right is a kitchen done up in earth tones. Above the sink is a painting. A snake curled into a figure eight, chomping on its own tail.

Beyond the kitchen is a dining room. Beyond that are windows. Beyond them is Central Park, colored orange by the setting sun.

I'm still in the Bartholomew. I have been the whole time.

I start to move, my bare feet smacking the floor in hurried steps. I get only a few feet before a hand spins me around.

Nick. Lips flat. Eyes angry.

To his right is Leslie Evelyn. To his left is Dr. Wagner, a needle and syringe in his hand. A bead of liquid quivers on the needle's tip before he jabs it into my upper arm.

Everything instantly goes woozy. I let out a scream.

I'm still hearing it when everything fades to nothingness.

Chapter 12

Two Days Later

I WAKE SLOWLY. Like a swimmer uncertain about surfacing, pulled against my will from dark waters. My eyes stay closed.

Although there's pain in my abdomen, it's distant, like a fire on the other side of the room.

Soon my eyelids move, flickering, fluttering, opening to the sight of a hospital room. The same one as before.

No windows. Chair in the corner. Monet hanging from the wall. Despite the fog in my brain, I know exactly where I am.

A slow turn of my head to the left lets me see the IV stand by the bed, its thin plastic tube snaking into my hand.

I roll my head in the opposite direction. That's where the photo of my family sits, my wan reflection visible in the cracked frame.

I move my right hand across my hospital gown. Beneath the paper-thin fabric is a slight bump where a bandage sits. I can feel it on the upper left side of my abdomen. Touching it sends pain flashing through my body, cutting the fog like a lightning strike.

My hand keeps moving down my side. Just to the left of my navel is a different dreadful rise. Another bandage. More pain.

More smoothing my hand over my stomach, fingers probing, searching for yet another bandage. I find it in the center of my lower abdomen. The pain gets worse when I press down on it. A gasp-inducing flare. My weakling voice can only moan.

Outside the room, someone hears me.

A moment later, Nick enters the room. He feels my forehead. He strokes my cheek.

"The surgery was a success," he says.

A single question forms in my thoughts. *What surgery?*

I attempt to ask it, sputtering out half a syllable before the fog returns. I can't tell if I've once again been injected with something. I'm back to being a swimmer, sinking into the murky depths.

Before I go under, Nick whispers in my ear.

"You're fine," he says. "Everything is fine. Right now, we only needed the one kidney."

Three Days Later

HOURS pass. Maybe days.

I'm awake, although the mental fog makes it difficult to know for sure. Everything has the feel of a dream.

I hear voices just outside the door. A man and a woman.

"You need to rest," the man says. I note the accent. Dr. Wagner.

"What I need is to see her," the woman says. "Now push me in there." That's followed by a hum. Rubber wheels on the floor.

A hand, leathery and rough, clasps my own. My eyelids part, and I see Greta Manville, small and frail in a wheelchair. Her skin clings to her bones. Veins zigzag beneath the papery whiteness. "I didn't want it to be you," she says. "I need you to know that."

I close my eyes and say nothing. I don't have the strength.

"It was supposed to be Ingrid. During her interview, they asked for her medical records, and she handed them over. Lo and behold, she was a potential match. But then she left, and there you were. Another match. I had no choice. It was you or certain death. So I chose life. You saved me, Jules. I will always be grateful for that."

I open my eyes again. I see that she's wearing a hospital gown similar to mine. Light blue. Near the collar, someone has pinned a golden brooch just like the one Marjorie Milton was wearing.

An ouroboros. I pull my hand away from hers and scream until I fall back to sleep.

I WAKE. I sleep. I wake again.

Some of the fog has burned away. Now I can move my arms, feel the painful intrusion of the IV and catheter that invade my body. I can even tell that someone's in the room with me.

I open my eyes, my vision blurred by whatever it was they gave me. He comes into focus slowly. Nick. A wicked bruise circles his right eye. The spot where my foot connected with his face.

He places a plastic tumbler full of water and a small paper cup on the tray beside the bed. Inside the paper cup are two chalky white pills the size of baby aspirin.

"I brought you something for the pain. We want you to be comfortable. There's no need to suffer."

I stay quiet, even though I *am* in pain. It burns through my abdomen—a fierce, throbbing agony. I welcome it. Pain equals clarity. Clarity equals survival.

Which is why I break my silence to ask the question I didn't have the strength to utter yesterday. "Why did you do it?"

Nick gives me a curious look. "Under normal circumstances, we prefer that donors know as little as possible. But I see no harm in trying to clear up some of your *misconceptions*."

He hisses the word with clear distaste.

"In 1918, the Spanish flu came out of nowhere, killing more than fifty million people worldwide," he says. "Right here in America, more than half a million people died. As a doctor, Thomas Bartholomew saw it strike down friends, family members. It didn't discriminate. It didn't care if you were rich or poor."

I remember that horrible picture I saw. The dead servants lined up on the street. The blankets over their corpses.

"What Thomas Bartholomew couldn't understand was how a millionaire could succumb to the flu as easily as a piece of tenement trash. Shouldn't the wealthy, by virtue of their superior breeding, be less susceptible than people who have nothing, come from nothing, *are* nothing? He decided his destiny was to build a facility where important people could live in comfort and splendor while he kept them safe from many of the ailments that afflicted the common class. That's how the Bartholomew was born. This building was willed into existence by my great-grandfather."

A memory forces its way into my mind. Nick and me in his dining room, talking over pizza and beer. *I come from a long line of surgeons, beginning with my great-grandfather.*

Another memory quickly follows. The two of us in his kitchen, having my blood pressure checked. After I told him the story behind my name, he shared the obvious fact that Nick was short for Nicholas. What he didn't tell me was his last name. Bartholomew.

"My great-grandfather's dream didn't last very long," Nick says. "His first task was to find a way to protect the residents in case the Spanish flu ever flared up again. But things went wrong. Some of the people he was trying to protect got sick. Some even died."

He doesn't mention the dead servants. He doesn't need to. I know they were test subjects. Infect the poor to heal the rich.

"When it looked like the police might get involved, my great-grandfather took his own life. But an ouroboros never dies. It's simply reborn. So when my grandfather left medical school, he chose to continue his father's work. He was more careful, of course.

More discreet. He shifted the focus away from virology to prolonging life. And the truly important people in the world deserve to live longer lives than those who are beneath them."

Telling his tale has left Nick energized. Beads of moisture shine along his hairline. He gets up and starts moving about the room.

"Right now, at this very moment, hundreds of thousands of people wait for organ transplants," he says. "Some of them are important people. Very important. Yet they're told to just get in line and wait their turn. What I do—what my family has always done—is provide options for those who are too important to wait like everyone else. For a fee, we allow them to skip that line."

What he doesn't say is that letting so-called important people move to the front of the line requires an equal number of unimportant people. Like Dylan. Like Erica. Like me.

Life from our deaths. *That's* the meaning behind the ouroboros.

"Cornelia Swanson," I say. "What was she?"

"The first transplant recipient," Nick says. "It went . . . badly."

So Ingrid and I had it wrong. This isn't about Marie Damyanov or the Golden Chalice or devil worship. It's just a group of dying rich people desperate to save their lives no matter the cost.

I can't resist asking a few more questions. For clarity's sake.

"What else are you going to take?"

"Your liver."

Nick says it with shocking indifference. Like he doesn't even consider me a human being.

I wonder what he was thinking that night in his bedroom, when I let him kiss me, undress me, make love to me. Even in that moment, was he appraising me, taking stock of what my body offered, wondering how much money I would make him?

"Who's going to get it?"

"Marianne Duncan," he says. "She's in need of one. Badly."

"What else?"

"Your heart." Nick pauses then. The only concession to my feelings. "That's going to Charlie's daughter. He's earned it."

I figured there had to be a reason people like Charlie willingly worked at the Bartholomew. Now I know. It's a classic quid pro quo.

For doing the dirty work, the little folks will get something in return.

"And Leslie? Dr. Wagner?"

"Our Mrs. Evelyn is a believer in the Bartholomew's mission," Nick says. "Her late husband benefited from a heart transplant during my father's tenure. When he died—later than expected, I might add—she offered to keep things running smoothly. As for Dr. Wagner, he's a good surgeon who lost his license twenty years ago after showing up for surgery drunk. My father, in need of assistance, made him an offer he couldn't refuse."

"I pity you," I tell Nick. "I pity you, and I hate you, although not as much as you hate yourself. Because you do. I'm sure of it."

Nick pats my leg. "Nice try. But guilt trips don't work on me. Now take your pills."

He grabs the paper cup and holds it out to me. I have just enough strength to knock it out of his hand. The cup drops to the floor, the pills bouncing into the corners.

"Please, Jules," Nick says with a sigh. "Don't become a problem patient. We can make the rest of your time here comfortable or extremely unpleasant. It's up to you."

He leaves quickly after that, letting the pills remain on the floor. The cleanup job falls to Jeannette, who enters the room a minute later dressed in the same purple scrubs and gray cardigan she wore when we first spoke in the basement.

She places new pills on the tray. When she bends down to pick up the ones on the floor, her cigarette lighter slips from her pocket and joins them. Jeannette curses before scooping it all up.

"Take the pills or get the needle again," she says while shoving the lighter back into her pocket. "Your choice."

Staring at the pills, those two tiny eggs in a white-paper nest, I can't help but think of my parents. They, too, had a choice—to continue fighting a battle they had no chance of winning or to willingly wrap themselves in the sweet embrace of nothingness.

Now I face a similar decision. I turn to their photo on the table, their faces crisscrossed by cracks in the glass. I look at them and know which choice to make.

I grab the paper cup and tip it back.

Four Days Later

THEY keep the door closed. It's also locked from the outside. During my rare bouts of wakefulness, I hear the click of the lock before anyone enters. Which is often. A veritable parade stomping through my drug-induced slumber.

First up is Dr. Wagner, who checks my vitals and gives me my pills and a breakfast smoothie. I dutifully put the pills in my mouth. I don't touch the smoothie.

Next are Jeannette and Bernard, who wake me with their chatter while they change my bandages and swap out the IV bag. From their conversation, I gather that there are three patient rooms, all occupied. I'm in one. Greta's in another. The third is occupied by Mr. Leonard, who only days ago received a new heart.

Although they never mention Dylan by name, I know where that heart came from. When I do eventually fall asleep again, it's with tears in my eyes.

Hours later, I'm roused from my deep slumber by Jeannette, who unlocks the door before carrying in food and more pills.

I look at her, groggy and dazed. "Where did Bernard go?"

"Home." She slides the tray in front of me. "Try not to talk."

Dinner is soup. Creamed spinach. Pudding. The pills have made me surly. Jeannette has a hard time scooping the soup into my mouth. I outright refuse to open my mouth for the spinach.

It's the rice pudding my pill-addled body craves. Willingly I open wide when Jeannette dips the spoon into it. But as she's bringing it toward my mouth, I change my mind. My jaw clamps shut, and I suddenly turn away, pouting. The spoon hits my cheek, sending pudding splatting onto my neck and shoulder.

"Look at this mess," Jeannette mutters as she grabs a napkin. "Lord forgive me, but I can't say I'll be sad to see you go."

I lie completely still as she leans over me to mop up the spilled pudding. Sleep is already threatening to overtake me again. I'm almost completely unconscious when she nudges my shoulder.

"You need to take your pills," she says.

My mouth falls open, and Jeannette drops the pills into it, one at a time. Then I'm asleep, closed fists at my sides, riding the narcotic fog until my mind is empty and blissful and at peace.

When I hear the door's lock click into place, I wait. After a full minute, I stuff the fingers of one hand into my mouth and fish out the pills. They emerge softened, slimy with saliva.

I sit up, wincing with pain, and lift my pillow. Beneath the case, in the pillow itself, is the small tear I created yesterday after talking to Nick. I shove the spit-slick pills into it, where they join the others. Eight of them. A whole day's worth of little white pills.

I replace the pillow and lie back down. I then unclench my other fist and examine the cigarette lighter I snatched after it fell from Jeannette's cardigan pocket while she cleaned me.

It's made of cheap plastic. The kind you can pick up at a gas station for a dollar. Jeannette probably has more in her purse.

She won't miss this one.

I TOSS the blanket aside and slide my legs over the side of the bed, even though it hurts to move, hurts to breathe. Three sets of stitches pull at the skin of my abdomen.

Before placing my feet on the floor, I pause.

I'm not sure standing's a good idea. Even if it is, I'm not sure I can. My legs tingle from disuse. The back of my hand is bleeding where I plucked out the IV. Removing the catheter was even worse. Soreness pulses through my core.

Yet I attempt to stand anyway, sucking in air to steel myself against the pain before pushing off the bed. Then I'm up, somehow standing on these weak, wobbling legs.

I take a step. Then another. And another.

Soon I'm staggering across the room, the floor seeming to rock like a ship's deck on a stormy sea. I keep walking, all the way to the door, where I try the handle and discover it is indeed locked.

So it's back to the side of the bed, where I grab the photograph of my family. I press it against my chest with one hand while gripping Jeannette's lighter in the other.

With a flick of my thumb, there's a flame, which I touch against the fitted sheet in the center of the bed. It ignites in an instant—a fire-ringed hole that grows exponentially. Expanding circles of fire spreading into each other and then outward, all the way to the pillows, which pop into flame. I watch, squinting against the smoke, as the entire bed is engulfed. A rectangle of fire.

Then, just as I had hoped, the fire alarm starts to blare.

It's Dr. Wagner who enters the room first, drawn by the fire alarm's call. Jeannette follows right behind him. They unlock the door and burst inside. Jeannette screams when she sees the flames on the bed. Because they're focused on the fire, neither of them sees me standing just behind the recently opened door.

Nor do they see me slip out of the room.

By the time they turn around to notice me, it's too late.

I'm already closing the door behind me and, with a quick turn of my wrist, locking them inside.

I walk as fast as I can, which isn't very fast at all. Behind me, Dr. Wagner and Jeannette pound on the door from inside my room. In between their frantic knocks I hear the sounds of Dr. Wagner coughing and Jeannette shrieking.

To my left is a darkened doorway. Inside I see Mr. Leonard, dead to the world despite the racket coming from the room next door. Surrounding him is all manner of equipment, the lights disconcertingly festive. Like a strand of Christmas bulbs.

I make my way to the nurses' station, where I allow myself to pause to catch my breath. Just beyond it is another hospital room and the short corridor I took the first time I left this place. The corridor ends at a door that leads directly into Nick's apartment. From there, I need to make it down the twelfth-floor hallway to the elevator. In my condition, taking the stairs isn't an option.

I push off the nurses' station and am on my way to the corridor when the door at its end starts to open. I duck into the room to my left and press myself against the wall by the open doorway, hoping I haven't been spotted.

Outside, I hear the rapid click of heels. Leslie Evelyn.

While waiting for her to pass, I scan the darkened room.

That's when I see Greta. She sits up in bed, startled, staring at me in fear. Her mouth drops open, on the knife's edge of a scream.

One sound from her could give me away. I stare back, silently begging her to stay quiet. I mouth a single word. *Please.*

Greta's mouth stays open while Leslie hurries past the door. She waits a few more seconds before finally speaking.

"Go," she says in a hoarse whisper. *"Hurry."*

I WAIT to move until Leslie pushes open the door two rooms down. Smoke pours from the room, gray and heavy. I use it as cover while heading down the corridor. I need to keep moving.

And I do. To the corridor's end. Through the door left open by Leslie. Into Nick's apartment.

I close the door behind me, remembering how heavy it is, using a shoulder to nudge it back into place. When the door is finally closed, I spot the dead bolt in its center.

I slide it shut. Satisfaction swells in my chest, although I harbor no illusions that Leslie and all the rest are now trapped. Surely there's another way out of there. But it will certainly delay them, and I need all the time I can get.

I hobble onward, exhaustion, pain, and adrenaline dancing through me. When I reach Nick's kitchen, the whole place seems to be spinning. The cabinets. The doorway to the dining room and the night-darkened park outside the windows. The only thing not spinning is the painting of the ouroboros.

The snake's flickering-flame eye watches me as I shuffle to the knife block on the counter and grab the biggest one.

Having the knife in my hand chases away some of the disorientation. I need to escape this place. I owe it to my family.

I look at the photograph still clutched to my chest. When faced with the decision, I knew what my choice had to be. To live. To be the one member of my family who doesn't vanish forever.

I keep going, out of the kitchen, back into the hallway, where thin strands of smoke have started to make an appearance. Here the noise of the fire alarm is distant yet audible. A system separate from the rest of the building.

The sound fades slightly as I head down the hallway. At the other end is Nick's study, the bookcase at the far wall still open. Beyond it is 12A. The study. Then the hallway. Then a way out.

But as I stagger toward the open bookcase, I feel a sudden heat at my back. I whirl around to see Nick standing in a corner of the study. In his hands is Ingrid's gun.

He lifts it, aims it my way, and pulls the trigger.

I close my eyes. In that fraught, fearful darkness, I hear a metallic click. Then another. Then two more.

I open my eyes and see Nick continuing to pull the trigger of the unloaded gun. Like it's a toy and he's just a kid playing cowboy. He smiles, pleased with himself.

"Don't worry, Jules," he says. "I can't shoot you. You're too valuable." He takes several steps toward me, the gun now lowered. My grip tightens around the knife's handle.

He takes two more steps, closing the gap between us.

I lift the knife, barely aware of what I'm doing.

He takes two more steps.

One slow, the other a startling leap toward me.

I thrust the knife forward until it makes contact with Nick's stomach. There's a pause. A breath of resistance.

I gasp as I yank the knife away.

Nick can only moan as blood soaks his shirt. Then he hits the floor. A swift, uninterrupted drop.

I back away from him. That backward shuffle takes me through the bookcase passage into the study of 12A. There I do another shoulder nudge to close the bookcase. Before it lumbers into place, I take one final glance into Nick's apartment. He's on the floor, still bleeding, still alive. But probably not for long.

I let the bookcase fall back into place.

Inside 12A, all traces of my existence are gone. The apartment looks just as it did when I first set foot inside it. Uninhabited.

But it's also a trap. I know that now. This perfect apartment with its perfect views inside a perfect building. The only reason the building exists is to serve the rich and trap the poor.

Those servants laid out like firewood. Cornelia Swanson's maid.

Dylan and Erica and all those other men and women without families who were lured here with the promise of a reset button for their sad lives. They deserve closure. Even more, they deserve vengeance. Which means only one thing.

This whole place needs to be burned to the ground.

I START with the study, pulling books at random from the shelves to form a pile in the middle of the floor. When I'm done, I grab the copy of *Heart of a Dreamer* Greta signed for Erica and hold the lighter to a corner of its dust jacket.

Fire tears across the book. I drop it onto the pile and walk away.

In the sitting room, I remove the cushions from the crimson sofa. One is shoved under the coffee table, where I use the lighter to set it ablaze. In the dining room, I repeat the process—place a cushion under that ridiculously long table, light it, leave. In the kitchen, I stuff the cushion into the oven and crank up the heat.

Sitting on the table in the breakfast nook is another copy of *Heart of a Dreamer.* I turn to the page Greta signed for me and, with a flick of my thumb, light it up. I wait for a flame to bloom before dropping it down the dumbwaiter shaft.

After that, it's up to the bedroom. On the nightstand is one final copy of *Heart of a Dreamer.* My real copy, first read to me by Jane as we lay on her bed.

I scoop it up and carry it back downstairs.

By the time I've reached the foyer, the apartment has filled with smoke. Already the fires have grown out of control. Satisfied, I open the door and leave 12A for the last time.

I keep the apartment door open as I move down the hallway, letting smoke billow out behind me. I press the button for the elevator. While waiting for it to arrive, I go to the nearby trash chute. I then flick the lighter and hold it just below the last copy of *Heart of a Dreamer.* My hand resists bringing the flame any closer.

This isn't just some random copy of the book. It's my copy. *Jane's* copy.

But I also understand that she'd want me to do it. This isn't the Bartholomew of her dreams. It's something dark and rotten to its core. If Jane knew the truth about the Bartholomew, I'm sure she'd despise it as much as I do.

Without another moment's hesitation, I place the book against the lighter's white-hot flame. As fire leaps across its cover, I drop the book down the trash chute, where it hits the dumpster below with a soft sizzle.

The fire alarm in the rest of the building goes off just as the elevator reaches the twelfth floor. I step into it, ignoring the shrieking alarm, the flashing emergency lights, the smoke rolling out of 12A in sinuous waves.

The elevator starts to descend. On my way down, I see that the residents have already started to evacuate. They move down the stairs in rushed packs. Rats scurrying from the sinking ship. Between the sixth and seventh floors, Marianne Duncan sits on the landing, jostled by others coming down the staircase. Tears stream down her face. "Rufus?" she screams. "Come back, baby!"

Our eyes lock for a moment, hers yellowed from jaundice, mine aflame with vengeance. The elevator sinks to the next floor.

None of the retreating residents tries to stop my descent. All it would take is a press of the elevator button on a lower floor. But they see the look on my face and the blood-stained knife in my hand and instinctively stay away.

As the elevator comes to a stop in the lobby, I spot a small dark shape streaking down the steps. Rufus, making his escape. I yank open the grate and step out of the elevator, lowering my aching body just enough to scoop him up. He shivers in my arms and lets out a few yaps that I hope are loud enough for Marianne to hear.

Together, we approach the door. Charlie is there, helping the Bartholomew's population of old and infirm get outside. He sees me and freezes, shocked, his arms dropping to his sides. This time, he doesn't try to stop me. He knows it's all over.

"I hope your daughter gets the care she needs," I tell him. "Do the right thing now, and maybe one day she'll forgive you."

I continue on, limping out of the Bartholomew as police and fire trucks start to arrive. It's a firefighter who spots me first, although it's hard not to. I'm a girl in a hospital gown with bare feet, a frightened dog, a cracked family photo, and a blood-slicked knife. Immediately, I'm swarmed by cops, who pry the knife from my hand. I refuse to give them Rufus or the picture of my family.

I'm allowed to keep hold of them as I'm wrapped in a blanket and guided first to a waiting patrol car and then, when it arrives, to an ambulance. Soon I'm on a stretcher, being carried to the ambulance. "Is anyone else inside hurt?" a cop asks me.

I give a weak nod. "A man on the twelfth floor—12B."

I'm then loaded feetfirst into the ambulance with two EMTs. Through the open rear door, I get a view of the Bartholomew itself. I look to the northern corner, where George sits, stoic as ever, even as flames start to leap in the window just behind his wings. I'm about to give him a whispered goodbye when I notice movement on the other side of the roof.

A dark figure emerges from the smoke, stumbling toward the roof's edge. I can tell it's Nick. He has a towel pressed to his stomach. When a smoke-filled breeze kicks up, the towel flutters, flashing bits of red.

Two more people join him on the roof. Cops. The smoke blows across him in malevolent strands, bringing him in and out of my vision. When it clears, I see that he's reached the edge of the roof. Even though he must be aware of the cops, he ignores them. Instead, he looks outward, surveying the park and the city beyond.

Then, like his great-grandfather before him, Nicholas Bartholomew jumps.

Chapter 13

Six Months Later

"Lo mein or fried rice?" Chloe says as she holds up two identical cardboard containers of Chinese food.

I shrug. "You pick. I'm fine with either."

We're in her apartment in Jersey City, which has, for the time being, become my apartment. After I was released from the hospital, Chloe handed me the keys and moved in with Paul.

"But what about rent?" I had asked.

"I've got it covered for now," she said. "Pay me what you can when you can."

I'm sitting next to Chloe on the couch as we open our takeout lunch containers. Joining us this afternoon is Ingrid, fresh from her new job at a midtown Sephora. Although she's dressed in black, her nails are a vivid purple. The bad bus station dye job is long gone, replaced with a relatively demure strawberry blond.

"Rice for me, please," she says.

Chloe hands her the container. If they gave out Nobel Prizes for patience, she'd certainly be in contention for one. She's been a saint since the moment I was released from the hospital with a clean bill of health. I haven't heard her complain once.

Not about the reporters who spent a full week camped outside the building. Not about the nightmares that sometimes leave me so shaken that I call her in the wee hours of the morning. Not about Rufus, who yaps at her every time she enters the apartment.

And certainly not about Ingrid, who's here more often than not, even though she now shares an apartment with Bobbie in Queens. Chloe knows that Ingrid and I are now bound together by what happened. I've got Ingrid's back. She's got mine. As for Chloe, she looks out for us both.

The two of them first met while I was being held against my will in the Bartholomew. When I never came back to the shelter, Ingrid went to the police, claiming I was taken by a coven living at the Bartholomew. They didn't believe her.

The police didn't think anything was amiss until Chloe, returning from Vermont early after eventually receiving the texts I had sent, also contacted them. A friendly cop put the two of them in touch. After Chloe went to the Bartholomew and was told by Leslie Evelyn that I had moved out in the middle of the night, the police got a search warrant. They were on their way to the building just as I was setting fire to 12A.

The fire ended up doing less damage than I intended. Yes, 12A was burned beyond repair, but the blaze in the basement was contained by the dumpster. Still, there was enough damage to make me worry that I could face criminal charges. The detective on the case remains doubtful that will happen. I was fearing for my life.

WHAT took place at the Bartholomew was insidious in its efficiency. People in need of a lifesaving organ were tipped off, usually by a former Bartholomew resident. They then used a dummy corporation to purchase an apartment, paying as much as a million dollars more than its market value.

There they waited for an apartment sitter who'd be a suitable donor. After the surgery, the resident spent a few more weeks in the Bartholomew to recuperate. The body of the apartment sitter, meanwhile, was quietly removed via a freight elevator and taken to a crematorium in New Jersey with Mafia ties.

Almost everyone involved was brought to justice, thanks to Charlie. He took my advice and did the right thing, providing police with valuable information about how the Bartholomew operated, who worked there, who lived there, who died there.

Those who managed to escape during the fire were slowly rounded up, including Marianne Duncan, the other doormen, and Bernard. All of them copped to their respective roles in the enterprise and were sentenced accordingly. Marianne began her ten-year stint in prison yesterday. She's still waiting for a new liver.

Marjorie Milton hired the best defense lawyer in Manhattan to represent her—until it turned out he had also used the Bartholomew's services. Both eventually entered guilty pleas.

Even more shocking was the participation of Mr. Leonard. Also known as Senator Horace Leonard from the great state of Indiana. Police found him crawling across the floor of the room next to mine. He probably would have died were it not for Dylan's heart pumping in his chest. Although he won't be sentenced until next month, even his own attorneys expect him to get life in prison. Thanks to Dylan's heart, that could mean a lot of time behind bars.

Then again, Mr. Leonard could always kill himself, which is

what Dr. Wagner did after Leslie freed him and Jeannette from the burning room. Once the three of them escaped out a back exit of the Bartholomew and went their separate ways, he spent two days at a Sheraton in Flushing, Queens, before putting a gun to his temple and pulling the trigger.

Jeannette went the opposite route, going home and sitting with her husband until the police arrived.

Leslie Evelyn was apprehended at Newark Liberty International Airport as she was about to board a flight to Brazil. Prosecutors pummeled her with charges ranging from human trafficking to aiding and abetting to tax fraud. She received multiple life sentences.

Out of everyone I encountered at the Bartholomew, only one person is neither dead nor facing years in prison. Greta Manville.

She was nowhere to be found when cops stormed the Bartholomew. The police searched her apartment and the basement storage cage, finding them mostly intact. No one has seen or heard from her, a fact that messes with my emotions more than it should. While I have a burning desire to see her brought to justice, I also know that I never would have escaped without her help.

Then there's the fact that she literally has a piece of me with her everywhere she goes.

As for me, I'm still adjusting to my new life as a celebrity victim—two words, by the way, that should never be used together. Yet that's what I was called during those few weeks when I was a media darling. Chloe took a two-week leave of absence from work to help me deal with all the interview requests. I did the bare minimum. A few phone interviews. Nothing in person. Nothing on camera. I ended each one by talking about Jane, imploring anyone with the slightest bit of information to come forward, anonymously if necessary. So far, there have been no new leads.

But people have been generous in other ways. There's the GoFundMe page Chloe set up to help pay for my medical expenses. Although I wasn't keen on accepting charity, I didn't have a choice. When your sole possession is a broken picture frame, you come to terms with relying on the kindness of strangers.

And I've received so many clothes that Bobbie and I have started handing things out at the homeless shelter. Same thing with shoes and phones and laptops. Everything I lost has been replaced threefold.

That's in addition to the money I've received. More than sixty thousand dollars in five months. The amount got to be so high that I begged Chloe to close the account. It's more than enough, especially considering that on Monday I'll be starting a job at a nonprofit group that helps people locate missing loved ones. They asked if I wanted to work for them after I used some of my GoFundMe money to make a donation in Jane's memory. I said yes. The office is small. The salary is even smaller. But I'll get by.

I'm feeding Rufus a barbecued sparerib when I notice the time. Quarter after one. "We need to go," I tell Ingrid.

Ingrid brushes rice from her lap and jumps to her feet. "We definitely don't want to be late for this."

"Are you positive you want to do this?" Chloe says.

"I think we need to," I tell her. "Whether we want to or not."

"I'll be here when you get back," she says. "With wine."

INGRID and I reach the Bartholomew just before two, finding the block closed off to cars. The crane and its wrecking ball have already arrived, parked in the middle of Central Park West like some giant metal beast. A temporary fence has been erected around it, presumably to deter onlookers.

It doesn't work. The sidewalk is mobbed. Many in the pack are from news outlets, their cameras aimed at the building across the street. Others are the morbidly curious who want to boast that they were there when the infamous Bartholomew was demolished.

The real estate conglomerate that bought the building is fully aware no one would buy an apartment that had been used in an organ-transplant black market. Now the Bartholomew faces its final minutes, and half the city has come out to watch it die.

Ingrid and I push our way into the fray. We go unnoticed, thanks to the knit caps and sunglasses we donned after emerging from the subway.

I peer through the chain-link fence. It's the first time I've laid eyes on the building in six months. Seeing it again brings a fearful chill that shoots through my bones even after I tighten my jacket.

Missing from the corner of the roof is George. At my request, he was removed and put into the care of the New-York Historical Society. The plan is to put him on display as a monument to the people who died. I hope it happens. It might be nice to visit him.

The crowd around us goes silent as a worker climbs into the cab of the crane. Once he's in place, an alarm sounds. So loud I feel it in my chest.

I start to cry, the tears sudden and unstoppable. Most of them are for those who never left the Bartholomew. Dylan especially, but also Erica, Ruby, and so many more.

I cry for my family. Jane, who may or may not still be out there. My parents, beaten down by life until they simply gave up.

But a few of those tears, I know, are reserved for myself. The younger, more hopeful person who saw the Bartholomew on a book cover and believed the promises it offered were real. That girl is gone now, replaced by someone wiser but no less hopeful.

Ingrid sees the tears streaming out from beneath my sunglasses and says, "Are you okay?"

"No," I say. "But I will be."

Then I wipe away the tears, grip Ingrid's hand, and watch the wrecking ball swing.

AfterWords

Riley Sager is a believer in new beginnings. He started his career as a journalist, working for a newspaper in New Jersey. While the job exposed him to interesting situations and he learned that "people are strange and do strange things," his real dream was writing fiction.

The author switched gears and began writing fiction under his real name, Todd Ritter. Unfortunately, those early books didn't sell well. Sager worked even harder, and when he finished *Final Girls*, his agent predicted it would be his breakthrough novel. "We wanted to give it the best opportunity to thrive," said Sager. "My agent decided it would be best to 'hit the reset button' on my career and start from scratch with a new name." The pseudonym Riley Sager was born, the book became a bestseller, and two more bestsellers followed.

Lock Every Door features Jules Larsen, a young woman desperate for a new beginning. For inspiration into her character, Sager looked inward. "I wanted Jules to be relatable," he says. "She's just had a long string of bad luck, and so she's really financially struggling through no fault of her own. I was in that boat not too long ago. I was laid off from my job, dropped from my publisher . . . It was terrifying."

Clearly those days are over. Today, the successful author lives in Princeton, New Jersey, and is at work on his next thriller.

SHAMED

A NOVEL
OF SUSPENSE

LINDA CASTILLO

Prologue

No ONE WENT TO the old Schattenbaum place anymore. No one had lived there since the flood back in 1969 washed away the crops and swept the outhouse and one of the barns into Painters Creek. Rumor had it Mr. Schattenbaum's 1960 Chevy Corvair was still sitting in the gully where the water left it.

Even in its heyday, the house had been run-down. The roof shingles were rusty and curled. Mr. Schattenbaum had talked about painting the house, but he'd never gotten around to it. Sometimes, he didn't even cut the grass. Despite its dilapidated state, once upon a time the Schattenbaum house had been the center of Mary Yoder's world, filled with laughter, love, and life.

The Schattenbaums had six kids, and even though they weren't Amish, Mary's *mamm* had let her visit—and Mary did just that every chance she got. The Schattenbaums had four spotted ponies, after all; they had baby pigs, donkeys, and too many goats to count. Mary had been ten years old that last summer, and she'd had the time of her life.

It was hard for her to believe fifty years had passed; she was a grandmother now, a widow, and had seen her sixtieth birthday just last week. Every time she drove the buggy past the old farm, the years melted away.

159

Mary still lived in her childhood home, with her daughter and son-in-law now, half a mile down the road. She made it a point to walk this way when the opportunity presented itself. In spring, she cut the irises that still bloomed at the back of the house. In summer, she came for the peonies. In fall, it was walnuts. According to Mr. Schattenbaum, his grandfather had planted a dozen black walnut trees. Every fall, the trees dropped thousands of nuts that kept Mary baking throughout the year—and her eight grandchildren supplied with walnut layer cake.

The house looked much the same as it did all those years ago. The barn where Mary had spent so many afternoons cooing over the ponies had collapsed a few years back. The rafters and siding were slowly being reclaimed by a jungle of vines.

"Grossmammi! Do you want me to open the gate?"

Mary looked over at the girl on the seat beside her, and her heart soared. She'd brought her granddaughters with her to help pick up walnuts. Annie was five and the picture of her *mamm* at that age: Blond hair. Blue eyes. A thoughtful child.

At seven, Elsie was a sweet, effervescent girl. She was one of the special ones, curious and affectionate, with a plump little body and round eyeglasses with thick lenses. She was a true gift from God, and Mary loved her all the more because of her differences.

"Might be good to stop the buggy first, don't you think?" Tugging the reins, Mary turned into the gravel lane. "Whoa."

She could just make out the blazing orange canopies of the trees behind the house, and she felt that familiar tug of nostalgia.

"Hop on down now," she told the girls. "Open that gate. Watch out for that barbed wire, you hear?"

Both children clambered from the buggy. Their skirts swished around their legs as they ran to the rusted steel gate, their hands making short work of the chain.

Mary drove the horse through, then stopped to wait for the girls. "Come on, little ones! Leave the gate open. I hear all those pretty walnuts calling for us!"

Giggling, the girls climbed into the buggy.

"Get your bags ready," Mary told them as she drove past the house. "I think we're going to fill all those baskets we brought."

She smiled as the two little ones gathered their bags. Mary had made them from burlap for just this occasion. The bags were large, with double handles easily looped over a small shoulder.

Mary drove the buggy around to the back of the house and stopped the horse in the shade of a hackberry tree. Picking up their gloves and her own bag, Mary climbed down. For a moment, she stood and listened to the whisper of wind through the treetops.

"Girls, we've chosen a perfect day to harvest walnuts," she said.

Bag draped over her shoulder, Elsie followed suit. Annie was still a little thing, so Mary reached for her and set her on the ground. She handed the two girls their tiny leather gloves.

"I don't want to see any stained fingers," she told them.

"You, too, Grossmammi."

Chuckling, Mary walked with them to the stand of trees.

"Look at all the walnuts!" Elsie said with exuberance.

"Are we going to make walnut cakes?" Annie asked.

"Of course we are," Mary assured her.

"And pumpkin bread!" Elsie added.

"If you girls picked as much as you talked, we'd be done by now." She tempered the admonition with a smile.

Mary knelt and scooped up a few walnuts, looking closely at the husks. They were green, mottled with black, but solid and mold free. It was best to gather them by October, but they were already into November. "Firm ones only, girls," she said.

Out of the corner of her eye, she saw little Annie squat and drop a walnut into her bag. Ten yards away, Elsie was already at the next tree, leather gloves on her little hands. Such a sweet child.

Mary worked in silence for half an hour. Before she knew it, her bag was full. Hefting it onto her shoulder, she walked to the buggy and dumped her spoils into the bushel basket.

She was on her way to join the girls when something in the house snagged her attention. Movement in the window? She didn't think so; no one ever came here. Probably just the branches swaying in the breeze and reflecting off the glass. Then she saw it again. She was sure of it this time. A shadow in the kitchen window.

She set her bag on the ground and made her way to the back

porch. The door stood open a few inches. "Hello?" she called out.

"Who are you talking to, Grossmammi?"

She glanced over her shoulder to see Annie watching her from her place beneath the tree. Behind her, Elsie was making a valiant effort to juggle walnuts and not having very much luck.

"You just mind those walnuts," she told them. "I'm taking a quick peek at Mrs. Schattenbaum's kitchen. I'll only be a minute."

Mary waited until the girls resumed their task and then pushed open the door. "Hello? Is someone there?"

Memories assailed her as she stepped inside. She recalled peanut butter and jelly sandwiches at the big kitchen table. The old Formica counters were still intact. The stove was gone; all that remained was a gas line. Some of the linoleum had been chewed away.

Mary was about to go to the cabinet, to see if the old cookie jar was still in its place, when a sound from the next room stopped her. Something—or someone—was definitely in there.

She went to the doorway that opened to the living room. It was a dimly lit space filled with shadows.

"Who's there?" she said quietly.

A sound to her right startled a gasp from her. She saw movement from the shadows. Someone rushing toward her . . .

The first blow landed against her chest. She reeled backward. A shock of pain registered behind her ribs. The knowledge that she was injured. All of it followed by an explosion of terror.

Something glinted in the periphery of her vision. A silhouette coming at her fast. She saw the pale oval of a face. She raised her hands. A scream ripped from her throat.

The second blow came from above. Slammed into her shoulder and went deep. Pain zinged; then her arm went numb.

Mewling, she stumbled into the kitchen. Her attacker followed, aggressive and intent. The light hit his face, and recognition kicked.

"You!" she cried.

The knife went up again, came down hard, hit her clavicle. Pain arced, like a lightning strike in her brain. And in that instant, she knew. Why he'd come. What came next. The realization filled her with horror. She tried to run. But she slipped and fell to her knees.

She twisted to face him, looked up at her assailant. "Leave her alone!" she screamed. "In the name of God, *leave her alone!*"

Her attacker raised the knife.

She scrambled to her feet, threw herself toward the window above the sink, and smashed her hand through the glass. Caught a glimpse of the girls.

"Run!" she screamed. *"Da Deivel!"* The Devil. "Run! *Run!*"

Footfalls sounded behind her. She looked over her shoulder. A flash of silver as the knife came down, slammed into her back. Her knees buckled, and she went down. Above, her attacker bellowed like a beast. *Da Deivel.*

Another knife blow jolted her body. Using the last of her strength, she looked up at her attacker.

Run, sweet child, she thought. *Run for your life.*

The knife arced. The blow rocked her body. Once. Twice. No more fight left. She couldn't get away, couldn't move.

She was aware of the linoleum cold and gritty against her cheek. The sunlight streaming in through the window. A crow cawing outside. Finally, the sound of his footfalls as he walked to the door.

Chapter 1

You SEE A LOT OF THINGS when you're the chief of police in a small town. Things most other people don't know about—don't want to know about—and are probably better off for it.

My name is Kate Burkholder, and I'm the police chief of Painters Mill. It's a pretty little town of about fifty-three hundred—a third of whom are Amish—nestled in the heart of Ohio's Amish country. I was born here and raised Plain, but I left the fold when I was eighteen. I never thought I'd return. But after twelve years—and after I'd found my place in law enforcement—my roots called me back. Fate obliged when the town council offered me the position of chief. I'm good at what I do. But I know my being formerly Amish—my familiarity with the culture, the religion, and being fluent in *Deitsch*—played a role in their decision.

It's a little after four p.m., and I'm riding shotgun in the passenger seat of my city-issue Explorer. My newest patrol officer, Mona Kurtz, is behind the wheel. She's all business this afternoon, wearing her full uniform. Her usually unruly hair is pulled into a ponytail. She works dispatch most nights, but recognizing the importance of patrol experience, I've been spending a couple of hours with her every day when our schedules align.

It's a sunny afternoon; cool, but pleasant for November in this part of Ohio. We're cruising down County Road 19 when we spot the dozen or so bales of hay scattered across both lanes.

"Looks like someone lost their load," Mona says, slowing.

"Driver hits a bale of hay doing fifty, and they're going to have a problem."

Hitting the light bar switch, Mona pulls over. "Set up flares?"

I look ahead, and sure enough, an Amish wagon piled high with hay wobbles on the horizon. "Looks like our culprit there. Let's toss the bales onto the shoulder and go get them."

We spend a few minutes lugging bales onto the gravel shoulder, and then we're back in the Explorer heading toward the wayward driver. It's an old wooden hay wagon with slatted side rails.

"Shall I pull him over, Chief?"

"Let's do it."

Mona tracks the wagon, keeping slightly to the left. We can't see the driver because the bed is stacked ten feet high with hay. It's being drawn by a couple of equally old draft horses. Slowly, the wagon veers onto the shoulder and stops.

Taking a breath, Mona straightens her jacket, shoots me an I-got-this glance, and gets out. Trying not to smile, I follow suit and trail her to the left front side of the wagon.

The driver isn't what either of us expected. She's fourteen or fifteen years old. An even younger girl sits on the bench seat next to her. Between them, a little boy of about six grins a nearly toothless smile. I can tell by their clothes that they're Swartzentruber Amish; the boy is wearing a black coat over jeans. A flat-brimmed hat sits atop the typical "Dutch boy" haircut. The girls are wearing blue dresses with black coats and black winter bonnets.

The Swartzentruber Amish are Old Order. They forgo many of the conveniences other Amish use in their daily lives. Things like running water and indoor plumbing. They don't use windshields in their buggies or rubber tires. The women wear long dark dresses. Most wear winter bonnets year-round. The men don't trim their beards. Even their homes tend to be plain.

The kids are uneasy about being pulled over, so I move to set them at ease. *"Guder nochmiddawks,"* I say, using the Pennsylvania Dutch words for "good afternoon."

"Hi." The driver's gaze flicks from Mona to me. "Did I do something wrong?"

"No, ma'am," Mona tells the girl. "I just wanted to let you know you lost a few bales of hay."

The girl's eyes widen. "Oh, no. How many?"

"Ten or so," Mona says. "About a quarter mile back."

Now that I've gotten a better look at them, I realize I've seen these children around town with their parents.

"You're Elam Shetler's kids?" I ask.

The driver shifts her gaze to me. "I'm Loretta." She jabs a thumb at the younger girl sitting beside her. "That's Lena. And Marvin."

I gauge the size of the wagon. It's a big rig that's overloaded. I'm about to suggest she go home to unload and return with an adult when she gathers the reins and clucks to the horses.

"Kumma druff!" she snaps. *"Kumma druff!"* Come on there!

The horses come alive. Their heads go up. Ears pricked forward. Listening. *Old pros,* I think.

"Are you sure you can turn that thing around?" I ask her.

"I can turn it around just fine," the girl tells me.

I watch as she skillfully sends both horses into a graceful side pass. The animals' heads are tucked, outside forelegs crossing over the inside legs in perfect unison. Within minutes, the wagon faces the direction from which it came.

"I have a whole new respect for Amish girls," Mona whispers.

I cross to the wagon, look at the girl. "Nicely done," I tell her.

She looks away, but not before I see a flash of pride in her eyes.

I motion toward the fallen bales of hay. "Pull up to those bales, and Mona and I will toss them onto the wagon for you."

The children giggle at the thought of two *Englischer* women in police uniforms loading their fallen hay, but they don't argue.

I've just tossed the last bale onto the wagon when the radio strapped to my duty belt comes to life. "Chief?"

I hit my shoulder mike, recognizing my dispatcher. "Hey, Lois."

"I just took a call from Mike Rhodehammel. Says there's a horse and buggy loose on Township Road 14 by the old Schattenbaum place."

"On my way," I tell her. "ETA two minutes."

I slide into the Explorer. "You hear that?" I ask Mona.

"Yep." She gets in and puts the vehicle in gear.

A few minutes later, we make the turn onto the township road. There are two houses on this swath of road. Ivan and Miriam Helmuth own a decent-sized farm, growing hay, soybeans, and corn. The other property is the old Schattenbaum place, which has been abandoned for as long as I can remember.

I spot the buggy and horse ahead. The animal is still hitched and standing in the ditch against a rusty, tumbling-down fence. The buggy sits at a cockeyed angle.

"No sign of the driver." Mona pulls up behind the buggy and hits the switch for the light bar. "What do you think happened?"

"The Helmuths have a lot of kids." I shrug. "Maybe someone didn't tether their horse." I get out and start toward the buggy.

The horse looks at me as I approach. I peer into the buggy, find it unoccupied, three old-fashioned bushel baskets in the back.

"Well, that's odd." I look around and spot a red F-150 rolling up.

"Hey, Chief." Local hardware store owner Mike Rhodehammel lowers his window. "Any sign of the driver?"

I shake my head. "Might belong to Mr. Helmuth down the road. I'm going to head that way now and check."

He nods. "I thought someone should know."

"Thanks for calling us, Mike."

"Anytime, Chief."

I watch him pull away and then start back toward the Explorer. "Let's go talk to the Helmuths."

I'm in the process of sliding in when I hear the scream. I go still, listening. Another scream splits the air. It's high-pitched and goes on for too long. The hairs at the back of my neck prickle.

Mona's eyes meet mine. "What the hell, Chief?"

"Where is it coming from?" I say.

I step away from the Explorer, trying to determine the direction from which the voice came. This time, I discern words.

"Grossmammi! Grossmammi! Grossmammi!"

Terror echoes in the young voice. I glance at the Schattenbaum house, spot a little Amish girl running down the gravel lane.

"Grossmammi! Grossmammi!"

Mona and I rush toward her. I reach the mouth of the lane. The gate is open. The little girl is twenty yards away, running fast, darting looks over her shoulder as if she's seen a ghost. She's about five years old. She looks right at me, but she doesn't see.

"Sweetheart. Hey, are you okay?" I ask in *Deitsch*.

When she's ten feet from me, I notice the blood on her hands. On her dress. A lot of it. *Too much.* A hard rise of alarm in my chest. I glance at Mona. "I got blood. Keep your eyes open."

The girl slams into me. Mewling sounds tear from her throat.

"Easy." I set my hands on her little shoulders. "It's okay."

"Grossmammi!" Screaming, she claws at my clothes, looks over her shoulder toward the house. "*Da Deivel* got her!"

"What happened? Are you hurt? Tell me what happened."

"*Da Deivel* hurt Grossmammi!" the girl cries. "She's bleeding. He's coming to get me, too!"

"Where is she?" I ask firmly.

Choking, she lifts a shaking hand, points toward the old house. "In the kitchen. She won't wake up!"

I look at Mona. "Get an ambulance out here. Call County and tell them to send a deputy." I ease the little girl over to Mona. "Stay with her. I'm going to take a look."

I hear Mona hail Dispatch as I jog toward the house. I notice the buggy-wheel marks in the dust as I run. A burlap tote someone must have dropped.

I reach the back of the house. No movement inside. I go to the porch, spot a single footprint in the dust. The door stands ajar. The hinges squeak when I push it open the rest of the way.

I smell blood an instant before I see it. An ocean of red covers the floor. Spatter on the wall. Adrenaline burns my gut. I slide my .38 from its holster. A female lies on the floor. She's Amish. Blue dress. White *kapp*. Older. Not moving. There's no weapon in sight. All I can think is that this was no accident or suicide and I may not be alone.

"Damn." I hit my radio. "Ten-thirty-five-C. Ten-seven-eight." They are the codes for homicide and "need assistance."

I train my weapon on the doorway that leads to the next room. "Painters Mill Police! Get your hands up and get out here! Now!"

Keeping my eyes on the door, I go to the woman, kneel, and I get my first good look at her face. My brain kicks out a name: Mary Yoder. She lives with her daughter and son-in-law, Miriam and Ivan Helmuth, at the farm down the road. Even before I press my index finger to her carotid, I know she's gone.

I rise and sidle to the doorway, peer into the living room. It's dark; curtains drawn. I yank the mini Maglite from my belt. I shine the beam around the room. No sign of anyone.

"Chief?"

I spin, see a Holmes County deputy come through the back door. He does a double take upon spotting the victim.

"Place isn't cleared," I tell him. "Victim is deceased."

Drawing his sidearm, he moves past me, into the living room.

"Holmes County Sheriff's Department!" The voice comes from outside an instant before the front door flies open. A second deputy enters, shotgun at the ready.

"House isn't cleared," I say. "Deceased female in the kitchen."

The men exchange looks. The first deputy strides to a casement doorway, peers into an adjoining room. "Clear!"

The other deputy calls for additional units. Together, they start up the stairs to the second level.

I go back to the kitchen, stop in the doorway, bank a swift rise of revulsion. I've seen a lot of bad scenes. Traffic accidents. Knife fights. Serious beatings. Even murder. I can honestly say I've never seen so much blood from a single victim. What happened?

"Chief?"

I look up to see Mona come through the back door. She spots the victim and freezes. A tremor passes through her body.

My newest deputy is not ready for this.

"Mona." I say her name firmly. "Get out. I got this."

She backs away onto the porch and throws up in the bushes.

That same queasy response bubbles in my own gut. I shove it back, refuse to acknowledge it.

"Where's the girl?" I ask Mona.

"She's with a deputy, in the back seat of his cruiser." Hands on her hips, she looks at me. "Chief, kid says a man took her sister."

The words land a solid punch to my gut. "Did you get names?"

"Helmuth."

"I know the family," I say. "They live down the road."

"What do you think happened?"

I shake my head. "Hard to tell. Looks like she was . . . stabbed."

Butchered, a little voice whispers.

I hit my lapel mike and hail Dispatch. "Possible ten-thirty-one-D," I say, using the ten code for kidnapping in progress.

If we were dealing solely with a likely homicide, my first priorities would be to protect the scene, limit access, set up a perimeter, canvass the area. The possibility of a kidnapped child changes everything. The living always take precedence over the dead.

"Did the little girl say anything else?" I ask Mona.

"Couldn't get much out of her, Chief. She's pretty shaken up."

I take a final look at the victim. "Let's go talk to her."

I FIND the girl huddled in the back seat of a Holmes County Sheriff's Department cruiser. Someone has draped a Mylar blanket across her legs and given her a teddy bear to hold.

I make eye contact with the deputy as I approach. I've worked with him before; he's a good guy, a father himself, and a decent cop. We shake hands. "She say anything?"

"Been crying mostly, Chief. Said something in Dutch." He shrugs. "Wants her mom, I think."

I tell him about the possibility of a missing sister. "Best-case scenario, she got scared and ran home."

The door to the back seat stands open. I go to it and kneel so that I'm eye level with the girl. "Hi there," I say. "My name's Katie, and I'm a policeman. Can you tell me what happened?"

She looks at me, her face wet with tears. "I want my *mamm*."

She's a tiny thing. Blue dress. Blue eyes. Light hair. Blood on baby hands. She's shaking violently beneath the blanket. I switch to *Deitsch*. "Who did that to your *grossmammi*?"

"*Da Deivel*." The devil.

The words put a chill between my shoulder blades. "A *mann*?"

She nods.

"Do you know his name? Have you seen him before?"

She shakes her head.

"Is your sister with you?"

"Elsie." She whispers the name. "He took her."

"What did he look like?"

She stares at me. "I want my *mamm*."

"Sweetheart, do you know where he went?"

She shakes her head and begins to cry. Huge, wrenching sobs.

I reach out and squeeze her little knee. "I'm going to go get your *mamm* and *datt*."

Rising, I turn to Mona and the deputy. "We've got a male subject who's possibly taken a little girl. I want all hands on deck." I address Mona. "Tell T.J. and Pickles to canvass the area," I say, referring to my officers by their nicknames. "Tell Glock and Skid to clear the barn and outbuildings and fan out from there. Call the sheriff's department, see if they have someone with dogs. I want the property searched and everything marked and preserved."

"Got it."

Yanking out my phone, I hit speed dial for John Tomasetti and start toward the Explorer. He's an agent with the Ohio Bureau of Criminal Investigation. He's also my significant other and the love of my life. Painters Mill falls within his region. We've worked together on several cases, and I'm glad I have someone like him to count on.

He picks up on the second ring. "I hear you've got a body and a missing juvenile on your hands," he says without preamble.

"Word travels fast." I lay out what I know. "I think the five-year-old saw the killer and may have seen him take her sister."

"One man?"

"I think so. This kid is traumatized, so I need someone good to come down and talk to her. I need to know what she saw."

"I'm on it," he says. "I'll be there in twenty minutes."

I hit END and drop the cell into my pocket. I've just opened the car door when I spot the Amish man running toward me, a boy of about nine or ten hot on his heels. I recognize him immediately as Ivan Helmuth. More than likely he heard the sirens or saw the police vehicles pulling in and came down to see what happened.

"Chief Burkholder!" he calls out.

I go to him. "Mr. Helmuth—"

"What happened?" he says. "Why are all of these police here? Where are my children? My mother-in-law?"

"I've got one girl in the car, sir. She's okay."

"One? But . . ." Leaving the sentence unfinished, he rushes to the vehicle, pushes past Mona and the deputy, and looks into the car. *"Annie."* He pulls the girl into his arms.

"Datt!" Sobbing, the little girl clings to him.

"Where is your *shveshtah?*" he asks. Sister. "Your *grossmammi?*"

"Da Deivel got Grossmammi!" she cries. "He took Elsie!"

"What?" The Amish man is so startled that he stumbles back. "Took her? *Da Deivel?*" His eyes find mine. "Where are they, Chief Burkholder? What's happened here?"

I set my hand on his arm. "I need to speak with you privately."

He looks down at the boy who'd followed him over. *"Bleiva mitt die shveshtah."* Stay with your sister.

He lets me lead him a few feet away. When we're out of earshot of the children, I turn to him. "Mr. Helmuth, Mary Yoder is dead. She's inside the house." I motion toward the structure a hundred yards away where half a dozen deputies mill about.

"What?" He blinks, disbelieving. *"Dead?* How—"

I struggle to find the right words. "All I know at this point is that Mary is dead and we haven't been able to locate the other girl."

"Elsie?" He struggles for calm. "We need to find her," he snaps. "She's got to be around here somewhere."

"She's not in the house. We're searching the property now. Is it possible she's at home?"

"No, she was with her sister and grandmother."

"Mr. Helmuth, there was foul play involved—"

"You mean someone did this thing?"

I nod. "Annie told me a man took Elsie. We have reason to believe it was the same man who attacked your mother-in-law."

"Took her? *Mein Gott.*" My God. He begins to shake. "Who?"

"I don't know."

"We must find Elsie," he says. "She's just a child." His entire body is vibrating with terror. "Chief Burkholder, what happened to my mother-in-law? How did she . . ."

I fudge. "I'm not sure, but it's bad."

He nods. "Miriam will want to know."

"Mr. Helmuth, is it possible Elsie got scared and ran home?"

"I didn't see her, but . . ."

"We need to check." I motion toward the Explorer, and we start toward it. "Do you have a phone at your house?"

"No."

"I know this is a lot to take in. But time is of the essence. We need to hurry. Grab Annie and come with me."

Snapping out of his fugue, the Amish man looks at the boy. *"Bringa da waegli haymet,"* he tells him. Bring the buggy home.

"Take the horse," I tell him. "Leave the buggy. I need to check it for evidence."

The man nods at the boy, and then we're off.

A minute later, I pull into the gravel lane of the Helmuth farm and park in the driveway behind the house. Helmuth opens the passenger door and scrambles from the vehicle.

"Miriam!" he calls out as he rushes toward the back porch. *"Finna Elsie! Finna Elsie!"* Find Elsie.

The screen door squeaks open. A heavyset Amish woman with a

kind, tired face looks out at the man running toward her. *"Was der schinner is letz?"* What in the world is wrong?

"Elsie is missing," he says. "Did she come home?"

"No," the woman says, looking startled. "She went with—"

He cuts her off. "Search the house. I'll look in the barn."

He trots toward the barn. The woman shoots a worried, questioning look my way, then disappears inside.

I get out of the Explorer and open the door for the girl in the back seat. She's not making a sound, but her cheeks are shiny with tears. "Let's go inside, sweetheart."

Taking her hand, I walk with her to the back door. We enter a mudroom with a wall of windows to my right. An old wringer washing machine squats in the corner. A clothesline bisects the room at its center, half a dozen pairs of trousers hanging to dry.

Annie and I have just stepped into the kitchen when the screen door slams. Footsteps pound, and then Ivan Helmuth enters the room. "She's not in the barn," he says breathlessly.

I hear shoes in the hallway, and then Miriam enters the kitchen. "Elsie's not upstairs. What's happened? Where's Mamm?"

"Elsie's missing." Ivan's voice breaks. "Mary is . . . gone."

"Gone? What do you mean?" The Amish woman's gaze lands on Annie; her eyes go wide when she spots the blood. *"Mein Gott."* She rushes to the child and takes the girl into her arms. "Are you hurt? How did you get that blood on you?" she asks in *Deitsch.*

"Da Deivel," the little girl whispers.

Miriam pales. "What is she saying? Whose blood is this?" Her eyes dart to me. "Chief Burkholder? What's happened?"

"Mrs. Helmuth, I need to speak to you and your husband privately." I let my eyes slide to the little girl.

Taking the girl by her hand, the Amish woman rushes from the kitchen, goes to the base of the stairs, and calls out. "Irma!"

A girl of ten or eleven clatters down the steps. "What's wrong?"

"Take Annie. Get her cleaned up."

The girl's eyes widen when she sees the blood. "Oh!"

"Go on now. Get her washed up. Quick."

When the children are gone and we're seated, I tell them everything.

"Mamm passed? But . . ." Miriam covers her face with her hands. "*Elsie*. Gone? *Mein Gott*. It's too much. I can't believe it."

Ivan looks at me. "Who would do this terrible thing?"

"Did your mother-in-law have any enemies?" I ask.

The couple exchange looks. "No," Ivan says after a moment.

"Has anything unusual happened to Annie or Elsie recently?"

The Amish man shakes his head adamantly. "No."

"Any problems with family members? Or neighbors? Any arguments or bad blood? Money disputes?"

"No," he tells me. "Nothing like that."

"Have you had any workers here at the farm? Day laborers?"

"I do everything myself," Ivan says.

I shift gears. "How many children do you have?"

Miriam raises her head. "Eight."

"Any problems with any of them?"

"Of course not," Miriam snaps. "We are *Amisch*." As if that explains everything. In a way, it does.

"Have you noticed any strangers in the area?"

Ivan gives another head shake. "No."

"I just want my baby." Miriam begins to cry. "Please, Chief Burkholder. Elsie is . . . special. Sweet and innocent. She won't understand what's happening."

The word "special" gives me pause. "Elsie is special needs?"

"She's a slow learner. She was diagnosed with Cohen syndrome when she was four. Please, we've got to find her."

Cohen syndrome is a rare gene disorder that's slightly more common among the Amish. It carries a host of problems, including delayed physical development and intellectual disability.

I set my hand on the Amish woman's arm. "Do you have a photo of Elsie?"

"We do not take photos of the children."

"Can you tell me what she looks like? What was she wearing?"

She describes the girl—seven years old, blue dress, brown hair and eyes. Slightly overweight. Thick, round eyeglasses. I jot everything in my notebook. All the while, the urge to get back to the scene is powerful. Find the evidence. Churn it. Answer the questions pounding my brain. No one does something like what was done to Mary Yoder without leaving something behind.

More than anything, I want to find the girl. That need is tempered by the knowledge that the information-gathering phase of the investigation—speaking with family, friends, and possible witnesses—is critical. The majority of homicide victims know their killers. Most kidnappings are committed by family members. If either of those statistics is true in this instance, the most vital information I receive will come from the people closest to Elsie: her family, right here and now.

"Mr. and Mrs. Helmuth, you mentioned Mary and your two daughters went to the house to pick up walnuts. Has Mary ever had any problems there? Any strangers hanging around?"

Miriam shakes her head. "She never mentioned anything."

I pause. "Look, I know Annie has been through a lot. But I need to ask her some questions."

Miriam rises. "I'll fetch her."

A few minutes later, the four of us are seated at the kitchen table. Annie is sitting in her mother's lap, wearing a fresh dress. Miriam supplied me with the soiled one, which I'll send to the BCI lab to have the blood tested. Chances are it belongs to Mary Yoder, but you never know.

"Hi, sweetheart," I begin.

The little girl puts her thumb in her mouth and starts to suck. Miriam gently takes the child's hand and lowers it. "Chief Katie has a few questions for you, my little peach."

I need to be gentle, to not frighten this child.

"My *grossmuder* used to call me little peach." I tilt my head. "Your cheeks kind of look like peaches."

A ghost of a smile floats across the child's expression.

"Makes me want to pinch them."

This time, a full-blown grin.

I jump on it. "Can you tell me what happened when you and Elsie and your *grossmammi* were gathering walnuts?"

The little girl buries her face against her *mamm*. "I'm scared," she whispers.

I try again. "Was there someone else there?"

"*Da Deivel*," she mumbles.

"Can you tell me what he looked like, sweetie?"

"I can't remember," she whispers. "Just a man."

I pull a lollipop from my pocket and offer it to her.

An almost-smile, and then the girl reaches for the lollipop.

"What was the man wearing?" I ask matter-of-factly.

When Annie doesn't respond, I try another tactic. "How about if we play a game? I'll guess what he looks like, and you tell me if I'm right or wrong."

Nodding, she slides the lollipop into her mouth.

"Was his hair blond, like yours? Or brown, like mine?"

"Like yours," she says in a small voice.

"Okay." I pretend to think for a moment. "Was his skin the color of mine? Or was it the color of chocolate pudding?"

The mention of pudding elicits the whisper of a smile. "Yours."

"Was he Plain or English?"

"Plain."

"Good job." I say the words with a little too much enthusiasm. "Were his eyes blue like your *mamm*'s or brown like your *datt*'s?"

Her brows knit, and she shakes her head.

"Was he old? Like Bishop Troyer? Or young, like your *mamm*?"

"Kind of in the middle."

"Was he tall or short?"

"Tall. *Grohs*." Big.

"So you, Elsie, and Grossmammi were gathering walnuts." I switch to *Deitsch*, so she doesn't clam up. "What happened next?"

"Grossmammi went in the house to look at Mrs. Schattenbaum's kitchen. We heard something break and then yelling, so me and Elsie went in to find her."

"What did you see when you went inside?"

"Grossmammi was on the floor. She was all bloody. She was making noises. Elsie tried to help her. Then the man came."

"He came into the kitchen?"

"*Ja*." Her foot begins to jiggle. "I thought he was going to help Grossmammi. But he grabbed Elsie. Real rough. She got scared."

"Did he say anything?"

Her eyes fill with tears. "I got scared and ran."

"What about Elsie?" I ask. "Did she say anything?"

"All she did was scream."

Chapter 2

One hour missing

THE SCHATTENBAUM PLACE is teeming with activity when I pull into the driveway. I see a Holmes County Sheriff's Department vehicle. An Ohio State Highway Patrol Dodge Charger. Two Painters Mill cruisers tell me my own department has arrived.

I park behind Tomasetti's Tahoe and call my dispatcher.

"I need you to get me the names and addresses of all registered sex offenders in Painters Mill and all of Holmes County," I say. "If the offender has an Amish-sounding name, flag it. Let me know if any of them live in close proximity to the Schattenbaum place."

I hear her typing in the background, noting everything. "Got it."

"Run Ivan and Miriam Helmuth through LEADS. Run Mary Yoder as well as her deceased husband. See if anything comes back." LEADS is the acronym for the Law Enforcement Automated Data System, which stores information such as criminal records and outstanding warrants.

"Okay."

"Did you call Doc Coblentz?" I ask, referring to the Holmes County coroner.

"He's on his way."

"I need an aerial map of the Schattenbaum property and the surrounding area. Call the Holmes County auditor. Ask them to fax it to you. Tell them it's an emergency and I need it yesterday."

I end the call and hit my shoulder mike as I slide out of the Explorer. "Mona, what's your twenty?"

"Glock, Skid, and I cleared the barn and the small outbuilding."

"Anything?"

"Negative."

"I need you to ten-fifty-eight," I tell her, using the ten code for "direct traffic." "I want the road in front of the Schattenbaum place blocked off at both T's, flares and cones. No one comes in or goes out. I'll get County out there to help you."

"Roger that."

"Tell Glock and Skid to search the back of the property. It's a big spread. Grab some deputies, set up a grid, and get it done."

"Ten-four."

"Pickles? What's your twenty?"

"T.J. and I are talking to neighbors, Chief. No one saw a thing."

I blow out a breath of frustration. "Keep at it."

As I near the house, I spot a Holmes County deputy standing just off the back porch. He looks my way, and I recognize him. He was the first deputy to arrive on scene.

"Chief." He crosses to me. "Damn, this is bad."

"Anyone else in the house?" I ask as we shake hands.

"BCI guy ordered everyone out. Their crime scene truck is on the way."

Tomasetti, I think, and I'm thankful he got here so quickly. "House is clear?"

"Yep."

"Outbuildings are clear." I look toward the field. "I just sent two officers to search the back of the property. If you can spare a couple of deputies to help with the search, I'd appreciate it."

"You got it." He reaches for his shoulder mike.

"Chief Burkholder."

I turn to see Tomasetti come out of the house. I go to him, and we shake hands, a ridiculously formal greeting considering we're living together. Since it's not common knowledge among our peers, we're ever cognizant of appearances.

He holds on to my hand an instant too long. "Any word on the kid?"

I shake my head. "I talked to the parents. She's not there. I need to put out an Amber Alert."

"We meet the criteria." He pulls out his phone, thumbs something into it. "I need a physical description. Photo, too."

"Seven-year-old white female. Brown eyes. Brown hair. Three feet nine. About sixty pounds. Tomasetti, she's special needs."

"Damn."

"No photo." I describe her clothing—a white *kapp* and light blue dress—and he types all of it into his phone.

"You have anything on the suspect?" he asks.

I recite the particulars from memory. It isn't much.

"Vehicle?" he asks.

"I don't know. The sister said he was Amish."

"Still, he could be driving a vehicle. He could be disguised as an Amish person. But we'll go with it for now. I'll get this put into NCIC," he says, referring to the National Crime Information Center system. "I'll call the coordinator over at DPS." The Department of Public Safety. "Amber Alert will go out within the hour."

The crunch of tires on gravel draws our notice. I see the BCI crime scene truck pull into the driveway. Tomasetti and I start toward it. Normally, I'd stick around for the collection of evidence. But with a child missing, my efforts are best used looking for her.

I look at Tomasetti. "You got this?"

"Got it covered, Chief. Go."

I leave him with the crime scene unit. I'm on my way to locate the fence line to the east when I run into Glock and Skid along with two Holmes County deputies.

"You been to the back of the property?" I ask.

"Heading that way now," Glock tells me.

"I think the Schattenbaums owned about sixty acres," I tell them. "Ran cows for a while, so it's fenced."

Skid motions right. "Woods are pretty thick along that creek on the east side."

"Got some deep pools in that creek," Glock adds. "Water runs swift in a couple of areas."

"All right." I relay a description of the girl. "Name is Elsie. Seven years old. Amish. Special needs." I motion toward the rear of the property. "Set up a loose grid. Glock, you take the east woods.

Keep your eyes on the brush and water, especially any deep pools. Skid, you got the fence line. Keep your eyes west." I look at the two deputies. "Can you guys handle the pasture?"

Both men nod.

"Keep your eyes open for blood," I tell them. "Stay cognizant of evidence. Mark anything suspect." I motion toward the greenbelt. "I'll take the creek in front. Eyes open. Let's go."

The four men head toward the back of the property. I cut toward the woods. The grass is hip high as I pass through a microforest of saplings, most of which are taller than me. It's a huge, overgrown area. From the look of things, no one has been this way for a long time. No broken branches. None of the grass is laid over.

Fifty yards, and I reach the fence that runs front to back along the east side of the property. Rusty barbed wire is propped up on a combination of cedar posts and steel T-posts. I make the turn, head south toward the road.

The house is now behind me and to my right. I stick to the fence line, ducking beneath branches. I hear the rush of water over rocks to my left, telling me I'm not far from the creek.

I'm thirty yards from the road when I spot a patch of disturbed grass. A path, I realize. It starts at the house, weaves through a dozen trees, and leads to the fence. From there, it follows the fence line toward the road. If someone left the house in a hurry and didn't want to be seen, this would be the perfect route.

I move right, as not to disturb the path. Upon closer inspection, I see that the tall blades of grass are broken in places. I'm no tracker, but it looks fresh.

I've gone another dozen yards when I spot the shoe. It's a girl's sneaker. The laces are still tied. Canvas. Cheap. The kind of footwear a growing Amish girl might wear. I travel another ten feet, and a glint of red on the grass stops me cold. Blood.

I check my duty belt for something with which to mark the location. I come up with a yellow sticky note. I skewer it on a stick and poke the length of wood into the ground. I move on.

I find more blood. A footprint. Adult size with visible tread. There's no way to tell whose blood it is. There was a copious amount inside the house; it's likely the killer carried it out on his clothes or shoes or both, and it transferred to the grass. It's also possible he cut himself during the attack. Worst-case scenario, the blood belongs to the girl. . . .

I snap several photos and then call Tomasetti. "I got blood. And a decent footprint."

"Where are you?" he asks.

I can just make out the roof of the house through the trees. "A couple hundred yards southeast of the house, near the fence line."

"I'll get another agent out here. We're running out of light."

He's right; dusk is fast approaching. If the clouds to the west are any indication, we've probably got rain on the way, too.

I'm walking toward the road, looking down at the ground, when I spot tire marks in the moist soil. "I got tire imprints, too."

A thoughtful moment and then, "Tread?"

I pull the mini Maglite from my duty belt and kneel. "Yup. Tomasetti, if these marks get rained on, we'll lose this."

"I'm on my way."

A few minutes later, his Tahoe rolls up on the road and stops. Leaving the engine running, he gets out and starts my way. "An agent with some plaster should be here in twenty minutes."

"Rain isn't going to wait," I tell him.

"That's why they invented garbage bags." He snaps open a large trash bag. "Might work if it doesn't pour."

I take him to the tire-tread marks. He squats.

"Looks like he came down the road, heading east," I say. "Pulled over here. Left that imprint." I shift the Maglite beam to the falling-down fence at the edge of the property. "From there he went to the fence, used the trees for cover. Walked to the house, sticking to the fence line, and then cut over, keeping out of sight."

His gaze jerks to mine. "You got guys out canvassing?"

I nod, but we know the man we're looking for is probably gone.

"If this guy knew Mary Yoder and those kids were coming, if he knew their routine, he may have gone inside and waited for them," he says.

"If they were already here," I say, "all he had to do was sneak up to the house along this fence line and make entry."

"If he knew the victim, he's likely local." Tomasetti looks around. "Were they targets, or did they surprise him?"

"If he targeted them, who was he after?" I murmur. "Mary Yoder? Or the girl? Both?"

Kneeling, he spreads the bag over the tire-tread imprints.

"How's it coming along inside?" I ask.

"It's a mess, Kate." He anchors the plastic with a couple of stones, rises, and sighs. "Mary Yoder wasn't just stabbed. She was butchered. Defensive wounds. She put up a hell of a fight."

"You think this is personal? That he knew her?"

"Or he's a psycho, or both."

"You guys get anything?"

"Footwear imprints. Large. Definitely male." He reaches into the pocket of his jacket. "Crime scene agent found this on the victim." He pulls out a clear plastic bag containing a sheet of notebook paper. "We've still got to log it, but I wanted you to take a look to see if it means something that might help us find the kid."

I shine my flashlight on the bag. White notebook paper. Lined. From a spiral binding. Printed in pencil by an inept hand.

> Food gained by fraud tastes sweet, but one ends up with a mouth full of gravel.

"Mean anything to you?" he asks.

"It's from the Bible," I say. "A proverb, I think. Something to do with deception."

"Any idea how this might fit with any of this?"

I shake my head. "No clue."

We fall silent. I look around the property, the dilapidated house. "How did he know they'd be here?" I say, thinking aloud.

"Could be a crime of opportunity. He was in the area. Saw them." He shrugs. "Or maybe he's a stalker. Had his eyes on the kid for some time. Followed them. Figured this was his chance."

"You think he lives in the area?"

"I think that's the most likely scenario." His expression darkens. "We need to find that kid."

The knot in my gut draws inexorably tighter. All children are innocent, but for this to happen to a child with special needs heaps on another cruel layer of urgency.

My cell vibrates against my hip. It's my dispatcher. "Hey, Lois."

"I got two registered sex offenders within a ten-mile radius of the Schattenbaum address, Chief. One of them is Amish."

I pull out the small notebook I keep in the back pocket of my trousers. "Give me the Amish guy first."

"Lester Nisley. Twenty-two years old. Convicted of rape of a thirteen-year-old girl in 2015. Got out on parole last September. Current address 5819 Township Road 4."

Less than five miles away . . .

"What about the other guy?"

"Gene Fitch. Fifty-seven years old. Convicted of rape of a nine-year-old girl in 1992. On parole since 2016. Home address 9345 County Highway 83, Painters Mill."

"Thanks, Lois."

A SHORT time later, I'm in the Explorer with Glock in the passenger seat. I've just made the turn onto Township Road 4 when my cell chirps. I glance at the display. T.J.

"Chief, I'm out at Dick Howard's place on Township Road 14 and Goat Head Road," he says. "Dick says he saw a pickup truck he didn't recognize drive past his place right about the time the kid went missing."

My interest surges. That intersection is just down the road from the Schattenbaum place. "Make or model?"

"No and no."

I think about the tire-tread marks. "Full-size pickup?"

"Yeah. White or tan."

"Did he get a look at the driver?"

"No, ma'am."

"Tell him to call if he remembers anything else. Glock and I are talking to RSOs. Keep at it."

"You got it."

I tell Glock about the call. "We're on our way to see Lester Nisley," I say. "He's an RSO and Swartzentruber. Still on parole."

"Sounds promising."

"We'll see."

Lester Nisley lives with his parents on a hog farm four miles south of the Schattenbaum place. The smell of manure hits me as I make the turn into the lane. Next to me, Glock mutters something unseemly and rolls up his window.

Most Swartzentruber Amish don't use gravel for their lanes, and the Nisleys are no exception. We bump down a rough dirt road fraught with ruts. A quarter mile in, the lane opens to a clapboard farmhouse and two barns. The one to my right is a low-slung hog barn. Farther back is an old white bank barn with its front sliding door standing open. The plain farmhouse is to my left.

Movement at the door of the hog barn snags my attention. I see a man in a flat-brimmed hat standing in the doorway watching us. We start that way.

A second man has come up beside him. A younger version of the older man. They watch us approach. Father and son, I think.

I've seen the elder Nisley around town. He's got angular features, an unkempt beard. A thin mouth. Neither of them looks concerned about the police showing up at eight in the evening.

Glock and I reach them. "I'm looking for Lester Nisley," I say.

The elder man jabs his thumb at the younger man. "Found him."

I turn my attention to the younger man. "Lester, is there a place we can speak privately? I need to ask you some questions about your whereabouts earlier today."

The older man straightens. He's realized this isn't a routine visit.

The younger man shrugs. "I reckon we can talk right here."

"Where were you between noon and five p.m. today?"

"I was here all morning. Went to the feed store around noon."

"Were you with anyone?" I ask. "Or were you alone?"

"I went by myself."

"Can anyone corroborate that?"

"My *datt*," he says. "Guy at the feed store."

The older man nods. "He worked out here in the barn all day. Midday I sent him into town to pick up feed."

"Do you know the Helmuth family?" I ask, aware that Glock has quietly made his way into the barn for a look around.

"Ivan and Miriam?" Lester says. "Yeah, I know 'em."

"Not well," the elder Nisley cuts in. "I helped when the wind blew their barn down. That is all."

I don't look away from Lester. "What about the children?"

He laughs. "They got a bunch, that's for sure."

"Do you know them?" I ask. "Have contact with them?"

"No."

I add a harsh note to my voice. "You sure about that, Lester? I know you're a registered sex offender."

The young man's eyes widen. "She wadn't no little kid!"

"You were convicted of having a sexual relationship with a thirteen-year-old girl when you were nineteen."

"The *Englischer* police don't understand our ways," the elder hisses. "They were going to marry."

As if that makes any difference whatsoever.

I look at Lester. "Let me see your hands," I snap.

Looking bewildered, he puts out his hands. No blood or cuts.

The old man's eyes narrow. "Why are you asking my son about the Helmuth family? Why are you interested in his hands?"

I give them the basics of what happened at the Schattenbaum farm, watching them closely for reactions. The elder's mouth falls open. "Mary Yoder?" he gasps. *"Doht?"* Dead?

"Elsie Helmuth is missing," I tell them.

Comprehension flickers in the elder man's eyes; he knows why I'm here. "Someone took a child?" he asks.

I turn my attention to Lester, who has fallen silent. "Lester, did you see any of the Helmuth family earlier today?"

"No!"

"You were convicted of sexual misconduct with a minor. I'm obligated to ask you about Elsie Helmuth. Do you understand?"

Lester looks at me, frightened now. "Yes, but . . . that was different. Edna was young, but . . . we're married now!"

As much as I despise what transpired between him and a minor six years his junior, I understand how and why it happened. It was immoral; it was against the law. Unfortunately, some of the Old Order Amish don't see it that way.

The age of consent in Ohio is sixteen. Most Amish couples marry in their late teens or early twenties. Some of the Swartzentruber and Old Order marry younger. Even with Ohio's "Romeo and Juliet" law, which would have protected Lester from prosecution if he was less than four years older than the minor female, the six-year age difference made the courtship a crime, hence his two-year stint in the Mansfield Correctional Institution.

The elder Nisley moves forward. "They're married now, in the eyes of the Lord. Edna is sixteen. A grown woman."

"When's the last time you spoke to Elsie?" I ask Lester.

"I don't even know which one she is," Lester says.

I pause, let the silence ride. Out of the corner of my eye, I see Glock approach from the shadows of the barn.

"Mr. Nisley, do you mind if I take a look inside your house?"

"We have nothing to hide."

"Thank you." I send Glock a nod. He starts toward the house.

Over the next minutes, I take both men through several more questions, but they've nothing to add. By the time I'm finished, Glock has exited the house and joins us.

"If you think of anything that might be important, I'd appreciate it if you'd let me know." I hand the elder man my card.

Neither man says anything, so Glock and I head to the Explorer.

Chapter 3

Four hours missing

A MISSING ENDANGERED CHILD is the kind of scenario in which a cop needs to be in a dozen places at once. Searching. Talking to family, witnesses, and suspects. Doing something—whatever it takes—to find a child in imminent danger and bring her home. Glock and I spent half an hour talking to registered sex offender Gene Fitch. He's a drunken slob, but he had a solid alibi.

It's excruciating to know a little girl is out there, frightened and alone and in danger. I'm consciously trying not to become too entangled in my own emotions when a call comes in from Tomasetti.

"I'm on my way to the Helmuth place," he begins. "I'm with a colleague. She's trained to interview young children. I thought we might have another go at the five-year-old."

"I can be there in a few minutes," I say.

"She's wondering if you can bring a toy for the girl. Something a kid her age will like and be comforted by."

"I know just the thing."

I MAKE it to the Carriage Stop Country Store just as the manager is locking up for the night. Some fast talking gets me in the door and to the toy aisle. I was never a doll lover as a child; much to my *mamm*'s chagrin, I was a tomboy. Still, I manage to find an Amish-made doll I think a five-year-old girl will like.

In keeping with the Amish tradition of avoiding any type of graven image, it's faceless and made of nude-colored fabric. She's wearing a blue dress, a black apron, and a bonnet. The clerk rings up the sale, and I'm through the door and back in the Explorer.

I pass six buggies as I near the Helmuth farm, Amish men armed with flashlights or lanterns and the resolve to find one of their own. These men have organized search parties. More than likely, the women are cooking and cleaning for the Helmuth family. As always, the Amish community has rallied to support those in crisis.

The farm glows with lantern light. Tomasetti's Tahoe sits adjacent to a chicken coop, the headlights on, engine running. I park and start toward it. I'm midway there when Tomasetti and his passenger get out. He's wearing creased trousers, a button-down shirt, and a suit jacket with a tie I bought him. He looks tired and grim.

"Agent Tomasetti." I extend my hand, and we shake.

"Chief Burkholder."

I offer my hand to the woman standing next to him. She's pe-
tite, about fifty, with silver hair cut into a sleek bob. She's wearing khaki slacks. Practical shoes. A navy windbreaker embellished
with the BCI logo. She's soft-spoken and self-assured.

"Mackenzie Upshaw." She gives my hand a squeeze. "Everyone
calls me Mackie. Agent Tomasetti was just filling me in on the
case. I wanted to get your take before we speak to the child."

She's ready to get down to business. I like her already.

Tomasetti motions to his Tahoe, and we gather around for a
quick huddle. "Kate, Mackie is trained in the forensic-interviewing
protocol RATAC—rapport, anatomy identification, touch inquiry,
abuse scenario, and closure," he tells me. "It's a questioning process
most often used with child victims of sexual abuse."

"It's a terrific protocol," she says. "Effective and nonintrusive. It
basically means I'll be asking nonleading questions, using terms the
little girl will understand. I'll keep it nice and slow since most children that age have pretty short attention spans."

"I talked to Annie immediately after the incident." I relay to her
our exchange. "I didn't get much out of her."

"Kids younger than six or seven make for difficult interview subjects," she says. "I understand this child is Amish. Is there anything
you can tell me that might help me relate to her?"

I get my thoughts in order. "Generally, Amish kids are more
sheltered. She will probably see you as an outsider, not because
you're a cop, but because you're not Amish."

"What do you suggest?"

"Win her trust." I hold up the doll, pass it to her. "Bribery."

Mackie takes the doll and grins. "Cool. If I sense she's clamming
up, I want you to jump in. Any thoughts on that?"

I shrug. "*Deitsch* might help."

"Excellent." Mackie looks at Tomasetti. "Would you mind sitting this one out? The fewer people present, the more comfortable
she'll be."

"No problem."

"You're a good sport, Agent Tomasetti." Mackie looks at me.
"Shall we?"

As we cross the gravel to the sidewalk, I notice a young boy carrying a bucket of water to the buggy horses. I recognize him as one of the Helmuth children. Even in times of turmoil and stress, the parents keep the kids busy with responsibilities.

I knock, and we enter. We're midway through the mudroom when Ivan Helmuth rushes through the door to greet us. "You bring news of Elsie?"

"We're here to speak with Annie," I tell him.

His brows furrow. "This way." He leads us into the kitchen.

Two Amish women stand at the sink, washing dishes. A third mans the stove, stirring a steaming Dutch oven with a spoon.

Mackie extends her hand to Helmuth and recites her name. "I'm with BCI," she tells him.

"Sit down." He motions to the wooden table. "I'll get Annie."

A minute later, Ivan and Miriam Helmuth appear with their daughter. The girl is pale, with circles beneath her eyes. She's wearing a light green dress with sneakers and her *kapp*. Upon spotting us, she turns and buries her face against her *mamm*'s skirt.

"You remember Chief Burkholder?" Ivan asks.

The girl doesn't turn around, but nods.

"You can call me Katie," I tell her in *Deitsch*.

She turns her head, peeks at me out of the corner of one eye.

"My friend's name is Mackie," I tell her.

The BCI agent raises the doll. "I'm hoping we can come up with good name for her. Do you have any ideas, Annie?"

The girl looks up at her *mamm* as if asking for permission to speak. Tugging out a chair, the Amish woman settles into it and pulls the child into her lap. Ivan leans against the doorjamb.

"What do you think about Willie?" Mackie says mischievously.

Annie smiles shyly. "That's a boy's name."

Mackie laughs. "Do you have any ideas?"

The girl nods, but she's not engaged.

"I always liked the name Susie," I tell her. "What do you think?" For the first time, the girl gives us two eyes. "I like it."

"Susie it is then." Mackie looks longingly at the doll, giving an exaggerated frown. "I think I'm a little too old for dolls."

"Annie's just about the right age," I put in.

Mackie perks up as if she hadn't thought of it. "What a great idea! Annie, would you like her?"

Again, the girl looks up at her *mamm*. Asking for permission to accept the gift. The woman nods, encouraging her to interact.

The girl gives an enthusiastic nod. *"Ja."*

Mackie passes it to the child. "There you go."

A smile crosses the girl's face as she hugs the doll against her.

"Maybe Susie can keep you company until we find Elsie," Mackie says. "Did you and Elsie find lots of walnuts today?"

"Two bags," Annie says in a small voice.

"What happened while you were picking up walnuts?"

The girl turns away, sets her face against her *mamm*'s dress.

"Was there someone else there?" Mackie asks gently.

The little girl puts her thumb in her mouth and begins to suck.

"I wonder if the stranger was picking up walnuts, too?" Mackie asks of no one in particular.

The thumb comes out. "He was in the house," Annie tells us. "Grossmammi was in the house, too."

Mackie looks toward me. "'Grossmammi' is 'Grandmother'?"

"Yes." I wink at Annie and say, "She doesn't know *Deitsch*."

Mackie continues. "I wonder why your *grossmammi* went into the house." A pause and then, "Did she hear something?"

"She likes it because she used to play there when she was little."

"I see." Mackie gives an exaggerated nod. "Did she go in through the front door or back?"

"Back."

"What were you and Elsie doing?"

"Putting walnuts in our bags."

"So you and Elsie were picking up walnuts," Mackie says. "And Grossmammi was in the house. What happened next?"

"We heard Grossmammi yelling. We thought she fell or saw a mouse, so we went in to find her."

"What did you see when you went inside?"

Her breaths quicken. "Grossmammi. On the floor. In the kitchen. She was bleeding and . . ." The girl stops speaking.

"Was there anyone else in the kitchen?"

"Not at first, but then the Plain man came out."

"What did he look like?"

The girl takes us through much the same description as the one she gave me. White male. Old—at least in the eyes of a five-year-old. Brown hair. When she's finished, she presses her face against her *mamm* and whispers, *"Ich bin fashrokka."* I'm scared.

Miriam pats her daughter's back. "God is with you."

Mackie is soft and sympathetic but maintains a gentle level of pressure. "Everything you tell me might help us find Elsie."

The girl turns to look at her. "Elsie was scared," she whispers. "We ran out the back door."

"Did the man follow?"

"Ja."

"What happened next?"

"I don't know. I just ran."

"Did he say anything?"

She takes a moment to think. "He said, *'Sie is meiner.'*"

It's the first time I've heard the words. Mackie looks at me for translation, raises her brows.

"It means 'She's mine,'" I tell her.

"You're a very brave little girl." Mackie pats the girl's hand. "Just a few more questions and we're all done, okay?"

Over the next twenty minutes, Mackie covers every conceivable question with the child. Some the girl answers readily; others she veers away from. Mackie is good at what she does. Is it enough?

When we're finished, I thank the parents and then Mackie and I walk to the Tahoe, where Tomasetti is waiting.

"I feel confident that child told us everything she can recall at this time," Mackie says with a sigh. "It's possible she'll remember new details over the next few days. But I think we got most of it."

"Anything new?" Tomasetti asks.

I nod. "When Mackie asked Annie if the man said anything, she responded with, *'Sie is meiner,'* which basically means 'She's mine.' It's an odd thing for an attacker to say."

Tomasetti grimaces. "As if he feels . . . entitled to her."

Mackie shrugs. "Or he's mentally unhinged. Confused."

"Do you think she's credible enough for us to get a facial composite?" Tomasetti asks.

"I think it's worth a shot."

"I'll get permission from the parents." I look at Tomasetti. "It would be helpful if the composite artist can come to the house."

"I'll get it done," he says.

I glance at my watch. "I'm going to talk to the Helmuths, find out who Mary Yoder was close to."

"I'll work on getting a composite artist down here," Tomasetti says. "Probably first thing in the morning."

Mackie extends her hand to me. "I'll email you a transcript of our interview with Annie as soon as I get it transcribed."

We part ways, and I head back into the house. I find Ivan and Miriam and five of their children in the kitchen. Both parents look frazzled and exhausted and utterly miserable.

I pull a prepaid cell phone from my pocket and hand it to Ivan. The Amish man doesn't take it. "We do not need a phone," he says. "All we need is our daughter."

"Take it," I say firmly. "If there's an emergency and you need to talk to me quickly."

When he doesn't accept the phone, I go to the counter and set it down next to the sink. "Keep it handy," I tell them.

The Amish woman looks away, but I see the assent in her eyes.

"I'm going to look for her." Ivan Helmuth's gaze is defensive, defiant. "She's out there somewhere."

"It's going to be cold tonight." Miriam puts a hand over her mouth, tears streaming. "Elsie doesn't have a coat. She'll be cold."

Rising abruptly, she rushes from the room.

I look at Ivan. "I need to ask you about Mary Yoder."

"I'm finished with your questions. All this talking . . . it's not helping." He buttons his coat and strides through the door.

I become aware of the children sitting at the table. Five pairs of eyes pin me, expressions apprehensive and confused.

"Mamm says God will take care of Elsie," says a girl of about eight or nine.

"Grossmammi isn't coming back." The youngest girl closes her eyes and begins to cry.

A girl of ten or eleven puts her arm around her. "Shush now. Grossmammi's in heaven with God."

"No one knows where Elsie is." The little boy speaks up for the first time. "Mr. Miller said someone stole her."

Realizing the conversation is about to go in a dark direction, I move to refocus them. "What are your names?" I ask.

The oldest girl straightens. "I'm Irma."

A girl with strawberry-blond hair and eyes the color of spring grass says, "I'm Becky, and I'm seven."

I look from child to child; each mutters their name and age, polite but reluctant. Red-haired and freckled, Elam is eight. Gracie is nine and very pretty. At ten, Bonnie is thin and gangly, nearly as tall as her *mamm*.

"Luke and Annie are sleeping," Becky says.

"I'm Katie Burkholder, the chief of police," I tell them. "I want you to know we're doing everything we can to find your sister."

A shower of measured responses sound. They don't believe me— the *Englischer*—I realize.

Becky begins to cry. "I want Elsie to come home. She always kisses me good night. Sometimes she tickles my belly."

"I'll kiss you good night," Bonnie says. "But I'm not tickling your belly."

"Shush now." Irma sets her hand over Becky's. "It's like Mamm says. God will take care of her. And He will send her back to us."

"Mamm says Elsie was a gift," Becky says.

Bonnie's expression softens. "I've known that since the day Bishop Troyer brought her—" She cuts off the words. Her eyes skate away from mine.

I'm curious what Bonnie had been about to say.

"What about the bishop?" I ask.

Bonnie swallows. "Nothing," she mumbles.

Next to me, Irma and Becky exchange a look. What the hell? Something I can't quite articulate niggles at the back of my brain.

Miriam enters the kitchen, and the moment is gone. The Amish woman brings her hands together. "Come on now. Up to bed. All of you." She shakes her head with exaggerated admonition.

Chairs scrape against the floor. The little boy goes to his *mamm* and throws his arms around her hips. "Night."

She sets her hand on his head. "You say a prayer for Grossmammi and Elsie," she says to all of them.

When the children are gone, Miriam goes to the nearest chair and collapses into it. I pull out the chair across from her and sit.

"We'll be searching through the night," I say.

She raises her gaze to mine. "I don't know what to do, Chief Burkholder. I keep searching the house, thinking she'll be there."

I'm still pondering the odd moment with the children a few minutes ago. Something Bonnie said. "Are Elsie and Becky twins?" I ask. "They're both seven years old?"

"They're not twins. The children came . . . quickly."

I wait a beat, my thoughts circling back to Mary Yoder. "Was your mother close to anyone? Did she have a best friend?"

"Mamm spent most of her time with us, here at home. But she liked to visit with the widow down the road, Martha Hershberger. She was friendly with the bishop's wife, too. Sometimes the three of them would sew together after worship."

I pull out my notebook and scribble the names. "Your *mamm* was a widow?"

Miriam nods and cocks her head. "I don't see how Mamm's friends could have anything to do with what happened."

"It's helpful to know the backgrounds of everyone involved. You never know when something from someone's past can come back to haunt them."

"We're *Amisch*. We've no ghosts to speak of."

Over the course of my career, I've heard a thousand variations of those words. Experience has taught me they're rarely true, even among the Amish.

Six hours missing

THERE were too many people around—police and Amish alike—for him to risk taking the road, so he cut through the field on foot and ran until he could go on no more. Ivan Helmuth couldn't remember the last time he'd cried. Now, alone and under cover of darkness, he fell to his knees and wept. He'd never felt such agony. He'd never been so frightened in his life.

Sweet Elsie.

Please deliver her back to us.

He knew God always listened, but he couldn't help but wonder: Was he finally being punished for what he'd done?

Rising, Ivan trudged to the edge of the plowed field, which put him on the township road that would take him to the Troyer place. The bishop had been at their farm most of the day. He'd prayed with them. Comforted them. But they hadn't had the chance to talk. Not privately. Ivan needed to be alone with the bishop. He needed to show him the note.

By the time Ivan reached the house, he'd regained some semblance of control. He went directly to the back door and knocked.

The door swung open. Bishop Troyer stood there, gripping the walker he used these days, wearing his sleep shirt. His ancient face was gaunt. He'd been the Amish bishop since Ivan was a boy.

Ivan didn't bother with a greeting. "We must talk," he said.

"You are alone?" Bishop Troyer asked. "No one followed?"

"I'm alone."

"Kumma inseid." Come inside.

Glancing over his shoulder, Ivan walked into the house. The two men went to the kitchen. The bishop lowered himself into the chair. Ivan reached into his pocket, fished out the letter. He set the note on the table and slid it over to the old man.

Anyone who steals must certainly make restitution, but if they have nothing, they must be sold to pay for their theft.

Bishop Troyer took his time, trying to make sense of it. But Ivan could tell he knew exactly what it was. What it meant.

"Exodus," the bishop said. "When did you get it?"

"It was in the mailbox this morning." Ivan looked at the note.

"Did anyone else see it?" the bishop asked.

"Miriam."

The old man stared at him. "This is the work of the devil."

"Ja," *Ivan said. "Someone knows. About that night."*

"Unmeeklich!" *Impossible! "No one has spoken of it. No one!"*

Ivan saw through the bishop's veneer. The truth of that terrified him anew. "All these years." He whispered the words, fighting tears. "I need the truth, Bishop. All of it."

Seven hours missing

It's midnight when I pull into the gravel lane of the Troyer farm. Despite the hour, I'm not surprised to find the windows aglow with lantern light. The bishop may be getting up in years—last time I saw him he was using a walker—but neither age nor his arthritis has slowed him down. I pull up to the house, park next to the bishop's buggy, and start toward the door.

Gas hisses in the lamppost as I take the steps to the small porch. The door stands open, but the screen is closed, which is odd. I knock, wait a full minute, and tap the wood jamb with my key fob.

"Bishop Troyer?" I call out. "It's Kate Burkholder!"

I finally see a woman's form approach. Freda Troyer shoves a lantern my way and glares at me through the screen. *"En hand foll funn geduld is veaht may vi en bushel funn der grips,"* she mutters. A handful of patience is worth more than a bushel of brains.

The bishop's wife is barely five feet tall and a scant hundred pounds, but the force of her persona adds both height and weight. She's wearing a gray dress and a white *kapp,* all draped with an oversized cardigan she's thrown over thin shoulders. Both she and the bishop are well into their eighties.

She's looking at me as if I'm some vermin that's wandered onto her porch from the barn. I suspect I woke her.

"This won't wait," I tell her. "You heard what happened to Mary Yoder?"

"Of course I heard." A shadow of anguish darkens her expression. *"Gottlos."* Ungodly. "You're here for the bishop?"

"Actually, I'm here to speak with you."

Her eyes narrow behind wire-rimmed glasses with thick lenses. "I reckon you ought to come in then."

The Troyer home is a hundred-year-old Amish farmhouse.

Wood plank floors. A big kitchen with a gas stove and a propane refrigerator. I take one of six chairs at a rectangular table covered with a red-checkered cloth. A lantern flickers in the center.

"Have you found the girl?" Freda Troyer asks as she shuffles to the table.

"No."

"Poor, sweet child."

"I understand you and Mary were friends."

"I've known Mary for years. She was a good friend."

"Can you think of anyone who might've wanted to harm her?" I ask. "Did she have any enemies? Any trouble in her life?"

She shakes her head. "Lord, no. Mary Yoder lived her life the way an Amish woman ought to, full of kindness and faith."

"Did she ever mention having any problems with anyone?"

"No."

"What about Ivan and Miriam?"

"They're a good Amish family, Chief Burkholder. Not the kind of people who invite trouble into their lives."

"If you think of anything, will you let me know?"

"Of course I will."

"I'll see myself out." I'm midway to the door when I stop and turn to her. "Mrs. Troyer? When I was at the Helmuth place, one of the children told me Bishop Troyer was there the day Elsie was born. Is that true?"

She dismisses the statement with a wave. "Those little ones are confused and missing their sister is all."

She raises rheumy blue eyes to mine, and for an instant, I see the pain, the burden of the things she hides behind a tetchy veneer.

UNDER normal circumstances, it would be far too late for me to be rousing citizens from bed to question them about their association with Mary Yoder or the Helmuth family. With a little girl missing, I don't have a choice.

I call Tomasetti as I make the turn onto Threadgill Creek Road. "Any luck with those impressions?" I ask.

"We got decent plaster on both the footwear and the tire tread," he replies. "Footwear has a waffle-type sole. Probably a men's work boot. Size thirteen."

"Big guy."

"Where are you?" he says.

"I'm talking with Mary Yoder's known associates."

"At midnight?"

"So sue me." Rain begins to patter the windshield, so I flip on my wipers. "What about you?"

"I'm still at the Schattenbaum place. CSU is about to wrap up."

I hear voices in the background, telling me the place is still bustling, that he's busy, and I miss him. "I'll do my best to make it home tonight."

"Me, too."

Smiling, I drop my cell back into my pocket.

MARTHA Hershberger lives in a mobile home a few miles from the Helmuth place. As I pull into the driveway, I don't see any lights on inside.

Rain and wind lash me as I go up the steps to the porch. I've just knocked when I feel something brush against my ankle. Startled, I see a couple of cats come out of a small doghouse.

I'm in the process of shooing them back inside when the door to the mobile home opens.

"What are you doing to my cats?" comes a voice in *Deitsch*.

I pluck my badge from my pocket. "Martha Hershberger?"

She eyes me up and down. "What is it?"

Holding the badge, I introduce myself. "I'm the police chief of Painters Mill. I need to—"

"Do you have any idea what time it is?"

I guess Martha Hershberger to be in her mid- to late seventies. She's wearing a flannel sleeping gown with white socks. A blue scarf covers her silver hair.

Her question tells me she probably doesn't know about Mary Yoder or Elsie Helmuth. "I need to talk to you about Mary Yoder."

She cocks her head. "Has something happened to Mary?"

"She was killed earlier today," I tell her.

"*What?* Mary? Killed?" Pressing her hand to her mouth, she staggers back, looking aghast.

"May I come in?" I ask. "I'd like to ask you a few questions."

"Of course." She motions me in, grappling for her composure. "What happened to Mary?" Bending, she turns on a lamp.

Dim light illuminates a small, cluttered room that smells of nail polish and last night's TV dinner. That's when it strikes me that either she's left the Amish way or she's not big on all those rules. . . .

"She was murdered," I reply, watching her.

The only thing that comes back at me is complete shock. "Murdered? Oh, dear Lord. Mary? Who would—I just can't believe it."

"You were close?" I ask.

"I knew her most of my life. She was one of the few who stuck with me after I became Mennonite. I loved her like a sister." The grief on her features intensifies. "How is her family coping?"

I tell her about the missing girl.

"Oh, that just makes me sick. Who does something like that?"

Neither of us has the answer, so we fall silent.

After a moment, she seems to shake off her shock and motions toward the kitchen. "You want some coffee?"

"That would be great. Thanks."

I trail her to a tiny, jumbled kitchen. Every square inch of the countertop surface is strewn with kitchen items.

"Sorry about all the junk." She opens a can of Folgers and scoops grounds into a stovetop percolator.

There's a collage of photos on the wall. Martha Hershberger with four teenage girls. Granddaughters. Heads thrown back in laughter. The photo makes me think about familial connections. The lengths to which people will go to protect their own.

She clears the surface of a small table for two, and we sit. The coffee is weak, but I'm desperate for caffeine, so I drink.

Over the next ten minutes, I go over the same questions I covered with Freda Troyer. Martha Hershberger answers them in much the same way. Everyone loved Mary. She had no enemies. No problems with her family or anyone else.

"How did you meet her?" I ask.

"Back when I was still Amish, we were in the same church district." Her laugh is a sad sound. "I was a midwife, you know, delivered their babies."

I take a sip of coffee. "So you delivered Elsie."

The woman's brows snap together. "Now that you mention it, I think she's the only one I *didn't* deliver."

An odd ping sounds inside my head. "Is there a reason why you didn't deliver Elsie?"

"Miriam told me the baby came quickly. There was no time."

I finish my coffee. "Did Mary Yoder have any other children?"

"She has a daughter in Indiana, I think."

"What about sisters? Brothers? Extended family?"

"I do recall her mentioning a sister." The Mennonite woman assumes a thoughtful countenance. "Younger, I think. They were close once but had some sort of falling-out."

I flip the page on my notebook. "Do you remember her name?"

"Started with an M. Marsha. Marie. Marlene, I think."

"Last name?"

Martha shakes her head. "I don't know."

"Did she live around here?"

"Down south somewhere. I couldn't say for sure. I don't even know if she's still alive. Mary didn't talk about her much."

I nod, disappointed. I pluck my card from my pocket and slide it across the table to her. "If you think of anything else, will you get in touch with me?"

"Of course I will."

I rise, and she takes me through the living room. I'm opening the door when I think of one more question. "Mrs. Hershberger, do you know who delivered Elsie?"

"I'm not rightly sure. Miriam never said. They had so many children. I never thought to ask."

Chapter 4

Fourteen hours missing

IT'S SEVEN A.M. BY THE TIME I make it home. There's nothing I'd like more than to fall into bed for a few hours of sleep. But I'm going to have to settle for a shower and food.

The house smells of coffee and toast when I walk into my big farmhouse kitchen. The air is warm, and for the first time, the full weight of exhaustion presses down on me. I hear the TV in the living room, tuned to cable news.

Tomasetti appears in the doorway between the kitchen and the living room, in sweatpants and an ancient Cleveland Division of Police T-shirt. He's carrying a towel; his hair is wet.

He crosses to me. I smell soap and aftershave as he puts his arms around me, presses a kiss to my mouth.

"You get any sleep?" he asks.

"I just need a shower."

"Uh-huh." He shifts me to arm's length and tilts his head. "Got time for breakfast?"

"Give me ten minutes."

Later, over scrambled eggs and toast, he updates me on everything he's learned since we last spoke.

"Was the lab able to type the blood found in the yard of the Schattenbaum house?" I ask.

He grimaces. "Same as the girl's."

I wince inwardly, knowing what that means: that the girl could have been stabbed or cut—or worse.

"We don't have DNA back yet, but the lab matched the type. The kid had a tonsillectomy. She's O-negative—"

"But it's possible the blood belongs to the killer."

"Maybe. We're running DNA now, but the lab is backed up. It's going to take a few days."

"What about the footwear impressions?" I ask. "The size-thirteen work boots? Any unique marks on the sole?"

"We got tread, but not enough detail to pick up unique marks."

I nod, disappointed.

We eat in silence. When I walked into the house twenty minutes ago, I wasn't hungry. Now I'm starving, and I eat with relish. After the shower and a clean uniform, I feel human again. As I down my second cup of coffee, my thoughts take me through the conversations I had overnight. The one exchange that keeps coming back to me is the odd commentary between the Helmuth children, Becky and Bonnie, about their missing sister.

Mamm says Elsie was a gift.

I've known that since the day Bishop Troyer brought her—

When I asked them to clarify, they clammed up. Why? And what about Elsie being the only baby in the family that Martha Hershberger didn't deliver?

"You're thinking about something awfully hard," Tomasetti says as he takes dishes to the sink. "Anything you want to share?"

"I think there's something going on with the Helmuth family." I tell him about the girls' comments. "Bonnie, who's ten, cut off mid-sentence. It was as if she knew she'd broached a subject she wasn't supposed to discuss."

"You think the parents are withholding information?"

"I think they're not telling us something."

I tell Tomasetti about my conversations with Miriam Helmuth and, later, with the midwife, Martha Hershberger.

"She delivered all of Miriam's babies, except for Elsie."

"So what aren't they telling you?" Tomasetti asks.

Between the caffeine, the food, and the shower, my brain has clicked back into place. "The Helmuths have eight children."

"That's not unusual for an Amish family, though, right?"

"Two of the girls are seven years old."

"Twins?"

I shake my head. "Miriam says no."

"Could be Irish twins. It's technically possible."

My mind is already racing ahead. "Tomasetti, I took the physical description of Elsie. Brown hair. Brown eyes."

"Okay."

"I didn't think much about it at the time. But when I walked into the Helmuth house and got a look at the other children . . . they're strawberry blond and green-eyed. Not all kids look like their parents or siblings. But there's something there."

I pick up my cell, hit the button for the station.

Mona picks up on the first ring. "Hey, Chief."

"Get me vital statistics on the Helmuth children," I say. "Birth dates. Place of birth. All eight of them." I rattle off the names from memory. "I need it yesterday."

"Warp factor one."

"Who's on duty this morning?" I ask, pulling out my notebook.

"Everyone. I mean, in light of the missing kid . . ."

"I'm heading that way. Briefing in my office in an hour."

"I'll let everyone know."

I glance down at my notebook, flip the page. "Mona, one more thing. See if you can find anything on Mary Yoder's sister. First name is Marlene. I think she lives south of here. No city."

"You got it."

I end the call to find Tomasetti's eyes on me. A look I'm all too familiar with. "You think I'm barking up the wrong tree," I say.

"I think if those two seven-year-olds were born any closer than nine months apart, the parents have some explaining to do."

We fall silent. I see the wheels of his mind working.

"When we talked to the witness child, Annie, do you remember what she told us the man who took Elsie said?" I ask.

He nods. "'She's mine.'"

"I didn't think of the statement in terms of a literal meaning," I tell him. "Maybe I should have. What if, for whatever reason, this male subject *thinks* that girl is . . . his."

"I think there's a higher probability that he's a nutcase."

"I know that. I do. Still, I'm going to do some poking around." I can tell by his expression he doesn't concur. It's not the first time we've disagreed on a case. Fortunately, both of us are confident enough to admit it when we get it wrong.

"In the interim," he says, rising, "I'm going to round up that composite artist. She's in Parma, so give me a couple of hours."

I get to my feet, pick up my duty belt from the table, buckle it around my hips. "Call me, and I'll meet you at the Helmuths'."

"You got it." Leaning close, he kisses me. "Don't spend too much time looking for ghosts."

"Wouldn't dream of it," I tell him, and start toward the door.

ONE of the pitfalls of being a cop is that you look at the things people say with a healthy dose of skepticism. It's not that you think everyone is a liar; you just happen to know from experience individuals lie with more frequency than most people realize.

I'm thinking about Miriam Helmuth and motives for lying when I enter the station. Mona Kurtz, who still spends most of her time working dispatch, stands at her station, speaking into the headset, waving a stack of pink message slips at me. Tugging the slips from her hand, I make tracks toward my office and unlock the door.

I've just booted up my laptop when Mona taps on the jamb. "Chief?"

"Morning," I say as I log in. "Any luck with the stats on the Helmuth children?"

She takes the visitor chair adjacent to my desk. "The clerk at the Holmes County General Health District is going to courier birth certificates for the Helmuth children by day's end." She glances down at a sheet of paper in her hand. "Seven of the Helmuth children were delivered by a local midwife, Martha Hershberger. The midwife filed for birth certificates shortly after birth."

"Is the remaining child Elsie Helmuth?"

Her eyes flash interest. "Get this: There's no birth certificate on file for Elsie. No social security number. No paperwork was ever filed."

"Well, that's interesting as hell."

The majority of Amish women use midwives to deliver their babies at home. In the state of Ohio, most midwives are certified and, as a matter of course, file the appropriate paperwork with the local registrar for birth certificates and social security numbers.

So why doesn't Elsie Helmuth have a birth certificate?

"Anything on Marlene, the sister?"

"Still looking."

"Chief?"

I glance up to see my first-shift dispatcher, Lois Monroe, standing in the doorway. "Everyone's in the war room," she tells me.

"Be right there."

Lois rushes back to reception, and Mona heads out the door.

A few minutes later, I'm in the "war room," which is a storage room turned meeting room. I'm standing at the half podium Lois has set up. She's taped a map of Holmes County to the dry-erase board behind me, with Painters Mill circled in red. A red X marks the Helmuth farm. A second X marks the Schattenbaum place.

I look out at my team. "I appreciate everyone working double shifts," I say. Then I outline the facts of both cases and where we are in terms of the investigation.

I look at Lois, who's standing in the doorway. "You get the stats and description of Elsie Helmuth typed up?"

"Right here, Chief."

Mona jumps up and passes a sheet to everyone in the room.

"Since the girl is Amish, we do not have a photo. We believe the suspect is a white male. Likely Amish. Thirty-five to fifty years old. Brown hair. Size-thirteen shoe, which would likely put him at six two or six three. He likely wore a work boot with a waffle-type sole. We suspect he may be using a vehicle for transportation."

"Covers a lot of ground," Glock says beneath his breath.

I nod. "None of that is set in stone." I point at the nearest officer sitting to my right. "Reports. Pickles."

Roland "Pickles" Shumaker is seventy-five, but you'd never know it. His hair is mahogany with no gray in sight. His uniform is creased, his trademark Lucchese boots buffed to a burnished patina. He went part-time a few years ago and spends mornings and afternoons working the crosswalk at the elementary school.

This morning, Pickles is looking at me with the attitude of a man half his age. "T.J. and I hit every house within a five-mile radius of the Schattenbaum place, Chief. That's nine homes. Four

Amish. Five non-Amish. We talked to multiple individuals inside each home. Aside from Dick Howard, no one saw anything."

I address T.J. and Pickles. "Before you guys call it a day, I want you to talk to them again. Expand your canvass to ten miles."

"Yes, ma'am."

I look at my female officer. "Mona, there's a service station two miles down the road from the intersection of Goat Head Road and CR 14. Stop in on your way home and see if they have security cameras. If they do, get a copy of the last seventy-two hours."

"I'm on it," she says.

I go to the next man. "Glock."

Rupert "Glock" Maddox is the first African American to grace the Painters Mill PD, and he's my most solid officer. With two tours in Afghanistan, a calm demeanor, and a boatload of common sense, he's my go-to guy when I need a job done right.

"Skid and I cleared the outbuildings at the Schattenbaum place. No footprints. No disturbed dust. Nothing. CSI with BCI looked around as well and concurred." He glances at his notes. "We walked a grid of the back pasture, but there was nothing there."

"Anyone go out there with dogs?" I ask.

"County did," he tells me. "No hit in the back of the property, but the dogs *did* hit on a scent in the front, near where you found the tread marks and blood. BCI jumped on it. Took those plasters. Sent blood samples to the lab."

"Glock," I say, "where did the dogs lose the scent?"

"At the road, a few feet from where you spotted tire tracks."

Which means our subject may have put the girl in his vehicle and fled the scene. The thought makes me sick to my stomach.

I look at Skid. "Get with the IT guy who does the website for our department. Tell him to create another page, something promi-nent, and put out a call for the public's assistance. Tell them they can remain anonymous."

Skid nods, thumbing notes into his cell. "You got it."

I consider filling them in on the mystery surrounding Elsie Helmuth's birth certificate, but since nothing has been substantiated, I opt not to muddy the waters. "I'll be speaking with the Helmuths again this morning. My cell is on day and night. Mandatory OT until we find that girl or catch this son of a bitch."

Seventeen hours missing

On the drive to the Helmuth farm, I pass Amish men and boys who've saddled their buggy horses to search the ditches and wooded areas near the Schattenbaum place. Men clad in camouflage jackets ride ATVs through open fields, searching rugged terrain not easily accessed by vehicle or on foot. It warms me to see that the community—Amish and English alike—has come out in force to find a missing girl.

I've just pulled into the Helmuth lane when my cell erupts. I glance at the display: holmes cnty coroner.

I take a breath and brace. "Hi, Doc."

"I'm about to start the autopsy on Mary Yoder."

"Anything preliminary you can tell me?"

"She was stabbed twenty-two times. Probably with a large knife. She sustained many defensive wounds."

"She fought back. Cause and manner of death?"

"I suspect she died from blood loss. That's not official yet." He sighs. "There's no doubt it's a homicide. I'll be able to answer those questions definitively once I get her on the table."

"I'd like to be there." I look toward the back door of the house, where three Amish women carrying grocery bags stare in my direction. "Can you give me half an hour?"

"She's not going anywhere."

The Amish women on the back porch don't speak to me as I ascend the steps; they move silently aside as I enter the house. I find Miriam Helmuth sitting at the kitchen table.

"You bring news of Elsie?" she asks.

"No news." I go to the table, lower myself to the chair next to her. "Miriam, I need to ask you a few more questions. Do you have a birth certificate for Elsie?"

She stiffens. "Why would you ask such a thing? Some silly piece of paper isn't going to help you find her, is it?"

"It's part of the process." The words aren't exactly true.

"I don't have a birth certificate for Elsie. We were going to file the paperwork. But . . . we just haven't gotten around to it yet."

"Where was she born?" I ask.

Her eyes meet mine. "Here. At the house."

"You used a midwife?"

"I would have." She looks down at her hands. "Elsie came fast. There was no time. Mamm was here. She helped me through."

"Which midwife were you going to use?"

"The one I used with the other children. Martha Hershberger."

"Did you get prenatal care with Elsie?"

"These questions are not going to help you find my girl." Impatience flares in her voice.

"Mrs. Helmuth," I say gently, "I'm not the enemy. I want to bring her home, too. If there's something you haven't told me—"

"I've told you everything."

I give her a moment before moving on to my next question. "How well do you know your aunt? Mary's sister, Marlene?"

The woman stares at me. "Aunt Marlene passed away years ago. I don't see what she has to do with any of this."

"Why don't you let me decide what's relevant?" I say firmly.

She looks down. "I met Marlene once or twice when I was a girl. She was . . . a delicate thing. Didn't come around much."

"Delicate?" I ask. "You mean physically?"

"That was my general impression."

"Did Marlene have kids?"

"Not that I know of."

"What was your aunt's last name?"

"Her maiden name was Byler, of course, same as Mamm's. If she ever got married . . ." She shrugs. "I wouldn't know."

"Do you have any idea where she used to live?"

"I don't know. I told you. *I don't know!* If you really want to find my little girl, Kate Burkholder, get out there and look for her."

I CALL Lois on the way to Pomerene Hospital. "I need you to dig up everything you can find on every member of the Helmuth family. There may not be much out there, since they're Amish.

But . . . I need for you to dig around a little, see if anything pops."

"Can you give a hint what I'm looking for?"

"Anything to do with children. Deaths in the family. Marriages. Divorces." I think about that a moment. "I've got Mona looking at Miriam's sister, Marlene. She's deceased, but I have a last name: Byler. Tell Mona to take a look, see if there's anything out there. Lois, I want you to look at the midwife, Martha Hershberger, too. See if Hershberger has any problems with her certifications."

"I'll get right on it. Oh, before I forget, that courier package from Holmes County General Health District came for you."

Copies of the birth certificates. "Put it on my desk, will you?"

"You got it."

I end the call as I slide into a parking space near the Emergency entrance. I go through the double glass doors and take the elevator to the basement. I enter the reception area of the morgue.

"Hi, Chief."

I look up to see Doc Coblentz's administrative assistant rise to greet me. "Hey, Carmen."

"He's waiting for you."

I barely notice the smell of formalin as I pass through the doors. The autopsy room is ahead. Left is Doc Coblentz's glassed-in office. The mini blinds facing the hall are open. Inside, Doc and a second man clad in scrubs are staring at the laptop on his desk.

"Kate."

Doc Coblentz is a corpulent man, about my height, with a balding pate. This morning, he's wearing his usual green scrubs.

He offers his hand for a shake. "Looking a little worse for wear this morning," he tells me.

"Long night," I murmur. "Sorry I'm late."

The other man in his office rises. He's African American, tall, with hair the color of steel wool and keen, intelligent eyes.

"This is Dr. Larry Blake," the coroner says. "He's the deputy medical examiner for Cuyahoga County and specializes in forensic pathology."

Blake and I shake. His grip is firm, but not crushing.

"I'm here at the behest of BCI," Dr. Blake tells me. "I understand you've got a missing child on your hands."

I give him a condensed version of the case. "I'm hoping we'll learn something today that will help us find her."

"In that case, let's get started," Doc Coblentz says.

The three of us walk to the alcove and gear up. A paper apron for me. Face mask. Shoe covers. Hair cap. Once I'm dressed, I follow the men through the double doors to the autopsy room.

The room is so cold, I half expect to see a coating of frost on the gray subway-tiled walls. I follow the men to the gurney, where I see a body draped with a pale blue sheet. Doc Coblentz pulls on a headset with a small mike and recites the date and time, case number, the names of everyone present, and the name of the deceased.

He pulls the cover down. "Sixty-year-old female Caucasian. One hundred and fifty pounds. Five feet four inches. Dr. Blake has taken all possible evidence present on the body. It has been photographed extensively. Once that was done, the body was X-rayed." Doc Coblentz looks at me. "One of the more interesting things we found was that the victim had gravel in her mouth."

I stare at him, surprised. "Any idea how it got there?"

"I'd say someone put it there. Postmortem."

"Any idea where the gravel came from? The driveway?"

Dr. Blake chimes in. "We sent a sample to the BCI lab. They'll run a comparison to the material in the driveway."

I find myself thinking about the note found on Mary Yoder the day she was killed. *Food gained by fraud tastes sweet, but one ends up with a mouth full of gravel.*

I make a mental note to see if Tomasetti has the resources to match the gravel to a specific area.

"Moving forward." Doc Coblentz repositions the light. "As you can see, the decedent suffered multiple sharp-force trauma. Defensive wounds present on both hands and arms."

"Do you have any idea what kind of weapon was used?" I ask.

"A knife with a serrated blade. I would estimate the length at six to eight inches. I'll know more once I make the Y-incision. But I'm comfortable telling you now, preliminarily, that the cause of death is massive hemorrhage. The manner of death is homicide."

Chapter 5

Twenty-three hours missing

You put in the hours. You do all the right things. All of it with vigor and hope. Still, a little girl is missing. A grandmother is dead. A community is on edge. And the cops don't have a clue.

Wind and rain thrash my office window. Though it's not yet closing time for most businesses, Main Street is deserted. The first major cold front of the fall season blew through around noon.

"Chief?"

I glance up to see my second-shift dispatcher, Jodie Metzger, come through the door, a carafe of coffee in one hand, a stack of paper in the other.

I shove my cup toward her. "Thanks."

She pours and sets the stack in front of me. "Ladies' Club of Painters Mill had these flyers printed. Volunteers put out nine hundred of them all over the county."

I glance at the top sheet. "Have you seen me?" There's no photo of Elsie Helmuth, just her name and a physical description. "Seven years old. Female. Special Needs. Born: March 14, 2012. Brown hair. Brown eyes. Height: 3 feet 9 inches. Weight: 60 lbs."

It's well done, with all the right information, including the tip line number and the number for the Painters Mill PD.

"I think we could probably use a miracle, too," I say.

She shoots me a sympathetic look. "Anything else I can do?"

"Check the tip line again, will you?" I ask.

"Sure." Jodie looks at me as if she wants to say something else, but she goes through the door without comment.

Earlier, I talked to Tomasetti about the gravel discovered in Mary Yoder's mouth. He agrees it's likely some extension of the note found at the scene. He can have the lab run a comparison to see if the gravel came from the Schattenbaum driveway. If the gravel didn't come from the driveway, we start checking with aggregate dealers in the area. It's a long shot, but worth pursuing.

I open the folder in front of me and look at my copy of the note.

Food gained by fraud tastes sweet, but one ends up with a mouth full of gravel.

The original is printed in pencil. The words are from Psalm 94, which has to do with the ills of receiving something undeserved through deception. What does it mean in terms of the case?

Tucking the note back in the folder, I read the police report again. My description of the girl: "Elsie Helmuth. Age 7. Brn. Brn. Ht: 3 feet 9 inches. Wt: 60 lbs."

A caution light flares inside my head. I try to pinpoint what set it off. I glance at the Missing flyer again. Nothing there. I reach for the envelope from the Holmes County General Health District and, for the second time, I skim through the birth certificates of the Helmuth children. Names. Birth dates. County of birth.

Irma. 5-11-2008. Holmes Cnty.
Bonnie. 8-4-2009. Holmes Cnty.
Gracie. 9-19-2010. Holmes Cnty.
Elam. 11-13-2011. Holmes Cnty.
Becky. 10-27-2012. Holmes Cnty.
Luke. 9-1-2013. Holmes Cnty.
Annie. 8-31-2014. Holmes Cnty.

Why the hell isn't there a birth certificate for Elsie?

I go back to the Missing flyer, trying to figure out what had caused that flutter in my brain. "Have you seen me? Elsie Helmuth. Seven years old. Female. Special Needs. Born: March 14, 2012. Brown hair. Brown eyes. Height: 3 feet 9 inches. Weight: 60 lbs."

"Wait," I mutter. I look at the birth date. March 14, 2012. I go back to the birth certificates and look at the birth dates of the other children. If Elam was born in November of 2011 and Becky was born in October of 2012, there's no way Miriam could have given birth to Elsie in March of 2012.

"Jodie?" I call out to reception.

She appears at the door to my office. "Yeah, Chief?"

"Call the Ladies' Club and find out who put together the information for the Missing flyer. I'm specifically looking for Elsie Helmuth's birth date. Find out where they got the information."

"Sure."

Leaning forward, I rub my temples, trying in vain to jump-start a brain in dire need of sleep. I look down at the yellow legal pad in front of me, filled with theories and a summary of what I know.

I've just finished writing the names of the children and their birth dates when Jodie appears in the doorway. "I just talked to Kelly Hernandez with the Ladies' Club. She got the girl's birth date from Miriam Helmuth."

I PULL into the driveway of the Helmuth farm and barrel down the lane. Though it's dark and pouring rain, I pass several men on horseback braving the weather, still looking. I wonder if they know that Miriam and Ivan Helmuth are keeping secrets.

If my suspicions are correct, Miriam Helmuth didn't give birth to Elsie. But if not Miriam, then who?

I park a few yards from two buggies, and I hightail it to the door. I enter the house without knocking. The smells of lye soap and bleach greet me as I pass through the mudroom, where two Amish women are operating the old wringer washing machine. I nod at them as I head for the kitchen.

I find two of the children sitting at the kitchen table. Miriam is at the stove stirring something in a saucepan. She looks exhausted.

"Hi, Chief Katie!" Annie calls out.

"Did you bring Elsie?" Luke asks simultaneously.

"Hello back at you." I muster a smile that feels plastic on my face. "We haven't found Elsie yet, but we're looking hard."

"We miss her!"

"She's probably hungry! And cold!"

The words strike like punches. I look at Miriam to find her eyes already on me. "I need to talk to you," I say. "Privately."

The woman twists off the burner knob and sets down the spoon.

"Pudding's just about done," she tells her children. "Go wash your hands and faces. Luke, go get your brother in the barn."

The kids scramble from their chairs.

"That'll buy us a few minutes." Grabbing a mug, Miriam walks to the table and sinks into a chair. "You bring news?"

I take the chair across from her and get right to the point.

"Elam was born in November of 2011. Becky was born in October 2012. Miriam, there's no way you could have had Elsie in between."

"But . . . she came early, you know. Just four pounds of her."

"When was Elsie born?"

For the first time, she looks flustered. "The babies came so close together, sometimes I lose track. . . ."

"Stop lying to me." I smack my hand against the table. "Your little girl's life is in danger, and all I'm getting from you are lies."

"I'm not. I just . . . I got a little confused on the dates is all."

I rise, go to her, bend, so that my face is a foot away from hers. "Elsie isn't your biological child, is she?" I say quietly.

The flesh of her cheeks begins to quiver. Her body follows suit, shaking so violently I'm afraid she's going to vibrate off the chair.

"She's mine," she whispers. "In every way."

Miriam Helmuth has reached her breaking point. Her child is missing. Her mother is dead—violently murdered. If I'm going to get anything out of her, now is the time to do it, so I push.

"The choice you make at this moment may be the only thing that saves your daughter's life," I say. "Think about that before you lie to me again. Do you know where she is?"

"No."

"Do you know who has her?"

Closing her eyes tightly, she shakes her head. "I don't know," she cries. "I don't know why they did what they did."

"Who are 'they,' and what did they do?" I ask.

A sob escapes her. "They brought her to us," she whispers. "In the middle of the night. This screaming, red-faced little baby."

"Elsie?"

She nods. "She was a tiny thing. Just hours old. Hungry. Frightened. Wanting her *mamm* and some milk."

The reality of what I'm hearing strikes me with the force of a blow. I almost can't believe my ears.

"Who brought her to you?" I ask.

"The midwife. The bishop from Scioto County."

"I need names."

She scrubs her fingertips over her eyes. "I don't know."

Lowering myself into the chair, I pull out my notebook.

"Who's the baby's mother?" I ask.

"No one said, and I didn't ask. They were secretive about it."

"Who else was involved?"

"The bishop. The midwife." She hesitates. "Bishop Troyer."

"Bishop Troyer?" I echo the name dumbly. A man I've known my entire life. A leader admired not only by me, but by the entire Amish community. But he's tough, too. When I was a troubled teen and didn't follow the rules set forth by the *Ordnung,* my parents put me before him. It was an experience I never forgot. Tonight, I can't help but wonder: How is it that a man who had judged me so harshly could commit his own sin with absolute impunity?

"Why did they bring the baby to you, Miriam?"

"I don't know. You have to understand, Chief Burkholder, it was the kind of thing that wasn't to be discussed or questioned."

"What can you tell me about the midwife?"

"She wasn't from around here. She was older. I didn't recognize her. I assumed the bishop brought her along to care for the baby."

"I need more. Surely they told you *something.*"

"They said nothing to me, but I listened. From what I gathered, the baby's *mamm* was . . . troubled. I think there was something wrong with her. So much that she couldn't care for her own baby."

"Do you mean health problems? Mental problems? What?"

"I wish I knew."

I stare at her, trying to come to terms with what was done. "Why did you agree to take the baby?" I ask. "Didn't you wonder where she came from? Why she was being given to you? Did you think about the parents? That it might cause problems down the road?"

"We did it because the bishop asked us to. Adopt her, I mean. Children are a gift from God, and I knew that little girl was in trouble. She's one of the special ones, you know. She needed us. I figured her *mamm* might have some problem, too. I thought we were probably helping her, as well." She shrugs. "If she was sick or dying. If she didn't have a husband or family."

"Does Ivan know all of this?"

"Yes."

"Was your mother involved?" I ask.

"I think she knew about it. I don't know how much. I asked later, but she wouldn't speak of it."

"Did Elsie's biological parents agree to relinquish her? Or was Elsie . . . taken? Removed from the home?"

"No one said."

We fall silent, the only sound coming from the tap of rain against the window.

"Do Elsie's biological parents know where she was sent?"

Fear tears across her face. "You think they did this?"

Sie is meiner. She's mine.

"I think it's a possibility we have to consider."

She begins to sob. "Oh, dear Lord, how could this happen?"

I don't know what to say. What to think. "Is there anything you can tell me that might help me figure this out?"

She raises her gaze to mine. "The notes," she whispers. "I didn't tell you . . . Ivan thought it best if we didn't say anything."

"What notes?" But I'm thinking about the note found on Mary Yoder's body. A detail that was not made public.

Miriam goes to the kitchen drawer, pulls out a devotional book, opens it, and pulls out some papers. "Three of them. The latest this morning, in the mailbox." She slides them across the table to me. The same type of paper as the note found on Mary Yoder.

> Ill-gotten treasures have no lasting value, but righteousness delivers from death.

As I read, I'm thinking about evidence. Fingerprints. The possibility of DNA. Matching the paper to a specific notebook or manufacturer. A retailer. The prospect of CCTV.

I go to the second note.

The Lord is a God who avenges. O God who avenges, shine forth. Rise up, Judge of the earth; pay back to the proud what they deserve.

And the third.

Anyone who steals must certainly make restitution, but if they have nothing, they must be sold to pay for their theft.

"I should have told you." Miriam begins to sputter. "I was scared. Ivan didn't want to tell. He didn't—"

"Who has handled these notes?" I ask, my voice sharp.

"Me. Ivan. That's it."

"Do the passages mean anything to you?"

The Amish woman shakes her head. "The first is a proverb. The second is a psalm. Ninety-four, I think. The other . . . Exodus."

I let my anger come through. "What else haven't you told me?"

"That's it. I promise." She looks down at her hands. "Chief Burkholder, I don't know who the parents are. I don't know why they did what they did. All I know is that when I took Elsie into my arms, she was mine. She was home." A sob escapes her. "I want her back. My sweet baby girl. Please. Find her."

Twenty-five hours missing

My HEAD is reeling on the drive to the Troyer farm. I need to talk to the bishop, find out if he was involved, and get all the facts.

Why would a child be taken from her birth mother and placed with another family? Was the mother afflicted with Cohen syndrome, too? Usually, if there's some kind of disability—mental or physical or both—the Amish take care of their own without question. But if that was the case, why all the secrecy?

A hundred questions pound my brain as I park in the gravel area behind the Troyer farmhouse. It's after six p.m., fully dark, and a steady rain falls. I take the sidewalk to the back door and knock.

A moment later, the door opens and I find myself looking at Bishop Troyer. He's always seemed ancient to me, especially when I was a kid. His hair is silver. His beard reaches the waistline of his trousers. He's dressed in black—shirt, suspenders, jacket, and a flat-brimmed hat. He's smaller than I remember, his body a little more bent. He's using a walker now. None of those things detract from the power that radiates from those steely eyes.

"Katie Burkholder?"

"Bishop Troyer." I look past him to see his wife standing at the kitchen table. "I need to talk to you. Alone. It's important."

"Kumma inseid." Come inside.

Gripping the walker, the bishop turns and trundles to the table. I follow him into the kitchen.

"Sie bringa zeiya funn da kind?" his wife asks, eyeing me with anticipation. She brings news of the child?

I give her a hard look. "No."

"Ich braucha shvetza zu Chief Burkholder," he tells her. I need to speak with Chief Burkholder. *"Laynich."* Alone.

The woman lowers her gaze in submission. *"Voll."* Of course. She leaves and disappears into the shadows of the living room.

I make no move to assist as the bishop struggles into a kitchen chair. Before he's seated, I say, "I know Elsie isn't the biological child of Miriam and Ivan Helmuth. I need to know what happened and who was involved. Right now. Do you understand me?"

When the old man is seated, he sighs. "I don't know what you think you know, Kate Burkholder, but chances are you are wrong."

"What I know," I say, "is that you and Ivan and Miriam have been lying to me. Elsie's abduction and the murder of Mary Yoder are likely related to what happened with Elsie seven years ago. You need to tell me everything so I can do my job and find her."

"Miriam told you?"

"She didn't have a choice. Neither do you. If you refuse to help me, I will arrest you for obstructing justice. You got that?"

"I can tell you what I know, Katie. It isn't much."

"Start talking."

The old man isn't rattled, but I see the wheels turning behind those eyes. "Seven years ago, I received a letter from the bishop in Scioto County, Noah Schwartz. He asked for an emergency meeting. I agreed, and the next day he came to Painters Mill. He said the

Deiner had made an important decision and they needed my help."

Deiner is the *Deitsch* word for "servants," which is how the elected officials—the bishop, ministers, and preachers—are referred to. "Tell me about the meeting."

He looks down at the tabletop. "Noah asked me if I knew of a couple who could take in a child and raise it as their own."

I tug out my notebook and write down the bishop's name. "Why would an Amish bishop become involved in something like that?"

"According to Bishop Schwartz, the child had no one. *No one.* She needed a family. Parents. A safe place. A home."

"You didn't question him? Or wonder about the parents?"

"I trusted in the wisdom and goodness of the bishop."

"Who else was involved?" I ask.

"The midwife."

"What's her name?"

"I do not know."

"Noah Schwartz brought you the baby?"

The old man nods. "Two days later. Noah and the midwife brought the girl child. We took her to Miriam and Ivan late in the night. We prayed. And it was done."

"Who are the parents?" I ask. "What are their names?"

"I do not know."

"Where did the baby come from? What town?"

"Scioto County. That's all I know."

I write it down. Scioto County is in the southern part of Ohio. I recall Martha Hershberger telling me that Mary Yoder's sister, Marlene, was from "down south somewhere."

"Do you know Mary Yoder's sister, Marlene?" I ask.

The bishop shakes his head. "No."

I struggle to make sense of everything. "Why did Bishop Schwartz take the baby? Was the mother sick? Injured? Dying?"

"I did not ask," he tells me. "All I can tell you is that Noah Schwartz did this thing in the name of the Lord and the church."

I stare at him, my heart pounding. I don't want to believe the story I've been told. That two Amish bishops participated in what is at best an illegal adoption. At worst, a kidnapping. But in my heart of hearts, I know it's the truth. Bishop Troyer is not a liar.

"Where do I find Bishop Schwartz?" I ask.

"I heard Noah passed a couple of weeks ago."

Disappointment tings in my chest. "What about the midwife?"

"I do not know."

"Where are they from?"

"Most of the Amish live in Crooked Creek, I think. A few hours south. Down by the river."

"Who else knows about this?" I ask.

"Just the bishop and me. The midwife. Miriam and Ivan."

"What about Mary Yoder?"

"I can't say for certain, but I think she knew. Noah mentioned speaking to her, but he didn't go into detail."

"Is it possible someone else knows about what happened?"

He shrugs. "I don't know."

"What about the parents of the baby? Do they know what happened? Do they know where the baby was taken?"

"I do not know."

"Does your wife know?"

"She was here that night, of course. As the wife of a bishop, she does not question."

"Bishop, I believe Elsie may have been taken by someone who knew about or found out about what happened all those years ago. Her birth parents. A relative. Someone who wanted her back."

"I don't see how, Katie. Bringing that baby here was done in the night. We were careful. It was never spoken of again."

"Someone spoke of it." I sigh. "Bishop, you can't just take a baby from one family and give it to another. Even if your intentions were honorable. You likely broke the law."

"It was done in the eyes of the Lord. His law is above man's law. You know this, Katie. Or have you strayed so far from your roots that you no longer believe?" He says the words in a voice like iron. "If what we did is against English law, then so be it."

I DRIVE back to the station in a state of shock. By the time I park and head inside, I've come up with a loose plan.

I find Mona, still in uniform, sitting at the reception desk.

"Oh, hey, Chief."

"Dig up everything you can find on Noah Schwartz. I think he lived in Crooked Creek, Ohio. Scioto County. No middle. He was an Amish bishop. I believe he's deceased."

She's already jotting everything down. "Got it."

I head toward my office. "Get me a list of midwives in Crooked Creek and Scioto County," I say over my shoulder. I realize that because we're dealing with the Amish—many of whom stay off the grid—the information may be hit-or-miss.

"Chief, you still interested in Marlene Byler?" she calls out.

I turn to find her holding out a purple folder. "There's not much out there. Just a newspaper story and an obituary," she tells me. "That's how I found her. Mary Yoder is listed in the obit."

I take the folder. "Anyone ever tell you you've got a great detective's mind?"

She grins. "All the time."

In my office, I open the folder and read her obituary.

Marlene Byler, 29, of Crooked Creek died unexpectedly on March 17, 1990. She was born in Scioto County on May 11, 1961. She was a member of the Old Order Amish Church. She is survived by her sister Mary Yoder of Painters Mill.

I go to the next page in the file. It's an article from the *Scioto County Times Record* newspaper dated two days after her death.

SCIOTO COUNTY WOMAN JUMPS TO HER DEATH

Sheriff Kris McGuire tells the *Scioto County Times Record* 29-year-old Marlene Byler died after jumping from the Sciotoville Bridge into the Ohio River about 5 p.m. Thursday. McGuire said her death is an apparent suicide.

I read the article twice. It's a troubling, unusual story. Not only was Marlene Byler Amish, but she was evidently distraught enough to jump to her death. Is any of it related to the murder of Mary Yoder or the abduction of Elsie Helmuth?

Shoving the questions aside for now, I cruise out to the National

Center for Missing and Exploited Children website, seeking information on infant abductions in Scioto County seven years earlier. There's nothing there.

At the same time, Mona ferrets through various Internet sites for information on Noah Schwartz, the bishop. The only thing she finds is a single piece on the buggy accident that took his life two weeks earlier and an obituary in *The Budget*.

"Here's the list of registered midwives for Scioto County." She passes me a printout from one of the national registries. "None listed for Crooked Creek, Chief. Several from Scioto County."

I take the list. "You got your Google hat with you?"

She grins. "Never leave home without it."

"I'm looking for information on a newborn that went missing seven years ago. If you strike out in Scioto County, expand your search to contiguous counties."

"I'm all over it."

For three hours Mona and I probe the Internet, searching for mention of a missing child, first in Crooked Creek, and then Scioto and surrounding counties. A couple of cases meet our general criteria, but further investigation proves they couldn't have been Elsie.

Tomasetti calls at midnight. "DNA from the blood found in the yard of the Schattenbaum farm belongs to Elsie Helmuth," he says.

I close my eyes. "Damn it."

He sighs. "Yeah."

"What about the notes I gave you?" I ask. "Anything come back? Prints? The paper or notebook manufacturer?"

"We got zilch. No prints. No DNA." A buzz of silence. "Kate, you sound wiped out."

I laugh, but it rings tired and phony. I tell him about my conversations with Bishop Troyer and Miriam Helmuth.

"That changes everything," he says. "Do you think any of this could have something to do with the girl being special needs?"

"I can't imagine. The Amish consider special needs children a gift from God. They're never considered a burden. Any Amish person with a physical or mental handicap is well cared for."

"What if, for some reason, the mother couldn't care for her?" He lets the thought trail. "Would that be enough for the Amish to step in?"

"Maybe," I say. "Family."

"Were you able to find Mary Yoder's sister?" he asks.

"Dead," I say. "Suicide. Tomasetti, the bishop who brought the baby to Painters Mill is dead. Buggy accident."

Silence ensues. "Kate, why the hell would a bishop get involved in something like that? It doesn't make sense."

"I don't think a bishop would without some compelling reason." It's the most honest answer I can give.

Silence ensues.

"So what are you going to do?" Tomasetti asks.

"There's only one thing I *can* do. Go to Scioto County. I'll only be gone a day," I tell him. "Two, tops."

"Famous last words." He sighs. "If it's not too much trouble, come home and get some sleep before you go."

"On my way."

Chapter 6

Forty-two hours missing

DAWN USHERS IN THE FIRST frost of the season, a sky the color of slate. I'd planned on an early start but ended up spending several hours at the station. I didn't pull out until after nine a.m. to make the four-hour drive to Crooked Creek. I'm southbound on Ohio 23 when the call comes in from Tomasetti.

"The tire-tread plaster casts captured at the scene were viable," he tells me. "Manufacturer is Goodyear. Wrangler radial P 235/75R15 105S SL OWL."

"Best news I've had all day. Does that tell us the type of vehicle?"

"Light truck or SUV."

"Pickup truck," I say. "Covers a lot of territory."

"The good news is the tires are worn. The technician says there are markings from wear. In this case, some minor damage, a slice on the outer edge that's unique to this tire."

"So if we produce a suspect, we'll be able to match the tire."

"Yeah. Look, I've got to run. Keep me posted on how it's going. And if it's not too much to ask, stay the hell out of trouble."

ANY time a cop pokes around in an outside jurisdiction, it's prudent to check in with local law enforcement, so I make my first stop in Portsmouth. The Scioto County Sheriff's Office is housed in a redbrick building that also accommodates the county jail. I called ahead, hoping to meet with the sheriff, but he wasn't available, so I spoke with one of the deputies. I briefed him on the case and asked him to check for reports of a missing child six to eight years earlier. He promised to take a look and let me know.

Deputy Martin Harleson meets me inside the reception area with a welcoming smile, then shepherds me to a small meeting room.

I lay out the fundamentals of the case. "We believe he may be Amish and has connections to Crooked Creek. I wanted to let you guys know I was in town."

"Any way I can help?" he asks.

"Do you know who replaced Noah Schwartz, the Amish bishop who was killed?"

He shakes his head. "No idea."

"Do you have the names of any of the ministers?" I ask. "Or preachers? Elders?"

"We don't deal with the Amish much here in Portsmouth. Most of them live east of us. A lot of buggies on the road in that area. Bishop Schwartz was the first fatality. Hit-and-run."

The term "hit-and-run" gives me pause. "What happened?"

"Driver hit the buggy from behind. Had to be doing fifty. Killed Schwartz instantly."

"You guys make an arrest?" I ask.

"We didn't have much to work with. There were no witnesses. Nothing left behind. Not even a skid mark."

I stare at him. "The driver made no attempt to stop?"

"We assumed he was probably under the influence. Drugs or alcohol or both." Grimacing, he shakes his head.

"Where did it happen?"

"River Road area. We call it the Bend. East where the road runs along the river, then doglegs north."

"The bishop lived in the area?"

"He actually lived to the east a ways." He cocks his head. "Why the interest?"

"I think the bishop knew the family in Painters Mill." I shrug, trying to keep it nonchalant. "Did you have a chance to double-check on any missing infants reported six to eight years ago?"

"I did a search, and there's nothing there." He shifts, looking a little miffed because he knows I'm not telling him everything. "Do you mind if I ask why you're interested in missing children?"

"The Helmuth family has relatives down here. Since most kidnappings of minor children are perpetrated by a family member or someone known to the family, I thought I'd sniff around."

His eyes narrow. "You think some Amish person from Crooked Creek took that little girl? Most of the Amish down here are Old Order. Painters Mill is four hours away. That would be a difficult trip to make by buggy."

"They hire drivers when they need to travel a distance."

"You know a lot about the Amish."

"I was born Amish," I tell him. "I left when I was eighteen."

"Oh. That's interesting." He offers a sheepish grin. "Never met an ex-Amish chief of police."

I smile back. "I thought talking to some of the Helmuths' relatives might be helpful."

"Wish I could be more help, Chief Burkholder. The Amish keep to themselves. They do some work for folks around here in Portsmouth. Fences. Sheds. Stuff like that. One of the local guys built a workshop for me last summer. Nice dude." He studies me intently. "I think I've got his name and address around here somewhere. Might be a good place for you to start."

"That would be great."

Pulling out his phone, he taps the screen. "Got it right here. Name's

Adam Fisher." He recites an address, and I thumb it into my phone.
I rise and extend my hand for a shake.

"If you need anything from us, Chief Burkholder, you let me
know and we'll help out if we can."

I thank him for his time and head for the door.

DRIVER *hit the buggy from behind. Had to be doing fifty. Killed*
Schwartz instantly....

The deputy's words echo in my head as I drive toward Crooked
Creek. Sadly, buggy accidents are a fact of life in Amish country.

No witnesses. Nothing left behind. Not even a skid mark....

While his assertion that the lack of skid marks can indicate an
intoxicated driver was true, it's not the only conclusion that might
be drawn. If Bishop Schwartz was involved in the illegal adoption
of an infant, who's to say some enraged parent or relative didn't
take it upon himself to mete out a little retribution?

Crooked Creek is a tiny village with a population of 623, according to the sign at the corporation limit. The small downtown
area is lined with historic buildings. As I make the turn onto River
Road and idle down the brick-paved street, it becomes apparent
that hard times have fallen upon this pretty little town. At least
half of the once-grand buildings are vacant.

I leave the downtown area and head east on the Ohio River Scenic Byway. Even with the economic downturn, this part of the state
is beautiful. Light rain falls from a glowering sky as I pass quaint
farms, some of which are Amish. Occasionally I catch a glimpse of
the river, a shimmering, muddy blur through the trees.

A few miles east of Crooked Creek proper, the voice of my GPS
tells me to turn left on Stephen Road. Another mile, and the name
on the mailbox tells me I've reached my destination.

The Fisher farm is set on lush bottomland. At the top of a rise,
the lane veers toward a two-story brick house that's been painted
white. Green shutters. There's a bank barn twenty yards from the
house. Black Angus cattle graze in a pasture.

I park in the rear of the house and take a walkway to the front.
I've just stepped onto the porch when the door swings open. A

plump Amish woman of about forty is holding a broom in one hand, a dustpan in the other. White apron and *kapp*. Sneakers. She startles upon spotting me and drops the dustpan. "Oh."

"I didn't mean to frighten you." I pick up the dustpan and hand it to her. "I'm looking for Adam Fisher."

"That's my husband." She glances at my badge as if she's not quite sure she believes me. "What's this all about?"

"I'm working on—"

"Was der schinner is kshicht?" What in the world is going on? I look past her to see a tall, thin Amish man approach. He's wearing typical garb: blue work shirt, dark gray trousers with suspenders, a navy jacket, and a flat-brimmed hat.

I introduce myself. "I'm working on a case in Painters Mill that involves an Amish family with connections to Crooked Creek." I recap, sticking to generalities. "I was wondering if you could tell me how to get in touch with Bishop Schwartz's widow?"

"That would be Lizzie. Put the house up for sale just last week."

"Do you have an address?"

"The old one." He recites a Crooked Creek address. "Not sure where she moved to."

I pull out my notebook and write it down. I direct my next question to Mrs. Fisher. "Do you know the midwives in the area?"

Mrs. Fisher answers readily. "Well, Sadie Stutzman was the only midwife around for years. I used her with our seven children. But she's getting old, you know. Had a stroke a few months back."

"Narrisch," the Amish man mutters beneath his breath. Insane. His wife bites her lip. "Most of the Amish ladies use Hannah Beachy over to Portsmouth these days. She's *Mennischt*, you know." Mennonite. "She's a nice girl, certified by the state."

I write down both names. "Where can I find Sadie Stutzman?"

"She still lives out to that old house by the river."

She rattles off an address, and I write it down.

Forty-eight hours missing

I PLUG the address for Sadie Stutzman into my GPS, but quickly discover that some of the roads aren't on the map. Half a mile from the river, I realize why. The road isn't really a road at all, but a narrow dirt track crisscrossed with tire ruts.

Mud pings inside the Explorer's wheel wells as I approach a small frame house covered from foundation to roof with vines. At first, I think the place is abandoned. Then I spot the loafing shed at the rear; a horse and several goats graze in a tumbling-down pen. An Amish buggy sits at the back side of the shed.

The mailbox slants at a precarious angle. There's no name, just two numbers. I glance at my GPS. The two numbers match, so I pull in and park next to a big clump of pampas grass.

I take the cracked sidewalk to the porch. A storm door hangs by a single hinge, so I ease it out of the way and knock.

I wait a full minute, but no one comes. I've just started descending the steps when a sound tells me there's someone in the backyard. Pulling up my collar against the wind and drizzle, I walk around the side of the house. There I get my first good look at the river, a vast expanse of shimmering brown water. A few yards away, a diminutive woman is at work on some earthen project. I start toward her.

She's Amish. Small in stature. White *kapp*. A charcoal-colored dress that reaches nearly to the ground. Gray barn coat. Black muck boots. No gloves, even though she's got a shovel in hand.

"Hello?" I call out. "Mrs. Stutzman?"

The woman shovels dirt from a wheelbarrow onto a pile of earth that's about three feet high. Her coat and head covering are soaking wet. Upon hearing my voice, she stops and turns to me.

"Who might you be?"

She's barely five feet tall, with a voice like rusted iron. Her face is deeply wrinkled. Gold, wire-rimmed glasses cover viscous eyes.

I introduce myself. "I'm from Painters Mill. I'd like to talk to you about something that may have happened here in Crooked Creek a few years ago that involves a child."

"Painters Mill, huh? Never heard of it."

The left side of her face sags slightly, and I recall Mrs. Fisher telling me this woman suffered a stroke a few months back.

"Are you sure about that?" I ask.

"If I wasn't sure, I wouldn't say it now, would I?" Hefting the shovel, she jams it into the dirt in the wheelbarrow and dumps it onto the mound. I'm not exactly sure what she's doing.

"What are you working on?" I ask.

"Levee," she tells me. "Storm comin'."

I was raised to respect my elders. You don't let them exert themselves while you do nothing. "Big job. Can I help?" I ask.

"Only got one shovel." She hands me the tool and grins. "Don't mind if I take a breather, though."

I take the shovel and toss a glob of mud onto the mound. "I understand you're a midwife."

"Was till the stroke got me. Don't do much anymore."

The handle of the shovel is muddy and wet. I'm not wearing gloves. But I keep going. "You knew Bishop Schwartz," I say.

"Everyone knew the bishop."

"Did you ever travel with him to Painters Mill?"

An emotion I can't identify flickers in her eyes. "Can't say I did."

"Are you sure about that, Mrs. Stutzman? I understand you and Bishop Schwartz transported an infant to Painters Mill."

"Don't recall anything like that." She holds out her hand for the shovel. "Give it here."

I ignore her, keep working.

"Do you know Bishop Troyer in Painters Mill?" I ask.

She looks at me over the top of her glasses. "You think you're pretty smart, don't you? Coming here and asking nosy questions."

I set down the shovel. "A seven-year-old little girl is missing," I tell her. "She's Amish. Someone took her two days ago. I think it's related to something that happened here seven years ago."

"I don't know anything about that."

I bank a rise of irritation, and put the energy into filling a wheelbarrow with dirt. For the span of several minutes, the only sound comes from the grate of steel against wet earth.

"They killed him, you know."

I stop digging, turn to her. "What? Killed who?"

"Bishop Schwartz. That's who we're talking about, isn't it?"

"Bishop Schwartz was killed in a buggy accident."

She stares at me as if I'm dense. "*Was* it an accident?" she asks.

"Are you saying someone did that to him on purpose?"

"I'm saying I knew something wasn't right all along," she whispers. "Knew it for a long time. Everyone did. Kept their mouths shut like good Amish. Sin piled atop of sin. I couldn't abide by it." The old woman hobbles to the wheelbarrow. "He said I was never to speak of it. So I held my tongue."

"Mrs. Stutzman, do you know who was driving the vehicle that struck Bishop Schwartz's buggy?"

"The police said it was druggies." She hefts a harsh laugh. "That ain't who done it, and it wadn't no accident. I told them, but they wouldn't listen. I'm just a crazy old woman, after all."

"Who killed him?"

A light enters her eyes. "The father of the child."

The earth seems to tremble beneath my feet. "Give me a name."

"I may be old, Kate Burkholder, but I still value my life. If he finds out I'm talking to you, he'll kill me, too. Just like the others."

"I can keep you safe," I tell her. "I'm a police officer."

"The way you kept that girl safe? The bishop? You can't stop him. No one can. It's in God's hands now."

I try another tactic. "Tell me about the baby. Who is her *mamm?*"

"They shamed her. She couldn't handle it. Those poor babies." The woman makes a sound that's part grief, part disgust.

"What babies?" I ask. "Who are you talking about?"

Ignoring me, she takes the shovel and jams it into dirt.

"What about Marlene Byler?" I ask.

"They shamed her to death. That's why she jumped. They shamed her." Repeating the words like a mantra, she begins to dig, frantically. "Like mother, like daughter—both were bad eggs."

"Why did they take the baby?" I ask.

The woman tightens her mouth, doesn't look at me.

"Who are the parents? Please, all I need is a name."

She raises a shaking hand and wipes rain from her face. "You speak the devil's name too often, and you'll hear the flap of his wings. You'd be wise to remember that, Kate Burkholder."

Throwing down the shovel, she starts toward the house.

For an instant, I consider going after her. But I think the stroke must have affected her mental state. Might be better to try in the morning.

My boots sink into mud as I walk back to the Explorer, trying to get my head around what just transpired.

. . . it wadn't no accident.

Is it possible the hit-and-run that killed Bishop Schwartz wasn't some random, tragic accident? Did the sheriff's department interview Sadie Stutzman? Did they listen to her claims? Or did they simply write her off as an eccentric old woman?

"Damn it." I climb into the Explorer and pick up my phone.

The last thing any cop wants to be subjected to is some cop from an outside jurisdiction coming in and questioning the way they handled an investigation. That's exactly what I'm about to do.

I get put on hold twice, and then Deputy Harleson comes on the line. "Hi, Chief Burkholder. What can I do for you?"

"I got plaster on some tire-tread impressions related to the case I'm working on, and I realized I forgot to ask if you were able to pick up any tread on the hit-and-run that killed Noah Schwartz. I thought it might be worth running a comp."

"We didn't get any tread marks. There was heavy rain that night. Anything left behind by the driver got washed away."

I make a sound of disappointment. "I was just talking with some of the local Amish. There are some individuals who believe the bishop's death was not accidental."

He chuckles. "Ah, you talked to the Stutzman widow."

Busted. "Yes."

"I should have warned you. She's a nice lady and all, but she's crazy as a loon. Half the stuff she says . . . you can't believe it."

"Can you tell me where the accident happened?"

"Intersection of Hayport Road and Burkes Lane. Driver blew the stop sign at a high rate of speed. Hit the buggy from behind."

"What time did it happen?" I ask.

"Nine p.m. Schwartz had no reflective signage on the buggy. It was dark. Perfect storm for a wreck." He pauses. "Mind telling me what that hit-and-run has to do with your case in Painters Mill?"

"I'm not sure just yet," I say honestly. "If I figure it out, you'll be the first to know."

Chapter 7

Fifty hours missing

THE HOUSE WHERE Bishop Schwartz had once lived is vacant, with a "for sale" sign in the front yard. I call the Realtor's number and get the address for the widow, Lizzie Schwartz.

It's a scenic drive that takes me past picturesque farms and forest. The mailbox is well marked, so I make the turn onto a nicely maintained lane. The residence is a sunny yellow farmhouse.

I park in the gravel pullover at the side of the house. Two huge black dogs bound up to me, their tails wagging, so I get out. Luckily, the dogs are friendly, and they accompany me onto the porch.

I knock and take a moment to scratch one of the dogs behind a floppy ear. The door opens, and I find myself looking at a pretty Mennonite woman. She's wearing a pink print dress with a white apron and sneakers. I guess her to be about forty. She's got red hair pulled into a ponytail and eyes the color of a mossy pond.

She looks from me to the dogs and grins. "You lost?"

"I hope not." I show her my badge. "I'm looking for Lizzie Schwartz."

"I'm Rachel, her daughter. Is this about the buggy accident?"

"In part," I say honestly.

She looks at me thoughtfully. "After Dad was killed, my husband and I brought Mom here. I don't know if you saw it, but we've got that cute little *dawdi haus* out back."

Dawdi haus is *Deitsch* for "grandfather's house," which is basically a cottage some Amish build next to their home so their elderly parents can live nearby.

I follow her out the back door. The *dawdi haus* cottage is more Victorian than Plain. White board-and-batten siding, a steeply pitched roof, wood shutters stained a dark walnut, and a tiny stone porch crowded with clay pots overflowing with fall mums.

"Mama?" Rachel doesn't knock but calls out as she enters.

"In the kitchen!" comes a spry female voice.

Rachel sniffs the air. "She's making apple butter."

We find Lizzie Schwartz at the counter, peeling apples, mason jars lined up on the counter, and a big pot sitting on the stovetop.

"Didn't know we had company." The woman turns to us. She's substantially built and clad in black, since she's in mourning.

"She's a police, Mama. Here to talk to you about Datt."

Her expression darkens. "You caught the man who hit him?"

"No, ma'am." I tell her about Mary Yoder and Elsie Helmuth. "I want to talk about something that happened a few years ago."

A few minutes later, the two of us are seated at the table, a cup of steaming cider in front of each of us.

"Noah was a good bishop," she tells me. "A good man. Father."

"Did he ever travel to Painters Mill?" I ask.

"I believe he did, in fact."

"How long ago?"

"Years, I think."

"Did he know Sadie Stutzman?"

"Anyone who's had a baby around here knows Sadie."

It's the longest run of straight answers I've received in Crooked Creek. "Did your husband transport a baby to Painters Mill?"

Her eyes flick away, then return to mine. "Maybe."

"An interesting answer. Do you know the circumstances?"

"No, But I probably know more than I should." She gives me a sage look. "The little girl you were telling me about. The missing one. Do you believe they're one and the same?"

"I think that's a possibility."

Bowing her head slightly, she rubs her temples. "Oh, Lord."

"Mrs. Schwartz, do you know who the parents are?"

"I do not," she tells me. "But I overheard something I never forgot. I knew it would come back to haunt me. I just had this feeling . . . that it was *wrong*."

"Your husband told you about it?"

"Not exactly." Her smile is sad. "Noah took his position as bishop very seriously. He never burdened me with knowledge of the things that troubled him."

"How did you find out about the baby?"

This time, her smile contains shame. "I eavesdropped on a conversation between Sadie Stutzman and my husband. I'm not proud, and it bothered me for years. What I heard kept me up nights."

"Tell me about the conversation."

Her mouth tightens. "Sadie came to our door. It was the middle of the night. She was . . . distraught. That was odd for her because that lady is coolheaded and not prone to high emotion. I assumed one of her young mothers had lost a baby. I was wrong."

The Amish woman wraps her hands around her mug. "Noah went out to the porch, and they spoke for a long time. I went to the kitchen and made coffee, but when I took the cups to them, I heard Sadie say something about taking a newborn from its *mamm*."

"Did she mention a name?" I ask.

The Amish woman shakes her head. "The thing that surprised me was that Noah already knew about it. They'd discussed it before. He was the one who suggested Painters Mill. I think he knew someone or had someone in mind for that poor little baby."

"Did you have some sense as to why they did it?" I ask.

"There must have been a good reason. That, I know for certain."

"Like what?"

She shrugs. "I couldn't say. But my husband was a good and decent God-loving man. This must have been an urgent situation. If the baby wasn't being fed or cared for. Something like that."

"Did you ask your husband about it?"

"I did. He wouldn't speak of it. Said he didn't want to burden me. He went to Painters Mill the next day. Came home very late. I knew they'd done it. I never broached the subject again."

We sit in silence, the smells of cinnamon and cider lingering.

She raises her gaze to mine. "Chief Burkholder, do you think my husband's death is related to what happened with that child?"

"I think it's a possibility."

Tears glimmer in her eyes. "Why now? After all this time?"

"I don't know," I say honestly.

Another cumbrous silence, and then I ask, "Mrs. Schwartz, do you know of any women who were *ime familye weg* in the weeks before the conversation you overheard?" "In the family way" is the Amish term for "pregnant." "Anyone you can think of?"

"I wondered, of course. Was she unmarried? Was she too young?" She gives another shake of her head. "I didn't dwell."

I think about everything that's been said and what it could mean in terms of finding Elsie Helmuth. "Do you know Marlene Byler or Mary Byler?" I ask, using Mary's maiden name.

"I didn't know either of them, but I heard about what happened to Marlene. What she did all those years ago. Jumped off that big bridge up near Portsmouth. I don't know if it's true, but I heard she took her infant daughter off that bridge with her."

A rush of interest engulfs me. "A baby?"

"The police never found the body, so no one knows if it's true."

"What can you tell me about her?"

"Not much." The woman shrugs. "She was Amish. Had some mental or emotional issues, I think. There were rumors. Eventually the bishop excommunicated her."

"Do you know why?"

She shakes her head. "She killed herself shortly afterward."

"Who's the new bishop?" I ask.

"They just nominated Melvin Chupp."

"Do you know where he lives?" I ask.

"Near Wheelersburg, I think."

I reach into my pocket and set my card on the table in front of her. "If you think of anything else, will you let me know?"

"I will." Giving me a sad smile, she reaches out and pats my hand. "You'll do the same, Kate Burkholder?"

"Bet on it."

I DRIVE to Wheelersburg, but there's no one home at the Chupp house, so I head back to Crooked Creek. I find the one and only motel, the Sleepy Time Motel, which is a mid-century modern dive. I'm desperate for a shower and a bed, so I park and check in.

The room is exactly what I thought it would be. There's a sway-back queen-size bed with a tattered spread. Bad wall art from the 1970s. The bathroom fixtures are rusty, loose tiles on the floor. But the room is clean and will do just fine for a shower and sleep.

I brave the shower and crawl into a lumpy bed that smells of scorched cotton. A mix of rain and sleet pounds the window.

Pulling the spread up to my waist, I fire up my laptop. I run a few searches on Cohen syndrome. The symptoms include a host of problems—developmental delay, intellectual disability, muscle weakness, eye problems. It's a rare genetic disorder, slightly more prevalent among the Amish. Both parents have to have the gene, but usually don't show signs of the disorder themselves.

It's eleven p.m. when I call Tomasetti. I summarize my conversation with Lizzie Schwartz. "She overheard Bishop Schwartz and the midwife conspire to bring a newborn to Painters Mill."

"You talk to the midwife?"

I take him through my exchange with Sadie Stutzman. "She suggested Bishop Schwartz's death wasn't an accident."

"Did you look at the police report?"

"I talked to the deputy who investigated the accident. They have no idea who was responsible and attributed it to a drunk driver."

"Was the midwife able to make a case?"

"That's the problem. She's . . . eccentric. She'd suffered a stroke recently, and the general consensus is that she may be in the early stages of dementia."

"Is she completely diminished mentally?" he asks.

"Not so much that I felt I needed to discount everything she said. And I got the distinct impression she's afraid."

Tomasetti falls silent, digesting; then he asks, "What's your gut telling you? Do you think it's possible someone killed him because of what happened with the kid seven years ago?"

"I think the timing of it and the circumstances are suspect."

"Why now?" he asks. "After so much time?"

"Maybe the parents or even a family member recently found out what happened and who was involved, and they decided to . . . take back what had been stolen from them." I pause, thinking about the notes. "I'm going to try the midwife one more time tomorrow before I leave, talk to the new bishop; then I'll head back."

After hanging up with Tomasetti, I go back to the file I brought with me, rereading every report, every interview transcript, and my own personal notes. One name that keeps popping up is Marlene Byler, Mary Yoder's sister. I think about the rumors surrounding her death. Is there some nexus I'm not seeing? I flip the page, seeking something I missed before, all to no avail.

By the time midnight rolls around, I can't keep my eyes open. I shut my laptop cover, and exhaustion drags me into a hard sleep.

Sixty-four hours missing

THE *river moved with an uneasy restlessness. Wind whipped the surface into waves more befitting a lake.*

Something coming, she thought.

Sadie Stutzman stood on the back porch and watched the water slither past the bank. Dawn teased the horizon to the east. She loved the river. She'd been born here, raised in this very house. This morning, watching the water that was as cloudy and troubled as her own mind, she knew she'd probably die here, too.

Taking a final look at the river, she pushed open the door that took her into her kitchen. She'd pulled mint from the little patch that grew along the side of the house. Tearing off a few leaves, she dropped them into a mug and poured hot water from the teapot she kept simmering on the stove. Mint tea always calmed her.

She couldn't stop thinking about the English policewoman who'd come, asking questions. If she wasn't careful, Kate Burkholder was going to unearth something awful. Something dangerous. Dummkopp, *she thought. Idiot. It was a harsh judgment; the woman was just doing her job. She had no way of knowing the truth would only make things worse.*

The exchange haunted her throughout the night. If only she could erase the memory of that night, of what she'd done. What they'd done. Thanks to Kate Burkholder, it was all coming back.

Clutching the mug of tea, Sadie shuffled down the hall and entered her bedroom. She set the cup on the night table and opened the drawer. The sight of the notes sent a shiver through her. She picked them up and read.

It is mine to avenge; I will repay. In due time their foot will slip;
their day of disaster is near and their doom rushes upon them.

*The Bible quote was from Deuteronomy 32:35. She'd found it in
her mailbox the morning after Bishop Schwartz was killed. Sadie had
known right away who'd written it, and why.*
She flipped to the second note.

If a thief is caught breaking in at night and is struck a fatal
blow, the defender is not guilty of bloodshed . . .

*The threat was not lost on Sadie. The question in her mind was: How
did they find out? Only a handful of people knew what had been done.
None of them would have talked about such a thing.*
*Sadie cursed herself for what she'd done. She tucked the notes into the
envelope. Picking up her mug, she left the bedroom.*
*She knew the policewoman would be back. Kate Burkholder didn't
have a timid spirit. Next time, Sadie would tell her the truth.*
*Sadie was midway down the hall when she felt cold air around her
ankles. She stopped.* Door's open, *she thought, and she knew.*
"Du dauerte iahra," came a whispered voice from the living room.
You took her.
She saw him. A mountain of a man, standing there, stone still.
*"I saved her life." Despite the fear crawling over her, Sadie held her
ground. "You'd best take her home."*
"She is home." He started toward her. Purpose in his strides.
Sadie turned and ran. But two steps, and he was upon her.
*The first blow fell upon her, sent her to her knees. Pain streaked across
her scalp. Head reeling, she looked up at him.*
"Thou shalt not steal," he said.
*Before she could retort, he raised his foot, brought it down hard, and
the night swallowed the day.*

Sixty-five hours missing

I WAKE a little before seven a.m. to two inches of snow and a sun-
rise of monochrome gray. By eight a.m. I'm back on the road. I
swing by a small grocery store, grab a cup of coffee, and an extra

for Sadie Stutzman along with a dozen blueberry muffins; then I take the county road south toward the river.

Muddy tire tracks mar the driveway of the Stutzman place. As I pull up to the house, I wonder who's already been here so early.

Grabbing the coffee and muffins, I wade through snow and take the steps to the front porch. A dusting of snow on the concrete reveals footprints. Judging from the size, they belong to a male and they haven't been there long.

I knock. "Sadie?" I call out. "It's Kate Burkholder."

There's no sound from inside, and no one comes to the door. Undeterred, I head around to the rear and take the steps to the tiny porch. I find the door open a few inches.

"Sadie? Hey, it's Kate Burkholder. Is everything all right?"

No answer.

I stand there, holding the cardboard tray, thinking about the tire tracks in the driveway, the footprints on the porch. Setting the tray on the concrete, I push open the door. The interior is dimly lit and quiet. The smell of something burning floats on cold air.

"Sadie?"

I step into the small kitchen. Something sizzles to my right. There's a low-burning blue flame beneath an old-fashioned teapot. The water has boiled over. The source of the smell. Evidently, it's been burning for some time. I twist off the gas.

The house is a boxy structure with low ceilings. I pass through the kitchen, pause in the doorway that opens to the living room. Lanterns, paperback books, and knitting projects are scattered atop a rustic coffee table. An afghan is draped over a green sofa.

"Sadie?"

Shadows fill the room, so I go to the front window and open the curtains. Dim light seeps in. I glance into the hallway to my left.

I see the Amish woman lying on the floor, unmoving.

"Oh, no." I go to her and kneel. She's sprawled on her right side. A smear on her *kapp* snags my attention. Blood, I realize. A dribble of it runs from her ear to her throat. Horror burgeons when I realize one side of her skull has been crushed.

"Damn. Damn." Rising, I slide my .38 from the holster.

The floor creaks behind me. I spin, catch a glimpse of the rocking chair an instant before it crashes into me. Pain sears across my scalp. The force sends me to my knees. My .38 clatters to the floor.

A jet engine of adrenaline roars through me. A dozen thoughts register at once. My attacker is male. Tall. Heavily built. Beard.

I dive for the .38. An instant before I reach it, a hand yanks me backward with such force that I land on my back. He comes down on top of me, straddles my midsection, draws back to punch me.

I bring up both knees, drive them against his spine. He rocks forward, unfazed, but it buys me an instant. I ram the heel of my hand into his face. The cartilage in his nose crunches.

His fist careens off my cheek. Pain zings. I bring up my right leg, hook it over his head, my heel against his throat, and send him backward. He growls like an animal. He's off balance, halfway off me. I bring up my other leg and stomp his chest. The force drives him back. Not for long. He lunges at me, throws a wild punch.

"I'm a cop!" I scream. "I am armed! Get the hell off me!"

His fist bounces off my knee as I bring it up. I kick at him wildly. I roll, launch myself at the .38. My hand finds the butt.

He comes down on top of me, a boulder slamming against my back. I'm facedown, my right arm extended, gripping my weapon. A fist comes down on my head like a sledgehammer. My chin slams against the floor. My teeth clack together.

Viselike fingers clamp around my throat.

I yank the .38 toward me, bend my arm at the elbow, aim over my shoulder, and take a blind shot. The explosion rocks my brain.

My attacker goes rigid, and an animalistic howl tears from his throat. I pull the trigger again. He rolls off me. I twist, crabwalk back, bring up the gun. "Police! Get on the ground!"

I see his silhouette against the window, coming toward me, and I pull off another shot. I hear a whoosh! A chair flung at me, hitting my arm. Another zing of pain. I kick it aside, hear it clatter across the floor. He's nowhere in sight, but I hear him moving around in the living room. "Get your hands up!" I scream. "Get on the ground, or I will shoot you dead! Do it now!"

The chair flies at me from the mouth of the hall. I block it with my foot. I catch a glimpse of him as he sprints to the kitchen. I follow, round the corner, see him go through the back door.

"Police! Halt!"

The man jumps from the porch, streaks across the yard. Then I'm through the door. I level my .38 at the man. But he's gone.

THE deputy with the Scioto County Sheriff's Office arrives on scene in fourteen minutes. I'm sitting in the Explorer, which I've moved to the road's shoulder in front of the house.

The deputy isn't happy with me. For letting myself into the house. For corrupting a crime scene like some backwoods rookie. He's not shy about letting me know.

"You make a habit of walking into other people's homes when they don't answer the damn door?" he asks.

"She was elderly. I figured a welfare check was in order."

It's a good reason to enter a residence. He's still not pleased.

"Do you need an ambulance?" he asks.

"I'm fine."

Within minutes, another deputy arrives on scene, followed by an ambulance from Portsmouth. In the last two hours, I've been questioned by three deputies and a female trooper. I've relayed the turn of events half a dozen times. I expect I'll tell it a dozen more.

"Chief Burkholder."

I turn to see Deputy Martin Harleson approach. He's frowning at me, but his hand is outstretched, so I shake it.

"You've certainly had bad luck in Crooked Creek," he says.

"I'm not sure it has much to do with luck."

I tell him everything I know about the case, my suspicions about an infant being taken from the area seven years ago.

"That's why you were asking about missing kids," he mutters.

I nod. "And Noah Schwartz."

"You think that hit-and-run has something to do with all this?"

"I do."

"Holy cow." He blinks. "So are we talking about a stolen baby?"

"Or an illegal adoption of sorts involving Noah Schwartz and Sadie Stutzman."

"And now both of them are dead. Any idea who?"

I shrug. "A relative. Biological parent or parents."

We watch a white Suburban with Scioto County Coroner emblazoned on the doors pull into the driveway.

"Maybe I ought to take another look at the hit-and-run that killed Noah Schwartz," he says after a moment.

"I'd appreciate it if you did." I watch the technician open the rear door of the Suburban and roll a gurney out of the back. "I thought I might talk to the new bishop before I head back to Painters Mill. See if he can shed some light on any of this."

He nods, interested now. "I'll do what I can to send you on your way, but someone in our investigations division is going to want to talk to you; they're going to want a statement." He motions toward my sidearm. "They're going to need your weapon, too."

I don't relish the idea of being without my .38 for the remainder of the trip, but I don't argue. "That's fine."

"Hang tight, Chief Burkholder, and I'll get things rolling."

Bishop Melvin Chupp lives on a dirt track off of Hansgen Morgan Road near Wheelersburg. It's pretty land with a brick farmhouse and two red barns in the back. The woman who answers the door tells me I'll find her husband in the barn. She hands me a plate heaped with oatmeal cookies to take to him.

Carting the plate, I take a stone path to the barn. The big sliding door stands open, so I take the ramp and go inside.

"Hello?" I call out. "Bishop Chupp?"

"Who wants to know?" comes a whispered voice.

"Chief of Police Kate Burkholder."

"I like the sound of that name. Come on back."

I start toward the sound of the voice and find the bishop in the first stall. He glances at me and puts his finger to his lips. "Shhh."

I look past him to see a goat in the throes of kidding. For an instant, I'm living in the moment, enthralled, watching three tiny creatures enter the world. As the doe begins to lick her offspring, I find myself thinking of the bond between a mother and her offspring. I think about the woman who gave birth to Elsie Helmuth, and I wonder: How far would a parent go to get their child back? I look at the bishop and motion toward the aisle outside the stall. *"Kann ich shvetza zu du e weil?"* I ask. Can I talk to you awhile? *"Kannscht du Deitsch schwetze."* You can talk Dutch. The Amish man grins. "That's two miracles in one day," he exclaims. "First triplet goats, and then an *Englischer* speaking *Deitsch!"*

Breaking into laughter, he follows me from the stall. Once we're in the aisle, I hand him the cookies. "From your wife."

Smiling down at the plate, he selects the biggest one.

Noticing the bruises on my face, he proffers the plate. "You look like you could use a little kindness."

I take a cookie. I don't know this man, but I find myself liking him. He's got gentle eyes filled with jollity and intelligence.

"I'm working on a case, Bishop, and I need your help," I say, and tell him about Mary Yoder and Elsie Helmuth. "I think Bishop Schwartz may have been involved in . . . an unofficial adoption of a newborn infant seven years ago."

His expression sobers. "Unofficial adoption?"

"I have reason to believe a baby born here in Scioto County was taken from her mother and transported to Painters Mill to be placed with another Amish family. Bishop Schwartz and a midwife, Sadie Stutzman, were involved." I pause. "As you know, Bishop Schwartz was killed a couple of weeks ago. Sadie Stutzman was murdered sometime this morning."

"Sadie? *Mein Gott."* The Amish man steps back, presses his hand to his chest.

I watch him carefully, gauging his responses. The only emotions that come back at me are shock and grief.

"I believe someone living in this area knows what happened seven years ago," I tell him. "I believe that person traveled to Painters Mill, murdered the girl's grandmother, and took the child. I think this individual may be a family member or parent. That little girl is in grave danger."

The bishop lowers the cookie he'd been nibbling and sets the plate on a bale of hay next to him. "I will pray for her safe return."

"Does the name Marlene Byler mean anything to you?" I ask.

He sags, as if the memory is a physical weight. "Her story is a terrible one." He raises his gaze to mine. "Do you think what happened to Marlene has something to do with this missing child?"

I tell him what little I know. "She was Mary Yoder's sister."

The bishop sighs. "I didn't know Marlene, but I heard stories. She was . . . disturbed." He taps his temple. "Here. She thought she was possessed by the devil. *Narrisch*, you know." Insane. "There were all sorts of rumors."

"What kind of rumors?"

"About men. English, Amish. She wasn't living a godly life."

"Does she have any children?"

"Rumor had it when she jumped from that bridge, she took her last child with her."

It's a tragic, haunting tale.

"Do you know if Bishop Schwartz kept any writings?" I ask.

He shakes his head. "I've not seen such a thing. You've checked with Lizzie?"

I tell him as much as I can without revealing anything she wouldn't want disclosed.

The smile that follows is so filled with grief that I feel the weight of it in my own heart. "There's a saying among the Amish. *Wu schmoke is, is aa feier.*" Where there is smoke, there is fire. "I will ask around. If I find something, I will let you know."

Chapter 8

Seventy-four hours missing

IT WAS NIGHTS LIKE THIS that tested a man's faith. Bishop David Troyer didn't know how it had come to this.

He left the Helmuth farm ten minutes ago. Miriam and Ivan had spent most of the day praying for the safe return of their daughter. The bishop thought maybe they should pray for forgiveness, too—all of them—but he didn't say it.

This evening, Bishop Troyer was questioning the decision he'd made seven years ago regarding the fate of an infant at risk. Had he done the right thing? He had no answers.

Clucking to the horse, he sent the gelding into a trot. At the intersection of County Road 150 and Township Road 104, he made the turn toward home and headed north.

He was thinking about the notes when pain exploded in his side. The breath left his lungs, and he slumped forward. One of the reins slipped from his hands. Then he was falling. The cold grit of dirt and wood against his face. Blood on his hands, running like rain.

The buggy stopped. He couldn't move. Wasn't sure what had happened. Footsteps sounded on the asphalt. The bishop opened his eyes. Relief washed over him when he saw the Plain man. He tried to speak, but he managed little more than a gurgle.

The man came to him. "If thou do that which is evil, be afraid; for he beareth not the sword in vain," the man said in Deitsch.

Only then did the bishop realize the man wasn't there to help. Words flared in his brain. He had to stop this terrible thing he had helped put into play. "Forgive them," he said. "For they know not what they do."

"Avvah shpoht," came the voice. Too late.

The bishop tumbled into the waiting darkness.

Seventy-five hours missing

I'M EASTBOUND on U.S. 62 west of Killbuck when my Bluetooth jangles. Glock's name pops up on the screen, so I hit ANSWER.

"Chief, I'm out at David Troyer's place. He's been shot. Wife found him twenty minutes ago. It's bad."

"Shot?" I repeat dumbly. "Bishop Troyer?"

"He's alive. Ambulance just left for the hospital. I'm at their farm, trying to figure out what happened. Tomasetti's on the way."

"My God." Bishop Troyer has been a constant in my life—for better or worse—for as long as I can remember. "I'm ten minutes out." I hit my emergency lights, crank the speedometer to eighty.

I arrive at the Troyer farm to an ocean of emergency vehicles.

As I barrel up the lane, I see an Ohio State Highway Patrol Dodge Charger. Tomasetti's Tahoe is parked behind a buggy to which a horse is hitched. There's an ambulance and a fire truck. Glock's cruiser is parked a few yards away. Half a dozen cops mill about.

I park behind the Tahoe and throw open my door. I spot Glock standing next to Sheriff Mike Rasmussen. Both men give my bruised face a double take as I stride toward them.

"Chief?" Glock says, looking concerned.

"What happened to Troyer?" I ask, making an effort to yank back my emotions.

"All we know is that he was shot," Rasmussen tells me. He motions toward the buggy a few feet away. "Wife said he was over at the Helmuths'. He was late getting home. She walked out here and found him in the buggy, unconscious. It looks like he was shot elsewhere and the horse brought him home."

"His wife ran to the neighbors and called nine-one-one," Glock adds.

Beyond him, I see Tomasetti; he's talking to a trooper, but he's caught sight of me. Abruptly he ends his conversation and heads my way. "Chief Burkholder."

I start toward the buggy. I'm midway there when he sets his hand on my shoulder and turns me around. Concern sharpens his features, tightens his mouth. "What happened to your face?"

"I got jumped," I say. "I'm fine."

"Kate . . ."

"I can't talk right now."

"You need to see this," he snaps.

I waver, turn to him. He reaches into his coat pocket and pulls out a clear plastic bag. The ground dips beneath my feet when I recognize the eyeglasses inside. They're small and round with thick lenses. Lenses that are cracked and covered with blood.

"They're Elsie's," I manage. "Where did you find them?"

"Buggy. On the seat." He shakes his head. "We don't know if Troyer had them for some reason or if the shooter left them."

"He left them for us to find," I say. "The son of a bitch."

"I'm going to rush them to the lab. Have the blood analyzed."

"Dear God, if he hurt that child," I hear myself say.

He grimaces. "I'll have Ivan confirm they belong to the girl."

It's not going to be easy. I want to be there, I realize. But I can't leave. "I need to talk to the bishop's wife."

"Go," he says. "I'll take care of this."

I start toward the buggy. I'm ten feet away when I spot the pool of blood on the gravel. There's more inside the buggy.

I look over my shoulder toward the men. Glock and Rasmussen have followed me over. "Where did this happen?" I ask.

"We're trying to figure it out," Rasmussen says. "We've got a trail of blood. Deputies are tracing it now."

"Where's his wife?" I ask.

"Inside," Rasmussen says. "I talked to her. She didn't see anything."

"I want a go at her."

His eyes narrow. "You think she's not being forthcoming?"

I lay out my theory. As implausible as it seems, I know I'm right. "I think Bishop Troyer was involved with this . . . adoption."

"If there was a newborn stolen, why wasn't it reported to the authorities?" he asks, incredulity thick in his voice.

"Because they wanted to handle it on their own. Because they didn't want to involve Children Services. They knew someone would try to stop them. All of the above."

I turn away from him and start toward the house.

"Where are you going?" he asks.

"I'm going to talk to Freda Troyer."

"She's already been interviewed, Kate. That poor woman is trying to get to the hospital to be with her husband."

"I'll take her," I say. "You need to trust me on this, Mike. Freda Troyer knows more than she's letting on."

I WALK into the Troyer home to find Freda pacing the kitchen. She's wearing a charcoal-colored dress, a black cardigan, practical shoes. She's put a black winter bonnet over her prayer *kapp*.

"Freda?" I say as I enter.

She startles and turns to me. "Kate." I see anguish in her face. Dried blood on hands she didn't think to wash. "How is he?"

"I don't know. Ambulance took him to the hospital." I approach her. "Get your things. I'll take you."

While Freda gathers her things—a canvas bag filled with what looks like knitting supplies, a devotional book—I radio Glock and tell him that I'll be driving the bishop's wife to the hospital.

"You guys figure out where the shooting took place?" I ask him.

"Deputy followed the blood trail," he tells me. "Looks like it was where County Road 150 intersects with Township Road 104."

It's a rural area, not many houses. "Anyone see anything?"

"We're canvassing now."

"I'll be there as soon as I can."

I drop the cell into my pocket, turn to see the bishop's wife standing in the doorway, clutching her bag. "Let's go," I say.

She follows me outside, and we make our way to the Explorer. I open the passenger door for her, and then I round the front of the vehicle and get in. We start down the lane.

I only have a few minutes to ask questions. I have no idea what we'll find when we arrive at Pomerene Hospital.

"I know Bishop Schwartz from Scioto County brought a newborn baby to Bishop Troyer seven years ago," I say. "I know the baby was taken to Miriam and Ivan Helmuth."

She looks over at me, anguish churning in her eyes. "I don't know what that has to do with what's happened to my husband."

"It has everything to do with it, Freda." I tell her about the eyeglasses, my trip to Crooked Creek. "Look at my face. I was ambushed and beaten. Bishop Schwartz is dead. The midwife who helped bring that child up here was murdered. Your husband was shot. If you care about that little girl, you need to start talking."

The Amish woman doesn't make a sound.

I hit her with the coup de grâce. "If Elsie Helmuth is killed, it's on your shoulders, Freda. You got that?"

Silence reigns for the span of several minutes. Neither of us speaks until I'm stopped at a traffic light in Millersburg.

"You have to understand," she says in a strangled voice. "Being the bishop's wife . . . I see things. I hear things. That doesn't mean I'm told what's going on."

"Tell me what you know."

"I was there the night they brought her," she whispers. "David told me I was to never speak of it. I took those words to heart."

"Who brought her?"

"Bishop Schwartz and a midwife. They brought her here to the house. A tiny little girl. Hours old. She was desperately hungry. I fed her, held her in my arms . . ."

"Do you know who the parents are?" I ask.

"No." She shakes her head. "They did not say, and I did not ask. It was a night filled with worry and tears and things left unsaid."

"Why did they do it?"

"There is a saying. *Die besht vayk zu flucht eevil is zu verfolgen goot,*" she whispers. The best way to escape evil is to pursue good. "The bishop, my husband, and that midwife were pursuing good. All they wanted was to place that innocent baby in a loving home, where she would be safe, and so she would be raised Amish."

"The baby came from an Amish family?"

She shrugs. "I assumed so."

"Freda, why did they take her?"

"I don't know, Katie." The woman shrugs. "I suspected there was something wrong in the home. Something bad, or they never would have done what they did."

"Was the baby brought here with the blessing of the family?"

"I do not know."

Everything she's told me I already knew or suspected. What I need more than anything is a name. That's when it occurs to me that Crooked Creek is four hours away by car. There's no way they would have transported a baby in a buggy.

"Freda, did they use a driver?"

She nods. "They came in a van."

"Did you see the driver?"

"No. He stayed outside."

As I turn into the hospital parking lot, the Amish woman tosses me a look. "You believe the parents or some relative of the baby is responsible for the bad things that have been done?"

"I do."

She thinks about that a moment. "I'm glad I told you, Katie. It was the right thing to do. God willing, David will give you the name you need when we talk to him."

ACCORDING to the emergency room physician, Bishop Troyer was rushed to surgery upon arrival. He sustained a single gunshot wound to his abdomen; it's a life-threatening injury. All the doctor can tell us is that the bishop is in extremely critical condition.

I walk with Freda to the surgical intensive care waiting area.

"I can't stay," I tell her. "I have to get back out there and try to find the person responsible."

She nods. "Thank you for bringing me to be with my husband."

She may be alone at the moment, but word of the shooting will spread through the Amish community like wildfire. I know that even as we speak, half a dozen buggies are already en route.

"Freda, is there anything else you can tell me that might help me find the person who did this?"

She shakes her head. "I've told you everything I know."

I walk away, leaving her with her anguish.

I ARRIVE at the intersection of County Road 150 and Township Road 104 to find Glock's cruiser blocking traffic, his lights flashing. He's set out flares, but he's nowhere in sight. A quarter mile ahead, a Holmes County cruiser is parked in the same fashion.

I call Skid. Last I heard, he'd gone home to get some sleep. I'm loath to call him back to work, but I can't spare him.

He answers with a groggy, "Yeah."

"Sorry to wake you."

"I wasn't asleep." We laugh because we both know it's not true.

I tell him about Bishop Troyer.

"Damn, Chief, the *bishop?* Is he—"

"He's alive, but critical. The problem is I don't know if the son of a bitch who shot him is finished. I need you to go out to the Helmuth place and keep an eye on things. Wear your vest."

A thoughtful silence, and then, "You got it."

I end the call, and I'm reminded that I'll need to pick up another sidearm when I get back to the station. Around me, the area is heavily treed, except to the south where yellow cornstalks shiver in a brisk wind. The temperature is falling fast.

Hitting my emergency lights, I park behind Glock's cruiser, grab my Maglite, and go in search of him. I spot the cone of a flashlight just inside the tree line and start that way.

I call out to him. "Find anything?"

Glock motions toward the road, where there's a smattering of tiny orange cones. "Got blood on the road, Chief. Starts where I'm parked. I'm pretty sure this is where the shooting took place."

"Brass?"

"Nada. County arrived a few minutes ago. Pickles and T.J. started a canvass."

We both know with the neighboring houses separated by miles of fields, the chances of finding a witness are slim.

We reach the cones. Glock shifts his Maglite. The yellow beam reveals the red-black gleam of blood on the asphalt; additional spatters stand out against the yellow line. We study the blood, trying to figure out exactly where the shooting took place.

"According to his wife," I say, "the bishop was on his way home from the Helmuth place." I set my beam on the ground, find a spot of blood that's been run over by a buggy wheel.

Glock drops a cone next to it.

"He would have been traveling north," I tell him.

"That helps." Glock motions to the woods where the trees are thick. "If I wanted to ambush someone and I thought they might be coming this way, I'd take cover in those trees over there."

I follow his gaze to the place where I'd found him when I arrived. "He would have had decent cover."

"And a clean shot," he adds.

We traverse the ditch and reenter the woods. The underbrush is thick, making it difficult to maneuver. We reach a clearing and split up, moving slowly, our beams sweeping left and right.

I step over a rotting log, veer left toward the road. I've gone about twenty yards when a speck on the ground snags my attention. A tiny white scrap of what looks like tissue paper or fabric is nestled beneath a bush. I kneel for a closer look, and my heart begins to pound. The piece of paper is about the size of a dime. It's actually gray in color. Darker and tattered around the edges. Burned, I realize. I've seen these scraps of paper before. My *datt* was an avid hunter. His rifle of choice was a muzzleloader.

I hit my shoulder mike. "Glock, I got something."

"On my way."

I stand, shine my beam in a circle. I find a freshly broken branch on a sapling. A tuft of grass that's been crushed beneath a shoe. Six feet away, there's the faint shoe imprint with a waffled sole.

Brush rustles as Glock approaches. "Brass?"

"Partial shoe imprint." I shift my beam to the scrap of paper.

"What the hell is that?" he asks. "Wrapper of some sort?"

"Wadding from a muzzleloader," I tell him.

He laughs. "Damn good find, Chief."

We kneel for a closer look. "My dad had a muzzleloader," I tell him. "I saw plenty of those little scraps of paper when I was a kid."

"So our shooter is probably Amish. I wonder if there's any way we can use that wadding to ID the weapon," he says.

"Firearms guy at BCI might know."

He pulls an orange cone from his coat and sets it on the ground next to the scrap of paper. "Hopefully, it'll help us stop this guy."

IT'S ten p.m., and the Painters Mill PD bustles with activity. Everyone except Skid and my off-duty dispatcher is here, including Tomasetti, Sheriff Mike Rasmussen, and an Ohio State Highway Patrol trooper. The task force is meeting, and I'm five minutes late, so I snag my legal pad off my desk and head that way.

I enter the war room to find Tomasetti standing at the head of the table. He nods at me when I enter.

"The technician was able to lift a plaster of the shoe imprint out at the intersection where we believe the shooting took place," he says. "Preliminarily, we got a men's size thirteen. Tread matches the plaster taken at the scene of the Yoder murder and the abduction of the Helmuth girl. I think it's safe to assume we are dealing with the same individual. We believe he is a white male. He may be Amish or presenting himself

as an Amish person. Judging from the shoe size, well over six feet tall."
He flips a page. "We did not get DNA from the killer at the
Schattenbaum farm. Both sets belong to Yoder and the Helmuth
girl. The tire tread was identified, as most of you know. We believe
this person drives or has access to a pickup truck or SUV."
He looks at me. "Chief Burkholder, you want to talk about that
wadding you found at the scene of the Troyer shooting?"
I speak from my place at the door. "We believe David Troyer
was traveling north on Township Road 104 when he was shot. The
wadding was in the woods east of the road, ten yards in. That's
where we think the shooter stood. The wadding is consistent with
a muzzleloader or black-powder-type rifle. For those of you not familiar with that kind of weapon, they do not use regular cartridges.
According to the surgeon who removed the projectile from Troyer,
the projectile was a lead ball, which is commonly used and has been
sent to the BCI lab. What's significant about the muzzleloader is
that the Amish use that type of rifle for hunting."
"Makes sense in light of the victim and abducted girl being
Amish," Sheriff Rasmussen puts in.
"Unless he wants us to *believe* he's Amish," Tomasetti adds.
I nod in agreement and continue, summarizing my theory
about the illicit adoption of an infant seven years ago and hitting
the highlights of my trip to Crooked Creek. "The two people
from Crooked Creek who I believe were involved, Bishop Noah
Schwartz and the midwife, Sadie Stutzman, are both dead."
A barely discernible stir goes around the room.
I relay the details of my being ambushed and follow up with a
physical description of my attacker. "Male. Six three. Two twenty.
Dark hair. Beard." I look at my audience. "I don't believe the timing of any of this was coincidental."
"You believe the bishop and midwife were targeted because of
what they knew?" the trooper asks.
"Or because of what they did," I reply. "I think the hit-and-
run that killed the bishop in Crooked Creek and the murder of
Stutzman are directly related to the crimes here in Painters Mill
and were perpetrated by the same individual."

"Why would an Amish bishop—*two* Amish bishops—and a midwife take a baby?" Rasmussen asks.

"No one I've talked to has been able to give me an answer," I tell him. "What they have told me is that the people involved must have believed they had a good reason. If they were concerned about the safety of the baby, for example. Or if, for whatever reason, the mother was unable to care for a newborn."

"What about the timing of all this?" Glock asks. "Seven years is a long time."

"We don't know," I say.

"So the murders are likely revenge-motivated," Tomasetti says.

"Probably." I nod. "As for the abduction of the girl, I believe we have to operate under the assumption that they wanted her back."

"Is there a possibility Mary Yoder was part of it seven years ago?" Tomasetti asks.

"According to Miriam Helmuth, her mother knew about it. I don't believe she was a major player."

"What about Ivan Helmuth?" Tomasetti asks.

"We've gone easy on the parents due to the circumstances," Rasmussen says. "Maybe it's time we stepped it up."

Tomasetti nods in agreement. "We can pick up Ivan first thing in the morning, bring him in for formal questioning."

"I'll take care of it," Rasmussen says.

I close my notebook and look out over the group. "We're hoping that as David Troyer recovers, he'll be able to give us a name. As it stands now, he's in critical condition and on a respirator."

I nod at Tomasetti to let him know he has the floor.

He stands. "I spoke with Sheriff Dan Pallant down in Scioto County earlier. He's on board with the task force and taking a second look at the hit-skip that killed Noah Schwartz as well as the murder of Stutzman." He gives me his deadpan expression. "Chief Burkholder and I are going to head that way in the morning."

"Do you think the Helmuth girl is being held in Scioto County?" Rasmussen asks.

"We don't know," Tomasetti says. "But in light of everything we now know, I think there's a possibility we'll find some answers there."

"Keep me updated," Rasmussen says.

"Bet on it," Tomasetti replies, and the meeting is adjourned.

Chapter 9

Seventy-nine hours missing

MIRIAM HELMUTH SAT AT *the kitchen table by the light of the lantern and sobbed. When she had no tears left, she prayed.*

Please return her to me, O Lord God.

It was the first time she'd been alone all day. The police had left half an hour ago. The children were finally sleeping. Ivan, unable to bear the waiting, had saddled the plow horse for the second time that day. He'd been gone for hours.

For the thousandth time, she wondered about her sweet Elsie. Was she warm and dry? Had she been fed? Was she afraid?

She couldn't help but wonder if she was being punished for what they'd done all those years ago. If this was God's way of telling her they'd taken the wrong path.

"Please forgive me my sin, Father, for I didn't know—"

The shattering of glass followed by an odd thwack! *tore her from her prayer. Miriam got to her feet, her heart beating hard.*

"Ivan?" she called out.

She strode to the mudroom, but her husband wasn't there.

Where had the odd sound come from? What had broken?

Miriam went back to the kitchen and looked around. The sight of the hole in the refrigerator froze her in place. Her datt *had been a hunter; she recognized a bullet hole when she saw it.*

Frightened, she ran to the living room. The curtains were open, darkness peering in. A hole the size of her thumb marred the glass. And she knew he'd finally come for them.

Spurred by panic, Miriam bolted up the stairs, tore down the hall, threw open the first door, and dashed to the beds. Bonnie and Irma slept soundly, snoring softly.

"Miriam?"

Gasping, she spun, saw her husband silhouetted against the door. She rushed to him, went through the door, closed it behind her. "Someone shot through the window," she said.

"What?" His face paled. "The children—"

Not waiting for him to finish, Miriam hurried to the next room. Her legs went weak with relief when she found her two sons sleeping.

Ivan met her in the hall, his eyes frightened and large. "The girls are fine," he said. "Sleeping."

"It's him," she whispered. "He's come for us."

Ivan stared at her. He knew, just as she did.

"Lock the doors and windows." He started toward the stairs.

Miriam choked out a sob, set her hand over her mouth. "Go to the phone," she whispered. "Call Chief Burkholder."

I'M ON my way home for a shower and a few hours of sleep when the call comes in. Uneasiness ripples through me when I recognize the number of the prepaid cell I left with the Helmuths.

"Chief Burkholder!" Ivan says with a breathless cadence to his voice. "Someone shot into the house. We need you to come."

"Is anyone hurt?" I ask.

"No, but we're afraid. The children!"

"I'm on my way. Stay inside. Stay away from the windows."

I make a U-turn and call Skid. "I got shots fired at the Helmuth place."

"Holy crap, I'm there. Goat Head Road. Didn't see a thing."

"I'm ten-seven-six," I say, letting him know I'm en route. "Drive the block. I'll meet you."

"Roger that."

I pick up my radio. "I've got a ten-forty-three-A," I say, the code for "shots fired." I recite the address. "Ten-seven-six. Expedite."

It takes me three minutes to reach the Helmuth farm. Ivan stands on the porch, a lantern in front of him.

"Get inside," I say as I take the steps two at a time to the porch.

He leads me into the kitchen. Lantern light reveals terror on their faces. I spot the hole in the refrigerator door.

"How long ago did this happen?" I ask.

"Less than five minutes. There's a hole in the front window." Miriam is already striding that way.

Ivan and I follow. The window covering is open about a foot. Sure enough, a bullet hole stares back at me. I check the angle, realize it could have come from someone sitting in a vehicle on the road in front of the house. Or the woods across the road.

"Where were you when this happened?" I ask.

"Kitchen table," Miriam replies.

"I was walking in from the barn," Ivan says.

"Were the curtains open?"

"Yes," Miriam tells me.

The shooter likely saw her, but she couldn't see him.

"Stay away from the windows. Do not go outside until I give you the go-ahead. Do not turn on any more lanterns. I'll be back."

I go out the back door, slide into the Explorer, and pick up my radio mike. "Skid, what's your twenty?"

"Township Road 14. Went around the block. I got nothing."

"Someone shot through the front window. Drive to the back of the property. You see anyone, make the stop. I got the front."

"Roger that."

I zip down the lane, too fast, and head east on the county road. The woods across the road are an ocean of impenetrable blackness. I stop in front of the Helmuth farmhouse, which puts me a hundred yards away, and I get out. The night is dead quiet. The only sounds come from the wind through the trees. All the while I'm keenly aware that there's likely someone nearby with a rifle.

My replacement .38 presses reassuringly against my hip as I look toward the house and the window through which the bullet passed. I think about the angle to the kitchen. If the projectile went into the refrigerator, the shooter likely stood exactly where I'm standing now or else just beyond in the woods.

I scan the darkened forest on the other side of the fence. The vague outline of the Schattenbaum farm down the road. I speak into my lapel mike. "County?"

"I'm ten-sixty," comes a male voice—the sheriff's deputy, meaning he's in the vicinity.

"Can you ten-eight-five?" I say, asking him to look for an abandoned vehicle.

"Copy that."

Tugging out my Maglite, I shine the beam on the gravel shoulder, looking for tire tracks, footprints, or spent casings, but there's nothing. I cross the road, check the other side, but the gravel is undisturbed. Turning off my Maglite, I cross through the ditch and climb the tumbling-down wire fence. Chances are, the shooter made the shot and fled in a vehicle.

Then it occurs to me he could have parked on the county road south of here and walked through these woods unseen. After taking the shot, he could have run back through the woods and reached his vehicle in two minutes.

Darkness closes around me when I enter the woods. Fifty feet in, I stop. I can just make out the silhouette of the Helmuth farmhouse behind me. It would take a good marksman to make the shot from this distance, but it could be done.

I'm reaching for my shoulder mike to hail Skid when something rustles in the leaves. I freeze, squint into the darkness. Twenty yards ahead, I can just make out the silhouette of a man. He's stone still, looking at me. For a second, we stare at each other.

"Police! Get your hands up!" Sliding my .38 from its holster, I start toward him. "Do not move! Get your hands up now!"

The man spins and runs.

I hit my lapel mike, give the code for suspicious person. "Ten-seven-eight." Need assistance.

"Stop! Halt! Police!" I sprint after him while I shout into my lapel mike. "Ten-eighty! Subject is on foot! Southbound, approaching County Road 79. Male. Dark coat."

I'm no slouch when it comes to running, but the man is faster and putting space between us at an astounding rate. Branches whip my face. I fling myself over a fallen log, splash through a shallow creek.

I'm thirty yards from the road when I see the flash of a dome light.

"Police!" I scream. "Stop!"

An engine roars. I hear the screech of tires. I see the glint of a vehicle through the trees. Moving fast.

I hit my shoulder mike. "Subject is in a vehicle," I say, breaths puffing. "Eastbound. No headlights."

My police radio lights up with a dozen voices. The sheriff's department. Ohio State Highway Patrol. My own department. Still, Holmes County is a labyrinth of highways, back roads, and woods.

I burst onto the road, my breaths labored; I see the red flash of taillights to my left. Then the vehicle disappears into the night.

Eighty-seven hours missing

I DIDN'T get much sleep last night. I spent most of it with the Helmuths and on the roads surrounding the farm. The sheriff's department searched for the shooter and collected what little evidence they could find, which boiled down to a single tire-tread mark that may or may not have been from the perpetrator's vehicle. There was no brass. No sign anyone had been in the woods with a rifle at all.

This morning, Tomasetti and I are on our way to Crooked Creek. We've spent most of the drive talking about the case.

Our first stop is the Scioto County Sheriff's Department. It's nine a.m. when Sheriff Dan Pallant ushers us into the same interview room where I met with the deputy two days ago.

Pallant is a middle-aged African American man with a quick smile and a booming voice. He's cordial, but once the niceties are out of the way, he's ready to get down to business.

"I pulled some files after speaking with you last night, Agent Tomasetti." He sets a stack of folders on the table, opens the one on top. "The hit-and-run that killed Noah Schwartz. We originally wrote it up as a hit-skip, possibly involving an intoxicated driver. I went through the file, and there's nothing to indicate otherwise. No skid marks, no tire-tread imprints. Only interesting thing I ran across was a homeowner who claimed to see a light-colored pickup truck in the vicinity a few minutes before it happened."

Tomasetti says, "Pickup truck fits with the type of vehicle that left the tire-tread imprint we took at the Schattenbaum place."

"Dick Howard on Goat Head Road says he saw a light-colored pickup truck—white or tan—in the area around the time Mary Yoder was murdered and the girl taken," I say.

"I'll get the ROs of all vehicles matching that description, starting in Scioto County, expand from there, and see if anything pops," Tomasetti says.

The sheriff rattles off the contiguous counties. "Adams. Pike. Lawrence. Jackson. Might check Greenup in Kentucky, too."

Tomasetti thumbs the information into his phone.

"I had my night clerk make you guys copies of everything." Pallant shoves a green folder across the table to us.

"Anything new on the Stutzman case?" I ask.

"We don't have much." Pallant slides a second folder toward us, then opens the official file in front of him. "Initially, we investigated the incident as a probable home invasion–robbery. Some scumbag looking for money or drugs or guns. There were no signs of forced entry. That means either Sadie left the door unlocked or she knew him." He flips the page. "There were signs of a struggle, but some of that occurred when Chief Burkholder was attacked later. Overall, the place wasn't too torn up."

"Prints?" I ask.

"Just yours." The sheriff leans back in his chair. "I appreciate your sending the BCI crime scene unit," he says to Tomasetti. "It was a big help. Your guy photographed and videotaped everything. Dusted for prints. Tried to get plaster on the tire treads, but snow melted too fast. He did, however, get a shoe imprint."

"Men's size thirteen?" I ask.

The sheriff's eyes narrow on mine. "Yes, ma'am."

"You guys have anyone in mind?" Tomasetti asks.

Pallant shakes his head. He taps the folder with his index finger. "That's everything we got on Stutzman."

I page through the folder. "The house was searched?" I ask.

"I had a couple of deputies look around. The woman was somewhat of a hoarder. The place was so messy, we couldn't tell if it had been ransacked. Our search was inconclusive."

"So you were unable to tell if anything had been taken?" I ask.

The sheriff nods. Leaning forward, he goes to the final two folders, slides one across to me and opens the original. "That brings us to Marlene Byler. Had to dig into the archives for this one."

I open the file to find bad copies from what looks like microfiche—police reports, an autopsy report, witness statements.

The sheriff squints at the paper through his bifocals. "Twenty-nine years ago, twenty-nine-year-old Marlene Byler jumped from Sciotoville Bridge. Death was ruled a suicide. Cause of death, drowning. Witness said she had a baby with her. Sheriff's department searched the river, but the infant's body was never found."

He looks from Tomasetti to me. "Do you think that case has something to do with what happened up there in Painters Mill?"

"Marlene is the sister of the woman who was murdered," I say.

"A lot of tragedy for one family," he says.

We fall silent. Everything that's been said, the information that's been passed along to us running through my head. I find myself thinking about Sadie Stutzman.

"Sheriff Pallant, would it be possible for us to go back to the Stutzman home and take a look around?" I ask.

"You mind telling me what you're looking for exactly?"

I give him the rundown of Sadie Stutzman's involvement in the Elsie Helmuth case. "We're hoping she kept something—letters or a diary—that might help us fill in the blanks."

"A lot of damn blanks." He jots a set of numbers onto a sticky note and passes it to me. "Deputy put a combination lock on the back door to keep out the thieves. Let me know if you find anything pertinent to either case."

"You got it," Tomasetti tells him.

THE sun plays hide-and-seek behind cumulus clouds when we pull into the driveway of the house where Sadie Stutzman lived. Already the place looks abandoned, sitting by the river.

We get out of the Explorer and make our way to the back porch. Bending, Tomasetti works at the combination lock. I think about the old woman, hearing her voice, her words.

I knew something wasn't right. Everyone did. Kept their mouths shut like good Amish. Sin piled atop of sin.

The lock snicks open, and we go inside.

The kitchen looks much the same as the last time I was here. Cluttered. Slightly dirty. Several of the drawers stand open. Muddy shoe prints mottle the floor. Dozens of people have been in the house since Sadie was killed. Deputies. Crime scene technicians. The coroner.

I go to the living room and look around. It's too dark to see much. I open the drapes, and crepuscular light pours in.

I hear Tomasetti moving around in the kitchen, opening and closing cabinets and drawers. "There's a little pantry to your right," I call out to him. "I'll take the bedrooms."

The house has already been searched by Scioto County deputies as well as BCI. Even so, they probably weren't looking for the sort of thing that I'm interested in. Most Amish correspond with letters. Any kind of writing. A diary. If we're lucky, she kept some kind of record of the babies she'd delivered over the years.

I go to the first bedroom. There's a twin-size bed covered with a ratty blanket. A closet. A desk with a single lantern. I check under the bed, beneath the mattress, but there's nothing there.

I move on to the next room. I know immediately this is where Sadie slept. There's a full-size bed with an iron headboard. A night table contains a lantern and a book titled *Prayers for Difficult Times*. Across the room, a narrow chest is piled high with newspapers.

I kneel next to the nightstand. I open the top drawer, find a tube of lip balm. The next drawer is filled with books and newspapers, all Amish publications. I page through the newspapers, checking the dates, which go back to last summer. I find nothing of interest.

"Come on, Sadie," I whisper.

The final drawer contains a manila folder. I flip it open. Dozens of newspaper clippings stare back at me. Obituaries. Births. Accidents. Church happenings. I'm about to close the drawer when I spot the brown envelope in the back. I reach for it. My heart stutters when I see the familiar white notebook papers inside.

"Good girl," I whisper.

I pull out two notes and carefully unfold them.

It is mine to avenge; I will repay. In due time their foot will slip; their day of disaster is near and their doom rushes upon them.

I go to the second note.

If a thief is caught breaking in at night and is struck a fatal blow, the defender is not guilty of bloodshed . . .

Though I still don't have a name or a suspect, for the first time, I can definitively tie the murder and abduction in Painters Mill to at least one murder in Crooked Creek.

Ninety-one hours missing

AFTER leaving the Stutzman place—the manila folder and a boatload of newspapers in hand—we head toward Wheelersburg. As we drive, I tell Tomasetti about my conversation with Freda Troyer. "The night they brought the baby to Painters Mill, they used a driver. Freda remembers seeing a van in her driveway."

"Does she have a name to go along with the van?"

"She didn't see the driver, but some of the Amish drivers, fondly referred to as 'Yoder Toters,' are hired out on a regular basis and are well known by the Amish community. The bishop is usually well-connected. I'm betting we can get a name."

"You thinking this driver overheard something?"

"Or he might be able to give us a name we don't already have."

We park in the same spot as last time I was here. I notice the barn door standing open, so we head that way. We find Bishop Chupp mucking stalls.

"You're back," he says by way of greeting, and his eyes slide to Tomasetti. "With a friend."

Tomasetti introduces himself and extends his hand.

"Any luck finding that missing girl?" the bishop asks.

I shake my head. "Did you have a chance to ask around to see if anyone is aware of what may have happened with the newborn seven years ago?"

The bishop sets the pitchfork on the ground. "I spoke with several reliable people. No one knows of an infant."

I block my disappointment and move on to my next question. "I think Bishop Schwartz and Sadie Stutzman may have hired a driver the night they traveled to Painters Mill. Do you know of someone who was driving for the Amish about that time?"

The bishop's eyes widen. "Elmer Moyer has been driving the Amish around for as long as I can remember. He's a nice fellow. A Mennonite. I've hired him a few times myself." Chupp looks from me to Tomasetti and back at me, his expression grave. "Chief Burkholder, I heard just last week that Elmer Moyer left town."

My heart does a weird patter against my ribs. "Do you know where he went or why he left?"

He shakes his head. "Word around town is that Elmer had some debt. A tab at the feed store. A bunch of credit cards. It was common knowledge he was having money problems."

"How long ago did he leave?" I ask.

"Recently." He shrugs. "A couple of weeks maybe."

"Do you have any idea how to get in touch with him?"

The bishop shakes his head. "Cell phone is disconnected. Several people I know have tried to contact him when they needed a ride. Elmer hasn't returned a single call."

"Sounds like he doesn't want to be found." Tomasetti thumbs something into his cell phone. "Let me see if he's in the system."

"Does Moyer have family in the area?" I ask the bishop.

"I don't believe so. He courted the waitress down at the diner for a while. Patty Lou. She still works there. Little place on Buckeye Street downtown called Foley's."

"When's the last time you saw him?" I ask.

"He drove me to Cincinnati for a doctor's appointment a couple of months ago." The bishop's eyebrows furrow. "Didn't know that would be the last time I saw him."

When we're back in the Explorer, Tomasetti says, "Moyer is not a missing person. He's not in any of the databases. No warrants."

"Record?"

"One conviction on misdemeanor drug charges two years ago. Paid a fine. No time served. Speeding ticket last summer."

"So he's not Scarface," I say. "I guess the question now is: Did he leave of his own accord? Or did someone do away with him?"

"Or is he somehow involved in the abduction?"

I think about that a moment. "Moyer used to date the waitress down at the diner. You hungry?"

"Starved."

FOLEY'S is more bar than diner and has Hard Times written all over its redbrick facade. I park the Explorer, and we head inside.

The interior is a dimly lit, narrow space with booths to the right and, on the left, an ornate bar. Two men in coveralls sit at the bar, sipping beer. A couple sits at a booth by the window. We make our way to the nearest booth and sit.

A woman wearing snug jeans and a purple sweater hustles over. "Evening, folks," she says. "Can I get you something to drink?"

She's tall and thin, with a face that had once been pretty. She's a fast mover, a woman used to getting things done quickly. I'm betting she's waitress, bartender, and manager.

"I'll have a Killian's Irish Red," Tomasetti tells her.

"Same." Before she can turn away, I ask, "Can you tell us where we can find Patty Lou?"

Her gaze alters between curiosity and caution. "You cops?"

I lay down my badge. "We're looking for Elmer Moyer."

She looks at my badge a moment too long, getting her response in order. "What makes you think I know where he is?"

"You're a friend of his."

"Was. Past tense. He left, so I guess we're not friends anymore."

"When was that?" I ask.

"Little over two weeks ago." She narrows eyes swathed with makeup. "What'd he do?"

"We're just trying to find him."

"Uh-huh. Right. And I'm here because I like the benefits. Give me a break."

"How long were you friends?" I ask.

"Ten years, on and off. Mostly on toward the end."

"Can you tell us why he left?" I ask.

"Hell if I know. One minute he's Mr. Let's-Get-Married, and

the next he's gone." For a second, I catch a glimpse of the woman who'd been happy with a man she loved. "If you figure it out, let me know. I'll be back with your beers." She goes to the bar.

"Sounds like she wasn't expecting Mr. Perfect to skip town," Tomasetti says.

I look at him. "What do you think?"

"I think I want to find Elmer Moyers."

The waitress returns to our booth, sets two beers in front of us, and slaps down menus. "Turkey and gravy is the special," she says as she pulls out her order pad. "Chicken-fried steak is better."

"I understand Elmer did some driving for the Amish," I say.

"Yeah, they hired him sometimes. You know, for long trips."

"Did he work anywhere else?" Tomasetti asks.

"Worked over to the hardware store for a while. But he was on disability. Hurt his back when he was working construction."

"Where did he live?"

"Little furnished apartment above the furniture store."

"Did he ever make a trip to Painters Mill?" I ask.

"Not that I know of."

"Did he ever take a trip with Bishop Schwartz?"

Something flickers in her eyes. "I think he did. Like, years ago. Why are you guys asking all these questions about Elmer?"

"Did anyone else go with them on that trip?" I ask.

"Look, I don't know anything about it. I just remember it was a long drive and the bishop paid cash."

"Did anything unusual happen during that trip?" I ask.

"He didn't say. Y'all have me pretty curious, though."

"Can you sit a moment?" I slide over to give her room.

"I reckon I can spare a five-minute break." She lowers herself into the booth. "What's this all about? Is Elmer all right?"

I give her the basics of the case in Painters Mill, not relaying any information that isn't public. "We think Elmer may have driven Bishop Schwartz and Sadie Stutzman to Painters Mill."

Her mouth opens. "Sadie Stutzman," she whispers. "That old lady who was murdered the other night?"

I nod. "Bishop Schwartz is dead, too. Killed in a hit-and-run."

She falls silent. "What does that have to do with Elmer?"

"Do you remember what day Elmer left town?" I ask.

"The twentieth of October."

The day after Noah Schwartz was killed.

Tomasetti steps in. "Patty Lou, did he seem upset or worried about anything in the days and weeks before he left?"

"Or scared?" I add.

Patty Lou looks down at her hands. "I figured there was another woman. I mean, we were getting along great. I wasn't expecting him to just pick up and leave me."

"Did he—" I start to speak, but she cuts me off.

"Look, he was . . . weird the last couple of days." She heaves a sigh. "Elmer was a talker. Except for when he was worried, and then he just kind of clammed up."

"Any idea what he was worried about?" Tomasetti presses.

"I thought he was going to pop the question. I figured he was nervous. Big step and all." She chokes out a laugh that holds not a smidgen of humor "After he left, I figured he had another woman in another town."

"Any idea how to get in touch with him?" I ask.

"His phone is disconnected." Tears fill her eyes. She slides from the booth and swipes at her face with the backs of her hands. "I gotta get back to work. You guys know what you want to eat?"

WE'RE nearly to the motel when the call comes from Dispatch.

"Hey, Chief," comes Mona's voice. "Any luck down there?"

I keep my eyes on the road as I tell her about Elmer Moyer.

"We're not sure if he's part of this, a witness, or a possible victim, but we're going to take a hard look at him," I say.

A too-long pause, then, "Chief, I thought you should know . . . Bishop Troyer lapsed into a coma a little while ago. The doc is giving him a fifty-fifty chance of making it through the night."

I grip the wheel harder. "How's Freda holding up?" I ask.

"T.J. swung by their place earlier. He said the Amish are holding vigil at the hospital. Her family is there, too."

"Skid still out at the Helmuth place?"

"Glock relieved him so he could grab some sleep and dinner, but he'll be back out there at midnight when he comes on."

"Tell him thanks, will you?"

"Sure."

"You, too, Mona."

I punch off the button, slant a look at Tomasetti, and I'm profoundly relieved the cab is dark and he can't see my face.

"I don't think the bishop is going to make it," I whisper.

It will sadden me in a profound way if Bishop Troyer dies, especially if his death is caused by an act of violence. While the Amish are certain he will be going to a better place to rejoin loved ones and be with God, I'm not quite so certain. At times like this, the loss of that kind of faith is hollow and cold.

"He's been tough on you," Tomasetti points out.

"I was what the Amish call 'disobedient.' I committed some serious transgressions—in the eyes of the Amish, anyway—and I got into a lot of trouble. I didn't realize it at the time, but Bishop Troyer never gave up on me. Not even after I left."

"So don't give up on him." He reaches across the console, and I put my hand in his. "He's strong. If he still has something important to do before he checks out—like save your soul from eternal damnation—that might be enough to get him through this."

I can't help it; I laugh. "Thank you for that perspective."

"Anytime, Chief."

Chapter 10

One hundred and four hours missing

I SHOULD HAVE KNOWN this would be the night my old friend insomnia drops in for a visit. For two hours I lie beside Tomasetti, staring into the darkness and listening to the sounds of the Sleepy

Time Motel. I can't stop thinking about an innocent little Amish girl whose life hinges on my finding her, the possibility that I may not succeed, and the reality that it may already be too late.

At one a.m., I slide from the bed, make my way to the desk, and open my laptop, along with the files I've amassed over the last few days. I read the files on the deaths of Noah Schwartz and Sadie Stutzman given to us by Sheriff Pallant, but neither offers anything new. Frustrated, I go to the cardboard box where I stowed the pile of newspapers and clippings and the manila folder we retrieved from Sadie's bedroom. I pull out the first stack.

I spend twenty minutes looking through copies of *The Budget, The Connection,* and *The Diary.* I look for familiar names or stories that could be related to the Helmuth family or a missing child. I pay particular attention to births and obituaries. At three a.m., I've gone through four months of newspapers, all to no avail.

"Damn," I mutter.

Scooting my chair back, I dig into the box, spot the folder at the bottom, and pull it out. Dozens of newspaper cutouts spill onto the desktop. I page through them, trying to determine if they are relevant or could somehow be helpful.

Nothing.

I skim the last article and shove it back into the folder. That's when I notice the dozen or so obituaries and birth notices that slipped out and scattered on the desktop. Tiny cutouts, just an inch or two in length. Beneath the obits is a folded half-page tear sheet from the *Portsmouth Daily Times.* I unfold it and skim. There's an advertisement for a local funeral home. Another for a new hospice center going up in Sciotodale. A few more obits, which I scan.

Nettie Mae Detweiler was born on March 14, 2012, at 3:32 a.m. and passed peacefully in the loving arms of her parents. She entered the house of the Lord at 6:53 a.m. Nettie was the daughter of Rosanna and Vernon Detweiler.

A resonant *ping* sounds in my brain. I stare at the date, knowing it's somehow significant. I've seen it before. But where?

Energized, I pull out the file on Elsie Helmuth. I set it on the desktop and page through. My fingers freeze on the Missing flyer published by the Painters Mill Ladies' Club.

Have you seen me? Elsie Helmuth. Seven years old. Female. Special Needs. Born: March 14, 2012. Brown hair. Brown eyes. Height: 3 feet 9 inches. Weight: 60 lbs.

I go back to the obit and look at the date. March 14, 2012. My mind scrolls through conversations I've had over the last few days. *They brought her to us. In the middle of the night. This screaming, red-faced little baby.*

They're Miriam Helmuth's words, recalling the night the two bishops—Troyer and Schwartz—and midwife Sadie Stutzman brought them a baby from Scioto County. Is it possible Nettie Mae Detweiler and Elsie Helmuth are the same girl?

I grab the file and tread to the bathroom. I'm hitting the speed dial for Dispatch even as I close the door.

"You're up late," Mona says.

"Get me everything you can find on Rosanna and Vernon Detweiler." I spell the last name. "Check Scioto County. See if you can find an address. If there's nothing there, try the adjoining counties. Run them through LEADS. Check for warrants."

"Got it."

"And check with the Scioto County Auditor website. Do a property search to see if they own property. A house or acreage."

"I'm on it."

Ending the call, I swing open the door. I startle at the sight of Tomasetti standing there, looking grumpy. He frowns.

"You're looking bright-eyed and bushy-tailed for a woman who's been up all night," he growls.

"I think I found something," I say.

He groans. "Lay it on me."

HALF an hour later, Tomasetti and I are sitting at the desk, my laptop in front of us. He's been on his cell, trying to get BCI and the local jurisdiction on board. I've got Mona on my cell.

"I ran Rosanna and Vernon Detweiler through LEADS," she

tells me. "No warrants. No record. But I have an address from the county auditor tax roll for a property owned by Vernon Detweiler. 8184 White Oak Road, Bracks Hollow."

I type the address into my laptop maps software. It's a rural area a few miles east of Ironton, north of the river. "Do either of them have a driver's license? ID card?"

"Vernon Detweiler has a driver's license."

"Physical description?"

"Six feet four inches. Two twenty. Brown. Brown."

"What do you have on the property?"

"A hundred and fifty-two acres."

"Can you get me a plat?"

"You got it."

"Look, I'm with Agent Tomasetti. We're in Crooked Creek, twenty minutes from Bracks Hollow. He's working on an affidavit for a warrant. We're going to move as soon as it comes through. None of this is for public consumption."

"Roger that. Anything else, Chief?"

"A prayer for the girl might help."

"Done."

I hit END and turn to Tomasetti. "Vernon Detweiler is six four. Two hundred twenty pounds. I bet the farm he's a thirteen shoe."

"Amish?"

I nod. "We need that warrant yesterday."

"Sheriff Pallant and the judge are golf buddies. He's on his way."

I think about Elsie Helmuth. The violence her abductor is capable of. The number of days she's been missing. "How long?"

He shrugs. "Hard to tell. An hour. You believe this couple are the parents of Elsie Helmuth?"

"There's no way those dates are coincidental."

"What's the connection to Miriam and Ivan Helmuth? And how does Mary Yoder play into this?"

I stare at him, my mind blinking back to my exchange with Sadie Stutzman when I asked about Marlene Byler, Mary's sister.

They shamed her to death. That's why she jumped. They shamed her. Like mother, like daughter—both were bad eggs.

Maybe Sadie Stutzman was a hell of a lot more cognizant than anyone gave her credit for. . . .

"A name that has come up repeatedly in the course of this case is Marlene Byler," I say. "She lived in Scioto County."

"Mary Yoder's sister." His eyes narrow. "Miriam's aunt. Elsie's great-aunt."

"It's a familial connection." I tell him about Marlene Byler's suicide. "Rumor has it she took her baby with her when she jumped."

"Does Byler have other children?"

"Not that we've found."

"If she does," he says, "they might be worth a look."

"I'll get with Mona, tell her to keep digging."

A sharp rap sounds at the door. Tomasetti and I exchange a look, and for the first time, I realize Pallant will know we shared a room. Nothing we can do about it now.

Growling beneath his breath, Tomasetti yanks the door open. Sheriff Pallant and another deputy are standing there, looking in.

"Morning." Pallant's eyes slide from Tomasetti to me and back to Tomasetti.

"Any luck with that warrant?" I ask.

Pallant slaps a stack of papers against his palm. "Got it."

Tomasetti steps back, all business. "In that case, come in."

The two men enter the cramped confines of our room.

"What does the warrant cover?" I ask.

"The house and property," the sheriff tells me.

"Which means we can basically go in and look at whatever we want," Tomasetti says.

Pallant nods. "That's about the size of it."

"Do either of you know Vernon or Rosanna Detweiler?" I ask. "Have you met them? Dealt with them?"

The sheriff shakes his head. "We've never had any dealings with them." He grimaces. "How sure are you these people have the kid?"

I recap what I know and explain the significance of the dates. "Add to that the plaster from the size-thirteen work boot and Detweiler's height, and we've got probable cause."

Pallant doesn't seem convinced. "The judge bought it."

"Anyone know the layout of the property?" I ask.

The two men shake their heads.

"It's a big spread," the sheriff says.

"They run cattle," the deputy adds. "A couple dozen head."

I go to the desk, pull up an aerial view on my laptop, and zoom in. "In addition to the house, there are at least three outbuildings."

"Lots of places to hide," Tomasetti says.

The sheriff squints at the screen. "Any other buildings?"

"Not on this aerial, but it's over a year old." I indicate what looks like an excavated area at the rear of the property. "Not sure what that is." I zoom in with my mouse. "A pond that's gone dry?"

"There's a quarry on the northwest corner of the property," the deputy says. "It's defunct now. There used to be a lot of gravel trucks coming and going through a gate at the back."

The sheriff indicates a greenbelt that bisects the property. "Creek runs through there, too."

"A lot of trees," I murmur.

"So what's the plan?" Tomasetti asks.

The sheriff looks at his watch. "It's six a.m. Let's execute the warrant. I've got two more deputies en route. Once we execute the warrant, my guys will enter the property through that back gate and work their way to the front." He addresses me and Tomasetti. "Before we do anything, might be a good idea to talk to the couple, feel them out, and then search the house and outbuildings."

"I think we're good to go," Tomasetti says.

"Let's do it." The sheriff brings his hands together. "My deputy and I will ride together. You two follow."

I snatch up my shoulder holster and .38, shrug into it. I grab my jacket out of the closet. I gather the file. My laptop.

Tomasetti reaches for the keys, and we go through the door.

One hundred eleven hours missing

It's still dark with drizzle and fog as Tomasetti and I follow the sheriff's cruiser to the Detweiler property, which takes twenty minutes. The lane entrance is overgrown, and we drive by twice before realizing we've arrived at our destination.

The brake lights flash as they make the turn. Tomasetti follows, wrestling the Explorer through hip-high weeds. A hundred yards in, we pass by a hog barn that looks abandoned. A quarter mile farther in, we climb a hill, and a small house looms into view. The downstairs window glows with light. Someone is awake.

Beyond the house, a falling-down bank barn leans precariously. A chicken house stands next to the barn. There's a smaller hog barn with an attached pen where several dozen hogs mill about. Two horses stand inside a loafing shed, munching on a bale of hay.

Tomasetti parks next to a black buggy, our headlights revealing the lack of a slow-moving-vehicle sign. But it's the lack of a windshield and the sight of the dual kerosene lanterns that confirm what I already know. The Detweilers are Swartzentruber.

"Interesting that he's got a driver's license and a buggy," I say.

"I guess all those Amish rules are a pain in the ass when you have a kid to abduct and she lives four hours away." Tomasetti jams the Explorer into park and looks at me. "You got a vest?"

"Didn't think I'd need it."

Giving me a dark look, he gets out. "Keep your eyes open."

The four of us meet next to the sheriff's cruiser. I'm keenly aware of the silence. The totality of the darkness pressing down.

The sheriff slaps the warrant against his palm, then addresses his deputy. "Stay here, keep an eye on things. Get on the radio, tell those guys in the back to stand by." He looks at me and Tomasetti. "Let's go serve this bastard."

We take a stone path around the side of the house to the front. There's a single large window that's covered with a dark pull-down shade. Standing slightly to one side, Sheriff Pallant knocks on the door. Tomasetti and I stand behind him and to his right.

Footsteps sound, and the door swings open. An elderly Amish woman blinks owlishly at the sight of us. "Oh my. What's this?" She's wearing a gray dress. A *kapp* covered with a black bonnet. Black apron. Practical black shoes. A dish towel in her hands.

I know immediately this woman isn't Rosanna Detweiler. If Rosanna Detweiler had a child in 2012, there's no way she could be much over fifty. This woman looks to be around seventy.

"Is something wrong?" she asks. "Has something happened?"

Pallant has his ID at the ready. "Are you Rosanna Detweiler?"

"I'm Irene Detweiler. What's this about?"

He identifies himself. "We're looking for Vernon and Rosanna Detweiler. Are either of them here?"

"No."

"Do they live here, ma'am?"

"No. This is my home."

"Are you related to the Detweilers?"

"Vern's my son. Rosanna is my daughter-in-law."

"When's the last time you saw them?" Pallant asks.

"I haven't seen my son or his wife for several years. Not since the bishop put them under the *bann*. Said they were backsliders," she tells him, using the Amish term for someone who doesn't follow the rules set forth by the *Ordnung*. "I always hoped they'd change their ways, but they didn't and they never came back."

This isn't what I expected. "Your husband's name was Vernon?" I ask.

"Yes."

It hadn't occurred to me that the property deed might be in her husband's name, not her son's. A rookie mistake.

Stepping back from the door, Pallant frowns at us and lowers his voice. "Someone get their information wrong here?"

"She could be covering for them," Tomasetti says.

Pallant holds his gaze for a moment, then goes back to the door and passes the warrant to the Amish woman. "I've got a warrant to search your house and your farm, ma'am. I suggest you read it."

"A warrant? But . . . what on earth are you looking for?"

"Everything you need to know is in the warrant." Opening the door wider, the sheriff pushes past her. "Is there anyone else here at the farm this morning, ma'am? Family member? Farmhand?"

"It's just me."

I follow the sheriff into the house, with Tomasetti behind me.

"Are there any firearms in the house or on the property?" Pallant asks, his voice amicable.

"Just that old muzzleloader that belonged to my husband."

The three of us exchange looks. "Where is it?" I ask.

"The mudroom." The Amish woman starts toward it.

The sheriff reaches out and touches her arm, stopping her. "I'll get it, ma'am. Why don't you just have a seat and relax?" He starts toward the kitchen and the back of the house.

My eyes adjust to the dimly lit interior. We're standing in a living room with battered hardwood floors. Dark blinds hang at the windows. In the light of a single lantern, I see a quilt wall covering above a ragtag sofa. A coffee table. An oval braided rug. There are stairs to our right. A darkened stairwell that goes to a second level.

The sheriff returns to the living room. He's wrapped the long gun in a dish towel. "We'll tag it and start a return sheet," he says.

"You can't just walk into someone's home and take things," Irene Detweiler says. "What on earth do you want?"

"Everything you need to know is in that warrant, ma'am," the sheriff tells her. "Why don't you take a seat and read it?"

He stares at her until she acquiesces, then speaks into his lapel mike. "Warrant has been executed." He gives the go-ahead for the deputies at the back of the property to enter through the rear gate.

Pallant looks at me. "Chief Burkholder?"

I look at the woman, address her in *Deitsch*. "Mrs. Detweiler, we're looking for a missing child. A seven-year-old little girl. Is it possible she's somewhere here on the property?"

"A little girl? Lord, no. There's no child here."

"Is it possible she's with your son or daughter-in-law?"

"What on earth would they do with a child?"

I translate for the sheriff.

"All right." Pallant looks from me to Tomasetti. "I've got a female deputy on the way to look after Mrs. Detweiler while we search the place. If you'd like to start, I'll stay with her."

"Sure." Tomasetti turns and takes the stairs to the second level.

I start toward the kitchen. A table is covered with a plain tablecloth. A lantern flickering in the center throws off a dim glow. There's a sink to my right. There's no refrigerator. Pulling my mini Maglite from my pocket, I move on to the mudroom.

It's a narrow space. Hooks for coats on the wall. A door that leads outside. I run the beam of my flashlight along the hanging coats. A barn coat. A woman's slicker. There's a pair of dirty, adult-size sneakers on the floor. Rubber muck boots. None are large enough to be a men's size thirteen.

I walk back to the living room to find a female deputy standing next to the sofa where Irene Detweiler sits. She's a big woman, tall, with blue eyes and buzz-cut blond hair.

I introduce myself, and we exchange a quick shake.

"Sheriff went out to help search the barns," she tells me.

Tomasetti jogs down the stairs. "Upstairs is clear," he says, and crosses over to me. "You want to take a look around?"

Anxious to get outside, I'm already striding toward the door.

THE gray light of dawn hovers atop the tree line as Tomasetti and I make our way to the hog barn. Two more cruisers are parked in the driveway. We find Sheriff Pallant and two deputies, flashlights in hand, running a dozen or so hogs from the barn. The smell of manure hits me when I walk in the door. To my left, one of the deputies wades through muck, arms spread, herding the last of the hogs through the lower half of a Dutch door and into the muddy pen outside. None of the men look too pleased to be here.

Pallant saunters over to me. "You still think this mystery couple has a kidnapped child somewhere on this property?" he asks.

"I don't think I'm wrong. It's the best lead we've got," I say.

After a moment, the sheriff sighs. "Well, we're here. We got the warrant. Let's do our jobs. If there's a kid here, we'll find her."

While the deputies and sheriff continue their search of the hog barn, Tomasetti and I move on to the bank barn. It's a massive structure. The interior is dark and dusty and full of ancient farming implements—a wooden wagon, a manure spreader, a harrow.

I raise my Maglite. There's a row of horse stalls, the boards covered with cobwebs and dust. To my right are the stairs to the loft. Beneath them, burlap bags of grain have been torn open by rodents.

"I'll take the horse stalls," I say.

"I got the loft."

I check all four stalls, even the floor for trapdoors, but it's obvious no one has used this place for years.

A few minutes later, I meet Tomasetti in the aisle. He doesn't say anything as we make our way toward the door, but I can tell he's thinking the same thing I am: The missing girl isn't here.

"Tomasetti, what if I'm wrong about this?" I say as we go through the door.

"We don't always get it right, Kate. We do our best." He slants me a look. "Let's finish this. Walk out of here with the certainty that we've done our jobs and the girl isn't here."

It's eight a.m. by the time Tomasetti and I reach the back of the property. A Scioto County cruiser is parked on the other side of the gate, but the deputies are nowhere in sight. More than likely they followed the fence line due west to the property line and then turned south toward the house and outbuildings.

Tomasetti looks around. "If you were going to stash a kid outside, where would you put her?"

"A cave. A defunct mine. Storm shelter. Root cellar."

"Didn't someone say there was an old quarry on the property?"

I nod. "I saw it on the aerial view. It's west, past the creek."

"Let's head that way and then cut south toward the house."

We slog through grass and mud for twenty minutes until we're standing on a high point of the property. Ahead, the ground drops away steeply. At the base of the hill, a creek churns south toward the river. Beyond are the house and barns. Disappointment presses into me when I realize we've covered the entire property.

"I hate to point out the obvious," Tomasetti says.

"She's not here," I mutter.

We take in the scene for a moment. "We did our best," he says.

"A seven-year-old little girl is still missing, Tomasetti. The statistics are not in her favor."

"Screw the statistics," he growls. "Let's talk to the old lady again, see if she has anything to add."

Heart heavy, I start down the hill and head toward the house.

Chapter 11

One hundred and fourteen hours missing

I FIND SHERIFF PALLANT and two deputies standing next to their cruisers, the engines running, headlights on, emergency lights off. Waiting for us. One of the deputies has already left.

"There's no child on this property," the sheriff says as we approach. "We searched the house, the land. I've got deputies talking to neighbors, and no one has seen either Detweiler in the vicinity. No one recalls seeing a light-colored truck in the area."

"Did you get anything from Irene Detweiler?" I ask.

"We talked to her at length," he tells me. "She doesn't know anything about a missing child. And she doesn't know where her son and daughter-in-law are."

"Do you mind if I speak with her?" I ask.

The sheriff sighs. "Do what you need to do." He looks at his watch. "We're going to take off. All I ask is that you not overstep."

"Of course," I say.

Tomasetti and I watch them pull away, and then we go back to the house. He knocks on the door. Irene Detweiler peers out at us. "I thought you were finished," she says.

"Just a couple of quick questions," I say in *Deitsch*.

She opens the door and ushers us inside. At some point, she's lit another lantern, and the living area glows with golden light.

The woman shuffles to the sofa, lowers herself onto it, and picks up a knitting project. Tomasetti holds his ground near the door. I sit in the chair next to the sofa.

"Did Rosanna have any children?" I ask.

"The Lord never blessed them with little ones. She was *ime familye weg* once or twice, but . . . no babies." She gives a shrug. "I know it was hard on her. The women used to gossip about poor Rosanna and her not having any little ones. Some said worse."

"Worse like what?"

"Cruel nonsense mostly. Gossipmongers saying she wasn't fit to be a mother. It must have hurt her something awful."

"Why would they say such a thing?" I ask.

"Rosanna was a quiet thing. Serious, you know. Different. Some of the Amish thought that was odd. I suppose I did, too."

"Why were they put under the *bann?*"

"Vernon bought a truck." She makes a sound of disapproval. "I didn't have them over anymore after that. You know how it is."

"Do you know what kind of truck it was? Color?"

"Never saw it. I wouldn't let him bring it on the property."

I nod, thinking about a woman without children, isolated from her family, and how both of those things could affect someone who is part of a community in which children are so highly valued.

"Did you know Mary Yoder?" I ask.

"I don't know who that is."

"What about Marlene Byler?"

The knitting needles go still. "I know the name. She's the woman who killed herself all those years ago. Jumped off the bridge. What she did . . . such an awful thing."

Her eyes don't meet mine. She stares at her knitting.

"Marlene Byler and Mary Yoder were sisters," I tell her.

The woman stares at me. I see the wheels of her mind spinning. I get the impression she's struggling with some internal dilemma.

"A little girl's life is at stake," I say quietly. "If you know something that might help me find her, I need to hear it."

For the span of a full minute, the only sound comes from the hiss of the lantern, the patter of rain against the window.

The woman tightens her mouth. "Chief Burkholder, Rosanna told me a strange story once. You have to understand, she was . . . a peculiar girl. Always saying odd things. You never knew if it was true or make-believe."

"What did she tell you?"

"She told me that Marlene Byler was her *mamm.*"

My pulse jumps at the possibility of yet another familial connection. "So Marlene Byler had more than one child?"

"Oh, no. You misunderstand. Marlene only had *one* child."

My mind scrambles to make sense of what I've just been told. "Rosanna is the baby that went off the bridge with Marlene?"

"That's what Rosanna said. I don't know if it's true."

"Did she tell you how she survived the fall?" I ask. "Did she say who raised her?"

"Her grandmother."

I pull the spiral pad from my pocket. "Do you have a name?"

"Rosanna only mentioned her once or twice." Closing her eyes, she presses her fingers to her temples. "Ruby something." She massages her temples. "Mullet." Her eyes open. "Ruby Mullet."

I hear Tomasetti move. "Does she live in the area?" he asks.

"Last I heard, she owned a farm down south, on the other side of the river. Eads Hollow, I think."

TEN minutes later, Tomasetti and I are back in the Explorer. "If she's right about Rosanna being Marlene Byler's daughter, then Mary Yoder was her aunt," I say.

"There's your connection. Might be why the bishop chose the Helmuths. To keep the child with family."

"What does it mean in terms of the case?" I ask.

"It means we have one more place to look for that girl." He puts the Explorer in gear and starts down the lane. "I don't have to tell you we're going to be light-years out of our jurisdiction."

"I'm aware." I type "Eads Hollow" into my phone. "We're twenty minutes away."

He sighs as he makes the turn onto the highway.

I call Dispatch. "Lois, can you pull up the tax roll for Boyd County, Kentucky, and do a property search for Ruby Mullet?" I spell the last name. "I'm looking for an address."

"Sure."

Keys clack; then Lois tells me, "It looks like Ruby Mullet owns a thirty-acre tract in Eads Hollow." She rattles off an address.

I enter it into my GPS. "Any news on David Troyer?"

"He's still in a coma but holding his own."

"Let me know if anything changes." I end the call and recite the address to Tomasetti.

"Get the Boyd County sheriff on the line," he says.

I'm already dialing the number. It takes a few minutes, but I finally get connected with the chief deputy, who agrees to have a deputy meet us at the Mullet address.

We cross the Ohio River at the Twelfth Street Bridge and enter Kentucky. I'm thinking about the things I've learned about Rosanna Detweiler and all the dark possibilities they present. My conversation with her mother-in-law hovers in my mind.

The women used to gossip about poor Rosanna and her not having any little ones.

Gossipmongers saying she wasn't fit to be a mother.

It must have hurt her something awful.

I'm so lost in my thoughts I don't notice when Tomasetti makes the turn onto Johnson Fork Road. Another mile, and he takes an unnamed dirt track. A half a mile in, we reach our destination.

The property has the look of a place that's been abandoned for years. A gray house sits fifty yards off the road in a thicket of trees. There's no sign of the Boyd County sheriff's deputy's cruiser.

Tomasetti parks the Explorer, and we get out. It's so quiet I can hear the rattle of tree branches against the steel-shingled roof.

My boots sink into mud as I walk to what was once a driveway. It's little more than an impression in the weeds. It looks driven upon, but any tire tracks have long since been washed away.

There's a dilapidated barn to my left. Farther back, a corn silo squats on the side of a hill. There's a sorrel horse standing in a small pen behind the barn. Beyond, a dozen or so goats graze.

"Someone lives here," I say.

We reach the crumbling sidewalk and take it to the front porch. Dark curtains on the windows are closed.

I reach the door and knock. "Hello?" I call out. "Ruby Mullet?"

A diamond-shaped window is set into the door. Cupping my hands, I put my face to the glass and peer inside. I see a living room, plainly decorated. A coffee table with a lantern in the center. An oval rag rug. A wicker basket loaded with dried flowers.

"Looks occupied," Tomasetti says.

The crunch of tires on gravel alerts us to an approaching vehicle. I glance over my shoulder to see a Boyd County Sheriff's Department vehicle roll up behind the Explorer.

We meet the deputy in the driveway. He's about thirty, with the build of a heavyweight boxer, a bald pate, and eyes the color of a bruise. He's wearing a crisp uniform and chewing gum vigorously.

Introductions are made.

"I understand you're looking for Ruby Mullet?" he says.

Tomasetti lays out the fundamentals of the case. "Do you know who lives here?" he asks.

The deputy shakes his head. "I've patrolled this area for almost a year now. Used to see Amish people out here every so often."

"A couple?" I ask.

"Older lady." He motions toward the house, and we start that way. "Haven't seen anyone in a while."

We walk to the porch, and the deputy knocks on the door. "Boyd County Sheriff's Office!" he calls out. "Ruby Mullet?"

No one answers.

The deputy knocks with a little more vigor. "Sheriff's department! Mrs. Mullet? Can you come to the door, please?"

He leans closer, peers through the window. "No one's home."

"Can we do a welfare check?" Tomasetti says.

The deputy tilts his head and speaks into his lapel mike. "This is three-nine-two. I'm on scene 2292 Johnson Fork Road. No sign of the homeowner. I'm going to ten-thirty-four-C," he says, using the code for a well-being check.

"Roger that," comes a staticky female voice.

The three of us leave the porch and walk back to the driveway. "We can't do much since this is just a welfare check," the deputy tells us. "I'll take a quick peek in the barn, see if there's a buggy."

I look at Tomasetti. "Maybe we ought to try the back door."

He shrugs. "If she's elderly, she may be hard of hearing."

The deputy heads toward the barn. Tomasetti and I start toward the back of the house. There are no curtains on the window set into the back door. I peer through the glass into a small room. There's a wood bench against the wall. A rocking chair in the corner. A pair of boots. Farther, a doorway leads to what looks like a kitchen.

"Hello?" I call out loudly as I rap my knuckles against the glass. "Ruby Mullet? I'm a police officer. Is everything okay in there?"

We wait a couple of minutes, but no one comes.

I stand there a moment, looking out over the property, and notice the small fenced area twenty yards away. The enclosure is about thirty feet square, with an arbor-type gate.

I hear Tomasetti talking to someone on his cell as I start that way. I'm midway there when I realize it's a family cemetery plot. There are five markers—small wooden crosses—arranged in two rows. The hinge screeches as I let myself in. I go to the first marker and kneel. The cross is covered with lichens. Reaching out, I brush the surface with my fingertips and read aloud.

"Ruby Marie Mullet. Born May 22, 1938. Died February 2, 2019."

The owner of the property. Rosanna Detweiler's grandmother. If she's been dead since February, who's been living here?

I go to the next marker.

MARTIN ROY MULLET
Born April 30, 1932. Died November 23, 2012.

The next marker gives me pause.

AMOS WAYNE DETWEILER
Born July 17, 2008. Died August 19, 2008.

An infant, I realize, and my conversation with Irene Detweiler floats through my mind.

The Lord never blessed them with little ones. She was ime familye weg *once or twice, but . . . no babies.*

Or were there? I go to the next marker.

BONNIE ANN DETWEILER
Born October 2, 2010. Died January 3, 2011.

The final marker slants at an angle. The grave has been disturbed; the earth freshly turned. I look into the shallow hole. There's nothing there. I kneel next to the marker and read.

NETTIE MAE DETWEILER
Born March 14, 2012. Died March 14, 2012.

For the span of a full minute, I ponder the possibilities.

"Warrant is in the works."

I turn to see Tomasetti standing at the gate, just outside the cemetery. His eyes moving from me to the markers and back to me.

"I never understood why an Amish bishop, an Amish midwife, would remove a baby from its mother," I say.

He comes through the gate and reads the nearest marker.

"According to Irene Detweiler, the Amish community was suspicious of Rosanna. The women said she was unfit to be a mother."

Tomasetti says nothing.

"I don't want to be right about this." I look around. "If Sadie Stutzman was concerned about the welfare of the children, if she thought Rosanna was somehow unfit, I can understand her going to the bishop. I can see the bishop stepping in."

He looks away. "We don't know what happened here."

"No, but we have a theory." A theory that's so hideous, neither of us says the words aloud . . .

Tomasetti's phone chirps. He looks at it. "Kentucky Department of Criminal Investigation. Hang tight." He turns away and sets it to his ear.

I glance toward the barn. The big sliding door stands open. There's no sign of the deputy. I leave the cemetery and walk back to the house. The curtains at the window are parted by a couple of inches, so I peer inside. I see light blue cabinets. Gas stove. Farther, I can just make out the corner of a kitchen table. I'm about to turn away when I hear a resonant thump from inside the house.

I hold my breath and listen. The faint sound of pounding reaches me. Muttering a curse, I try the knob, find it unlocked. I push open the door and step inside.

"Hello?" I call out. "I'm a police officer. Is someone there?"

The house reeks of mildew and dust and day-old garbage. I enter the kitchen. It's tidy, with a table and four chairs. A dozen or so mason jars sit on the counter. A towel is draped over the edge of a sink.

The sound of pounding startles me. It's muffled; I'm not sure where it's coming from. I move to the living room. Beyond is a hall with two doors. One opens to a bathroom. The other door is closed. There's a padlock, shiny and new.

The pounding sounds again.

Senses on alert, I go to the door. "Who's there?"

"Let me out!" A little girl's voice, high-pitched and panicked.

"Elsie?"

"Let me out! Let me out! I promise to be good!"

A hundred thoughts tear through my brain. I lift the lock, but it's engaged. I look around for the key, but it's nowhere in sight.

Caution makes me hesitate. I don't know if there's anyone else in the house. I don't know if the girl is alone. If there's someone with her. If they're armed . . .

"Are you alone?" I call out.

"Yes! Pleeeeeease lemme out! I promise not to run away!"

"I'm a policeman," I tell her. "Stay calm and keep quiet, okay? We'll get you out."

Either the girl doesn't hear me or she's too panicked to comprehend. The pounding becomes frenzied. I hear her crying.

I spin and dash through the kitchen. I tug out my .38 as I go through the mudroom; then I'm on the porch. Tomasetti stands a few feet away, on the phone. "I got her!" I say to him.

He whirls, a collage of emotions playing in his expression. He's already moving toward me. "Anyone else in the house?"

"I don't know. She said she's alone."

He pulls his Kimber from his shoulder holster. "Let's get her."

We burst into the house. Tomasetti reaches her door first.

"Can I come out now?" comes a tiny voice. "I want my *mamm*."

"Stand back," he tells her. "I'm going to break down the door."

Silence.

"Are you away from the door, sweetheart?" I ask.

"*Ja!*"

Stepping back, Tomasetti slams his foot against the door. Wood cracks but holds. He kicks it again and the door flies open.

It's a tiny bedroom. Windows covered with plywood. Little Elsie stands a few feet away, tears streaming. I want to go to her, but we're not sure what we've stumbled upon, so I hold my ground.

Tomasetti enters the room, goes to her, bends to her. "We're the police," he says gently. "We're here to take you home."

The girl rushes to him. Tomasetti sweeps her into his arms.

"I want Mamm," she sobs.

For the span of several seconds, he holds her. He presses his cheek to the top of her head. "Let's get you out of here."

The sight of him with the child in his arms moves me so profoundly that for a moment I have to blink back tears.

Still wearing her dress and *kapp,* the little girl clings to Tomasetti, her arms around his neck, her legs around his middle. Tomasetti is holding her with one arm, the Kimber in his other hand.

"I'm going to take her to the Explorer and call this in." He flashes me a look, his expression a mosaic of relief and trepidation. "Get that deputy. Keep your eyes open."

I turn and jog through the kitchen, go out the back door, and sprint toward the barn. The door stands open, the interior dark.

"Deputy!" I call out.

No answer.

I reach the doorway, give my eyes a moment to adjust to the dim light. It's a huge structure. To my right are tumbledown stalls with sliding doors in the front, Dutch doors that likely open to the outside pens. To my left are stairs that lead to the loft.

Gray light slants in through grimy windows. A sliding door at the back of the barn stands open. I've just reached it when I spot the deputy outside, sprawled on the ground. Blood covers his jacket.

My .38 at my side, I start toward him. I'm midway there when I spot the pickup truck in the trees twenty yards away. Tan. A man stands on the other side of the truck, his rifle leveled right at me.

A gunshot sears the air. I run back to the barn, throw myself against the nearest beam. Another shot rings out. The wood inches from my face explodes. Shards pierce my cheek. Through the open door I see the man round the truck. Rifle at his side.

"Police!" I scream. "Drop your weapon!"

He doesn't obey my command.

I raise the .38 and fire three times.

The man goes down on one knee. He looks my way. Face a mask of rage. He raises the rifle. The gunshot sears the air. I sprint to the nearest stall, throw myself inside and to the floor. I speed-crawl to the front rail, peer between the wood planks. The shooter stands silhouetted at the door, rifle in hand. He's a large man, tall and heavily built. Black jacket. Vernon Detweiler.

He doesn't see me, but I'm not well hidden. Slowly, I shift into position for a shot. The light is bad; the angle is worse. He's forty feet away. I have two bullets left. I set the .38 between the planks.

If he looks in my direction, he'll spot me. I take a deep breath, release it slowly. He walks into the barn and stops thirty feet away.

He looks right at me, brings up the rifle. I pull off two shots. Blood blooms on his shirt, but he doesn't fall. I watch in horror as he starts toward me.

"The thief comes only to steal and kill and destroy," he says.

Panic slams down on me. I'm out of ammo and facing an armed killer. No place to hide. My only chance is to run.

I scramble to my feet, fling myself to the Dutch door that will take me to the pens outside. I slap off the hook latch. Hit the door with both hands. It doesn't budge. I ram my shoulder against it. The door refuses to open. Nowhere to run. Nowhere to hide.

I hear him at the stall door, just ten feet away. I glance over my shoulder, see him standing in the doorway of the stall, looking at me, the rifle at his shoulder, finger inside the guard.

Dear God, he's going to kill me.

A horrific sense of helplessness assails me. I turn to face him, raise my hands, knowing they won't stop a bullet.

"Ich vissa si nemma deim bobli!" I scream the words. I know they took your baby!

A tremor passes through his body. He lowers the rifle, cocks his head, stares at me as if I'm some apparition that can't be explained.

I don't know if it's my use of *Deitsch* or the mention of his daughter that kept him from pulling the trigger. I keep talking.

"I know they took Nettie." I'm shaking so violently, I can barely stand. "They shouldn't have taken her," I choke.

Confusion suffuses his expression. "They told us she died. Our sweet Nettie. But they took her. They left us to mourn the way we'd mourned the others. All this time. Such a wicked thing. They *knew,* and yet they said nothing. They let us suffer."

My mind races for the right words. "Vernon, I don't blame you for being angry. But this isn't the way to make things right."

"Some things cannot be made right. Too much time has passed. Too much grief." The muscles in his jaw flex. "The cruel things they said about my wife. All the talk. So vicious."

"Put down the gun," I say.

"I won't let you take her."

"I'm not going to take her. I'll help you. Please put down the rifle so we can talk." When he doesn't move, I add, "If you can't do it for yourself, do it for your daughter. Do it for Nettie."

"Too late for talk, Kate Burkholder. You should've stayed in Painters Mill." He raises the rifle, levels it at my chest.

His finger curls inside the guard. On the trigger. Tomasetti . . .

"No!"

The scream shatters the air. An Amish woman runs to him from behind. Forty years old. Gray dress. Black winter bonnet. Rosanna Detweiler.

"No more killing," she cries.

Detweiler looks at her over his shoulder. "They are going to take Nettie from us."

A gasp escapes her when she notices the blood on his jacket. "This is not the way," she says. "It's not our way. Not this."

When he doesn't lower the rifle, the woman steps around him. Tears streaming, she levers down the nose of the rifle.

"Those who use swords are destroyed by swords," she says.

"We are her parents." He shakes off her touch, raises the rifle. "They cursed our lives. Caused us untold grief."

"What about the grief you've caused?" she cries. "All this killing. When will it stop?"

"I did it for you, Ros. For us. All of it."

"It's too late." The words are the howl of a wounded animal. "That poor child has been crying for her *mamm* since the day she arrived. We're not her family. We are not the ones she loves."

The Amish man chokes out a sob. "It was God's will," he whispers. "The way things should have been all along."

"We have to let her go," the woman says.

A collage of emotion infuses his face. Grief. Resignation. Pain.

Movement at the door draws my attention.

"Drop the rifle! Do it now!" Tomasetti stands at the sliding door, his Kimber leveled on Vernon Detweiler.

For an instant, I think the Amish man is going to raise the rifle, kill his wife, finish me—or Tomasetti. For an interminable moment, he stands frozen, rifle steady in his hands.

He looks at the woman. "They shamed you."

"I am not ashamed," she whispers.

Another flash of emotion in his eyes, sharp edges cutting.

The rifle clatters to the ground.

"Get your hands up!" Tomasetti is halfway to us, crouched, moving fast, cautious. "Do not move! Get on your knees!"

Never taking his eyes from the woman, Vernon Detweiler raises his hands and drops to his knees. Beaten, he lowers his head.

I get to my feet. My body quakes with such intensity I have to grab on to the rail as I make my way to the stall door.

Weapon trained on Vernon Detweiler, Tomasetti nudges the rifle away with his foot, out of reach. "Get down on your belly," he tells the Amish man. "Spread your hands and legs."

Vernon Detweiler obeys.

Tomasetti casts a look at me. "You okay?"

"Yeah. The deputy is down."

He curses. "County is on the way."

I cross to the woman. "Rosanna Detweiler?"

"Yes." She raises shaking hands. "Where's Nettie?"

A hundred questions boil in my brain. But I'm a civilian here in

Boyd County, Kentucky. I can't Mirandize her. I can't ask the things I so desperately need to know. Conversely, neither can I keep her from speaking if she so wishes to do so.

"Safe," I tell her.

While Tomasetti puts the zip ties on Detweiler, I perform a cursory pat-down on Rosanna. Finding nothing, I motion to the ground directly in front of the stall. "Have a seat, and do not move."

She obeys.

Tomasetti walks over to me. "Keep an eye on him. I'm going to stay with the deputy until the paramedics get here."

I position myself so that both Detweilers are readily visible. While Tomasetti attends to the deputy a few yards away, I fish the speed loader from my duty belt, load the rounds into my .38, and I place the gun back in its holster.

"You treated the girl well," I say in *Deitsch*.

"Of course we did. We're not monsters."

The irony of the statement burns. I think about Mary Yoder. Noah Schwartz. Sadie Stutzman. Bishop Troyer. Three lives snuffed out, a fourth irrevocably changed. And for what?

The Amish woman looks up at me. "You're *Amisch?*"

"I was," I say, hoping she'll talk to me, *willing* her to talk.

In the distance, sirens wail. Vernon Detweiler lies prone and unmoving just a few yards away.

I look at Rosanna Detweiler. "I know what it's like," I say. "All those rules. All the expectations."

She stares at me, saying nothing.

"There's a lot of pressure to conform when you're Amish," I say slowly. "A lot of cultural norms. I couldn't do it. Couldn't abide. I couldn't be the girl they expected me to be."

"The Amish and all their morals." Bitterness rings hard in her voice. "How moral were they when they took my baby?"

I wait, hoping she'll continue.

Her gaze settles on her husband. Pain flashes in her eyes at the sight of him facedown in the dirt. "All he ever wanted was to have a family," she whispers. "Little ones, you know. It was the one thing I couldn't give him. I tried, but . . . He went to them, you know."

"The Helmuths?"

"Vern went to see Mary Yoder. A week ago in Painters Mill. He asked her to return the girl. The child that was rightfully ours." Her mouth tightens. "The old woman refused. She threatened to go to the bishop. The police, even." Her lips tremble. "I realize this must sound crazy now, but Vern would have been a good *datt.*"

It's an outrageous statement, but I let it go without a response.

"Sadie thought I was hurting the babies." She whispers the words. "She never said as much, but I knew. I didn't hurt them. I would never commit such a terrible sin. Maybe I wasn't as good a *mamm* as I should have been. You know, cooing and kissing. I think Sadie must have picked up on that."

She's thoughtful for a moment. "They were special, you know. Little Amos and sweet Bonnie. They were slow learners. Like Nettie. The doctor said it was too early to tell, but I knew."

"They had Cohen syndrome?" I ask.

Nodding, she raises her hands, brushes tears from her cheeks. "The doctor said it was SIDS that killed them. That didn't keep people from talking." A bitter smile plays at the corners of her mouth. "Vern and I heard every cruel word."

I think about Sadie Stutzman. The minutes I spent with her at her house on the river. *Those poor babies . . .* The midwife's concern had not been ambivalent. Were her suspicions correct? Or is this woman telling the truth or some version of it? Is it possible Sadie Stutzman and the bishop did something unthinkable?

"And Nettie?" I say.

"I barely remember the birth. It was difficult and long. Afterward, Sadie told me she was gone. We never got to see her. Or hold her. We were so grief-stricken it's all a blur."

"And the grave?" I ask. "The marker?"

She shrugs. "Someone dug the grave the night she was born. They put up the marker. I don't know who."

The sirens are closer now. I stare at the Amish woman.

"At some point, you realized the truth," I say.

"Vern was always suspicious. I mean, after Nettie. A couple of months ago, he ran into Elmer Moyer. They'd had a falling-out over money before. Elmer had accused Vern of shortchanging him. That night, Elmer was drunk and started taunting Vern, telling him he'd driven a baby up to Painters Mill. Vern came home in a state. Angry, you know. Furious, in fact."

She closes her eyes, tears squeezing between her lashes. "He dug up the grave later that night, and there was nothing there."

"What happened to Elmer Moyer?" I ask.

"He left town. Ran away. If Vern had found him, he would have killed Elmer, too. He's the only one who got away."

Putting her face in her hands, she begins to sob.

Chapter 12

FOUR DAYS HAVE PASSED since Tomasetti and I discovered Elsie Helmuth locked in a bedroom at the Mullet farm. Over several interviews, the girl revealed that Vernon Detweiler abducted her that day at the Schattenbaum place. After murdering Mary Yoder, he dragged Elsie to his truck and drove her to Crooked Creek.

In the following days, Rosanna Detweiler fed her, washed her clothes, cooked her meals, and took her for long walks in the woods. They'd called the girl Nettie, and they'd told her they were her family now and that she would never go back to Painters Mill.

According to Elsie, the couple didn't hurt her physically. But there are a lot of ways to harm a child. She'd been taken from her family and everything she'd ever known. When she tried to run away—and find her way home—the Detweilers had locked her in the bedroom for hours on end. All of it had frightened Elsie terribly. Last time I talked to Miriam Helmuth, she told me the girl was having nightmares and couldn't be left alone. I suspect little Elsie will be dealing with her fears for some time to come.

Life is slowly returning to normal. Painters Mill is blissfully quiet. The Harvest Festival started this morning. The merchants along Main Street are reveling in the influx of tourists.

I should be feeling celebratory. A little girl is safe and home with her family. The Boyd County sheriff's deputy who was on scene that day at the Mullet farm survived a serious stabbing. Bishop Troyer is recovering at home. I'm thankful for all of it.

But I didn't walk away from this case unscathed. I've spent too much time thinking about Rosanna and Vernon Detweiler, trying to answer the questions that continue to nag. According to the people who knew them, Rosanna Detweiler rarely left the property, venturing into town only to buy groceries. She spent her days tending her garden and walking in the woods.

Vernon Detweiler was a silent, brooding man. He doted on his wife. He also had a temper and a propensity for violence.

From what little I've been able to piece together, Rosanna was, indeed, the daughter of Marlene Byler—and likely the baby she held in her arms when she jumped from the bridge. No one knows how she survived the fall. An Amish woman who'd been close to Ruby Mullet confirmed that Rosanna was raised by her grandmother and inherited the farm when her grandmother passed away.

Rosanna and Vernon claim they are the biological parents of Elsie Helmuth. They claim Sadie Stutzman and Noah Schwartz convinced them their infant child was stillborn—and then transported that child to Miriam and Ivan Helmuth. At some point, DNA testing will be done to determine parentage.

There's one unanswered question that continues to keep me awake nights. According to Rosanna, she lost two newborns. The death certificates listed SIDS as the cause of death, but no autopsies had been performed. I can't help but wonder: Did Rosanna Detweiler harm her children? Or was Sadie Stutzman wrong? They are disturbing questions that may never be answered.

It's late afternoon when I take the Explorer down the lane of the Troyer farm and park next to the bishop's buggy. The smell of woodsmoke drifts on the air as I take the sidewalk to the door.

Freda Troyer answers. Emotion flickers at the sight of me. She says my name softly. "You're here to see David?"

I nod. "How is he?"

"He's a grouchy old goat. I'll be glad when he's up and about so I can put him to work outside." She pushes open the door. *"Kumma inseid."* Come inside.

I enter an overheated kitchen that smells of lavender and lye. Soapmaking items are spread out on the table.

"He's in the next room, resting." Freda goes to the counter and picks up a dishcloth. I'm midway to the door when she whispers my name. I turn to her, shocked to see tears on her cheeks. She swipes at them with the dishcloth, comes to me, takes my hand.

It's the first time in all the years I've known her that Freda Troyer has shown any kind of affection—toward me or anyone else. She grips my hand hard, trembling, her eyes holding mine. For a moment, I think she's going to say something. Instead, she releases me, stiffens her spine, and turns back to the sink.

"Don't keep him long," she says. "He gets tired."

In the living room, a gas lamp hisses, casting yellow light on a brown sofa, two rocking chairs, a rustic coffee table. The bishop lies on a cot, his head and shoulders propped on pillows, his legs covered by an afghan. He's dressed, less his usual jacket and hat. He looks fragile and pale as he takes my measure.

For the span of several heartbeats, we stare at each other.

"How are you feeling?" I ask after a moment.

"Stronger," he tells me. "Thankful."

I move closer. "Vernon and Rosanna Detweiler are being extradited to Holmes County. They'll face an array of felonies here, not the least of which is murder. I thought you should know."

"I will pray for them." The old man nods, thoughtful. "The Amish community will support them."

Forgiveness is one of the hallmarks of the Amish faith. I'm well aware that the capacity to forgive is a virtue, but I knew at an early age that it was a tenet I would never be able to put into practice.

"Bishop, I know what you did. I know Sadie Stutzman and Noah Schwartz took a newborn from Rosanna and Vernon Detweiler. I know they brought that baby to you. You took her to the Helmuths and asked them to raise her. I know that infant is Elsie Helmuth."

"*Es voah Gottes wille.*" It was God's will.

"How much did the Helmuths know?"

"I told them nothing."

"Bishop Troyer, you can't take a baby from someone and just give it to someone else."

"She was taken to a family member. It was up to them to work things out." His expression doesn't alter. "What we did, Katie, it was the only way to save the life of the child."

"You should have gone to the police. There are laws in place to protect children at risk."

"And have the child taken by the social services people? I think not. It was an Amish matter to be handled by the Amish."

I've heard the sentiment a hundred times over the years. Every time, it grates on my sensibilities. This man's rigid adherence to Amish doctrine may have contributed to the deaths of four people.

"Had you gone to the police, Mary Yoder would still be here," I say. "Sadie Stutzman. Noah Schwartz. That wasn't God's will."

His expression falters. "It's done, Katie. We can't go back and change it." Wincing, he leans forward. "I prayed to God for the wisdom to do the right thing. I did the best I could. We had no way of knowing this would happen. Had we not acted, Elsie Helmuth might have died before she ever had the chance to live."

The exchange drives home the myriad reasons I left my Amish faith behind. While I will always hold a great deal of love for the people, the culture, and the religion, I'm reminded of how far I've strayed, and that I made the only decision I could have.

I hold his gaze for a moment longer, words best left unspoken passing between us. After a moment, I turn and leave the room.

ONE of the most satisfying aspects of closing an investigation is that golden moment when the facts come together and you finally figure out the how and why. It's not always a pleasant moment, but rewarding nonetheless.

I'm trying hard to believe that as I make the turn into the lane that will take me home. I pull up behind the house to find Tomasetti's Tahoe parked in its usual spot. I sit there a moment, watching the snow fall, drinking in the simple beauty of my surroundings. The barn with its peeling paint. The farmhouse with its drafty windows and a porch that's in dire need of a new railing.

The snow is coming down hard when I get out and take the sidewalk to the back door. I find Tomasetti sitting at the kitchen table, his laptop open in front of him, a cup of coffee at his side.

His eyes find mine. "How's the bishop?"

"He's going to be all right, I think."

Rising, he crosses to me. "How about you?"

I turn to him. "I'm glad this godforsaken case is over."

He pours coffee for me and sets it on the table. "Have a seat."

I take the chair across from him. "The Helmuths didn't know."

"Bodes well for them." He sips coffee.

"The bishop chose them because they're blood relatives," I tell him. "Ostensibly, they could work out any custody issues among themselves. He knew they were a good, solid Amish family. Their home was a place where the baby would be safe and grow up with traditional Amish values, surrounded by family and community."

I think about the cemetery plot at the Mullet farm. "I don't know what Rosanna did or didn't do. Some of it may come out during trial. But I get the sense that, as an Amish woman, she felt pressure to conform to societal roles, to have children, raise a large family."

"That can be a lot of pressure."

"Especially for someone not equipped to handle it."

"As twisted as all of that is, it fits." Tomasetti sips coffee. "You've been dwelling in some dark places."

"I knew the truth was in there somewhere."

His gaze meets mine. In their depths I see comprehension and the insights of a man who has experienced the many facets of life, both good and bad. "You and I have been around long enough to know that Lady Justice doesn't always get it exactly right."

"Tomasetti, what they did was incredibly . . . misguided."

He takes my hand. "That's true, Kate. But however misguided or wrong, they may have saved the life of a child. All things considered, I don't think that's such a hard thing to live with."

Rising, I go to him. He gets to his feet. I fall against him. Something settles inside me when his arms wrap around me.

"Do me a favor?" Setting his fingers against my chin, he tilts my face to his. "Stay out of those dark places."

"I'm working on it."

My cell vibrates; the ring that follows tells me it's Dispatch.

Pulling away, I put the cell to my ear. "Hey, Lois."

"Chief, I just took a call from Mr. Shafer with the Buckeye Credit Union on the traffic circle. He says there are a bunch of teenagers parked in his customer parking spots." She sounds frazzled. "He says he asked them to leave and they refused."

"Let Mr. Shafer know I'll be there in a few minutes."

"Copy that."

Tomasetti sets our cups in the sink. "Sounds serious."

"You have no idea." I smile. "I have to go."

Behind him, outside the window above the sink, snow swirls down, lending a magical quality to the fading afternoon light.

"Want some company?" he asks. "I hear the Harvest Festival is in full swing. Once you're off, we could drink some hard cider and check out the new antique shop on the south end."

"Tomasetti, that's the best idea I've heard all day."

Standing on my tiptoes, I pull his face to mine and press my mouth to his. "Let's go."

AfterWords

For *New York Times* bestselling author Linda Castillo, the eleventh intallment of her Amish mystery series has allowed her to explore some new morally complex themes.

According to Castillo, in *Shamed*, she wanted to focus on human weakness as it plays out in a religious culture. "What happens when a member of a religious community such as the Amish makes a mistake?" ohe asks. "What happens if they do something really bad? Break the law? How do they feel about themselves and what they did on the inside?"

While Castillo has spent years developing the character of Kate Burkholder, the author admits she doesn't have much in common with the tough police chief. Except one trait: Castillo reflects that, like Kate, she "was very much a tomboy growing up." Like the families in her novels, her family had horses, cattle, pigs, and other livestock. She learned to swim in a nearby pond and loved exploring the woods and the one-hundred-year-old bank barn.

These days, Castillo constantly strives to find new ways to challenge Kate Burkholder. The next book in the series, tentatively titled *Outsider*, will deal with the emergence of someone from Kate's past and offer a closer look at the years before she returned to Painter's Mill.

Castillo currently lives in Texas with her husband, two rescued blue heelers, and two Appaloosa horses.

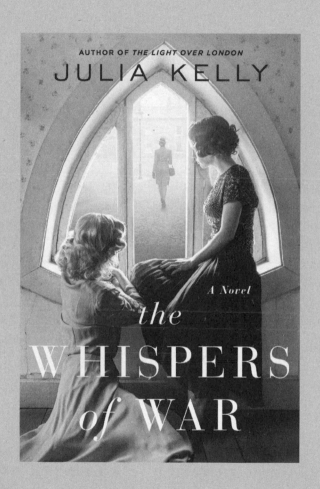

AUTHOR OF *THE LIGHT OVER LONDON*

JULIA KELLY

A Novel

the
WHISPERS
of WAR

Prologue

How QUICKLY MARIE *had become used to her new routine. Breakfast for two in the morning—porridge cooked on the hob with water since milk was already becoming scarce. On days when she wasn't working, she would tidy up before a small lunch. And, without fail, just around two o'clock, she'd listen for the brass flap of the letter box to squeak open and the second post to drop with a satisfying* thunk *onto the polished entryway floor.*

Now she sat wrapped in a blanket in the corner of the big rose-patterned sofa that faced the mews she'd come to think of as home. She'd somehow managed to forget everything—the war, her worries, her fears—and relax into her book. She was so caught up that it was only when the letter box flap rattled that she realized the post had arrived. Setting her book aside, she slipped her feet into a pair of slippers and rose.

Shivering, she pulled her cardigan tighter as she stepped into the corridor and scooped up the scattered letters. She began flipping through them, looking for her name. She may have been a guest in this house, but she still received a letter or two a day.

Marie set aside two brown envelopes on the little sideboard. Three large square envelopes followed those. Then she saw her neatly typed name on a slim white envelope. She ripped it open.

Her hand began to tremble as she stared down at the cheap paper,

willing the sentences to rearrange themselves. Desperate for them to say
something else. But there was no denying the words.

Her legs buckled under her, and she crumpled to the floor.

Chapter 1

Samantha
Now

SAMANTHA CLUTCHED HER passport as the line inched forward.
All around her, her fellow passengers from the red-eye to London
yawned and blinked against the fluorescent light of the immigration hall. She hardly noticed the jostle of bodies, her attention
fixed on the weight of the package and the half-scribbled notes in
her brown leather shoulder bag.

She should have made this trip earlier. "Never put off for tomorrow what you can do today," one of the posters in her third-grade
classroom read. It was stuck above the dry-erase board so her students couldn't miss the warning against procrastination. But teaching that lesson and living it were two different things.

She pulled out her passport as she approached the front of the
line. A guard behind a high desk checked it without comment, and
she couldn't help but be grateful she didn't have to explain why she
was in the country. What would she say? This trip wasn't business,
but it certainly wasn't bringing her any pleasure either.

After collecting her small suitcase, she navigated through the
customs gate past immigration and out into the bustle of Heathrow's Terminal 5. She focused on her first challenge: getting to
West London. It shouldn't be too difficult. She took the El from
her Lincoln Square apartment to school every weekday. She could
navigate the Tube. And then it was just a matter of finding the
streets that would lead her to the house.

Maybe it had been a mistake to accept Nora's invitation to stay with her. The woman was 103 years old—it was incredible she was still living at home—but Nora had been insistent from the moment Samantha called the number her grandmother's lawyer had provided. Every email exchange between Samantha and Nora contained some variation of *I won't hear of my dearest friend's granddaughter coming all the way from America and staying at a hotel. You'll stay with me. And you must meet David, too.*

Samantha tilted her head back to read the signs overhead. Trains to her right. She was adjusting her grip on her suitcase handle when she spotted a tall, dark-haired man holding a sign that read SAMANTHA MORRIS, CHICAGO. Her name. Her city. But she didn't have anyone here to pick her up from the airport. *Unless . . .*

"Excuse me, are you David?" she asked, stopping in front him.

"Samantha?"

She swallowed. "Yes."

David will meet you at Heathrow, one of Nora's emails had read. But she'd batted away the offer. Being collected by her grandmother's best friend's grandson was a step too far. Except now that he was here, she couldn't help but feel a tiny bit of relief.

"I thought that might be you. You look like your photograph." His hand dove into the pocket of his jacket and out came a photograph, a little bent at one corner. He handed it to her. "My grandmother gave me this to make sure I'd be able to spot you."

She stared at the photo. "This was taken when I was eighteen."

"I did point out that it might be a little out-of-date, but she insisted. She said that your grandmother hardly aged from eighteen to forty, and you wouldn't either."

"I had no idea Grandma had sent this to her," she said.

The left side of his mouth tipped up. "You should prepare yourself for Gran to know quite a bit about you."

She pressed a hand to the center of her chest and the guilt that had lodged itself there. She should know more about this woman who had clearly been dear to her mother's mother, but she had learned of Nora less than a year ago. So much of her grandmother's life remained a mystery, and it was her own fault.

"We should hop on the Tube. Gran has been tracking your flight since it was over Ireland and calling me every ten minutes to make sure I haven't forgotten that I'm to pick you up," David said.

"She sounds like quite the woman," she said.

The corner of his mouth kicked up again. "Oh, she is."

THROUGHOUT the entire trip into London on the Piccadilly line, David carried the burden of the conversation as Samantha's foggy brain tried to contend with being rocketed six hours into the future. They transferred at South Kensington and rode the District line three stops to West Kensington. David then led her out of the train station to a large street he told her was North End Road. A couple of schoolgirls in blazers and pleated skirts shrieked and ran, pursued by a pair of boys in maroon sweaters and navy trousers.

"They're still in classes?" she mused out loud.

David glanced over. "What was that?"

"I'm just surprised. I'm an elementary school teacher, so my life has always been dictated by academic year. It's actually the reason I'm here now. We let out the third week of June, but I gave myself a week off before traveling," she said, trying not to think about how she'd also let the academic year serve as an excuse to put off her trip until now.

"Then you have good timing. Schools don't let out here until closer to the end of July, which is when most people with kids go on holiday. It can become a little hectic traveling," he said.

They turned off the main road and stopped in front of a three-story white Victorian terraced house. David pulled out a key, opened the door, and stepped back to let Samantha pass him.

"David, is that you?" called a voice through an open door off the hallway on her right. "Is Samantha with you?"

"In you go," he said, nodding to the door with a smile.

Samantha edged through the doorway and into a wide room with two bay windows that looked out over the street. Deep blue curtains fell in graceful folds to the floor, and an iron fireplace topped with an elaborately carved mantel on one end of the room emitted a sense of grandeur and comfort all at once. And sitting near that fireplace in a high-backed wing chair was an old woman who sported a carefully combed snow-white bob and cherry-red lips. Nora Fowler.

Nora, who Samantha could see was tall even sitting down, was swathed in a gray cardigan with a colorful scarf tied at her throat.

"You must be Marie's granddaughter," said Nora, nudging her glasses up her nose to study Samantha with sharp pale blue eyes.

"Hello," said Samantha.

"My, you look like her. You have the same hair."

Samantha had to resist the urge to fuss with her shoulder-length blond hair.

"I'm glad David found you," Nora continued. "I should've known when he didn't text me."

David, who'd just rounded the door, swooped in to give his grandmother a kiss on the cheek. "I should've texted you."

"Yes, you should have. Come, sit with me, Samantha," said Nora, gesturing to the sofa across from her.

Samantha sank down into the spot. "Thank you for sending David. He has been a great help."

"I didn't want you lost and wandering around London. Not when you said you have something for me."

Samantha sucked in a breath. She had expected to have a little more time to . . . she didn't know. Make small talk and drink tea? But somehow Samantha doubted that small talk had ever interested the woman in front of her.

"When Grandma died, I found out that she'd made me the executor of her will," said Samantha, pulling out the packet she'd carried with her from Chicago. "She had three very specific instructions. She wanted a memorial service, not a funeral, and she was very clear that it should be celebratory, not sad."

A smile touched Nora's lips. "My generation has seen too much sadness to want to invite any more somberness into the world."

"She liked summer best, so the ceremony will be next month." A sudden wave of longing for her grandmother's soft accented words came over her. Samantha cleared her throat. "The next request was that she wanted me to deliver this to you. In her will, Grandma said it had to be delivered by hand."

"What is it?" asked Nora, eyeing the parcel in Samantha's lap.

"I don't know. All the instructions said was that it's meant for you. I'm sorry that it's taken me until now to bring it to you."

"She died last October," said Nora.

"I'm a teacher. I couldn't—" She stopped herself. "I could have asked for a leave of absence from my school. I could've made arrangements to come sooner, but I didn't."

"Why did you wait? I'm one hundred and three years old. Time isn't something I have a great deal of," said Nora, managing to sound teasing rather than sharp.

"It hasn't been easy losing her. We were very close when I was a girl, but then I went to college," she said.

"And life got in the way?" Nora finished for her.

Samantha nodded, the shame coursing through her.

"What was the third request?" asked David.

She started, realizing she'd forgotten he was there. "Oh, I'm supposed to give her eulogy at the ceremony."

"Not an easy thing," said Nora.

"No. I have a whole notebook of ideas in my purse, but nothing sticks. How do you eulogize a woman when all you really know about her is that she was a sweet grandmother who drank coffee all day and hummed Nina Simone songs while she mopped the kitchen floors? Her life was more than that."

Nora smiled. "Much more."

Tell me! It was on the tip of Samantha's tongue. Most of her memories of her grandmother were from her childhood. She remembered snowy winter afternoons hunched over a puzzle together at the dining room table. She recalled how Grandma Marie would sneak more marshmallows into her hot chocolate than her parents would allow. Then the memories became less personal. Samantha had started to grow up, and her relationship with her grandmother had slipped to the background of her life.

Now, sitting in a living room more than three thousand miles away from home, Samantha lifted up the package her grandmother had entrusted her with. "So here it is."

Carefully, she placed the thick manila envelope in Nora's lap. Samantha watched as the old woman began to draw out bundles of paper tied with string—six in total—and a velvet bag.

"What are they?" asked David.

Nora let out a long sigh. "My letters from the war. I sent them from all over, but you'll be able to tell the ones I wrote when I was on leave because I always marked that I wrote them from Cranley Mews. I was so proud of that house. I bought it before the war when young women did not own their own homes. David's uncle Colin lives there now."

Nora picked up the velvet bag, undid the drawstrings, and tipped it onto its side. Out into her wrinkled hand fell a thin gold chain and pendant set with a deep blue stone.

"That looks like yours," said David.

"David, will you go fetch my jewelry box?" his grandmother asked, her eyes still fixed on the pendant.

David slipped out of the room and returned with a black box fashioned in the style of a small steamer trunk. He set it down next to his grandmother and waited as she opened it and drew out a necklace on a gold chain from which hung the pendant's twin.

"I gave this to your grandmother," she said, gesturing to the necklace from the velvet pouch. Then she ran her thumb over the necklace she'd just retrieved. "This one was our friend Hazel's. And this"—she reached into the neckline of her sweater—"is mine. It's lapis lazuli. I had them made for us out of a bracelet I used to wear. I wanted to make sure that no matter what happened during the war, we would always have a piece of each other with us."

"Did you say Hazel?" asked Samantha.

"Yes. Why?" asked Nora.

"My middle name is Hazel. Samantha Hazel Morris. All I know about her is that she's a family friend I've never met. Who is she?"

"Was. She died about twenty years ago." For a long moment, Nora sat silent, but then she nodded, as though making up her mind. "David, will you go put the kettle on? I think we're going to need fortifications for this. A cup of tea will perk us all up.

"Now." Nora turned her attention back to Samantha. "I met your grandmother in 1928, when she, Hazel, and I were all put in a dormitory together. The Ethelbrook Misfits, we called ourselves that first term, although the name never stuck."

Chapter 2

Marie
August 1939 to October 1939

THE THREAT OF WAR hung heavy in the air. It was impossible to ignore as Marie shuffled around a newspaperman who stood outside the Hyde Park Corner tube station shouting, "Britain signs on to help Poland! Mutual assistance treaty!"

Marie ducked her head and hurried on, knowing that buying an evening edition of the paper would only delay her more. She'd stopped at the shop around the corner from work to pick up extra batteries after seeing the queue at lunch, and it had taken her twice as long as she'd thought it would. Still, she knew she'd made the right choice. If war came, there was sure to be a run on them.

She was nearly panting by the time the Harlan Club came into view, its proud redbrick face embellished with a cornice of white stone. Wallace, the doorman, stood tall in his oxblood uniform coat, ready and waiting for the arrival of any of the Harlan's ladies as they popped in for cocktails or supper before a Friday night at the theater. Marie may not have been a member, but she liked to think that she might one day be mistaken for the sort of woman who could walk up to this building knowing she belonged.

Wallace opened the door and, with a tug on the brim of his black top hat, folded into a half bow. "Good evening, Miss Bohn."

"Good evening. Has Miss Walcott arrived?" she asked.

"I'm afraid not, Miss Bohn, but I'm sure Mrs. Harper will make you comfortable while you wait."

Drat. Mrs. Harper, the club's receptionist, always glared at her as though Marie intended to filch the club's silverware.

"Marie!" called Hazel from the club's lobby with a cheerful wave that sent her strawberry-blond pageboy sweeping her shoulders. "I was just wondering where you'd gotten to."

"Batteries," Marie said, brushing her friend's cheek with a kiss. "That was me last Saturday. Forty minutes to buy two tins of potatoes and six boxes of matches."

The Harlan's grandfather clock chimed the quarter hour. "Is that really the time?" Marie asked.

"At least you're not as late as Nora. I feel as though we've been waiting for her to show up whenever we meet ever since we were at school."

"Because we have," said Marie.

"Well, Mrs. Harper and I have spent the last quarter hour becoming quite fast friends," said Hazel with a grin.

The receptionist glared from behind her desk. The stout, sour-faced woman had never approved of their band of three's habit of meeting at the Harlan on the last Friday of every month. Luckily, there was little she could do. Marie and Hazel were Nora's friends, and while she may not have been able to guarantee them membership to the exclusive—and expensive—club, Nora had enough clout to make sure they would always be welcome as guests.

Wallace swung the door open again, and Nora rushed in.

"I know, I know. I'm late," she said as she stooped to kiss each of them on the cheek. "I'm sorry."

"Marie was late, too," said Hazel.

"No one likes a tattletale," said Marie.

"Like the time you told Miss Burford that I was sneaking sweets in the back of math class?" Nora asked.

Hazel shrugged. "In my defense, I was thirteen, and it was only because you never shared your sweets—a character flaw, I will point out, that has not improved with age."

"If we're going to start the evening by pointing out all of my bad qualities, can I at least be armed with a drink?" asked Nora.

The Harlan's bar shared much of its design with the rest of London's Clubland properties. The chandeliers were heavy brass and crystal, and gilt-edged mirrors lined the walls. The Harlan, however, was a woman's domain. The Founding Few, including Nora's grandmother, had started it in the waning years of the last century.

Marie knew Nora relished telling the story of the ladies all sitting together in a drawing room after a dinner party, talking about what an injustice it was that their husbands could swan off to their clubs whenever they felt like escaping their families. Then one enterprising lady asked, "Why can't we do the same?"

Determined, the ladies had drummed up a membership, secured dues, and signed a lease in the space of three months. From its opening, the Harlan offered respectable rooms to distinguished ladies for whom staying in a hotel without a chaperone was simply too scandalous. By all accounts, it had been a little bit home, a little bit meeting place, but mostly it had been a sanctuary.

Now, decades later, the three friends claimed the small cluster of armchairs closest to the Harlan bar's iron-fronted fireplace.

"I swear the Underground is worse every day. I was stuck on a train that wouldn't move for ten minutes," said Nora.

"It's only going to be worse if they decide to institute the blackout. Just think of it, not a single light allowed on the trains aboveground at night or in the stations," said Hazel.

"We'll be living by torchlight," said Marie.

"What does Nathaniel think of all this?" Nora asked.

Hazel rolled her eyes at the mention of her husband. "He thinks that all of this is just Hitler grandstanding and that the Munich Agreement will be enough to keep him at bay."

The prime minister, Neville Chamberlain, had held off Hitler with the Munich Agreement almost a year ago, and much of Britain had breathed a collective sigh of relief. There would not be another war, they'd assured themselves. Now it looked less and less like a guarantee of "peace in our time," even if many people, like Hazel's husband, clung to it with all their might.

"Any word from your mother, Marie?" Hazel asked.

She dipped her chin, wishing her friends didn't know her so well that they'd spot a lie from one hundred paces. "Yes." She unsnapped her handbag and pulled out the letter. "Here. It's in French." All of her letters over the years had been in French. Hannah Bohn acted more like a nineteenth-century Russian princess than a German businessman's wife, forsaking her native language for the elegance of French.

"You read it," said Hazel, nodding to Nora. "Your French always was better than mine."

"'Dear daughter,'" Nora read, translating as she went. "'You know that nothing bores me more than these questions you ask about politics. We did not send you away to school for you to cultivate an interest in things that are no business of a young lady.' Well, that is rich."

"Keep reading," said Marie.

"'It's fortunate for you that your father is more amused than insulted by all of this,'" Nora read. "'He tells me to write that he would never do anything to sacrifice the health of the business or our life here in Munich. He doubts there will be any war at all and that the very best thing for him to do is to remain a friend to everyone.' So they're taking a stance of neutrality?"

Marie plucked the letter from Nora's grasp. "So it would seem."

"And you still don't think they would ever join the Nazi Party?" Nora asked. "There are all sorts of stories . . ."

"No," said Marie firmly. "Vater has too many foreign contracts at the factory to want Germany at war, cut off from the rest of Europe. Honestly, can't we talk about something else?"

Nora's eyes darted to Hazel. "Can I ask how you're doing?"

The gentleness of Nora's voice—usually so direct and forceful— belied the importance of the question. Marie could see Hazel digging her fingers into her thigh, grounding herself.

"I'm as well as can be expected," said Hazel.

Marie lowered her voice. "Did you go to the doctor?"

Hazel bit her lip and nodded. "He says there's nothing more that can be done. We just need to keep trying, but we've been trying for six years. Ever since . . ."

Marie and Nora each picked up Hazel's hands.

"I'm sorry, I shouldn't have asked," said Nora.

Hazel shook her head. "I want you to ask. It's just difficult. I should know by now not to become excited, but this one was almost three months along. I thought we might have a chance."

The yearning in Hazel's voice tore at Marie's heart. She knew how badly her friend wanted a baby. How elated she'd been the three times she'd realized she was pregnant. How each of the miscarriages had knocked Hazel back, threatening to plunge her into the darkness that had swallowed her when she'd lost her first baby, just weeks after marrying Nathaniel.

"Enough," said Hazel, blinking rapidly. "There's too much depressing talk in the world right now. It's Friday. Let's enjoy it."

Pierre, the Harlan's bartender, set down their usual drinks in front of them, and each woman took a sip.

"Tell us what happened at the agency this week," said Nora.

"You won't believe me when I tell you," said Hazel, a little glint in her eyes. "The Repeater is back."

Nora snorted, "Doesn't that man have any pride?"

"Clearly not," said Hazel.

Tales of the Repeater had been a staple of their monthly suppers since the man had first shown up at the door of the Mayfair Matrimonial Agency, where Hazel worked as a matchmaker. The third son of a baronet, the Repeater had seemed promising enough. But Hazel soon learned that no matter whom she matched him with, the woman would never be good enough. The lady would be too talkative, too tall, too blond. He was impossible to please.

"Heaven help the poor girl who ends up with him," said Nora.

"Do you know, it's funny, with all of this talk of war you would think that business would be slowing down. Instead, it's never been better. I had three new clients today," said Hazel.

"Anyone interesting?" asked Marie.

Hazel scrunched up her nose in thought. "One. A widower. Actually, Nora, you might know him. His late wife's family runs with your mother's set."

"What is his name?" asked Nora.

"You know I don't share names," said Hazel.

"What are Marie and I going to do with his name?" Nora argued back. "Plus, if I do know him, I might be able to help."

Hazel sighed. "Mr. Richard Calloway."

Nora cocked her head in thought. "It doesn't ring any bells."

"What happened to Mr. Calloway's wife?" asked Marie.

"Cancer. It all sounds very tragic," said Hazel.

"Poor man," said Marie.

"He's good-looking in a quiet, elegant sort of way. Smart, too. A civil engineer," said Hazel. "I think he's going to be one of the considered ones. Hard to place, but when he knows, he'll know."

"That's better than jumping into things feetfirst," said Nora.

"If you're interested . . ."

Nora scowled at Hazel. "Don't you dare."

Hazel sighed. "I wish you would let me match you up. Either of you. Marie?" asked Hazel hopefully.

"Oh, no, thank you," she said in a rush. "I—"

"Maybe she already has a man in mind," Nora teased.

Marie's mouth opened, then shut again. Was she that transparent? She couldn't lie to her friends, but there were things she kept from them, and Neil was one of them.

"Don't worry, Marie. You needn't tell a soul until you're ready," said Hazel, leaning over to pat her arm.

"There's no one," Marie insisted.

"Mmm-hmm. Marie's the kind of dark horse who won't tell us that she's seeing a fellow until two weeks before there's a ring on her finger," said Nora.

"And you're the kind who would telephone the day before her wedding and invite everyone around without letting them know what the celebration is for," Marie shot back.

Nora pointed to herself. "I'm not planning a trip to the altar, remember."

Hazel slumped into her chair. "I don't know why I bother."

"Frankly, darling," said Nora, "neither do we."

THE mornings were Marie's favorite time of day. Rising an hour earlier than anyone else, she could pretend that she had the flat to herself, except for Frau Hafner, who came before any of them awoke. Her aunt and uncle's housekeeper would set out toast for Marie along with the tall stoneware coffeepot. Even after years of school breakfasts and teas while boarding at Ethelbrook, Marie couldn't understand the British devotion to the insipid brown water that was tea.

Steam curled up off the coffee as she poured it into her cup. A twinge of guilt gripped her, as it did every morning. Her aunt and uncle lived a comfortable life, although it didn't touch the grandeur that Nora had given up when she'd left the family home after her father's death. Still, Marie knew that if Neil ever found out that the Müllers employed a housekeeper, he'd disapprove.

So when Marie left her aunt and uncle's home every day, she became a different woman. No longer was she the devoted niece who'd spent months helping Tante Matilda work intricate lace for the antimacassars that covered the sofa in the sitting room of their Bloomsbury flat. She became Marie the university secretary, and every other Monday, she'd take the bus to Tottenham and become Marie the comrade. That version of herself could walk into a Party meeting next to Neil, head held high. That Marie felt special.

Neil had asked her twice before she'd agreed to attend her first meeting of the Communist Party of Great Britain. Even then she wouldn't have said yes if it hadn't been for Anna, the secretary to the Russian Department. Her offices were just two doors down from the German Department, which Marie kept running in perfect order. Anna often came for a chat at midmorning, cup of coffee in her hand. She enjoyed stirring the pot just because she could.

Anna had been leaning against Marie's desk when Neil walked out of Herr Gunter's office. As the graduate student who seemed most likely to obtain the one vacant role in the department after completing his dissertation, Neil had the run of the place.

On that day, he stopped in front of Marie's desk. "Do you want to come see me speak tonight?" he asked.

"Speak?" Anna asked.

"At a meeting of the CPGB—sorry, the Communist Party of Great Britain," said Neil. "I've been asking Marie to come with me for months, but she always says no."

"Is that right?" Anna asked, casting her a sly look.

"It isn't easy to get away on a Monday night," Marie protested.

"I think what's really the matter is that her aunt and uncle disapprove of radical politics," Neil told Anna.

Anna's eyes narrowed. "I'm sure Mr. and Mrs. Müller wouldn't mind if you were to attend meetings of the Women's Institute. Such a good Christian organization," she said.

Marie stared at her. "You want me to lie to my aunt and uncle?"

Anna shrugged. "People do it all the time."

That might be the case, but Marie didn't. Not to Tante Matilda and Onkel Albrecht. How could she risk their disappointment when they had done so much for her? They'd given her a home, a family, a life here in London.

"I couldn't lie to them," said Marie.

Neil laughed. "You sound horrified, *kleine Maus.*"

Little mouse. It was the sort of endearment a man might bestow on his girlfriend—or a parent on a child. But there was something about hearing *him* say it that made her believe that maybe one day he, Neil Havitt, prodigy of Herr Gunter and one of Royal Imperial University's bright stars, might see her as something other than the department's diminutive secretary.

"I'll go."

Neil and Anna looked at her. "What will you tell your aunt and uncle?" he asked.

Marie pressed her lips together. "I will think of something."

Faced with her commitment to Neil, Marie had, in fact, told her aunt and uncle the fib about the Women's Institute. Tante Matilda had been delighted Marie had decided to join the respectable group of do-gooder women, which had made Marie's stomach clench, but she smiled through the discomfort. On the following Monday evening, she'd met Neil for the bus to Tottenham.

The Party meeting had been a crush of people. Neil seemed to know everyone and introduced her around as she hung close to his side until it was time for the speeches.

Neil had spoken fourth out of a lineup of six and had come off the stage wearing a light sheen of sweat and a triumphant glow.

"How was it?" he asked.

"You were brilliant," she said, although in truth his speech had been shorter than she'd expected.

He'd leaned down and kissed her on the cheek, pausing long enough to say quietly, "Thank you, *kleine Maus.*"

She'd let him persuade her to come to the next meeting two weeks later, and then the next. That had been four months ago.

A door creaked open somewhere in the flat as Marie spread butter on a roll. She sat up straighter. Then the dining room door swung open, and she relaxed again. It was only her cousin, Henrik.

"Why do you always wake up so early?" he asked in German, squinting in the glare of the overhead lights.

"Good morning to you, too," she said, watching him drop into his chair with a wince. "Do you have a hangover?" She clacked her cup hard on its saucer.

Sure enough, he winced again. "Not so loud."

Marie rolled her eyes but said, "Here," and lifted the heavy coffeepot, pulled his cup closer, and poured. "Drink this."

He gripped his cup tightly and drained it.

"Are you going to work today?" she asked him.

"It's Monday, isn't it?" he shot back.

She leaned on the table. "It really is fortunate that you work under your father, Henrik. Who else would tolerate you showing up late on a Monday morning stinking of schnapps?"

"I don't stink of schnapps," he said. But then he gave the air a sniff. "I will bathe before I go."

"What exactly were you doing yesterday evening?"

"I was out with like-minded men," he muttered.

Drunken fools who like the sound of their own voices is more like it, she thought, but kept her opinion to herself. They'd had this quarrel before, and it wouldn't be long until Henrik would snarl and remind her that she was his cousin, not his sister, and therefore a guest in this house no matter how long she'd been living there.

She sighed and pulled the newspaper set at her uncle's place toward her. All she could see of the headline was Britain to—

"Should you be touching that?" he asked. "It's my father's."

Her gaze flicked up. "Onkel Albrecht encourages me to read the paper. He says it's best that we all know what is happening in the world. He doesn't trust Hitler," she said.

That earned her a grunt and nothing else.

She pushed back from the table. "I should finish getting ready." She left, but not before unfolding her uncle's paper so she could see the full headline: Britain to Germany: We Stand by Poland.

"Our cause is the cause of the people. We must do everything we can to quell the spread of fascism. It is time for the people to rise up against the fascist state that has infected Germany!"

The hall exploded into applause as the barrel-chested man barking his speech brought his remarks to a thunderous close.

The woman sitting next to Marie nudged her. "You'll write to your friends in Germany, won't you? Tell them we are with them."

Marie started, but Neil leaned over her. "Of course she will. Marie is as dedicated to the cause as any of us."

"Neil," Marie whispered to him.

He shrugged. "We all have to do what we can, Marie. I've told you, it isn't just about attending meetings."

She bit her lip. She was doing more than attending meetings. He, more than anyone else, should know that.

After her first two visits to CPGB meetings, Neil had asked her to look over one of his speeches before he delivered it. She'd marked up the text, scribbling suggestions and swapping out phrases with ones she thought would have more impact.

The next time he'd stopped by her desk, she'd handed the papers back to him. He'd glanced at them, thanked her, and walked away. For a week, she'd been crawling with nerves, but when he took the stage she heard her words coming out of his mouth. The next time he had a speech, he appeared again, set the typewritten sheets on her desk, and walked off. She'd edited him again, and again his speech had shone.

"Come on," Neil said as the applause around them died down. He grabbed her and tugged her along the row of seats as people began to stream out of the hall. Clear of the seats, he looped her hand through the crook of his arm.

"Did you enjoy the speech, *kleine Maus?*" he asked.

"It was . . . illuminating," she said softly.

Neil glanced around. "Let's go to the pub a different way this time."

Breaking off from the crowd, they walked in silence. Marie relished the heat emanating from Neil's body and how it warmed her gloveless hands. He steered them down Scales Road, the lights in a few windows of the row houses diffused by cheap curtains.

"My friend works in the Air Raid Precautions Department. She says that the entire city will be under blackout orders if we end up at war," she said.

"My mum remembers the blackout from the Great War." Neil fell silent for a moment before saying, "The speaker tonight was right. Hitler won't be kept back with diplomacy."

Marie swallowed. "We don't know that."

"I do," Neil insisted. "I can see it everywhere. The Germans want to knock us back, and the people need to be prepared for it."

Marie stopped abruptly, and Neil's heel ground against the road as he swung around so they were facing one another.

"What?" he asked.

"Can't we talk about something else? All anyone can do is mention the war, and we aren't even in it," she said. "I'm tired of it."

He laughed. "What else are we supposed to talk about, silly girl?"

"Do not call me a silly girl," she bit out.

She saw Neil's mouth open. After a moment he said, "I'm sorry. I shouldn't have called you that."

"It's just that, well, I wasn't born here," she started to say.

His concern softened into a smile. "Is that all?"

She searched his face. "Do you know what happened during the last war? Thousands of Germans living here were forced to leave their homes. Put in camps. They lost their freedom."

"That won't happen to you. You were practically born here."

"Practically born here" was not "born here," but how did she explain that to him? He might be a student of German, but Neil wasn't actually *German*.

Neil reached out a hand and tucked a wisp of her stick-straight hair behind her ear. "You worry too much," he said.

"I don't," she whispered.

"I think perhaps . . ." But instead of finishing the thought, he kissed her. Their first kiss—soft, careful, and measured. She leaned into him in answer, gripping at the lapels of his jacket.

Finally, Neil pulled back. "Well, that was unexpected."

She flushed. Unexpectedly good? Unexpectedly bad?

Then he leaned in again and kissed her swiftly and softly.

Good enough. It must have been good enough.

Neil scooped up her hand, tucked it back onto his arm, and gave her a smile. "Come on, *kleine Maus*. There's a glass of sherry waiting for you and a pint of ale for me at the Stag and Hound."

Chapter 3

THE SCRAPE OF METAL CHAIRS against the cheap laminate floor of one of the Royal Imperial University's many teaching rooms pierced Marie's ears as she flipped her notepad closed. She rocked her head side to side, seeking relief for the headache that throbbed against her right temple. She'd been sitting in this room for nearly six hours now, but Herr Gunter was bound to march her back to the department offices to take dictation.

With a sigh, she hauled herself to her feet. Without a glance back at her, Herr Gunter began to make his way out of the symposium room.

In the corridor, the stale scent of cigarette smoke dissipated and her headache eased a bit. It was nearly six o'clock, and Royal Imperial's main campus was empty save for a few undergraduates hurrying through the lightly misting rain.

"Fräulein Bohn, I wish to dictate my notes from the symposium," Herr Gunter threw over his shoulder as they approached the department offices.

"Of course, Herr Gunter."

From inside the department office, a telephone began to ring. Herr Gunter opened the door, and Marie saw that it was the phone on her desk. "I'll just be one moment," she said, hurrying around to pick up the receiver.

"German Department."

"Marie! Finally!" Hazel's voice came out sharp across the line.

"Hazel, what's the matter?" she asked as Herr Gunter unlocked his office and disappeared inside.

"You don't know?"

"Don't know what?" she asked with a frown.

"It's happened. Germany marched on Poland."

Marie's notepad slipped from her hands. "What? When?"

"Early this morning. The news broke a few hours ago. Turn the radio on. The prime minister is due to speak any moment now."

"Maybe it isn't an invasion. Maybe it was just—"

"The Germans are bombing Polish cities. Troops are marching. There are tanks." Hazel's voice cracked. "I'm so sorry."

Marie sank onto the edge of her desk. It was happening.

Herr Gunter stuck his head out of his office. "Fräulein Bohn."

"Hazel, I need to go," Marie said.

"No, you need your friends. Meet us at the Harlan."

Herr Gunter was glaring at her, so she agreed and carefully set the phone down in its cradle.

"I thought I made it clear that there are to be no personal calls in this office, Fräulein Bohn," he said.

Marie pushed by him and made straight for the small radio sitting on a card table to the right of his desk and switched it on. The radio gave a crackle and then came to life.

"This is the BBC World Service," a presenter intoned.

"What is the meaning of this?" Herr Gunter raged behind her.

The presenter continued. *"Prime Minister Neville Chamberlain is due to speak to Parliament after reports of the German invasion of Poland before dawn this morning."*

Marie turned to see the blood drain from Herr Gunter's face. He knew just as well as she did what this all meant. Britain had signed a treaty with Poland. Any act of aggression against that country would mean war for Britain.

"That was my friend calling to tell me. We're at war," she said.

"Not yet," he said, his eyes locked on the radio. "Not yet. The British will give Hitler a chance to withdraw."

"Hitler won't withdraw."

"You don't know that," Herr Gunter barked so sharply she started. "I am sorry, Fräulein. Please turn that off."

She switched the dial off. Herr Gunter began muttering to himself.

He pulled his briefcase up onto the desk and began to open his drawers. In went a few papers and a leather-bound notebook.

"Is there something I can do, Herr Gunter?" she asked.

"Call Emily. Tell her I must cancel dinner."

Marie frowned. "I'm sorry, sir, I don't know who Emily is."

Herr Gunter froze for a second, his eyes wide, but then he again dropped his attention to his bag. "Never mind, never mind." He shut the briefcase. "You may go. I will see you on Monday."

Marie walked quickly to her own desk and pulled on her coat. She jammed her hat on and left.

Outside on the street, a bus pulled up to the stop. Marie sprinted and managed to make it just in time, huddling in the back corner until her stop. The rain had begun to pick up, and her hat and coat were soaked by the time she made it to the Harlan's front door.

"Miss Bohn," said Wallace, springing forward to hold the door open for her. Just inside the doorway stood Nora and Hazel. They both rushed to envelop her in a hug.

"Come," said Hazel. "Sit down right here."

Her friends maneuvered her onto a red velvet sofa. "Let's get this off of you," said Hazel, lifting Marie's hat from her head. Nora unbuttoned Marie's coat and helped her ease out of the wet fabric.

"When did you find out?" asked Marie quietly.

"I came to work at the Home Office, and the place was already in chaos. Sir Gerald was called into an emergency meeting to assess our preparedness, and I sat in to assist him. I rang you and then Hazel as soon as I could catch a moment," said Nora.

"I see," said Marie.

Hazel covered Marie's hand with one of her own. "It could still be stopped. The prime minister has given Hitler until Sunday to withdraw his troops from Poland."

She shook her head. "He won't withdraw. We're going to be at war soon, and I don't know what that means for me or my family."

"Miss Bohn." They all looked up to see Pierre standing before them, crystal glasses of whiskey balanced on a tray. "If I might be so bold as to suggest a little refreshment might be welcome."

"Thank you, Pierre. That's very kind of you," said Nora.

Marie was just reaching for a glass when Mrs. Harper descended on them. "No drinks in the foyer. Club rules."

Pierre straightened. "Given the circumstances, I thought an exception might be made."

"No exceptions," said Mrs. Harper. "And no need for any bowing and scraping to her kind either," she muttered.

Nora shot to her feet. "I beg your pardon, Mrs. Harper?"

Mrs. Harper stared straight down her nose at Marie.

"I said that her kind should never've been welcome in a place like the Harlan. Now more than ever," said Mrs. Harper.

Marie grabbed at Nora's hand. "It doesn't matter."

"It does," said Nora, not looking at Marie. "Miss Bohn is my guest. I expect her to be treated with the same courtesy that you would extend to any other guest of this club. Am I understood?"

"Young lady, I don't care if you're a Founding Few's granddaughter. I won't be told what to do by some jumped-up deb thirty years my junior." Mrs. Harper turned to Marie. "You may put on airs, but you're still a bloody kraut, and they should lock you up."

"What is the meaning of this?" The commanding voice of an older woman froze the foyer. At the head of the club's stairs stood Lady Dora, Countess of Dartman and Harlan Club chairwoman.

"Lady Dora, I must insist on making a complaint about the treatment of my friend. Miss Bohn came to the club at my invitation, and Mrs. Harper verbally attacked her," Nora exclaimed.

"And I say that her kind shouldn't be allowed past these doors. There is a war on," said Mrs. Harper with vitriol.

Lady Dora arched a snow-white brow. "Mrs. Harper, unless you know more than the prime minister, I believe you will find that we are not yet at war. I would also remind you that you are not employed to impose your opinions upon the Harlan."

"But—"

"Miss Bohn is German?" Lady Dora preempted as she began to descend the stairs, elegantly austere in a prim olive suit. "Of that I'm quite aware. You will also remember that Miss Bohn is the very good friend of Miss Walcott, which means that she is welcome at this club as long as Miss Walcott is."

When the countess reached the bottom, she turned to Marie. "I have no doubt that you will encounter your fair share of ugliness if this nonsense with Germany is not called off. However, I hope that you will find the Harlan always to be a place of comfort, good manners, and rationality in what will no doubt be irrational times."

"Thank you, Lady Dora," said Marie, rising from the sofa.

"Good, now I expect you ladies may need something fortifying. Pierre will escort you to the bar." Lady Dora looked over her shoulder. "Mrs. Harper, you will come see me in my office."

As they followed Pierre, Hazel let out a long, slow breath. "I don't think I've ever been so in awe of someone in my life as I am of Lady Dora right now."

"I should've just left," Marie murmured.

"No," said Nora firmly. "You have every right to be here."

"You're almost as British as British can be. You've been here since we were girls," said Hazel.

"That doesn't matter," said Marie. "Everyone knows I'm foreign. I still have to register at the police station if I move. And—"

"It does matter. This is Britain. We're nothing if not logical. You've nothing to worry about," said Hazel.

But Marie couldn't miss the wariness in her friend's eyes.

SUNDAY morning, with the deadline for Germany's withdrawal inching ever closer, Marie and her aunt and uncle sat in the front room, the only sound Tante Matilda's knitting needles. Finally, Tante Matilda clucked her tongue and muttered in German, "It cannot be. All that we've done. Everything we gave up to come here. It could all be gone in a moment."

"We left for Henrik," said Onkel Albrecht. "That was reason enough."

Marie had heard the stories in bits and pieces. Her aunt and uncle had lived through the Great War only to face hyperinflation as Germany tried to pay off its crippling war debt. While Tante Matilda's sister, Marie's mother, had married a man wealthy enough to survive on their foreign investments, the Müllers didn't have that luxury. Seeking a better life, they'd moved to London.

Marie's aunt and uncle continued to send Henrik back for the summers to stay with Onkel Albrecht's family. That is, until August 1933, when over breakfast with her aunt and uncle in their flat, Marie had watched Onkel Albrecht open a letter from his brother.

"Henrik is at a Hitlerjugend camp?" Onkel Albrecht had asked, stunned.

Tante Matilda snatched the letter. "But we told your brother—"

"He sent Dieter and Willi, and he writes that he couldn't see us having an objection to sending Henrik, too."

Marie watched as her aunt lurched to standing, leaning heavily on the table. "Telephone your brother right now."

"But Matilda, the cost of calling Germany—"

"I want him out! I don't want our son anywhere near any of this. Bring him home, Albrecht," Tante Matilda finished in a whisper.

Henrik had arrived on their doorstep a week later, sour-faced and sullen, and Marie had watched for the next six years as Hitler grasped for more power. After Chamberlain's deadline passed at eleven o'clock, there would be no turning back.

She cleared her throat. "May I put the radio on?"

"Where is Henrik?" asked his father, folding his paper.

Tante Matilda's lips thinned. Marie knew her aunt had also heard her cousin stumble into the flat around two that morning.

Onkel Albrecht sighed. "I'll wake our son. I cannot imagine anyone sleeping through this morning."

Marie turned the dial of the large radio that stood in the corner of the room, just as the doorbell rang. She jumped, but Tante Matilda put her hand up. "Calm, *mein Liebchen*. I will answer it."

Marie sank down into a seat, her hands folded in her lap.

The drawing room door swung open, and Henrik shuffled in.

"You look terrible," said Marie automatically.

He scowled at her. "Where's Mutter?"

"She just went to answer the door," said Marie.

"Marie," called Tante Matilda, "your friends are here."

Nora and Hazel burst into the room, their hats still perched on their heads. Her aunt followed them, a pleasant smile on her face.

Marie shot up out of her chair. "Oh, I'm so glad you're here."

"Miss Walcott, Mrs. Carey, it is always a pleasure to see you," said Onkel Albrecht, switching to English.

"And you, Mr. Müller," said Nora.

Prime Minister Chamberlain's voice crackled over the radio.

"I am speaking to you from Ten Downing Street. This morning the British ambassador in Berlin handed the German government a final note, stating that unless we heard from them by eleven o'clock that they were prepared at once to withdraw their troops from Poland, a state of war would exist between us.

"I have to tell you now that no such undertaking has been received, and consequently, this country is at war with Germany."

Slowly Onkel Albrecht rose to switch off the radio, his hand hesitating over the dial before turning back around to face his wife.

"Mein Liebchen," he started as tears began to roll down her face.

"You said it would not happen again," Marie's aunt said in German. "You said that if we moved here we would have a new life and no more war."

"I don't know what to say," Onkel Albrecht murmured.

"Twenty-six years, Albrecht!" Tante Matilda's voice rose. "Now we're enemies. They'll send us away to those horrid camps they put people in like during the last war."

Henrik slammed his fist on the arm of the sofa. "Who cares if Hitler runs the entire German army over Poland's borders?"

"Henrik," his father said sharply.

"I'm going to my club," Henrik spat in German.

"To do what?" Marie asked.

"What do you think?"

Suddenly the unmistakable, high-pitched wail of an air-raid siren cut across London.

"Is it real?" Tante Matilda asked through her tears. But it was very real. They were at war.

Nora snapped into action, whipping around to face Marie. "Do you have an air-raid shelter in the building?"

"The basement."

All at once, everyone was hurrying out of the flat, snatching up their gas masks as they went. The stairwell was filled with the muffled fall of footsteps against carpet as the entire building wound their way down.

"Everyone in!" Mr. Thompson from the third floor was shouting at the basement door. "Hurry up! Find a seat."

The basement was lit with a line of bare bulbs that hung on thick wires from the ceiling. Wood benches lined three walls.

Nora and Hazel grabbed space on the far left wall, while Tante Matilda and Onkel Albrecht huddled in the corner. Henrik made a point of skulking near the stairs, arms crossed and frowning.

Marie tucked into the space Nora and Hazel made for her between them as the now-faint wail of the air-raid siren continued.

"Perhaps it will just be a brief conflict," said Hazel hopefully. "Germany was crippled by the reparations. How much money can they really have to spend on an army?"

But Nora shook her head. "I haven't seen any of the reports—they're top secret—but everyone at the Home Office says that Germany will be a tougher fight than the press is making it out."

"What about your parents?" Hazel asked Marie. "Have you heard from them?"

The question knocked her back. What about her parents? She'd hardly thought of them at all. Which made her wonder: Did they have a thought for her? Her last letter had been the one she'd shown the girls in the Harlan the previous week.

"I'll try writing, although I don't know if the letter will make it through," said Marie.

Hazel and Nora exchanged a glance. "You don't think they'll want you to come home?"

She huffed a laugh. "I expect Vater will be too busy trying to figure out how to make sure the factories aren't requisitioned by the government, and Mutter will be strategizing how best to appear neutral in case popular opinion turns against the Nazi Party."

"Marie, I heard something at work I think you should know. It's about registered aliens," said Nora.

Marie's chest squeezed so tight she could hardly breathe, but before Nora could say more, a soft voice asked, "Where do you work?" It came from a sweet older woman Marie recognized as Mrs. Scherer, one of her aunt's friends from the third floor.

"I'm at the Home Office. Air Raid Precautions, but I sit in meetings with the man who leads the Aliens Department," said Nora.

Marie knew in an instant what Nora's news was. "We're being classed as enemy aliens now, aren't we?"

"Yes," said Nora.

"It's what they did last time," said Mrs. Scherer with a sigh.

"What does that mean?" Hazel asked.

"It means any of us who are German could be arrested and interned," said Marie.

From her spot, Tante Matilda said, "I'm sorry, Mr. and Mrs. Scherer. You shouldn't have to go through that again."

Marie sent the older couple a questioning look.

"They interned Harald in one of the camps in the last war," said Mrs. Scherer, looking at her husband. "We spent so long apart."

"At first it was just people they thought might be dangerous," said Mr. Scherer, "but then more arrests started."

"I still remember when the police came to take Harald away while we were eating dinner," said Mrs. Scherer, touching her husband on the arm. "It was the worst night of my life. I managed to avoid being deported, but many of my friends were. I knew families who lost their businesses, their homes, everything."

"But you stayed," Marie blurted out. "After, I mean."

Mr. Scherer patted his wife's hand. "This is our home."

"It won't be like last time," said Nora. "They're planning to do things differently. They're setting up tribunals. All of the Germans and Austrians in Britain who are registered aliens will have to be processed. There will be hearings before the tribunals, and they'll categorize people based on how much of a threat they might be. Category C will be people who are no threat and free to go about their business. Category B will have some restrictions placed on them. Category A will be considered a threat and detained."

"Will men and women both be interviewed?" Marie asked.

"Yes," Nora admitted.

She tried to calm herself, but it was impossible. Months of fears she'd kept bottled up now had nowhere else to go.

"What's going to happen to me? What's going to happen to my

family and Mr. and Mrs. Scherer and our friends?" asked Marie.

"I don't know," said Nora softly.

"Nothing is going to happen. We won't let it," said Hazel.

"How can you say that?" Marie asked, her voice rising. "You don't know! We could all be taken away tomorrow."

"Marie," said Tante Matilda from her spot down the bench.

Marie clapped a hand to her mouth. "I'm so sorry. I'm—"

"Miss Bohn," said Mr. Thompson, using his cane as leverage to push himself out of his seat. "I hope that you know that, at least in this building, you and your family will always have friends."

Tears pricked her eyes as most of the people lining the benches nodded. "Thank you," she whispered.

Nora leaned in to her to whisper, "We'll always be."

"Just us three," Hazel finished the silly phrase they'd started saying to one another their first term of school at Ethelbrook.

Marie nodded weakly.

Through the silence came the faint wail of the all clear. People began to stand cautiously and file out.

"I'm sorry if it seems as though I didn't understand why you're worried. I just don't want you to lose heart," said Hazel.

"I know," said Marie.

"No matter what happens, we'll do everything we can to make sure that nothing happens to you," said Nora.

Marie wanted to believe her friends, but she knew in her heart that there was nothing they could do if she came up category A.

Chapter 4

MARIE SWAYED AS THE BUS swung out to take a lazy corner. It was the same bus she always took to work, but for the last few weeks she'd found herself surreptitiously eyeing her fellow passengers.

It was her accent that was the problem. A dead giveaway. She could look every inch the young British woman, but if she were to speak, the entire bus would know.

Still, she would rather take her chances here than cower at home. Tante Matilda spent too much of the day wringing her hands for her relatives who remained in Germany. Onkel Albrecht pored over the family's bank accounts again and again, trying to predict whether they'd be able to hold on to the flat if he lost his job in a wave of anti-German sentiment.

Henrik seemed content to waste his hours away in his club. Twice she'd found him in the early morning, facedown on the sofa in the living room, sleeping off his drink. The first time she'd woken him up and then walked straight to the dining room, having no interest in or sympathy for his behavior. When it happened again last week, however, she'd stayed rooted in the spot.

"Your mother is worried sick over the war. I would think the last thing you'd want to do is add to her misery," she said.

Her cousin threw an arm over his face. Several papers covered in German scribbling came loose and floated to the floor when he moved his arm. The scent of stale beer wafted up to her nose.

With a sigh of disgust, she turned to leave, but he said, "You act as though you're a part of this family."

"I am a part of this family. I have been for years."

His scoff sounded like sandpaper. "You're not a Müller."

"My mother is your mother's sister. That makes us blood." But even she couldn't deny that those words rang hollow. Her mother had foisted Marie on her sister. Tante Matilda and Onkel Albrecht were compassionate and caring, but Marie had always wondered if some part of them couldn't help but resent her a little bit.

Taking perfect aim for the heart of her vulnerability, Henrik said, "You've been living off of my parents' charity for too long, pretending to be a lost little girl whose family doesn't love her. What did you do that your own parents sent you away, anyway?"

Slash after slash after slash. The cuts wounded deep.

The bus doors opened, and Marie pushed through the crowd. She hurried through the tall iron and redbrick gates of Royal

Imperial University's south entrance and made her way down the campus courtyard, through the door to the humanities building.

The door to the German Department offices was unlocked. Marie put her handbag into her desk drawer and took off her hat and jacket. Before sitting down, she knocked on Herr Gunter's door. No sound. She checked her watch and frowned. That was odd.

She knocked again. When there was no answer, she twisted the doorknob, edged the door open, and stopped in her tracks.

Herr Gunter's usually impeccable office was a mess. Desk drawers were pulled open. Papers were strewn everywhere. Half the books were missing from their shelves. The prints that lined his walls were all still there, but the oil painting of a ship by a minor nineteenth-century artist was gone.

"What on earth . . ."

Neil stood a few feet behind her, peering at the ransacked office.

"The door was unlocked when I came in, and when I opened it . . ." Marie looked in dismay at the office.

"Was he robbed?" Neil asked.

"I don't know."

Marie snuck a glance at Neil. She'd hardly seen him since the night he'd kissed her. After war had been declared, Tante Matilda had been nervous about Marie going anywhere in the evenings.

"What if he was taken?" Neil asked. The letters ordering Germans living in Britain to attend tribunals had starting coming out of the Home Office, just as Nora had warned.

Still, something nagged at Marie.

"Half of his things are missing. Far too many to fit into a simple briefcase. I think he left it because he had to," she said.

"Very astute, Miss Bohn." A deep voice made both Marie and Neil jump. Behind them, a man in a nondescript gray suit came through to the main office, trailing Dr. Bertram Hughes, the dean of humanities at Royal Imperial University. The two men stopped, their eyes fixed on Marie and Neil.

Marie folded her hands. "Dr. Hughes, good morning."

"Good morning, Miss Bohn," he said. "This is Thomas Dennison, from the Home Office."

Marie's hand flew up to the base of her throat. The Home Office didn't come out to German professors' offices for no reason.

"Miss Bohn. And you are?" Dennison asked, looking at Neil.

"Neil Havitt." He stuck out his hand, and Dennison examined it a moment before gingerly shaking Neil's hand.

"Herr Gunter was Neil's adviser," said Dr. Hughes.

Dennison pulled a handkerchief out of his pocket and began to methodically wipe the hand he'd used to shake Neil's. "I see."

"Miss Bohn is Herr Gunter's secretary," said Dr. Hughes.

"Yes. Miss Bohn, I'd like to speak with you," Dennison said. It was not, Marie noticed, a request.

"Of course," she said.

Neil stepped back toward the main door as Dennison and Dr. Hughes rearranged chairs in front of Marie's desk. She looked up and sent him a silent plea not to leave her, but he must not have registered it because he quietly opened the door and slid out.

Dennison gestured to Marie's desk chair. "Please sit."

She sat and smoothed her skirt.

It was Dr. Hughes who started the conversation. "As you'll have deduced, Herr Gunter is no longer with the German Department."

"What happened, if I might ask, sir?"

"I received a phone call this morning from the professor. He told me that he was leaving the country. He doesn't believe that Britain will be safe for Germans now that there is a war on, and he has chosen to go to live with his sister in America," the dean said.

She frowned. "It doesn't seem like Herr Gunter to leave without word. And without all of his things—some of his papers and books. He is very particular about them," she said.

"That, Miss Bohn, is why the Home Office is interested in him," said Dennison. "The Home Office has reason to believe that Mr. Gunter may have connections to the Nazi Party."

"What? But that's impossible," she said.

"Did he ever say anything to you that made you suspect his loyalties?" Dennison asked.

"No. In fact, I'd say he was almost apolitical," she said.

Dennison reached into his jacket pocket and pulled out a notebook and a silver pen. He flipped the notebook open. "How long have you been Herr Gunter's secretary?"

"I'm the secretary for the German Department," she said. "He is—*was*—the head of the department, but I also assist Herrs Lange, Fuchs, and Vogt."

Dennison scribbled something and, without looking up, asked, "When did you begin working in the German Department?"

"In 1935," she said.

"And when did you meet Herr Gunter?"

"Last year. A little more than a year ago," she said.

"In that time, did you ever see Herr Gunter act in a suspicious manner?" he asked.

She scrunched up her nose. "I'm surrounded by academics every day, Mr. Dennison. You will have to be more specific."

Dr. Hughes cleared his throat, but Dennison didn't look up.

"Miss Bohn, were you aware that Herr Gunter kept a personal diary for his appointments in addition to the one that is on his desk?" he asked.

"No, he didn't."

"He did," said Dennison, drawing a green leather book out of his jacket pocket. The book was no larger than a cigarette case.

"I've never seen that before," she said.

He handed it to her. "Could you please look at last week's appointments and verify that they are the same that appear in the diary you have?"

Picking through the mess of papers, Marie went to Herr Gunter's desk and retrieved the large leather desk diary that she left there each night. Back at her desk, she flipped to the last week and began checking the dates against the one in the green book. Everything seemed in order until she reached last Thursday.

"This," she said, tapping on an entry in the green book. "'Emily, half past seven, American Bar.'"

Dennison nodded. "And do you know who Emily is?"

She hesitated. "I don't, no, but he did mention an Emily once."

"When was this?" asked Dennison.

Herr Gunter was her employer, but she wasn't going to lie, and so she said, "The day that Germany invaded Poland."

Dennison's eyes narrowed. "Is that right?"

"Herr Gunter was upset—we all were. He asked me to call Emily and cancel his dinner with her. When I told him I didn't know who that was, he said that he would do it himself."

Dennison sat back. "Miss Bohn, were you aware that in the last few months, Herr Gunter had begun to see a woman?"

"No," she said. Herr Gunter had never so much as made a murmur about his social life outside of Royal Imperial.

"Then you did not know that your employer had used an agency to arrange to meet a woman?" Dennison asked.

Marie braced herself. "What kind of agency?"

Dennison looked down at his notes before fixing her with a stare she felt to her bones. "The Mayfair Matrimonial Agency. Now, Miss Bohn, I think you'd better come with me."

DENNISON bundled Marie into the back of a large black Morris that was parked in front of the university gates. She sat with her hands clasped tightly. Herr Gunter had never mentioned that he had been to Hazel's agency, but it couldn't be a coincidence. And why had Hazel never mentioned that Marie's boss was a client?

Of course she wouldn't, Marie reasoned. Hazel might tell stories from the agency, but she rarely used names.

Dennison drove like a man who expected traffic to part like the Red Sea for him. When they reached Mayfair, he swung the Morris into an open spot just a few doors down from Hazel's building and killed the ignition. He looked over his shoulder at Marie.

"This is the building of the agency Gunter visited," he said. "We're going to go speak to the proprietor. Miss Bohn, I want to remind you that this is an investigation. When we go inside, you'll only answer questions that I put to you. Is that clear?"

Then why bring me at all?

He didn't know. The realization struck her like lightning. However he'd found out about Herr Gunter, the matchmaking agency, and Emily, Dennison hadn't put together the fact that Marie might be the connection between her boss and Hazel's agency.

Dennison opened her door and led her into the building. They climbed the stairs just as Marie had done so many times before.

The light was on behind the frosted glass panel of the agency's door. Dennison leaned on the small brass doorbell, and a moment later Nancy, Hazel's secretary, opened the door with a smile.

Marie inched back from Dennison and shook her head emphatically, praying that Nancy wouldn't reveal that she knew Marie.

"Hello," said Nancy brightly, looking from Dennison to Marie. A flicker of doubt flashed over the secretary's face, but just as fast she turned her smile back to Dennison. "Welcome to the Mayfair Matrimonial Agency. How can I help you?"

Dennison pushed forward. "I need to speak to Mrs. Carey."

"I'm afraid Mrs. Carey is with a client," said Nancy.

"Perhaps we should come back at another time," said Marie, stepping into the reception.

Dennison glared at her. "I'm here on Home Office business. It's a matter of great importance."

"I can see if she—"

Hazel's door opened, and she appeared, a laugh on her lips as she looked over her shoulder at the client following her. He was a good-looking, solid sort of man with light brown hair.

"Mrs. Carey, a gentleman from the Home Office is here to see you," said Nancy.

Hazel's laugh died as she took in the players in the room. Marie hoped that her friend would pick up on Nancy's discomfort.

"The Home Office, you said?" Hazel asked.

"Thomas Dennison. I have some questions for you about a client." He pulled the notebook out of his jacket pocket.

Hazel put her hand up. "Mr. Dennison, will you please allow me to see Mr. Calloway out first?"

Calloway . . . Calloway . . . Marie turned the name over in her head until it snapped into place. Richard Calloway, the widower with the wife who'd died tragically young.

"I'll see myself out," said Richard, shaking Hazel's hand.

"We'll find you a more suitable match. Sometimes it simply takes a few attempts," said Hazel.

"I place myself entirely at your mercy." Richard said goodbye to Nancy and nodded at Dennison. When he came to Marie, he offered her a kind smile. "You're in good hands with Mrs. Carey."

"Thank you. I would certainly hope so," she said.

Over Richard's shoulder, she could see Hazel tilt her head in question. But by the time he gathered up his coat and hat to leave, Hazel's usual composure was back in place.

"If you'd like to come through, Mr. Dennison," said Hazel, gesturing to her office door.

Dennison gestured for Marie to lead, and they settled themselves into the chairs angled before Hazel's desk.

"Mrs. Carey, this is Marie Bohn. She is the secretary of Pieter Gunter, a professor of German at Royal Imperial University," said Dennison.

Marie's heart pounded as Hazel slowly said, "It's a pleasure to meet you, Miss Bohn."

"The pleasure is mine, Mrs. Carey," she managed.

"Yesterday, Miss Bohn's employer fled the country. We believe that he booked a place on a ship out of Southampton. It's likely that he is going to America, but we've wired all passenger ships at sea, and he doesn't appear on any manifest. In all likelihood, Gunter is using a false name and false papers," said Dennison.

"Why are you looking for him?" asked Hazel.

"When he was a university student, he was intimate friends with several men who now hold positions of some power in Berlin. We have reason to believe that he is still in contact with them and may be sympathetic to their cause," said Dennison. "A name came up in our investigation: Emily Boyne. I believe Mr. Gunter met her through this agency."

"I don't usually speak about clients, but given the circumstances, I can say that Mrs. Boyne is an older woman, quite respectable. Her husband died eight or nine years back."

"What nationality is Mrs. Boyne?" asked Dennison.

"British."

"When was the last time you made an arrangement for her?"

"When I introduced her to Herr Gunter," said Hazel. "But that was some time ago."

"You are remarkably confident about your answers without referring to any notes," said Dennison.

"I've often been told that I have a remarkable memory, Mr. Dennison. It's useful in my trade," said Hazel.

Dennison grunted. "Did Gunter ask for Mrs. Boyne?"

"No. He wouldn't have known her identity until I had secured permission from the lady to make the introduction."

"Are you aware that her father is a government official?"

"Yes," said Hazel.

"And you don't think it suspicious that a woman with a father in government was being courted by a man who is a German sympathizer?" asked Dennison.

"Unless your investigation is a foregone conclusion, I believe you mean to say *if* he was a sympathizer." Hazel folded her arms. "I find it strange that you should consider this match suspicious. Mrs. Boyne and Herr Gunter met months before war was declared. I never mentioned the lady's parentage, and he did not make any request to be matched with her. I believe you're chasing ghosts."

Dennison grunted again and turned to Marie. "Miss Bohn, you were Herr Gunter's secretary."

"I was the department's secretary," Marie said.

"Yet you claim to have no knowledge of Mrs. Boyne?"

"Except for the one time he mentioned an Emily right after we'd found out about the invasion," Marie replied.

"Did you ever make bookings for Gunter? Arrange any of his domestic duties?" Dennison asked her.

"Yes. I did on occasion," she said.

"And yet he did not see fit to use your services when he was going to see Mrs. Boyne," said Dennison.

"He was a private man," said Marie with a shrug.

"I think that we can assume that Gunter was taking pains to cover up his relationship with Mrs. Boyne," said Dennison.

"That's rather a stretch, Mr. Dennison," said Hazel with a laugh.

"I'd like to see your records, Mrs. Carey. The ones you claim you don't need in order to remember a client you matched so many months ago," said Dennison.

"No," said Hazel.

"I'm sorry?" asked Dennison.

"No," Hazel repeated.

"It is not wise to say no to the Home Office," said Dennison.

"And yet here I am, doing just that," said Hazel. "If you would like to complain, you may speak to my employer, Lady Moreton."

Dennison looked thrown. "The wife of Sir Gregory Moreton?"

Marie smiled at the way the prominent banker's name seemed to shake the man.

"That's right," said Hazel.

"Then you are not the owner?" he asked.

"No. I am the primary matchmaker and run the day-to-day business, but Lady Moreton owns the establishment," said Hazel.

Dennison snapped his mouth shut, and for a moment Marie thought he might let all of this go, but then he straightened his shoulders. "Mrs. Carey, I'll be frank with you. Agencies such as this one have come under scrutiny by the Home Office due to the nature of your business."

"What is that nature?" Hazel asked.

"Engineering marriages."

Hazel threw her head back and laughed. "Some would say that we're in the business of love and happiness, but if you must insist on calling it engineering . . ."

"We are at war, Mrs. Carey. This is not a time for bright-eyed idealism. The Home Office has identified a number of ways that enemy agents may try to infiltrate Britain."

"Are you really that worried about German men marrying British women?" Hazel asked.

"I believe that Gunter was attempting to marry Emily Boyne in order to avoid any restrictive designation when he went before his tribunal," he said. "This would allow him to continue to operate as an informant for his friends back at home in Germany."

"I can assure you that we vet all of our clients," Hazel said.

"How?" he asked.

"References. Identification cards. Service records. University degrees. We want to ensure that everyone is being honest."

Still, Dennison said, "I would like to see your record books and your correspondence. As Miss Bohn is Gunter's secretary, she should be more than equipped to identify his handwriting."

Hazel smiled. "I'm afraid that will be rather difficult."

"Why?" Dennison asked.

Outside in the reception, a woman's bright, "Wonderful day to help people fall in love, darlings!" rang out.

"Who is that?" Dennison asked.

Hazel's lips twitched. "That would be Lady Moreton. Perhaps you would like to make your request to her yourself."

All the years that Marie had been coming to the agency, she'd never met Lady Moreton. Part of it was her own doing. There was something intimidating about a regular girl meeting a baron's wife. But in that moment, Marie couldn't have been happier for Lady Moreton's elevated status because it unsettled Dennison. Lifting his chin, though, he said, "I shall do just that."

Dennison was the first through Hazel's door, giving Marie just enough time to grab Hazel's hand as she rounded her desk. "I haven't told him that we know each other."

"I gathered as much. I think it's best to keep him in the dark. I don't like the things he's hinting at one bit," whispered Hazel.

Out in the reception, Dennison appeared already to have introduced himself to Lady Moreton, because she was staring him down as though he were lower than pond scum.

"Does the Home Office not have enough to do without involving itself in the personal lives of British citizens?" asked Lady Moreton with a sniff.

"It is precisely because there is a war on that I'm here, my lady," said Dennison.

"What is it that you want, then?" Lady Moreton asked.

"I would like you to open your records for our inspection."

"Lady Moreton, I've already informed Mr. Dennison that we will not do that," said Hazel.

"Well, what do you have to say to that, Mr. Dennison?" Lady Moreton asked as she removed a cigarette from a gold case.

"I will need to see *all* of your records. Matches, correspondence, receipts," he pressed.

Lady Moreton lit her cigarette. "No, I think not."

"I'm sorry?" he asked.

"I refuse to have you snooping around without a judge's order."

Dennison stiffened. "I can compel you on legal grounds."

"Then I suggest you do that, or else I shall have to pay a visit to the Lord Chief Justice. He was up in the country with us in June, you see. He's mad about cricket."

"You have a duty to your country, madam," he said.

"I am acutely aware of my duty, and it does not include helping men like you persecute people when you cannot produce solid evidence of any wrongdoing. Good day, Mr. Dennison."

Dennison clenched his hands into fists, but nonetheless made a small bow. The door slammed behind him.

Lady Moreton let out a long breath. "If ever there was a time for a stiff drink, this is it. Still, if we start drinking before luncheon, where will we be? Nancy, if you would brew a pot of tea?" Then the agency owner turned to Marie. "Now, who are you?"

Marie would've laughed if she hadn't been quite so shaken by the events of the morning. "I'm Marie Bohn."

"Oh, the friend from boarding school," said Lady Moreton. "It's all coming back to me. Now, Hazel"—she turned to her head matchmaker—"what is all this nonsense about?"

Hazel filled her employer in on Dennison's visit.

"Do you know Herr Gunter?" Lady Moreton asked.

"Yes, I matched him with Mrs. Boyne," said Hazel, her eyes sliding to Marie. "I'm sorry I didn't tell you. He contacted me ages ago and said that he had heard you mention me and the agency when you were talking to one of your friends in the office."

"What's happened to the man?" Lady Moreton asked.

"They think he set sail on one of the passenger ships under a false name. I doubt they'll ever find him," said Marie.

"Well, what's done is done," said Lady Moreton.

"What shall I do if Dennison comes back?" Hazel asked.

"Ring round to the house. I'll speak to our solicitor," said Lady Moreton with a nod. "War or not, I refuse to be ordered around by a man who's clearly never even heard of a good tailor."

Chapter 5

A LIGHT MIST OF RAIN drifted down on Tottenham, dancing in the dim light of the streetlamps nearly entirely covered in accordance with the blackout. Marie tugged her coat closed at the throat.

She would've come to the Party meeting with Neil, only he had headed off early from campus, telling her he was determined to arrive well ahead of the start. He was supposed to speak that evening, so it made sense, except a selfish part of her wished that she'd traveled with him as they usually had.

She hadn't been able to shake the unsettled feeling that had crept under her skin since the day of Herr Gunter's disappearance. Everywhere she looked, she expected Dennison to pop out from hiding and arrest her even though she'd done nothing wrong.

But you don't need to do anything wrong, do you?

On Wednesday morning, the Müller family and Marie's tribunal hearing letters had come in the morning post. Tante Matilda had been waiting when Marie came home, her own letter already open on the sofa next to her. She'd handed Marie her own envelope and began to cry. Marie opened it carefully and slid the letter out. She was required to report to her hearing on October 26 at half past two. She would be permitted to bring character witnesses who were not related to her. She telephoned Hazel and Nora to ask them to stand with her. They'd both said yes.

Arriving at the CPGB's meeting hall, she spotted Neil near the stage. He started when he saw her, as though he'd forgotten that they'd agreed she would meet him. But then he gave her a little smile.

"I didn't think you'd actually come," he said.

"I told my aunt and uncle I was having dinner with a friend and her mother. They worry whenever I leave the house now, but they also know that they can't keep me locked up," she said.

"Like Cinderella in her tower?" he asked.

"You mean Rapunzel?" He frowned, so she clarified, "The damsel locked in her tower was Rapunzel."

"Yes," he said.

Something hung between them, heavy yet unacknowledged. She didn't know what it was, but she didn't like it.

"Are you ready for your speech?" she asked, attempting to find something that would once again forge the connection that she'd felt the night he'd kissed her.

He gave her a little smile and let out a long, shaky breath.

"As ready as I'll ever be, *kleine Maus*," he said.

If Marie was being honest, Neil's speech was adequate. He'd asked her to look over the draft a few weeks ago, before the entire world had gone mad. She'd rewritten large parts of it, coaxing poetry out of the prose. However, as she watched him deliver the words on the stage, it was clear that the written word could only do so much. While Neil had passion, he didn't have the charisma that made it impossible to look away from him when he spoke.

He was nearing the final page, when suddenly he veered wildly off course from what she'd edited.

"This organization has long stood up to the tyranny of the British government, ruled by corrupt politicians with no greater aspiration than to sit in Parliament and tell us how to live our lives," Neil said. "Well, it is time for that to end. Just as our brothers and sisters in Germany and Russia are struggling in the wake of war, we must demand an end to the government's warmongering!"

Marie sat up straight. Just a few weeks ago, at her last meeting, they were raging against the scourge of fascism spreading across Europe. Now Germany was their brother and the British were the ones agitating for war?

"Responsibility for this war lies at the feet of Prime Minister Chamberlain. We must stand up against the government. Stand up against those who would bring war to our doorsteps!"

People were on their feet applauding. Neil pushed back from the podium, triumphant, waved to the crowd, and stepped off the stage. He shot her a grin. "I made some changes."

"Neil, you were asking the people here to rise up against the government. In a time of war!" she shouted over the din.

He shrugged. "We *want* the government overthrown. 'Workers of the world unite; you have nothing to lose but your chains.'"

People around them had begun to sit down, drawing attention to the fact that the last speaker seemed to be having an impassioned conversation with a young woman. The attention would've made her uncomfortable on any given day, but now, with things as they were, she wanted to hide.

"Can we step outside, please?" she asked, her voice low.

Neil looked around, realizing how many eyes were on them. "Come on," he said, pulling her toward a side door.

They pushed outside into the night. It was pouring, and they huddled under an awning.

"Why did you change the speech?" she asked. "In August, all anyone could talk about was how we needed to defeat Germany and the fascists. Now the war is Britain's fault and Germany is our brother in arms?"

He scrubbed a hand over his face. "You're deliberately misunderstanding the politics of the situation. You don't know—"

"I'm not misunderstanding things, Neil. I'm fully capable of understanding." *I practically write your speeches for you.*

"Moscow decreed that we were no longer meant to focus on Germany as the enemy. We should be striving for peace."

"You changed your politics because Moscow told you to?"

"It's what I have to do, *kleine Maus*. You understand that, don't you?" he asked. "Sometimes doing things you don't want to?"

He tucked her into his chest so he could rest his chin on the top of her head. But even as they stood there, a question with hazy edges formed in her head.

"Or else what?" she asked.

"What?"

"You said, 'It's what I have to do,' as though someone is going to take something from you if you don't follow instructions."

He peeled away from her and smoothed his hand over his hair.

"A man I've been talking to thinks I could have a career in politics after the war," he said.

"Neil, that's wonderful!"

"Yes," he said, his head hanging down. "Yes, it is."

She frowned. "Why aren't you happier about this?"

"I'll have to join up. Probably the army. That way I'll have a service record and all of the respect that comes with it. No one will vote for a man who didn't fight if he was capable, not even if his politics mean he disagrees with it," he said.

"You don't want to fight," she said slowly.

"I'll do my bit, but there are other things I'd rather be doing. And there are things I would have to give up. People."

"I don't understand," she said.

"You're German, *kleine Maus.*"

Immediately she understood, bile rising in her throat. "You're saying you need to put me to the side just so you can maybe stand for office if you make it through this war. You *kissed* me, Neil."

He toed the ground with his brogue. "Just once. And this is my career. I could become one of the youngest members of Parliament ever to serve the North London boroughs. But not if there's anything that will make voters think twice about me."

"And I'm something to make people doubt your judgment."

It was as though the man who'd stopped by her desk to flirt and make her blush had dissolved and the true Neil stood before her. One who was as ambitious as he was craven.

"I thought better of you," she said.

She turned to leave, but he grabbed her arm. *"Kleine Maus."*

Through gritted teeth, she ground out, "Why do you call me that? It's a nickname people use when they feel affection for one another." *Not when they see someone as a burden.*

He spread his hands before him. "The first day I saw you, you were sitting behind that big desk looking so small. Just like a little mouse. It just popped into my head."

The cracks around her heart shattered. That nickname—the one that had made her hope for so long—had been nothing more than a joking acknowledgment that he thought her small and meek.

"Marie, I *do* like you."

"But not enough to fight for me," she said.

He threw up his hands. "I don't know what you want me to say. That I've secretly been in love with you for years and that I'd marry you no matter whether there's a war on or not?"

All she could do was stare.

"Oh, Marie." He chucked her under the chin. "You're a great girl. You have no idea how much I'll miss your cups of coffee when I'm at the front."

All of her memories of him reshuffled, and she saw with clarity what should have been right in front of her since she'd met him. He didn't care for her. All she was to him was the girl who fetched the coffee, edited his speeches, and told him he was brilliant.

"I can't believe I thought you would ever be good enough for me," she whispered.

"Well, there's no need to be mean-spirited about it."

"Goodbye, Neil." She walked around him and out into the rain.

MARIE spent three days furious at Neil, but it turned out that the best way to overcome a man's rejection was to have a tribunal hearing to worry about. She spent most of her free time at Hazel's office, where her friends were helping her study her own biography. For hours the three would go over the details of her life, making sure that nothing the panel might ask would trip her up.

"Are you sure Nathaniel doesn't mind us taking you away from him for so many evenings?" she asked Hazel one night over sandwiches from the shop around the corner.

Hazel waved her hand. "The agency has been so busy he hardly notices when I'm not home these days. It's been like this for months."

Marie frowned. It was difficult to imagine the man who had been madly in love with her friend during the first flush of their marriage not minding his wife spending so much time away at night.

"Back to it, then," said Nora. She put on a deep male voice. "Tell us about your employment history, Miss Bohn."

"I was a switchboard operator at Lindwood hotel," said Marie.

"When did you begin working there?" Hazel asked.

"June 1932."

"What were you doing before that?" Nora asked.

"I was at school in Herefordshire."

"Why didn't you return to Germany after school?" Nora asked.

"England had become my home," Marie said.

Hazel leaned forward, her chair squeaking in protest, and asked in a gravelly voice, "But what about your parents?"

"You know about my parents," said Marie, shifting in her seat.

"I don't know anything," said Hazel. "I'm Lawrence Humperdinck, underpaid, overworked civil servant who thinks that this whole thing is a waste of my time. But my supervisor is watching my every move, so I'm vigilant in my job."

Marie drew in a breath. "Well, Mr. Humperdinck, the truth is that my parents and I were never close. They sent me away to school in England and never visited. I stayed with my aunt and uncle during breaks."

Marie could still remember the day she met Tante Matilda. She was conjugating French verbs under her governess's watchful eye when a maid slipped into the nursery and whispered in her governess's ear. All at once, the French exercise books were put away, and Marie found herself being hurried to Mutter's morning room.

Mutter was not alone. Marie recognized Tante Matilda from her photograph, a little older but still the same pretty woman with thick blond hair caught up in a chignon.

"Marie, say hello to your aunt, Frau Müller," Mutter said.

Tante Matilda laughed at the formality and said in a low, warm voice, "Please, call me Tante Matilda."

"Hello, Tante Matilda," Marie said, holding back a grin.

Tante Matilda stretched out her hands to Marie. "Oh, let me look at you." Her aunt's gray leather gloves had felt divine, and the light floral scent of Tante Matilda's perfume hugged her.

"You've grown into quite the young lady, haven't you?" Tante Matilda looked back at Marie's mother. "The last time you sent me a photograph, she was barely at her father's knee."

Mutter selected a cigarette from a box. "We keep such a social calendar, it's nearly impossible to find the time to write."

Even at twelve, Marie saw the tightening around Tante Matilda's lips.

Everything moved in a flash after that. Marie's mother explained to her that she'd been enrolled in a girls' school in England called Ethelbrook. On holidays, she would stay with Tante Matilda and Onkel Albrecht in London. When she was finished with school, she would return to Munich. The words washed over Marie. She didn't understand. What had she done to be sent away?

When she arrived in London, there had been shopping for seemingly endless things Marie would need for school. Most of it felt like a fog until the morning they drove up to Ethelbrook.

A soft-spoken lady told them that the headmistress expected them and showed them into an office. The headmistress, Mrs. Osborn, strode in a few moments later and immediately began firing questions at Tante Matilda, who answered them all in her gentle voice. Yes, it was highly unusual to enroll a foreign girl in school midterm, but Marie was bright and would catch up quickly. Yes, Marie did have a full command of English, as she had been tutored by an English governess.

And, just like that, twelve-year-old Marie was officially an Ethelbrook girl. Tante Matilda kissed her on the cheek.

"Make friends, and make your mother and father proud, *mein Liebchen*," said her aunt before leaning in. "But don't forget that who you are is always good enough for Albrecht and me."

After her aunt left, Mrs. Osborn introduced her to the matron, who rattled off everything Marie needed to know as they walked. Class schedules, bathing schedules, dining schedules.

Finally, they reached a room tucked away in one of Ethelbrook's four turrets. "We already had an odd situation with a girl coming in a week into term, so we might as well put you in with her and the scholarship girl she's housed with."

Without knocking, the matron opened the door. Two other girls jumped off their beds. A book clattered to the floor on the raven-haired girl's side of the room.

"Miss Walcott, pick that up," the matron barked.

The gangly girl Marie would soon learn was Nora bent to scoop the book up, but not before shooting Marie a cheeky grin.

"This is Marie Bohn. German. She'll take the third bed. Your trunk will be up when the porter gets around to it."

Then the matron was gone, and Marie was left staring at her two new roommates.

"Well, come in," said the pretty strawberry blonde with a laugh. "I'm Hazel Ricci. Thirteen years old, which I suspect means I'm a year older than you. And before anyone else can tell you, yes, I'm a scholarship girl and, yes, my mother has a *reputation*."

"And I'm Nora Walcott. Are you twelve? I am. I like your hair. It's so blond. Are you really German?"

Marie blinked a few times at the onslaught of words and realized she could be friends with these girls.

Now, eleven years later, they were still her confidants, her champions, her best friends. Yet she knew she wasn't being completely honest with them. She'd been holding parts of herself back—the Party meetings, the speeches, Neil.

"I need to tell you something," Marie said, her voice halting. "It's nothing *bad*. It's just . . . Do you know how I could rarely go to the cinema on Monday nights? Well, I wasn't working late."

Nora's eyes widened. "Marie Bohn, you have a man."

"No, it isn't anything like that," said Marie quickly. "There wasn't a man involved. At least, not really." She took a breath. "I was attending CPGB meetings."

Her friends stared at her openmouthed.

"Commie meetings?" Nora asked.

"A graduate student in the department invited me," said Marie.

"His name?" Hazel prompted.

"Neil Havitt. He was speaking one night, so I went along. Then I just sort of kept going back."

"How often?" Nora asked.

Marie winced. "Every other Monday for months. Neil asked me

to read over his speeches. I would rewrite them, and I liked watching him say them out loud to all of those people. Sometimes, when they were clapping or yelling, I felt like they were applauding for me even though they had no idea who I was or what I'd done."

"Are you a Communist?" Nora asked.

"No, I don't think so. I listened to the speeches, and I agreed with things the speakers said. People should be paid more fairly. There should be better conditions. But I don't think the government is all wrong. I don't think there should be a revolution."

"You went because you liked him, didn't you?" Hazel asked.

"Yes," she admitted. A blush colored her cheeks. "I thought he might actually like me. He was always asking me to join him when he spoke, and then giving me his writing to look at. I was flattered. It turns out, he was never truly interested in me at all."

"Oh, Marie." Hazel sat next to her. "How did you find out?"

"We kissed just before the invasion, but then I went to a meeting the other day, and he told me he would have to drop me. He has political aspirations after the war, you see."

"He dropped you?" Nora asked at the same time Hazel said, "You kissed him?"

"It doesn't matter," said Marie. "It's all over now."

"Oh, Marie. It might not be," said Nora. "Did you register for membership? Did you march?"

"I never marched, but the membership . . . Maybe? They were asking people to put their names down at my first meeting."

"Then you'll be on the rolls, and you can be sure that the Aliens Department will have record of that," she said. "Between this and Herr Gunter's behavior . . ."

"I might not get a category C classification," Marie said.

"I'm sorry, darling," said Nora.

"Well." Marie took a deep breath. "I think we've been at it long enough."

"I would encourage you to stay, but in all honesty, I'm beginning to feel as though I live here," said Hazel with a yawn.

Nora glanced at her watch. "I should be going anyway. It's impossible to navigate the mews in the blackout."

They all put their coats on and made their way to the street. Nora peeled off toward Hyde Park Corner, and Marie was about to turn north to her bus when Hazel gripped her arm. "Wait."

"What's wrong?"

"I don't know if you remember, but there was a gentleman in my office that day Dennison brought you to the agency."

"Mr. Calloway?" Marie asked.

"Yes. He mentioned you the next time we spoke over the phone. He sounded quite taken with you. If you'd like to go to dinner with him, I could arrange it," said Hazel.

"I don't know," she said slowly.

"Here." Hazel pulled out the pencil and pad she always carried with her. "This is his exchange. You can ring him if you feel like it. It might do you some good to go out with a nice man."

Hazel ripped out the paper and handed it to her. Marie stared at it for a moment before taking it and stuffing it into her bag.

"I'll think about it."

Chapter 6

On the day of her tribunal hearing, Marie found herself in a crowded but eerily quiet waiting room. Nora sat on her right and Hazel on her left. They were surrounded by men in tired suits and women who looked as though they'd just walked out of a Parisian couturier. A handful of children squirmed in their seats.

Marie breathed deeply, trying to calm herself.

"Are you nervous?" Nora asked her.

"No," she said, but she was certain her friends could feel her whole body shake.

"It will be over soon enough," said Hazel.

A woman wearing a boxy blue suit stepped into the waiting area.

She glanced down at the stack of papers she held. "Marie Bohn."

The three of them walked through the door arm in arm, the woman with the papers leading the way.

Inside was a long table with three men sitting at the head. Two were balding, and one kept touching a handkerchief to his nose as he sniffled. They looked up in unison as Marie approached.

"Which of you is Miss Bohn?" asked one of the balding men.

Marie stepped forward. "I am, sir."

The sniffling man gestured to the hairless man on his left. "This is Mr. Renault. And to my right is Mr. Elliot. I am Mr. Perry. So, Miss . . . Bohn, what brought you to Britain?"

"I was educated at Ethelbrook School for Girls in Herefordshire. I arrived in the autumn of 1928," said Marie.

"And did you remain at Ethelbrook for the duration of your education?" Mr. Renault asked.

"I did. I left in June of 1932," said Marie.

"And what have you been doing since then?" asked Mr. Perry.

"First I was a switchboard operator. Then I took a job as a secretary at Royal Imperial University."

"Are you still employed there?" asked Mr. Renault.

"I am," said Marie.

"I have a note here that you were secretary to a Pieter Gunter, a man who is wanted by the Home Office," said Mr. Perry.

Breathe. It would do her no good to faint in the tribunal hearing.

"He fled the country shortly after Germany's invasion of Poland," she said in as steady a voice as she could muster.

"Your employer fled?" Mr. Elliot said, peering over his glasses. "That is most concerning."

Her heart rammed against her rib cage.

"To clarify, sir, I was the secretary for the German Department," she said. "There were several other professors in the department as well. I also performed administrative tasks for them."

The men looked at one another before moving on.

"Where are you currently living?" asked Mr. Renault.

"Number 5 Taviton Street with my aunt, uncle, and cousin."

"Who is your first witness?" asked Mr. Renault.

Marie gestured behind her. "My friend Nora Walcott."

"Miss Walcott, where do you reside?" asked Mr. Elliot.

"My house is at 22 Crawley Mews," said Nora.

"*Your* house?" Mr. Perry asked.

"Yes. I own it," said Nora.

"You mean your father owns it?" Mr. Perry asked with an indulgent smile.

Marie could feel Nora tense next to her. "I own it. My solicitor brokered the sale under my direction. After my father died."

"That is most unusual," muttered Mr. Elliot.

"If you're such a modern woman, I can only assume that you work, Miss Walcott?" asked Mr. Perry.

"I do."

"Where is it that you are employed?" he asked.

Marie cast a glance at Nora as her friend adjusted her glasses. The questions were meant to be for Marie. Nora's job at the Home Office was never meant to come into this; otherwise she never would have allowed her to come here and risk it.

"I am also a secretary," Nora finally said.

"All right, Miss Walcott. What have you to say about Miss Bohn's character?" asked the rather bored-sounding Mr. Elliot.

"I have known Marie since I was twelve years old. She has always been a dear friend, and one of the few people in this world I trust without reservation. She is no threat to me or this country."

"And am I to presume you will say more of the same, Miss . . ." Mr. Perry looked at Hazel.

"Mrs. Nathaniel Carey."

"You're married?" asked Mr. Renault.

"For five years, yes," said Hazel.

"Then I presume you're a homemaker," said Mr. Renault.

"I am not," said Hazel. "I am a matchmaker at Mayfair Matrimonial Agency."

"That is Lady Moreton's matchmaking business, isn't it? I've read of it in the papers," said Mr. Elliot, obviously a little impressed by Hazel's connection to the peerage.

"That's correct," said Hazel.

"And do you also feel as strongly about Miss Bohn's character as your friend does?" asked Mr. Renault.

"I do. Marie was a bridesmaid at my wedding. She attended my mother's funeral. She has been with me through every moment of celebration and struggle since we were schoolgirls."

"This is all very touching, but it really tells us nothing about whether Miss Bohn is a threat to this country," said Mr. Perry.

"Mr. Perry, Mr. Elliot, Mr. Renault," said Hazel, turning on her most brilliant smile, "Marie works at the German Department of Royal Imperial University because it was a natural place for a woman with such fluency. However, I know that her greatest ambition is to become a wife and mother. In fact, just the other week she asked me to arrange a connection between her and a well-respected gentleman who is also a client of mine."

Hazel's picture of Marie as a woman whose sole desire was for a life of domesticity seemed to be working. The men had sat back in their seats, and Mr. Perry and Mr. Renault were slowly nodding.

"Thank you, Mrs. Carey," said Mr. Renault.

The questioning continued, back and forth, for what seemed like an age. They wanted to know about Marie's habits, where she spent her time, the kinds of films she went to and books she read. The entire time, she held her breath, waiting for one of the men to mention the CPGB, but the meetings never came up.

Finally, the men declared that they were finished. Marie was directed to wait for her classification designation in the post.

As soon as they were released and the door shut behind them, Marie could feel all the energy drain from her.

"What on earth was that about wanting to find a man?" Nora hissed as they hurried out of the waiting room.

"They ate it up with a spoon," said Hazel.

Nora shook her head. "Sometimes I can't tell when you're being serious about that sort of thing."

"Oh, please. You know I don't believe in all that tosh, but I know what men want to think about women," said Hazel.

Her friends continued to bicker, but Marie had stopped listening. She had made it through the tribunal, but those men held her fate in their hands. One decision from them and she'd be confined to an internment camp. What if they found out about the CPGB? What if Herr Gunter really was as nefarious as Dennison seemed to think he was? She could be locked away, her freedom gone for the duration of the entire war. And if she was sent away, surely that would mean more scrutiny for her aunt, uncle, and Henrik. Would she be condemning them to a war spent in internment, too?

SINCE Herr Gunter's disappearance, Marie had begun to feel superfluous in the department she'd run for years. She'd never realized just how much of her day was occupied by the head of the department's demands. Already she'd tidied Herr Gunter's office. Last week she'd reorganized all of the department's files. And the day after Neil had told her that he didn't like her *in that way,* she'd set about cleaning the office from top to bottom.

Now, rag in hand, she gave the cabinet a good swipe. As she did so, the hinges on the office door squeaked, and she peered over her shoulder just in time to see Dr. Hughes stick his head in.

"Dr. Hughes, how can I help you?" she asked.

"Please sit," the dean said.

She hesitated but moved to her desk. Dr. Hughes sat opposite and began drumming his fingers on his chair.

"Dr. Hughes, is something wrong?" she asked.

He glanced at her. "I don't suppose there's any easy way to say this, Miss Bohn, so I'll just have out with it. There has been a great deal of scrutiny on this department after Herr Gunter ran out."

"I can imagine that it has set everyone on edge," she said.

"Precisely. And that is why we must be so very careful with what we do. We are at war, after all. I'm afraid that leaves us in the difficult position of what to do with you, Miss Bohn."

"Me?" she asked. "I don't understand, sir."

"I think, given the circumstances, it would be inappropriate for you to continue your employment at Royal Imperial," he said.

"The circumstances?" she asked, her mouth gone dry. "But I haven't done anything wrong."

"Come now, Miss Bohn. Think of what people are saying. Herr

Gunter's German-born secretary, a woman who was privy to all of his meetings, his diary, his correspondence, is bound to raise suspicions. It's time that the gossip be handled or we risk another investigation from our friend Mr. Dennison. No one wants that."

"But I haven't done anything wrong," she protested.

"You're German, Miss Bohn."

And with those words, he cut each of her arguments off at the knees. She was German, and nothing would change that.

MARIE sat on the now-empty bus, staring out the window at the unfamiliar bustle of a working day as she blinked back tears. This was the first time she'd been out of work for any reason other than holiday or sickness since she had left school. She'd been *sacked*.

She squeezed her eyes closed. What was she going to tell her aunt and uncle? What was she going to tell her friends?

The bus screeched to a halt, and Marie scrambled off. Desperate for the sanctuary of home, she fumbled for her keys to unlatch the door and ran up the stairs of her aunt and uncle's building.

"Tante Matilda," she called out as she shut the door behind her.

There was a shuffling from behind her bedroom door as she pulled off her coat. But when the door opened, it wasn't her aunt or Frau Hafner tidying up. It was Henrik.

"What are you doing?" she asked, taking in her bedroom. He'd clearly gone through her things, because a pair of stockings was hanging out of the side of a drawer that had been hastily pushed in, and he'd knocked over a pile of books on her desk.

Henrik straightened, a stack of papers in his hand. "I should ask you the same thing."

"What are you doing with those?" she asked, snatching the papers out of his hands. It was one of Neil's speeches.

"You're a commie," he sneered.

"It's just a speech a friend asked me to look over," she said, but even she could hear how unconvincing that sounded.

"You listen to that rubbish they spout?" Henrik asked.

"Not since Germany and Russia decided they were on the same side," she muttered.

His eyes narrowed. "What are you doing home?"

"I was fired today," she said.

His eyes bulged out. "Why?"

She told him about the investigation, unsure whether his parents had told him about the day when she'd come home pale-faced after Dennison and his questions. He simply stared.

"Leave."

"What?"

"If you were fired from your job because the Home Office is investigating you and you're a commie, the best thing you can do for this family is leave," said her cousin.

"The Home Office isn't investigating me."

"Don't be naive. The Home Office probably has a file an inch thick on you by now. Everything you've ever done wrong, ready for them to pull out when they need to rank your classification."

The classification. It hung over her head like an executioner's ax.

"They'll dig even deeper into the lives of everyone you know. Me. Mutter and Vater. Your parents," he said.

"They won't find anything. There isn't anything to find." She could say that about her aunt and uncle, but could she really answer for her parents? She hardly knew them any longer.

Henrik stepped forward until they were so close she could smell raw onion on his breath.

"I will not let any of this to chance. You will leave, or I will report you to the Home Office myself," he said.

"Report what?"

He tilted his head, a sick smile stretching his lips. "Does it matter? They'll believe anything about any of us."

"Henrik—"

"If you condemn your beloved Tante Matilda to an internment camp, will you be able to live with that guilt?"

How could this dolt of a man cut to the heart of her worst fears? She was the one putting the family at risk. If she became the reason they were interned, she'd never forgive herself. Still, part of her wanted to cling to the only home she had ever known.

"I can't leave. Where will I go?" she asked.

"I don't care."

"Why are you doing this?" she gritted out.

His nostrils flared. "I know what you all think. I'm lazy. I drink too much. But I see what's happening. I know what this war is going to bring. You aren't a Müller, and I'm doing what I need to protect my family. *You* are not my family." He walked to the door, but paused long enough to throw over his shoulder, "If you aren't gone in a half hour, I'll call the police myself."

The tears she'd held back on the bus began to streak down her face, but she wasn't going to stay and give him the satisfaction of seeing her pain. Instead, she hauled her suitcase from underneath her bed and began to transfer clothing from her chest of drawers. She would take only what she needed. Nora or Hazel could come for the rest and send them to . . . wherever she was going.

Marie latched her suitcase, gathered up her coat and purse, and made her way out to the street. It had started to rain, so she sheltered in the doorway of her aunt and uncle's building for a moment, peering up at the sky. She needed a place that was dry and safe where she could collect her thoughts and figure out how to pick herself up out of the ashes of this burning day.

A cab rolled by and inspiration struck her. She stuck out her arm, and the cabbie stopped. She told him she was going to Whitehall.

It didn't take long to cross to Central London. When the cab glided to a stop, she paid the driver and waved him off when he offered to carry her bag into the imposing building. Instead, she maneuvered the bag through the doors herself and gave her name to a guard at the front desk who telephoned up. Then Marie settled down into one of the chairs lining the lobby wall to wait.

Five minutes later, the rush of click-clacking heels across the marble floor jerked her to attention as Nora stopped in front of her.

"Marie, what are you doing here?"

She hauled herself to her feet. "After all this time, can you believe this is the first time I've been inside your office building?"

Nora looked at the floor. "Why do you have a suitcase?"

Marie mustered as much pride as she could. "I find myself between homes. I know it's an imposition, but could I please stay with you until I can find myself a place to live?"

Nora's mouth gaped open. "Between homes? What do you mean? What happened to your aunt and uncle? Are they all right?"

"Henrik threatened me, and I left."

"Threatened?" Nora shook her head. "Never mind that. There's plenty of time for you to tell me about it later. Of course you can come live with me as long as you like."

"Thank you," said Marie. And with that, all her resolve broke. She began to sob, and Nora gathered her up to hold her close.

Samantha
Now

"I think," said Nora, "that is enough for today."

"There's more?" asked Samantha.

Nora offered her a weary grin. "We're only at the beginning, but I'm an old woman, and it's my prerogative to be tired."

Samantha sank back into the sofa. She'd had no idea about any of the story Nora was unwinding for her. She knew her grandmother had gone to school in England. Simple math told her that Grandma would've lived through the war. But all the rest . . .

"David," said Nora. "Why don't you take Samantha to that pub down the road? The one with the garden."

"Of course," said David, straightening in his chair and looking to Samantha. "If you'd like to, that is."

"If you don't mind," said Samantha.

"Not at all. I'll just take these things back to the kitchen."

When he bent to gather up some of the mugs, Samantha stole another look at him. He was tall with dark—almost black—hair and blue eyes much like his grandmother's. A touch of stubble covered his jaw. He wore a moss-green sweater, and a crisp white shirt poked out from the V at his neck.

He moved off, revealing his grandmother watching her knowingly. Samantha blushed and asked, "Won't you join us?"

Nora laughed. "It's good of you to ask, but it's a production to take me anywhere these days."

David returned holding Samantha's green military-style jacket. He held it out and helped her slip it on. Then they said their good-byes to Nora and made their way down the road to the pub.

"If you'll let me know what you'd like and find a table, I'll get us drinks," said David.

"Since I'm in Britain, I feel as though I should have a pint of ale."

"Good choice. I'll just be a minute."

He disappeared through the pub doors, and she wove her way to the back of the garden, where a table stood empty. When David arrived, he set their beers down along with two menus.

"It's just pub food, but it's good," he said.

"That sounds perfect," she said, studying her menu even though she knew that she would have the chicken and leek pie.

"So your grandmother never told you any of that story . . ." he started as soon as she picked up her beer.

"I can't believe that I didn't know any of it." She paused. "I grew up just a few miles from her house. I used to go around after school at least once a week, especially after Grandpa died when I was thir-teen. I know all about her childhood in Germany, but she always told me she'd tell me the rest later. My biggest regret is not follow-ing up on that promise. And now I have a eulogy I don't know how to write about a woman I feel like I hardly knew."

"I've been thinking about your eulogy," he said. "Do you think it would help to see some of the places where Marie spent her time during the war? I'm sure I could find the Müllers' house in Bloomsbury. And Royal Imperial University is simple enough."

"I'd love to see them."

"Then we'll go on Wednesday. I'll come around to pick you up around two if that's all right with you," he said.

Samantha beamed. "That would be great," she said.

"Good, good. If you're feeling up for it, we could go to dinner as well," he said. He smiled that crooked little smile she'd come to like. "I wouldn't want you to come to London and never venture out of West Kensington for food."

"Yes, that would be a shame," she agreed with a grin.

Chapter 7

Hazel
November 1939 to March 1940
DINNER WAS, WITHOUT A DOUBT, Hazel's least favorite meal. If she wasn't working late, she usually rushed home from Mayfair in a desperate dash to get something on the table. The rush was exhausting, but at least it came with the satisfaction of a perfunctory thanks from Nathaniel at the end of the meal. Late nights, however, meant rising early to make something he could reheat for his supper. All she got out of that was guilt, heightened by the tiniest drop of relief to have an evening to herself.

That Tuesday, Hazel rose, unpinned her hair from its curlers, powdered her face, put on her dress, retrieved the paper from the front walk, and pulled on an apron to begin cooking.

She'd heard some women enjoyed cooking, but it had never been anything but a chore to her. Between her mother's modeling work and the settlement from Hazel's father, they'd had more than enough money to spare when she was growing up. Mundane tasks like cooking and cleaning were left to Mrs. Macmillan, their housekeeper who came in every day. So while some girls might've been encouraged by their mothers to learn a few basic homemaking skills, Penelope Ricci had other ideas about what constituted an appropriate education for her daughter.

Until Hazel turned twelve, Penelope would sweep her off to the theater, opera, concerts, and even portrait sittings. It had been heaven, but then there had been the other nights—ones where Hazel woke up and wandered into late-night parties of people sloppy on champagne and whatever drug was fashionable that month.

Then Hazel's father died, and the decadent whirlwind abruptly stopped. Penelope had come back from a meeting with her solicitor pale faced. Hazel's father's family had declared that his obligation to keep Penelope and her had ended with his death; there would be no more money.

The parties dried up, and all the people who'd crashed through their lives moved on. Penelope's modeling work soon went the same way, for there were younger beauties to paint and photograph. Thus mother and daughter moved south of the Thames into a flat that Penelope learned to clean herself.

Hazel had hoped that their lives would settle down into a quieter existence, but her mother, always full of surprises, had done something extraordinary. Using every connection she could, she'd secured a place for Hazel at the prestigious Ethelbrook School for Girls—with a scholarship to boot. The happiest day of Hazel's twelve-year-old life had been when she'd boarded the train and sped off to the countryside and a new life of normalcy.

Of course, no one at Ethelbrook had thought to teach the schoolgirls about cooking or cleaning either. It had generally been assumed that the girls would have some sort of help, because most of their families paid the breathtaking fees to board and educate their daughters. In turn, they were expected to marry a man of at least enough ambition to advance his career every few years while they kept a small household and had several children.

Hazel had needed a job after Ethelbrook and found one working as a secretary at the Mayfair Matrimonial Agency while she lived with her mother. It had taken several months before Hazel realized her mother was becoming gaunt and sickly. When Hazel finally convinced her mother to see her doctor, he told them that it was cancer of the stomach. Her mother's death had been slow and painful, and it had torn Hazel to pieces.

A creaking above Hazel's head announced that Nathaniel was awake. She set about laying things out for breakfast. By the time Nathaniel shuffled into the kitchen in his house slippers, she had the kettle on the boil and eggs frying in the pan.

"It'll all be ready in a minute, dearest," she said brightly.

He nodded and brushed by her. She turned back to the stove.

"The paper was wet again this morning. Could you speak to the boy about tossing it onto the step so it's out of the rain?" she asked.

"I thought you were going to say something the next time you paid him," he said around a deep, hacking cough.

"Are you ill?" she asked.

He grunted. "Just my usual cough," he said as he reached into his pocket for his cigarettes and shook one out of the packet.

She frowned. "I wish you wouldn't smoke at the table."

He looked up, a match poised in his hands. "What?"

"Please don't smoke at the table," she said.

His face contorted, but his expression was gone so quickly she must've imagined it. He took the cigarette out of his mouth and unfolded the paper to hold it to block his face from view. FIRST BRITISH DESTROYER LOST IN WAR: HMS *BLANCHE* SUNK BY MINE IN THAMES ESTUARY read the headline, but all Hazel could see was the bloom of a wet stain running down the middle of the paper.

"THE ship was accompanying her sister, Basilisk, when they entered a minefield laid the night before by German destroyers," droned the radio bulletin as Hazel tried to focus on the agency's accounts at her desk that afternoon. The war had brought with it a surge in lonely hearts looking for companionship, and with the clients came long hours of interviews and late nights making matches. But today Hazel was struggling to focus.

The look on Nathaniel's face as he put away his cigarettes was to blame. It had followed Hazel like a specter the entire day. She thought about it as she called her matches that morning and received reports about how their previous evenings' dinners had gone. It had been with her while she'd interviewed two women and a man all looking for love. She couldn't keep her thoughts from turning back to the man she shared a life with.

It all seemed clear: Nathaniel resented her.

"Men are never true," her mother had told her, but Hazel hadn't listened. Nathaniel had appeared in her life like a beacon to guide her down the path of respectability, and she'd never looked back.

He'd asked her out, and one dinner became a string of dates.

She'd felt proud walking into the cinema on his arm or sitting across from him at a restaurant. Nathaniel was a clerk in the Ministry of Fisheries and Agriculture. A few years older than her, he had opinions and seemed to know about the world. He'd charmed her so utterly that it had taken hardly any persuasion for him to convince her to break one rule the daughter of an unwed mother knew by heart. Six weeks later, she'd found out she was pregnant.

Like mother, like daughter.

A man cleared his throat, and Hazel froze. Dennison, the man from the Home Office, pushed her door until it was fully open.

"Mrs. Carey," he said.

Carefully, Hazel closed the ledger she was working in and folded her hands across the top of it.

All of the matches were legitimate, she reminded herself. The agency had done nothing wrong. *She'd* done nothing wrong. But Hazel's heart pounded a little faster as Dennison walked through the door and took one of the seats in front of her desk, uninvited.

"I'm sorry," said Nancy, glaring at the man from the doorway. "I told Mr. Dennison you were occupied, but he came in anyway."

"It's fine, Nancy. I'm sure this will only take a moment."

"Yes, Mrs. Carey," said Nancy before shutting the door.

Hazel sucked in a breath. "Mr. Dennison, to what do I owe the pleasure of a visit?"

His eyes darted around the room. "I thought it might be prudent to stop by and remind you of your obligations."

"My obligations?"

"As a British woman. To report any suspicious foreigners trying to use your agency. I haven't heard from you since my last visit."

"Your last visit was just a few weeks ago," she said.

"It was September. Now it is November."

"Mr. Dennison, if I had seen anything nefarious, I should've telephoned," she said.

"Have any Germans attempted to use your agency?" he asked.

"I have had people of many nationalities and backgrounds come to me. I'm a matchmaker," she said.

"Have any of them seemed suspicious?" he asked.

"One man swore that he'd never been married, but his wedding ring fell out of his pocket when he stood up at the end of our interview. He had a hole in his trouser pocket, you see," she said.

"Your insistence upon making a joke of this is very concerning, Mrs. Carey," he said.

"It is not a joke," she said sharply.

Dennison leaned forward. "I need to see your records. I need to see how many Germans have used your agency."

Hazel mirrored him and tilted over her desk. "No."

He stood and buttoned his double-breasted suit jacket. "Don't be on the wrong side of this war, Mrs. Carey."

"I assure you, I'm firmly on the side of Britain," she said. But, she suspected, her Britain looked very different from Dennison's.

After Dennison left, Hazel strode back into the reception. "Time for us both to go home, I think, Nancy," she said.

The telephone rang. With a rueful smile, the secretary picked it up. "Mayfair Matrimonial Agency." Nancy's brow furrowed. "Yes, she's right here, Miss Walcott."

Hazel took the phone from her secretary. "Nora?"

"You need to come to the house. Now," said Nora.

"What's wrong? What's happened?" Hazel asked in a rush.

There was a pause, and Nora said simply, "It's Marie."

THE front door swung open before Hazel could raise her hand to the knocker. "What's happened?" she asked as Nora let her in.

"Marie's in the front room. She's upset. She got a letter today with her classification from the tribunal."

Hazel sucked in a breath. "It's an A." But Marie couldn't have a category A classification. It didn't make sense.

"She isn't A, thank goodness. She's category B," said Nora.

She closed her eyes and sent up a prayer of thanks. "A category B is good, isn't it? It means she won't be sent away."

But from the way Nora's lips pressed into a line, Hazel could see she had it all wrong. "I wouldn't say that to her."

Nora led her through to the small sitting room, where Marie sat on the sofa. She looked small as a schoolgirl.

"Marie," Hazel said.

Marie lifted her head, and Hazel was stunned. Her friend was pale enough that she could swear she saw the blue veins on Marie's neck even at a distance. In Marie's hand was a letter.

"May I?" Hazel asked, indicating the letter as Nora moved to the bar tray set on one of the built-in bookshelves to pour a finger of brandy into three snifters.

"I can tell you what it says," said Marie quietly. "They've decided to give me a category B classification. They say they have reason to believe that I should be restricted in my movements."

"What does that mean?" Hazel asked.

"I won't be arrested, but I can't travel without informing my local police station. I can't ride a bicycle." Marie looked at Nora. "We'll have to get rid of the radio. I'm sorry about that."

"I can find someone to take the radio," said Nora, handing around the brandy.

Marie lifted her glass and took a gulp. "As soon as I got the letter, I went to my aunt and uncle's. Only Tante Matilda was home. I found her sitting on the sofa, surrounded by all of the letters. I'm the only one who is category B. The rest are category C." Marie pressed a hand to her heart. "Henrik was right. I'm a risk to my aunt and uncle. I need to stay away."

"No," Nora said. "No, that is not what this means. Don't isolate yourself so much that you might as well be imprisoned. Avoiding the people you love is not what living is supposed to be about."

Marie's lip quivered just enough that Hazel knew her friend was fighting back tears. As she sat there trying to comfort one of her best friends, the guilt of holding back from these women tugged at her. Hazel set her glass aside and cleared her throat. "I think there's something I need to tell you both."

Marie and Nora looked at her expectantly.

"I haven't been entirely honest about that man Dennison."

"Dennison?" Nora asked. "What does he have to do with this?"

Hazel swallowed. "You know how I've been working such late nights? Business has gone up since the war started, but there's more to it than that. Before war was declared, I was working with a different set of clients. Refugees who were escaping Germany."

"You're matching them up with British citizens," said Marie, comprehension and then shock spreading over her face.

Hazel nodded. "Single men in particular were having difficulties with their applications because the government was most sympathetic toward families with children. We found that applications for asylum were processed faster if a refugee could say that they were engaged to someone already living in Britain. The matching was all done by letter, of course, although the British women I matched the gentlemen with came in just like other clients."

"Was Herr Gunter a part of this group?" Marie asked.

"He was the one who convinced me to start helping after I'd matched him. He was trying to help some of his Jewish colleagues escape because it had become clear that they weren't safe any longer. What I told you in front of Dennison was true. Mr. Gunter had heard you mention my name and the agency when you were talking to one of the other departmental secretaries. That was all."

"So you were doing exactly what Dennison accused you of?" Nora asked.

Hazel jerked back. "No! There's nothing nefarious about it. The people this group helped were all intellectuals, not spies. Professors, artists. It seems that in the last few years, the Nazis had begun to take exception to them. The stories Mr. Gunter told me when he approached me—I didn't see how I couldn't help."

"Was he the only one you spoke to?" Marie asked.

"There was one other man—a printer who sometimes made up false papers if a refugee's had been confiscated before they escaped. I contacted him after Mr. Gunter disappeared, but he didn't know anything. The whole group has gone to ground." Hazel turned to Marie. "I hate that I lied to you, Marie. I'm so sorry."

"You didn't lie to me." But before Hazel could feel absolved of her guilt, Marie added, "But you didn't tell me the truth either. You held this back from me. From us."

"I didn't tell you what I was doing, because to involve either of you would have been dangerous," said Hazel.

"You were shielding us," said Nora.

"Yes. I thought it would be best if you knew as little as possible—Marie, because of your connection to Mr. Gunter, and, Nora, because of your place in the Home Office. If you didn't know, you couldn't be held accountable," said Hazel.

"But then Dennison showed up, and I had to face him not knowing a thing about what was going on," said Marie, her voice rising. "When he took me out of work and put me in the back of his car, I didn't know what was going to happen to me. And now look at me. I'm hardly making money working a few mornings a week in the stockroom of a shop. I'm afraid all of the time, and I don't even know if I'm part of Dennison's investigation or not."

"I'm truly sorry, Marie," said Hazel quietly.

Slowly, she replied, "I know that you both must think I'm weak. I've cried about my classification. I've been afraid."

"You're not weak at all," said Nora fiercely. "We know that."

"And you cried because that's a normal thing to do," said Hazel.

Marie stared at the brandy glass in her hand, rolling it from side to side. "Then promise me you won't ever hide things from me because you think I can't handle hearing them. Let me decide for myself what is too much to bear," said Marie.

"I won't," said Hazel. "You have my word."

THE last of the Christmas crackers lay abandoned on the dining room table amid the remnants of the goose and all of the trimmings. After what was likely to have been their last lavish meal for who knew how long, Hazel, Nathaniel, Hazel's mother-in-law Gertrude, Nora, and Marie had all decamped to the front room of Hazel's house to exchange gifts.

Gertrude sat in the middle of the sofa, handbag in her lap. Nathaniel had barely been able to persuade Gertrude to take off her coat when she'd arrived, and she'd only relinquished her handbag long enough to pick at Christmas lunch and criticize Hazel for letting the goose dry out while overdoing the roasted vegetables.

Now Hazel held her breath as her mother-in-law opened the last package under the tree with her name on it. Gertrude untied the cheerful red bow slowly, as though suspicious. Finally, the wrapping paper fell and she opened the box to lift out a pair of chocolate-brown gloves.

Gertrude looked at the gloves and then up at her son. "They're beautiful, Nathaniel. Thank you."

Hazel's gaze flew to her husband, who lifted his head from the book on golf Nora had bought him on Hazel's recommendation.

"What's that?" Nathaniel asked with a frown. "Oh, the present. You're welcome."

Hazel's jaw went slack, and she stared down at her hands. She'd told Nathaniel how long she'd searched for the right pair of gloves for his mother, how many shops she'd been to. Yet he wasn't going to say a thing to correct his mother's assumption?

Before she could say anything, Gertrude asked, "The leather is so soft. Where did you find them?"

Nathaniel scrunched up his brow as though trying to recall. Finally, he admitted, "I think Hazel bought them. Didn't you?"

"Yes," said Hazel through gritted teeth.

"I see," said Gertrude, carefully setting the gloves back in their box and putting it aside. "Well, you really shouldn't have. I have a perfectly good pair of gloves that will last me an age."

"Just two more presents under the tree," said Nora quickly, saving Hazel from telling Gertrude exactly what she thought.

"I'll get them," said Marie.

"Good, because I happen to know that one is for you," said Nora. "The other is for Hazel."

Marie hunched over to pull two small boxes out from under the branches of the fir tree. "There aren't any labels."

Nora waved a hand. "They're both the same."

"Shall we open them at the same time?" Hazel asked as Marie handed her one of the boxes.

Marie nodded and began to count off, "One. Two. Three!"

Hazel laughed as she ripped open her wrapping. Inside was a small black box. When she opened it, she fell silent. On a black velvet cushion lay a delicate gold chain. From it hung a stunning round lapis lazuli in a gold claw setting.

"What is it?" asked Nathaniel. She held it up for him to see.

"Nora," said Marie, "where is your grandmother's bracelet?"

Hazel glanced up to see Nora pulling out the necklaces' triplet from her neckline. "I took it to a jeweler and asked him to break up the stones into three necklaces."

"But you love that bracelet," Marie said.

"And I want you two to each have a piece of it. We can't know what's going to happen in this war, but this way we'll always have a reminder of each other."

Hazel touched her heart. "I don't know what to say."

Nora laughed. "Don't say anything. Try it on."

Marie smiled shyly as she unclasped the chain and smoothed the pendant against her skin.

Hazel turned to her husband. "Would you mind helping me with the clasp, Nathaniel?"

She lifted her hair as Nathaniel's fingers brushed the back of her neck. The cool metal settled on her sternum. She'd carry her friends with her always.

"Now, I think it's time for cake and tea. Who would like some?" Hazel asked brightly, slipping on her hostessing mask once again.

"Cake at a time like this?" Gertrude said with a sniff.

Nora jumped in. "A time like what, Mrs. Carey?"

Gertrude's fingertips touched her throat. "Why, war, of course."

"What better time to celebrate what we have than when things are the most difficult?" Nora asked sweetly.

"It's a time to enjoy each other," said Hazel.

That earned her another sniff. "If you had children of your own, you would understand . . ."

The well-aimed insult plunged white-hot into Hazel's belly.

Moving deliberately, she stood, smoothed the skirt of her green dress, and excused herself. She was closing the front room door behind her when she heard Gertrude mutter, "She needn't be so sensitive about it, but then given her mother . . ."

Hazel pushed through the kitchen door and stopped by the sink.

A few minutes later the door swung open and Nora announced, "Your mother-in-law is terrible."

Hazel gave a short laugh and let her head fall back. "She is the nightmare that everyone warns you about when you marry."

Marie circled an arm around her waist and said, "She has no right to say those things to you."

"It isn't anything I haven't heard before," she said.

"Why doesn't Nathaniel say anything?" Nora asked.

Hazel hesitated. It was only for a second—but it was enough that she knew her friends noticed it.

"It's no bother," she finally said. "They're just words." Maybe if she told herself that often enough, she would begin to believe it.

"Perhaps this isn't the best time, but I wonder if I could ask a favor," said Marie quietly.

"Of course," she said.

A smile played over Marie's lips. "Richard Calloway wants me to come to dinner."

Hazel's eyes widened. "You telephoned him."

"When?" Nora asked.

"While you were at work," said Marie.

"You sneaky thing," said Nora with a laugh.

"What did you talk about?" Hazel asked.

"He told me he'd hoped that I would call," said Marie. "That you'd said lovely things about me—"

"All of them true," said Hazel.

"—and we talked about . . . Oh, I don't know. Everything? He's easy to talk to. I told him about going to school with both of you. I told him about what it's been like since the war broke out—how worried I am all the time."

"What did he say?" Nora asked.

"He just listened," said Marie. "And then at the end, he asked me if I would like to have dinner with him in the New Year."

"That's wonderful, Marie," Hazel said. "Did you say yes?"

"Yes and no." Marie winced. "I sort of panicked and said I would only go if you went."

Hazel's brows popped. "Me?"

"You and Nathaniel. You . . . you'd offered to," said Marie.

Of course she had. But that was before the cracks in the foundation of her marriage had become too deep to ignore. Still, this was Marie asking. She would do anything to see her friend happy.

"We'd love nothing more than to have dinner with you," she said. She would figure out a way to explain it all to Nathaniel.

Marie blew out a breath. "Thank you."

"We'll have a wonderful time, don't worry. I'll ring around with a date next week. You could come, too, Nora," Hazel said.

Her friend snorted. "Who would I bring? Joseph from work?"

Hazel arched a brow. This wasn't the first time she'd heard Nora casually throw out that name.

"In that case, we'll keep it dinner for four." Hazel planted her hands on her hips and stared at the fondant-covered cake on her cake stand. "Now I suppose it's time to serve my sinful cake."

"Is it sinful or decadent?" Nora asked.

She shrugged. "Either way, I can promise you that Gertrude will have a second slice."

"I don't know how you can stand her," said Marie.

"I hide in the kitchen as often as possible," said Hazel with a laugh, but there was more truth in that statement than she wanted to admit.

Chapter 8

"I STILL DON'T UNDERSTAND why we're here," said Nathaniel, patting down his tie before passing a hand over his hair.

They stopped on the street corner for a turning bus, and Hazel prepared herself to explain yet again because, she suspected, he saw dinner with Marie and Mr. Calloway as an inconvenience. That was part of the reason that it had taken so long to arrange. Hazel had rung Mr. Calloway in the first week of January. He'd been delighted that Marie had asked her to arrange dinner, but then Marie had fallen ill with a head cold. Then Nathaniel had rejected three weeks' worth of Hazel's suggestions for an alternative night.

But the night was finally here, and Hazel was determined to be excited for her friend even if Nathaniel wasn't.

"It's just a double date, dear," she said.

Nathaniel rolled his shoulders back as though uncomfortable in the navy suit that came out only for church services.

"And who is the chap you've set her up with?" he asked.

"His name is Richard Calloway. He's a widower, and I've been trying to find him the right woman for months now, so be polite."

"I'm always polite."

They'd reached La Vieille Maison, a little French restaurant tucked into a side street in Marylebone. Nathaniel opened the door for her, and she nearly walked into Marie.

"Oh!"

"Hello, dear. We must have perfect timing," Hazel said, kissing her friend on either cheek.

"Hello, Nathaniel," said Marie as he bent awkwardly to kiss her on the cheek.

"How long have you been waiting?" asked Hazel.

Marie turned a tortured look to her. "Five minutes. I was hoping you would all arrive before me."

Nathaniel helped Hazel slide off her jacket. As soon as he was occupied with checking their coats, Hazel leaned in to Marie. "What's the matter?"

Marie bit her lip. "I don't know if I can do this. My dress is all wrong, and I'm nervous."

"You look perfect," said Hazel, giving the plum silk dress with a deep V at the neck a once-over.

She gave her friend's hand a squeeze just as Nathaniel came back. "Ready?" he asked.

Marie nodded. "Yes."

The dining room was half full, just as Hazel had hoped it would be. She'd wanted a location with enough patrons that they could speak freely, but not so many that they needed to shout.

She spotted her client at the back of the restaurant. When they were a few feet away, he looked up and his eyes crinkled into a smile as he rose to greet their party. "Hello," he said.

Hazel stole a glance at Marie, who looked up at him cautiously through her lashes.

"Mr. Calloway, this is Marie Bohn, one of my dearest friends, but of course you already know that," she said. "And this is my husband, Nathaniel."

Everyone shook hands and then took their seats. Mr. Calloway waved the maître d' away so he could help Marie with her chair, checking that she was comfortable before sitting down himself.

"I'm so pleased you agreed to dinner, Marie," he said. "I'll confess, I was pleased when Mrs. Carey offered to introduce us. She spoke very highly of you."

"Hazel is generous with her praise," said Marie with a blush.

"Marie and I have known each other for years. We went to school together," said Hazel.

"I came at midterm. I don't think the headmistress knew what to do with me, so they stuck me in the first room they could find," said Marie.

"Even though I was a year ahead of the other girls," said Hazel.

"So there's more than just the two of you?" Richard asked.

"Oh yes, they come as a trio," said Nathaniel. "You can't have Hazel without Marie and Nora."

"Well, I should very much like to meet your friend Nora one day as well," said Richard.

"She's quite something," murmured Nathaniel.

Hazel fought the urge to kick him under the table.

Nathaniel cleared his throat. "She's a good sort, but she is one of those forceful women one half expects to be running a unit in a women's auxiliary service."

"She's already doing her part. She used to be a deb, but now she works for the Home Office," Hazel clarified.

"Not exactly where one pictures a society girl," said Richard. "How would you spend your days, if you had a choice, Marie? Painting still lifes of fruit while listening to Wagner arias?"

Marie laughed. "To begin with, it wouldn't be Wagner."

"I must beg your apology," he said, hand over his heart. "I should've known that you would only listen to Verdi."

"American jazz records when I can get them, but thank you," said Marie, accepting the gentle teasing.

"Very modern," said Richard.

Hazel could hardly contain her grin as the feeling around the table settled. Marie was smiling openly now.

"I'm so pleased you said yes to dinner, Marie," said Richard. "When we first met, I had come in to see Mrs. Carey a second time after a dinner that didn't get off the ground. You were wearing a green dress, and I hoped that Mrs. Carey would match us."

"It did take some convincing," Marie admitted.

"It's a matchmaker's curse that her own friends always seem the most cautious about using her services," said Hazel.

"Well, I'm very glad that you did, Marie." Richard grinned. "Perhaps this is as good a time as any to lay my cards out on the table, as our American friends might say."

"Hardly our friends if they keep neutral," Nathaniel grumbled. Hazel pinched his leg under the table. He winced.

"I told you before that I'm a widower." Richard paused. "I have no children, but I would like them one day if I found a woman who wants to be a mother. I have a good living, and I'm fortunate enough to be doing work that is helping our men in Europe, even if it means I can't join them because mine is a reserved occupation. I have a sister I see every other month for Sunday lunch and a brother-in-law who I tolerate. I have a little house in Belsize Park and a car. That is about the sum of my parts."

Out of the corner of her eye, Hazel watched Marie stare at Richard quite openly until, without warning, a laugh bubbled up.

"I'm sorry." Marie slapped a hand over her mouth.

He gave her a smile. "I don't think I've ever made a lady laugh with so little effort before. My life must truly seem uninteresting."

"It's not that at *all*. It's just . . . Why should you feel you need to be blunt about any of this?" asked Marie.

"If the last few years have taught me anything, it's that nothing is gained by concealing my faults."

"*Your* faults? Ever since we spoke, I worried that you would decide you weren't interested in someone like me," said Marie.

"Someone like you?" Richard asked.

"A German."

Hazel held her breath, hardly daring to move.

"Whether you're German or not doesn't matter to me." Richard sounded so genuine Hazel could've kissed him for it.

"Just yesterday, a pair of boys called me a dirty Jerry. I've been told by women that their husbands were off to kill my kind."

"Did you make the decision to invade Poland?" Richard asked.

"Of course not," said Marie.

"And do you support what Hitler is doing in Europe?" he asked.

"Absolutely not."

"If women were able to fight, who would you fight for?"

"Britain."

"That's all the answer I need," he said. "And no one should be allowed to speak to you the way those people did."

Hazel watched her friend's expression soften.

"Thank you for saying that," said Marie.

"I'm not just saying it. I mean it. Now, I think we can begin with some of the conversational prompts that Hazel recommends to her clients," said Richard, tilting his head to her.

"Oh, don't do that," said Hazel. "I'll die of embarrassment."

"In that case, I think we should certainly go through Hazel's questions," said Marie with a laugh.

"Right, then. Miss Bohn," said Richard, folding his hands in front of him and assuming an overly serious expression. "I would love very much to know what the last book you read was."

SOMEHOW, after dessert was served, Hazel managed to maneuver things so she and Nathaniel sat at the long bar of La Vieille Maison and Marie and Nathaniel were alone at their cleared table.

"They seem to be getting along well," said Hazel.

"Are they?"

"He's been so attentive, following everything she says."

Nathaniel threw a look back over his shoulder. "I suppose."

She frowned. She wanted him to be more enthusiastic than this. This was her work. She brought people together. She wanted people to love the way she'd loved Nathaniel when they'd first met because it had felt incredible, like a gift.

"You fascinate me," he'd whispered to her after he'd kissed her for the first time. He'd wanted to know everything about her, quizzing her endlessly about Ethelbrook, her job, and her childhood, which he'd told her seemed wild and a little wonderful.

"My father was a gentleman painter, one of those men who have the privilege of painting for pleasure and not to survive," she remembered telling him. "He fell in love with my mother, his model, but he was Catholic. He wouldn't leave his wife, not even when my mother told him she was pregnant.

"He came to the house just once after I was born. My mother says that he spent a long time looking down at me in my cradle, and then he left without a word. The next week, she received a letter from his solicitor. He had decided that it was time for them to end their affair. He'd arranged an income for her for the duration of his lifetime. And then he was gone. I've never met him."

She remembered Nathaniel had picked up her hands and tenderly kissed the backs of them. That was the moment when Hazel knew she was in love. That she would marry this man.

She reached for his hand now, her fingers brushing his knuckles. He didn't pull away, but neither did he offer her his palm.

"How are things in the ministry?" she asked.

He gave her a weary smile. "You don't have to try to make small talk with me. This is the way it is with married couples sometimes. It's the way my father and mother were."

But she didn't want what his father and mother had. It meant nights sitting together in the front room, barely speaking to each other while trying to squash the insidious pull of loneliness.

"I can't imagine you would understand that," he added, "given that your mother never married."

"Nathaniel," she said sharply. "I cannot believe you would say something so callous."

"It's simply the truth," he said with a shrug.

His words stung. *How have we come to this?*

She'd once felt proud walking on his arm, knowing that he was a sturdy sort of man. One who would never abandon his responsibilities. And sure enough, when she told him she was pregnant just four months after they'd met, he'd proposed immediately.

She'd quit her job as a secretary at the Mayfair Matrimonial Agency, and as she'd stood in her wedding dress, a white satin bias-cut confection, surrounded by her best friends, she was *happy*. She was going to be Nathaniel Carey's wife. She was going to be a mother. She would have the life she wanted.

Then, just weeks later, it all shattered.

She'd been home alone. There had been blood—so much of it— and she'd pounded on a neighbor's door. They'd taken her to the hospital, but the doctors could do nothing except make her comfortable. Nathaniel had sat by her bed, squeezing her hand, but his face betrayed nothing as he stared at a spot on the far wall.

When Hazel had returned from the hospital, everything seemed to slow. She couldn't make herself leave the house, couldn't make herself stop crying. It had been like that for months until one day Lady Moreton had shown up at her door and offered her a purpose. Not her old job as a secretary, but a different one. One that would make use of talents she never knew she had. Matchmaking gave Hazel her life back.

"I went to the recruitment office today," said Nathaniel, yanking her attention around.

"What?"

"It was the army, in case you're curious."

Her heart skipped. "You enlisted? But you never said—"

"I tried to enlist. They won't have me," he said, toying with his half-empty glass. "They say that my lungs aren't strong enough."

"Your cough," she said, finally understanding.

"They think the pneumonia I had as a child tore up my lungs. They don't want a defective soldier."

"Nathaniel." She placed a hand on his leg, but he shifted to knock her touch away.

"We're in public."

Her hand clenched. He didn't want her to touch him.

"Do you want to know the worst of it?" he said. "I came out of the recruitment office, told I was a broken man, and all I wanted to do was go home to my wife. But your friends always come first."

"Nathaniel," she said sharply.

"No, no, you're right. The real problem is that we're here because you're a matchmaker at that bloody agency."

She swallowed. "Don't make this about the agency."

He lifted his head. "Maybe it's time for you to stop working."

She gasped for breath. "Why would you say that?"

"There's a war on. People have worries other than finding husbands," he argued.

"This is *exactly* the time that the agency should be working harder than ever. And that's what we're doing," she insisted.

"Then leave it to Lady Moreton. She owns it. Let her do the work while you come home to be a proper wife."

"Nathaniel, I don't want to stay home. I never did." The words were out of her mouth before she could think to stop herself.

His eyes narrowed. "You did when there was a baby on the way."

It had been true then, but now . . . She wasn't going to have a child. For all of her hope and all of her denial, she knew that.

"I understand that you're frustrated and angry, but you needn't be cruel, Nathaniel," she said as firmly as she could.

"Why shouldn't I be?" His voice was starting to rise. "Is it too much to expect my shirts to be clean, my dinner to be ready when I get home, and to know that I'm no longer the laughingstock of my office because I can't keep my wife from working?"

"Lower your voice. People are staring," she hissed.

Between gritted teeth, he said, "My mother thinks that if you stopped working, the pregnancies wouldn't be at risk."

"Your mother is not a doctor. And I'm not surprised she disapproves, given that she hates everything I do," she said.

"What does that mean?"

Hazel sighed and rubbed her temple. "I don't want to argue about this. Marie is doing so well tonight."

Her husband looked over his shoulder at her friend, who was laughing at something Richard had just said.

"Was that ever us?" Nathaniel asked after a long moment.

"Yes," she said. "And I loved you for it."

Nathaniel dropped his gaze to his glass, the fight gone from his body. "Forgive me. I'm not myself."

She forced a smile. "Everyone is on edge these days."

"It's not your fault that I couldn't pass my medical," he said. "And I really do want you to consider staying home, but I know that there isn't a single person on this planet who can make you do something you don't want to do."

It wasn't an apology, but Hazel wasn't going to stretch out a fight that was already beginning to cool. Instead, she took a sip of her drink and let the moment slip by, just like so many others.

THE next morning, Marie wasted no time calling Hazel before Nancy had even arrived for work.

Hazel rushed out of her office to pick up the telephone. "Mayfair Matrimonial Agency. How can I direct your call?"

"Hazel, I'm so glad you're in. I've been waiting to ring you since half past six. Thank you," Marie said in a rush.

"You're welcome." She laughed. "I take it this means you approve of my match."

"I like him. I like that he's kind and interesting and listens to other people when they talk. Thank you and Nathaniel for coming. I hope it wasn't too dull for you both," said Marie.

"We didn't mind at all," she lied.

"Are you sure? I didn't mean to impose upon Nathaniel's time. I know he's busy at work," said Marie.

It was an opening—a way for her to finally tell her friend what was going on in her marriage. Hazel shifted in her seat, but as soon as she opened her mouth, Nancy came through the door.

"Nathaniel wants to see you happy. He's very fond of you and Nora," she said firmly. "I should go. Nancy's just arrived."

The friends said goodbye, and Hazel settled into her routine of preparing for her first appointments of the morning. She'd just seen out a young woman when Nancy's telephone rang. Nancy answered it, then covered the receiver. "It's Mr. Calloway."

"I'll take it in my office," said Hazel.

She hurried back to her desk and picked up.

"How are you this morning, Mr. Calloway?"

"Richard, I really do insist." He laughed. "And it sounds as though you've been expecting me."

"I'd suspected you might call, yes," she said.

"Now I'm wondering if I've called too quickly, but I don't care. I'd like to take Marie to dinner again. Whenever she likes."

A huge smile broke out over Hazel's face. "Maybe this time you'd like to be alone," she said as Lady Moreton slipped into her office. She held up one finger, and the proprietor made herself comfortable in one of the chairs facing Hazel's desk.

He laughed. "Yes. Yes, if she's willing."

"I think that if you ring around to Marie's today, you'll find that she'd be happy to accept an invitation."

"I'll do that. And, Mrs. Carey? Thank you, sincerely."

As soon as Hazel hung up, Lady Moreton said, "Was that your friend?"

"The man I matched her with. The dinner was a success."

"I'm glad to hear that. Your friend deserves a bit of happiness."

"I think so, too. They seemed to get along so well."

Lady Moreton paused. "You were at the dinner?"

"That's right," she said.

"With your husband?"

Hazel tilted her head a little in question.

"How did he enjoy it?" Lady Moreton's voice was too high, as though she was fighting to keep her tone light.

"Why do you ask?" Hazel asked.

"You've been working very late for months," said Lady Moreton, picking at the hem of her simple black suit skirt.

"Your business is thriving."

"Perhaps we should take on another matchmaker."

"No! That is, if we need to take on another matchmaker, we should, but I don't need less work."

Lady Moreton arched a brow. "Perhaps the problem isn't the work, then. You're avoiding going home."

Hazel began to protest, but Lady Moreton wasn't done.

"I know that the agency is important to you. After you, well, returned to work, it seemed to give you some life back," said Lady Moreton. "But now I'm worried that it's becoming the problem."

"It's Nathaniel. Or maybe I'm the problem," said Hazel, rubbing her forehead. "Maybe it all happened too fast."

"Do you know, even with this mess with Germany, I'm grateful for the time we live in. Do you know why?" asked Lady Moreton.

"Tell me," said Hazel.

Lady Moreton leaned in. "Women can petition for divorce."

"I'm not going to divorce my husband."

Lady Moreton inclined her head slightly. "If any one of my grandmother's or even my mother's friends had the slightest hint of a rumor of divorce whispered about her, her social life would be over," said Lady Moreton. "But things are different now. Look at Ginger Rogers in that *Gay Divorcee* film, darling."

"It's just a film," said Hazel.

"It's a sign." Lady Moreton gathered her purse. "I just think you should consider the advice I've heard you give to your clients."

"What's that?" she asked.

"Don't let yourself believe that there's only one ending for your life's story."

The proprietor stood to leave, when Hazel blurted out, "Lady Moreton, I need to tell you something."

"I beg your pardon?" Lady Moreton said.

"Do you recall that man Dennison? He was here a few days ago, snooping around. If he's taken up the investigation into the group that was bringing refugees into Britain and trying to expedite their applications, he's going to dig deeper into the agency's records."

"So let him dig," said Lady Moreton. "What is the worst that he could find?"

"That I was arranging marriages for German refugees to help ease their applications along," said Hazel.

A long pause stretched between them. Finally Lady Moreton asked, "Did you do it because you wanted to help German spies?"

"No!"

"To your knowledge, were any of them sympathizers?"

"Of course not," she said.

"And did you match them with people you thought they might actually get on with?" Lady Moreton asked.

"The only thing different from the norm about these matches was that a network of people contacted me with a list of names, and the couples corresponded by letter. If they decided to marry, it was their decision," she said.

"Then what's the matter?" Lady Moreton asked.

"If Dennison finds out, he's going to twist what I did into knots. It could mean trouble for all of us."

The woman laughed. "If I was worried about every little man who thought he was more important than he is, I would have pulled the duvet over my head and given up long ago. You thought you were doing the right thing, and that is enough for me."

"Thank you," said Hazel.

Lady Moreton paused at the door. "Next time, perhaps let me know before launching a one-woman rescue mission from this office. I'd like to be involved. There's nothing like a little seditious do gooding to keep the spirits up in wartime."

Chapter 9

DESPITE HER EXCITEMENT, Marie was cautious by nature, and it was two weeks before she agreed to have dinner with Richard again—this time on their own. Afterward she'd done little more than blush at Hazel and Nora's interrogation.

"But what did you *do?*" Nora had asked as they entered the cinema one early spring evening.

"We talked," Marie replied.

"About what?" Nora demanded.

"Oh, leave her alone," Hazel stepped in with a laugh. "If she wants to tell us, she will."

Marie had looked gratefully to her, and Hazel had forced herself to follow her own advice. Marie would tell them what she wanted about her time with Richard. Slowly Hazel pieced together the story of their courtship as it progressed through dinners and a picnic in Regents Park on a fine day in March. There had been a trip to the cinema to see a Hollywood romance, and just last week, Marie had haltingly told them that Richard had given her a gift.

"A typewriter," Marie had said.

"A typewriter? That's unorthodox," said Hazel.

"It's secondhand," said Marie quickly. "We were walking by a shop, and I stopped to admire it. He insisted upon going in to look at it. Before I could protest, he'd bought it."

"But why?" Nora asked, clearly stumped.

Marie stared at her hands. "I told him that I used to help edit speeches for someone in the German Department—and, no, I didn't mention Neil's name. I found myself admitting that I've always wanted to try my hand at writing something of my own."

Hazel sat back. "I didn't know you had literary aspirations."

"I don't know that I do, but I think it's worth a try," Marie had said. "And it is a beautiful typewriter."

Now, as the days stretched into mid-April, Hazel wondered whether she should ask Marie for a more frank conversation about Richard. She snuck a glance at Nathaniel, who sat in his wing chair across from her in their front room. They sat in silence, Hazel with Stella Gibbons's *Cold Comfort Farm* forgotten on her lap while Nathaniel had his nose buried in a Graham Greene novel.

With a sigh she closed her book. "I think I'll head to bed."

Nathaniel's gaze flicked up, he gave her a weak smile, and then he lowered his eyes to his book again. "Good night."

This was absurd. All of this tiptoeing around each other.

Perhaps the problem isn't the work, then. Lady Moreton's words had been following her around for weeks, twisting and turning in her mind and always coming back to the same conclusion: He didn't love her anymore. As for her own mind, she questioned whether she ever had loved him, or if she'd merely loved everything he'd represented.

"Nathaniel, do you ever wonder—"

A knock cut through the quiet house.

"What the devil? It's nearly eleven," said Nathaniel, glancing at the clock.

She surged up out of her chair. "I'll get it."

"No, no, I'll go. You stay here," he said.

Another round of knocking sounded through the house, and she heard Nathaniel call out, "I'm coming!"

She followed a few steps behind him, her heart lodged in her throat. People did not knock on doors in the middle of the night unless there was something wrong.

Nathaniel opened the door, but his wide shoulders blocked the view so she couldn't see who it was.

"Can I help you?" he asked.

"Mr. Nathaniel Carey? I need to speak to you on a matter of great importance. It's about your wife."

Dennison.

Anger pushed her fear away, and she stepped into full view of the door. "It isn't enough that you badger me at my place of business? Now you insist on coming to my home?"

Nathaniel turned to cast a look over his shoulder, and she saw Dennison illuminated by their front light.

"Mrs. Carey, it's a pleasure as always," said Dennison.

"You have no right to come here in the dead of night," she said.

"Hazel, who is this man?" Nathaniel asked.

"Thomas Dennison of the Aliens Department. I am investigating the disappearance of a German national we suspect of wrongdoing, and your wife has blocked me every way I've turned."

"Don't be absurd. I've done nothing of the kind," said Hazel.

Nathaniel put a hand up, confusion etched on his brow. "I don't understand. My wife is a matchmaker. What business does the Home Office have with a marriage agency?"

"Were you aware, Mr. Carey, that for months before the war, your wife was helping Germans marry British citizens so they could live in this country?" asked Dennison. "And we have reason to believe that she has not stopped. In fact, she's graduated from matching refugees to matching sympathizers."

"What?" Nathaniel asked.

"I've never had a Nazi sympathizer in my office," she said.

Dennison pointed at her. "You've been playing a dangerous game, madam, and it has only become more dangerous."

Across the way, a light went on. Nathaniel must've seen it, too, because he said, "Maybe it would be best if we sat down inside."

Clenching her fists, she led the men into the front room, sitting back down in her armchair. Dennison perched awkwardly on one end of the sofa while Nathaniel sat bolt upright in his chair.

"You said that Hazel has been blocking your efforts in this investigation. That does not sound like my wife," said Nathaniel.

"She refuses to divulge her client list," said Dennison.

"That is because it is a violation of my clients' privacy and completely unreasonable. You have no reason to believe that any of them are German spies or whatever you're looking for," she said.

"Other investigators have made progress in the investigation into a group of Nazi sympathizers believed to be living and operating in London. This new information means that it is possible my investigation dovetails with—"

"Possible? Is that how you're justifying harassing me in my home? Where is your evidence, Mr. Dennison?" Hazel asked sharply. "Where is your order compelling me to comply?"

The man went bright red.

"You don't have one. You're grasping at straws," she said.

Dennison turned to Nathaniel. "I'd like to search your house. If your wife has nothing to hide, surely she won't try to stop me."

"No."

Hazel jerked her gaze to her husband. His jaw was set, and he was glaring at their interloper. She could feel his anger simmering.

"Excuse me?" Dennison asked.

"My wife has said no to your requests before. I would be a sorry excuse for a husband if I were to override her wishes simply because you told me to," Nathaniel said.

Dennison obviously thought that changing tactics might help, because he affected a chummy smile and said, "I know the feeling. Wouldn't want to make the wife angry."

"My wife's never displayed a particularly volatile temper, Mr. Dennison," said Nathaniel.

"Mr. Dennison." Hazel rose from her chair. "If you are finished trying to bully me using my husband, I will ask you to leave."

Dennison shot to his feet. "You're putting yourself in a dangerous position, Mrs. Carey." He stuck his finger in her face. "Soon people like you will have to cooperate or face the consequences."

A shiver ran down her spine, but still Hazel leaned in, hands on her hips. "Who, exactly, are people like me? Because I have never done anything but act in the best interest of my country, Mr. Dennison. Now leave my house."

Dennison, beet red, rounded on Nathaniel. "I would suggest that you control your wife, sir."

"Why would I want to control her? I think she's rather spectacular," said Nathaniel.

Hazel caught a little smile playing at the corner of his lips. It was the first genuine smile he'd given her in months.

"This is not over," said Dennison.

The Home Office man marched out the door and slammed it.

Nathaniel and Hazel stood there for a moment, eyeing each other. "Are you going to tell me what's going on?" he asked.

She looked at him, and it all came spilling out, from helping the refugees to Dennison's first visit to Marie's connection to it through Pieter Gunter. When she was done, he sat silent.

"Aren't you going to say something?" she asked cautiously.

"What should a man say when his wife is defying the government and going against orders from a Home Office official?"

"Dennison thinks I've been helping spies, which couldn't be further from the truth."

"He doesn't care. If he finds a connection from you to this group, he will put you in jail," said Nathaniel.

Hazel breathed deep. "He won't find out. The rumor is that the network has all gone to ground since war was declared."

"Hazel, I don't know what to say—"

"Then don't say anything," she cut in.

"If you'll let me finish, you'll find that I was going to say that

I don't know what to say when my wife has been working to help people so many others would ignore, and I couldn't be prouder."

She stilled. "What?"

"I couldn't be prouder." He offered her a little smile. "Is that so hard to believe?"

"Yes."

His hand rasped over his chin. "I suppose that's my fault."

"No. No, it's not."

He shook his head. "This hasn't been a marriage for a long time, has it, dear?"

His question sliced through her, even if she'd been thinking the same thing just a half hour before.

"It's my fault," he said again.

Tears started to brim in her eyes. "I've been neglectful. If I were the sort of wife you deserved—"

"Stop that," he said. "You've been nothing but the best wife a man could wish for. I've been the one who's come up short. It's just . . . after the baby, I couldn't think."

There it was, this hurt they'd skirted around for years.

"I wasn't the husband you needed me to be," he said quietly. "When you were grieving, I tried to help, but then you seemed to heal without me, and I couldn't stand the thought that you didn't need me. I pulled away, and by the time I realized what was happening, you'd become this woman I hardly knew."

"I didn't know what else to do," she said, tears falling. "I needed you once. I wanted to love you so much when we met."

He was across the room, arms around her, before she realized he'd moved. She leaned into him, unable to stop wanting comfort and contact. It had been so long since he'd just held her.

"I know. I know that now," he said, stroking her hair.

They sat like that until her crying slowed to shuddering breaths. Finally, she looked up. "I can't do this any longer. I'm not happy. I haven't been for years."

He closed his eyes but nodded. "Neither have I," he admitted.

She gave a laugh through her tears. "And it's as simple as that?"

He sighed. "Nothing is ever simple, but for the first time since we met, I think we're finally being honest. We should've done this before things became so broken they couldn't be fixed."

"I just think we got carried away," she said quietly.

"I wanted to do the right thing."

"I need more than that now," she said, the truth sending prickles throughout her entire body. She wanted more. She deserved more.

"Do you know, the first night that we met, I saw you making your way around the room," he said. "You were so beautiful."

"My mother was beautiful, not me," she said.

"You're beautiful. You still are."

He kissed her on the temple, then stood and crossed the room to the record player. After a moment, a dance band filled the drawing room with the sweet notes of "Deed I Do." Extending his hand to her, he said, "One last one? For old times' sake?"

Slowly, Hazel placed her right hand into his left. "I would love to."

He pulled her close. She tucked her head onto his shoulder and felt at honest peace for the first time in years.

IT WAS nearly half past two in the morning when Hazel rang Nora's doorbell. The door opened to Nora in a dressing gown.

"Hazel! What's wrong?" Nora asked in a rush.

She lifted her two suitcases. "Do you think you could stand a second houseguest?"

"What's going on?" Marie asked, appearing at the bottom of the stairs. "Hazel?"

"I'm leaving Nathaniel. Or rather, we're leaving each other," she said with a frown. The words still felt strange in her mouth.

"Isn't that his car?" Nora asked, nodding over her shoulder.

"Yes. He insisted on driving me. He wanted to be sure that I made it to your house safely, since it's so late."

Nora opened her mouth, but instead of the barrage of questions Hazel was expecting, Nora snapped it shut and nodded firmly. "Well, you'd better come in, then. We'll get you settled, and then you can tell us whatever you want to tell us in the morning."

"Yes, a good night's sleep is what you need," said Marie.

"Thank you," she said.

Nora let her through the door. As soon as she was inside, Nora waved to Nathaniel and called, "Don't worry! We have her now!"

Hazel looked back at her husband. He'd rolled down the window and now lifted his hand. She returned the gesture; then he put the car into gear, and the man she'd once loved drove away.

Samantha
Now

SAMANTHA stood in front of 5 Taviton Street, looking up at the brick facade. Poured concrete detail formed a cornice over the front door with a set of brass buzzers to the right of the door handle. This was the third stop on their tour of her grandmother's life.

After her morning session with Nora, David had come to pick up Samantha as planned. They'd started in Chelsea, where Colin had given them a tour of Nora's old mews house. The second stop had been Royal Imperial University, interesting enough but impersonal in comparison. But this. Standing on the Bloomsbury street next to David in front of the building her grandmother had called home for so long felt different.

"Do you think we can go inside?" she asked, glancing at David.

"We can try," he said, stepping forward to the buzzers. "What was her flat number?"

"She was in flat C," she said.

David leaned on the bell and stepped back to wait. Nothing.

"I'm sorry," he said. "Why don't I take you to the Harlan?"

He placed a gentle hand on her elbow to guide her back down the street. But just as they turned, the door to the building swung open, and an older woman with dyed black hair shuffled out.

"Excuse me," said Samantha, "do you live in flat C?"

The woman stopped. "No. I don't. Why do you ask?"

"My friend's grandmother used to live in the building before the war," said David. "We had hoped we might be able to meet the owners and see the flat."

"They won't be back until next week," said the woman. "I sometimes take in their post for them, and they told me they'd be around to collect it on Wednesday. You might come back then."

"I'm afraid my flight is tomorrow afternoon," said Samantha, unable to hide her disappointment. "But thank you for your help."

She and David got three steps down the street before the woman called, "Will you not be wanting to see the air-raid shelter, then?"

Samantha and David exchanged a look.

"Air raid shelter?" he asked.

"Well, it's really a basement, but they fitted it out to be an air-raid shelter. Many places did. In you go, then, and I'll open it up for you." The woman pulled out a key and unlatched the front door, letting David hold it open for her. "I'm Joan, by the way."

"I'm Samantha, and this is David."

Joan led them to a painted metal door with a large bolt keeping it shut. "Here it is."

David undid the bolt and opened the door. After searching for a moment, he found the light switch, illuminating a set of stairs.

"I'll wait for you up here if you'd like to have a look," said Joan.

Samantha followed David down the stairs. It was cool and a little musty down in the basement. A wall of bunks stacked with boxes stood on one side. On the other was a row of benches.

"This must be the place your grandmother was telling us they went after the air-raid siren went off," she said.

David sat down on one of the benches as he watched her. "What she's told you over the last few days—it seems incredible. I can't imagine London during that time."

Samantha wandered over to the bunks and ran her fingers over them. "They must've been terrified."

"Your grandmother more than most, I think."

"I just hate to think that she was so afraid of what might happen to her and her family," she said.

David didn't say anything, instead letting her stand in silence, absorbing everything she'd learned over the last few days.

Finally, she sighed. "I wish I could stay for longer. There's so much more that I'd like to ask Nora."

"She's not done, then?" he asked.

"She told me I'll get the rest of the story tomorrow morning and not a moment sooner," she said.

"She never was one to shy away from a dramatic moment." He paused. "I'm glad you came to London."

"I am, too."

"Do you think you might come back one day?" he asked, something in his voice telling her it was more than just a polite question.

"If I had a reason to come back," she said.

The fingers on his right hand twitched, and she thought for a moment that he might reach for her. Instead, he stood, his head nearly touching the low ceiling. "Shall we go on to the Harlan?"

Samantha glanced around the basement one last time. "Let's."

SAMANTHA's things were stacked in the hallway and her boarding pass downloaded when she sat with Nora for the last time.

"Your final morning," said Nora as Samantha folded the ends of her cardigan around her. "How has your trip been?"

"I wish I could stay longer," she said truthfully.

Nora peered over her spectacles. "Is that a testament to my riveting storytelling or to a certain grandson of mine?"

A blush crept up the back of Samantha's neck.

"David has been very kind to me these last few days," she said.

"Yes. He has, hasn't he?"

"I appreciate the time he took to show me around London. Seeing the places where Grandma used to go made it feel more real."

"Do you know, I never thought I would marry?" Nora said. "I managed to make it through the entire war without a man, got myself a job at the BBC in the programming department, and then when everyone thought I was too old to possibly be a bride, I was reintroduced to my husband at a party."

"Reintroduced?" Samantha asked.

"Yes." Nora smiled slyly. "I married Joseph Fowler, who I'd worked with before the war. He'd become a radio reporter after VE Day. He'd just been transferred back from Hong Kong and was supposed to go back, but then a well-meaning friend cornered us and told us we'd both worked in the Home Office before the war, so we should have plenty in common. I've never seen a man more shocked in my life than Joseph was when he saw me again.

"We left the party and went to a little Cypriot restaurant for dinner to catch up. We talked for so long that the waiters had to tell us to leave. The day after that party, he put in a request to transfer to London. We were married six months later."

"What made you change your mind about getting married?"

"Joseph was the first man I'd ever met who didn't tell me what I was supposed to think or do. We could fight like cats and dogs sometimes, but he always respected what I had to say and listened. He didn't balk when I told him I didn't want to stop working. He didn't think it was 'unnatural' for a woman to love both her work and her children, because that was the kind of father he wanted to be. How could I not have fallen in love with him? All this is to say sometimes you don't plan for things. They just happen."

But even as Nora said it, Samantha knew it wouldn't be true for her. There were so many reasons it wouldn't work, but she liked knowing that she'd always remember David as the kind man who had gone with her on the most seemingly unremarkable sightseeing trip around London because the places were important to her.

"Then there's what Joseph did for Marie," Nora added.

"What he did for Marie?"

Nora's lips hitched up just a little on the left side, and she nodded slowly. "I think it's time for you to hear the end of the story."

Chapter 10

Nora
May 1940 to June 1940

"Good morning, Miss Walcott." Sir Gerald's booming voice filled the reception of the Air Raid Precautions Department. "An early start for you today."

Nora looked up from the brief she was writing. She was not,

in fact, particularly early, having come in at half past eight, like she normally did. Not only did she oversee the typists assigned to the department, but she also managed much of the flow of work between the department's twelve regional commissioners and the main office, training in local councils across the country, and communication with the other four departments that made up the Ministry of Home Security in the Home Office. And yet, Sir Gerald still walked in every day surprised that she had shown up for work.

Pushing away from her desk, Nora grabbed the small diary with Sir Gerald's appointments in it. "Good morning, sir. Messages are on your desk. You may want to return Mr. Grant's call first. Another shipment of gas masks sent to Leeds are defective."

"Defective?" he asked.

"Cracks in the rubber seals."

"Handle it, Miss Walcott, if you would," he said.

She placed a tick mark next to the item on her list. "You have a meeting with Mr. Elroy at one o'clock."

"Thank you, Miss Walcott. Is that all?"

She hesitated. "You mentioned that you might look at my proposal for the Ministry of Information."

Sir Gerald leveled a direct look at her for the first time that day. "What was it about again?"

"A new group of recruitment materials aimed at women. The proposal is on your desk. I've included an estimate of costs for both color and black-and-white printing. There's also a suggestion for a media campaign that could run in conjunction—"

"A media campaign?"

"Yes." She hated that he suddenly made her doubt what she'd been sure only moments ago had been a very good idea. It *was* a good idea. Newsreel features and advertisements in women's magazines would reach far more women than the simple bus posters Huw in the department had suggested last week.

"There will be questions of budget around that," Sir Gerald said, a hint that budget would be the reason he didn't back her proposal strongly enough to pass it along to the Ministry of Information.

They'd been down this path too many times before. Nora's ideas were good. Sometimes they were taken up—when one of the young men in the bullpen twisted them just enough so it couldn't be called stealing and pitched them. It made her want to put her heel through Sir Gerald's frosted glass door.

"I would appreciate your thoughts on the proposal, sir. If adjustments are needed, I would be happy to make them," she said.

"If there is time, I will give it a look. But only if there is time."

Nora's shoulders sagged. There was never time. She understood the importance of her work. Keeping a department like Air Raid Precautions running was vital, but it didn't feel like enough. She wanted to do more, to be challenged.

"Is that all, Miss Walcott?" Sir Gerald asked.

"You're due at a meeting of the department heads of the Ministry of Home Security in fifteen minutes," she said. "Will you be wanting tea before you go?"

"No time. I'll need you for notes. Go and secure us seats." He shuffled to his office and shut the door.

Nora gathered up her steno pad and pen and hurried out of the office. Inside the meeting room, some of the most powerful men in the Home Office sat around a large table. Lining the wall behind them, their secretaries sat ready with steno pads in hand. She sat down behind an empty spot Sir Gerald took a few minutes later.

Voices droned as her hand flew across the page to record the meeting's proceedings. Her mind began to wander, until she heard a man say, "And then there is the matter of the camps."

She started, her notepad nearly falling to the floor.

"Mass internment came up again in the last Cabinet meeting," said Sir John Anderson, home secretary and minister of home security, from his seat at the head of the table.

"Yes, sir," said Mr. Gilman, the undersecretary who headed the Aliens Department. "We're ready for the internment of all German and Austrian men in the south if the Home Office should order it."

"And the women?" a man Nora didn't recognize asked.

"Not yet, but the Cabinet isn't ruling it out," said Gilman.

As the men continued the discussion, Nora forced herself to start taking notes again, but the way they spoke about the internees set her on edge. The internees would lose their livelihoods, their homes. They would be locked away within camps with barbed wire–topped walls for the duration of the war.

That couldn't be Marie. She wouldn't let it be.

BY THE end of the meeting, Nora had chewed the inside of her right cheek so raw it stung. As heads of departments stood to stretch their legs and secretaries gathered their things, she glanced at Sir Gerald, but he was engaged in a discussion with Mr. Williams. If he wanted her, he could find her back at her desk.

But first, a little fortification. Nora made her way down the hallway and into the canteen. She nodded to the tea lady, who wore a bright white nurselike uniform.

"White tea, no sugar, love?" the woman asked.

"Yes, thank you," she said, taking the cup.

"That isn't your lunch, is it?" She turned to find Joseph Fowler, one of the civil servants from her department, standing behind her.

"Is it lunchtime?" she asked, checking her wristwatch and finding, to her surprise, that it was nearly one.

"Will you be joining the young lady for a cup of tea, sir?" the tea lady asked Joseph.

"Yes, thank you."

As the older woman fixed Joseph his cup, Nora couldn't help but notice that he didn't have to confirm how he took his tea.

"Was there anything interesting in the meeting you just came from?" Joseph asked, nodding to a small table in the corner.

"Internment," Nora said as they sat down. "They're going to issue the order to detain German men in the south next week."

"And I take it from your tone that you don't agree."

"I don't believe in internment," she said.

He chuckled until he saw that she wasn't doing the same. "You're serious? Even those who are category A?"

"I understand the need to find and jail sympathizers and those who are actively working against Britain, but mass internment? Of course not. Even if you set aside the morality of it, consider the expense. There are far better things for the government to be doing in the middle of a war than funding what is essentially the imprisonment of tens of thousands of people."

"On the other hand, what is expense when you consider the safety of British citizens and the state?" he shot back.

"And what of the last war? We interned thousands of innocent people in camps that were ill run and exposed them to disease."

"We couldn't risk the possibility that some of those people would've done us harm if given the opportunity," he said.

"But Joseph, what about the little matter of what it means to be British? If we begin to lock people up purely because they happen to have been born in a different country—"

"A country we're at war with," he interjected. His eyes narrowed. "Why do you care so much about this?"

The sudden question threw her off balance a little. "What?"

"This isn't merely a philosophical argument. You're invested."

She caught herself shifting in her seat and forced herself still. "You know I have a German friend," she said.

"One of the girls you went to school with. Yes, I remember you mentioning her," he said.

"She's living with me now."

Joseph's mouth fell open. "Living with you?"

"She has been for months. She had a disagreement with her family and had nowhere to go," said Nora.

"Nora, you know it's not wise to have a German woman living with you," he said. "Think of where you work. How it looks."

"It looks as though I've helped a friend in a time of need," she said. "I have a divorcée living with me now, too, if you find that morally objectionable."

"Nora, this is not a joke. You're making a mistake."

"If helping a friend is a mistake, it's one I'm happy to make. Now, if you'll excuse me, I think it's time to return to work."

"You still haven't eaten lunch. At least let me bring you a sandwich," he said.

"I'm not hungry," she announced, and walked deliberately out of the room, leaving him and their cold cups of tea behind.

NORA THREW DOWN HER KEYS on the entryway table when she got home. It had been a rotten day, and now she was going to have to tell Marie the bad news about the internment plans.

Keys rattled in the door, and Hazel pushed through.

"Evening," Hazel said. "Did you get stuck in the storm?"

"Just as I was coming off the Tube," said Nora. "Fancy a drink before dinner?"

"Oh yes," said her friend.

"Dinner's at seven," Marie called from the kitchen.

Nora's heart twisted as she set about making their usual drinks. She was just dropping an olive into Hazel's glass when Marie came through, pushing her hair back from her face with a smile.

Nora handed drinks around, and then slipped off her shoes and settled onto the sofa. She watched her friends take up their favorite spots—Hazel in a chair that caught the late afternoon sun and Marie on the other end of the sofa, a blanket tossed over her legs.

"Marie, there's something I need to tell you, but you can't tell anyone else. It'll cost me my job," she said.

Marie froze. "What's wrong?"

"The Home Office is going to order the internment of German men living along the south coast."

Marie's hand covered her mouth. "When?"

"Next Tuesday."

"How can they do that? Those people all received their classifications and were found not to be dangerous," said Hazel.

"This is exactly what I worried would happen," murmured Marie. "Who will be taken away?"

"All men between seventeen and sixty who aren't infirm. The police will begin to arrest them on the seventh," she said.

Marie set down her glass. "I think it's time."

"For what?" Nora asked.

"To make a plan."

"What do you mean?" Hazel asked.

Marie looked between them. "I don't want to be interned. I will do whatever I can to make sure I'm not arrested and locked up—even if that means leaving."

The word hit Nora like a swift kick to the stomach. "Leaving?"

"I've heard of some Germans and Austrians trying to leave the country. They go to Canada, Australia. There are still ships sailing out of British ports," said Marie.

"You're restricted in how far you can travel," Hazel pointed out.

"That's a problem, yes. I will need to book my passage under a false name. And I'll need a new passport," said Marie.

"I may know someone who may be able to help with the passport," said Hazel quietly.

"You do?" Nora and Marie asked in unison.

Hazel held up her hands. "Don't become too excited. I don't know if the man I'm thinking of is still in the business of false papers. He could've been arrested, for all I know."

"Was he the printer working with your refugees?" Nora asked.

"That's the one," Hazel said.

"Will asking put you in danger of being arrested?" Marie asked.

Hazel shrugged. "I'm happy to take the risk for you."

"I'll find what I can in the way of ships' schedules," said Nora.

"Is there anything else that we can do?" asked Hazel.

Marie shook her head, but Nora wasn't so sure. She worked in the Home Office. Surely that must be worth something.

Still, she kept her thoughts to herself for now.

"Marie, when will dinner be ready?" she asked instead.

Marie glanced at her watch. "Thirty minutes?"

"Then I propose we sit here and enjoy our cocktails and let Hazel regale us with the latest stories of her clients," she said, lifting her glass to her friends.

Marie mirrored her, but before she took a sip, she said, "Your mother called earlier."

"She didn't say anything cruel, did she?"

Marie smiled. "She sounded a little taken aback when I told her that I was staying with you now," she admitted.

"Did you mention me?" asked Hazel with a laugh.

"I didn't," said Marie.

"That's probably for the best," said Hazel. "We wouldn't want to give Mrs. Walcott an aneurism."

NORA WALKED DOWN THE hallway from the Air Raid Precautions Department, arms full of files from Sir Gerald's office. When she whipped around a corner, she collided straight into a tall, solid object. Her files cascaded to the floor, and she lunged for them.

A hand flew to her elbow. "Nora, Nora, wait. Let me help you."

She shot Joseph, the solid object himself, a glare. "I'm fine."

His other hand went to her elbow, stilling her enough that she was forced to look at him fully. The expression he wore was appropriately contrite. "I'm sorry for walking into you."

She shook her head and breathed. This was Joseph. Even if they didn't always see eye to eye, they were friends. "No, I should've looked where I was going."

He handed her back her files, his hand lingering when it brushed hers. Her gaze jerked up to his, and she found he was smiling down at her in that particular way—the one she'd catch a glimpse of when he thought she wasn't looking. She took a step back.

Joseph tapped the files. "What are these?"

"Authorizations. Sir Gerald's sending me down to Records."

"I was just down there a couple of weeks ago. The amount of paperwork this war has generated is incredible, and they're storing as much of it as they can here."

"Why?" she asked.

"They're worried the usual storage facilities might be bombed. They're all aboveground. It's not a permanent solution, but at least it keeps all of the important things safe for now," he said.

"Like what?"

He shrugged. "Personnel records, invoices, tribunal hearing documents—"

She straightened. "Tribunal hearings?"

"The London ones, yes. The hearings meant a lot of paperwork because each classification justification had to be recorded, in case of an appeal. Why are you interested in—" He froze. "Nora, no."

"No, what?" she asked sweetly.

He grabbed her elbow. "Nora, you can't go to the Records Department to look at your friend's file."

She shifted her elbow out of his reach. " Joseph, we still don't know why Marie was given her classification—"

"I know you're worried for your friend," he interjected, "but you can't go rooting around in the Records Department."

"Why not?" she demanded.

"Dennison!" a man called out from over Joseph's shoulder before Joseph could respond. Nora whipped around, catching sight of a little man in a cheap gray suit. *That* was Dennison?

Dennison looked up, and their eyes locked across the hallway. Without thinking, Nora spun around and made for the stairs.

"Nora, what's wrong?" Joseph's question pulled her back.

"There's a man I don't want to see," she said.

Joseph peered over his shoulder. "You're not running from Dennison, are you? Has he asked you out to dinner, too?"

Nora nearly tripped over her feet. "Asked me out to dinner?"

Joseph sighed. "The girls in the typing pool were talking about it the other day. Apparently he's been after all of them. He has a reputation of working from department to department."

"But he was wearing a wedding ring." He stared at her, and quickly she added, "That's exactly what he did. Before Christmas. I've been trying to avoid him ever since. You know him?"

"Cambridge man," Joseph said, as though those two words declaring their shared alma mater was all she needed to know.

"I'll have a word with him," he continued.

She let out a breath. She could tell Joseph everything, and at one time she might have, but something had shifted since war had broken out. Loyalties weren't as simple as they once had been.

"There's no need, but thank you," she said.

"None of this changes the fact that you haven't promised me not to go snooping around the Records Department," he said.

She smiled at him. "Why would you ask me to make a promise I'm not going to keep?"

He sighed and shook his head. "No, silly me. Come on, then."

"What do you mean?" she asked.

"It'll be faster with two of us looking."

She blinked. "You're going to help me?"

"Yes. And one day I'm going to remind you of this," he muttered. Then he grabbed her hand and began to lead her down, until they reached the lowest floor of the building. They stopped in front of a set of doors with RECORDS written on a plaque over the frame.

Joseph held open the door for her, and she nearly walked straight into Mrs. Stowe. Nora'd crossed paths on occasion with the stern white-haired lady who had ruled over the Records Department for the past forty years. Seeing her now turned Nora's blood cold.

"Miss Walcott," said Mrs. Stowe. "Mr. Fowler, what brings you here? It isn't often that the gentlemen of Air Raid Precautions grace us with their presence twice in one month."

Nora could've kicked herself for not realizing that Joseph would likely send up red flags. Filing was an act reserved for secretaries.

"He's helping me," said Nora. "On a project. At Sir Gerald's request."

"And what project would that be?" asked Mrs. Stowe.

Nora looked at Joseph. He stared back at her in panic. Sweet, useless man. So Nora said the first thing that came to her head. "Shipment records. For air-raid wardens' helmets."

"Yes, I made an error and three thousand were lost in transit," said Joseph. "Completely my fault. I made quite the hash of it."

"And Sir Gerald thought I might be able to sort it out for him," Nora finished.

Mrs. Stowe huffed. "Go along, then. The Air Raid Precautions Department's supply records are on the right, halfway down."

As they walked away, Nora was acutely aware of her footsteps' echo in the large space filled with metal boxes. Neat printed signs were pasted onto the ends of all of the columns, surely the work of Mrs. Stowe. There were personnel records, purchase orders, meeting minutes. Then, on her left, something caught her eye.

"There are the tribunal records," she said, nudging Joseph.

"We can't," he said out of the corner of his mouth. "She could be watching."

"But Joseph—"

"On your right, Miss Walcott. Over there," called Mrs. Stowe. Nora's jaw clamped shut.

"I told you, she's watching too closely," Joseph whispered.

"This could be my one chance. I think it will help Marie, and that's the most important thing to me in the world."

He blew out a breath. "I will figure something out. I promise."

"Why are you helping me?" she asked.

He looked at her for a long moment. "I had hoped you wouldn't need to ask that question."

"Joseph . . ." But she didn't know what to say. She knew that if she could give him more, he would take it. If she let him say what always seemed on the tip of his tongue, he would willingly. But that wasn't what she wanted. Not yet. Not before she'd had a chance to prove that she could be the woman she'd always hoped she'd become, independent and loyal. Someone who *mattered*.

"I will figure something out," he repeated. "I promise."

Chapter 11

NORA COULD HARDLY be accused of being the sort of girl who sat at her desk and stared at the wall clock ticking its monotonous way until the hands read five. But with the wind rattling the windows of her office and clouds threatening rain on the dull Tuesday afternoon, she couldn't help but will time to move a little faster.

The morning had been a rush of activity. The internment orders had gone out, and all day the Home Office had been abuzz with updates from the roundup of Germans and Austrians living along the coast. When Nora finally made it back to her desk, Sir Gerald had kept buzzing her intercom. Around teatime, however, she'd heard his phone ring and he'd shut his office door, making it clear she would not be needed.

Nora was just pulling out her handbag and gloves when the telephone rang. Unclipping her right earring, she picked up the receiver with her other hand. "Air Raid Precautions Department."

There was a pause, and then she heard her mother's voice. "Nora, is that you?"

She pressed two fingers to her right temple. "Hello, Mother."

"Good, you are there."

"I almost wasn't. It's nearly five."

"What does the time matter? You never take my calls anyway."

Nora winced. "What can I do to help you?" she asked.

Her mother paused. "I wanted to see how you are."

The way her mother hesitated gave her pause. Caroline Walcott was nothing if not certain. About everything.

"Why do you ask?"

"No reason," said her mother quickly.

"Mother, why did you call me?" Nora asked slowly as the melodic tones of the Walcotts' Hanover Terrace doorbell sounded on the other end of the phone.

"That will be Rosamunde Kilkern now," said her mother. "She's come for drinks. Says she's worried sick about Robert. You remember Robert. He's a lieutenant in the navy now."

"Mother—"

"I'll tell Rosamunde to tell him to give you a ring when he's on leave. Goodbye, darling," trilled her mother, disconnecting.

Nora pulled the phone back from her ear to stare at the receiver.

"Miss Walcott."

She glanced over her shoulder to see Sir Gerald filling the doorway of his office. She set the phone down carefully.

"If you are finished taking that personal call, would you care to join me?" He nodded toward his desk before retreating inside.

She collected her paper and pencil to join him.

"Close the door," said Sir Gerald. She did and took the seat in front of his desk.

"Miss Walcott, it has come to my attention that there is a very grave matter about which we must speak," said Sir Gerald.

"I assure you, Sir Gerald, that I will be the soul of discretion."

"I'm afraid the time for your assurances has passed." He folded his hands on the table. "I find myself concerned about your current living situation."

"My living situation?"

"You have taken in a houseguest, I believe, who some might consider inappropriate," Sir Gerald clarified.

"I actually have two houseguests at the moment, sir, and I can assure you that both are respectable women."

"I'm speaking of your German friend. She is not an appropriate housemate for a woman working at the Home Office."

His words crashed down on her. "Surely you can't be suggesting that my living with Marie is a problem for my job."

"She is German," said Sir Gerald.

"So is Marlene Dietrich, but the United States didn't seem to take issue with her becoming a citizen," she argued.

"That is America, a country that is not at war with Germany. You must see how this looks. A German woman with a category B classification attached to her name living with a woman who is the secretary to a high-ranking official in the Home Office."

"I won't turn her away. Marie has nowhere else to go."

That drew a patronizing little smile. "Even if you did, it wouldn't make a difference at this point in time. This office must be beyond reproach. I'm afraid I have no choice but to let you go."

The entire world tilted on its axis. "You're sacking me?"

"I'm afraid there's no helping it. If what you've done were to get around this building—"

"I've done nothing wrong."

"And yet, even the slightest whiff of scandal could compromise all of the good work we're doing here."

The work I'm *doing here.* She stood, but before she could turn to leave, a thought struck her. "How did you know that Marie is living at my home?"

Sir Gerald was visibly taken aback by the question. "I've looked at her tribunal file."

"Marie was not living with me when the tribunal happened."

Sir Gerald's mouth opened and closed, making him look absurdly like a flounder. Finally, he said, "I received a phone call informing me of your arrangement with Miss Bohn."

"Who called you?" she asked.

"If you must know, it was your mother. Mrs. Walcott asked that I not tell you if I could possibly help it, but I suppose you have a right to know who brought this to my attention," he said.

"Thank you," she said curtly.

"You won't tell your mother that I mentioned this to you, will you?" asked Sir Gerald. "My wife sometimes plays bridge with her crowd, and I shall never hear the end of it if she's cut."

Nora snorted in disgust. "Goodbye, Sir Gerald."

She walked straight out, letting Sir Gerald's door bang shut behind her. Joseph, who was standing by her desk, looked up.

"What's wrong?" he asked immediately.

"I've been dismissed," she said, tugging on her coat.

"What do you mean you've been dismissed?"

It all came out. Marie, her tribunal, the judgment, her mother's phone call, and the dismissal. Joseph sat listening to all of it, nodding once or twice but never stopping her.

"I don't suppose you understand," she said at the end.

He crossed his arms. "Why wouldn't I?"

"All of our arguments about internment—"

"That doesn't mean that I can't be sympathetic to what your friend is going through. Nora, you must know I care." The way he said it, with a hint of longing, gave her pause. But this wasn't what she wanted. She wanted to do something that mattered. Joseph was a good man, but he wasn't what she needed. Not now.

"You could look for me," she blurted out.

"What?"

"Sir Gerald has Marie's file. If you found it, you could see what's written there. Maybe there is something we could use in an appeal, to get Marie's classification lifted."

"How am I supposed to find this file? It's probably on his desk," said Joseph. "And besides, that won't help you with your job."

She stared at him. "I'm not the one who needs help."

"Your friend will be fine. Category B women aren't being sent away," he said.

"Yes, but for how long? If this war takes a turn, how long until women are caught up?"

He sighed. "I don't know."

"And you still think mass internment is the best way to win this war?" she asked.

"Not to win the war, no, but to keep us from losing it," he said.

"I believe you think you're doing the right thing, Joseph, but I hope that one day you'll understand how wrong you are."

Without another word, she walked out the door.

THE heavy black lacquered door to the Walcott family home creaked open, and Mrs. Phillips, the Walcotts' housekeeper, peered out. "Miss Nora," said the older woman in surprise.

"Is my mother at home, Mrs. Phillips?" she asked, her voice barely masking her anger.

"She's just having tea with Mrs. Kilkern in the drawing room."

"Thank you," said Nora, maneuvering around the housekeeper.

She tore through the short corridor that led to the formal drawing room. Not bothering to knock, she yanked open the door and stopped. Her mother and Mrs. Kilkern looked up from their tea.

"Nora, it's lovely to see you," said her mother.

"Why did you do it?" she said through clenched teeth.

"I'm sorry?" asked her mother.

"Tell me why you tattled to Sir Gerald about Marie."

Her mother's back straightened, and her face became serene. "I telephoned him because it was necessary. I cannot stand by and let you compromise your reputation by letting that girl live in your house. The government decided she's dangerous."

"She has a B classification. She's been charged with *nothing*—no wrongdoing. Do you understand that?" asked Nora.

"Marie Bohn is German," said Nora's mother. "Think of the things you expose yourself to by continuing to associate with her."

"She's one of my dearest friends! She attended Papa's funeral!"

Her mother sniffed. "I did what's best for you, just as any mother would. I know you enjoyed playing at work—"

"I don't play at working!"

"Nora Walcott, you will not use that tone when you speak to me," her mother snapped. "There is a war on. You should be

doing things that matter, like charitable work for the war effort."
Nora straightened. "You want me to do war work, do you?"
"Well, yes. Of course I do," said her mother, taken aback.

Turning to Mrs. Kilkern, Nora said, "I want you to listen carefully and remember this so you can tell all the awful women you
two call friends. You tell them that Mrs. Walcott deliberately sabo-
taged her daughter's job working in the Home Office in a department that is doing its best to keep people safe when the Germans
begin to bomb us. All of the air-raid shelters, air-raid warnings,
and air-raid wardens who will help protect you when it starts? My
mother thought they were less important than proving a point."

Mrs. Kilkern slowly began to nod, still shocked but with a tiny
glint in her eye at the prime gossip she was witnessing.

"Mother, if you ever intervene in my life again, you will not see
me again," she said.

"Nora . . ." But her mother's voice faded as Nora walked out of
the room.

As soon as Nora was out of the house, she turned right and began to walk. She had no doubts that she'd done the right thing in
offering Marie a home. Even so, she couldn't deny the pain of losing her job. She hadn't always loved it, but it was still her job. She'd
felt as though she was making a difference.

What she needed was to find a way to contribute to the war effort without becoming the debutante her mother wanted her to be.

And then she saw it. Painted high on impeccably polished glass:
Women's Royal Navy Service. The WRNS.

Without a moment's hesitation, Nora abruptly changed course
for the door and walked in. A woman with sandy hair looked up
from a large ledger. "We're closing soon, miss."

"I won't take much of your time," she said. "You see, I'd like to
become a Wren."

NORA knew she had to tell her friends that she'd joined up. The
woman at the recruitment office had taken her details and told her
that the WRNS would be in touch shortly with instructions on
where to report for training. Until then, it was a waiting game.

Still, every time she sat down to tell her friends, Nora froze. She'd been leaving the house every day, holing up at the Harlan or spending hours reading books at a tearoom on Piccadilly. But every time she returned home and fended off questions about how her day at the Home Office had been, she wanted to sob. And so, that evening, she'd suggested dinner at the Harlan—her treat, especially since it was still weeks before their regular Friday evening.

Once they were seated, she forced herself to say the words.

"I have some news, and I've been waiting to tell you both until the time was right," she said. "I've decided to join the Wrens."

"What? Why?" Marie asked.

"Does it seem so strange that I'd want to do my bit?"

"But you've always said you were doing your bit in the Home Office," said Hazel.

"I was dismissed from my position," said Nora.

"Was it because of me?" Marie asked.

Nora wished that she could take back this entire conversation, but how could she avoid it?

"My mother called Sir Gerald after she found out that you were living with me. He told me that it wasn't acceptable for Home Office employees to have Germans living in their homes," she said.

Marie covered her face with her hands. "Nora, I'm so sorry."

"No," she said fiercely. "Don't be sorry. You are more important to me than that job. And being a Wren will be exciting."

"You're sure this is what you want?" Hazel asked.

"Yes." She had almost convinced herself of it.

"When do you leave for basic training?" Hazel asked.

Nora swallowed. "I don't know. I'll get a letter. It could be anytime. I don't know where I'll eventually be posted or when I'll be granted leave, but I'll be coming here as soon as I can. London is my home." *You are both my home.*

"I suppose we won't have many more dinners like this," said Marie with a weak smile. "We haven't missed a Harlan dinner in seven years."

Looking between the girls, Nora felt a lump rise in her throat. This was going to be harder than she'd expected.

408 | Julia Kelly

Suddenly Pierre approached their table with a silver platter and a folded note on it. "Miss Walcott."

"Thank you, Pierre." Nora waited until he was halfway across the dining room before opening the note. The moment she saw what was written inside, she bolted up from her seat.

"What's wrong?" Hazel asked.

But she was already speeding out of the dining room.

"Nora, slow down," Marie called out behind her.

Halfway down the stairs to the lobby, Nora locked eyes with Joseph, who waited below.

"Did you mean it?" she asked, raising the note aloft.

He took the steps two at a time, his suitcase whacking against his leg, until he stood before her. "I wouldn't lie, not to you."

"This way. Come on, girls." Nora grabbed him by the arm and hustled him up the rest of the stairs. She bustled them all into one of the club's drawing rooms. As soon as Hazel and Marie slipped inside behind her, she shut the door and whirled around.

"I want to see it," she demanded.

Joseph fought a smile. "It's good to see you, too." He glanced at Hazel and Marie. "I'm Joseph Fowler."

"Hazel Carey." Nora watched her friend stick out her hand and give Joseph a quick assessment, knowing that the matchmaker would have him sized up in a matter of seconds.

"It's a pleasure." He turned to Marie. "You must be Marie Bohn."

Marie was a little slower to shake his hand. Nora had noticed that her friend seemed to be more cautious with strangers since the headlines had become more urgent, and it broke Nora's heart.

"Enough with the introductions," Nora said, holding out the note Pierre had delivered. "Does this mean what I think it does?"

He gave a tight nod. She dropped the note onto the table, and her friends leaned down to read it.

I have what you were looking for.
—J

Joseph opened his briefcase and pulled out a manila file folder. "Nora, what's going on?" Hazel asked.

"It's been bothering me for months that we don't know why you were given your classification, Marie. A few weeks ago, when I was still at the Home Office, I thought maybe I could find out."

"How?" Marie asked.

"Joseph told me that records were being held in the basement of the Home Office's building."

"What sort of records?" Hazel asked.

"Tribunal records," said Joseph with a glint in his eye.

"You have my file?" asked Marie. When Joseph nodded, she sat down on one of the sofas. "Tell me what it says."

He crouched down to Marie's level and spoke to her in a soft voice. "British intelligence has reports that your father is manufacturing parts for the German military. His brother, your uncle, is a high-ranking official in the Nazi government at Munich."

"I don't understand," Marie whispered.

"There's more, I'm afraid. The reason that the Foreign Office was able to make that connection was your cousin," Joseph said.

"Henrik?"

"It might be best if you read it yourself," said Joseph.

With a shaking hand, Marie took the file and spread its contents out on her lap. Nora and Hazel both read over Marie's shoulder.

Nora's gaze jumped down the page, where it listed Marie's occupation and assigned her to category B. But that wasn't all. Attached to the tribunal notes was a sheaf of papers, with bold type at the top: Supplemental Investigation Findings.

"Why would they want a supplemental investigation of me?" Marie murmured.

Nora leaned a little closer.

Certain irregularities have appeared in the investigation into MARIE BOHN. Although an initial investigation found nothing to indicate Miss Bohn, a German national, poses a threat to Britain's security, recent revelations of her connection to a deputy of the Nazi Party in Munich have cast doubt on her claims to be without threat at this time.

Miss Bohn's father, HERMAN BOHN, is the owner of a

factory on the outskirts of Munich specializing in the production of automotive parts. His brother, PIETER BOHN, has risen up through the ranks of the local Nazi Party and now serves as adviser to the gauleiter, Adolf Wagner, in the Munich-Obergavern Gau. In his role as governor of this state, Wagner has direct communication with Hitler's cabinet. It appears that Herman Bohn has not only fully aligned himself with the Nazi Party through deals struck by Pieter Bohn, but he has facilitated the correspondence between Pieter Bohn and a known sympathizer to the German cause living in Britain. (A translation of an intercepted letter is included in exhibit A.)

"A letter?" Nora asked.

Marie began flipping through the pages until she landed on a piece of paper marked with *Exhibit A*. It was a transcription of a translation of the letter, typed up from the original.

> *Dear Uncle Pieter,*
>
> *I hope that I do not offend you by addressing you in such a familiar manner. Although we are not related by blood, the bond of marriage is strong enough that I can hope that you will believe the earnestness of my appeal.*
>
> *I have been in contact with your brother because I am desperate to do all that I can to help the fatherland's cause. Although I have lived in England since I was a child, I have never felt any love for this country. It is a land that is impossible to love, filled with people corrupted and blind to everything that has gone on around them. I am determined to do all that you need of me here to help the fatherland in any way I can. There is a group of us, small but passionate, who await your orders.*

The rest of the letter was brief, filled with praise for the führer. Nora's eyes skimmed over it until they reached the bottom, where they stopped. Clear letters spelled out the name Henrik Müller.

"Oh, Henrik, you fool," Nora murmured.

Marie said nothing as she flipped back to the investigation notes.

At this time, this office has not been able to determine that the group of sympathizers mentioned by HENRIK MÜLLER in his letter to Pieter Bohn has been successful in the gathering and transition of information to Germany. However, the decision was made to allow Müller to continue to live under a category C classification in the hope that he may reveal more of his compatriots and their plans.

Additionally, there has been no evidence of a reply being sent from Pieter Bohn to his nephew; however, the possibility that such a connection was made through secretive means cannot be ruled out. It is the recommendation of this office that a restriction and close monitoring be placed upon Marie Bohn, as she is the link between Henrik Müller and Pieter Bohn.

Nora let out a long, slow breath. Henrik was the reason that Marie was now living with restrictions on her movements.

"Stupid, careless boy!" Marie flipped her head up, her eyes blazing. "What did my aunt and uncle's files say?"

"I couldn't risk it. It was hard enough to take yours," said Joseph.

"I need to tell them," said Marie, scrambling to her feet.

Nora's hand shot out to stop her friend. "You can't."

"Why not?" Marie demanded.

"You know why not," said Nora. "If you tell them, they might try to do something to help Henrik. They might tip someone off that they know he's being watched."

"What am I supposed to do, then?" Marie exploded. "They're my only real family! I haven't seen my parents in seven years. Now I find out they lied to me. They lied to me in their letters and told me that they didn't have anything to do with the Party. I knew they didn't love me, but I didn't think they'd lie to me."

"They're not your only real family," said Nora quietly.

Marie stopped and stared at Nora. "What?"

"Your aunt and uncle. They aren't your only real family."

Hazel nodded. "We are, too."

Marie crumpled back down to the sofa. Hazel eased herself onto the sofa and folded Marie into her shoulder.

"They're all so selfish," came the muffled sobs. "They don't care about us. And Henrik. Tante Matilda and Onkel Albrecht could be sent away for this. What he's doing is treason."

"Shhh." Hazel rubbed Marie's back. "It's going to be all right."

"How can you say that?" Marie gasped.

"Because Nora and I would never let anything happen to you."

"But we don't know anything about the investigation into Henrik. The police could come tomorrow and arrest all of us," said Marie through her tears.

"We are not out of options yet. There may be something we can do," said Nora.

"I should go to Canada," said Marie as her sobs slowed.

"Marie's passport arrived at the matchmaking agency yesterday. It looks as good as real," said Hazel.

Nora slid her gaze to Joseph, who had been standing quietly in the corner of the room, his hands folded behind his back.

"I can't hear a thing all the way over here," he said.

Nora mouthed *thank you* to him.

"Let's not hear any more talk about Canada," said Nora, coming to sit on the other side of Marie. "Don't be silly."

"This doesn't feel silly. It feels as though I need to be prepared for the possibility that I could be interned, or worse," said Marie.

Nora didn't want to lose her friend, but she'd never be able to forgive herself if her selfishness led to Marie's imprisonment.

"Just take a moment to think about all of this. There must be something we can do to help your cause," said Hazel.

"Yes, Hazel's right. And no one can know that you took Marie's file, Joseph," Nora said.

"I'll put the file back in place as soon as I can," he said.

"Good," she said, as though it was the end of the matter, but she had a sinking feeling that this was only the beginning.

Chapter 12

Nora couldn't help but feel like she was in limbo. She was going to be a Wren—if they'd ever call her up. Until then, she was to be Hazel's assistant, because Hazel had told her in no uncertain terms that she was driving them crazy moping around the house.

Four days in, Nora had a new respect for her friend and her skill.

"Do you really think you'll be able to find someone for Mr. Newsom?" Nora asked that Thursday. They were on a bus rolling down the Kings Road in order to collect Marie for lunch.

"Why wouldn't I?" Hazel asked.

"He's so painfully shy. You could hardly get a word out of him," Nora said, pulling on the cord to call for their stop.

"Some women find that sort of reticence appealing," said Hazel.

The bus doors clattered open, and Nora and Hazel clambered down to the street. Before Nora could put the key in the latch, the door swung open.

"Hungry for lunch?" But the question died on Nora's lips as soon as she saw Marie in the hallway. Her friend was chalk white.

"What is it? What's wrong?"

"Come," Marie said. Nora and Hazel pushed into the house and followed her into the front room. Marie's aunt sat on the sofa.

"Hello, Mrs. Müller." But Nora stopped when she saw the older woman's eyes were red rimmed and puffy from crying.

"They've taken them," Mrs. Müller sobbed.

"Who?" Hazel asked.

"Onkel Albrecht and Henrik," said Marie. "Onkel Albrecht's secretary rang Tante Matilda an hour ago. They were both arrested at the office."

Mrs. Müller rattled off a long stream of German.

"She says that his secretary said four police officers came and put Henrik in handcuffs," Marie translated. "They told him he was being arrested under Defense Regulation 18B. Onkel Albrecht tried to stop them, but they put him in handcuffs, too." Marie took a deep breath. "This has to be because of the letter. They must've found whatever they were looking for about the group, and now they don't need to watch Henrik any longer."

"I must find my son and my husband. I need to know that they are unharmed," said Mrs. Müller, switching back to English.

"I'm so sorry, Mrs. Müller," said Hazel.

Marie's aunt's head snapped up. "You said something about a letter, Marie. You said they found what they are looking for. Who are they? Why would they be watching my boy?"

"Tante Matilda, I'm so sorry. Henrik is a sympathizer. He was trying to help Germany," said Marie gently.

"But that's absurd. Henrik left Germany when he was a boy," Mrs. Müller said, a desperation to her denial, as though deep down inside, she knew. "He's lived in this country for years."

"Tante Matilda, think of all the things Henrik has said. You know he hasn't been happy here for years. He tried to push you to go back to Germany at the start of the war," said Marie.

"He romanticizes Germany because he only remembers what he knew as a child. He doesn't recall how hard it was then."

Marie took her aunt's hand in hers. "Henrik believes the things that Hitler says. That isn't being nostalgic. It's dangerous. Nora's friend in the Home Office found out that Henrik tried to get a letter out of the country to Germany offering support for Hitler. Henrik wrote that he and a group of other men were sympathetic to what is happening in Germany. They want to help."

Mrs. Müller hunched over. "Who did he send this letter to?"

Nora watched Marie swallow around her emotion. "My father's brother. Onkel Pieter. He is a member of the Nazi Party and a deputy in the Munich government. Henrik has offered to help."

Mrs. Müller's rage broke like a tidal wave. "*Dummkopf.* Reckless, stupid boy! What was he thinking? We've never said a word while he drinks and spends money without a care. But this—" Mrs. Müller's voice broke. "If he is the reason Albrecht is interned, too, I'll never forgive him."

Marie wrapped her arms around her aunt and sat with her, rocking her gently back and forth.

"When you left the house and moved here, was it because of Henrik?" Mrs. Müller asked.

Marie stopped rocking. "It was complicated."

"It wasn't Marie's choice," Hazel said.

"Henrik told her to go," Nora added quickly.

"Marie, why didn't you tell me?" Mrs. Müller asked. "I thought you wanted to leave. That you regretted agreeing to stay with us when you could've gone back to your own parents."

"Henrik told me that I couldn't tell you. He threatened me," said Marie quietly.

"But what could he threaten you with?" said Mrs. Müller.

Marie's hands knitted in her lap until finally she said, "You. He threatened to make you choose between the two of us."

"And you thought we wouldn't fight to keep you with us? Albrecht and I love you."

"He's your *son*. He's your flesh and blood," said Marie.

"And you are, too."

"I'm not your daughter."

Mrs. Müller stiffened. "Albrecht and I have *always* loved you like a daughter. You are precious to us. When my sister wrote to me and told me that she wanted us to send you home after Ethelbrook, it nearly broke my heart. But then you decided to stay, and I couldn't have been prouder. I felt as though you had chosen us."

"I did choose you," said Marie softly.

Nora could see tears shimmering in the corners of Marie's eyes.

Mrs. Müller gathered her niece against her side. "Marie, I couldn't love you more if I tried. If Henrik would've tried to make me choose, I wouldn't have been able to. I love you both so much it feels sometimes as though my heart is too full to contain it all."

"I love you, too," Marie whispered.

Mrs. Müller kissed Marie on the forehead. "And that is why you cannot stay in London. You must leave."

"But I can't. You'll be all alone," said Marie.

Mrs. Müller laid a palm on her niece's cheek. "You *must*. Germany keeps advancing, and everything will become worse for us. You cannot risk staying here, although I don't know where you will go," said Mrs. Müller, worrying her lip.

"Mrs. Müller," said Hazel, "Nora, Marie, and I have spoken about this before. As a precaution, I was able to arrange for Marie to have new papers made."

"Is that legal?" asked Mrs. Müller.

"Not in the least bit," Nora piped up.

The older woman nodded. "Where will you go, Marie?"

"Canada. All we have to do is arrange for passage on a ship."

"That will be my job," said Nora.

"What will you do, Mrs. Müller?" Hazel asked.

"I am category C. I'm safe for now," said the older woman. "If Albrecht is interned here, I'll want to be close by."

Nora could see Marie wanted to argue but nodded nonetheless.

"Marie, did you give this address to the police?" asked Mrs. Müller, becoming businesslike.

"Yes," said Marie.

"Then you'll need another place to hide until you can get on a ship," said Mrs. Müller.

"I don't know where I'll go. I won't put anyone else in danger."

An idea popped into Nora's head, so obvious she could've smacked herself on the forehead for not thinking of it earlier.

"Marie," she said. "I know exactly where you can stay."

"NEARLY ten o'clock," said Nora, looking at her watch.

The three of them had been sitting at the breakfast table, nervously sipping at a round of sidecars. None of them really felt like drinking, though. There was too much at stake.

"Are you nervous?" Hazel asked.

Marie pulled her cardigan closer around her. "Yes, but if I have to hide out somewhere, I trust you two more than anyone else."

The faint chiming of the carriage clock in the front room drifted through the open kitchen door. It was time.

Nora nudged Marie with her shoulder. "Are you ready?"

Marie nodded, and they all went to put on their coats.

They hardly spoke on the bus ride over. It was only when they were a block away from the Harlan that Nora stopped them.

"All right, remember, you two stay in the service entrance around the side while I go inside," she instructed. "Pierre said the top floor was under renovation when the war started, and all the builders left to join up. Between that and the lift that's been broken for a month, no one will be trudging up there. He'll let me around behind the bar, and I'll slip down the back stairs and collect you from the service entrance."

"Are you sure this will work?" Marie said.

Nora looked her friend in the eye and said, "What I can promise is that Hazel and I will do everything we can to make sure that you're on a boat to Canada as soon as I can find you passage."

"Thank you both," whispered Marie.

Hazel smiled. "You don't need to thank me. You two are the closest thing I've ever had to sisters."

"You know I feel the same way," said Nora.

Marie gave them each a hug, and then nodded. "I'm ready."

Nora's heels clipped the pavement with purpose as she pulled away from her friends. She didn't look back at Hazel and Marie. For now, it was her turn to perform.

It was late enough that no doorman stood at the doors. Instead, she leaned on the brass buzzer to the right of the door handle and waited for a reedy young woman to let her in.

"Good evening, Miss Walcott," said the woman.

"Evening," said Nora, whipping off her chocolate coat and revealing a silver lamé evening dress. "Is Pierre still at the bar?"

"I believe he is," the young woman said, taking the coat.

"Thank you."

Without another word, she marched herself through the lobby, up the center stairs, and into the bar.

It was mercifully empty except for an ancient woman sitting in front of a half-full glass of sherry. Pierre stood behind the bar.

"Miss Walcott, what a pleasure," he said.

"Thank you, Pierre. I was passing by after a concert and realized

I meant to look in earlier. I believe I lost an earring the other day."

Pierre gamely tilted his head. "Perhaps you would like to look at the box we keep for lost items . . ."

She let her eyes slide over to the old woman in the corner as she nodded. The woman appeared to be falling asleep.

"That would be very helpful, Pierre. Thank you," said Nora.

He inclined his head, and she followed him through the door to the side of the bar. As soon as they were through, they scuttled along a passageway to what had once been the servants' staircase.

"Come," said Pierre. "We'll let Miss Bohn and Mrs. Carey in."

"Yes, I expect they're wondering what's taking so long and—"

"Miss Walcott, what are you doing below stairs?"

Nora and Pierre froze like naughty children. Slowly, Nora turned to face Lady Dora, who was standing on the landing above them in a long black satin evening dress, diamonds at her throat.

"Lady Dora," she breathed.

"Pierre, you know that members are not permitted in this area of the club." The Harlan's chairwoman slid a sharp glare at Nora.

Pierre looked frightened, and Nora's stomach churned with the knowledge that she'd likely cost him his job.

"Pierre was only doing what I asked. To help a friend," she said.

Lady Dora arched a brow.

"My friend Marie—"

"The German girl," said Lady Dora, her tone unreadable.

Nora sucked in a breath. She was going to have to trust that she could appeal to Lady Dora's decency.

"The police are arresting category B enemy aliens," said Nora.

"*Male* category B aliens. Miss Bohn is not a man, is she?"

"No." She hesitated. "But we believe she is in danger nonetheless. She could be arrested."

"Arrested?"

"Not for anything she did," Nora added quickly. "Because of something her cousin did. Her uncle and father, too. I can't stand by and let her be punished for their mistakes."

The club chairwoman studied her for a long moment. "I take it that Miss Bohn is somewhere on the club's premises?"

"She's waiting at the service entrance with Hazel," said Nora.

"Mrs. Carey? Why am I not surprised?" Lady Dora began to descend the stairs.

"Where are you going?" Nora asked.

"To see to your friends. Pierre, I suggest that you return to the bar. I believe you'll find Mrs. Thorborough is in danger of knocking over her glass," Lady Dora threw over her shoulder.

Pierre scrambled back through the door. Then Nora clambered down the narrow stairs behind Lady Dora. At the lower ground floor, Lady Dora whipped open the door.

"Good evening, Miss Bohn, Mrs. Carey," said Lady Dora.

Nora saw the blood drain out of Marie's face.

"L-Lady Dora," Hazel stammered.

"I don't usually find guests skulking outside of the service entrance. However, Miss Walcott assures me that there is an excellent reason for your presence here," said Lady Dora.

Nora watched Marie swallow and nod. "I need a place to stay."

"I told Lady Dora about your uncle and cousin's arrests," Nora said. If only the chairwoman would see how serious this all was.

"Then you'll know that I have reason to be frightened for my freedom," said Marie. "I had hoped that I'd be able to stay hidden at the Harlan until I could secure passage on a ship to Canada."

Lady Dora fixed them with a long stare. Finally, she stepped out of the doorway. "Well, you had better come inside before the air-raid warden yells at us for breaking the blackout."

The three friends exchanged nervous glances, Marie moving first. Hazel stopped just on the threshold.

"What happened?" Hazel whispered.

"She caught Pierre and me on the stairwell."

"Does she seem willing to help?"

Nora shrugged. They didn't know whether Lady Dora was planning to welcome them into the club or lock them in her office and telephone the police to report them for suspicious behavior.

Nora shuffled ahead to keep up with Lady Dora, who swept her skirts into one hand, the other draping elegantly on the banister.

"Are you going to let Marie stay?" Nora asked her.

Lady Dora stopped on the first-floor landing. "Of course Miss Bohn can stay. We're a women's club, not the police. And we understand that sometimes there are things more important than law and order, especially when men's foolishness is to blame."

As they resumed their ascent, Lady Dora turned to Marie. "We'll see to it that you're made comfortable, Miss Bohn, even if you won't be able to leave your room very often."

"Thank you. You have no idea what a relief that is," said Marie.

"I will tell the staff that one of our country members fell ill when she was in town, and the doctor has ordered that she should rest in complete silence, so we've installed her on the top floor. I will arrange for Pierre to bring your meals," said Lady Dora.

They reached the top floor, and Lady Dora pulled out a brass key. She fitted it into a door and let it swing open. Inside was modest but comfortable, with a double bed and a large armoire that loomed on one side of the room. The closed door next to the armoire, Nora assumed, must lead to the en suite bathroom.

"I will leave you to settle in, but if you should need anything, don't hesitate to call down to my office," said Lady Dora.

"Thank you," said Marie.

Lady Dora waved a hand. "Think nothing of it. You're Miss Walcott's friend, and you are in need. That's enough for me."

IT WAS well past midnight when Nora and Hazel stumbled through Nora's front door.

"I'm too worried to sleep but too exhausted to stay awake," moaned Hazel.

Nora bent to collect the post they'd neglected that afternoon. "Go up to bed. I'm just going to lock up."

As Hazel pulled herself up the stairs, Nora began sorting through the post. When she reached the last letter, she ripped open the envelope, pulled out the letter, and unfolded the single sheet.

Miss Nora Elizabeth Walcott to report at 0800 hours on June 1, 1940, to RNC Greenwich for training.

She exhaled with relief at finally knowing—in less than a month's time, she would be a Wren.

NEARLY a week after installing Marie in the Harlan, Nora unhooked her umbrella from the rack in the shared lobby of the Mayfair Matrimonial Agency's building. The rain fell heavy outside.

"You were right when you said to bring them," said Hazel, shaking her own umbrella out.

"Let's hope that the bus isn't too crowded. I hate the smell of wet wool coats," she said.

Hazel nodded and pushed open the door, when a man appeared on the front steps. "Mr. Calloway? What are you doing here?"

Nora peered around her friend's shoulder at the man. Water dripped from the brim of his hat as though he'd been waiting for a long time. He wore a sheepish smile. "Hello, Mrs. Carey."

"Come in out of the wet. Please," Hazel said, opening the door wide while Nora reversed into the entryway to let him in.

"Thank you." He shook off the rain that had clung to his coat.

"Nora, this is Richard Calloway," said Hazel.

"Nora Walcott," she said, sticking out her hand.

"I've heard a great deal about you, Miss Walcott," he said.

"And I you. You'd better call me Nora," she said, peering at him wide-eyed. He had a strong jaw and a piercing blue gaze.

"You're soaked through," said Hazel.

"I've been walking around, trying to convince myself not to come see you," he said.

"Why?" Nora asked.

"Because I'm not sure it's my right to ask what I'm about to ask you," he said.

She stole a glance at Hazel. The day Nora had purchased Marie passage on a ship, the three of them had quarreled over whether or not it was safe for Marie to telephone Richard. Hazel was for it, Nora against. Finally, Marie announced that she would call Richard and explain. Now, looking at Richard's slumped shoulders, Nora wondered if she'd been wrong to argue the side of caution.

"I can't stop thinking about her," he said. "She telephoned and said she couldn't see me any longer. That it was best this way."

"I'm sorry," said Hazel.

"Do you think— Did I do something wrong?" He stared down at his hands. "It's only that I thought there might be something between us. I haven't felt this way about anyone since my wife died."

"Sometimes things don't work out between people," Hazel said, laying a hand on his forearm.

"I just want the chance to speak with her one more time. To be sure. I miss talking to her. Would you tell her that, for me?"

With a sigh, Hazel said, "I can't make any promises, but if you'll come with us, I might be able to arrange something."

He nodded and opened up the door. Nora put up her umbrella, and the three of them plunged out into the rain.

NORA breathed a sigh of relief when the young woman at the Harlan's front desk put down the receiver and said that Lady Dora would be down to see her in five minutes.

They'd left Richard in the booth of a restaurant two streets over. If Marie agreed, they would telephone him and give him the club's address. If not, he was to consider that his answer.

"Miss Walcott, Mrs. Carey, I trust you're well."

Nora looked up and saw Lady Dora approaching.

"Might we speak somewhere private?" Nora asked.

Lady Dora led them to the club chairwoman's office. It was a serious woman's room with a large Queen Anne desk in the bay window, bookshelves lining two walls, and a sofa and chairs under a large painting of a group of distinguished-looking Victorian women—the Founding Few, including Nora's grandmother.

"Do make yourself at home," said Lady Dora, gesturing to the sofa. "I take it you're here about our mutual friend on the top floor. I feel for her. It must be terribly dull being locked up, even here."

"She won't have to stay hidden for too much longer. I've booked her passage on a ship bound for Canada on the twenty-seventh," said Nora. Just days before she had to report to the Wrens, a fact she still hadn't told her friends.

"It's Marie's departure that we wanted to speak to you about," said Hazel. "You see, before it became clear that she would not be able to remain in this country, I introduced her to a gentleman."

"And I take it he wasn't satisfied with letting her go?" Lady Dora asked. "He wants one more chance to fight for her."

"Well, yes," she said.

"Good. I can't abide a man with no backbone," said Lady Dora. "Does Miss Bohn wish to speak to this gentleman?"

"I don't think we can be sure yet," said Hazel.

"You haven't asked her?" asked Lady Dora.

Nora shook her head. "We wanted to speak to you first. To see if it would be possible to arrange a place for her to see him here."

Lady Dora tilted her chin and then asked, "Where is this man?"

"He is at a restaurant nearby, waiting for our call," said Nora.

"Well, I suppose we should find out how Miss Bohn feels about the matter. I was already planning to ask her to my office for an hour to allow housekeeping to tidy her room."

"Thank you, Lady Dora," said Hazel.

The older woman excused herself. Ten minutes later, a side door hidden in the paneling swung open, and Marie emerged.

"Why didn't you come up to the room?" Marie asked, hugging them each in turn.

"We had to speak to Lady Dora first. Marie, we didn't just come here to see you. Richard came to see us at the agency this evening," said Hazel.

Marie sank down onto the sofa. "What did he want?"

"He's worried. He wants to see you," Hazel said.

Her friend shook her head. "That's not a good idea."

"Do you not trust him?" Nora asked.

"We've known each other for such a short time. Are a few dinners and a handful of telephone calls enough to truly know someone?" Marie asked.

"He wants to see you," Hazel repeated.

"I want to see him," said Marie. "If only to explain."

"Tonight?" Hazel asked.

"He's here?"

"Close by. I can tell him to come now if you're ready."

Nora could see Marie worrying the inside of her lip, but her friend nodded.

Nora telephoned Richard at the restaurant and told him they were collecting him. They used the service entrance so they could use the discreet door to the chairwoman's office.

Marie rose to her feet as soon as they walked in. "Richard."

A smile broke out over his face. "I didn't think that seeing you would require so much subterfuge, but I'm happy regardless."

Nora and Hazel stood half in, half out of the room.

"We'll just leave you two—"

"No!" Marie hugged her arms across her midsection, as though holding herself together. "Please stay. I'm sorry, Richard, but this was a mistake. You shouldn't have come."

"Why not?" He took a step forward.

"You just shouldn't," said Marie, her voice rising.

"If this is a bad time, I'll come back—"

"I'm leaving!" Marie blurted out.

Richard took a step back. "Leaving?"

"I'm sailing for Canada from Liverpool on Monday."

"Why?" he asked.

"I have to leave London. My cousin and my uncle have been arrested. I might be arrested, too. I don't want to be sent to an internment camp for crimes that I didn't commit," said Marie.

"But if you didn't do anything wrong, why should you worry?"

Marie fixed him with a hollow stare. "I told you that I had been given category B status."

"Category B women weren't arrested last week."

"But you must see that it's only a matter of time," said Marie.

"That's why you telephoned and told me that you couldn't see me any longer?" he asked.

"Well, yes," said Marie.

"But none of that changes who you are—who you are to me. You should've—"

"Done what?" Marie asked fiercely. "Rung you and said I might be taken away by the police because I'm German, and it looks as though my family may be a bunch of Nazis? That my cousin is an idiot sympathizer? My uncle's been arrested, and now I have to leave behind the woman who was more of a mother to me than my own mother, and you think you can somehow *fix* this?"

Without hesitation, Richard wrapped his arms around her.

Marie turned her face into his chest. "I feel as though I'm being punished, but I'm a good person."

"I know that. I know that," said Richard, stroking her hair.

"I thought if I did everything right, I would be safe," said Marie.

"It's not fair. It's never fair," Richard murmured, dropping a light kiss to the top of Marie's head.

"I wish that there was no war, no internment. I wish we'd just met and that you might come to . . . like me one day."

He leaned back so he could lift Marie's chin with a crooked finger. "I think I've come to like you already."

Marie squeezed her eyes shut and stepped away. "We should say goodbye."

Richard seemed to stiffen, but he nodded. "I suppose."

Marie gave a shuddering breath as Richard leaned down to kiss her on the cheek. He lingered, just a moment, and Nora watched longing, regret, anger, sorrow break over her friend's face.

"Goodbye, Marie," he said as he stepped back.

"Goodbye."

"Let me see you out," said Nora quietly.

"I'll make my own way," said Richard.

She stepped aside, but he stopped, his hand on the door frame. "Perhaps we'll see each other again, Marie. After the war."

Through her tears, Marie nodded.

"Take care of her," said Richard, leaning close as he passed Nora. "I don't want to lose her."

"I will," Nora promised, even though she would be losing Marie herself in just a few days' time.

Chapter 13

THE DOCKS WERE MOBBED with people bustling around the ship's gangways as the five-minute warning blast echoed across the water. Little clusters of families said teary-eyed goodbyes to loved ones while porters pushed carts of luggage. Above them all, the massive ship towered, a wall of steel painted stark black.

"Here we are," said Nora, putting down Marie's suitcase. Marie's hands were wrapped around the handle of the typewriter case.

"Thank you," said Marie. This was the moment when they were supposed to all say goodbye, but how did you start to say goodbye to one of the most important people in your life?

"I . . ." Marie looked at her friends, her eyes beginning to brim.

Nora pulled Marie into a hug. "I can't believe you're leaving."

"I can hardly believe it either," said Marie. "We'll always be."

"Just us three," said Hazel and Nora at the same time.

Marie clasped each of their hands. "I'll never be able to tell you how much I love you."

Over Marie's shoulder, Nora saw a flash of silver. She squinted. Badges. The badges on police constables' helmets. Three of them. And they were making their way right for her friends.

"I think we have a problem," she said, pointing.

Hazel craned her neck as a fourth man stepped out from behind the constables. "Is that— Oh no, it's Dennison!"

"What?" Nora grabbed her arm.

"Marie, if I led him to you—" Hazel began.

"I don't care how he figured out about Marie leaving; we need to make sure that he doesn't stop her from sailing," said Nora as the boat blasted its final warning whistle.

They shouldered through the throng, trying to make it to the gangway. But no matter how they pushed, they were nothing compared to the broad shoulders of the four men barreling down on them. When Marie looked back, Dennison was twenty feet away.

"Oh, this is ridiculous," muttered Nora, before whipping around to face Dennison.

"What are you doing?" cried Hazel.

"Dealing with him," said Nora.

"Nora, please. I have to leave now," said Marie as attendants hurried the last stream of passengers onto the gangplank.

But it was too late. Dennison bore down upon them until he was three feet from Nora, who put her hands on her hips and said, "Good morning, Mr. Dennison."

"Out of my way. This is a matter for the Home Office and the police," said Dennison gruffly. "An order has been issued. All category B women are to be arrested, processed, and interned." He stretched out a hand. "You're to come with me, Miss Bohn."

Marie pressed back as he tried to advance, but Nora stepped in front of him. "I would stop that if I were you."

"Out of my way, or I'll have you arrested, too," he said.

"Thomas Dennison," Nora said. "You're having affairs with two women in the Aliens Department, despite being married. And who knows how many others there are in the Home Office."

Dennison stopped abruptly. "How do you know that?"

Nora's eyes sparkled. "It's a wonder that the women you're cavorting with haven't figured you out yet. Does your wife know about them? I'm going to guess no."

Dennison swallowed. "H-how, how . . . ?"

"Secretaries talk. You really should be more careful."

Dennison seemed to relax. "You want to blackmail me. Is that it? And who would believe you?"

"I don't have to blackmail you. All it would take is three calls to make your life hell. The first one would be to your wife. The second and third would be to the two women in your department."

"They wouldn't believe you," Dennison said.

Nora laughed. "Do you really want to test that theory? And then, of course, there is the undersecretary, who would hate for scandal to distract from the important work he's doing in the Aliens Department. It would look very bad indeed if there was an investigation into gross misconduct at a wartime Home Office."

Dennison swallowed but still pointed at Marie. "She's under investigation."

"For something she didn't do," Hazel said. "Marie is no more of a threat to this country than you or I."

"At the end of this war, do you want to be the sort of man who did his job or the sort of man who showed compassion when it was necessary?" asked Nora.

"Please," said Marie.

The man didn't move. His gaze locked on Marie.

"You'll have to come with me, Miss Bohn," he said.

Nora gave a strangled cry and fainted dead away, crashing into Dennison and knocking him into an empty luggage cart being pushed by two porters. The metal cage crashed to the dock, knocking the feet out from underneath the police officers—as well as about half a dozen bystanders. Shouts and cries went up as women crowded around Nora. One of the porters jumped at Dennison, who was climbing to his feet, knocking him to the ground again with an angry yell. Hazel and Marie stood frozen, watching in horror, until Hazel saw a smile twitch Nora's lips.

Hazel whipped around to Marie, pulled her into a hug, and whispered, "Be happy." Then Hazel pushed her in the direction of the gangway. She watched Marie race up, pausing only to show her ticket and passport to the man at the entryway to the gangway. He already had the rope in his hand, but he shrugged and let Marie through. Then he pulled the rope over the gate, and as soon as Marie was on deck, the gangway was pulled away.

The ship gave a triumphant whistle, and its giant engines roared to life. Slowly, the ship began to pull away from the dock.

Hazel searched the crowd of people crammed against the railing, waving down to their loved ones on the dock below. Behind her, she heard Nora say, "I'm fine. Just a little dizzy still. My sister is on that ship, you see. I don't know when I'll see her again."

Hazel searched and searched. At last, she saw a head of wheat-blond hair push between the shoulders of two women.

"There she is," she murmured, putting up her hand to wave.

Marie waved back.

"She made it," Nora said, joining her.

"She did. What happened to Dennison?" Hazel asked.

"He slunk off once he realized that Marie'd gotten away. He's not going to tell his superiors that he let three women outsmart him and three constables."

As the ship made for open sea, it became impossible to tell which member of the thinning crowd was Marie.

Hazel dropped her hand to her side. "Everything's changing."

"I should think so. I don't think I'd be able to bear it if it all went on just as it was, only without Marie."

"Things are moving forward with the divorce," she said.

Nora pressed a hand to her forearm. "And I've received my call-up. I'm off to basic training on the first."

"You are?" she asked in surprise. "Where?"

Nora nudged her. "RNS Greenwich. Not so far away. And you know I'll be back whenever I have leave."

But Hazel knew that it might as well have been a world apart. Their lives *were* changing. Marie was off to Canada. Nora was in the Wrens now. And Hazel . . . Well, she was beginning to figure out what she wanted her life to look like when she was the only person she would need to worry about pleasing.

Nora hooked her arm through Hazel's. "Now I think it's high time we stop somewhere for a cup of tea. You can tell me all about what you have to do for the divorce, and then make me promise fifteen times that I won't get myself torpedoed at sea."

"I think you're right," she said as they took their first steps together as two.

Samantha
Now

THE day of Grandma Marie's memorial could not have been more beautiful, without a cloud in the sky that stretched over Lake Ontario.

A gentle breeze picked up Samantha's blond hair. All around her, friends and family gathered each with a unique memory of the woman who had touched lives for more than one hundred years.

"How are you, sweet pea?" Samantha's mother asked, coming to stand next to her. Her father tucked himself into her other side, his hand a solid comfort on her shoulder.

"I'm glad we're doing this," she said.

"It's what Mum wanted," said her mother. "A beautiful day and not a stitch of black in sight."

"Are you ready?" asked her father.

"I am," she said.

Her parents nodded and walked off to gather the crowd. She tilted her head up, enjoying the July sun. Her parents were right. It was exactly what her grandmother would have wanted.

Her only regret was that Nora, the person who'd known Grandma Marie the best all those years ago, couldn't be there. Samantha had sent one of the programs her parents had had printed, and she'd received a long email back from Nora five days later telling her she was touched and virtually demanding that Samantha come back for another visit.

Don't spend too long thinking about another trip either. I'll remind you that I am 103 years old.

Samantha had laughed so hard at the imperious, yet matter-of-fact point that she'd nearly cried.

Now she closed her eyes and took a deep breath. It was time.

Suddenly she froze. Standing on the edge of the crowd of well-wishers was a tall man in a navy jacket.

"David," she murmured.

He lifted his hand, and since she couldn't think of anything else to do, she did the same.

Then her father stepped into her view. "Ready, Samantha?"

Shaking her head to rattle her focus back into place, she stepped in front of the people forming a semicircle around her family.

"Thank you all for joining us to celebrate the life of my grandma Marie," she started. "When she passed away last year at the impressive age of one hundred and three, it felt like the kind of loss you never recover from. But Grandma Marie was clever. She found a way to bring us closer even after she passed away. She left me a task. She sent me to London, where she'd lived as a young woman, to return something that had once belonged to a friend of hers. That's where I met Nora, one of her closest friends. Nora knew things about my grandmother no one else did. She told me wonderful stories about a woman I thought I'd known so well, a woman who always had a moment for me, whether I was bored or scared or just a little lonely. Maybe some of you knew her to be that woman, too—quiet, strong, and generous. But I've learned since her death that my grandmother was so many other things as well.

"Born in Germany and educated in England, she made her home in London with an aunt and uncle who loved her. But equally important were what we would call her 'found family.' Nora Walcott and Hazel Carey were her best friends and confidants for years until the war came and changed everything.

"During the war, my grandmother's friends showed who they really were. She was German, and the British had interned Germans during the First World War. They would do it again, locking up thousands of German-born people in internment camps.

"But Nora and Hazel weren't going to let that happen to their friend. They bought her forged papers, smuggled her into hiding, and outran a Home Office agent and three police officers to get her onto a ship bound for Canada.

"My grandmother built herself a new life here. Trenton is where she married my grandfather, had her children, and made new friends. Although she left behind a hole in our lives that will never be filled, I find comfort knowing that she's always been loved fiercely by people who do extraordinary things for their friends."

Samantha's father, aunt, and uncle stepped forward and carefully unclasped the urn containing her grandmother's ashes at the water's edge. As they released the dust into the wind, she couldn't help smiling. At last, Marie was at peace.

After the scattering, people began to file by and pay their respects. She tried to look around for David, but it was impossible with all the hugs and kind words about her eulogy. She finally gave up, hoping that he would follow the cars leaving the parking lot.

When most of the well-wishers had shuffled by, her uncle Charles clapped his hands together. "Everyone, we're going to be adjourning to my house for a champagne toast, plenty of music, and a good party, just like Mum would've loved."

Samantha turned to her parents. "I'll follow in a few minutes."

Her mother nodded as her father kissed her on her forehead, and Samantha headed down to the water's edge. She slipped her shoes off and stood with her toes in the grass.

"You figured out your eulogy."

She couldn't stop her smile as she turned and found David just a few feet away. "I had no idea you were coming."

"Well, I've been given the responsibility of hand-delivering this," he said, pulling a little silk pouch out of his pocket.

She took it from him, undoing the drawstring. When she tipped it into her palm, her grandmother's necklace tumbled out.

"Gran felt you should have it after all. She said she was happy your grandmother wanted you to return it, because it brought you into her life, but the necklace belongs to you now," he said.

She closed her fingers around the pendant, almost unable to speak. "David, did you come just to give me this necklace?"

He squinted at her, looking unsure. "I wanted to pay my respects to your grandmother, but that's not the only reason I'm here. I understand if this isn't an appropriate time, but I wanted to know if you'd have dinner with me on Wednesday. As a date."

Her heart sank. "Oh, David, I want to more than anything, but I go back to Chicago tomorrow morning." She hesitantly reached out to touch his wrist. "Our timing is terrible, isn't it?"

But instead of pulling away, he flipped his hand so his fingers slid down hers and laced together. "Oh, it isn't that bad. Not when I made the reservation in Chicago."

She startled to look in his eyes. "Chicago?"

"I've been put on a project, working on overhauling digital marketing for a retail chain in Chicago." He grinned. "It's a big job. At least six months. I'll probably need an extension. Or two."

"You're moving to Chicago?" she whispered.

"As soon as my visa is sorted out. I have meetings with the client, and I'm looking for a flat this week, but I wanted to be sure I was here for your grandmother's remembrance ceremony."

She went up on tiptoe and kissed him. It was light, just a brush, but then he pulled her to him and they sank into the kiss.

When finally she pulled back, she murmured, "I think I can squeeze in dinner on Wednesday night, but first you might have to meet my family. They're expecting me."

He laughed and grabbed her hand. "I can't wait to meet them. Let's go together, shall we?"

Epilogue

June 12, 1943
Trenton, Ontario

MARIE'S BACK ALWAYS ACHED by the time she made her way to Mrs. Franklin's boardinghouse, but it was a good sort of ache. A useful one. She'd arrived in Ontario frightened and unsure but determined. She'd been given another chance and her freedom, and she wasn't going to squander those gifts.

She'd found herself a place to live and signed on to work at the local munitions factory in Trenton, doing the dangerous work of handling the explosives that would be loaded onto airplanes and flown to the front. She'd learned quickly. Last October, she'd been promoted to manager of her own line.

She pushed through the front door of the boardinghouse and hung her coat. On the sideboard, in her little mail slot, stood a letter addressed to her in Hazel's looping hand. From behind the parlor door came a burst of laughter, but instead of going to join in, she plucked up the letter. Tonight she wanted news from home.

Marie retreated up the stairs to the room she shared with her roommate, Josie. It was only a little larger than her bedroom in her aunt and uncle's house—just enough space for a pair of beds and armoires. Under the window was a writing desk upon which stood the typewriter Richard had given her.

Marie sat on her bed, tore open the letter, and began to read.

Dearest Marie,

I've been sitting here, wondering how to tell you all of the news I've had. I suppose I should start with the most important. In a few short weeks, your uncle should be back at home. The government has been releasing those detained under Regulation 18B in larger and larger numbers. The last I saw Mrs. Müller, she seemed almost like a young bride, unable to contain her impatience as she waits for her husband to return so they'll be together again.

Henrik, of course, will remain jailed. Even your aunt recognizes that there can be no hope for his release when he was caught so openly conspiring against Britain.

If you haven't had a letter from Nora in some time, don't fret. She wrote to me to say that her unit with the WRNS had been reassigned, and she couldn't yet say where she was being deployed. However, I know that as soon as she can make it back to London, she will.

I truly didn't know what to expect when conscription for women was implemented and I found myself an army nurse. However, I find the work fulfilling. I am, I've found, tougher than I thought.

I know you must be—

A knock sounded at the door. She glanced up. "Who is it?"

"Marie, can you come out here?" Josie's voice was muffled by the oak door.

She got to her feet, the letter drifting to her bed as she crossed the room. She pulled the door open, and her jaw dropped.

"Richard?"

"Hello, Marie," Richard said, smiling shyly, his uniform cap crushed between his hands.

Josie bounced on her toes looking pleased with herself. "He just showed up on the porch, ringing the bell like any other man."

"What are you doing here?" she asked, ignoring her roommate.

"You look as lovely as the last time I saw you," he said.

There was a clatter on the stairs, and Mrs. Franklin rounded the corner. "Miss Bohn, you know that I don't allow gentlemen to visit my young ladies—especially not above stairs."

"Mrs. Franklin, this isn't just any gentleman," said Josie.

"He's my Richard," Marie breathed. Because that was what he'd become over all of their months apart.

Mrs. Franklin peered at Richard with curiosity. "This is him?"

Marie nodded.

"Well, in that case, I think an exception can be made," said Mrs. Franklin. "But keep the door open."

The landlady took Josie by the wrist and practically dragged her back down the hall, leaving Marie and Richard alone.

"Would you like to come in?" she asked, her whole body shaking as she gestured behind her.

"I would," he said.

She walked slowly into the room, acutely aware of the 738 days that had passed. So many things had changed, and yet here he was. In her room in Canada. It didn't make sense.

"Would you—"

But before she could fully turn, he'd crossed the space between them and kissed her.

Marie melted into Richard's arms. The feeling of his lips against hers was the best sort of shock. The weight of his hands around her waist. His kiss was full of longing and need and felt like home.

When finally he inched back, he breathed a sigh of contentment, his eyes closed. "I've been thinking of nothing but that since I found out that my transfer was accepted."

She leaned back from him. "Your transfer?"

He nodded. "I put in for RCAF Trenton to work training airplane engineers as part of the British Commonwealth Air Training Plan. I didn't tell you because I didn't want to say until I was here. The Royal Air Force can change its mind sometimes, and I didn't want you to be disappointed if they did." He hesitated. "Was I presumptuous to have put in that request without consulting you first? Is there—" He cleared his throat. "Is there someone else?"

It was all she could do not to burst out laughing.

"There's no one else, Richard."

"When I saw the shock on your face . . ."

"Because I can't believe you're here," she said.

He breathed out, resting his forehead against hers. "I'm sorry. I should've said hello rather than grabbing for you the moment you walked through the door. I didn't know—"

"I'm happy you kissed me," she said, smiling. "Our first kiss."

He grinned. "A first kiss after nearly two years of letters."

"I was so nervous when I first wrote to you. I almost didn't put the letter in the post," she admitted.

"I'm glad you did. When you left, I felt sure I'd lost you."

She shook her head. "It was the hardest thing in the world to leave my friends and my aunt and uncle behind. Leaving you only made it hurt more."

"But now I'm here."

"And a very dashing RAF man, too," she said, touching his tie.

He caught her hand and kissed it. "Now, I have a very important question, and I want you to think carefully about this," he said.

"Yes?"

"Miss Bohn, will you do me the honor of joining me for dinner on my first night of leave?" She laughed, and he grinned, adding, "I thought it would be best to carry on where we left off."

She slipped her arms around his neck, tilting her face up to bask in the happiness of having him near. "If you're ready to run the gauntlet that is meeting every single woman in the boardinghouse, then I would love nothing more. Let's go to dinner, Richard."

AfterWords

Julia Kelly describes herself as an author who writes about ordinary women doing extraordinary things. This is certainly true of the three friends in *The Whispers of War*, her second foray into historical fiction.

Kelly started writing fiction as a sideline "distraction" during graduate school. By the time graduation rolled around, she was hooked. Initially she wrote romance novels, but she had always been interested in history. It seemed logical to marry her romantic storytelling skills with her fascination with World War II, an era ripe with drama, heroism, and endless fodder for plot ideas.

There was no specific moment when the author got the idea for *The Whispers of War*, but she did grow up near the Santa Anita Racetrack in California, which was an internment camp for Japanese people during the war. Later she learned that England had interned thousands of people during the war as well. This sparked the general concept for the book.

Kelly enjoys doing research for her historicals. To get the details right for this one, she read a book called *Marriages Are Made in Bond Street*, about a matrimonial agency that thrived during World War II. She also learned about blackouts, air-raid drills, bomb shelters, and other aspects of wartime London.

Kelly, who was born in America but now lives in London, is working on a new novel.

A NOVEL OF SUSPENSE

CAREFUL WHAT YOU WISH FOR

HALLIE EPHRON

NEW YORK TIMES BESTSELLING AUTHOR

Chapter 1

Saturday

EMILY HARLOW WASN'T convinced that her sock drawer sparked joy. Her socks had once been a jumbled mess, stuffed in the top drawer of the mahogany bureau she'd inherited from her grandmother. She'd tried to follow the decluttering guru's mantra, keeping only those socks that "spoke to her heart" and arranging them so that they stood at attention, paired and folded just so (starting at the toe) and sorted by color. Months later, bright and early on this muggy August morning, as she stood in her sunlit bedroom in shorts, a tank top, and flip-flops, the message those socks whispered to her heart was more about privilege than joy. Who on earth needed so many pairs of socks?

Still, sock sorting had been life-changing. On a whim, as she'd done it, she took a sequence of snapshots, then assembled the stills into a stop-motion video, a herky-jerky animated progression showing the transformation from chaotic to tidy, with a few socks saluting the camera in the process, and ending with a selfie of her grinning as she deposited a bag of discards in a Goodwill collection bin. Dissolve to a final shot of her newly ordered sock drawer.

Watching that video *did* spark joy. She'd posted it on Instagram.

Thousands of views and shares later, the *Boston Globe* ran a human-interest story on Emily and her sock-sorting video. A local morning TV talk show invited her on. And before she knew it, she had people reaching out and asking her to help them declutter their drawers and closets and film the process.

That had been just before the school year ended, at a time when she was susceptible to any excuse not to go back to teaching the next fall. Once upon a time, she'd loved teaching. Loved setting up her classroom in September. Meeting twenty-five fresh-faced third-graders and introducing them to the wonders of fractions and *Charlotte's Web*. But after eight years of the East Hartwell school system's relentless focus on tests, along with well-meaning parents who valued grammar and spelling over creativity and problem-solving, teaching itself no longer *spoke to her heart*. Not in the uncomplicated way that her sock-sorting did.

The outpouring in response to her video and the prospect of a stream of clients willing to pay for help decluttering their living spaces felt like a minor miracle. In short order Emily had tendered her resignation and given away a ton of school supplies.

She'd been pleasantly surprised when her husband, Frank, encouraged her to go for it. *Give it a year and see what happens.* Even though they were still paying off loans they'd taken out when Frank and his best friend, Ryan Melanson III, started their private-practice law firm. Compared to the emotional roller coaster that she and Frank had been on trying to conceive a child, launching a business seemed like a walk in the park.

The only thing that made Frank uneasy was her going alone into strangers' homes. So he'd set up location sharing on her phone so he'd know where to look if she didn't come home and bought her a stun gun, baby blue. She'd fired it once. The sparks and lightning crackle had scared her half to death. She'd dropped the gadget into her gear bag and hoped she'd never have to use it.

Emily had partnered with her best friend, Becca Jain, a nurse turned social worker turned life coach, who was perfectly equipped to hold clients' hands and nurture them through the peeling away of personal property. Turned out people could part with that beloved herd of plastic horses they'd collected when they were eight if they had its image saved digitally. Emily made the freeze-frame videos capturing vanishing possessions. She and Becca called themselves Freeze-Frame Clutter Kickers, their logo a high-heeled boot kicking an unspooling reel of videotape.

Emily's sock-sorting had gotten them off to a good start. Now she was creating a closet-sorting video to grab the attention of more potential customers.

"Emmy, I'm off!" Frank shouted up to her. She'd left him downstairs in the kitchen, poring over yard-sale ads printed off Craigslist and Facebook. Every Saturday he plotted a route, then left the house no later than seven thirty, because, according to Frank, no one meant it when they advertised "No early birds."

Emily left the bedroom and crossed the upstairs hall. When she got to the landing, Frank was at the foot of the stairs, grinning up at her. He went to weekend yard sales looking distinctly unlawyerly in a pair of grungy Levi's and a T-shirt.

"Need anything?" Frank said.

"No bedroom sets," she said. "But I could use a salad spinner."

Frank saluted and clicked his heels.

Emily returned to the bedroom. *No bedroom sets* was only half joking on her end. She suspected Frank had several headboards and bed frames, not to mention bureaus, stashed in their garage and basement. Lighter fare—radios and small appliances—he'd sneak up into the attic when he thought she wasn't looking. Even when Emily was shut away in her tiny upstairs office with its jar of freshly sharpened pencils and well-ordered files, she could feel Frank's finds restively revving up, like a phalanx of *Sorcerer's Apprentice* brooms mustering to invade the main house.

It wasn't all junk. Only last week he'd scored the original cover art for an issue of one of his favorite 1960s horror comics, *Creepy*. The signed watercolor had been tucked between the pages of a scrapbook priced at two dollars. Emily looked up the artist. Individual pieces of his cover art sold for tens of thousands of dollars.

Emily recognized the sound of the back door slamming shut. She crossed to the window and looked down at the driveway. Frank's

Chevy Suburban (he didn't take his BMW Z4 to yard sales) backed out into the street. The irony of her upstairs, sorting and culling, and Frank out hunting and gathering was not lost on her.

But there was no point dwelling on it. There were worse hobbies than compulsive yard-sale-ing. Besides, she had to get busy. She and Becca had an appointment to meet a new client this afternoon, and it would take Emily hours to get this video done.

First, she needed an establishing shot. She looked at her closet interior through her camera's viewfinder. Her clothes were hanging packed together on a single rod, winter at one end, summer at the other. Shoes and handbags were heaped on the floor.

She snapped a picture. Next, she mounted the camera on a tripod in the corner of the room and set up a pair of LED light pads on either side of the bed to cancel out shadows. Closed the window shades. Lit a scented candle on the windowsill.

Stage set, Emily pulled out clothing by the armload from the closet and mounded the pieces on one side of their king-size bed. She set three empty plastic trash bags on the floor for discards.

She looked at the pile through the viewfinder, then pressed the camera's remote control. She had her opening shot—the big mess.

Emily snagged the top item, a pair of wool trousers. She spread them out on the bed. *Keep or toss?* Easy decision. Moth holes and a disintegrating lining did not spark joy. She crossed the trouser legs. *Click.* Crumpled them up. *Click.* Threw them into a garbage bag and took a final picture of the empty spot on the bed.

She made short work of three double-breasted blazers. After that, she whipped through a pile of dresses, dumping them all.

She was stuffing the last dress into the garbage bag when she heard gravel crunch in the driveway. She stepped to the window and raised the shade. Frank's SUV was parked in the driveway below her. The driver's-side door opened, and Frank got out.

From above she could see the bald spot that he took pains to comb over. He must have bought something, because he popped the trunk and was bending down, reaching for the bulkhead door to their basement. The metal door creaked open.

Before Frank turned back to his car, he glanced up and waved.

She waved back and dropped the shade. She really didn't want to see what he was bringing in.

She picked up a turquoise jumpsuit that she'd bought in Venice Beach. She'd been a different person back then, just out of college and getting her teaching degree. Frank was an idealistic, newly minted attorney, committed to human rights, about to start work in the Massachusetts public defender's office. Venice Beach had been fast changing from a neighborhood of aging hippies to one with hipsters and yoga studios. She wondered if Frank remembered the amazing sex they'd had, camped out on a friend's porch. Sex-without-checking-the-calendar-and-taking-your-temperature sex.

That had been years ago, back when she assumed that having a baby would just happen. Never dreaming how fast Frank would fill their house with more and more stuff. If only he'd let her work her organizing magic on his clutter, Emily thought as she eyed the bulging drawers of his bureau. But there was an ironclad rule of decluttering: You're only allowed to declutter your own stuff.

She threw the jumpsuit on the bed. Took a picture.

Had it been inevitable that Frank would become a rabid collector? At their wedding Frank's mother had confided to Emily that Frank's first word had been "Mine." Back then Frank's redeeming features seemed to far outweigh what Emily then thought of as his quirky passion for collecting. He was handsome, with that million-dollar smile. He laughed at her jokes. And he didn't screw around like his law partner, Ryan, who'd divorced wife number two and was already cheating on his new girlfriend.

She turned her attention back to the jumpsuit. *Keep or toss?*

She was considering, when she heard a thud. Probably the steel bulkhead door to the basement slamming shut. She looked out the window in time to see Frank climbing into his car. No sooner had he pulled out of the driveway than there was a loud, discordant crash from the bowels of the house. Echoes sent a chill down Emily's spine. What on earth had he dragged home this time?

Emily stood on the upstairs landing, listening. There was a quieter, almost musical reverberation, but it was the sound of breaking glass that propelled her down the stairs. She doubled back from the foot of the stairs to the kitchen, her turf, and continued through the laundry room. She hesitated at the door to the basement. Unless a fuse blew, she had no reason to go down there. She pulled open the door and flipped on the light. Clearly, Frank wasn't using these stairs for speedy access to the basement: The risers were crowded with boxes and bags.

She cleared a pathway, descended the stairs, and picked her way across the basement. She passed a rockerless rocking chair, occupied by the skeleton they put out every Halloween; a pair of life-size ceramic cats; a grinning glass clown; and a pile of three-ring binders. Emily had put the binders, clown, and cats out for a charity donation pickup. Apparently, Frank had had other ideas.

So far, nothing to account for the crash she'd heard. She spotted what looked like a gold-painted person-size harp. On closer inspection she recognized it as a gracefully arched piano frame. Too small to have come from a grand piano, it was still formidable. It was leaning against a utility table, the floor around it littered with broken glass and china. She tried to shift it, but it was too heavy for her to manage. Frank could deal with it when he got home.

Emily climbed the stairs and returned to the kitchen. Sitting on the counter in the drying rack was a blue plastic salad spinner. Frank must have picked it up for her. He'd even washed it. She felt a pang of guilt. If Frank could bag her a salad spinner, the least she could do was sweep up the mess in the basement.

Emily went back with a broom, a dustpan, and a paper bag. Crouching beside the piano frame, she reached across to sweep up pieces of glass and china. It was maybe a vase and some wine-glasses. She crouch-walked farther in. Swept up more pieces.

She was straining forward, trying to reach the last shards, when the bulkhead opened. Light streamed in. Emily glanced up to see Frank silhouetted in the opening. He came down the stairs, his fair hair a nimbus of light, peering into an oversized brown portfolio. She recognized that covetous look. He'd scored.

"Hey, Frank," Emily said.

Startled, he looked up from the portfolio. "Emily?"

"What did you get?"

"What are you doing down here?" he said, closing the portfolio and fastening it shut. Emily recognized the dodge. Maybe he'd overpaid.

She stood. Or tried to, but lost her balance. She reached out for the utility table to steady herself. That's all it took. The table cracked and buckled. The piano frame that had been resting against it toppled sideways. Emily threw her arms over her head and crouched, cringing at the sound of more breakage, followed by the same discordant reverb she'd heard from upstairs.

When the dust settled, Emily looked up. Frank was staring in stunned silence. Finally he said, "Are you okay?"

"I think so." Emily rose slowly to her feet. That's when she realized her flip-flop had come off and her bare foot was wedged firmly between the piano frame and what looked like a four-person church pew that had been lying on its back under the utility table. She tried to wiggle her foot loose but only succeeded in pinning her foot more tightly. "Ouch! Dammit." She looked across at Frank. He was picking through the broken pieces that she'd swept into the bag. "Frank, can you help me here? I'm stuck."

Frank's phone pinged. He slid it out of his pocket and looked at the readout, probably an alarm reminding him not to be late for the next yard sale. He smiled.

"Frank! Please? I can't—" Emily tried to inch her foot free, but the piano frame slipped again, slamming down onto the pew and her bare foot. Emily screamed in pain and yanked her foot free. The piano frame thudded onto the concrete floor.

"Ow, ow." Emily collapsed in a heap, cradling her injured foot.

"Emmy!" Frank dropped the portfolio and rushed over, pulling her away from the piano frame. "Are you okay?"

No. Emily shook her head. Her foot throbbed.

"What were you doing down here, anyway?" he said.

"I heard a crash, and I came to see what happened."

A pause. "And what did . . . happen?" Gently he examined her foot. Already it had turned angry black and red across the instep.

"It hurts like hell." She winced as she tried to flex her foot. At least it didn't seem as if any bones were broken.

Frank helped her to her feet. She set her injured foot on the floor and applied a little pressure. No pain shooting up her leg. "You need to get some ice on that right away," Frank said. He looped his arm around her waist and helped her to the stairs.

She leaned against him and climbed one step. Then another. "I heard a crash," Emily said again. "I came down to make sure everything was okay. When I saw the mess, all I did was—"

"I know. Clean. Straighten," he said, helping her up another riser. "It's what you do."

Emily stopped midstep. "You're the one who dragged that . . . that useless monster of a thing down here and left it propped up. Precariously. An accident waiting to happen." She turned and stared at the piles of stuff that crowded the stairs and basement. "Who needs this much crap? There's so much. It's a sickness."

Frank looked stunned. "So now *I'm* sick?" He pushed past her into the laundry room and then turned back. "I'm fine. You're the one who's allergic . . ." His voice died.

Was he really dragging their fertility test results into an argument about his crap? Emily's eyes brimmed with tears as she managed the last few steps on her own, following Frank into the kitchen. He got out an ice-cube tray from the freezer, slamming it into the sink. He grabbed a towel and scooped up a handful of cubes. He offered Emily the makeshift ice pack. She stared at it.

"Just so you know," Emily said, "I hate your crap. And it makes me crazy knowing how much of it you've dragged into our attic. Into our garage. Into our basement. It feels like it's growing. Breeding!" She took a ragged breath. "Even if we're not."

Chapter 2

FRANK REARED BACK AS if he'd been struck. Emily was stunned, too. Those final words had burst out raw and uncensored. Frank dropped the ice pack on the table and stormed out of the house.

Emily sank into a chair, picked up the ice pack, and pressed it to the side of her face. She held it there until the cold stung.

Gingerly she lifted her leg, resting her foot on the seat of another kitchen chair. Her instep was bruised and swollen, but she could rotate her ankle. She rested the ice pack on the sorest spot.

She shouldn't have torn into Frank like that. Hating his crap was like hating his smile. And his collecting came as no surprise, not after eight years of marriage. But his crack about their fertility issues—*her* fertility issues—had been mean and thoughtless. When they'd gotten the latest test results a few weeks ago, Frank had seemed relieved, maybe because there really was something wrong and it turned out not to be his fault. Emily was producing antibodies that were killing Frank's sperm. She'd been trying to get Frank to talk about what to do next, but he kept brushing her off. Too tired. Too busy. But not too busy to go to yard sales.

Maybe he'd been relieved, too, because, when it came to having a family, he wasn't as *all in* as he claimed to be. Or maybe it was their marriage that he wasn't that *all into*. That brought Emily to a full stop, and she choked up.

A half hour later Emily was in her bedroom with the makeshift ice pack tied around her foot. As she finished sorting her closet, she thought about Frank. Yes, he had his shortcomings. But he remembered that she needed a salad spinner.

Her eyes misted over after she pulled her wedding dress—a short white sleeveless silk dress with a V-neck—from the much diminished clothing pile. She glanced across to her bureau at a wedding picture of her wearing that dress with Frank beside her, staring into her eyes with goofy affection.

Emily had known full well that Frank wasn't perfect when she'd married him, and she'd loved him anyway. Surely she was never going to wear that wedding dress again, but still she set it aside to hang back in the closet, swallowing the lump in her throat.

It was three o'clock when her phone pinged. Becca, punctual as always.

Meet you at the Park 'n' Ride in thirty.

Emily texted back: *Leaving in 5.*

She shucked off her top and shorts and grabbed a freshly laundered pale blue collared T-shirt with their company logo embroidered on one side and a pair of matching cotton drawstring pants. Her dorky matching baseball cap was in her gear bag. She tried to slip on one of the blue sneakers that were part of their official ensemble, but her foot was too sore. No way could she wear them for the next few days at least. Instead, she put on a pair of roomy purple Crocs that she used for gardening. She took a test step. They'd get her through the on-site consult that she and Becca did together before committing to work with a client.

She ducked into the bathroom and put her hair up in a ponytail. Then she went downstairs. She left Frank a note—a frowny face with tears and below it a row of X's and O's.

Then she grabbed the canvas bag where she kept her gear, tucked her little purse and cell phone into it, and left the house.

EMILY's white Honda Civic hatchback had been the last 2006 on the lot in December of that year, the model so basic that it didn't have automatic door locks. A month ago she had the Freeze-Frame Clutter Kickers logo stenciled on the doors. The car started right up. It always did. For Emily dependability far outranked flash. It was an easy ten-minute drive to the Park 'n' Ride on a Saturday afternoon, and when Emily arrived, there were plenty of empty spots. She pulled up alongside Becca's car, a white Kia whose door was also stenciled with their logo.

Becca lowered her car window. "Come on, let's roll."

Becca looked exactly the same as she had in elementary school, her Little Orphan Annie curls barely tamed. On through high school and college, she and Becca had been best friends, a pair of otherwise unaffiliated geeks whose friendship only grew from the days when they shared a trove of Barbie clothing and built a massive Barbie castle from cardboard boxes and tubes.

Emily grabbed her gear bag. She got out of her car, freezing for a moment as pain sparked across her instep. She locked her car and got into Becca's. A former ER nurse, Becca still had a scrubbed-clean nursey feel about her. Her Clutter Kickers shirt and pants were freshly ironed.

"You okay?" Becca asked. "You look—"

"I'm fine." Emily really didn't want to talk to Becca about her fight with Frank. Or their fertility test results. Becca was married to one of the kindest men on the planet, and she'd pumped out two adorable children without breaking a sweat.

"You're limping." Becca turned in her seat.

"I was in the basement. Frank's piano guts assaulted my foot. You know, that thing inside a piano that looks like a harp? Weighs a ton? It wasn't his fault. Really."

"Really?"

Emily looked at her watch. "Let's go. We're running late."

She was grateful that Becca let it go at that. They were on the highway when Emily said, "So tell me about this client."

"Ruth Murphy," Becca said. "Retired bookkeeper."

Fifteen minutes later Becca pulled up in front of Ruth Murphy's split-level home. Dandelions thrived on the front lawn, and the yews under her front window needed clipping. Emily put on her cap, threading her ponytail through the opening in the back. Then she got out of the car and followed Becca up the walk.

Becca rang the bell. *Young or old?* This was a game Emily played, trying to imagine the person who was about to greet her. Short, stout, and elderly, she decided.

Emily was two-for-three. With a white dandelion puff of hair, Mrs. Murphy had to be past seventy, and she came up to Emily's chin. But she was slender as a reed. She ushered them into a living room filled with stuffy Victorian-style furniture. The scalloped wood valances over the windows were pure 1950s, like the ones in the house Emily's parents had sold before moving to the Cape.

This seemed like a house with a place for everything and everything in its place. What was there to organize?

Emily took a clipboard and pen from her bag and shot Becca a questioning look. Becca tipped her head toward a leather recliner in the corner that was leaning back, its footrest raised as if someone were still sitting in it. On the floor beside it sat a pair of men's bedroom slippers and a drift of newspapers. On a nearby end table sat an empty cut-glass tumbler and an ashtray with a cigar stub.

Mrs. Murphy picked up a silver-framed photograph from on top of an upright piano. The picture was of a young bride and groom, standing stiffly together. The bride wore a high-necked silk gown. Alongside her stood a much taller man, his thick, dark hair parted and slicked down. He wore a military uniform.

"Me and Murph," Mrs. Murphy said. "Nineteen sixty. We were married at Fort Bragg."

"He was handsome," Becca said.

"He was that and more. Cunning devil one minute, saint the next. I just don't know—" She dabbed at her eyes with a Kleenex. "It's been hard. Sometimes I feel so lost I want to disappear."

Becca touched Mrs. Murphy's arm. "When did you lose him?"

"A year ago. Massive heart attack. Just weeks after he retired from his dental practice." She reached for another framed picture on the piano. The older man in the picture was still handsome, his hair now a lush white pompadour over defiantly dark eyebrows. Mrs. Murphy held the picture to her chest, then laid it facedown on the piano. "Went, just like that. Doctors said even if he'd been in the hospital when it happened, they couldn't have saved him."

"I'm so sorry for your loss," Becca said.

Emily sidled over to the pile of newspapers on the floor. The date of the one on top was July 14, 2018. More than a year ago.

"So," Mrs. Murphy said, taking a breath. "It's time for me to deal with Murph's *things*. But there's so much stuff. I pick up one thing and try to decide what to do with it, and then another thing catches my eye and there's a memory . . ." She hiccupped. "It's exhausting. And where will it all go? We have no children, so . . ." Emily imagined herself in Mrs. Murphy's shoes—childless, widowed, staring into the abyss that was Frank's basement. "So I called you. I thought, if only I had help and some way to remember the things that were his. The picture-taking seemed like just the ticket."

"If you invite us in to help you," Becca said, "how and what we do will be up to you. We can stop whenever you've had enough. Because this is your life. Your home. Your memories."

Mrs. Murphy took that in. She pursed her lips and nodded.

"So let's have a look, shall we?" Becca said.

Mrs. Murphy led the way down a hallway to a closed door. She pushed it open, then stepped aside so Becca and Emily could go in first. The room smelled of dust and old paper. At its center was a massive oak desk, its top piled with mail and a drift of auction catalogues. Sotheby's in Boston. T. E. Kalmus in Hyannis. The return address on an unopened envelope to Dr. Charles Murphy, DMD, was the American Dental Society.

"Okay if I take some pictures?" Emily asked.

"Be my guest," Mrs. Murphy said.

On the desk sat a pad of paper, its top page half written on in red pencil. It was a list that began "FA LIBRARY" followed by *Twelve Months of Flowers, The Pinetum Britannicum,*" and a dozen more titles. It looked as if Charles Murphy had been planning to go to the library when he died. A red pencil lay beside the pad, along with a cup, the bottom coated with dried coffee. Emily took a few pictures. The room was a perfect time capsule.

"I never come in here. I can't bear . . ." Mrs. Murphy said.

"May I?" Becca asked, indicating the desk.

"Help yourself."

Becca opened the desk's file drawers. They were packed with hanging files, each with a typed label. Emily started a list titled "Husband's Office," writing down the categories of things they'd be sorting through. She took more pictures of the room, the desk, the bookcase, zooming in on the procession of carved wooden birds lined up, tail to beak, across a topmost shelf. Duck decoys. Long-legged wading birds. Smaller birds. Delicately carved and carefully painted, they had to be worth something to a collector.

"And"—Mrs. Murphy fished a ring of keys from an ashtray on the desk—"there's this." She removed a key, handing it to Emily. Written in flaking red nail polish on the key was the number 217.

"I think it's to a storage unit," Mrs. Murphy said. "He must have paid a year in advance. The first bill I saw was this." She reached into her pocket and pulled out a folded sheet of paper. Her hands trembled as she unfolded it. "It came weeks ago."

Emily tucked the key into an inside pocket of her gear bag. The bill was dated June, and the amount due was for twelve months. It was from Inner Peace Storage. Emily was familiar with the outfit. They rented storage units in a nearby industrial park on the river.

"You paid the bill?" Emily asked.

"I did. Solved the mystery of what the key was for."

"Do you know what he'd been storing there?" Becca asked.

"No idea whatsoever."

"We'll need to see what's in there before we can give you an accurate idea of what it will take to sort it out. Do you want to come with us when we check this out?"

"I'd rather not. I'm curious about what's in there, but I don't need to see for myself. You'll tell me, won't you?"

"Yes, of course. We'll check it out and then put together an estimate for you. We can have that done by . . ." Becca paused, waiting for Emily to fill in the blank.

"In a week?" Emily said.

"A week?" Mrs. Murphy moaned. "Can't you do it sooner than that? It took me forever to get up the nerve to call you."

"As soon as possible," Becca said, taking out her cell phone and thumbing through her calendar. "Let's see. . . . Wednesday?"

"Couldn't you do it any sooner?"

"Sure," Emily said. "Assuming we get into the storage unit, we'll try to email you an estimate Monday."

Mrs. Murphy beamed.

"MONDAY?" Becca said. It was nearly half past five, and Emily was sitting in the passenger seat of Becca's car in front of Mrs. Murphy's house. "What were you thinking? We'd have to get over to that storage unit tomorrow."

Emily's foot hurt. She slipped off a Croc, pulled her foot to her lap, and massaged it. "I thought you wanted *as soon as possible*."

"I know, I know that's what I said. But I didn't mean tomorrow. It's Sunday, and I've got Makesh's family coming for brunch." Becca's husband had a large extended Indian family, brothers and sisters and their children. "And Sophie has a piano recital."

"Based on what we've seen so far, this doesn't look like it's going to be too complicated. Ballpark, three days to sort."

"And whatever's in that storage unit. That's the wild card."

"Don't worry," Emily said. "I'll check it out tomorrow." As she spoke, she realized that tomorrow she was supposed to go to a PawSox game with Frank and his college buddies. She'd have to tell him that she couldn't go. After their fight, he'd assume her bagging it was some kind of passive-aggressive payback. But the truth was, Emily never looked forward to hanging out with Frank's odious law partner, Ryan Melanson, and the rest of their gang, overgrown frat boys who reeked of self-confidence. By the third inning, they'd be drunk and squinty-eyed.

Becca started the car but then sat staring at the house. "Did it strike you as odd that Mrs. Murphy didn't seem all that curious about what was in that storage unit? Wouldn't you want to know?"

Emily laughed. "If it were Frank's storage unit? I'd pay double if you promised to nuke everything in it, sight unseen."

Becca didn't laugh. "Are you sure everything's okay?"

Emily forced a smile. "Don't worry. When it's not, you'll be the first to know."

EMILY dreaded telling Frank that she had to bail on the ball game. On the drive back to the Park 'n' Ride, she decided it would be less fraught if she did it by phone. Becca let her off at her car. She got in, started the engine, and waited for the AC to kick in. Then she dialed Frank's cell. He picked up after four rings.

"Hey," he said. "I got your note. Thanks."

Emily felt a rush of remorse. "I felt terrible after you left. I wasn't being fair."

"I don't get why you care what I collect. It's not in your face."

"I meant the fertility test results. We need to talk about it. We need to decide what to do, even if that means doing nothing."

She heard some shuffling on his end. "I know. I'm just not ready. I need to think about it," he said. "I'm not sure about kids."

"Isn't that why I stopped taking the pill? We always said—"

"No. *You* always said. I just listened."

That was a lie. Frank had even joked that he wanted to name his son Neuman after Alfred E.

"Well, I need for us to talk about it," Emily said.

"Okay, okay. We'll talk. Just not now. How'd it go with the new client?" Changing the subject. But it gave her a lead-in.

"That's why I called." She rushed on. "Turns out this is a big project, and I need to come back tomorrow to do more prep." Emily tried to sound apologetic. "So I can't go to the game."

"Becca can't do it?" Frank sounded annoyed.

"She's tied up with family. All day and into the evening."

"Can't this woman just tell you what's in there?"

"She doesn't *know* what's in there. Her husband rented it—"

"And *she's* cleaning it out?" He snorted. "Typical."

The dig wasn't lost on Emily. "Her husband's dead."

That left a hole in the conversation.

"Anyway," Emily said, "we promised an estimate Monday, so I have to get in tomorrow and make an inventory. Maybe you can find someone to use my ticket?"

"You know it's not about the ticket," Frank said. "I like having you there." After a pause, he asked, "How's your foot?"

It was swollen and throbbing. "It's better," she said.

"Glad to hear. I'm sorry you got hurt."

Emily felt vindicated. "I'm sorry I took your head off," she said. "It's just that . . ." It was just that his crap made her see red. "Really, I'm sorry about missing the game."

That's when she realized he'd already disconnected the call.

FRANK'S Z4 was gone when Emily got home. A note on the kitchen counter read "Don't wait up, client meeting."

She heated some leftover mac and cheese. After she ate, she went upstairs to her office and uploaded images for her closet-sorting video. She put them in order and synced them to Scott Joplin's "Pineapple Rag," watching as her clothes took turns lying on the bed, then folding themselves or jumping into a garbage bag. She'd have to wait for the final image, her clothes arranged on shelves and racks that she'd purchased but had yet to install.

Three hours after she'd started working on the video, she heard the front door slam. "Frank? Is that you?" she hollered.

Moments later he stood in her office doorway. He looked tired and drained. "Long meeting?" Emily asked.

Frank nodded and dropped his briefcase on the floor.

She stood. "You know I didn't mean to mess with your things."

"I know that," Frank said. "It wasn't your fault. I should have been more careful about how I left them." He pulled her into his arms and nuzzled her neck. He smelled of beer and cigar smoke. "I know I can be a jerk." Emily choked up, sideswiped by tears that filled her eyes. Frank snagged a tissue from the box on her desk and handed it to her. "Just not too much of a jerk too much of the time. Right?" He sat in her desk chair and pulled her into his lap, turned on the gooseneck desk lamp, and aimed the light at her foot. "Let me see. Has it gone Technicolor?" He eased off her Croc and ran fingertips gently over her bruised instep. Emily shivered with pleasure. "Can you wiggle your toes?"

Emily wiggled her toes. "I'm okay. How was your meeting?"

"Productive." He smiled. "Want to hear the gory details?"

She didn't. "You smell like cigar. Celebrating?"

"I like the way you smell." He ran his hand up her leg. Emily shivered again. "But you're right. I smell of cigar smoke. And lousy Chinese food. I need a shower. But first tell me more about your new client."

Emily was surprised. Frank often asked about the stuff she was decluttering, but he rarely wanted to know about the person behind the clutter. "Mrs. Murphy? Her husband died a year ago. She hasn't been able to throw away any of his things. He'd been renting a storage unit she knew nothing about until the bill came."

Frank chuckled. "Don't get any ideas. I like my stuff where I can hang out with it." He stood slowly, and she slid off his lap. "So how much of a mess did her husband leave her with?"

"I won't know until I check out the unit tomorrow."

"Ah, right, tomorrow." He narrowed his eyes at her. "You don't need to make up excuses not to go to our games. I thought you liked them. Makes no difference to me if you take a pass."

Was that a trick? Because Emily had been under the impression it did matter. At first she'd enjoyed the games. Now it felt as if it took too long to drive there and the game went on endlessly. Plus his friends drank too much and they'd get handsy. Some of them.

She hesitated. "Actually, it's not my favorite thing."

"No big deal. I absolve you from having to attend this and all future games." Frank grinned. "All you had to do was say so."

"Tomorrow I really do have to work."

"I know." Frank sniffed his armpit. "And I really do need a shower." He picked up his briefcase and left the room.

She shut down her computer. Before she changed for bed, she shifted the folded piles of clothing from the bed to the floor. The empty closet needed to be vacuumed. She stretched her aching shoulders and envisioned the new rods and shelves she'd bought.

Frank came into the bedroom wearing his bathrobe. He looked into her empty closet and gave his head a little shake. He'd encouraged her new venture, but Emily could tell from his expression that, for him at least, nothing about it sparked joy.

Chapter 3

Sunday

FRANK LEFT THE NEXT morning wearing his Pawtucket Red Sox cap and carrying a cooler loaded with six-packs of Sam Adams.

Emily spent the better part of the morning preparing her new closet—taking down the old rods and unpacking new wire shelves, rods, and assorted organizers. It was early afternoon by the time she was ready to head over to Inner Peace Storage.

She checked her gear bag to be sure she had all the supplies she might need. Clean rags and a roll of paper towels. Spray cleaner. Rubber gloves and dust masks. An extra camera.

It didn't take long to drive to the sprawling complex of modular prefab units that squatted on the banks of Mariscotta River. Emily wondered if the color scheme at Inner Peace—the metal overhead doors to all the units were saffron orange—was supposed to remind customers of the robes worn by Buddhist monks.

She parked in front of the office, a boxy, glassed-in room. The hours painted on the door confirmed that the office wasn't staffed on Sundays, so Emily continued into the complex, through the narrow alleys between units. When she found 217, she parked and got out. In the heat of the day, the macadam seemed to shimmer.

She approached the Murphys' unit. A padlock secured the door. As with the key, 217 was painted on the padlock in peeling red nail polish. It took not-so-gentle pressure to get the lock to open. She grabbed the door handle and started to raise the door.

The *beep-beep* of a horn stopped her. She turned as a golf cart pulled up alongside her. Security.

"Back again?" the driver said. She must have looked puzzled, because he did a double take. "Sorry, I thought you were someone else. My mistake. Is this your unit?"

Emily wiped away a trickle of sweat making its way down the side of her face. "The owner gave me the key." How had this security guard even known she was here? She spotted a CCTV camera mounted on the roof one unit away, aimed down at her. "You said someone was in and out of here? You sure it was this unit?"

"Yup. Seen her a few times. Not my business, of course."

Her? Before Emily could ask what the woman looked like or how recently she'd been here, the driver took off.

She raised the door of the storage unit. The interior was in shadow. A blast of hot air drove her back, and she gagged on the smell—mildew and general rot. She returned to her car to get a face mask from her gear bag.

Back at the storage unit, face mask strapped in place, Emily felt for a light switch and flipped it. Fluorescent lights flickered on. The readout on a thermostat hanging beside the light switch was blank. So much for the climate control Inner Peace advertised.

The space was narrow and twice as deep as it was wide. Lining both sides were metal shelves. Emily noted that most shelves were stacked with books and boxes. Some were loaded with document tubes. Everything was sorted with the kind of precision that Emily's mother, a retired librarian, would have relished. Books were shelved one deep. Boxes and tubes were labeled.

On one shelf sat a set of leather-bound books: *Les Misérables,* Volumes I–V. The lower part of the book spines looked as if they'd been dipped in white powder. Beside them was a pair of taller books, their spines so blackened that their embossed titles were illegible. Emily tried to pull one from the shelf. Its spine broke, releasing a cloud of what were probably mold spores. In her hands the book felt fragile. She peeked at the title page: *Hakluyt's Voyages.* Beneath that it read, *Anno 1599.*

Emily took photos of the spine, the cover, and the title page, where the paper was sprinkled with black dots. She and Becca would need a book dealer to advise them whether in this condition it was worth saving. She slid the fragile book back into its spot.

She ventured to the far end of the unit. Across the back was a sturdy wooden workbench. Behind it shelves were loaded with glues and adhesives, cleaning supplies, and paintbrushes.

Emily took a series of pictures. Then she turned to the rows of containers that lined the shelves. She raised the lid of a plastic bin labeled DOORKNOBS. As promised, it was filled with them. Crystal octagons. White porcelain. This was not junk. It was a collector's collection. She lifted the lid of a shoe box. Inside was a vintage thermostat with lovely filigree work.

Emily replaced the lids. Murph and Emily's Frank would have been soul mates. She could imagine their poker game: *I'll see your 1936 thermostat and raise you a World War I copper fan.*

She counted the books on a length of shelving (twenty-six), counted the number of shelves loaded with books (twenty-four), and multiplied. Around six hundred. Next, she counted boxes: thirty, ranging in size from shoe boxes to liquor boxes. Judging by the labels, they contained all manner of building hardware.

Then she turned her attention to the document storage tubes. There were at least sixty of them. She pulled out a tube at random and was about to open it when she noticed an unlabeled black hat-box. She tucked the document tube under her arm and pulled the hatbox from the shelf. It was light—not filled with hardware.

Her phone chirped. Becca. Juggling the hatbox and document tube, she stepped outside and removed the mask to take the call.

"Where are you?" Becca sounded breathless. In the background, Emily could hear a piano laboring.

"The Murphys' storage unit."

"I'm glad I caught you. I just talked to a potential client. She asked if we could go over and see her. Now." Becca paused. "I told her no. We don't work Sundays, and we don't work nights. She said there were extenuating circumstances."

"What extenuating circumstances?"

"I think it's about her husband. He's out of the house. I told her no. We can't turn on a dime. Then, after I hung up, I get a call." Becca lowered her voice, *"This is Ryan Melanson the Third."* It was a good imitation of Frank's law partner's resonant bass. "He was call-ing on that woman's behalf, begging us to reconsider. He says she lives in Mandarin Cliffs and she'll pay double whatever we usually charge and that he personally vouched for us."

"Ryan recommended us?" Emily was shocked, because she and Ryan Melanson had barely spoken since the last time she and Frank had had Ryan and his then wife over to dinner. Emily had been in the kitchen chopping onions when she smelled Ryan's whiskey-scented breath and felt his hand cup her behind. She'd whirled around and jabbed the knife point into his belly and told him to back off. Surely even thick-skinned Ryan would know that his personal recommendation wouldn't cut any ice with her.

Maybe Becca's caller was a new woman in Ryan's life. Whoever she was, it sounded as if she shared his sense of entitlement. On the other hand, she and Becca did need more clients.

"She'll pay double?" Emily said.

"Exactly. I thought I'd run it by you before I left it at no."

With its fancy homes, Mandarin Cliffs might have been another universe, but it wasn't far from Emily's neighborhood. "We didn't say *when* on Monday we'd get back to Mrs. Murphy."

"Right. You could finish up the storage unit in the morning and head to Mandarin Cliffs now. Okay?" It was ten after five, and Emily was, at most, twenty minutes from Mandarin Cliffs. Taking her silence for yes, Becca added, "I'll call her back and let her know. And I'll text you her name and address. You're the best."

"I guess. I hope this doesn't turn into a regular thing."

"It won't if we don't let it. What's it look like there?"

"It looks like"—Emily stepped to the doorway of the unit and looked in—"old books. Vintage hardware. And—" Just then she lost her grip on the document tube that she'd tucked under her arm. When she tried to catch it, her phone clattered to the concrete floor. The hatbox had tumbled, too, spilling papers and cards.

Emily grabbed her phone. Not broken, thank goodness. "Mr. Murphy was paying for climate control, and he wasn't getting it," she said to Becca. "Looks like rodents have been having a banquet in here. Mrs. Murphy should bring in an insurance appraiser before we clear this out, and possibly an attorney, too." Squeezing the phone between her shoulder and ear, she stooped and began to gather the pieces of paper that had spilled from the hatbox.

Becca said, "We'll include coordinating that in our estimate."

But Emily almost missed the suggestion. The slip of paper in her hand was a bookplate engraved with an image of a table laden with books. Below the picture were the words "Middlebury College Library." And below that "Gift of Silas M. Pearson 1910."

"Talk to you later," Becca said. In the background, Emily heard Sophie coming down hard on piano keys. The call disconnected. A few moments later Emily's phone pinged with a text.

Quinn Newell 55 Ardmore Ln

Emily picked up another slip of paper. This one was card stock, yellowed with age. Typewritten at the top, it said, "This book should be returned to the Library on or before the last date stamped below." The date stamped was NOV.-1 '79.

She shuffled through the rest of the papers. Library book pockets. Bookplates. Due-date slips. There were hundreds of them . . . in a storage unit that contained hundreds of old books.

Emily stuffed the cards and bookplates back into the hatbox, set it on a shelf, turned off the light, and pulled the storage-unit door closed. It took several tries to force the padlock to snap shut. As she backed away, she stumbled over the document tube she'd been holding when Becca called. She picked it up and went to return it, but when she tried to unlock the padlock again, it wouldn't give. She didn't want to break the key, so she gave up, making a mental note to bring a can of WD-40 when she returned.

She put the key in her pants pocket and tossed the document tube on the passenger seat of her car.

On her way to Mandarin Cliffs, Emily mulled over what she'd found in the storage unit. She was certain Mr. Murphy was a serious collector. But the hatbox full of library slips raised the question: Had he legitimately purchased his books, or were they on "permanent loan"? And what about the documents in those tubes?

Stopped at a red light, Emily gave a furtive glance at the tube on the passenger seat. What happened when a client's clutter consisted of *potentially* stolen goods? It was an issue that Becca and Emily wouldn't have chosen to touch with a ten-foot pole.

Emily pushed the tube to the floor and nudged it under the seat.

THE entrance to the enclave of Mandarin Cliffs was marked by a gold sign. The street, its houses set back on generous lots rife with blooming hydrangeas, curved and forked. Quinn Newell's house was at the far end of a cul-de-sac.

It was nearly six o'clock when Emily parked and got out of her car. She took in the house. Make that *château*, clad in beige stucco. Its grand entrance featured massive double doors. The house dwarfed its neighbors. Mandarin Cliffs was, after all, still New England, where conspicuous consumption was considered wretched excess. These people must not be New Englanders.

Emily grabbed her gear bag from the car and went up to the front door. She pressed the doorbell and waited.

Young or old? From the house, and from the fact that Ryan had referred this client to them, Emily expected Quinn to be blond and impeccably dressed.

Wrong on all counts. The woman who came to the door was a thirty-something brunette, shoulder-length hair held back with a banana clip. The clothes—black yoga pants with a black tank—were probably Lululemon. If she was one of Ryan's conquests, she was an outlier in terms of looks. Not that she wasn't attractive; she just wasn't flashy. Maybe money made the difference.

The woman blinked at Emily. "Are you from Clutter . . ."

"Clutter Kickers. Here." Emily fished a business card from her bag. "Freeze-Frame Clutter Kickers. You must be Ms. Newell."

"Quinn," the woman said, studying the card. "Thank you so much for coming. I'm afraid I had a bit of a meltdown on the phone. But I'm not a nut or a princess, I swear."

No, Quinn did not strike Emily as a nut. The not-a-princess part she was less sure about. For sure she was a bit jittery. But Emily knew better than to ask the obvious question: Why the fire drill? She'd worked with new clients often enough to know that answers would emerge. Instead, she said, "So you know Ryan?"

"We're"—Quinn hesitated—"friends." She rushed on with, "He speaks highly of you. Says you're trustworthy. Dependable."

"He works with my husband," Emily said. She looked around. "Well, this is quite a house."

"No kidding. My husband's taste."

The two-story foyer dwarfed its spare furnishings. The floor was a patchwork of Oriental carpets in pastels and cream. And, of course, there was a grand staircase. The walls, on the other hand, featured prints and posters hung haphazardly, along with old advertising signs.

Quinn must have followed Emily's gaze, because she said, "Furniture's not my taste, either. And that stuff on the walls belongs to my husband. Wally's big into vintage advertising. In fact, that's where he is right now, at an auction of the stuff in Hyannis."

A brightly colored sign for laundry detergent, the paint flaking at the edges, hung crooked at the bottom of the grand stairs. Emily couldn't stop herself from going over to straighten it. When she did, she realized it was covering a fist-size hole in the wall. She glanced back at Quinn. At what was surely a bruise under her eye.

Emily was startled by a creaking sound overhead. Was someone else in the house? Quinn looked up, on the alert, too. A *pad-pad-pad* revealed itself to be a fat calico cat, sauntering down the stairs. It rubbed its head against Emily's leg. She reached down to pet it.

Quinn said, "Wally's a pack rat. You wouldn't believe the stuff he's got down in the basement."

Actually, I would. Emily was sure she hadn't said it out loud, but still Quinn asked, "Don't tell me, you're married to one, too?"

Emily felt her face grow hot. Her role was to listen and take notes. Be supportive and professional. *It's not group therapy.*

"Does your husband know you're consulting us?" Emily said. How ugly would it get if he returned and found her here?

"I told him, but does he *know?*" Quinn laughed. "That's practically an existential question. He's not the world's best listener."

"I ask because it's one of our rules. I can't help you declutter someone else's stuff."

"Don't worry, I wouldn't dare touch any of his stuff. Come out to the garage. I'll show you what I need your help dealing with."

Emily followed Quinn through an airy open kitchen. On the granite counter sat a massive espresso machine. Stuck to a bulletin board were a dozen business cards. Emily foraged in her bag for another business card. "Mind if I pin this up for you?"

"Sure," Quinn said. "Thanks."

Emily used an orphaned pushpin to post her business card alongside a class calendar for the women's fitness center in East Hartwell. Morning vinyasa yoga classes were circled in red.

Quinn opened the refrigerator and took out a bottle of prosecco. She grabbed a pair of balloon shaped wineglasses from an overhead rack, filled them with prosecco, and offered one to Emily.

Emily hesitated.

"What, you don't like prosecco?"

"It's not that," Emily said. Actually, Emily and Frank drank prosecco whenever they had something to celebrate.

"You're not supposed to drink on the job?" Quinn said slyly.

No drinking on the job was another of Becca and Emily's rules. That was an enormous glass Quinn was waving, and prosecco went straight to Emily's head. Especially on an empty stomach.

"You probably aren't supposed to work weekends or after five, either. And yet here you are." Quinn held out a glass to Emily. "Come on. In for a penny, in for a pound."

Emily couldn't help smiling. She took the glass.

Quinn raised her own glass in a toast. "Cheers!"

Emily held up her glass. "What are we celebrating?"

"Me. Calling Clutter Kickers for help. Finally." Quinn took a sip and waited for Emily to do the same. The wine was ice-cold and not too dry. "Here's to taking care of business." She clinked Emily's glass, drank some more, and carried her glass and the bottle out the kitchen door and into a garage. Emily took one more small sip and then picked up her gear bag and followed Quinn.

The garage, like the rest of the house, was oversized. It had four bays. Nearest to the kitchen door was an empty bay where Emily presumed the absent Wally parked his Ferrari, or whatever muscle car he drove. In the next spot sat a sporty red Miata convertible. Probably Quinn's. Marking the boundary between these two bays was a row of orange traffic cones.

"Those cones?" Quinn said. "He's afraid I'm going to sideswipe his precious car. What does your husband drive?"

"A BMW Z4," Emily said.

"And he'd die before he'd let someone else drive it. Right?"

Of course she was right.

The remaining two bays in the garage were a jumble of furniture, storage boxes, and assorted junk. "See all that?" Quinn said. "That's all I owned before I moved in with Wally." She hit a button that raised both of the garage's double doors. "When I moved in, he promised he'd make room for my things. Guess I didn't know him as well as I thought, because here we are, three years later, and my junk's still in the garage. And you know what? I don't even care anymore." She splashed some wine on the floor. "I gave up my job. My name. Why not give it all up?"

"That sucks." At least Frank had never begrudged Emily her own space and, for the most part, kept his crap out of it.

"People see the big house." Quinn's eyes brimmed with tears. "The fancy car. And they think, wow, she's got everything."

Emily felt a flash of guilt, because that was exactly what she had thought. She took a swallow of wine. "You must have been in love with him."

"I suppose so." In a whisper, "But if I got a do-over?" Quinn gave a bitter laugh. "I was thirty-five; my biological clock was ticking; I wanted to be married in the worst way. I should never have married Wally, but I did. I have no illusions about the bargain I've made. Most days I get up and do my thing. It's okay."

Emily could have said the same thing about her own marriage. She and Frank let each other do their own thing. And her biological clock was set to run out.

"But this," Quinn went on, gesturing to her belongings. "It's so disrespectful, don't you think? Makes me feel worthless."

"Quinn, you're not your things." The minute Emily said that, she realized it wasn't true. To a very real extent, people could be defined by the things they kept, each one a choice, even if it was not a conscious one. Emily was her sock drawer, both before and after. Frank was his piano guts.

As if on cue, Emily's foot throbbed. She reached down to rub it, and when she straightened, Quinn was looking at her. She had a pale intensity about her, repressed rage that Emily sometimes saw when she unexpectedly caught her own reflection in a mirror.

Emily shivered. Quinn topped off Emily's glass and her own.

"Seriously," Quinn said, "how would you like to be married to a guy who goes to auctions and brings home prosthetic limbs?"

"Mine's into rotting church pews," Emily said. "And horror comics." She raised her glass.

"Autographed Dwight D. Eisenhower bobblehead dolls," Quinn said. "Preserved piranha fish." She lifted her own glass.

Emily clinked and took another drink. "At least your husband's stuff's right out in the open. He's not hiding it."

Quinn emptied her glass. "Yours has a secret stash?"

"Define *secret*. I know where it is, but I try not to look. Today I met a widow whose husband left her a jam-packed storage unit that she knew nothing about until the rental bill showed up a year after he died." She reached into her pants pocket, pulled out the key, and flashed it at Quinn. "Turns out it's packed with old books and prints."

Quinn put her finger to her lips. "Please don't tell Wally."

"You know what storage company he's been using? Inner Peace. She was far more serene before she knew about that storage unit. When she finds out what's in it, she'll be a wreck."

"What's wrong with the old books and prints?" Quinn asked.

Emily stopped herself from answering. The wine was talking. She wished she could put the words back in her mouth as she tried to slip the key back into her pocket. But she missed, and the key dropped onto the floor. When she bent to pick it up, blood rushed to her head. As she staggered sideways, she managed to kick the key under a chest of drawers.

Quinn put out a hand, and Emily grabbed it to steady herself. When the dizziness passed and Emily straightened, Quinn scooped up the key for her and dropped it into Emily's gear bag.

Emily set her wineglass on the floor, trying to collect herself. Becca would have been apoplectic if she'd witnessed this performance. "If it's okay with you, I'll take a few pictures. And you'll need to think about whether you really want to dump all of it. You don't get a day-after do-over."

"I'm not going to need one," Quinn said firmly. "Now that I'm ready to deal with this, I want to be done with it."

Emily assessed the pile. This would be manageable, especially if Quinn was committed to getting rid of everything. Shoe boxes were filled with CDs. Stuffed animals—Care Bears, each a different pastel—were stuck in a cardboard liquor box on a bureau.

"I see you still have your Care Bears," Emily said. When they were kids, Emily and Becca had each had her own set. Months ago Emily had packed hers in a box. Leaving them on her front steps for charity donation pickup, she'd felt as if she were abandoning beloved pets.

"Care Bears are just the tip of the iceberg." Quinn reached into the pile for a brown Bloomingdale's bag, pulling out a hooded red T-shirt with BOSTON emblazoned in white letters down the sleeve. Emily recognized it as a BU Terriers basketball T-shirt.

"You went to BU?" Emily asked.

"I did," Quinn said. "Undergrad."

Frank and Emily had met at BU when they were in graduate school—she in education, he in law. He'd had a T-shirt just like the one that Quinn was holding up as Exhibit A of useless sentiment. Emily had slept in the shirt when she'd stayed at the apartment that Frank shared with Ryan, long before the pair had started their law firm. Emily wondered what had happened to the shirt.

Emily picked up her wineglass. She knew she shouldn't have more to drink, but she wanted to swallow the bittersweet memory.

"But this shirt wasn't mine." Quinn held it up to her face and inhaled. "Or Wally's." *Another BU boyfriend?*

"Was T-shirt man the one that got away?" Emily asked.

"Not exactly," Quinn said, her cheeks coloring slightly. "But Wally knows the shirt's not his. He goes off the rails, crazy jealous, if I mention any of my old boyfriends. It's silly, really."

Emily set her glass down. Holding her cell phone high over her head, she took a picture, then checked the viewfinder to see what was there. Was that a papasan chair? Quintessential dorm furniture. Lying across this chair's frame was a rolled-up area rug.

"You think I'd be able to sell some of this?" Quinn asked. "Not that we need the money."

There was no point in sugarcoating it. Emily indicated a pair of pre–World War II mahogany chests of drawers. "That's sturdy and nice-looking, and thirty years ago you might have found a buyer. But these days it's what people refer to as"—she drew air quotes—"'brown furniture.' Frankly, it's hard to give away. But there'd be a ready buyer for that kitchen set if you put it out at a yard sale." She pointed to a 1950s kitchen table and matching chairs with their aluminum tubing and yellow vinyl seats.

"Goody, a yard sale! Let's not invite Wally." Quinn laughed.

"Or you could donate. There's a ton of charities, and you'd get a tax deduction. I can find one that will pick up."

"What I really should do is stuff all of my stuff down Wally's—" Quinn broke off, put her head back, and drank from the bottle. "Think there are any charities that will come and pick *him* up? Or maybe I should just chuck him off the roof instead."

Emily had picked up her glass and just taken another sip of prosecco herself when something about the matter-of-fact way that Quinn said *chuck him off the roof* struck her as hilarious. She laughed so hard, wine came fizzing out her nose.

"Or slip poison mushrooms into his lasagna," Quinn went on. "Or accidentally back over him." She held up her hands as if she were holding on to a steering wheel. "*Rrrmm.* Oops! My bad."

Emily imagined the piano frame falling from their bedroom window onto Frank's head as he dragged a church pew through the bulkhead door. She raised her glass. "To *'Til death do us part.*"

"To accidents waiting to happen." Quinn raised the bottle. Then slowly lowered it. Her look turned somber. "Or maybe it's safer to hire a hit man, a complete stranger, and be done with it." She gave Emily an appraising look. "So . . . could you?"

"Could I what?" Emily said, though she knew what Quinn was asking. She could never kill anyone, and certainly not Frank.

"I'll bet you would. In a heartbeat." Quinn winked. "If you thought you could get away with it."

Chapter 4

EMILY SPENT THE NEXT HOUR in a wine-infused haze, taking more photos of the piles and scribbling nearly indecipherable notes.

Finally, Emily quoted Quinn a fee for their organizing services, inflating her guesstimate by 50 percent. To double it felt like price gouging. She gave Quinn a PayPal account to which she could transfer a $500 deposit "If you decide to move forward."

"Of course I'm going to move forward." Quinn gave Emily an awkward hug. "I feel good about this. I just know I can trust you."

Emily was jotting down the best times for her or Becca to return—

when Quinn's husband wouldn't be there, of course—when Quinn slipped her cell phone from her pocket and looked at the readout. "Not mine. That must have been yours."

Emily got out her phone. Sure enough, she'd missed a text from Frank.

Em, could you stop at JC & bring me coffee? :-x

"Your partner?" Quinn asked.

"My husband. He wants me to pick him up a coffee on the way home. I've got just enough time to stop in the Square."

"They say jump, we say how high," Quinn said.

"It's not like that." Frank was usually the one who picked up a coffee for *her*. He even tried to get to the coffee shop before they ran out of her favorite cider donuts dusted with cinnamon sugar.

"Whatever," Quinn said, giving Emily a skeptical look.

Emily had just enough time to do a quick pee and make it to Java Connection before it closed. As she was leaving, Quinn offered her a black plastic controller. "Here's the garage-door remote. You'll be able to get in and out when I'm not here."

Emily hesitated. "Let's wait until after we have a signed agreement." Even then, she doubted that she'd want to come back when Quinn wasn't here. She didn't want to run into Wally.

"It's a spare. Give it back when we're done." Quinn dropped it into Emily's gear bag and walked Emily out to her car.

Emily knew she'd have to find a way to keep Quinn from steamrolling her. Right now she was too woozy to push back.

EMILY started her car and pulled away from the curb. Feeling the effects of too much wine, she opened the car windows to let in some fresh air. She turned onto the main road. She and Frank had always had their differences. But was his acquisitiveness pathological hoarding? Was her aversion to chaos obsessive nitpicking? Would she end up, years from now, bound to a man she'd once loved but with whom she no longer shared much in common? Maybe that was okay. Case in point: her parents. Lila Laubenstein had been a librarian whose passions were books, art, and more books. A retired cop, Bert loved golf, a football game, and more golf. Emily was the one thing they had in common.

Without a child to bring them together, would Emily and Frank still *spark joy* for each other? Because trying to "fold" Frank and tidy him up would prove futile. She'd fallen in love with his smile and intellect, even if he drove her around the bend with his auctions. At least he didn't screw around. Or tell her what she couldn't bring into their house. Only what she couldn't take *out* of it.

EMILY pulled up in front of the lone car parked in front of Java Connection. The neighboring sandwich shop and insurance office were closed. Java Connection was a recent addition to what residents referred to as the Square. Its plate-glass windows dated back to the sixties. A sign in the front door read WELCOME.

As Emily got out of her car, she called Frank. "I'm here," she said when he answered. "What do you want me to get you?"

"Thanks, doll. Americano with an extra shot of espresso."

Emily pocketed her phone and pushed through the door of the coffee shop. The tables were empty, and a single customer stood at the front register. The top shelf of the glass cabinet that usually held the cinnamon-sugar cider donuts was empty. Of course there wouldn't be any left at this time of day.

Emily was approaching the counter when the man there wheeled around and crashed into her. His coffee splashed all over. "I'm so sorry," Emily said, even though it wasn't her fault.

The man cursed. He wore a baseball cap and aviator glasses with yellow lenses, and he had a well-tended beard and mustache. He looked down at his coffee-stained yellow polo shirt and lidless venti, then bent farther to see the coffee pooling on his butterscotch leather loafers. Under his breath he spat, "Stupid cow."

Emily recoiled. But before she could come up with an equally hateful epithet, he'd brushed past her, striding out the door. Then, making eye contact with her through the coffee shop window, he overhanded his coffee cup against the back of her car.

What an ass. Too late, apt retorts came to her.

The barista, a young woman with a rich mocha complexion and

long dark hair, was already at Emily's side with a roll of paper towels. It was only then that Emily realized coffee had splattered all over her shirt and pants as well. As she patted her arms dry, she heard the screech of tires from outside. She looked out the window. The man and his car were gone.

"Charming fellow," Emily said. She handed the barista the coffee-soaked paper towels. "Thank you."

"You are sure you are not hurt?" The barista gave Emily a sympathetic look. Her name badge read ANA.

"I hope he's not one of your regular customers," Emily said.

Ana dropped a fresh wad of paper towels on the floor and bent to spread them around to sop up the spill. "I never seen him before." She wore a bracelet of colored macaroni. A mom.

"Needs to seriously chill out," Emily said.

"You think?" Ana laughed. She scooped up the towels and stood. "So what can I get you?"

"An Americano with an extra shot," Emily told her.

"On the house," Ana said when Emily tried to pay.

"No. Seriously," Emily said, offering a ten-dollar bill.

"Absolutely not. And I am so sorry."

"Not your fault." Emily stuffed the money into the tip jar and went out to her car. Coffee was splashed across her rear window and had run rivulets through the grime coating the white trunk lid.

Furious as well as shaken, Emily unlocked her car and got in. She hoped that guy's fancy shoes were well and truly ruined.

On the short ride home the smell of coffee evaporating off her clothing made Emily nauseous. She turned onto her street, pulled into the driveway, and got out of the car.

Inside, she made her way to Frank's office. He sat at his desk, his face lit by his computer screen. She crept up behind him. Startled, he jumped, nearly knocking the coffee from her hand.

"You're back," he said, snapping his laptop shut.

"What are you up to?"

"Working." He pushed his chair away from the desk.

"At this hour?"

"Okay. Sussed me out. I'm working, but I'm also bidding. Online auction ends in a half hour, and I need to stay sharp." Emily didn't want to know what he was bidding on. She held out the coffee. He took it, lifted the lid, and sniffed. "Thanks."

"How was the game?" she asked.

"We won. What about you? You said you had to work, but I didn't expect you back this late."

He looked up at her with that million-dollar smile of his, his look turning askance. "Looks like you're wearing some of this." He blew on the coffee and took another sip. "What happened?"

"Some guy ran into me at the coffee shop." All that remained was a fleeting impression of a big man with a trim dark beard and tinted glasses. *Stupid cow.* "Spilled his coffee and blamed me."

"That sounds unpleasant."

"It was." She looked down at her shirt and pants. "It'll come out in the wash."

Frank settled in his chair. "Other than that, how was your day?"

She perched on the edge of a two-drawer file cabinet. "I checked out that storage unit. Then I took a quick run over to meet a new client. Someone Ryan sent our way."

"Really?" Frank guffawed. "See, he's not such a bad sort."

"He knew better than to call me. He phoned Becca and begged us to go see the woman right away."

"I wondered what he was up to. He took a call and left the game early. What's her name?"

"Quinn. Quinn Newell. She lives in Mandarin Cliffs. Fabulous house. Married to a creep."

"A dead creep?"

The comment made her squirm. "No. It's the other client, the one with the storage unit, who's a widow. Becca and I should be able to help both of them, though I'm really not sure why the woman in Mandarin Cliffs needs our help at all. It's not like she's a hoarder. Because we know firsthand what *that* looks like."

Ignoring the dig, Frank said, "At least Mrs. Mandarin Cliffs will pay you what you're worth." He gathered the papers strewn across his desk.

"A new case?"

"Homeowner's suing over a smoke detector that she says short-circuited and caused her house to catch fire. She's not asking for a big payout. But it could open the door to a class action, so they're taking no chances." He took a drink of coffee. "Know what's the most common cause of smoke detector failure?" He smirked. "Dirt. People don't clean them." He opened his laptop.

Emily felt sympathy for the homeowner. Frank would probably annihilate her on the witness stand as he made the case against her housekeeping and for the company that manufactured the device. Once upon a time, he'd have been on her side, David dueling Goliath. Turned out, the satisfaction of winning for the underdog went only so far when you were making a paltry $50K a year. Though Frank didn't seem to miss it, he claimed working for the public defender had been great experience, standing up for people who more often than not had gotten themselves in trouble out of ignorance or impulsiveness. Emily wondered if she and Becca weren't doing that now, helping Mrs. Murphy get rid of her husband's trove when already there were red flags about how exactly he'd acquired it.

"Question," she said. "Purely hypothetical. As a former defense attorney."

"Uh-oh." Frank closed his laptop.

"Suppose I help someone declutter their house, and it turns out that the clutter they're getting rid of isn't theirs. Suppose that I suspect it's—I don't know—items that he or she borrowed . . ."

"Borrowed?" He sounded incredulous and cracked a smile. "In other words, hypothetically stole."

"Like I said, I'm not sure. Do I have an obligation to report my suspicions to the police?"

Frank thought for a few moments. "Well, it's not a crime to witness a crime. And it sounds as if we're not talking child abuse or murder, in which case you'd be obligated to report your suspicions. So no. You have no *legal* obligation to report a suspected theft unless you actually help the person get away with it. That's aiding and abetting, and you could be charged. But for just suspecting that it's stolen? That doesn't put you in jeopardy."

That was a relief. "What if I then help this client sell the stuff that I suspect may be stolen?"

"Then . . . well, now it gets more serious. You could be charged with fencing stolen property if the police have evidence that you knew it was stolen." He paused and looked at her. "What kind of value are we talking about? Hundreds of dollars or thousands?"

"Does it matter?"

"It matters. Emily, I don't like where this is going. Worst case it's a felony to be involved in the disposal of stolen goods worth two hundred fifty dollars or more. You could go to jail."

Going to jail was not among the goals Emily and Becca had scoped out for themselves when they'd started their business.

"Don't worry. I have no idea what it's worth or how he got it. So far, all I've done is look at some of the stuff."

"What kind of stuff is it?"

"Books. Doorknobs."

"Doorknobs?" Frank's face lit up.

"Boxes of them. You'd go nuts."

"Be careful not to remove anything. Taking possession—"

Emily cursed, remembering the document tube.

"You took something?" Frank said. He sounded astonished.

"I didn't mean to," Emily said. "I've got it in the car. I should run it back. I've got the key—" She tried to remember where she'd put the padlock key. She checked her pants pockets before remembering that it had fallen on Quinn's garage floor. Quinn had picked it up and dropped it in her gear bag. "I'll drive—"

"Drive? You get stopped, I doubt you'd pass a Breathalyzer."

"You can tell?"

"It's pretty obvious. Besides, it's late. No one's going to arrest you for holding on to it overnight."

Emily didn't need convincing. She was exhausted.

"And keep in mind," Frank added, "I'm being pretty cautious with my legal advice. If what's in that storage unit was acquired legally, you're good to go. If not, and it's worth a significant amount of money, you need to protect yourself. That's why you have insurance. And you also have free in-house counsel." Frank took another drink of coffee. "Thanks for this. I've got a few hours before I can turn in. You get in bed." He opened his computer. "When the auction's over, I'll come up and tuck you in."

UPSTAIRS, Emily peeled off her coffee-stained T-shirt and pants. She pulled on a nightgown and began to brush her teeth, thinking about the storage unit and its contents. There were plenty of reasons a man might not want his wife to know about his collections. She hoped that Mrs. Murphy's husband had acquired his treasures legitimately. But if he had, why keep them hidden?

She got in bed, trying not to notice her closet. Even more unsettling than a cluttered closet was one in the midst of becoming uncluttered. And speaking of unfinished business, she needed to alert Becca. She got out her phone and started typing a text:

Murphy's storage unit is complicated. Call if you're up.

She waited for the notification TEXT DELIVERED. But nothing came. Becca must have her phone turned off.

A text message pinged. Not Becca. Emily didn't recognize the number.

PAYPAL: Mission Accomplished! xxx ooo So what do you think? How soon? Please please please. Cheers!

That sounded like Quinn Newell. She must have deposited the advance payment into the Clutter Kickers account and kept right on drinking. This was not the start of a professional relationship. But what had she expected when she'd undoubtedly overshared?

Emily closed her eyes and tried to block out exactly how many gory details of her personal life she'd revealed.

"Here," Frank said from the doorway. He was carrying her favorite mug, gray with purple irises painted on. "Nonalcoholic."

The smell of hot cocoa wafted over. Emily set her phone on the bedside table. Frank hadn't made cocoa for her in ages.

He handed her the mug. "Drink. It will help you fall asleep."

Emily took a sip. Then another. Did cocoa really help you sleep? Or was it one of those things that people believed but turned out to be a canard? After all, wasn't chocolate loaded with caffeine? Or—

She stopped herself. Her brain was in overdrive, pinging from one inane thought to the next. She relaxed and inhaled. "Thank you. This is just what I needed," she said.

Frank picked up her cell phone. "Your battery's nearly dead. Want me to plug it in for you?"

"Thanks." She sank back into the pillows. "My charger's . . ." Where had she left it? "I think it's in my gear bag."

Frank kissed her on the top of her head, turned out the lights, and left the room.

She took one last sip and set the mug on the table and closed her eyes. Her phone's LOW BATTERY message flickered in her head. Plug herself in. That was what she needed to do. But she didn't have a plug, and the outlet was . . .

Chapter 5

Monday

IT SEEMED LIKE ONLY moments later the sun was shining in through the bedroom windows and Emily blinked awake. It was after nine, and Frank's side of the bed was rumpled but empty. She never slept this late. Her cell phone was on the bedside table, plugged in. She powered it on.

She tried to sit up but managed only to prop herself up on her elbows. It felt as if a fifty-pound weight shifted in her skull. She hadn't had a hangover this bad since college.

In the bathroom she knocked back aspirin and forced herself into the shower. Under the pulsing showerhead, her mind cleared.

She wrapped herself in a towel and padded out to her bureau. It still came as a surprise to find her underwear neatly rolled in the drawer. No more having to forage to find what she wanted. It might not spark joy, but it did spark serenity. Her foot was still too sore to lace it into a sneaker, so she put on her Crocs again.

When she got downstairs, she saw that Frank had gone to work. All she could stomach was weak tea. Frank's warning about the risks of handling stolen property made her anxious to get to the storage facility and return the tube. She took a can of WD-40 from under the kitchen sink for the lock and left the house. Fifteen minutes later she arrived at Inner Peace Storage.

She parked in front of Mrs. Murphy's unit and grabbed the document tube from under the passenger seat. Black mildew coated one end of the tube, and as Emily swiped it a few times against her pants leg, the plastic end cap came loose and fell on the car floor. She was putting the cap back on when she read the tube's handwritten label: "William Alexander Map of the Northeast."

Why not at least have a look at what was inside before she put it back? She slid the document out and smoothed it across the steering wheel. The paper was thick and slightly yellowed. "New France" was written in an elegant cursive hand across the topmost landmass. Below that, "New Scotland."

Emily was no expert, but it certainly looked old. With no tears, it was in pristine condition. She used her phone to Google the words on the label. Back came a link to an auction house that in 2012 had offered what looked like the identical map. According to the description, it was published in London in 1624. In "excellent condition" it had a value estimate of—Emily blinked—$12,000. If the map in front of her was worth that much and if it turned out to have been on permanent unofficial *loan*, she and Becca were catapulted into felony territory.

Carefully Emily rolled up the map and slipped it into the tube, anxious to put it back on the shelf where she'd found it. She got out of the car, feeling around in her gear bag for the storage-unit key. But when she went to use it, the padlock she distinctly remembered hanging on the door was gone. The padlock in its place was round, not square; brass, not silvery; and it had no nail-polish number painted on.

Someone had been here since yesterday and changed the lock.

What was she supposed to do now? She couldn't open the padlock and finish her inventory. Plus, she was now stuck in possession of a possibly antique map that could be worth thousands of dollars.

Emily got back in her car, banged the heel of her hand on the steering wheel, and called Becca.

"There you are!" Becca said. "I was just about to call you. What do you mean, it's 'complicated'?"

"I mean, it's possible the books in that unit are from libraries."

"Libraries," Becca said. "*Borrowed* from libraries?"

"Best case."

"Yikes."

"Exactly. At least I took a ton of pictures, so when we get back in, we should be able to tell if anything's—"

"Wait a minute. I thought you were already in."

"I was. Last night. But I couldn't get in again this morning. Someone's changed the lock. A security guard told me yesterday that he'd seen a woman going in and out of that unit."

"Mrs. Murphy?"

"Not likely. He thought it might have been me."

Silence from Becca. "Mrs. Murphy's going to have a fit. The sooner she knows, the better. Can you meet me over there?"

"You're done with family?"

"They'll survive an hour without me. I'll call Mrs. Murphy and tell her we need to see her right away. When we get back in there, we're going to need someone who knows their way around books to give us advice. Normally I'd call in a book dealer. But it sounds like we need an informal, confidential take on what we've gotten ourselves into. From someone we know. Personally."

Of course, Becca was suggesting Emily's mother. For years Lila Laubenstein had managed special collections for the library at Auburn Design School. She'd know how to handle the William Alexander map. How to tell if it was an original or a reproduction. She could also tell at a glance if repairs to Mr. Murphy's damaged books were even feasible and whether they were library copies.

As soon as Emily finished talking to Becca, she called her mother. Lila Laubenstein answered on the second ring with a bright "Hello, dear. Is everything all right?"

"We need your expertise," Emily said. "Becca and I."

"Of course you do." Emily heard her father's rumbling bass in the background. "It's Emmy," her mother said. Then, to Emily, "Your father says hello." More rumbling. "All right, all right. I'll take the phone outside." Back to Emily. "Your father's doing his crossword, and you know how he gets."

All too well. A creature of habit, Bert Laubenstein would be settled in his easy chair with his morning coffee, immersed in three newspapers' puzzles. Crosswords, sudokus, acrostics.

"There," Lila said a minute later. "I'm on the balcony. Which of my many areas of expertise are we talking about?"

"We're helping a woman deal with a collection she inherited from her husband. Some of the books and prints are in rough condition. Mold. Mildew. We're trying to figure out if they're salvageable and how many of them are library copies."

"That shouldn't be hard to tell. Libraries clearly mark their discarded books. Crooked book dealers know how to hide the evidence, but usually I can tell."

"That's why I called you. There's also a lot of documents. They're stored in tubes, and I think they're in good shape. One of them is a map. I Googled it and found one that looks the same. At auction it was estimated to bring twelve thousand dollars."

"Twelve *thousand?* No library would discard a twelve-thousand-dollar map. Did you look for a library stamp?"

Emily opened the tube and slipped the map out again. Sure enough, overlapping the lower right margin there was an oval stamped in black ink. Inside the oval it read PROPERTY OF BLAINE FREE LIBRARY. "Blaine Free Library," Emily said.

"The Blaine," Lila said. "That's in Maine. Let me get to my computer." Emily heard their balcony door slide open and shut. She imagined her mother crossing her living room to the guest bedroom that doubled as her office. A minute later, typing. Then, "Right. Private library set up in the thirties. A couple of Richardson buildings with a collection of fine books and prints."

"Google this. See if you can find what I did." Emily read her mother the label: "William Alexander Map of the Northeast."

Emily heard Lila's keyboard clicking. "That map . . . Oh, my." She was silent for a long time and then said, "It looks like it's a page from a four-volume collection of illustrated travel stories. *The Pilgrimage.* Published in 1625. I wouldn't be surprised if the one you found online realized a good deal more than twelve thousand dollars. Of course, the map's been reproduced, but if it's the real deal . . ." More clicking, then Lila said, "I'm in the Blaine catalogue. According to them, the book with that map is on their shelf."

"So the question is—" Emily began.

"—does theirs have a page missing. We'd have to go there and take a look."

"Of course. And that's just the first document I've looked at. There's dozens more. Will you come up and give us a hand?"

"Emmy, Boston's full of antiquarian book experts. I'm sure there are people who'd be happy to consult."

"You're as knowledgeable as anyone. And Mrs. Murphy will like you. She'll trust you."

"My eyesight's not what it used to be, and my back—"

"Hogwash. Admit it, you'd love to get in there and be the first to see what's what. You'll come, won't you?"

Lila laughed. "You know you had me at 'old books.' But I've got bridge this afternoon."

"Tomorrow, then. I'll make up the bed in the guest room."

"Please give Frank a heads-up. Tell him I'm looking forward to seeing him." She ended the call with her distinctive laugh.

"I WAS not expecting you ladies back so soon," Mrs. Murphy said an hour later. She seemed only mildly puzzled by Emily and Becca's unexpected visit.

Becca said, "We wanted you to know what we found in your husband's storage unit."

"Goodness. I hope nothing gruesome," Mrs. Murphy said with an uneasy laugh, "or embarrassing."

"Nothing like that," Becca said. She looked across at Emily.

"I got into the storage unit yesterday," Emily said. "It's packed with all kinds of stuff. Books. Prints. Doorknobs."

"Murph loved old hardware. His father was in construction. He used to talk about how when Big Charlie worked on an old house, he'd bring home thingamabobs, like doorknobs and hinges." Mrs. Murphy's eyes filled with tears. "I had no idea Murph kept any of it."

It sounded altogether plausible that Murph had moved his father's thingamabobs directly into storage. He certainly hadn't installed choice antique hardware in his own house. The pulls on the kitchen doors and cabinets were ordinary stainless steel.

"There's quite a collection of books," Emily said. "Climate control seems to have failed. Mold and moisture do a number on paper. But there's also document tubes, like this one." She showed Mrs. Murphy the one she'd taken. She opened it, slipped out the map, and unrolled it. "See, it's in excellent condition."

Mrs. Murphy looked perplexed. "I knew Murph had a thing about old books and maps. But I had no idea he collected them."

"The hardware won't be hard to sell," Emily said. "Folks who restore old buildings will be lining up to take it off your hands. Some of the books may be salvageable. And there may be significant value in the documents. But provenance is an issue."

"Provenance?" Mrs. Murphy sat forward, looking at Emily.

"How your husband acquired them. Who owned them before." Emily pointed at the library stamp in the map's lower margin. "That stamp. It's the Blaine Library's."

Mrs. Murphy's eyes widened. "In Portland?"

Emily nodded.

"Murph and I were there several times, if I remember correctly. He loved to visit libraries."

Emily hated what she had to say next, but plunged ahead. "The book that this map comes from is still listed in their collection."

Mrs. Murphy blinked. It took a few moments for the implication to dawn on her. "Surely he bought it from the library. Or from a reputable dealer. My husband would never . . ."

"This could be the only one like this," Emily said. "But I did also find a box full of bookplates and due-date cards that have been removed from library books."

Mrs. Murphy straightened. "Are you suggesting that my husband stole from libraries?"

"I'm saying that provenance is an issue," Emily said. "Maybe the books were discards. Maybe the map belongs to someone else and your husband was storing it. Figuring it all out will take time. Which brings us to another issue. When I tried to get back into the storage unit this morning, someone had changed the lock."

"Changed the lock?" Mrs. Murphy looked confused.

Becca said, "Do you have any idea who might have done that?"

"How in blue blazes would I know?" Mrs. Murphy shook her head. "I've never even been there. And now you tell me it's full of library books and stolen maps, and someone broke in."

"We're not sure any of it's stolen or that anyone broke in," Becca said, looking to Emily to continue.

Emily said, "The thing is, a security guard there told me that he's seen someone opening up the unit from time to time in the last few months. He said it was a woman."

Mrs. Murphy swallowed hard. "A woman? What are you suggesting? That my Charlie was a common thief? And on top of that, he was up to some kind of mischief with some . . . bimbo?"

"No one's suggesting—" Emily began.

"You most certainly are." After a frosty silence, Mrs. Murphy added, "He couldn't. He wouldn't."

"This must be confusing and upsetting." Becca gave Mrs. Murphy her most sympathetic smile. "It's possible, isn't it, that those books and prints aren't your husband's? Maybe he was storing someone else's things. A brother or sister—"

"Murph was an only child," Mrs. Murphy said.

Emily said, "Or someone he worked with?"

Mrs. Murphy looked stone-faced ahead. "He was retired." Her gaze turned angry, pinning Becca. "How do I know this lock business isn't just a cover for some kind of shenanigan? How do I know Charlie's things are even still in there?" Her chin quivered.

Emily was speechless. No one had ever doubted their integrity.

Becca said calmly, "I can see why you might think that. I can only assure you that we haven't taken anything and we haven't done anything that you didn't ask us to do. We're here now because we need to know what you'd like our next steps to be."

"What do I want you to do now?" Mrs. Murphy stood facing her husband's reclining recliner. "He could have explained. But unfortunately I can't ask him why he thought he needed books and maps. And why he needed to hide them from me. And why he canceled his doctor's appointment the day before he died. Said he had indigestion. Indigestion?" She dabbed at her eyes with a tissue. "This can't be happening. What am I supposed to do now?"

"Poor thing. My heart goes out to her," Becca said later as she and Emily stood on the sidewalk in front of Mrs. Murphy's house. "She's grieving. Stuck in denial for over a year. Anger comes next. I think she realizes that at some level all this rage is a step forward. Maybe that's why she didn't tell us to take a hike."

Emily opened her car door. She'd been surprised, too, that at the end of their meeting, Mrs. Murphy wanted to continue to work with them. She talked about returning anything in the storage unit that hadn't been acquired on the up-and-up. Before they'd left, Mrs. Murphy placed a call to Inner Peace Storage. She barely managed to explain the situation before breaking down again.

Becca had taken over. She told the manager that, by the way, climate control in the unit had failed some time ago. "There's mold and mildew. Very toxic. Disastrous for the valuable books and prints that were being stored there. Not exactly the conditions that your advertising promises." That sped up the discussion.

The manager had promised to investigate and arrange for a time when they could meet him there, as soon as possible, and he'd break open the unit. It might even be as soon as tomorrow.

Becca's gaze shifted to the Murphys' untidy front lawn. "No one expects to drop dead," she said. "Indigestion the day before? That was probably the start of a heart attack."

"Still," Emily said, "it would be nice if he'd cleaned up after himself before he checked out. He's left her with a big mess to figure out." She started to get into her car.

Becca looked at her watch. "I need to get back. But give me an update on our other new client. How'd it go? Tell me her husband doesn't collect doorknobs."

"He's a collector, all right," Emily said. "Vintage advertising. But what she wants to declutter is a garage filled with stuffed animals and forties furniture. When she married him, he wouldn't let her move her things into *his* house. Three years later she's ready to kiss them goodbye."

Becca blinked. "Sounds like she should kiss *him* goodbye."

"That thought occurred to me. But as you're fond of saying, we're not marriage counselors," Emily said.

"So you think the husband could be a problem."

The hole in the wall. Quinn's bruised face. "I think it was a big deal for her to call for our help. I'd rather be there when he's not."

"Sheesh," Becca said under her breath. "And I was so optimistic. Cleaning out a garage sounded like a tidy little project."

"Except for the load of emotions to unpack in the middle."

"That goes without saying. Though you'd think a storage unit would've been manageable. It's not even connected to a house." Becca shrugged at Mrs. Murphy's house, and Emily turned to look. The corner of a curtain in the front window dropped.

Chapter 6

AT HOME LATER THAT afternoon, Emily got to work on her closet, drilling holes for drywall anchors and installing brackets for shelving and rods. She took pictures as she went along. It was so satisfying at the end when she stood back and took in the results.

It took her an hour to put away her clothes. Summer clothes hung separate from winter. Tops hung above pants and skirts. When she was done, she went to her office to upload the pictures. She was finishing when she heard Frank come in. A few moments

later he was at her office door. "How's the trial going?" she asked.
"The trial. Right." A pause. "It hasn't started yet. What about
you? Did you return whatever you took from that storage unit?"

"I tried to, but someone changed the lock. And it turns out a
map I inadvertently took out of there could be worth thousands."

Frank's jaw dropped. "Thousands?"

"Mom thinks it's a page from a book. Possibly stolen from a library. So now, of course, I'm worried about what's in the rest of
those tubes. Mom's coming up to take a look. She'll be staying with
us for a few days, at least until we get this thing sorted."

Frank's usual response to one of her mother's impending visits
was a groan. Instead, he looked relieved. "Smart plan. She knows
all about old maps and libraries. And it will make her feel useful."

Before Emily could process his change of heart, their landline rang.
She went into the kitchen, where the answering machine kicked on
and her recorded voice played: "Sorry we can't take your call. You
know what to do." Then silence. Or, no, there was a sound. Breathing.

Then, "Emily? Are you there?" The quavery voice sounded familiar. "I need to talk to you. It's Wally. I—"

Frank watched from the doorway as Emily picked up the handset. "Quinn?" she said. "What is it?"

"Wally didn't come home last night. I didn't realize until I got up
this morning. I waited and I waited, and he still hasn't shown up. I
tried to call his cell. No answer. His office. He's not there."

Frank gave Emily a questioning look. She mouthed, *Mandarin
Cliffs.*

"Maybe the auction ran late and he decided to stay over," Emily
said. "Did you call the auction house?"

"I did. They told me last night's auction ended at six."

"Maybe something happened and he couldn't call you. Like a car
accident."

"That's what I thought. So I called every hospital I could find
between here and Hyannis. I was about to call the police when I
remembered what you and I talked about last night."

Last night. Emily felt her face flush.

"We were just kidding around, right?" Quinn went on.

Emily held the receiver away from her ear and stared at it. Quinn couldn't be serious. When she listened again, there was silence on the other end. Then, "Uh-oh."

"Uh-oh what?" Emily said.

"What?" Frank said.

"A police car just pulled up in front of my house." Quinn's voice was a whisper.

Emily put her hand over the mouthpiece. She told Frank, "Her husband didn't come home last night, and the police just pulled up in front of her house."

Frank asked, "What does she expect you to do about it?" at the same time as Quinn said, "Oh . . . my . . . God."

Emily shushed Frank. He moved alongside her, and she angled the receiver so he could hear.

"Two police officers." Quinn's voice was faint. "They're getting out of their cruiser. They're walking up to the door." A doorbell chimed. "Should I answer?" She didn't wait for Emily's response. "Go away, go away," Quinn whispered. "There's the bell again." A pause. "Now one of them's going around back."

Emily's heart was in her throat. The last thing she heard before the line went dead was what sounded like banging on a door.

Emily tried calling back, but the call went directly to voice mail.

Frank said, "So this is someone you met exactly once? Why is she calling you?"

Because they'd bonded? Because she'd shared her fantasy of what life would be like without her husband and then he'd disappeared?

"She sounds more than slightly neurotic," Frank said.

"Wouldn't you be upset? Her husband's missing, and the police show up on her doorstep?"

"Hysteria is not a good strategy when you're dealing with police. You want to help her? She shouldn't be alone."

Emily didn't need to be convinced—not with Quinn's *We were just kidding around, right?* echoing in her head. Quinn hadn't called her because Emily was her new best friend.

"I could go over there, but I'm not sure I'd be much help," Emily said. "I've never had to deal with the police."

Frank gave her a long, hard look. "Do you want me to come?"

Relief flooded through her. "Would you?"

"She needs to know that I can't represent her. I don't deal with police or missing husbands or—"

"But you'd know what to do if it comes to that. You could connect her with the right attorney." Emily grabbed her car keys.

"Let's get over there." Frank took the keys from Emily. "They're probably asking questions she shouldn't be answering."

EMILY hated it when Frank drove her car. Soon she was clutching the armrest as Frank accelerated down the street and ran a yellow light. Traffic was snarled, as usual, in the Square. Emily managed to text Quinn, saying she was on her way.

Once they were out of the Square, Frank put on another burst of speed. The car swerved around a corner and into Mandarin Cliffs and slowed as Emily directed him to Quinn's house.

No police cars were parked out front.

"They must have come and gone," Frank said, getting out of the car. He gazed across at the house. "This is quite a heap. Hope he got her to sign a prenup."

"Are you here to help or to snark?" Emily asked, getting out of the car. She started across the perfectly manicured front lawn. When she reached the front door, she rang the bell. "Quinn!"

When there was no answer, she turned to tell Frank that she was going to go around back. That's when she realized Frank was still at the curb, crouched behind her car and examining . . . something. She returned to see what. A broken taillight.

He squinted across at her. "You back into something?"

"Not that I remember."

"Then it looks like something backed into—"

"Emily?" They both turned around at the querulous voice. Quinn stood at the front door, holding the calico cat.

"What's her name again?" Frank said under his breath as they approached the house.

"Newell," Emily whispered back. "Quinn Newell."

Close up, Emily could see that Quinn looked exhausted. The

bruise was slightly faded but still livid. Her yoga pants and top might have been the same ones she'd been wearing Sunday night.

"What happened?" Emily said. "Where are the police?"

Quinn just stood there, staring at Frank. "Who is this?"

"My husband," Emily said.

"This is Frank?" Quinn seemed surprised.

"Huh?" Frank said, and shot Emily a questioning look.

"Don't freak," Quinn told him. "Emily and I talked about you. I just imagined . . . well, something different. Never mind."

Emily felt the prick of embarrassment. She couldn't remember exactly what she'd told Quinn about Frank.

"Frank Harlow," Frank said, flashing his smile. "Emily thought you might need legal advice." He offered Quinn his hand.

"Legal advice," Quinn said, eyeing his hand but not shaking it.

"Dealing with the police and all," Frank said. "Not something most of us do every day. I'm sorry to hear about your husband."

"He's missing. Not dead." Quinn shifted her gaze to Emily as she nuzzled the cat. "Right?" The cat squirmed from her arms, dropped on all four feet, and slinked back into the house.

"You still haven't heard from him?" Emily said.

Quinn shook her head.

"Emily asked if I'd come along to see if I could help," Frank said. That wasn't exactly how it had happened, but she let it pass.

Quinn gazed down at Frank's still extended hand. She shook it. "I'm sorry. I must seem rude and ungrateful. I'm just so upset by all this. I really appreciate both of you coming. Come in." She led them into the house and through to the kitchen. "Coffee?"

Coffee? It was just the kind of thing women did, offered a refreshment to guests when life had been upended. Emily was about to say no thanks when Frank said, "Sure. That'd be great."

Quinn pulled out the refrigerator's freezer drawer, got out a bag of coffee, and kicked the drawer shut. Hands shaking, she tried to scoop a measure of coffee into the top of the gleaming espresso machine, but a cascade of beans flooded the counter. She slammed the bag on the counter, scattering more beans.

Emily put her arm around Quinn. "You don't have to play hostess," she said. She felt Quinn go limp against her as Frank gathered the beans on the counter and scraped them back into the bag.

"Sit," Emily said, pulling out a stool from under the counter. "Tell us what happened."

Quinn perched on the stool, looking spent. Emily noticed a business card on the counter. EAST HARTWELL POLICE DEPARTMENT. From a lieutenant detective.

"There were two police officers," Quinn said.

"So you had reported your husband missing?" Frank asked.

"No. I was going to. And then they just showed up. They were looking for Wally, too. They said they were investigating a car accident. Last night." Quinn choked up. "No one was hurt, but it was a hit-and-run. I explained to them that he went to an auction yesterday and didn't come home. They wanted to see his car, but I told them it wasn't here. They asked if they could look in the garage."

"And?" Frank asked.

"What was I supposed to do?" Quinn said, straightening and scowling at Frank. "Tell them to get lost? The car's not here, so why not let them look? I didn't want them to think I was lying."

"It's a felony to lie to the police, but they can lie to you," Frank said. "They make things up to get you to reveal—"

"You *don't* think they came here to investigate a hit-and-run?"

"I believe that's the reason they gave you, but I have no idea what they really came for, and neither do you," Frank said. "Which is why we often advise people not to say anything."

"Well, I didn't have your sage advice. I told them the truth. Wally's car's not here. He didn't come home last night. I told them I hadn't reported him missing because"—she picked at a loose thread in her leggings—"well, because he sometimes gets back very late. I told them I was about to call the police when they showed up." Her voice turned shrill. "And that's the truth."

"All right, all right." Frank put up his hands. "You don't need to convince me. What else did they say?"

"That someone would get back to me."

"You can count on that. Take my advice," Frank said, his voice bullying. "When they come back asking questions, don't talk to them alone. Call a friend or, better still, an attorney. Because—"

A tear trickled down Quinn's cheek.

"Enough!" Emily said. "Can't you see she's upset enough without your haranguing her?" She turned to Quinn. "You have to excuse Frank. He spent time working as a public defender. He views the justice system as lose-lose for the average citizen."

A phone rang, a marimba playing a minor scale. It wasn't Emily's—her ringtone was crickets. Quinn slipped from her stool and picked up a cell phone from the counter. She glanced at the readout. Swallowed. "It's them again. East Hartwell PD."

Quinn put the phone to her ear. "Hello?" A pause. "Yes, that's me." A longer pause as she turned to face the wall. "Uh-huh. Okay . . . um-hmm . . ." She carried the phone into the next room.

"I'm sorry if I came on too strong," Frank said to Emily. "She needs to know what she's up against."

"You can't blame her for being upset."

"I get that. I'm not sure she understands how the real world—" Frank broke off when Quinn came back into the kitchen.

She was clutching the phone, and she'd gone even paler. "They found Wally's car."

Frank looked stunned. "Just his car?" he asked Quinn. Emily winced. Frank could be colossally insensitive.

"They found it," Quinn said, "in the commuter parking lot at the town wharf. They're going to start looking for him." She sounded like an automaton. "They want me to bring them—" She clasped her hand over her mouth and took a moment, then swallowed. "They want a photograph and something with his scent."

"Maybe something he recently wore?" Emily suggested.

"Yes. That would be the thing." But Quinn stood there, frozen.

"And a recent photo?" Frank tipped his head toward Emily.

"Upstairs?" Emily said. "Or maybe in his office?"

Emily followed as Quinn drifted out of the kitchen to a study in the back of the house. This had to be Wally's man cave. The Chesterfield sofa was leather. Overhead lighting was hidden in a red-glass hanging dome with BUDWEISER written in gold letters. A flat-screen TV hung on one wall, while the other walls were hung with framed magazine covers. *MAD. National Lampoon. Creepy.*

Quinn picked up a framed photo from the corner of a sleek modern desk. The picture looked like a selfie of Quinn and her husband standing on a beach with waves breaking in the background. Quinn stared at the photo, inhaling a ragged breath, then removed the back of the frame and handed the snapshot to Emily.

So this was Walter. He had dense dark hair that curled around his face, a mustache, and a goatee. He squinted at the camera and grinned. Quinn, tucked into his side, rested her head on his chest.

"I need to explain," Quinn said, turning to face Emily. "I didn't, you know, *mean* any of those things I said the other night. Because I'd never. Ever. You didn't think—"

"Of course not. It was the wine. I said things I didn't mean, either. We were just being . . ." Emily searched for the right word. *Silly* wasn't quite right. Because how silly was it to dream up ways to get rid of your husband?

Quinn didn't wait for Emily to finish the thought. "Okay, great. I just wanted to be sure we're on the same page here. Because if something terrible has happened to Wally, I wouldn't want you to think—" Quinn gave Emily a long, hard look.

"It was just talk," Emily said. "Right?"

"And it was just between us."

Emily got it. Quinn didn't want her sharing what they'd talked about with the police. "Right."

Quinn gave a weak smile. "That's what I knew you'd say, but I had to ask. And I didn't want to ask in front of Fred."

"Frank."

"Whatever."

Emily followed Quinn upstairs to the master suite. It was enormous, of course. The bed was unmade, piled high with pillows.

Quinn entered a walk-in closet, though *closet* was a misnomer. You could have moved a twin bed and a bureau in there and called it a bedroom. Emily stared in awe at the neatly organized racks of men's shoes. High-top black sneakers. Cordovan oxfords. Walter probably had more pairs of shoes than Emily had socks.

Quinn tilted open a built-in clothes hamper. "Something with his scent," she said, sifting through laundry. She lifted an undershirt from the basket. "This should work."

Emily followed her back downstairs. In the kitchen, Quinn slid her husband's undershirt into a large freezer bag. She added the photograph and zipped the bag shut.

"Please, take my advice," Frank said. "Don't be alone when you talk to the police. You don't know what their agenda is."

"Their agenda," Quinn said, "is to find Wally."

"Right now that seems likely," Frank said, annoyed. "But it's smart to have someone with you. How could it hurt?"

Quinn looked at him. "Who would that someone be? You?"

Frank said, "I can. If you like. But—"

Quinn said, "Emily? Could you come with me?"

"You'd be better off with an attorney," Emily said.

"I'm better off with a *trusted* friend," Quinn shot back.

"You okay going with her?" Frank said as he stood with Emily in front of the house, waiting for Quinn to back her car out of the garage. "Because you seem, I don't know, distracted."

Freaked out was more like it. She barely knew Quinn, but in the short time they'd spent together, she'd felt a connection. Emily said, "She needs someone for emotional support."

Frank put his arm around her. "You're a good person. Promise me you'll call if things get weird. And remember, she doesn't have to answer any questions. Keep reminding her of that."

Emily eased herself free of his arm. The garage door opened, and a car engine turned over. Red taillights came into view.

Emily stood behind her own car, waiting for Quinn to pull up alongside. Frank touched her car's broken taillight. She was surprised that she hadn't noticed that before. And it wasn't just a broken taillight; there was also a dent on the rear bumper and a stain. She touched it, and dried flakes came off on her fingertips. She sniffed. It had a coffee smell.

Frank took one look at Quinn's Miata and rolled his eyes at Emily. As if he were in any position to comment on someone else's sports car. He opened the passenger door, and Emily got in. Then Quinn accelerated out of there.

Quinn drove up the street, past the entrance to Mandarin Cliffs. Before she pulled onto the main street, she turned to Emily. "If they ask where we were last night, I was with you."

"Of course. You were."

"From six on. You didn't leave until late."

Emily gave Quinn a sideways look. Quinn was gripping the steering wheel, tendons strained in her neck.

Quinn added, "Because we're in this together."

In what together? Emily's seat belt tightened, cutting into her neck. She shifted her position, working it loose.

"And just so you know," Quinn said, "I talked to Wally yesterday before I talked to your partner. He said he'd be home late and—" She choked up. "All I could think was that at long last I had a window of opportunity, so I called you guys. I thought . . ."

Quinn went on, her voice rising, but Emily wasn't listening. Walter Newell hadn't come home last night, but his car had been involved in a hit-and-run. Emily's car had been struck by a hit-and-run driver. Seemed like an odd coincidence.

Chapter 7

THE EAST HARTWELL police station dominated one corner of a busy intersection opposite a brightly lit Burger King. Emily's stomach rumbled as the smell of burgers and fries wafted over. It was past dinnertime, and she hadn't eaten.

The sky was black. The parking lot, in contrast, was brightly lit. Quinn pulled into a visitor parking spot and sat, her knuckles white. She gave Emily a tight smile before getting out of the car.

The police station looked old, its granite steps worn smooth.

Emily followed Quinn inside. The interior featured white walls, harshly lit by overhead fluorescent lighting.

A uniformed officer sat at a desk behind the counter.

Quinn inhaled deeply and approached him. "Sir?"

"Ma'am." The officer took in both of them.

"We're here to see Sergeant . . ." Quinn rummaged through her purse. She came up with a scrap of paper. "Stanley."

"And you are?"

"Quinn Newell."

"And Emily Harlow," Emily said.

"IDs, please."

Quinn fished out her driver's license and handed it to him. Emily did the same. The officer picked up the phone and spoke into the handset. He hung up and rotated a ledger book toward them. After Emily and Quinn signed, he gave them each a blank name tag. They wrote their names and pressed on the labels.

"Ladies." The deep voice came from a police officer who'd entered from behind the desk officer. "Mrs. Newell?"

"That's me," Quinn said in a whispery soft voice. She seemed to shrink under the short, stocky uniformed officer's gaze.

"And?" He tilted his head in Emily's direction.

"Emily Harlow," Emily said, hoping she sounded confident.

"Sergeant Brian Stanley," the officer said with a nod to Quinn. "I spoke with you on the phone."

"You found my husband's car? And asked me to bring these." Quinn offered him the bag with the photo and the undershirt.

He glanced at the bag and then handed it to the desk officer. Then he raised the hinged end of the countertop and ushered them through. "We have the car downstairs," he said. Quinn shot Emily a tense look. "Let's go take a look."

Emily hooked Quinn's arm and followed Stanley down two flights of stairs. The basement was a vast parking garage. Their footsteps echoed on the concrete as they continued past parked police cruisers, SUVs, and vans. Past taped-off boundaries surrounding cars that surely hadn't come in under their own steam.

In the farthest corner of the basement garage sat a silver Audi.

The car was barely damaged. The passenger-side headlight was cracked and the front fender scraped. There were no plates.

"Oh," Quinn said, dropping Emily's arm. "That looks like his car."

"It was left overnight in the parking lot at the town wharf," Stanley said. "That lot empties out after the trains stop running. It matches a car that was reported involved in a hit-and-run."

"Was there . . . Did you find . . ." Quinn began. "My husband didn't come home last night. I've been so worried."

"That's the only damage," Stanley said, pointing to the front. "We were hoping you could confirm that it's your husband's."

"May I look inside?" Quinn asked.

Stanley said, "Go ahead. But please don't touch anything."

Stanley lifted the tape barrier, and Quinn slipped under it. Stanley followed. He snapped on a latex glove and opened the driver's-side door. Quinn looked inside. Past her, Emily could see that the upholstery in the car was black leather.

Quinn bit her knuckle and started to cry. "It's his," she rasped.

"I'm sorry, ma'am. We'll find him," Stanley said. He closed the car door and raised the tape for Quinn to step out.

A blue tarp was spread on the floor next to the car. On it was a flashlight and a snow scraper. A pile of papers with an Audi owner's guide. And a pair of aviator glasses with yellow lenses.

Could this have been the car she'd parked in front of at the coffee shop last night? It might have been a silver Audi. She'd been distracted by the spilled coffee. All she remembered clearly was a mustache and a cropped beard, along with a baseball cap and yellow tinted aviator glasses, like the ones lying on the tarp.

"Mrs. Newell, when did you last see your husband?" Stanley asked.

Quinn was standing beside Emily again. She grabbed Emily's hand and squeezed. "Yesterday. He left the house at around noon. Or maybe one. I wasn't paying attention. I knew he'd been looking at an auction listing and planned to bid on some of the items."

Stanley slipped a pad from his pocket and jotted a note.

"Later he texted me to say he'd be back late and not to wait up." Quinn rummaged in her purse for her phone. She thumbed through, then turned the screen to face Stanley. "Here's his text."

"Do you mind?" Stanley said, taking the phone from her. He used his own phone to take a picture of her screen. "And he sent this text to you from the auction? Where was the auction?"

"Somewhere down the Cape."

"Hyannis," Emily piped up, remembering Quinn telling her that.

"Right. That's it," Quinn said, seeming flustered. "Stone Mills Auction Gallery. I called them. They couldn't tell me a thing."

"After he texted, what did you do?" Stanley said as he wrote.

"Nothing. I stayed home."

"Is there anyone who can vouch for you?"

Quinn pointed to Emily.

Emily said, "Right. We were together."

Stanley looked at Emily as if registering her presence for the first time. Eyed her name badge. "Miss Harlow?"

"Mrs." Emily was glad that she was married to a lawyer who'd prepared her for this interrogation. "I'm a professional organizer."

Quinn added, "She's helping me downsize."

"And you arrived at what time?" Stanley asked.

Emily looked at Quinn. "Around six?"

"Right," Quinn said. "I called her when I knew Wally would be tied up."

That caught Stanley's attention. "And why was that?" he said.

"You don't need to answer—" Emily began, but Quinn plowed ahead with, "He doesn't like strangers in the house. I wanted her to come when he wasn't there." Her look challenged Stanley to question that.

Stanley gazed at Emily. "And you stayed until when?"

Quinn answered. "I turned on the TV after she left, and the ten-o'clock news was on."

Emily squirmed. If she had left Quinn's house that late, the coffee shop would have been closed by the time she got there.

"And you got home at . . ." Stanley looked at Emily.

"I didn't notice the time." That was the truth. "It had to have been past ten. I live in East Hartwell. It's a short drive."

Stanley nodded. "So you ladies were there together for, what, four hours? From six until after ten? Then what?"

"I watched the news, then went to sleep," Quinn said.

Stanley narrowed his eyes at Quinn. "You didn't feel like you needed to stay awake? Wait for your husband to come back?"

Quinn took a step back. "Not really. He told me not to wait up. I thought he'd gone out with his buddies after the auction. He does that sometimes. To celebrate. Especially if he makes a kill." Stanley gave her a surprised look. "That's what he calls it when he scores a good buy."

"Well, here's what I'm trying to work out," Stanley said. "Our dispatch gets a call Sunday night at nine fifty-five. Hit-and-run in the Square. The description of the car matches your husband's, and this car has the dent to prove it.

"But that night, traffic was tied up coming back from the Cape. Summer Sunday. Accident on the Bourne Bridge and another one on the Sagamore. Hyannis to Boston, no matter what route you took, would have taken at least three and a half hours. He'd have to have left Hyannis by six thirty in order to be back here by ten."

Quinn stood there blinking. "All I know is, he said he'd be late. Don't wait up." She shook her phone at him. "You saw his text."

"You watched the ten-o'clock news? What station?"

"I . . . I wasn't paying attention," Quinn said.

Stanley came back at Quinn, challenging her to remember what had been on the newscast, but Emily barely listened. What had she and Quinn talked about the night before? Exactly how much wine had they each had to drink?

"Seriously?" Stanley stood there calmly, staring at Quinn. Quinn had gone rigid with rage. "What did you think when you got up the next morning and your husband wasn't there?"

"I sleep late," she said. "All right? He's usually up. When he wasn't downstairs and his car wasn't there, I assumed he'd gone to work. I didn't realize he was missing until I tried to reach him at work and they told me he hadn't come in."

Stanley's gaze shifted from Quinn to Emily and back to Quinn. "So let me repeat the timeline back to you." He looked down at his notes. "From six o'clock on, you two ladies were together. You left at around ten?" He looked to Emily for confirmation.

Any minute he'd drill down and ask Emily exactly where she'd gone after she left Quinn's house. She couldn't pretend that she hadn't stopped in the Square for coffee or that her unpleasant encounter with a man who could have been Walter Newell hadn't happened. She tried to imagine Frank's advice—beyond *Don't lie,* probably something on the order of *Pull a Hail Mary.*

Instead of answering Stanley's question, Emily said, "I'm really sorry. I desperately need to use the ladies' room. Do you mind? Just tell me where it is and I'll come right back."

Quinn shot her a terrified look that said, *Don't leave me alone.*

Stanley looked annoyed. "Up one flight. Turn right. Down the corridor. Why don't you meet us in the lobby when you're done."

Emily resisted the urge to break into a run as she made her way to the stairwell. She felt guilty about leaving Quinn alone with Stanley, but she had to get out of there before she found herself in his crosshairs.

EMILY checked under the doors to the two stalls in the women's room. No feet. She took out her phone. It was nearly ten o'clock. She called Frank. *Pick up, pick up, pick up.*

He answered on the fourth ring. "Where are you?" he said.

"I'm still at the police station. I need—" Emily froze at the sound of footsteps in the hall.

"Emily, if they—"

"Shhh. Stop. Just listen." Emily cupped her hand over the phone and lowered her voice. "Quinn's husband's car. It was in a hit-and-run at about ten o'clock last night in the Square."

"Isn't that where you . . ." Frank said. "Wait a minute. Are you saying he's the jerk you spilled coffee on at the coffee shop?"

"He spilled coffee on me," Emily corrected. "Quite a coincidence, huh?"

"Maybe." A long pause. "Or maybe not. What if he was in the house? Heard you take my call and knew where you were going?"

Maybe that creaking she'd heard from overhead wasn't the cat. If Walter had been upstairs listening to Emily and Quinn bitch about their husbands, he'd have been truly pissed. "Do I tell the police that I went to the coffee shop after I left Quinn's house?"

Frank didn't answer right away. "Did you tell the police that you *didn't* stop for coffee?"

"I said I went home. I didn't mention the coffee stop."

Silence on the other end.

Emily knew Frank was analyzing and weighing the options. But she needed an answer. What if Stanley came back at her with more questions? "If I don't tell them now and they find out later, won't that be worse?"

"Emmy, stop acting like you're guilty. You didn't do anything. You haven't lied. You've just—"

"Withheld information that I know could be pertinent."

"Really? They already know his car was in the Square, because someone reported the hit-and-run. What does it add to their investigation? Unless . . ."

"Unless what?"

"Unless it's your car that he hit."

Emily shuddered, remembering when the man had locked eyes with hers from outside and pitched his coffee cup at her car. How his tires had screeched as he drove off. "What if he did? And what happens when the police discover my car? My taillight."

"Easily fixed. I'll take care of it. I know a guy who owes me." Frank's voice sounded so reassuring. "Emmy, you know as well as I do that you had absolutely nothing to do with this man's disappearance. So why waste the detective's time?"

"What if I saw something that could help the police find him?"

"Emmy, for once think about what's in your own best interest." Frank sounded exasperated. "It will only open up a can of worms if . . . well, if, worst-case, that woman's husband never comes home and she says something that makes them suspect that you had something to do with his disappearance."

Emily swallowed hard. "Why would they think that?"

"Do I need to spell it out? He spills his coffee on you. Dents your car. Anyone would be ticked off."

"But I'd never—"

"I know normally you'd never. But you were drunk. I'm not saying that's what happened. Just showing you what can happen when you go offering information to the police. Promise me you won't go back and spill your guts to that officer. They'll hold you for questioning, and who knows what will happen after that."

LATER, as Emily and Quinn sat in Quinn's Miata in the police station parking lot, Quinn said, "Thanks for being here, Emmy."

Emmy? Only family called her that. Emily was somehow both annoyed and flattered by the familiarity of it. "Sorry I had to leave you alone with that detective," Emily said.

"I'm sure you had your reasons." Quinn closed her eyes in a long blink. "I can't believe this is happening. The parking lot where the police found Wally's car, do you know where it is?"

"The town landing?" Sure, Emily knew. Every fall, they held a neighborhood yard sale there that Frank never missed.

"Is it far?"

"A mile, maybe a mile and a half."

Quinn faced Emily. "Would you mind terribly," she said, using a little-girl voice, "if we stopped there on the way back? I need to see the place. *Feel* it. Does that sound crazy?" The wince Emily felt must have shown, because Quinn went on. "I know. You're probably desperate to get home. Last favor, I promise." Wasn't it enough that Emily hadn't contradicted the half-truths Quinn had sold the police? "I know you probably just want to get rid of me."

Quinn didn't wait for Emily's answer. She started the car and pulled out of the parking lot. "It's this way, right? You'll tell me where to turn, won't you?"

Ridding herself of Quinn really was difficult. But the landing *was* on the way back. Just a quick detour. Emily texted Frank to let him know she'd be another twenty minutes. She was about to put the phone away when it chirped. Becca. They'd reached the side street that led down to the boat basin and the light-rail station.

"Turn here," Emily said, and let Becca's call go to voice mail.

The commuter lot was half empty. Quinn parked and got out.

Emily remained in the car and listened to Becca's message. "Can you meet me and Mrs. Murphy at the storage place tomorrow morning at ten? They're going to break open the unit for her."

Emily texted back a quick okay and sent a second message, to her mother, asking if she'd be able to drive up early the next day. Then she got out of the car and joined Quinn under a streetlight at a railing that separated the parking area from the river.

A stiff breeze whipped Quinn's dark hair away from her face as she stared past the deep shadows into the inky darkness beyond the water's edge. Across the river on the opposite bank, Emily recognized the warren of storage units with saffron-colored doors that were lit up a short distance downstream. Inner Peace Storage.

Quinn said, "I thought I'd feel him here. But I don't." She scanned the lot. "Where do you think they found his car?"

Emily followed Quinn through the lot, from one pool of light to the next, and onto the boat ramp at the far end. There was no lighting there, and it took a few moments for Emily's eyes to adjust. Boats and kayaks were lined up nearby.

Quinn ventured down the boat ramp. The sky was dark. No moon. Quinn picked up a pebble and overhanded it into the water. Bits of light glinted where it splashed down. Quinn was reaching for another pebble when Emily noticed a white card caught in the weeds. It was blank except for a large 37 printed in bold type. It could have been a bidder card. Walter Newell had been to an auction.

"Quinn," Emily said, pointing to the card. "Do you see that?"

It took Quinn a moment to spot what Emily was pointing to. She reached for the card and plucked it from the weeds. "Oh, my God," she said as she stared at it. Turned it over and over. Then held it to her chest and started to sob. Emily stood beside her, feeling helpless. She didn't even have a Kleenex on her to offer.

Quinn let Emily walk her to a bench. Quinn wiped away tears with the heel of her hand. Water lapped against the shore.

As they sat there, Quinn talked about Wally. How they'd met at a ball game. Their over-the-top wedding, paid for by the groom's wealthy family. Their honeymoon, a Caribbean cruise.

Quinn's first inkling that this might not be the union she'd dreamed of was when Wally had spent hours in the ship's casino, gambling and drinking. When the honeymoon ended and she moved into his house, he wouldn't let her move in anything but her clothes and toiletries. She'd told herself he'd loosen up, but three years later he'd only become more controlling.

"Every once in a while I'd bring something into the house, just to see if he noticed. He did. Every damned time." Quinn bit the words off. "It's like my stuff was contaminated."

Emily felt a twinge of guilt. In her marriage, she played the spouse trying to keep her partner's beloved junk from invading their mutual living spaces. But surely she was nowhere near as toxic about it as Walter Newell had been.

IT WAS late when Quinn dropped Emily at her house. On the kitchen counter, Frank had left her a note: "Getting your car fixed. Pizza in the fridge."

Thank you, thank you, she said to herself. For the car. For the pizza. She warmed the slices he'd left her. As the microwave hummed, the kitchen filled with the irresistible smell. Standing at the sink, she wolfed down a slice.

The house felt empty. Emily went upstairs and changed into a cotton nightgown, opened the windows as wide as possible, and turned on the TV. Red Sox and Dodgers were tied at 1–1.

Usually a televised baseball game put her right to sleep. But tonight she kept listening for Frank. Thinking about Quinn *not* staying up and waiting for Wally to come home the night before.

It felt as if it had been days ago that she'd hurried to Inner Peace Storage to return that map, only to find herself locked out. Could it have been only earlier today that she and Becca had given Mrs. Murphy the disquieting news that someone had changed the lock? And once that fire had been put out, Quinn had called with the news that the police were on her doorstep.

At least Frank was getting Emily's car fixed. A manager would break open the storage unit tomorrow. And her mother was coming to give her expert opinion of exactly what Mr. Murphy had been up to with his so-called collecting.

But for every question that was being resolved, Emily had another that remained a mystery.

Chapter 8

Tuesday

BY THE TIME EMILY GOT UP on Tuesday morning, the temperature was already in the eighties. Too bad a meeting with the manager of Inner Peace Storage required a work uniform. She ironed pants and a matching polo shirt. Her foot felt better, but it seemed wiser to stick with Crocs for one more day.

When she got downstairs, it was nearly nine. Lila was already there, sitting at the kitchen table across from Frank, each of them reading a section of the paper and holding it up like a barrier. Lila's rolling suitcase and purse sat on the floor by the back door. In the month since Emily had last seen her, her mother had dyed her hair red and cut it short and spiky. As she'd told Emily, the problem with getting older was that women over sixty were treated as if they were invisible. At sixty-five, between the hair and a silk caftan in swirling shades of pink and purple, Lila showed the world just how determined she was not to disappear.

"You made it," Emily said, giving her mother an air kiss. "How was traffic?"

"I left at six." Lila got up and poured Emily a cup of coffee.

"And?" Emily took the cup and sipped.

"Just the usual congestion crossing the bridge."

Which meant—Emily glanced at the kitchen clock—Lila had probably been here for at least an hour. Alone. With Frank.

"Your car's back." Frank put down the paper, rising to his feet.

"Your car?" Lila said.

Emily and Lila followed Frank out to the curb where her car was parked. Emily walked all the way around it. The rear taillight had been replaced, the dent in the back erased, the spill washed away.

Good as new. You'd have to get out a magnifying glass to see—

"Oh, dear," Lila said. "What happened?"

"Where?" Frank said.

"There," Lila said, pointing at the back of the car. Spot-on. "It's obvious, isn't it?" She ran her hand over the offending area. "There's a dimple. And the paint's thicker here. Plus, one taillight's a lot cleaner than the other." She looked at Emily over the top of her rhinestone-rimmed glasses. "Might not be as noticeable if you got your car washed occasionally, dear."

Emily exchanged eye rolls with Frank. "A few dents add to the charm of an old car, don't you think?" she said.

"What I think," Lila said, "is that an amateur repair makes you look like you don't care." Lila looked up as thunder rumbled. "We're going to need umbrellas."

"I've got umbrellas in the trunk." Of course Emily knew where the car had been damaged, but would she have noticed if she didn't? Probably not. Which was the difference between Emily and her mother. That was why Lila had been good at her job and why Emily wanted her to have a look at Mr. Murphy's collection.

Emily checked her watch. "We should get going soon. We need to be at the storage place in thirty minutes."

WHILE Emily drove, her mother *tsk*ed her way through the pictures of the storage unit that Emily had on her cell phone. "This is going to be painful. The condition of those books." She shook her head. "And what about those tubes?"

"That one I talked to you about? It's in the back." Emily pointed over her shoulder. "See what you think."

Lila turned in her seat and reached for the tube. She examined the label. "I should probably be wearing gloves."

"In the back seat, too. In the bag that's on the floor."

Lila hauled the bag forward and rummaged around. "What's this?" she asked, showing Emily the baby-blue stun gun.

"It's a stun gun. Frank got it for me to carry for self-defense."

Lila examined the stun gun. "Looks dead to me. If you're going to carry one, you should at least keep it charged."

How did she even know? "Just put it in the bag," Emily said.

Lila rummaged around some more in Emily's bag until she found a pair of latex gloves. She put them on, then popped the lid off one end of the tube and upended it. The map slid out.

Lila gently flattened the paper across her lap. "New France, New Scotland." She whispered the words like an incantation.

"Do you think it's original?" Emily asked.

"I'd need to look at it with a magnifier, but the paper seems right. Of course, it could be giclée."

"What's that?"

"A really fine print copy. Digital technology so good it can fool an expert. But this appears to have been printed from a plate." Lila held the map up to the light. "It's been removed from a book. See how this edge is rough, where the others are sharp?"

"I'll take your word for it," Emily said as she drove past the turn-off for the town wharf. "You're saying it's been torn out?"

"Carefully. By someone who knew what they were doing." Lila held up the map. "This is a beauty. Really old. Historically signifi-cant. You can see why someone would want it." She sighed. "And the Blaine doesn't even know they're missing it."

BECCA and Mrs. Murphy were at the storage unit when Emily and Lila pulled up. Before getting out, Emily slid the map into its tube. As soon as the storage bin was open, she'd put it back.

Mrs. Murphy narrowed her eyes as they approached, and Em-ily wondered if she thought Lila might have been the woman the security guard had recently seen going in and out of her husband's storage unit. She looked puzzled when Lila hugged Becca.

"Mrs. Murphy, this is Lila Laubenstein," Emily said. "She's my mother, and she knows everything there is to know about books and prints."

"Your mother?" Mrs. Murphy's face relaxed into a smile. She shook Lila's hand. As different as they looked—Mrs. Murphy all in black like an Italian widow, her white hair and unvarnished face accepting her age; Lila in bright plumage, fighting it all the way—Emily realized that they were about the same vintage.

"My mother was a librarian," Emily said.

"*Is* a librarian," Lila said. She smiled at Mrs. Murphy. "You can take the girl out of the library, but it's not something you stop being, even after you've retired, and I haven't been retired all that long. I worked in special collections."

"Really?" Mrs. Murphy asked. "Where?"

"The Auburn Design School. It's in—"

"I know where it is," Mrs. Murphy said. "Murph and I visited. Beautiful Kahn building."

Lila's face lit up. "One of his first truly modern designs."

"We visited about every library he designed," Mrs. Murphy went on. "Murph used to say—" Her voice broke.

"I'm sorry," Lila said. "Really I am."

Mrs. Murphy gave a wan smile. "I think my husband would have liked to be an architect. Unfortunately, he grew up in a family that didn't nourish artistic talent. He made a good living as a dentist. But it was a job, not a passion."

Lila asked, "I wonder, have you gotten to the Blaine?"

Emily's ears pricked up.

But before Mrs. Murphy could answer, a security cart pulled up and a man got out. Not the security guard Emily had spoken with before—this man was young and looked bored. He wore a saffron-colored golf shirt with a name badge that read MANAGER. From the floor of the cart, he picked up a clipboard. "Ruth Murphy?"

"That's me," Mrs. Murphy said.

"Ma'am. Can I see some identification?"

Mrs. Murphy showed her driver's license to the manager.

"Thank you. I need your signature, authorizing us to remove the lock." He gave her the clipboard and a pen. Mrs. Murphy signed.

The manager tossed the clipboard onto the cart's seat and lifted an enormous bolt cutter from the back. He approached the unit's closed door, bent over, and angled the bolt cutter so it hooked the shackle. Then he set his feet apart and grunted as he pressed the handles together. There was a loud crunch as the metal caved. He wiggled the bolt cutter free, unhooked the shackle, and opened the hasp.

Emily held her breath as he reached for the door handle. He raised the overhead door, reached inside, and flipped on the light.

She had been afraid they'd find the interior cleared out, but everything looked more or less as she remembered. But she realized something *was* different. There'd been a sour smell before. Mold and mildew. But the stink now wafting from the interior was worse. Putrid. Perhaps an animal had gotten trapped inside?

The manager must have smelled it, too, because he scowled. "What are you storing in here?" He turned to face Mrs. Murphy. "Plants and animals aren't allowed. No food. No fertilizer."

"Fertilizer?" Mrs. Murphy said, drawing herself up. "You haven't the slightest idea what you're talking about, young man."

Emily said, "Maybe it's because the climate control isn't working."

The manager examined the thermostat on the wall. Raised his hand and felt a vent in the ceiling. Scowled. "I'll look into it and get back to you. Right away." He got in his cart and rode off.

Mrs. Murphy hung back with Becca as Emily stepped into the unit, with Lila behind her. Emily put the document tube on a shelf with other tubes and looked around for the source of the odor. Meanwhile, Lila moved slowly down one side of shelving, pulling down an occasional book, gently examining it, putting it back.

Taking shallow breaths, Emily pulled down the hatbox. She gave it to Lila, who opened the lid. Lila's frown deepened as she leafed through the library book pockets and due-date cards.

Emily noticed a red baseball cap on the floor near the workbench. She stooped to pick it up.

Under the workbench was a rolled-up area rug with burlap backing. She hadn't noticed it on her earlier visit. It was lying in a shallow puddle of water that hadn't been there earlier, either. Was the place leaking, too? Emily inched closer.

Standing at the workbench, Lila whispered, "This is quite a set of supplies he's got. Bleach pens, gum erasers, and sandpaper—"

"Mom." Emily interrupted Lila. "Look." She pointed to the rolled-up rug under the workbench. Her attention was riveted on what was poking out from one end. The fingers of a pale hand. Sticking out the other end were the toes of a pair of sneakers.

Lila bent over, took one look, and backed away.

Emily set the baseball cap on the workbench and picked up a document tube. She poked it at one of the sneakered feet. Stiff. She reached in and touched the fingers. They were cold.

Lila already had her phone out. "Hello, police?"

"WE FIND a dead body and you're sorting library cards," Emily said under her breath to Lila. They were in the office at Inner Peace Storage. Lila held the open hatbox in her lap and was organizing the cards, clipping groups of them together with paper clips she'd appropriated from the office desk. Becca and Mrs. Murphy stood looking out through the fogged-over window. Two police cruisers had arrived. The manager had gone back to the storage unit with the police, and the women had been told to wait in the office until they came back. Sheets of rain pelted the glass.

"What else can I do?" Lila whispered back. She added a card to a clipped group. "This is my way of coping. Stay busy. Focus on minutiae. Where do you think you get it from? Don't judge."

Emily whispered, "You think the collection is stolen?"

"Don't know yet," Lila whispered back. "I'm getting things organized for when we contact these libraries. Once Ruth understands what she's got, that's what I expect she'll want to do."

Ruth. Already her mother was on a first-name basis with Mrs. Murphy. Emily was glad she'd asked her mother to help out.

Headlights lit up the water-streaked windows as a white emergency van drove past, heading in the direction of Mr. Murphy's storage unit. Emily had no idea how long it took for a body to stiffen up, but the person rolled up in the rug could have been dead for some time. Had the body been there on Sunday? Was it possible she hadn't noticed it? The thought made her skin crawl.

She took out her phone and thumbed through the photos she'd taken inside the storage unit on Sunday. Found one of the workbench. She enlarged it, confirming to her relief that underneath there'd been no puddle, no rolled-up rug, no baseball cap.

Before long a man entered the office. He was not wearing a uniform, but an ID badge with the insignia of the Hartwell police hung from his neck. He was square-jawed and stern. His mere presence made Emily feel as if she should stand.

Mrs. Murphy marched right up to the man. Her puff of hair came up to his chin. "Please, can't you explain to us who that person is and what he is doing in my husband's storage unit?"

"Ma'am. That's just what we're trying to find out. I'm Detective Lieutenant Moran." The man pulled a pad from his pants pocket and flipped it open. "And you are?"

"Ruth Murphy," Mrs. Murphy said.

"You say that's your husband's storage unit."

"Mine now. He died," Mrs. Murphy said, her chin quivering.

Lila stood beside Mrs. Murphy. "Mr. Murphy died about a year ago," Lila explained. "We're here to help her clear out the unit."

"And you are?" Moran asked.

"Lila Laubenstein," Lila said.

"Emily Harlow," Emily said.

Moran looked from Emily to Lila and then back to Emily. "Mother and daughter," Lila said.

Then he looked from Emily to Becca, no doubt taking in their matching outfits. "I'm Rebecca Jain," Becca said. "Emily and I are business partners. We're professional organizers."

"Thank you," Moran said. "Which of you found the body?"

No one answered right away. Finally Emily said, "I guess I did. We all noticed the smell, but we didn't realize what it was until I looked under the table. The puddle of water caught my attention."

"When were any of you inside the unit before today?"

"I was here on Sunday. Alone," Emily admitted.

"And then you came back today."

"Actually, I came yesterday but couldn't get in. The key Mrs. Murphy gave me worked the first time I was here. But not when I came back the next day. Someone had changed the lock."

"And from the looks of it, they did a good bit more," Lila said.

"Apparently," Moran said. "So you all came back this morning?"

Becca said, "The manager needed Mrs. Murphy's signature giving him permission to break the lock. Which he did."

"So let me see if I understand," Moran said. "Sunday, Mrs. Harlow was here. She unlocks the unit. Looks around. Leaves. When she returns the next day, the lock's been changed. You're certain you locked up when you left here Sunday."

"Positive," Emily said.

Moran asked, "And when you were here Sunday, did you notice anything else unusual?"

Emily said, "Do you mean, was there a man's body under that table? No." She got out her phone and showed him pictures she'd taken, pausing on the one of the workbench.

"I wonder if any of you recognize him." Moran put away his pad and took out a cell phone. He held it out so they could see a photo of the man. His face was bloated. His eyes were closed. He had dark, close-cropped hair and a mustache and beard.

"I don't know him," Lila said.

"Nor do I," added Mrs. Murphy.

Becca said, "I don't recognize him, either."

Emily didn't say anything. She could feel everyone's eyes on her. Walter Newell had dark hair and a mustache and beard like this guy, but that was hardly enough to say it was him.

"Take your time," Moran said.

Emily tried to visualize the picture that Quinn had brought to the police, or the man she'd run into at the coffee shop. "There was no identification on him?" she asked.

Moran didn't answer. He opened the door to the office and beckoned her outside. Emily hesitated and then followed him.

Outside, the rain had turned to a fine mist. Moran tilted his head and looked down at her. "You recognize him, don't you?"

"No," Emily said. "But I know who he might be."

DETECTIVE Moran's car looked like your average black sedan, but inside, a metal grille separated the front seat from the back. Moran had let Mrs. Murphy, Becca, and Lila leave and had driven Emily to the storage unit, where he parked and got out of the car. He opened Emily's door. She emerged into spitting rain.

Moran reached into the front seat for an umbrella, raised it, and held it over her. Emily's heart hammered as she walked past what turned out to be a coroner's van, backed up to the unit's door. Moran raised yellow crime-scene tape, letting her come inside it.

"Just give us a minute," Moran said to two technicians working inside the unit. The two men stood and stepped away from the body of a man lying on his back on a thick plastic tarp.

Emily forced herself to look. The man was tall and muscular. The face was pale, and down one side was a deep red stain.

She said, "I don't recognize this man. I don't know him."

"But?" Moran said. He folded his arms and waited.

"He could be the husband of one of my clients. That man went to an auction Sunday night, and he's been missing ever since. The East Hartwell police found his car in the lot at the town wharf."

"The wharf," Moran said, turning his gaze in that direction.

Emily added, "Yesterday I went to the police station with his wife to identify the car. Like I said, I'm not sure if this is him. I saw the picture his wife gave the police. The hair seems right."

One of the technicians handed Moran a plastic bag with a wallet inside, open to a driver's license. Moran looked at it.

"Walter Newell?" Emily said.

Moran nodded. He took out his phone, turned his back to Emily, and placed a call. Although he spoke quietly, Emily caught some of it. "Walter Newell . . . Wife reported . . . Where?" His tone was decidedly pissed as his gaze shifted toward East Hartwell's town wharf. "Anything else I should know?" The last laced with sarcasm.

As Moran talked, the technicians wheeled a gurney to the edge of the storage unit. They folded the plastic tarp around Walter Newell's body like a cocoon and then lifted it up and onto the gurney. Moments later they'd loaded him into the coroner's van.

Quinn's husband was dead. Quinn would be devastated. Grief-stricken and no doubt guilt-ridden, what with all her talk about the many creative ways she'd have liked to dispose of him. And Emily had gone along, laughing, imagining ways she might go about dispatching Frank. She cringed at the memory.

"How well do you know his wife?" Moran asked Emily.

"She's our client. We're going to help declutter her garage."

"Anything that you can tell us about Walter Newell could help us find his killer."

"I don't know anything about him. I've never been introduced to him. I met his wife in a professional capacity."

"Really," Moran said. The back doors to the coroner's van slammed shut, and he turned to watch it drive off. Then he raised the crime-scene tape again, gesturing for Emily to precede him out. The rain had stopped. "So why do you think his body was dumped in a storage unit that you happened to be clearing out?"

It was a good question, one she'd been asking herself. "Do you think he was killed here?" she asked.

Moran's gaze dropped to the rug Walter Newell had been rolled up in. A technician was wrapping it in plastic. "We'll know that soon enough. But as far as how he got here . . ." The sun broke through as he pointed to the CCTV camera. "As soon as we view the footage, I expect we'll have an answer to that, too."

Chapter 9

DETECTIVE MORAN DROVE Emily back to the Inner Peace office. "I'd appreciate it if you'd come to the police station and give a written statement," he said after he opened the car door for her. "Today. While the details are fresh in your mind."

How long would it be before she could shake that nauseating smell or stop seeing Walter Newell's pale face, stained as if someone had smeared the side of it with Mercurochrome?

"I'll go now and get it over with," Emily said.

She got into her car. Moments later a police cruiser drove past. No lights flashing. No rush now. Emily followed it.

The surveillance footage would confirm that Emily had arrived and opened the unit on Sunday. Left after a few hours. It would show her trying to get back in the next day. But in between, what? Overnight someone else had opened the unit, dragged in a dead body rolled up in a wet area rug, shoved it under the workbench, and then left the unit fastened with a new padlock.

She reached the street entrance. Just beyond was parked a van with a satellite dish mounted on top. BOSTON 35 was written in block letters on the side. Emily gripped the wheel and accelerated past. She hoped they weren't already broadcasting the story.

Quinn would be waiting at home for some word of what had happened to her husband. Emily shuddered to think that Quinn could learn of her husband's death from a news crawl.

Maybe Emily could reach her and break the news. Then she'd be somewhat prepared when the police showed up on her doorstep. If Frank had been found dead, Emily would have been grateful for a small window of privacy in which to absorb the shock.

Emily pulled over to the curb, slipped her phone from her pocket, and called. Quinn picked up after a single ring. "Hello? Emily?" She sounded breathless.

Emily swallowed hard. How to begin?

"What is it?" Quinn said. "Have you heard something?"

"It's Wally," Emily managed. "He's dead."

A gasp from Quinn. "He can't be. You're sure?"

"I wanted you to hear about it before the police get there."

When she didn't say anything, Emily said, "Quinn?" No response. "I'm so sorry." More silence. "Are you okay?"

"I can't believe it." Quinn's voice was raspy. "It's just . . . How do you know?"

Emily realized how strange this was going to sound. "He was in a storage unit I was working on. We were clearing out the unit for another client and . . . Listen, is there someone you can call to be with you? Do you want me to come over?"

"No! No, I need to think. This wasn't supposed to happen."

"I'm so sorry." Emily knew she was repeating herself, but what else was there to say?

"Just remember," Quinn said. "Whatever happens? I've got your back. We're in this together."

IN *WHAT* TOGETHER? WHEN Emily disconnected the call, she tried to grasp what Quinn was suggesting. She started driving home.

Halfway there she remembered she'd agreed to go to the police station to give a statement. She drove there instead. She tried to call Frank but got his voice mail.

The officer at the desk at the police station asked her to sign in, then whisked her past the front counter, delivering her to a familiar uniformed officer waiting in the corridor. Sergeant Stanley.

"Mrs. Harlow? I understand you're back? This time to give a witness statement?" All business, Stanley escorted her to a small room with a table and four chairs. He pulled out a miniature recorder from a drawer and placed it on the table between them.

"Tuesday, August sixth, three twenty p.m., Sergeant Brian Stanley with Emily Harlow." He stopped and played back the recording. Satisfied, he pressed RECORD again. "Can you describe what happened this morning when you arrived at Inner Peace Storage?"

Emily reached across and shut off the recorder. "I thought this was supposed to be a written statement."

"No problem. If that's what you'd prefer." He reached into the desk and pulled out a form. "I was going to have someone transcribe your statement and have you sign it. Easier that way. But if you prefer to write it out yourself . . ." He offered her a pen.

It would be easier just to tell him what happened. "Okay." She waited until he turned the recorder back on, then began. "I left my house at nine thirty." She described her arrival at the storage facility, the manager breaking open the unit, and the moment she'd noticed the rug rolled up under the workbench and realized what it was. She ended with, "We immediately called the police."

"Thank you," Stanley said, nodding. Emily rose to her feet, thinking she was done, but he motioned for her to sit back down. "Just a few more details that we're hoping to get straight."

Emily waited, perched on the edge of the seat.

"Can you describe your whereabouts and actions going back to Sunday afternoon?"

Sunday afternoon? Why was he asking her that? "I thought this was about what happened today."

"We're trying to tie up a few loose ends. You spent Sunday late afternoon and evening with the victim's wife. Is that correct?"

Emily nodded. "I did."

"A witness reported that his car was involved in an accident that same night in the Square. He hit your car. Would it surprise you that we have that on CCTV?" He didn't wait for her to respond. "Why didn't you report the incident to the police?"

Emily felt her face flush. "I had no idea that it was Walter Newell who hit me. I'd never met the man. I didn't report it, because at first I didn't realize my car had been hit."

Emily could hear the clock on the wall ticking.

Stanley said, "By the next day you knew who he was, didn't you? You knew he'd hit your car. You knew all of that when you came here with his wife to report him missing."

She started to deny that but stopped herself. She knew what Frank's advice would be if he'd answered his phone. She stood and announced, "I came here to give a statement about finding a body. I've done that. I'm leaving."

"Of course you can go. But we'll be keeping your car."

"You have a warrant?"

"We can get one and hold your car until we do. Or you can give me the keys and we'll return it to you as soon as possible."

"How long will you need to keep it?"

"That depends on what we find," he said. "But I can guarantee that you'll get it back faster if you leave it and let us examine it."

What choice did Emily have? Reluctantly, she removed her car key from her key ring and handed it over.

EMILY was still shaking when she called her mother and asked her to come pick her up at the police station. She hung up before Lila could ask why, all the while kicking herself for coming alone to give what was supposed to have been a *written* statement.

She took a seat in the lobby. A couple was huddled together near the exit, their backs to her. When the woman turned, Emily recognized Quinn Newell. She was clutching a tissue, her face red. *She* knew better than to talk to the police without an attorney present.

The man she'd been talking to was Ryan Melanson, Frank's law partner.

"Mrs. Newell?" Sergeant Stanley held open the counter for Quinn and Ryan to pass through. "This way, please." Emily was worried about how Quinn's *I've got your back* would play out under Stanley's relentless questioning.

As Ryan escorted Quinn across the lobby, he spotted Emily. He came over to her, bent down, and rested his hand on her shoulder. "You missed a great game," he said quietly.

Emily recoiled from Ryan's touch. And if it had been such a great game, then why had he left early? He backed off and said, "I'm only here because Frank asked me to help out."

Please, Emily thought, don't do us any more favors. Without Ryan's referral, Emily never would have met Quinn Newell and she wouldn't have gotten tangled up in this mess.

Ryan returned to Quinn. She dabbed at her eyes. Attached once again to Ryan's arm, she followed Stanley past the front counter.

"So you just answered their questions and left your car there?" Frank said after he got home that evening and Emily told him what had happened. "Really?"

"He told me I had to—"

"He who?"

"Sergeant Stanley. He's the same officer that Quinn and I talked to after the police found her husband's car. He told me if I didn't leave the car voluntarily, he'd impound it while they waited for a court order." Emily's eyes filled with tears.

"That is such pure and utter bull." Frank cracked his knuckles. "I still don't get why they took your car."

"They have CCTV footage that shows Quinn's husband hitting my car while I was getting your coffee."

Frank sank down on a kitchen chair. "They *have* it on camera? Or he *told you* they have it on camera? Did you actually see it?"

"No. But—"

"They were fishing."

"I didn't tell them about the hit-and-run. Someone called it in.

Even if they don't have it on video, all they'd have to do is go to the coffee shop and talk to—"

"You have no idea who they're talking to, because you're the last person they'd tell. This is serious, Emmy." He pointed his finger at her. "Don't talk to the police again alone. Understand?"

Emily always found that tone and the finger-pointing irritating. She swallowed her annoyance. "They're going to let me know when I can come back for the car."

"Just to get your car?" He got up, opened a bottom kitchen cabinet, and pulled out a bottle of Maker's Mark. Got down a glass and poured an inch. "You watch. They're not done jerking you around." He sat down and knocked back the bourbon. Smacked the glass down on the table and pointed the mouth of the bottle at Emily. "Please, the next time you talk to the police, take me with you. And if I'm tied up in court, make them wait. So what if they end up impounding your car? Better that than impounding *you*."

Frank opened his mouth, about to continue his rant. Instead, he shook his head. "What am I doing? None of this is your fault. It makes me so angry when the police use their status to *con* unsuspecting people whose worst sin has been to try to be helpful. And here I am"—he stood, his expression softening—"taking it out on you. I'm sorry." Frank pulled Emily into his arms.

Emily surrendered to the hug. She closed her eyes. For the moment, at least, she felt sheltered and safe.

"I'm sorry you have to deal with all this," Frank said. "And I shouldn't have lost my temper." His reassuring words were warm in her ear. "I love you, and I don't want you to get hurt."

Emily broke down in tears.

IN BED that night, Emily tried not to let the panic bubbling in her stomach overwhelm her. Frank was right. She never should have spoken with the police alone. Her only sin had been to find Walter Newell's body, and how had he ended up in the Murphys' storage unit, anyway? There had to be some link between the Newells and the Murphys—a link other than Emily.

Emily turned on her phone and Googled *Walter Newell*. The

item that caught her eye was nearly three years old, a wedding announcement in the *Boston Globe* featuring a shot of the couple standing side by side and grinning. Quinn had been channeling a Kristen Stewart vibe, with shoulder-length platinum-blond hair, ironed straight, a dark inverse-skunk stripe lining the center part. Her face was pale, and her eyes were smudged with kohl.

Emily stared at the picture of the groom. She tried to overlay the features of this smiling hipster on either the face she'd glimpsed behind yellow aviator glasses at the coffee shop or the port-wine-stained face of the dead man. Frustrated, she turned her attention to the announcement below the photo.

> *Amanda Quinn and Walter Halsey Newell were married May 11 at Four Seasons Hotel in Boston.*

Amanda? The name lacked the panache of *Quinn.*

> *The bride is an associate at T. E. Kalmus Fine Art and Auctions. She was previously married to the late Michael Safstrom.*

Huh? Not only had Quinn been married before, she'd been *widowed*. And so much for Quinn being clueless about her husband's collections. She'd worked for an auction house.

Walter Newell, according to the announcement, was a graduate of Boston University and a real estate developer.

Emily rechecked the search results for more information. She tried *Walter Newell* and various permutations of Quinn. *Amanda Safstrom. Quinn Safstrom. Quinn Newell.* But all she came up with was some charitable giving in Quinn's name and a raft of real estate transactions in Walter's. They'd kept a low profile.

She turned on the television and tuned to the ten-o'clock news.

BREAKING STORY! streamed across the top of the screen, white letters against a band of red. Then, BODY FOUND IN STORAGE UNIT.

Voice-over, a woman newscaster: "A gruesome discovery today. Police are investigating a man's body found in a self-storage unit. Stay tuned for an update on this late-breaking story."

Emily pushed the pillow behind her and sat up in bed, waiting out what felt like an endless stream of ads until finally the same introduction ran, this time over video of the entrance to Inner Peace Storage.

Frank came out of the bathroom, toothbrush in hand, and watched as a police cruiser drove out of the storage facility.

"Isn't that your car?" Frank asked.

Emily cringed. Sure enough, there was her Honda, trailing behind the cruiser. At least the camera was angled so that viewers couldn't see the Clutter Kickers logo on her door.

"Good thing—" Their front door chimed, and Frank broke off. He looked at his watch. "What the hell?"

Emily went to the window and looked out. She fully expected to see Quinn's red Miata or a police cruiser in front of the house. But the vehicle parked in front was a dark green pickup truck.

Frank looked out the window behind her. "I'll go see who it is."

"Emily? Frank?" Lila's tremulous voice came from the other side of the bedroom door. "Do you want me to get that?"

"No, thank you, we do not want you to get that," Frank said, enunciating each word. He pulled open the bedroom door and brushed past Lila. "Stay up here, both of you." Delivered like they were a pair of dogs who'd mastered *sit* and *stay*.

Emily put on her robe and joined Lila in the hall. She couldn't see past the bend in the staircase, but she heard the front door open. Then Frank's voice, barely audible. "What do you want?"

Emily couldn't make out the reply, just a man's gruff voice. She crept down to where she could see Frank's legs.

"We're done." Frank's voice. "There's nothing left to discuss."

"You lied. You wouldn't want me to go public—"

Frank said, "I didn't lie. It's what you agreed to. You cashed the check and signed a nondisclosure."

The man spoke some more, but Emily caught only the tail end when his voice rose. "You can't seriously think—"

"Shhh. You'll wake my wife."

Her heart pounding, Emily backed up a few steps. She bumped into Lila. "Who's that?" Lila whispered.

"No idea," Emily whispered back.

Frank again. "You need to leave. Right now. We're done."

"We're not done," the man snarled.

A scuffling sound. Then a thud and a grunt.

"Take your hands off me," Frank said, his voice cold and steady. "You don't want to play this game." There was a long silence. Then Frank again. "You want to talk? In my office."

There was the sound of receding footsteps to Frank's office.

"Who is that man?" Lila said. "Shouldn't we call the police?"

"I have no idea who he is," Emily said. And, knowing how much Frank distrusted the police, she wasn't about to call them unless he'd specifically asked her to. She started down the stairs with Lila right behind her. She could hear the rumble of voices from Frank's office. It sounded as if they were arguing.

Emily tiptoed to the front door and peered out through its glass panel. The front yard was dark. The pickup was parked out there.

"We could at least take a picture of his license plate," Lila said. "Just in case he throws a chair at Frank."

It wasn't a bad idea. Emily ran upstairs for her phone, came down, and slipped outside. Lila watched from the screen door.

Emily approached the truck. She risked using the flash and snapped a close-up of the plate, then hurried up the front walk.

She was nearly to the screen door when she realized that Lila was no longer there. Frank's back filled the doorframe. The porch light came on. Before Emily could dart into the shadows, Frank moved aside, the door opened, and the visitor hurtled out.

He came to a halt within inches of running into her. Jeans. A black shirt stretched over a muscular gut. Dark, close-cropped hair. He glanced at her, surprised. *You?* he mouthed. Then he laughed. He turned and gave Frank his middle finger. When he wheeled around, Emily looked down, avoiding eye contact.

That's when she noticed his shoes. He was wearing loafers. Leather loafers the color of butterscotch. And they were stained.

The man pushed past Emily. He got into his truck and screeched off into the night. She stood there for a few moments.

Coffee-stained loafers.

Minus the glasses, the baseball cap, the beard, and mustache, was this the man who'd run into her at Java Connection, whom a witness had reported hitting her car and then driving off—not in a green truck—but in Walter Newell's car, which the police found abandoned later that night?

"Emily?" Frank called to her. "What are you doing out there?"

"Are you all right, dear?" Lila asked, coming up behind Frank. "You look like you've seen a ghost."

That was exactly what she had seen. Emily came back into the house. "Frank, how do you know that man?"

"He's one of our clients. Why?"

"I've seen him before. At the coffee shop when I went to get your coffee Sunday night. I think he's Walter Newell."

Frank's brow furrowed. "How could it be? Newell is dead. Didn't his wife identify his body?"

"I don't know," Emily said. "I haven't talked to her. Would they go on that? Just her say-so? Maybe she wants people to think he's dead. Sometimes wealthy people need to disappear. Maybe it was an act, her telling me how much she hated being married to him."

"Seriously?" Frank looked at her. "She said that?"

Emily squirmed. Her conversations with clients were supposed to be confidential.

Frank waved his hand as if it didn't matter. "Okay, so suppose the dead man's not Walter Newell. Then who is he? You can't just pick up a spare corpse at Whole Foods. Anyway, that guy who just left here? He's one of Ryan's clients."

"And Ryan's the one who recommended us to Quinn Newell."

Frank stared out to the street where the green truck had been parked. "You're sure that's the man from the coffee shop?"

Emily was about to explain about the shoes when her phone pinged with a text message.

Releasing your car tomorrow 10 am—E Hartwell Police

Chapter 10

THE NEXT MORNING, Emily was awake long before Frank or Lila. She'd barely slept. She had herself convinced that the man who'd come to their house was the man who'd run into her at the coffee shop. Those stained shoes, right? Plus *he'd* recognized *her*. But if he was, then the man who'd run into her wasn't Walter Newell, because Walter Newell was dead. Unless he wasn't.

At eight o'clock, moments after Frank came downstairs and poured himself a cup of coffee, Emily's cell phone chirped. The readout said NEWELL. Emily showed Frank and answered the call.

"This has been such a nightmare," Quinn said.

"Ask if she identified her husband's body," Frank whispered.

Emily shushed him. She couldn't lead with such an intrusive question. "I can't imagine what you must be going through. What with the police and all."

"Well, the police treated me with kid gloves . . . up to a point. Then they started in on whether Wally and I had gotten along. Did we have financial problems? Did he have anger management issues? Was he screwing around? Was *I* screwing around?"

"Fishing," Emily said. Sounded familiar.

"It was sort of a minefield. Because, well, I don't need to tell you, marriage is never uncomplicated, and with the police, honesty's not always the best policy." She sounded like Frank. "I was glad Ryan was there. He kept me from saying too much."

Emily said, "It must have been hard, identifying the body," cringing at how intrusive that sounded.

"It was hard," Quinn replied without skipping a beat. "And horrifying. I could barely do it." A long pause. "He died . . .

blunt-force trauma, they said. I don't even know what that means."

"But at least you got to see him," Emily pressed. She had to know if Quinn had identified the body. "How did he look?"

"I don't know, peaceful. You found him, so you know."

The rolled-up area rug had been lying in a puddle of water. All she could see were pale gray fingers. Then, later, the corpse mercilessly exposed under the spotlights. *Peaceful* would not have been the word Emily would have chosen.

Quinn added, "I felt terrible leaving him in the morgue. It was so cold there. I wasn't happy married to him, but I didn't want this."

"It must be hard," Emily said. Empty words, she knew.

"Emmy, we're still going to finish what we talked about, right? I don't want you to think I'm going to just let it go."

"I . . . uh . . ." Emily stammered, not sure what to say. She wanted as little as possible to do with Quinn. "Now's not the best time for you to make major decisions. I'll return your deposit."

"Not at all. Now we can do the whole house. I really don't care about any of it. Then I won't have to be reminded everywhere that I wasn't welcome. Wally hogged the bed. Hogged the comforter. Filled the medicine cabinet with his stuff—"

"Quinn." Emily interrupted the flow of bile. "I'm not a psychologist, but I think you should wait. A few weeks, at least—"

"I don't want to wait. I'm counting on the help you promised." A pause. "You'll call me, won't you?" When Emily didn't respond, Quinn pressed. "You've got the garage-door opener. You can come by when I'm not here. I want to get rid of everything."

"We'll see," Emily said. "Seriously, don't make any major decisions right now. Okay?" Without waiting for an answer, she disconnected the call, then stood there, looking at her phone.

"Well?" Frank's voice startled her. She'd forgotten he was in the room with her.

"You were right. She identified the body."

"What did I tell you? Walter Newell is dead. Satisfied?"

"Tell me again, who was the man who was here last night, and what were you talking about?"

"He's . . ." Frank took a deep breath. "Emmy, I really can't.

Attorney-client privilege and all that. But this much I can tell you. He's not my client. He's Ryan's. He's the son of a CEO we've worked with before. Guy's a jerk. Suing his neighbor, or I think that's what he's up to this time. All I know is, he agreed to the settlement and now he's balking at the nondisclosure."

"What's his name?"

"Come on. You know I can't tell you that."

"If he's Ryan's client, how come he wasn't at Ryan's house, threatening him?"

Frank poured some more coffee into his cup, took a sip, and grimaced. "He wasn't threatening anyone."

"He was. I heard him."

Lila appeared in the doorway. "I heard him, too. We almost called the police." She crossed the kitchen and poured herself a cup of coffee.

"There was no need to be concerned. The guy just needed to vent." Frank put his cup in the sink and left the room.

Lila watched him go. "I'm afraid I underestimated your husband. Either he's much tougher than I imagined, or he's a superb liar."

AT TEN Frank drove Emily to the police station to get her car. He stuck to the speed limit. But his manner was anything but calm as he pounded the steering wheel and issued orders.

Just go in there and get your car.

Do not trust the police. They want information, and they'll do whatever they need to do to get it.

And most of all, *Check with me before you say anything.*

He kept looking at her, making sure that she was paying attention. She folded her arms and waited for him to run out of steam.

Sergeant Stanley was in the lobby waiting for them. "And who's this?" he said, eyeing Frank in his power suit.

"Frank Harlow," Frank said. He offered his hand to Stanley, who was at least a head shorter than him. "Attorney."

Stanley shook the hand and gazed up at Frank. "Harlow?"

Emily felt her face flush. "Frank is my husband."

Stanley's gaze shifted to Emily. "Lawyered up?" A smirk tugged at the corner of his mouth. "Interesting."

"I'm just here to pick up my car. My husband drove me."

"Of course. Right this way." Stanley led them into the back and downstairs. Walter Newell's Audi was still at the far end of the basement. Emily's car was parked nearby.

"The keys?" Frank said.

Stanley faced Emily. "Don't you want to know what we found when we examined your car?"

"I—" Emily began. She looked at Frank.

"She just wants her car," Frank said.

Stanley ignored him. "We can tell your car had recent body-work." He pointed to the back. "And traces of paint we found on the front bumper of Walter Newell's Audi match your car's. Why were you in the Square?"

Frank nodded for Emily to answer. "I was getting coffee. I guess he was getting coffee, too."

"We've also examined the surveillance camera's footage from the storage facility the night your friend's husband disappeared."

"She's my client. Not my friend," Emily said.

"Would it surprise you that the surveillance video shows you unlocking the unit on Sunday? Going inside?"

"I told you—" Emily began. Frank shushed her.

"Right," Stanley said. "Then you left. But hours later, after midnight, you're back."

Emily was speechless. Frank scowled and shook his head. "Enough," he said under his breath. "She's just here for the car."

"No problem." Stanley went over to a red metal lockbox on the wall. He punched in some numbers and opened it, then fished out a key and closed the box. He tossed Emily the key and pressed a button on the wall. With a loud clank an overhead door rose on the adjacent wall. "You can leave now. Or you can come upstairs and look at the surveillance footage. See what *you* make of it."

Emily took a step back. "I didn't go back to the storage unit Sunday night. I went home. I went to sleep."

"The surveillance footage says otherwise."

Frank hooked Emily's arm and tugged her toward the car.

"What doesn't your husband want you to see?" Stanley said.

"Why not look at the tape? You don't have to say a word. Or maybe you'll be able to help us out by identifying the person."

Emily said to Frank, "What harm can it do, just to look?"

"This is not a good idea," Frank said back.

"I need to see what they have. I won't say anything."

"Then I'm coming with you."

"Sorry," Stanley said. "This offer is just for your wife. She comes alone or it's off the table."

"This is extortion. Don't go." Frank squeezed her arm. "For all you know, there are no pictures. It's a ploy to get you alone."

"We have pictures," Stanley said. "Mr. Harlow, your wife's a grown-up. She can see what's on the tape and judge for herself. Though I have to wonder why you're so adamant that she shouldn't." He gave a little salute and strutted off.

Frank dropped her arm and opened the door of her car.

Emily glanced back. Stanley stood in the stairwell doorway.

"Get in!" Frank said, gesturing for Emily to get in the car.

How long had they been married, and still he hadn't learned that ordering her around in that tone of voice was counterproductive? Why not look at the surveillance video? She could keep her mouth shut. Emily bumped the car door shut with her hip.

As she walked toward the stairwell, Frank called after her, "Emily, don't. This is not a good idea."

She turned back. "I get that. I appreciate that you're trying to protect me, but I need to see what they have."

"Okay, okay. Go. But *don't say anything*. Understood?"

The advice was for her own good, Emily told herself. When she reached Stanley, she followed him up the stairs.

SERGEANT Stanley led Emily to an office. He waited for her to sit across the desk from him. Then he pulled out a folder and opened it. Inside was a stack of photos. On top a grainy black-and-white shot showed an alley lined with storage units. Painted in white on the driveway of the closest unit was the number 218.

Stanley tapped the time stamp at the bottom of the frame. It had been taken at 1:16 a.m., hours after Emily had conked out after much too much wine and a soothing cup of hot chocolate. Stanley indicated a dark shadow with two pinpoints of light that, on closer inspection, looked like parking lights of a car facing the camera.

Stanley showed her the next picture. The time stamp was a minute later, 1:17 a.m. In this photo a car was sideways to the camera, backed up to the door of the unit next to 218. The car's hatch was raised. "That's your car, isn't it?"

Emily's stomach turned over. The car was light-colored. Clear as day, the Clutter Kickers logo was stenciled on the door.

"Here you are again." The next photo showed a shadowy figure hunkered down on the far side of the car from the video camera, presumably opening the padlock.

Emily bit her lip.

"But you were home, right? So maybe you were sleepwalking." Stanley put down another picture. "Because here's you again, crouched inside your car and pushing something out the back."

It was a compelling narrative, but the picture didn't actually support it. Nothing was clear but the side of the car.

"You crawl out the back," Stanley went on. "Disappear into the unit. Ten minutes later you're locking up." He placed another picture on the desk. This one showed the car's hatchback shut and someone hunched over the lock again. Her top and pants looked like Emily's work uniform. A ponytail hung out the back opening of a baseball cap. "That is you, isn't it?" Stanley asked.

Emily caught one detail proving, to her at least, that it wasn't her. She pointed to the person's shoes, which were not open-backed Crocs. "I hurt my foot. I would've been wearing these." She stuck out her foot for Stanley to see her Crocs.

"You're saying that's not you? Not driving your car?" Stanley said. "License plate QVC838? And perhaps you can explain something we found in your car. Carpet fibers. I don't need to remind you that Walter Newell was rolled inside a rug."

It wasn't possible. Emily leaned forward, head in her hands.

"And about the person," Stanley said, "who called in the hit-and-run? We traced the call. It came from Walter Newell's cell. We know he registered at the auction in Hyannis at about two. We know he didn't buy anything. The call reporting the accident came in from his phone eight hours later. I can play it for you. Maybe you'll recognize the voice."

He picked up the phone on his desk and punched a few buttons. Listened. He turned on the speakerphone, and Emily heard a beep.

First, in a robotic voice: "Call received August four, twenty-one fifty-five." Then a woman dispatcher's voice: "This is nine one one. Please state your emergency."

"Hello?" This voice was also a woman's. Low and raspy. "I just witnessed a hit-and-run in East Hartwell Square. Car pulled out of a parking space. Hit the car in front of it. Didn't stop."

"What is your name?"

"He's gone now. The car was a light-colored Audi. He hit a Honda hatchback with printing on the door."

The dispatcher asked, "Is anyone injured?"

"No. The other car was parked." The caller gave the location in front of the coffee shop and the license plate of the Audi.

Emily closed her eyes, trying to place the caller's voice. The person who'd most likely have had access to Walter Newell's phone was Quinn. But how could Quinn have known about the accident when Emily had left her at her home minutes earlier?

After the recording ended, Stanley hung up. "The caller says she saw the accident. But here's the thing about it. No one in the coffee shop remembers serving you."

That seemed highly unlikely. Her nasty run-in had been witnessed by the barista.

"Did you pay with a credit card?"

Emily said nothing.

"Cash, then? Did you get a receipt?"

She hadn't, because Ana—Emily remembered the barista's name—had given her Frank's coffee on the house.

Don't say anything. Frank had been so right.

"Shall I tell you how Walter Newell died?" Stanley didn't wait for an answer. "Blunt-force trauma to the front of the legs. Trauma to the back of the head. Finally, his chest was crushed. It looks like he got hit by a car. He was knocked to the ground; then the vehicle ran over him. Twice. An accident? What do you think?"

Emily shuddered. She was trying not to think.

"After that—and now I'm guessing based on the fact that his car was found parked at the wharf and his body was wrapped in a water-soaked rug—the killer rolled his body down the ramp and into the water. That staining on his face? Tells us he was left lying facedown after he died. Blood pools at the lowest point.

"After he dented your car, did you follow him to the wharf? Or maybe you dented his car when you parked and *he* followed *you.* One way or another, you both end up at the wharf. It's late. Quiet. You argue. Maybe he threatens you. You get in your car. Start the engine." Stanley stood, leaning toward her, his palms on the desk. "He's angry. He's standing in front of you, daring you to . . ."

Emily resisted the urge to put her hands over her ears. None of that had happened.

"You'd have needed help," Stanley went on. "A dead body's heavy—even heavier when it's wrapped up in a wet rug. Gravity works in your favor getting it into the water. But getting it out? That's a two-person job." Stanley sat down. "So who helped you?" He stared at Emily for a few moments. "Let's leave that for a minute. You could have done the rest by yourself. Driven to the storage unit. Rolled the body out of the car. Pushed it under that table. And changed the lock, buying at least another day before the body could be examined. Guaranteeing that there'd be even more uncertainty when we tried to estimate Mr. Newell's time of death."

Emily couldn't hold back. "I don't care what you think those surveillance images show. That is not me."

Stanley collected the photos and slapped them in the folder. "Then you have nothing to worry about. Our officers won't find the original padlock to that storage unit in your house, will they? Because that's where they are now, executing a search warrant."

EMILY left Stanley's office, her stomach in a knot. Frank was waiting for her in the lobby. He jumped to his feet and followed her out the door. She didn't break down until she got out to the parking lot, where Frank had parked her car alongside his.

Emily was expecting a big told-you-so. Instead, Frank opened his arms. Emily collapsed against him and sobbed, surrendering to anger and frustration. But this was no time to fall apart.

She pulled away from Frank. "We need to get home. The police are probably already there, searching our house."

Frank cursed. "What are they looking for?"

"The padlock to the Murphys' storage unit."

Frank gave her a long look. "Are they going to find it?"

"Frank!"

"Just asking. You're sure they won't?"

Emily wasn't sure of anything after seeing the picture of a car that looked like hers pulled up to the storage unit. She opened her car's back door, touching the dark carpeting that lined the hatchback's cargo bay. It was damp, and when she smelled her fingertips, she gagged on the whiff of sulfur, like decaying plant matter.

"What?" Frank said.

"Stanley said they found carpet fibers back here. Walter Newell was rolled up in a rug."

Frank gave her a pitying look. "They'd find carpet fibers in the back of *my* car. It's like saying they found hair in your bathroom."

Emily's gear bag was on the floor. She opened the bag. Everything seemed to be in order. The only thing that wasn't there was the key to the old padlock on Mrs. Murphy's storage unit.

"What did he tell you?" Frank asked.

Emily closed the bag. "He said they think that the body was in the river. They have surveillance photos they say show me driving his body to the storage unit in the middle of the night, leaving it there, and changing the lock. And they say I'm not strong enough to have done it on my own. I had to have had help."

"Huh." Frank was quiet for a few moments. "Did he actually show you the pictures? Because they talk a good game—"

"Frank, he showed me. It looks like my car." She slammed the car door. "But it's not me."

"Surveillance pictures are notoriously lousy. Low resolution. Nine times out of ten, CCTV footage doesn't stand up in court."

"Please tell me it won't come to that. Because he made it sound as if they think I killed Walter Newell. That after he hit my car, I followed him to the wharf, confronted him, and ran him down."

"Whoa." Frank held up his hand. "They think you ran him down, and now they're letting you drive off in the murder weapon? How likely is that?"

Emily paused. It was true that didn't seem too likely. She let Frank's words wash over her. His confidence was bracing even if his words weren't all that reassuring.

"I'll meet you at home," Frank said, getting into his car.

Emily nodded and got into her car, too. Her hand shook as she started the engine. She lowered the window.

Frank leaned out his car window. "Sure you're okay driving?"

"Just keep me in your rearview."

"No worries. I've got your back."

Emily repressed a shudder. She'd heard something like that before. Recently. From Quinn Newell.

EMILY drove, following Frank back to the house. The more she thought about the evidence the police had gathered, the angrier she got. The person in the grainy CCTV footage was barely visible, and the car might have been hers, or it might have been any light-colored compact car with their logo painted on the door. But the person, indistinct as she was, did seem to be wearing an outfit like Emily's work uniform, and she had a long ponytail.

Emily shivered. This was not a case of mistaken identity. Whoever it was had been *trying* to look like Emily. What Emily couldn't understand was why the barista refused to confirm she'd been in there. That, at least, she could discover for herself later.

Emily turned onto her block. She gripped the steering wheel even tighter when she saw that a police van was backed into their driveway and a cruiser was parked in front. The bulkhead doors to the basement were open, as was the front door.

Lila, wearing a broad-brimmed straw hat and sunglasses, a gold tunic, and white leggings, sat in a folding chair on the front lawn watching the house as if she were watching a movie. When she saw Emily, she jumped up, waving some sheets of paper at her. Emily reached out for them. Across the top page it read: "Search Warrant."

Frank, who'd parked his car down the street, joined them.

"I'm sorry," Lila said. "I didn't know how to stop them."

"You couldn't have stopped them," Frank said. "And if you'd tried, you'd have gotten yourself arrested."

"Why are they here?" Lila asked. "They can't possibly think that Emily had anything to do with that man who—" She broke off as a police officer emerged from the front door, wearing blue rubber gloves and carrying a pile of clothing. He laid the items down on a plastic tarp behind the police van. Emily could see several of her work uniforms, including her sneakers and cap.

"Can they take whatever they want?" Lila said. "Isn't there something in the Constitution about illegal search and seizure?"

"Lila," Frank said, "this is what legal looks like. They can only take what's in the warrant." He eased the stapled sheets of paper from Emily's grasp, looked them over, then handed them back.

Emily read the warrant herself. It listed the places the police were allowed to go. The house. The garage. The yard. Vehicles on the property. All in search of *any property that is or has been used as a means of committing a criminal offense.*

Below that, written in by hand, was a list of items. It began, *padlock.* After that, *women's clothing per photo.* Stapled to the search warrant was a copy of one of the surveillance stills—the woman in a baseball cap and a Clutter Kickers uniform.

A uniformed officer emerged from the house. He stopped at the back of the police van to write on a clipboard. Frank went over to him, and Emily followed. The officer kept on writing.

"Officer," Frank said. "Are you almost done?"

"We'll let you know," the officer said without looking up.

Another officer emerged from the basement, carrying a medium-sized cardboard box. He set the box beside the tarp.

Emily drew closer. The plastic label stuck to the side of the box read LOCKS. Inside were old padlocks, keys, and keyhole escutcheons. One padlock was emblazoned with a Celtic cross. Emily could see these were old, more collectible than functional.

"Those are mine," Frank said.

Of course they were. The padlock the police were looking for—the one that had hung outside Mr. Murphy's storage unit, the one with a flaking 217 painted on it in red nail polish—would have stood out like an ugly duckling in this pack of swans.

Frank was staring at the box of padlocks, his fists clenched. That's when Emily realized: This was the first moment her misadventure had touched *his things*.

AFTER the police left, Emily pulled her car into the driveway and picked up her gear bag. She hoped she'd find the padlock key. But after she'd emptied everything onto the passenger seat, she couldn't find it. What she did find was her stun gun. Lila had proclaimed it dead. Was it? Emily took it out and pressed the trigger.

No bug-zapper snap. All she got was a tiny spark and a dead-sounding clicking. Emily had no idea where she'd stashed the charger. She returned the stun gun and the rest of the contents to her gear bag and put it back in her car. Then she entered the house.

The police had turned the place upside down. Lila was in the living room, restoring order: plumping sofa cushions and straightening piles of mail, lining up photos and books on their shelves.

Emily went up to her bedroom. Bedding was pulled back. Bureau drawers were open, the contents spilled onto the floor. The clothes she'd carefully folded and hung in her newly installed closet system were a jumbled mess. The clothing she'd bagged to give away had been dumped on the floor.

Emily scooped up her socks and underwear and hurled them into the laundry basket. If there'd been room, she'd have added everything the police had laid hands on. In the room. In the house.

"Emmy?" Her mother stood in the doorway. "Can I help?"

"No." Emily yanked a pillow from its case. "Thanks."

"Okay," Lila said, but she came into the bedroom anyway. She went to the closet and grabbed an armload of clothes from the floor. Dumped them on the bare mattress and started to fold.

"Stop," Emily snapped. Lila dropped the pants she'd been folding. "Sorry," Emily said. "It's just that I was giving those away."

"So what can I do?" Lila asked, hands on her hips.

"Nothing. It all feels contaminated." Emily's throat closed. She tried to swallow. "I have to do laundry."

Her mother came over and put her arms around her. "It's all right," Lila said. "Sometimes we all need to do laundry."

Emily sat on the bed, and Lila sat next to her. "I see they gave you back your car," Lila said.

"Yes, they did," Emily said. "But they think I used it to kill that man in the storage unit and move his body."

Lila's jaw dropped. "Why on earth would they think that?"

Emily told her about the CCTV stills taken in the dead of night. When she finished, Lila said, "Darling, from the moment you opened up that storage unit the first time, there's been a chain of bad events. I know you feel as if you did something to trigger the chain, but you didn't. So the question is, what did?"

"And the answer?"

Lila thought. "I'd go back to that storage unit. It began there, didn't it? The police are allowing us to go back in, and I promised Ruth that I'd meet her there in the morning. Becca's meeting us there, too. If nothing else, getting out of here will do you a heap of good, or before you know it you'll be power-washing the driveway."

Emily laughed weakly. "I need to take care of something first. I'll meet you at the storage unit. I'll bring coffee and donuts."

"Donuts?" Her mother made a sour face.

"Trust me. You'll like these donuts."

Chapter 11

Thursday

THE NEXT MORNING, Emily drove to Java Connection. The day hadn't heated up yet, and the door to the café was propped open.

She entered the coffee shop. The air was filled with thumping percussion and jazzy guitar riffs along with the whir of beans grinding and the sucking sound of an espresso machine. Three registers were open, fed by a single line of customers.

Emily looked for the barista who'd come to her rescue the other night. Not at any of the registers. Then Emily spotted her behind the counter twisting a coffee scoop onto an espresso machine. She wore the same macaroni bracelet.

Emily got in line and, when it was her turn, ordered three iced lattes and a dozen cider donut holes. Her mouth watered as she watched the clerk dust the donut holes with cinnamon sugar and scoop them into a bag. She paid and then waited off to the side. Minutes later Ana put three tall lidded cups into a cardboard carrier and set them on the counter. "Emily," she called out.

"Ana?" Emily approached the counter. Ana's eyes flickered with recognition and morphed into a blank stare, like a wall had gone up. Emily took the coffees. She said, "Excuse me, Ana?"

Ana turned her back to Emily and switched on the grinder.

Emily raised her voice. "Ana? Remember me? I was in Sunday night before closing? A man ran into me and spilled his coffee?"

The bean grinder shut off, and Ana turned to face Emily, avoiding eye contact. "Sorry. I no remember," she mumbled.

"You were here," Emily said. "I'm sure it was you." She lowered her voice and pointed to Ana's macaroni bracelet. "You were wearing that bracelet. I thought it was so sweet."

Ana put her hand behind her back.

"You have a daughter?" Emily asked.

"Sobrina." Ana whispered the word. *Niece.*

"You recognize me. I know you do. I wouldn't be here bothering you if it weren't important." When Ana didn't respond, Emily pressed. "Do you remember the man that ran into me a few nights ago? The police came and asked about him?"

Ana's eyes widened. She said, "Please. Go. Away."

"I just want to know what you remember about him," Emily said. "It turns out that it matters. A lot. Maybe the police—"

Ana squeezed her eyes shut. That's when Emily realized Ana wasn't afraid of Emily. She was terrified of the police.

"No police. I promise," Emily said. "Just talk to me. No one will know. Please. I'm begging you."

Ana opened her eyes and took a deep breath. She went over to one of the other clerks and whispered to her. Then she returned to Emily and motioned her through a back door. Emily followed her into the shadowy alley behind the store.

Ana folded her arms across her chest. "Okay? So?"

"Did you talk to the police?"

Ana pressed her lips together. Emily took that for a no.

"But they were here? And they asked about me and that man?"

"I don't talk to police. Never. I have family. You understand? If they send me back, what will they do?"

"I won't tell the police I talked to you. But I need to know what you saw. The man was so nasty. He hit my car. And then"—Emily paused until Ana met her gaze—"he was killed."

Ana's eyes widened. "Killed?"

"He was found in a storage unit near the town wharf. But you saw him. He must have gotten here right before I did."

Ana gave her head a tiny shake. "No right before. He waited."

"You mean, he'd been here awhile?"

"No drinking. No other customers, so I noticed. He's making me uncomfortable just sitting there, watching out the window."

"Like he was waiting for someone? How long?"

"Twenty minutes. Maybe more, even."

"But he was at the counter when I came in."

"I'm cleaning up. Ready to close the accounts. He come back up to me and ask how much for coffee beans. What kind do we have. I show him the shelf. Next thing, he's shouting at you."

"And you helped me. That was so kind of you. You told me that he wasn't a regular customer."

"No." A whisper. "I never seen him before."

"Thank you. Thank you so much," Emily said.

So the man who'd spilled coffee all over Emily hadn't simply run into her. He'd been waiting for her to get there. Which meant he'd been tipped off that she'd be stopping there.

"So who was he?" Emily murmured the words to herself. She

asked Ana, "You said you closed the accounts that night. Could you look up whether he paid with a credit card?"

Ana shook her head. "I'm not supposed to—"

"But you could. Right?" Emily paused.

Ana flinched.

"All I need is a name," Emily said. "Then I won't have to ask the police to look into it." The minute the words were out of her mouth, Emily regretted saying them. Ana looked stricken. "I didn't mean that. I'd *never* sic the police on you. Just think about it. And *if* you feel comfortable looking up who it was, call me." She offered one of her business cards to Ana.

Ana hesitated. Then she took it.

As EMILY drove from the coffee shop to Inner Peace Storage, her face went hot with shame. There was no excuse for bullying Ana. On the other hand, she felt satisfaction that at last she'd discovered something: The man in the coffee shop had been waiting for her to get there. She hadn't been a victim of chance. She'd been set up by someone who knew she'd be stopping there on the way home.

Walter could have been upstairs listening as Emily and Quinn rhapsodized about killing their husbands. Heard Emily say she'd be stopping for coffee on the way home. Or Quinn could have alerted him. Though why would she have done that?

The only other person who knew Emily would be stopping at the coffee shop was Frank. All he had to do was ask and he knew she'd stop on the way home and pick him up a coffee. He'd even know when she'd be likely to get there, since the coffee shop closed at ten. It was Frank—and putting this together felt like peering into an abyss—who'd insisted that the guy who came to their house wearing coffee-stained loafers was Ryan's client, even though the man was clearly pissed off at Frank.

She desperately hoped that her soft sell had worked and Ana was looking up whether Mr. Congeniality had paid with a credit card. She needed a name to go with those shoes.

When Emily got to the Murphys' storage unit, it was open and Lila's car was parked in front. Emily got out of the car.

The hum she heard when she entered the unit turned out to be the ventilation system. The thermostat was now reading seventy-two degrees. Cool air was pouring in from the ceiling vent.

At a glance, Emily could see about a quarter of the shelves had already been cleared. Books had been transferred to stacks on the floor. Mrs. Murphy sat in a folding chair at the worktable, looking like she was playing solitaire with due-date cards and library pockets. Lila stood on a cinder block and eased a thick volume from the topmost shelf. She gently opened the book. "Morris, William," she called out. "*The Wood Beyond the World.*"

After a pause Mrs. Murphy said, "Got it!" She held up a due-date card. "Francis Lewis Memorial Library."

Becca, who was sitting cross-legged on the floor with her computer on her lap, repeated the title and the library as she typed.

Lila sniffed at the book and riffled the pages. "It's in rough condition, but they'll be happy to have it back where it belongs. She walked over and picked up the card from Mrs. Murphy, tucked it into the book, and set the book on top of one of the piles.

"Hey, guys," Emily said. "How's it going?" She sidestepped around the stacks to give Lila, Becca, and Mrs. Murphy each a coffee. "I have cider donut holes." She handed one to Lila, who sniffed it suspiciously, took a nibble, then popped it into her mouth.

"We're turning back history," Becca said. "It's satisfying."

"Can I help?" Emily asked.

"You can help by not helping." Lila snagged another donut hole. "Please. It's tight quarters in here. And we have a system."

"Really, we've got it under control," Becca said.

Emily examined the unit. They'd made good progress. Once the books had been sorted, they'd have to do the document tubes—at least it looked as if those were clearly labeled and properly sealed. And after that the boxes of hardware. Was it Emily's imagination, or did there seem to be fewer of those?

"Oh, I need to send you the combination to the new padlock." Becca began typing on her laptop.

"Thanks," Emily said. But her attention was focused on Mr. Murphy's dozen or so remaining boxes. Stuck to each of them were green plastic labels, punched with white capital letters: HINGES. KNOBS. BRACKETS. They reminded her of something.

But before Emily could follow the thought, her cell phone pinged. She'd missed a call and had a voice message waiting. Caller ID read ANA PEREZ. The barista at Java Connection.

"Catch you later, guys," Emily said.

Becca waved. Emily pushed the last box of discarded books across the floor and out to the curb. Then she got in her car and listened to the message.

In a lightly accented voice, "That man. He charged his coffee." Emily waited for the name she expected: Walter Newell.

Instead, Ana said, "Rafe Bartok." She spelled the name and then hung up.

WHO was Rafe Bartok? And why had this stranger been waiting for Emily to enter the coffee shop? And had the same man shown up at her house threatening Frank two days later, clean-shaven but still wearing coffee-stained loafers?

Emily typed the name into the Google app on her cell phone. She narrowed the search to images. The first photos that came up were of a man in his forties. Thick dark hair. Intense eyes. He looked like the man who'd driven the green pickup to their house.

She tapped one of the images, and up came a record from IMDb. Turned out Mr. Bartok was an actor. He'd been at it for decades, struggling, it seemed, from the list of parts he'd played. Coroner's assistant on *CSI*. Delivery guy in *Gone Baby Gone*.

Emily also found a photograph that was a whole lot less flattering than his headshot: a mug shot from a news story dated May 2017. The text said, Bartok, forty-five, a "local actor," had been arrested for OUI outside a restaurant for being intoxicated. He'd attempted to leave the parking lot with his truck's emergency brake engaged. Sounded like a down-on-his-luck guy who'd be willing to take a sketchy gig if the price was right.

Emily hurried home and ran upstairs to her office. She logged on to her computer and found one of Bartok's more recent headshots. She pasted it into Photoshop. Next she captured a photograph of

Walter Newell from the wedding announcement she'd found earlier and pasted it into Photoshop, too.

You'd never have mistaken Rafe Bartok for Walter Newell. Bartok had a blocky face with deep-set eyes. Newell was more of a
pretty boy with a devilish heart-shaped face. On the other hand,
they had the same general build, dark hair, and dark features.
Tweak the hair, add a few accessories . . . She Photoshopped a
beard and mustache onto Bartok's face. Then gave both men
yellow-tinted aviator glasses and baseball caps. Emily gazed with
satisfaction at the doppelgängers she'd created. It wouldn't have
taken much for Rafe Bartok to pass himself off as Walter Newell.

She was so immersed in Photoshop that she was startled when
she heard Frank's voice. "I'm back."

She whipped around. Frank stood in the doorway, dressed in
a dark suit—his court clothes. "I didn't hear you come in." She
checked the time on her screen. One. "What are you doing back?"
She snapped her laptop shut.

"Court's recessed. What are you up to? Can I see?" Frank reached
past her and opened her laptop. The screen bloomed with the images of the two Photoshopped faces, side by side. "Who's that?"

"It's supposed to be Walter Newell," she said.

"That's the guy who ran into you at the coffee shop?"

Not *That's the dead guy in the storage unit.* Instead, Frank was
reminding her that the man in the coffee shop had been Walter
Newell, though she was now convinced that he wasn't.

"Doesn't he look like your visitor from the other night?"

"Ryan's client," Frank said quickly. Too quickly. He stared at the
screen. "Nah. This guy looks nothing like him. You told me you
only got a brief glimpse of Walter Newell before his coffee spilled
all over you. You were a bit . . . more than a bit compromised. I'm
surprised"—Frank's tone softened—"the police haven't charged *you*
with hit-and-run and driving under the influence."

Emily recognized Frank's tried-and-true technique: *If a witness
gives you a hard time, make him look like a jerk.* Still, his comment
struck a nerve. She had behaved like a rank amateur, drinking with
Quinn. Oversharing. Toasting dead husbands.

Emily knew she should let it drop, but she couldn't help herself. "According to the police, Cape traffic was so bad on Sunday that Walter Newell couldn't have gotten back in time to run into me if he left when he told Quinn he was leaving. So maybe he wasn't the man at the coffee shop. Maybe Newell was already dead."

Frank put up his hands. "*If* he left when he said he did? That's a big *if.* Isn't it possible that he was lying to his wife? Emmy, think about it. What do you actually know about Walter Newell?"

FRANK left Emily in her office. The two faces on her computer screen stared at her from behind matching aviator glasses. Frank was right. Again. What *did* she know about Walter Newell? He collected retro advertising signs and magazine cover art. According to Quinn, he was a control freak. And something that Quinn had neglected to mention: He was her *second* dead husband.

Full stop. That felt like lightning striking the same spot twice. Emily pulled up Quinn and Walter's wedding announcement. It named her previous husband, "the late Michael Safstrom."

Emily Googled his name and got hundreds of hits. Articles that Michael Safstrom had written for *Collectors' Quarterly* caught her eye. "Collecting Original Cover Art." "The Disappearing Art of Porcelain Advertising Signs."

Safstrom's article on signs began, "Perhaps the most recognizable advertising medium of the late 19th century was the porcelain sign." It extolled their durability and weather resistance, their bold colors, and eye-catching graphics. As collectibles, they were sought after because they were rare. The article was illustrated with pictures of signs "from the author's collection."

Safstrom's columns on collecting had been published every few months, from 2005 until 2011. A news article in the *Nassau Times* dated March 2012 explained why they'd stopped: HERMÈS CRUISE SHIP PASSENGER REMAINS MISSING. Forty-three-year-old Michael Safstrom had been on his honeymoon cruise when he went overboard from the eighth deck of the ship on its way to Bermuda. His wife, Amanda Quinn Safstrom, had reported him missing two days later when the ship reached Nassau.

Four years after Safstrom's death, his widow, Amanda/Quinn, married Walter Newell, a man she claimed was so controlling that he wouldn't let his wife bring so much as a stuffed toy from her past into their home. And yet all over the house, he'd displayed porcelain signs and magazine illustrations that looked suspiciously similar to what her first husband collected.

Similar to or identical?

Emily needed to take a closer look at those advertising signs. How likely was it that a controlling husband would have allowed himself to be surrounded by items coveted by his wife's ex?

Getting into the Newells' house wouldn't be a problem. Quinn had given Emily the garage-door opener, inviting her to use it *whenever*. But it would be better if Emily got in and out when Quinn wasn't there. But when was that? Then Emily remembered the morning yoga classes circled on the fitness center calendar in Quinn's kitchen.

It took a minute for Emily to find the schedule of the local fitness center on its website. A yoga class was scheduled for tomorrow morning at eleven. It was worth a try.

Friday

LILA was in the kitchen eating a bowl of cereal when Emily came downstairs. She had on a dark blazer and skirt, her red hair despiked. A black coat was draped across the back of her chair.

"Good morning, dear. There's a pot of coffee," Lila said.

"Good morning," Emily said, eyeing her mother. That outfit she had on looked all too familiar. "You look—"

"I know. Boring."

"Stand up so I can see."

Lila stood. She looked surprisingly chic, given that Emily's skirt was too short and that boxy blazer was at least ten years old.

"I didn't think you'd mind," Lila said. "You *were* getting rid of them, weren't you? I needed something that looked professional and conservative. And, yes, boring. What do you think?"

"I think you nailed it on all counts." Emily poured herself a cup of coffee and added an inch of milk.

"I'm going to South Hadley with Ruth and Becca to return some lithographs to their District collection. Folios from Gould's hummingbirds. We'll be back early afternoon." Lila sat down.

"Unless you get arrested."

"And if that happens, I'll be counting on you to bail us out."

"You don't seem overly concerned." Emily sipped her coffee.

"I'm not. I've known their director for years. I thought it would be a safe place to start. If I'm right, they have no idea what they're missing. You can't inventory the contents of every book. I'm hoping a discreet return will be in everyone's best interest. Especially since the thief has already gone to meet his maker.

"By the way, I thought you'd appreciate this." Lila twisted around and lifted the black coat on the back of her chair. "Ruth found it in her husband's closet." She opened the coat. "Here's how he got away with it." A patchwork of pockets had been sewn inside. She showed Emily a hook in the lining. Hanging from it was a black-felt pocket. From it Lila drew out an X-Acto knife.

Emily took the coat from Lila. She draped it over her own shoulders, then threaded her arms through the sleeves. She buttoned two top buttons. The coat fit snug across her shoulders but loose, almost tentlike, in the middle. Plenty of room for whatever you wanted to slip into those deep pockets. "Do you think Mrs. Murphy knew what he was up to?" Emily asked.

"It's possible. But then why would she bring us his coat?" Lila carried her empty bowl and cup to the sink, then turned around and leaned against the counter. "More likely she was the naïve magician's assistant, chatting up librarians. Lowering their guard. Not realizing that he brought her along to divert attention while he made things disappear." Lila glanced at her watch. "Time to face the music." She picked up her purse and left the house.

Alone in the kitchen, Emily unbuttoned the coat and started to take it off. That's when she realized something else odd about it. The buttons were on the left side, buttonholes on the right.

Emily ran to the door, hoping to catch Lila, but her car was gone. She sent a text that she hoped Lila would understand:

It's a woman's coat. Let Becca know.

EMILY PULLED INTO THE parking lot across from East Hartwell's fitness center thirty minutes before the eleven-o'clock yoga class was to start. She watched as the lot filled and women in leggings got out of their cars and crossed the street. At eleven Emily was about to give up when Quinn's Miata pulled in. As Quinn raced to the fitness center, Emily headed for Quinn's house.

Mandarin Cliffs felt deserted. Few cars were parked in front of the houses. Emily made a U-turn in the cul-de-sac and parked.

With her gear bag over her shoulder, she rang the bell, making sure no one was home. Then she crossed to the garage, took out the controller that Quinn had given her, and pressed the button. One of the garage's two double doors rose, revealing the empty bays where Quinn and her husband's cars were usually parked.

Emily entered the garage. Off to the side, in the pair of bays behind the still closed garage door, sat the pile of possessions that Quinn had said she was ready to deep-six.

Emily heard a plaintive cat's meow coming from the kitchen. She closed the garage door and let herself into the house. The calico cat greeted her, rubbing its head against her leg.

Emily unfolded the printouts she'd made of the photos that illustrated Quinn's first husband's articles on collecting. The moment she entered the front hall, she found a match, the metal sign at the bottom of the stairs that advertised Sunlight soap. Halfway up the stairs, she found another match, a sign for Omega watches.

Emily photographed both signs. Then she made her way to Walter Newell's study. Hanging on the walls, she found many of the magazine covers reproduced in another of Michael Safstrom's articles. Not magazine *covers*, Emily confirmed when she examined them close up. They looked to be artist-signed original art.

Emily felt satisfied that she had evidence that the objects in Walter's house had been collected by his wife's previous dead husband. That meant Walter wasn't the jealous husband Quinn had made him out to be. Maybe he was just rich and inconvenient.

Emily hurried through the kitchen and into the garage. But before she could close the door behind her, the cat darted past and was instantly lost in the shadows.

Emily cursed her carelessness. If she didn't get the cat back in the house, Quinn would know someone had been here. "Here, kitty." She dropped her gear bag and fished out her cell phone. She turned on its flashlight and shone the beam from one end of the garage to the other. "Come on, you stupid cat." Emily made kissing sounds and held the kitchen door open, but the cat was having none of it.

Emily went back into the kitchen, poured a saucer of milk, and brought it out to the garage. She rattled the saucer. At last a faint rustling sound came from the pile of Quinn's belongings.

Emily shone the light, trying to penetrate the pile. The glassy eyes of a Care Bear gleamed back at her. It sat in a box of stuffed toys on the floor between the bureaus. Emily realized that box had been moved since she was last there. She thumbed back through the pictures she'd taken on her first visit. The stuffed animals had been on top of a bureau. And the dark stain that was now visible across the papasan chair's gold seat cushion had been hidden beneath a burlap-backed area rug.

Her heart racing, Emily stepped closer to the pile and examined it in the flashlight beam. The rolled-up rug had vanished.

That's when she heard it. A lapping sound. The cat was drinking from the saucer. Emily slipped her phone into her pocket, snuck over, scooped up the cat, and unceremoniously dumped it back in the kitchen. Raced the saucer to the sink, rinsed and dried it, put it in the cabinet, and then hurried back out to the garage.

She picked up her gear bag and got out the garage opener. But before she could activate the mechanism, it clanked and the door started to rise. When the door was inches off the ground, a red car bumper came into view. Quinn's Miata.

Emily could see silhouettes of a driver and a passenger in the car. She hid behind one of the bureaus as the Miata slipped in and stopped. The engine shut down, and the garage door descended. A car door opened and shut. Through a sliver of space between the bureaus, Emily could see the driver had gotten out. Quinn.

The passenger door opened, and moments later there was a click as it was pressed shut. Emily heard a man clearing his throat.

Emily clutched her gear bag to her chest, her legs trembling as she tried not to make a sound, not daring to raise her head.

The door to the kitchen opened. "Emily?" Quinn called into the house. Emily's hand flew to her mouth; she panicked before she realized Quinn must have spotted her car outside.

"Emmy?" Quinn called out again. *Don't call me Emmy!* Emily wanted to scream. "According to this," Quinn said to her companion, "she's here somewhere."

According to this? A chill went down Emily's back. The door to the kitchen closed. Emily heard the sound of crickets. Her phone. In the empty garage its chirp was like a clap of thunder.

Chapter 12

EMILY SLID THE PHONE FROM her pocket, her hand shaking. It felt radioactive, its screen lit up: QUINN NEWELL. She powered it off.

How could Quinn be tracking her location? When Frank installed the friend-finder app on Emily's phone, he'd explained to her that only people she'd specifically granted permission could track her, and only when her phone was turned on. He'd linked her to himself and Becca and Lila. So who'd added Quinn?

Emily had to get out of here *now*. It wouldn't take long for Quinn to realize that Emily wasn't still in the house. But activating the garage-door opener would be like triggering a burglar alarm. There had to be another way out.

That's when she noticed the standard door sandwiched between the two overhead doors. She picked up her gear bag and made her way over to it. She tried to turn the knob, but it was locked. Panicked for a moment, she felt for a lock in the handle. Bingo. She twisted it, opened the door, and slipped out.

She raced to her car, taking a quick look back. No one came after her. She jumped into her car, threw her bag and cell onto the passenger seat, and jammed her key into the ignition. The engine roared to life. Her tires squealed as she accelerated out of there.

Emily checked her rearview mirror, expecting the Miata to pull up behind her. As she drove, she reached for her cell, swerving to avoid oncoming traffic. How did you turn off the locator? She pulled over on a side street, switched the phone on, found LOCATION SHARING, and set it to OFF. Then she drove on.

Frank could have tinkered with her friend-finder app. But why would he have added Quinn? It seemed more likely that Quinn had added herself. She could have done it the night when Emily was drunk. They'd been in Quinn's kitchen when Frank texted, asking Emily to stop for a coffee. She'd left her phone on Quinn's kitchen counter when she'd gone to the bathroom before leaving. Quinn could easily have picked it up and made the change.

All roads seemed to lead back to Quinn. Quinn hadn't needed Emily's help decluttering her garage; she'd needed someone to declutter her life and take the blame for her husband's murder.

As Sergeant Stanley liked to point out, moving Walter Newell's body would have been a two-person job. Had Ryan helped Quinn, with an eye toward becoming her third husband? Or maybe it was Rafe Bartok, the actor in coffee-stained loafers. She swallowed. Or could it have been Frank?

Emily felt her thoughts spiraling out of control. So how did Wally's body get from the wharf to the storage unit? Emily wondered if she had time to drive to the wharf and look around before meeting Becca and Lila at the storage unit. . . .

As if on cue, her phone pinged with a text from Becca.

Heading back. See you at Inner Peace in about an hour

THE commuter lot at the wharf was full when Emily got there. She pulled over in a no-parking zone near the boat ramp.

She took a few deep breaths, trying to slow her heartbeat, when her phone chirped. The readout said QUINN NEWELL. Emily dropped the phone. It bounced onto the car floor and chirped again. In the silence that followed, Emily could hear her own labored breathing. When the voice-mail message chimed, she felt around on the floor for the phone and picked it up, staring at the red dot that said she had two new messages before playing them.

Quinn's voice: "I just got home. I thought you might be here, but it looks like I missed you. Call me as soon as you can." That was the call that had come when Emily was in the garage. The second message: "Me again. Did you get my message? There's something I need to show you. Can you come back right away?"

Emily had no intention of returning to Quinn's house. She pocketed her phone, got out of the car, and walked to the water's edge. Four days ago she'd pulled an auction bidder card from the weeds right here. It seemed bizarre that Wally had last been seen at an auction and that bidder card had washed up right under Emily's nose. Almost as if . . . she'd been meant to find it.

Auctions. They seemed to keep coming up. Wally had been attending one the day he was killed. According to Quinn's wedding announcement, she'd worked in an auction gallery. And hadn't there been auction catalogues on Mr. Murphy's desk?

Emily scrolled back through the pictures she'd taken the first time she and Becca had visited the Murphys' house. There were Murph's carved birds. And before that, his desk. Emily zoomed in. On top was a catalogue from Kalmus Fine Art.

Kalmus. That was the auction house where Quinn had worked. Maybe Quinn knew the Murphys. Maybe she'd helped them sell ill-gotten maps and books.

Emily looked across the water. It was supposed to look as if Emily had followed Walter here after he'd bumped into her at Java Connection. She'd confronted him. Run him down. Rolled him up in a rug. Stashed his body in the water for a while, then driven it to Inner Peace Storage. With evidence the police had collected— paint from her car on Wally's fender and CCTV footage of her car at the storage facility in the middle of the night—they had to be a whisker away from charging her with murder.

And yet, they hadn't.

EMILY GOT BACK IN HER CAR and returned to the Murphys' storage unit. As she got out of the car, the toot of a car horn announced Becca's arrival. Lila pulled in behind her with Mrs. Murphy.

"Hey, how'd it go?" Emily asked as Becca got out of her car.

Becca unlocked the unit as Lila and Mrs. Murphy exited, too. Lila's face was solemn. Judging from Mrs. Murphy's red face and the way she clutched a tissue, things had not gone well.

Lila said, "They knew exactly what they were missing."

"And they had a good idea who'd taken them," Becca added.

"They had our picture," Mrs. Murphy said, "like a pair of common criminals on a WANTED poster, pinned to a bulletin board in their work area." She dabbed at her eyes.

"They were happy to get back *some* of what they lost," Becca said. "But they gave us a list of more items that went missing." She opened the storage unit, then handed Emily a printout. Under her breath she said, "Mr. Murphy dropped an X-Acto blade the last time he was there. That's why they started looking for losses. A little over a year ago they alerted other libraries to what the pair was up to and had an attorney contact Mr. Murphy."

A little over a year ago. That was when Charles Murphy died.

Emily scanned the list of missing items. More bird prints. Maps. And three carved birds. Emily groaned, remembering the entire shelf of carved wooden birds in Mr. Murphy's study.

"Believe me when I tell you," Mrs. Murphy said, "I had no idea what he was up to." Her eyes filled with tears. "He wasn't a bad man. He was just"—she blew her nose—"weak."

Emily could tell from Lila's expression that she wasn't buying it. Emily went inside the storage unit, motioning Becca to follow.

"I said we'd help her inventory the rest of what's in here," Becca said quietly. "Lila's putting together a list of people for her to contact. But after that—" Becca sliced the air with her hand.

Emily got it. They'd cut their losses, hoping to keep their reputation intact. She remembered what Frank had told her: Knowing about stolen goods wasn't a crime, but helping to dispose of them could be. The line between the two wasn't that bright.

"And we've been making such good progress," Becca said.

"Amazing progress," Emily said, "given the circumstances."

Only a few dozen boxes remained on the shelves—Mr. Murphy's thingamabobs: Doorknobs. Hinges. Every box labeled.

But, looking at those boxes now, Emily felt unsettled. She'd recently seen a box of padlocks carefully labeled, just like Mr. Murphy's. It had been disinterred by the police from her own basement, and the sight of it had left Frank visibly shaken.

Frank, who claimed labels were for sissies. In his basement, attic, and garage, he had no need to impose the orderliness Mr. Murphy had apparently craved. He knew where everything was.

So why had that box of padlocks the police pulled out of her basement been tagged with labeling tape? The obvious answer: It wasn't Frank's. It was Mr. Murphy's. Emily remembered how Frank had lit up when Emily had described the contents of the storage unit. Emily had told Frank that she had a key, and—

"What are you thinking?" Becca asked.

"Nothing," Emily said. When Becca looked skeptical, she added, "It's just this whole situation is such a mess."

"Your mother was amazing. I think we'd all be in jail if she hadn't been with us."

"Emily? Becca?" Lila called from outside. "You all okay if I drive Ruth home now?"

Becca looked relieved.

"Sure," Emily called back. "I'll see you at home."

Becca held Emily's gaze until Lila and Mrs. Murphy had driven off. "She knew," Becca said. Her mouth was set in a taut line. "The library had pictures of the pair of them consulting a little notebook that she kept in her purse. Like a shopping list."

"I was afraid of that. After I saw the coat."

Becca said, "All those pockets, and it's not a man's coat."

"Not a man's coat," Emily repeated, but she was thinking about Frank. Had he taken the key and snuck into the storage unit after he was sure Emily was sound asleep? Had he helped himself? Had that been before or after Walter Newell's body was delivered to the storage unit and whoever delivered it changed the lock? Or had Frank helped Quinn move the body and helped himself to a box of hardware as a reward for services rendered? "I can't believe it," she said.

"I can't believe it, either," Becca said. "I knew that we'd have clients who'd make up excuses for what they hoarded. But I wasn't prepared for clients who'd outright lie and get us to help them break the law." Becca gave a wry smile.

"People can really fool you," Emily said.

Becca did a double take. "You're not talking about the Murphys now, are you?" Emily felt her face flush. "Quinn Newell?"

"Quinn told me her husband collected the advertising signs and magazine art that's in their house. But that collection belonged to her *first* husband, and he disappeared from a cruise ship off Bermuda while they were on their honeymoon seven years ago."

Becca's eyes widened. "Disappeared?"

"Jumped. Fell. Or was pushed. The rug we found Walter Newell wrapped up in? I think it came from their garage." Emily showed Becca the picture that she'd taken on her phone of the rolled-up rug the first time she'd been in the Newells' garage.

Becca looked at the picture and winced.

"Thing is, I was just in their garage," Emily went on, "and that rug's not there now. Should I tell the police?" When Becca didn't respond, Emily added, "I need a good reason not to."

"How about because we're up to our armpits in stolen goods and our clients are lying to us? Sometimes a rug is just a rug."

Emily looked across at the boxes that remained on the shelves. "We haven't done anything with the boxes of hardware that Mr. Murphy collected, have we? Because it seems to me there's not as many of them as there were when we first got in here."

Becca looked around. Emily swiped through the shots she'd taken of the storage unit. She showed Becca a picture. There was no question about it: Boxes were missing.

"Who would have taken those boxes?" Becca asked. "Too bad there's no surveillance cameras *inside* these storage units."

At least Emily could fix that. She marched out to her car, returning with the spare camera she carried in the gear bag. She set the camera to low light and programmed it to snap a picture every sixty seconds. She attached a power cord to the camera, tore a hole in the side of a small empty storage box, and set her camera inside, the lens looking through the hole and the cord snaking out the back. She set the box on a high shelf with the camera facing out, pointing down. She ran the power cord from the box to a wall outlet and plugged it in, then turned the camera on and waited.

Click. Emily cringed. The sound of the shutter was loud enough to alert any burglar. Maybe she could mask the sound. There was already white noise in the unit—the ventilation system hum that was blowing cold air on the back of her neck. She checked the thermostat and switched the fan from low to high. The hum grew louder. She waited for the next camera click. She heard it, but she might not have noticed it if she hadn't known it was coming.

"At least now we'll know if someone's coming and going when we're not here," she said.

BECCA drove off, leaving Emily to close and lock the unit. She hoped that Frank was in court. She didn't want him to come home and find her again in his basement, which was where she was headed now. When she turned onto her street, both her mother's and Frank's cars were gone.

She parked in front of the house and grabbed her gear bag. She hurried inside, heading straight for the basement. Dropping her bag, she turned on the light and picked her way down the stairs. She gave the piano frame a wide berth as she looked around for more stray boxes labeled with Mr. Murphy's labeling tape.

She was about to give up when she found them—two cardboard boxes with green plastic labels. They were hidden under a dusty crocheted afghan in the lap of the seated plastic skeleton. She picked up one box. It was heavy, and its label read DRAWER PULLS. The other box was lighter. It was labeled SWITCH PLATES.

No wonder Frank had been so upset when the police took the box of padlocks. *Those are mine,* he'd said. Only they weren't.

Frank had to have been in the storage unit Sunday night. Emily had come back from Quinn's house, shaken by the incident at the coffee shop and only slightly drunk. After she drank the cocoa that Frank had made for her, she'd conked out and slept soundly during the night. So soundly that she'd had trouble waking up the next morning. At the time, she assumed she'd been sleeping off the prosecco, but now she wondered if she'd been drugged.

Did Frank know Quinn? When Emily introduced them, Quinn had acted as if she despised Frank, as if the very notion of a male attorney gave her indigestion. They'd both made it seem as if they were strangers who couldn't even get each other's name straight.

One thing was for sure. Walter Newell had coveted Quinn's first husband's collections or he wouldn't have paraded them on his walls. Frank would have coveted them as well. She wondered what had been tucked into that portfolio he'd been carrying when he found Emily in the basement, about to be attacked by the piano frame. Another treasure he'd never have been able to afford? What would he have been willing to do in return? And was that all it was, a business transaction? Emily had written off Frank's recent indifference to sex as the stress of fertility testing, but maybe he'd been getting it somewhere else.

Just then car tires crunched in the driveway. Through the basement window, Emily caught a glimpse of Frank's car's mag wheels rolling past. A minute later she heard the back door to the house open. "Emily!" Frank called. "Emily? Are you here?"

Emily didn't answer. She heard footsteps overhead. The door opened, then slammed. Then, silence. Frank had gone back out.

Angrily, Emily stacked the box of switch plates on the box of drawer pulls, picked them up, and carried them to the top of the basement stairs. Frank came bursting in from outside, arms loaded with what looked like empty plastic bags.

"Hi, Frank," Emily said.

He jerked upright. "Hey, hon. I thought you were upstairs."

Looking at him, she felt cold, as if she were seeing him for the first time. "What are you up to?" she said, holding the boxes of hardware in front of her, daring him to notice.

"What am *I* up to?" He shook one of the plastic bags at her. "Look familiar?"

Emily dropped the boxes on the kitchen table and took the bag from him. The clear plastic was printed with blue letters: ICE.

"Why on earth did you need this much ice?" he asked.

"Me? What makes you think they're mine?" Emily asked.

"Because they were in the trunk of my car and I didn't put them there. You're the only person who's got a key besides me."

Emily sat down in a kitchen chair. "I don't know how those bags ended up in the trunk of your car. I didn't put them there."

He looked past her to the boxes she'd set on the table. "And I suppose you're going to tell me you didn't put those boxes in the basement, either." Emily was speechless. When she didn't answer, he went on. "Light-switch covers? Drawer pulls? Locks?"

"They're from the storage unit Becca and I are emptying out."

"I guessed as much. But I can't figure why you left them—"

"Whoa." Emily reared back. "I most certainly did not—"

"So I'm supposed to believe that those boxes just magically appeared in the basement?" Frank said. "Like these bags got beamed into the trunk of my car?"

Emily folded her arms across her chest. "It wasn't me."

Frank gave her a hard look. "If you didn't"—he blinked—"and I didn't, then *someone's* messing with us. Planting evidence—"

Before he could finish, the front doorbell rang.

Frank headed for the front hall. Emily followed. He looked through the peephole. "It's your mother."

Frank opened the door. Lila stood outside holding a pizza box. She looked pale and shaken.

"What's wrong?" Frank asked.

Lila stepped inside. Behind her stood two police officers. One of them showed his badge. "Emily Harlow?"

"Officer?" Frank positioned himself in the doorway, his arm wrapped around Emily's shoulders, keeping her glued to his side.

The officer said to Emily, "We'd like you to come with us to the East Hartwell police station to answer some questions."

"Police station?" Frank said. Emily felt his grip on her loosen a bit as he exhaled. "Okay, then. I'll meet you there." She looked at him, surprised. Then she realized how relieved he must be that the police weren't here to search the house. It would take two seconds for them to spot the boxes that were on the kitchen table.

Frank closed the door, leaving the police officers outside to wait for Emily.

Lila appeared in the kitchen. "I'm coming with you."

Lila's no-nonsense support would have been a godsend, and Emily was about to say so when Frank said, "We need someone here in case the police come back with another search warrant."

Sadly, Emily had to agree. "If nothing else, as a witness."

"But—" Lila began to protest.

Emily forced a smile. "I'll be okay. I just need my gear bag." She didn't want to have it confiscated in another police search.

Lila disappeared and returned a moment later with the bag. "You're sure?" Lila said. Emily gave her a hug.

Frank said, "Go on. Give me ten minutes and I'll meet you there. Meanwhile . . ." He put a finger to his lips.

EMILY wasn't surprised when the back seat of the police car felt like a cage. But it made her feel safe and gave her the space she needed to sort her thoughts. As the cruiser drove off, she felt as if her life, like a disordered closet, had been suddenly emptied out. What to toss? What to keep? As if she had choices.

This had all started with Ryan's call to Becca, begging them to help his wealthy friend. Emily had assumed that Quinn was one of Ryan's *wenches*, as he liked to call them. And yet, when Emily saw them together, he barely seemed to know her. Was Ryan a straw man, set up to receive Emily's distrust while more and more evidence piled up connecting Emily to Walter Newell's murder? Who had put the boxes from that storage unit in her basement and the empty ice bags in the trunk of Frank's car? The obvious answer: Frank. Or was she overreacting? Had all those months of futile fertility tests left her feeling estranged and paranoid?

By the time the police car pulled up to the station and one of the officers had herded her upstairs, Emily was no closer to deciding which pieces of her life to tuck back in place and which to jettison. It all came down to whether or not she trusted Frank.

They continued down a corridor. The door to the room where

she'd been taken to give a *written* statement was open. At first Emily didn't recognize the woman inside wearing dark glasses, a white coat, and a red head scarf. But on a second look she realized it was Quinn. Quinn glanced at Emily but remained poker-faced.

Then Ryan appeared from behind Quinn. He stepped through the doorway and looked past Emily and down the corridor, where Frank strode toward them with another police officer.

Emily's officer nudged her on. She looked back. When Frank got to Ryan, Ryan said, "Sidebar," and pulled Frank aside.

No. No sidebars! This wasn't some corporate lawsuit. This was their life. But Emily feigned indifference and followed her officer into another windowless interview room along the corridor.

She took a seat at the table. Frank joined her, closing the door. He paced the few steps that he could. Pent-up anxiety.

"What were you and Ryan—" Emily began.

Frank shushed her, raising his eyebrows in the direction of a mirror on the wall. Probably two-way glass.

"That's sturdy and nice-looking," announced a woman's voice, "and thirty years ago you might have found a buyer." It took Emily a moment to recognize the voice as her own, another moment to realize that it was coming from a small speaker that sat on the table. "But these days it's what people refer to as . . . 'brown furniture.' Frankly, it's hard to give away. But there'd be a ready buyer for that kitchen set if you put it out at a yard sale."

"What is this crap?" Frank said.

Emily stared at the speaker in horror. This was the conversation she and Quinn had had on the night they'd met, a conversation fueled by far too much prosecco. Quinn had *recorded* it?

"Goody." Quinn's voice. "A yard sale! Let's not invite Wally."

"Or you could donate." Emily. "There's a ton of charities, and you'd get a tax deduction. I can find one that will pick up."

"What I really should do is stuff all of my stuff down Wally's—" Silence for a few moments. "Think there are any charities that will come and pick *him* up? Or maybe I should just chuck him off the roof instead."

The laughter that followed was Emily's. Had she really found that so hilarious? Frank sank down into the chair beside her, staring at Emily in disbelief. Emily wanted to crawl under the table.

Quinn's voice picked back up. "Or slip poison mushrooms into his lasagna." A gagging sound. "Or accidentally back over him. *Rrrmm.* Oops! My bad."

The clink of wineglasses. ᵲThen Emily. "To *'Til death do us part.*"

"To accidents waiting to happen." Quinn's voice. "Or maybe it's safer to hire a hit man, a complete stranger, and be done with it?" After a pause, "So, could you?"

"Could I what?" Emily had sounded so matter-of-fact.

"I'll bet you would. In a heartbeat." Then, in a barely audible whisper, "If you thought you could get away with it."

There was a click, and the audio shut off. In the silence that followed, Emily stared at the tabletop. Slowly she let her gaze rise. Frank chewed on his thumbnail and scowled.

"Frank? I didn't—" She reached out to touch his arm. He pulled away and shushed her.

The door to the room opened, and Sergeant Stanley stepped in. He looked down at Emily, then at Frank with undisguised pity.

Frank crossed his legs, folded his arms across his chest, and leaned back. "That tape isn't evidence. My wife never gave her permission to be recorded. It's inadmissible in court."

"I wasn't aware that this is a courtroom, Counselor," Stanley said. "Still, it speaks to your wife's state of mind." He took a seat, addressing Emily. "Mrs. Newell knew she couldn't get away with killing her husband. But you, a stranger, could." He shifted his gaze to Frank. "Mr. Harlow, I'd watch my back if I were you. Because it sounds as if your wife and Mrs. Newell struck a deal."

Frank sat there, frozen. Emily could tell he was furious.

"Test results are back," Stanley went on, still talking to Frank. "Those carpet fibers that we found in the back of your wife's car? They match the rug that Walter Newell's body was wrapped in. The report confirms the CCTV camera footage that shows Mrs. Harlow delivering a body to the storage unit."

"All it confirms—" Emily began.

"Don't respond," Frank said.

"—is that the rug was in my car. Not that I put it there or even that I was driving. Frank knows. I was asleep."

"You're saying someone took your car and used it to transport Mr. Newell's body?" Stanley paused. "Let's run with that. Who could that have been? Had to be someone who had a set of car keys or who knew where to find them." His gaze shifted to Frank.

"Frank doesn't know anything about that rug," Emily said. "But I do. I can even tell you where it came from. It was—"

"Emily!" Frank's voice echoed in the room. He squeezed her arm and addressed Stanley. "Can my wife and I have a minute?"

"It's up to your wife," Stanley said. "Pardon me, your client."

Emily nodded to Stanley. Stanley got up and went to the door, glancing at his watch. "Five minutes." He started to close the door, then turned back. "Mrs. Harlow, I'm telling you this in good conscience. From my experience it's not a good idea to be married to your attorney." He left and closed the door behind him.

"What an ass," Frank said, muttering into his cupped palm.

Frank fished his cell phone out of his pocket and opened a newscast, turning the sound up. Then he put the cell phone on the table alongside the speaker, turned his chair away from the mirror, and waited until Emily had turned away from it, too.

With the news playing, Emily could barely hear Frank's low voice. "We don't know where he's taking this. Because, taken at face value, it mounts up. Boxes from that storage unit show up in my basement. And now we come to find out that the rug the body was wrapped up in actually *was* in your car."

"I know where that rug came from," Emily said in a whisper. "There was one like it in the Newells' garage."

"One like it?" Frank narrowed his eyes. "Is that going to help you? Taken together, it points to you being involved—if not in Newell's murder, then in the disposal of his body. If I were the police and heard that recording of you and that woman talking about getting rid of your husbands, it wouldn't be too big a leap to imagine the two of you coming up with a plan. Kill her husband and make it look like *I* did it. Two husbands for the price of one."

It took Emily a while to wrap her head around that logic. "I think the rug was planted in my car to incriminate me," she said.

"And the boxes of hardware? Planted to incriminate *me*."

Emily was speechless. "You can't think that I—"

"Of course I don't. "And you can't think that I . . ."

"That you what?" Drugged her so he could slip out at night? Took boxes from the Murphys' storage unit? Helped Quinn hire someone to kill her husband? Helped her himself?

"Do you think the police know about Quinn's first husband?" Emily asked. "That collection of advertising signs and illustrations hanging in her home? They belonged to him, not Walter."

He didn't say anything for a moment. "She was married before?"

"Married before. Widowed before. For all I know, she's already got number three waiting in the wings. Maybe that's how Ryan figures into all this. Or Rafe Bartok." *Or you?*

Emily was too focused on watching Frank's reaction to notice that the door of the interview room had opened. Behind her, Sergeant Stanley said, "Who's Rafe Bartok?"

"Rafe Barok," Emily said. "He's the man who showed up in a coffee shop, made up to look like Walter Newell and driving Walter's car. Just to guarantee that he'd be noticed, he hit my car and had someone report the incident to the police."

Chapter 13

STANLEY SAT IN THE chair across the table from Emily in the little interview room. He leaned forward. "Go on," he said.

"That's enough!" Frank looked like he was ready to explode.

"I'll answer your question about who's Rafe Bartok," Emily said, ignoring Frank, "if you'll answer a question for me first. When does your medical examiner think that Newell *could* have died? Forget CCTV cameras. What does the body tell you?"

"What are you thinking?" Stanley gave Emily a narrow look.

"I'm thinking that maybe your medical examiner would come to a different conclusion if he had all the facts. I want to know what's the earliest that Walter Newell *could* have died? What's the time range? Because at the time he was supposed to have been at an auction in Hyannis, and later when he's supposed to have been driving back in a major traffic jam, and later when he's supposed to have hit my car in the Square and then gotten run down at the town wharf, is it possible that he was already dead?"

Stanley propped an elbow on the table, rested his chin on his knuckles. "From the autopsy results?"

"This is crazy," Frank said. "Walter Newell was at that auction. He registered. So doesn't that mean—"

"It doesn't mean a thing," Emily said. "All you need to register at an auction is a credit card. If he had his credit card at the auction, why didn't he use it later that night to pay for his coffee?"

Stanley said, "You really think someone went to the auction pretending to be Walter Newell?"

"Maybe," Emily said. "What I want to know is, from the body, what's the earliest he could have died?" She looked at Stanley. At Frank. "Anyone have a problem with that?"

Frank shut down, his face drained of expression.

"Fair enough." Stanley stood. "Give me a few minutes."

As soon as he left the room, Frank turned to Emily and gave an exasperated huff. "I only hope you know what you're doing."

Emily shushed him, pointing to the mirror. She was banking on something from Stanley that would account for a whole lot of ice.

When Stanley returned, he was carrying a manila folder. He opened it and pulled out a stapled set of pages. "Here's the autopsy report. I'll read you the conclusions." He turned to one of the final pages. "Based on body temperature, rigor, and livor mortis, approximate time of death: eight o'clock p.m., Sunday, August fourth, to eight o'clock a.m., Monday, August fifth. Immediate cause of death: traumatic asphyxia due to blunt chest trauma."

Emily swallowed. "Eight o'clock Sunday to eight o'clock Monday," she said. "That's a twelve-hour window."

"We like it to be more precise. But the body had been in water. That delays the onset of rigor."

"So the time frame is really a guess," Emily said.

Stanley nodded.

"It allows time," Emily went on, "for him to have registered for the auction and for that witness to report him hitting my car?"

"The hit-and-run," Stanley said, "was the last time anyone but his killer saw Walter Newell alive."

"No, it was the last time anyone saw Walter Newell's *car.*"

He opened his hands, palms up, allowing that she had a point.

"Could Walter Newell have been killed earlier and his body packed in ice?" Emily said.

Stanley blinked. Narrowed his eyes. "It would take a lot of ice."

"It sure would," Emily said. "And if that's what happened, what does it do to the estimated time of death?"

"I'd have to ask an expert," Stanley said.

"Come on. You know as well as I do that it would shift the time frame earlier. How much earlier?"

Frank grabbed her. "Emily, this is outlandish."

She peeled his fingers from around her arm. "My husband is worried because someone stuffed the trunk of his car with empty ten-pound ice bags. He thought I put them there."

"But you didn't," Stanley said.

"Of course I didn't."

"Bags." Stanley sat back. "You have them?"

"I handled them," Frank said. "Emily handled them, too."

And so did the killer. "Aren't they in your car?" Emily asked him.

Frank swallowed. "I got rid of them on the way over here."

"You . . ." Stanley shook his head. "Where?"

"In a dumpster behind 7-Eleven."

Stanley faced the mirror, gesturing to whoever was watching from the other side. "I'm sending an officer over there now." He turned to Frank. "I'm hoping for your sake they're still there. Tampering with evidence in a murder investigation? That's a felony." He turned his attention to Emily. "So you're suggesting that Walter Newell got back from the auction early."

"Or wasn't there at all. Someone using his ID and credit card could have registered as him."

Stanley picked up the thread. "But he was already dead, his body packed in ice. Someone else drove his car to the coffee shop, created a stir, hit your car, and abandoned the car at the wharf."

"Rafe Bartok. That's who ran into me at the coffee shop."

"And you know that . . . how?"

Emily remembered the promise she'd made to Ana Perez. "You can check for yourself. Look up the purchases he made on his personal credit card. I'll bet he used it to pay for a venti. Hot. Black. At around nine thirty at Java Connection."

Stanley nodded, thinking. "So assuming Walter Newell died, let's say a day earlier, where were you on Saturday?"

Before Emily could answer, Frank was on his feet. "Enough. My wife has been more than forthcoming. Emily?" He was out the door before Emily had gotten up out of her chair.

Emily glanced at Stanley, catching a look of frustration on his face. "You have no idea who killed Walter Newell, do you?"

Stanley seemed taken aback. "Let's just say your information has been extremely helpful. Right now I have no more questions for you. Just one piece of advice. Watch yourself."

IT WAS dark when Emily found Frank in his car in the parking lot. He had his cell to his ear, talking animatedly. She caught his gaze through the windshield. He held up a finger. Then shifted to face away from her.

Finally, Emily heard a click—the doors unlocking. Frank's window rolled down. "Sorry," Frank said. "I didn't mean to abandon you. I just wish you hadn't told them about the ice bags."

"I wish you hadn't dumped them at the 7-Eleven."

"I didn't. I was buying time so we could destroy the bags and return those boxes to the storage unit." A police cruiser screamed out of the parking lot. "I think you're right. The bags. The boxes. The rug in your car. They were planted to implicate you. Or me. Or both of us." Frank reached across, pushed open the passenger door. "Get in. It won't take long before they realize there's no bags in that dumpster. They'll be back to search our house and cars. We need to make sure there's nothing for them to find."

Emily hesitated. "Who were you talking to on the phone?"

"Ryan. I wanted to give him a heads-up in case you and I both get pulled in again." He made it sound so routine.

Watch yourself. Stanley's warning came back to her. She said, "You're sure you can trust Ryan? He connected us to Quinn Newell in the first place. He left the ball game early. He could have helped Quinn kill her husband and hide his body."

"Emily, Ryan is the least of our worries right now. I don't think you realize how much trouble you could end up in. What if it turns out that everything in that storage unit is stolen?"

Emily swallowed hard. "But we're returning everything we can to the libraries they were taken from."

"What do you want to bet that your client will cut a deal in return for testifying against you?"

Emily stared at the open car door. Frank was right about Mrs. Murphy. She'd put her own self-interest first.

"We need to return those boxes now," Frank said. "If they're found anywhere but in that storage unit, you'll be facing charges of trafficking stolen goods. You, your mother, and Becca could get sent to prison. You know how to open the unit and where the boxes need to be put back. Come on. I can't do this without you."

He was right. Doing nothing could put all of them at risk. Emily got in the car.

"Which way?" Frank said.

Emily pointed, and Frank pulled out of the parking lot and accelerated onto the main street. "Keep on straight until you're past the wharf," she said. "Then right again over the bridge."

Emily got out her phone and texted her mother that she was almost done. Then she put her phone in the cupholder between the seats, closed her eyes, and thought about the evidence. An abandoned car with a dented fender. A rolled-up rug in a puddle of water. Empty ice bags. Boxes of vintage hardware. A cover-up that would have taken two people to pull off—two people with access to the Murphys' storage unit, Emily's car, and her house.

Emily opened her eyes as Frank drove through the main gate of Inner Peace Storage, continuing to the Murphys' unit. He parked just past it, beyond the CCTV camera. Fear prickled at the back of Emily's neck. How did he know which unit it was?

Frank popped the trunk and got out. Emily stayed in the car, panicked. He must have been here before. She realized that no one but Frank knew where she was. She should text Lila.

She reached for her cell phone, but it wasn't in the cupholder. She felt around on the floor. In her gear bag. No phone. The car jiggled as Frank rummaged in the trunk.

It slammed shut, and Frank emerged holding a long-handled windshield scraper with a plastic bag hanging off the end of it. In the other hand he held a pen. Not a pen. From one end of it shot a beam of green light. A laser pointer.

Frank aimed the laser at the security camera as he moved into its field of vision. Raised the windshield scraper and draped the bag over the camera lens. Then he went back to the trunk and returned carrying the two boxes containing Mr. Murphy's hardware. He rapped on Emily's window. "What's the combination?"

She picked up her gear bag and got out of the car. With not another human in sight, the storage facility felt like a cemetery.

"Frank, have you seen my phone?" she asked.

"Again? You're always losing it."

Emily didn't bother coming up with a response. She remembered the combination Becca had given her. She went over to the storage-unit door, bent down, and entered the code. The lock popped open. Frank raised the door and turned on the light.

She hung back as Frank entered.

"Where do these go?" he asked.

She pointed to one of the now half-empty shelves. He set the boxes down and was starting to turn away when he froze, hyperalert. Emily knew at once what had happened. Even on high, the fan in the unit hadn't kept him from noticing the shutter click.

At first he didn't spot the box where Emily had set up her camera. But when the shutter clicked again, he did.

"What the . . . ?" He reached for the top shelf, took down the box, and unplugged the power cord. Raised the lid. He emerged from the unit and thrust the box at her. "Did you set this up?"

"Of course I did," Emily said. She took the box, lifted out her camera, and detached the cord.

Frank stared at the camera. "Why didn't the police find it?"

Frank's jaw was tense. He thought the camera had been set up days earlier, when Emily had first opened the unit, before Walter Newell's body was dumped there and the lock was changed.

"I guess they didn't know what to look for," Emily said, playing along. "One of the security guards told me that he'd seen a woman coming and going from this unit. That's when I planted that camera. We didn't want to get accused of stealing anything."

"Did you catch anyone?" Frank reached for the camera.

"Let me have a look." Her heart was beating so hard she was surprised Frank couldn't hear it. She turned away and pressed PLAYBACK. One of the first images, that looked like a close-up of Frank's shirt, had been snapped as he'd taken the lid off the box.

"There you are," she said. Frank looked startled. "Just now."

"Let me see," he said in a harsher tone.

She turned the screen to face him and gave an uneasy laugh. "Your shirt and your thumb." She pressed PLAYBACK again. The previous image came up: Frank putting a box of hardware on the shelf. The one before that was a black exposure—the dark interior of the closed storage unit, taken before they'd opened it up.

She turned the screen away from him and scrolled back through a stream of pictures of the same dark nothingness.

"What?" Frank said, coming up beside her.

"Still just shooting blanks." She clicked back more until an image came up. "And . . . wait a minute." There was a silhouette backlit against the partially open unit door. The time stamp placed it a few hours ago. "I can't see who it is. Looks like a man."

"Emily." Beads of sweat had popped up on Frank's forehead.

In the next image, taken a minute before, the door to the unit was fully raised. In the foreground, Emily recognized Mrs. Murphy. She was standing by the workbench, opening a document tube. Several other tubes were lying on the workbench.

When Emily saw the next image, she almost dropped the camera. There was Mrs. Murphy again, but now a man stood beside her. The overhead light gleamed off his silver pompadour. He looked like the man in the framed photo that Mrs. Murphy had on her piano—her supposedly deceased husband. They had one . . . no, two documents on the workbench. Two maps, similar in size.

Emily zoomed in. Even with crappy resolution the maps looked identical. She remembered what her mother had told her about printing a forgery of an old map onto old paper using digital technology so advanced that even experts were fooled.

"What? What did you get?" Frank said.

Emily clicked back, then ahead again. Mrs. Murphy hadn't been opening the tube. She'd been closing it. And she'd slid one of those two maps inside, keeping one and sealing up the other. It wasn't hard to guess which copy she was planning to return to the library.

"People can really surprise you, can't they?" Emily said, looking at Frank. "And not in a good way."

Frank had gone pale. "You have to destroy those pictures." He grabbed for the camera, but Emily held on as she backed away. He tugged it his way; she tugged it hers. Finally it flew from their hands and landed on the pavement with a thud.

Frank lunged for it. Picked it up. A web of cracks in the lens lit up as he turned the camera over under the streetlight. He dropped the camera on the ground and stomped on it until the screen shattered. The case came apart, disgorging circuit boards and wires.

A wave of sadness swept over Emily. Not for the camera, which could be replaced. Not for the pictures that revealed Mrs. Murphy to be a thief and a fraud. She wasn't even a widow.

No, the grief Emily felt was for the Frank she'd married, who'd stood in his first pin-striped suit for their wedding as they faced the minister. When they'd kissed, he'd smelled sweet and musky. That lazy smile of his that could still take her breath away.

Back then, Emily knew that she was *the one* he'd chosen. Now he could barely meet her gaze. "Emily, I—" he began. For a moment it seemed as if he were about to break down. But if so, he was interrupted by a car that approached from behind her. His face was lit up by oncoming headlights as the car came to a halt. When Frank waved, Emily's heart sank. She wheeled around.

The car's headlights went out, but even in the dark Emily could see that it was a white Honda Civic hatchback with the Clutter Kickers logo stenciled on the door.

THE car door opened, and a woman got out. She wore a blue cap, its brim pulled down over her eyes. A long ponytail stuck out the back. She had on blue pants and a top, just like the ones that Emily and Becca wore for dirty work. It was Quinn Newell.

This must have been how she'd looked when she'd driven Emily's car to pick up her husband's body from wherever he'd been killed— not the wharf, Emily was pretty sure—and deliver it to this storage unit. Making sure that the CCTV camera got enough of a glimpse of her to convince the police she was Emily.

Now Quinn stood, arms akimbo, facing Emily.

"Shall I tell you how her first husband died?" Emily said to Frank. "The one she married before Wally. She killed him, too."

"Shut up," Quinn said, and lunged at Emily.

Emily backed up onto the apron of the storage unit. "On her honeymoon—" Before she could finish, Quinn backhanded her across the face. Emily staggered back, tripped over her gear bag, and landed on her behind on the concrete floor inside the unit. Winded, she sat there gasping as Quinn stood over her.

"Stop it!" Frank shouted. "This wasn't part of the deal."

Emily rolled over onto her stomach. "She's not good at deals, unless it's the part about 'til death do us part."

"I said, shut up!" Quinn said, and kicked Emily. Emily curled into a fetal position, pain like lightning searing her rib cage.

Above her she heard Frank. "You were married before?"

"What difference does it make?" Quinn snapped. She grabbed Emily under one arm. "Come on," she said to Frank. "Help me."

Frank hesitated before he grabbed Emily under her other arm. Together he and Quinn dragged her to the back of the storage unit. Quinn yanked the overhead door shut and turned on the light.

"Your first husband was killed?" Frank asked.

"So?" Quinn gave a slow smile. "Does it matter?"

"It matters, Frank." Emily took a painful breath. "He was a collector, like you. Those signs and prints in her house were his."

"They were Wally's," Quinn said.

"Know how her first husband died?" Emily said. "She pushed him off the deck of a cruise ship. Then she marries Wally. He's not a collector at all. Just—what?—wealthy? And now I guess she's in the market for an attorney to settle his estate. Someone who'd do anything to own all those fabulous magazine covers." Frank's cringe told her she was right.

"Shut up," Quinn reared back, about to kick Emily again, when Frank grabbed her around the waist from behind. "Seriously?" Quinn said to him. "You have to know it's too late to have second thoughts. You're up to your neck—"

"It's not too late," Emily said, struggling to sit up. "Frank?"

Frank looked lost. He'd always been so good at convincing himself that he was on the side of the angels, even when that meant representing a corporate pariah whose faulty engineering was killing people. But once upon a time, he'd defended people who didn't have any other options. That Frank had married Emily in a pinstriped suit. Maybe, just maybe, he was still in there.

"Frank, you don't have to—" Emily began.

"I told you the ride might get a little bumpy," Quinn said, shaking free of Frank's grasp. "You just have to hold on. Trust me."

"This wasn't supposed to happen," Frank said.

"What did you think was going to happen?" Emily said. "You'd set me up to be charged with murder and I'd roll over?"

She thought back over what must have happened. Quinn and Frank had waited for a night when Becca was busy and Emily would have to go alone to meet a new client. Becca had gotten Quinn's call. When Becca said they didn't work Sunday nights, a man who identified himself as Ryan Melanson had called Becca, begging her to accommodate a client who needed their help *now* decluttering. That caller must have been Frank, claiming to be Ryan. Becca wouldn't have been able to tell their voices apart.

Frank would have advised Quinn to complain about a husband

who was an out-of-control collector. To have a bottle of prosecco handy. To put the Care Bears atop the pile in the garage.

Quinn gazed at Emily. "In another lifetime we might have been besties. Now you need to disappear. The question is, how?"

"I guess you don't have the time to create an illusion," Emily said, "or the convenience of a ship's railing to push me over."

"He sat on the railing, you know. Like he was asking . . ." Quinn shifted her gaze toward the river. "Water," she said, mulling. "I wonder when it's high tide." She took out her phone. After a bit of fiddling, she frowned. "Not for a few hours."

Just then there was the sound of movement on the other side of the overhead door. Quinn and Frank traded surprised looks as, with a creak, the door started to rise. Frank raced over and slammed it shut. Quinn joined him, holding it down.

"Who's in there?" A woman's thin, reedy voice. "You don't belong in there. Get out!" Emily had never been happier to hear Mrs. Murphy at her most outraged.

"Friend of yours?" Emily said. Quinn glared at her. "I guess you knew her husband. Charles Murphy? Antique maps, sold at auction? You helped them out, didn't you? Did she know you were going to dump your husband's body in her storage unit?"

"Let me in!" Mrs. Murphy's voice came from outside.

Emily shouted, "Ruth! Call the police. It's Emily. I'm trapped." But her final words were drowned out by Mrs. Murphy banging on the door from the other side.

Quinn glared at Emily, but she couldn't hold the door shut and muzzle her at the same time. The door rattled as Frank and Quinn held it shut. They didn't notice Emily crab-walking inch by inch backward to her gear bag.

"What are you doing in there?" This time it was an older man's voice. Probably the white-haired Mr. Murphy. "Open the door."

Quinn and Frank were struggling to keep the door shut. Emily reached her gear bag, found her stun gun inside, then painfully rose. She held it in front of her and advanced toward Quinn.

"What's that supposed to be?" Quinn said, eyeing the stun gun, straining to keep the door down.

"Frank?" Emily said. "Why don't you explain?"

"It's a stun gun," Frank said. "But trust me, she'd never use it."

Emily put her thumb on the trigger. "You don't think so?" She took a step toward Quinn, and Quinn shrank back. "Don't worry. It won't kill you. But it'll knock you out cold for an hour or two."

Quinn kicked out at Emily, aiming for the stun gun. But she couldn't reach it and hold the door at the same time.

"Mrs. Murphy," Emily shouted. "Call the police. Do it now!"

"Emily? Is that you?" Mrs. Murphy asked. "Open the door."

Emily could only hope that Mrs. Murphy had been as surprised as anyone when Walter Newell's body turned up in her storage unit. The woman was greedy. But she was more amoral than evil.

"I know what you've been up to," Emily shouted. "Stealing and counterfeiting. Selling fakes. But you really don't want to be charged as an accessory to murder. I can help you, once I get out of here. But you have to call the police. Tell them to come. Now."

Emily heard low voices, Mrs. Murphy's and the man's. Sounded as if they were arguing. They wouldn't be eager to have the police back. There'd be no windfall from selling original old prints and returning their giclée copies to libraries from which the originals had been stolen. Emily hoped the loss was outweighed by the prospect of no charges, no trial, and no prison term.

Finally Emily heard footsteps. A car door slammed. An engine turned over, and tires sounded on the pavement.

Quinn released her grip on the door and inched away.

"She's calling the police," Emily said.

"Maybe," Quinn said. "But I'm guessing not. They've got quite a big investment to protect." She darted at Emily, reaching for the stun gun but missed.

"You sound as if you know them," Emily said. "They steal. You fence?" Emily backed away, running into the workbench.

Quinn kicked the stun gun from Emily's grip and sent it skittering across the floor. Quinn lunged for it and grabbed it. "This knocks you out for a few hours?" Quinn looked at the gun. "Really?" She rushed at Emily, pinning her against a bank of shelving, poking the gun hard into her neck and pushing the trigger.

Emily felt a tickle of electricity, the stun gun's feeble attempt at firing. She screamed, then slid to the floor, stiffening and shaking, her eyes open, going from rigid to slack. She had no idea if that was what would have happened if the gun had been charged, but she was banking on neither Quinn nor Frank knowing, either.

Out of the corner of her eye, she saw Frank raising the door. He came over and got down on one knee. He grasped her wrist and felt her pulse. She knew her heart was pounding.

"She's all right," Quinn said. "We need to get her out of here before anyone comes back." When Frank didn't respond, she said sharply, "Frank, you'll tell them that she was depressed. At her wits' end about the murder investigation. Her reputation shot—"

"How can you be like this?" Frank said. "So cold. It's as if she's just . . ." Frank seemed at a loss, but Emily would have supplied the rest: *an inconvenience.*

"You had no trouble helping me get rid of Wally's body," Quinn said. "This is no time to get sentimental."

Helping me get rid of Wally's body. Emily felt relieved that maybe Frank hadn't actually killed him. Without meaning to, she shifted her gaze. Her eyes locked with Frank's. He flinched.

"What?" Quinn said.

"I . . ." Frank stared down at Emily. Was he going to rat her out? She wanted to believe that he'd gotten into this situation not with a huge leap but inch by inch. An attraction. An affair. Emily knew how Quinn could hone in on vulnerability and lure you in.

Emily squeezed Frank's hand. She could only hope that he'd remember what they'd been to each other.

"Back the car up to the door," Frank said.

Quinn went out. Frank got behind Emily and dragged her out of the unit as Quinn backed the Honda up to them. Frank raised the tailgate. "Get her bag," he called. "The stun gun, too."

While Quinn was in the storage unit, Frank whispered, "Get in." Emily scrambled into her car through the open tailgate. "Stay down and hold on." She lay curled on her side as he closed the hatchback. Seconds later the front door of the car opened and shut. The car lurched in reverse; then it peeled out.

"Frank!" From outside, Quinn's voice pierced the air. "Where are you . . ." Her voice grew faint until it was gone entirely.

"Emmy, are you all right?" Frank said.

Emily's side throbbed. "I'm—" She heard the shriek of a siren. Blue lights screamed past in the opposite direction. Emily looked out the back window as the speeding police cruiser continued toward the storage facility. Mrs. Murphy, bless her heart. She must have called the police, after all.

"I'll be okay," Emily said.

Frank tossed her his cell phone. "Call Ryan. Tell him to meet us at the police station."

Tell me you didn't kill Quinn's husband. Did it really matter? Because what was clear was that this had been a twofer, as Frank had suggested. Only not two wives setting up one husband to take the blame for the other husband's murder. It was a pair of lovers, setting up his wife to take the blame for her husband's murder. When you looked at it that way, Emily had been Frank's savior. Because how long would it have been before Quinn tired of him? One look at what Frank collected would have been enough to curdle her rosy view of the life that he and she would share.

And he would have insisted on a prenup.

Chapter 14

Six months later Emily sat at her kitchen table with Becca and Lila, the front page of the *Boston Globe* spread out in front of them. "Looks like he's gained a little weight," Lila said. She was taking in a photograph of Frank testifying at the murder trial of Quinn Newell, aka Amanda Quinn Safstrom Newell.

Frank didn't look fat. He looked pasty-faced and miserable in a tie that seemed to be choking him. He'd been in custody since the night Ryan met them in the parking lot of the police station and walked Frank inside to cut a deal with the DA. Frank had agreed to turn state's evidence in return for pleading guilty to a lesser charge. Eventually, he hoped to be released on time served.

Emily would testify soon, the prosecution's other star witness. She was relieved that the tape of her and Quinn, apparently conspiring to kill their husbands, had been ruled inadmissible.

Rafe Bartok would take a turn in the witness box, too, testifying that Quinn and Frank had hired him to impersonate Walter Newell. His role was to drive Walter's car to the Hyannis auction, register as Walter, turn around, and drive back in time to run into Emily at Java Connection, where he'd make a scene, ding her car, and abandon Walter's car at the wharf, establishing multiple witnesses who'd swear that Walter was alive long after he'd been killed and put on ice in the Jacuzzi in the Newells' master bath.

The operation had gone off like clockwork until Rafe Bartok realized the face he'd been paid to make himself up to look like belonged to a murder victim. Emily felt it was entirely reasonable for him to feel shortchanged by a mere one thousand dollars' cash, which Quinn had withdrawn from the bank a few days earlier.

Frank was being held in what they called low-security detention. Emily was not paying him visits. She'd sold his BMW, then rented three storage units at Inner Peace Storage and hired movers to transport everything he'd stuffed into their basement, attic, and garage. Most of the time, looking at those newly emptied spaces sparked joy.

"So," Emily said, folding the newspaper, "back to work." On the table she placed a chart showing their current projects. "Looks like everyone has a full plate." Business was booming, with Lila rounding the staff of Freeze-Frame Clutter Kickers up to three and expanding their reach to Cape Cod.

Quinn's trial, along with the return of prints stolen from libraries, had catapulted them to national news. The Murphys' books turned out to be worthless. Most had been purchased as library discards. It was the prints, protected in special tubes impervious to mold and decay, that were priceless. The police had impounded scores of giclée copies that the Murphys had been prepared to "return" to the libraries from which they'd stolen the originals. They'd then sell the originals, netting over a million dollars.

Emily was convinced that Mrs. Murphy was protecting her husband. Apparently, he'd gone underground a year ago, around the time the District Collection had gotten wind of their losses. Mrs. Murphy wouldn't admit that he was still alive or that she'd known Quinn Newell, though it must have been Quinn who suggested Mrs. Murphy call Freeze-Frame Clutter Kickers and act the part of the clueless widow who needed help to liquidate—or the more accurate word would be *launder*—her husband's collection. Quinn must have had a key to the Murphys' storage unit. She'd probably been the woman the Inner Peace security guard had seen coming and going from the unit. She probably disabled the ventilation system before she and Frank dumped Walter's body there. Emily expected it would all come out at her trial.

"Any new leads?" Emily asked.

Lila said, "I got a call this morning from a woman who inherited her mother's collection of dolls. Hundreds of them. She and her three sisters are arguing about what to do with them." Lila laid out the project. The dolls, the dollhouses, the clothing. Emily envisioned the video that she could put together. Dolls marching around. Saluting one another. Doll parts sorting themselves.

"Four sisters?" Becca said, giving the project a thumbs-down. "It will be a mess, and it won't ever be about the dolls."

AfterWords

Hallie Ephron found inspiration for her latest novel close to home—in her own marriage.

The author, who describes her husband as a "world-champion yard sale-er," found plenty of material for *Careful What You Wish For* in his copious collections of old books, prints, and maps. Ephron, by contrast, is more organized. "When I found myself slavishly following Marie Kondo's instructions for decluttering my closet and folding my socks," she says, "I knew I needed to write about the kind of marriage where one partner is inured to clutter and the other is not."

Of course, she clarifies that the similarities between fact and fiction end there. Her husband, she is quick to point out, "sparks joy. He is not in the book, but his stuff is."

While yard sales may not be Ephron's passion, she has plenty of other interests that spark joy. For example, she enjoys working with unpublished authors and teaches writing at workshops and conferences across the country and abroad. Ephron is also an amateur birder. "Spotting a bird you've never seen before is like adding to a collection without adding to the clutter," she says.

Ephron is a *New York Times* bestselling author, Edgar Award finalist, and five-time finalist for the Mary Higgins Clark Award. The daughter of Hollywood screenwriters, she grew up in Beverly Hills and currently lives near Boston, Massachusetts.

The condensations in this volume have been created by Trusted Media Brands, Inc.,
by special arrangement with the publishers, authors, or holders of copyrights.
With the exception of actual personages identified as such, the characters and incidents
in the selections in this volume are entirely the products of the authors' imaginations
and have no relation to any person or event in real life.

ACKNOWLEDGMENTS

Page 157: © Michael Livio. Page 299: Pam Lary. Page 437: © Scott Bottles. Page 575: Lynn Wayne.
Jacket and title page image: Image Source/Getty Images.

The original editions of the books in this volume are published and copyrighted as follows:

Lock Every Door, published at $26.00 by Dutton, an imprint of Penguin Publishing Group,
a division of Penguin Random House LLC
© 2019 by Todd Ritter

Shamed, published at $26.99 by Minotaur Books,
an imprint of St. Martin's Publishing Group
© 2019 by Linda Castillo

The Whispers of War, published at $27.00 by Gallery Books,
an imprint of Simon & Schuster, Inc.
© 2020 by Julia Kelly

Careful What You Wish For, published at $26.99 by William Morrow,
an imprint of HarperCollins Publishers
© 2019 by Hallie Ephron

The volumes in this series are issued every two months.
Readers may receive this service by contacting us by mail, email, or company website.

In the United States:
Reader's Digest Select Editions
PO Box 50005, Prescott, AZ 86304-5005
bookservices@rd.com
rd.com

In Canada:
Reader's Digest Select Editions
PO Box 970 Stn Main, Markham, ON L3P 0K2
bookservices@rd.com
rd.ca

Some of the titles in this volume are also available in large-print format.
For information about Select Editions Large Type, contact us at
PO Box 433031, Palm Coast, FL 32143-3031 or selt@emailcustomerservice.com.